THE ROAD AND THE HILLS

Book One of
A WALK IN THE DARK

THE ROAD
AND THE HILLS

Book One of
A WALK IN THE DARK

by SPEDDING

London
ALLEN & UNWIN
Boston   Sydney

First published in Great Britain by Allen & Unwin 1986
This book is copyright under the Berne Convention. No reproduction
without permission. All rights reserved.

**Allen & Unwin (Publishers) Ltd,
40 Museum Street, London WC1A 1LU, UK**

Allen & Unwin (Publishers) Ltd,
Park Lane, Hemel Hempstead, Herts HP2 4TE, UK

Allen & Unwin Australia Pty Ltd,
8 Napier Street, North Sydney, NSW 2060, Australia

Allen & Unwin with the
Port Nicholson Press
PO Box 11-838 Wellington, New Zealand

© Alison Spedding 1986

British Library Cataloguing in Publication Data
Spedding
    The road and the hills.—(Book one of A walk
    in the dark)
I. Title   II. Series
823'.914[F]   PR6069.P3/
ISBN 0-04-823319-6

Set in 10 on 11 point Sabon by Columns of Reading
and printed in Great Britain by
Billings & Sons Ltd, Worcester

This book is dedicated to Alexander
(356–323 BC)
without whom, nothing

PART ONE

THE ROAD AND
THE HILLS

In the corner of a field stood two scrubby cabbages. The first time he passed them, Ogo let them be; they'd been in the ground too long, overgrown, woody-stemmed and yellow-leaved; but the Yakkas had scoured their fields before they left them, and he found nothing else. He uprooted them, beat off some of the earth and took them back to the wagon.

Garget was still sitting in the back of the cart, staring out over the camp; the oxen stood yoked together, heads bowed. The air echoed with voices, metal on metal and metal on wood, tents going up, dinners on to cook, animals being fed, water fetched – Ogo tossed the cabbages in at Garget's feet. He glanced up.

'God's teeth. They for the beasts?'

'Good for nothing! Did I not tell you to start a fire?' Ogo jumped into the wagon and reached under the driver's seat, pulled out cooking pot and tripod. Garget looked from side to side. 'Wood?'

'Think you, why did I tell you to go find some?'

'O.'

'Move, you lazy bastard!'

Garget shrugged, climbed slowly to the ground and shuffled off among the bracken and gorse bushes. Ogo rummaged among the baggage some more and brought out a carving knife, a ladle and a leather bag; he tipped out of it a few lumps of yellow rock salt, and crumbled a little into the pot. One of the oxen lowed, shifting its neck under the yoke. He put the salt in the pot, the pot on the seat and jumped down; as he reached up to unyoke the animals, one of them pushed back against the wagon. The pot tumbled off the seat into the grass. Ogo swore, lifting up the yoke; the freed oxen lumbered a few yards away, and fell to grazing. He climbed back in and picked up the waterskin tied on one side of the cart, up-ended it; a few drops of water dribbled out. He swore again, untied it and slung it over his shoulder, started down towards the river.

A couple of blue-daubed stakes had been driven into the river bank to mark the point above which drinking water could be drawn, below which animals could be watered and ablutions conducted; a group of women waited nearby. As Ogo squatted at the water's edge to fill the skin, one of them stood up and approached him, pulling her mantle tight across her body. He ignored her. She came up behind him and bent over so that her long hair brushed his shoulder.

'Good day, soldier. It seems that you need someone to . . . warm your supper . . .'

3

'Shameless whore,' grunted Ogo. He corked the skin, and turned away from her to go. She made the sign of the horns at him, 'May you die without sons.'

'Whore,' he said again, returning to the wagon. He stripped the cabbage leaves from the stalks, and chopped them up, put them in the pot with more coarse salt, water and oatmeal, kicked at a patch of ground until it was reasonably clear of grass and set up the tripod, ready to suspend the pot from it. Garget came back with a miserable bundle of twigs and bracken. 'Little firewood here.'

'I find nothing odd in that. No doubt people have taken what they need. We must be content with their leavings. Fetch me the fire bag.' It held chips of bark, dry moss and rotten wood, flint and steel in a tinderbox; in a few minutes there was a small fire under the pot. Ogo broke up the woody cabbage stalks and added them to the blaze. Garget sat with his back against the wheel, looking miserable. The dusk thickened; the oxen, drawing closer to the wagon, lay down and began peacefully chewing the cud. The stew bubbled in the pot.

'I see someone coming,' said Garget. 'Maybe they have news of Parrek. When is that ready?'

' 's ready as it'll ever be,' said Ogo, pausing.

'Well?' said Garget.

'Well?' said Ogo.

'Your pardon?'

'Bowls,' Ogo said politely.

'O.' Garget clambered into the wagon and began fumbling about; it was near full dark by now. The dark figure emerged from the furze bushes, into the firelight – 'Good day,' he said, and squatted down across from Ogo.

'Good day.' Ogo brought up a ladleful of stew and sipped it, looking under his brows at the stranger; no one he remembered – a much worn, heavy black winter cloak, a broad-brimmed black hat pulled down over his ears; between that and a black woollen scarf, only a beardless chin and a thin mouth, and the end of a long nose. In the wagon, a clatter and thump, and Garget cursing; Ogo looked over his shoulder. 'Son of a snake! Under the seat, in the right-hand corner.' The stranger grabbed the soup ladle, and sucked up a mouthful of stew. 'Ha! You intend to eat this?'

'If you leave us enough,' Ogo took back the ladle.

'Wait on.' The stranger reached inside his cloak and took out a leather pouch, and, from that, two or three little vials; he shook a

4

specky powder from one, a dark red dust from another, into the stew. Aroma of pepper and spices came up in the steam. Ogo went on stirring. 'Let it stew an hourtenth more,' said the young man; he was beardless, not clean shaven, and thin-voiced as though he might be only fifteen or so. Garget returned to the firelight, with two wooden bowls and horn spoons.

'Fetch another,' said Ogo.

The young man nodded, and settled down more comfortably.

They ate in silence; the hot spices did not make the cabbage any more tender or tasty, but the dish was filling enough. As soon as they had done, Garget was dismissed to wash the pots. Ogo looked after him in disgust as he dragged away.

'Fool that he is! He sleeps nine hours in ten and complains for the other. The sooner that Parrek returns . . .'

'I come for that.'

'What?'

'From Saripion. You'll not see Parrek back.'

'Eh? Has the fever —'

'In the morning, before camp was struck.'

'Yes? So he's gone?'

'Yes.'

'Eh. That's six years, that he and I were soldiering . . . eh, he was a good friend to me . . .' Ogo folded his hands, bent to rest his forehead on them; the young man said nothing, until he looked up again — 'Eh, then, God send he's in a better place than this . . . you're come in his place?'

'I'm sent to be second man to you. I'm told that your third . . .'

'Aye, a good for nothing. Are you long in the army? I think I've not seen you before.'

'No, I'm new come. But I know something of catapults, siegecraft. And I learn quickly.'

'We'll see . . . you know me, then — Master Ogo?'

'Aleizon Ailix Ayndra,' said the young man, extending his left hand. 'Your pardon?' said Ogo.

'Aleizon Ailix Ayndra,' he said clearly.

'Ah.' Ogo took his hand. 'I've not heard such a name before — your home? In the New Empire?'

'We all have homes in the New Empire, do we not? — no, but I come from Safi,' he said. Ogo could just see that he was smiling. 'Indeed. So Saripion says you're to be second here? We'll see about that. If you prove fit . . .'

'I hope I may,' said Aleizon, with sudden sincerity; he looked up, and Ogo saw his face clearly in the firelight: he had indeed a great beak of a nose, and wide, pale-lashed, stone-blue eyes. 'Then welcome,' he said, 'come with luck.'

'Perhaps,' said Aleizon, and stood up. 'I go to sleep, now.' He walked over to the wagon, and climbed into it as if he had been travelling in it for months. Ogo shrugged. Garget, he knew, would not be back for hours. He sat a while longer by the fire, then banked it with ashes and a couple of turves, and climbed into the wagon to sleep.

The marching order of the Grand Army of the Most Serene Lord and King of Safi, Ailixond eighth of that name, in the Fourth Month of the four hundred and sixty-first year of the city: entering the land of Biit-Yiakarak:

Ahead of the column, the hobilars, mounted and lightly armed, to scout the land ahead and survey passage for the mass of men.

In the vanguard, the Companion Cavalry; leading, the Royal Squadron, the great noblemen and Lord Ailixond. After them, the light cavalry, the Thaless horse, the mercenary cavalry.

In column of march, the infantry: the Silver Shields, the heavy-armed Safic levies, the archers, slingers, javelin-men; territorial levies of the New Empire, Lysmal, Purrllum, the Needle's Eye, the Land-beyond-the-Mountains, each in accustomed dress with weapons as they are used to bear.

In the rear: a squadron of the Companions.

Lightly-armed gallopers pass up and down the line, carrying messages from one commander to another and reporting incidents.

Behind, with its own scouts, mounted and foot-guards, the baggage and the siege train; the siege train leading. After them, at any distance behind or by another road altogether, the baggage.

The lumbering disorder of the baggage train bore military supplies that could not go on man or horseback, loot and clutter too much for its owners to bear with them, the ornate wagons of the wives, concubines and mistresses of the lords and captains, common soldiers' women and children packed in carts or on foot, merchants and their goods, mobile emporia and workshops, bands of slaves, brothels on wheels; the market there had no hours of closing, and it was said that if there was anything that could be had anywhere for a price, then it could find a seller or buyer there; the looted treasure of a dozen nations, a hundred cities; the baggage train was a city on the march.

On this, the seventh day of Fourth Month in the ninth regnal year of Lord Ailixond, the army was crossing the ill-defined marches of the principality of Biit-Yiakarak, rolling down a stony road over rough moorlands, into the mountains which ringed the heartland and the only city of the nation; the peaks reached no great height above the plateau, but they were whitened already with snow. The people who lived in the stonebuilt hamlets near the road and scratched a living in the poor fields had fled, some into the hills away from the road, but most gone to the city as the army approached.

'Little good will it do them,' commented Ogo. 'A worse fate in a sacked city than they would suffer here.'

'If we take the city,' said Aleizon Ailix Ayndra.

'There's not a city yet we've sieged and not taken.'

'No,' said Aleizon Ailix Ayndra idly; they sank back into the creak and grating of the wagon, the oxen plodding docile after the wagon before them, under the birdless arc of autumn sky. The day wore on; the young man said little, wrapped in his cloak and the hat which he did not relinquish even in sleep. Garget dozed in the back of the wagon; Ogo sat gazing at the beasts' heads, tugging now and then at the slack reins. He had not yet had a proper look at the new man; nor even found out whence he got his exotic name; but there was too little interest in his days to use up too quickly any fresh source of it. The road crossed a stone-paved ford, and began to climb; in the evening, the men from the supply train came round with a dole of hard-tack and musty hay for the oxen, since there was no forage beyond cloudberries in the land now. In the morning, white rinds of frost edged exposed surfaces; Leader Saripion came through the artillery column, ordering them to arm themselves, saying the pass was held against them. 'We must pass through a narrow defile, may be 'at they throw rocks from above.'

'Get out my helmet,' said Ogo to Garget, 'and my mail coat.' This was the name he used for a jacket of boiled leather studded all over with iron. He reached under the seat – where he kept all his belongings – and fished out his bone-hilted falchion. 'Have you anything to protect you?' he said to Aleizon Ailix Ayndra. It was hardly likely that he would own anything beyond a heavy knife; most young soldiers relied on a heavy jerkin until they had a chance to glean the battle-harvest of dead men's gear, or save up their pay – half a year's money for a short mail coat.

'O aye.' Aleizon Ailix Ayndra climbed to the back of the cart, and untied the grey canvas bundle that was all his luggage; he took out a long, thin, leather-wrapped item, and a large heavy package; under its wrapping, canvas on top of oiled silk, was bright silvery metal. When he shook it out, it was a thigh-length sleeveless mail shirt, so fine that he was able to fold it up like a tunic; the gear of an officer, if not a nobleman.

'Did you steal that?' said Garget.

'It's mine.' He undid the leather case on the long thing; it was what it had seemed to be, a sword, very well wrapped against wet, and looking new.

'You stole that,' said Garget. 'Infantry sword, is it? How did you come by it?'

'It's mine,' said Ayndra again. 'Have you a leather shirt?'

'There's Parrek's,' Ogo said. 'In the back, there. In the brown sack. Garget. I want my helmet.' The helmet was a double-thickness leather cap, with flaps protecting cheeks and neck, and strengthened by iron bands round the forehead and over the top of the head; a projecting metal brim kept blows and missiles off his face. Aleizon Ailix Ayndra pulled Parrek's stiff, long-sleeved leather shirt on over his tunic; it was not too large to be unwearable; Parrek had been short, and narrow-shouldered. Garget had a studded leather jerkin and a rusty iron cap which he took from a dead Lysmalish at the siege of Keesherran. The hills had closed in either side of the road; up ahead they could be seen to rise into rock walls, either side of a narrow cleft through which the road ran; originally river-cut, the Korhorn Gates. Water still ran there, either side of, and among, the stones of the road; the rock walls wept, dark and dank, and voices echoed.

Aleizon Ailix Ayndra had his cloak and hat on again, over his armour; it seemed that he had not got a boar's tusk helmet to go with the rest of his panoply. He sat with his head up, turning it from side to side, listening. The road bent around an outthrust knee of rock; only cliffs, the crowded road and the ribbon of sky above to be seen. Saripion had said nothing of where or when the enemy were thought to be; the road rang with the fall of hooves, creak of wheels and the chattering of the cold brooks.

'Do you hear that?' said Aleizon Ailix Ayndra.

'What?' Ogo took his falchion out of its sheath and laid it beside him.

'Shouting . . . up there.'

'Can't hear but the wagons and that.'

Above and ahead there was a long high yell – 'Ya-ya-yay-aay! Ya-ya-ya-Yiakarak! Hah-ki Yiakarai! Ya-ya-ya!' The noise echoed to and fro; it came from everywhere, nowhere; it was impossible

8

to tell. The oxen drew up; the driver behind shouted, 'Move on!' Cries like a battle sounded somewhere, shrieks, grating metal, made directionless by the echo-chamber of the cleft.

Weaving in and out of the vehicles, moving as fast as possible between the vehicles, came a horseback messenger; finding his way blocked, he reined in and yelled, 'Get that wagon aside! The rearguard is coming up!' He sat fuming until Ogo had moved on enough to get the wagon over to the side. 'And your helmets,' he said, 'they're throwing rocks up there.'

'Up where?'

'Ahead!' He dug in his spurs, and his horse leapt forward. The indistinct noise of battle seemed louder. Ogo jammed his cap down over his head. Aleizon Ailix Ayndra got up on to the driver's seat; he took off his black hat, and shook out a mop of wild dark-blond hair.

'Is not glued to your head, then,' said Garget, who was squatting down among the heaviest pieces of catapult timber. Someone behind shouted, 'Move on, move on!' Aleizon Ailix Ayndra took his sword in his right hand, and shoved the edge of the other hand into his mouth; he looked yellowish-pale. A heavy stone bounced over the edge of the cliff, and ricocheted past them; round the corner, careering in single file between the wagons, came the cavalry squadron from the rear, small round shields held up over their heads. The frightened oxen lowed and pulled against their traces; immediately overhead, a voice yelled 'Ha-ki Yiakarai!' and they tossed their heads in terror. A larger stone crashed down from above and struck the side of the wagon; the wagon in front leapt forward, and the oxen followed it, going faster, faster; creaking and bouncing, the wagon raced down the rough road, and boulders began to rain around it. 'Slow down!' gasped Aleizon Ailix Ayndra.

'Can't!' said Ogo. A stone the size of a clenched fist struck his shoulder, and fell to hit the nearside ox on its hindquarters; it bellowed and bucked, the wagon slewed round and rocked to a halt, wheel jammed behind a stone. The carts behind pulled up; Garget shrieked and fell over on to the timbers, struck by an apple-sized stone between the shoulderblades.

'Get out! Get out – move it!' Ogo almost pushed Ayndra off the wagon; he dropped his sword, tumbled down and set to heaving at the offending rock. 'Move!' yelled the men behind.

'Ya-aaa-ya-Yiakarak!'

'Safi! Safi!'

Ayndra heaved at the stone, heaved again, fell on to his back with it clasped between his hands; Ogo kicked out at the nearest ox, 'Go!' The wagon jolted forward; Garget groaned aloud; Ayndra leapt up on the wheel and tumbled in as they jolted forward again. Above the cliffs, voices cried 'Safi! Safi! Safi conquers!' and a skein of silhouettes appeared, dancing on the rock lips ahead against the sky, crossing swords and knives; one stepped back and leant too far over, screaming as he felt his balance go; the wagon raced on as he fell, bouncing off the cliffside; he struck the road, head down, a javelin's cast away. The back of his head split open in a smear of red; the other figures had gone out of sight again, and the shouts faded. No more stones fell. Coming up on the wagon in front again, the oxen fell back to a slower pace; the men above were shouting 'Victory!' now, and the cry spread down the column below. They passed one more corpse lying in the road; his throat had been slit. He did not wear Safic badges.

Ogo took off his cap as the road emerged into a wider valley.

'I've not seen such close action for a fivemonth,' he remarked.

'No,' said Aleizon Ailix Ayndra; he was observably trembling. Garget still lay in the wagon and groaned.

'What for you've got such fine things? A waste in the siege train,' said Ogo; he twitched at the hem of the other's mail shirt. Ayndra moved back, as if to get out of reach. 'Does no harm,' he said. 'If we go not to battle, still battle might come to us.'

'Ay! Ay!' moaned Garget. 'My ribs are broken . . . ay . . .'

'Go you, look at him,' said Ogo; he settled back into his sit-for-hours posture. They had entered a broad high valley; the road ran along one side; a marsh-fringed lake, the source of the river that had cut the pass, took up the floor. On its far side, several troops of cavalry and a large number of footmen were descending from the snow-scattered high ground above the pass. At their head was a rider all in white on a bay horse. Ogo looked over his shoulder, to catch the others' gaze; Garget was sitting propped against the backboard, arms clasping himself, shivering sullenly; Ayndra was looking out over the lake. 'There's Lord Ailixond,' Ogo said, 'there. Him in white.'

'They must have gone up from the ford,' Ayndra said, 'there was a track leading away . . .'

'Couldn't tell you,' said Ogo.

'Are those the Companions with him?'

'All those riders in the bright cloaks, they're the lords, the Council. Or some of them at least.'

'Who's the one in green?'

10

'Couldn't tell you. Lord Kadaron I see sometimes, he has charge of the artillery. The others, I couldn't tell you their faces, even an I know some of their names.' Ogo grinned. 'It's no very noble pastime, the siege train,' he said. 'No glory here.'

'I never thought so . . .'

'You've seen a battle before?'

'Was that a battle?'

'O aye. Battle of the Korhorn Gates, I do not doubt, in the Chronicles.'

'No, I've not.'

'Frightened?'

Ayndra gave a sort of twisted smile.

'A fool if you're not frightened,' said Ogo.

'Then I'm not a fool,' he said.

'You've not seemed it . . . aye, Aleizon, I think you'll do.'

'Ayndra.'

'What?'

'Ayndra. If you'll not call me my full name, call me Ayndra.'

'As you will, then.'

'As you will,' said Aleizon Ailix Ayndra, pulling on his hat again, and grinning.

A fine rain fell as the army of Safi descended the other side of the Korhorn. Yiakarak lay in a wide natural bowl, ringed by mountains; the Korhorn was the only road that wheeled traffic could go on, out to the south; a bridle-path road led out to the north and the land of Haramin. The land in the valley was wet and green, fed by many rivers; the Yiakarai exchanged corn for metals and artifacts. The road down zigzagged across a broad, bare slope; the carts went down at a slow walk, drags fixed, the road below them fading into the grey curtains of the rain; thicker grey smears hid most of the green fields far below. By the evening, they were low enough to smell smoke; the Yiakarai were burning off any crops that they had not been able to harvest in time. They bivouacked by the road, given a dole of bacon and biscuit; a necklace of campfires looped across the dark below them, but the lights of Yiakarak were too far away to see; although red stars scattering the valley floor showed where the fields still smouldered.

The air around the city of Yiakarak was sad and bitter with the smoke of lost crops, and ashes tainted the mountain water of the river that looped round the city's hill, leaving only a narrow neck

11

of land onto which the city's single gate opened. In two days since crossing the Korhorn, the Yiakarai had sent no envoys; finally, Lord Ailixond sent to them four heralds under the blue truce banner. A small door in the walls opened to admit them, but the main gate stayed barred; next day, when they had not emerged, he ordered the army to surround the city.

The siege machines which must have land approach forded the river on to the isthmus; the devices which threw missiles were set up on the far side of the river, while the soldiers encamped all around the city, but most facing the gate. The walls and rooftops of the city were crowded with staring people, as the wagons moved in a stream along the riverbank, marshalled by red-cloaked officers, and horses and men by the thousand waded through the river, while the camp-followers erected their shanty-town half a mile down the road, well out of reach of arrows. The pavilions of the lords unfolded like giant bloated blooms in a crescent facing the gate, the king's white tent in the middle, lesser tents and booths and shacks multiplying around them. Leader Saripion distributed the dozen catapults under his command at intervals around the curve of the river, told each master to set up his machine as he thought best, and departed in the direction of the already thriving market.

Ogo got down from the wagon and stamped around, testing the firmness and lie of the land, holding up his hands to take approximate sightings on the wall, until he found a gravelly rise which suited him. 'Here!' Garget was dozing, Aleizon Ailix Ayndra gawping at the city in a daydream. 'Wake up!' he bellowed. 'Over here!'

Ayndra roused sufficiently to flick the whip over the oxen; they lumbered over to Ogo. He hollered at a cart not far away. 'Master Varro! Let's have a hand from you!' It took six of them to heave the main timbers of the machine out of the wagon, and set up the base of the catapult; the wagon sat some way behind it, to provide a hut for the catapultmen. Ogo unyoked the oxen, and told Ayndra to find stones to chock the wheels. 'Garget! Go find where we're to pasture the beasts – ask Saripion.'

'Saripion's gone.'

'Go after him, then. Tell him his old friend Ogo sent you.'

'But he –'

'I care not what he may but. Go – and leave the beasts yet, you'll not be able to walk all over the camp with them behind you.'

Garget pulled a face and went, dragging his feet. Ogo squatted by the wheel where Ayndra was pushing rocks under it. 'At your age you know nothing of siegecraft, no doubt – why I should be cursed with a raw youth and a wittol, I know not, but . . . you see there the frame of the catapult. We fit in it the spoon, like this . . .' He took out his knife and started scratching a diagram on the ground. 'And the ropes, the springs, here. Takes a twothree of us to pull the cup back and hook it down, here, then a stone or whatever it may be in it –'

'And let it go, and it flies up and strikes on the upper beam, here. Like this,' said Ayndra, taking hold of the knife and adding to the diagram. 'And the load flies off . . .' He added a round object, pursuing a high trajectory away from the machine, and embellished it with two closed eyes, a line for a nose and an open mouth. 'Eh?' said Ogo.

'Enemy head,' he said. 'Set the range by tightening or loosening the ropes, or lifting or lowering the frame.'

'Luamis,' said Ogo. 'Am I to go home and leave you to do all?'

'O no. I know nothing about it, I've not even seen a catapult fired.'

'So what is this?'

'I read in a book . . .'

'A book on siegecraft? – where did you find such a book? And who read it to you?'

'No one . . .'

'Do you read? Do you write also?'

'Well enough.'

'Letters, do you write?'

'If I am paid.'

'Was that your trade?'

'No.' Ayndra got up and went to fill his cloak with another load of pebbles from the river bank. Ogo watched him carry them back, heap them around the wheels, fetch some more, push the wagon to see that it was secure; then he set down the tailgate, reached in and pulled out a rough stepladder, propped that up against it with a few more stones to steady its feet, and sat down on the lowest rung to stare off into the distance again. After a while he said, 'Why do you not take this back away from the machine – will we not get fire here?'

'We'll put up pavises,' said Ogo. 'Pays to guard the machine. Sometimes they come out of the city and cut the ropes, or steal them, or try to destroy everything.'

Ayndra nodded.

'Hoy there!'

13

Ogo spat. 'That fool Garget.'

Garget, strolling up, stared sullenly at them. 'A message.'

'From . . .?'

'Leader Saripion says, Catapultmaster Ogo should not presume on any link he may have with the Leader in times past, nor think himself deserving of special favour, for the Leader never does other than act with perfect justice,' Garget recited.

'Go, take the oxen! And return directly once you have done with them.'

Garget turned his back on them, reaching out for the patient animals. Ogo spat again.

'You are harsh to him,' said Ayndra.

'Hush! If you will be second man, it's no place of yours to tell me how to act.'

'Will you let me go to the market?'

'An you do not waste time there. Why do you wish to go?'

Ayndra shrugged. 'Buy things.'

'You will return promptly, and waste no time in wineshops?'

'I shall not set foot in any wineshop.' Ogo watched him crossing the rough grass; he was long-legged for his height, but small, scarcely five and a half feet, and thin-limbed; there was something odd, effeminate, about his walk. Most likely he still had some growing to do.

The gravel bottom of the ford had been churned to porridge by the traffic that had crossed it; a six-wheeled wagon was stalled in the middle, eight oxen straining to drag it out and half a dozen men waist-deep in the water around it. Piles of timber, ropes and stones lay about on the banks; a bridge was to be built there, and another one above the city.

Ayndra took off his battered boots and waded into the cold torrent. As he splashed across, a gorgeous young rider, on a stallion with a gold-bitted bridle, galloped out of the camp and straight into the water, casting sheets of spray over the people crossing; one man he almost ran down, who had to jump aside and fell over in the water. The young man went on without stopping. 'My lord!' cried the soaked man, furious, and then, 'God damn you, Lord Lakkannar!' when the rider was out of earshot. Ayndra climbed the ruts of the far bank, wiped his feet in the grass, tied his foot-rags again and pushed them into his boots before tramping into the camp.

The clerks of the government, when they were not taken up with the king's work, read or wrote letters, for a fee, and, for a further fee, arranged that they were sent with the royal message-

14

riders who travelled by relays of fast horses all over the Empire. A sign painted with a ribboned and sealed scroll showed where they received clients, though at present it hung from a pole among a heap of canvas, tent poles and five or six large iron-bound chests. One clerk was on his knees before an open chest. 'All ruined by rain! Only fit for mattress-stuffing – look at this!' He held up a mildewed sheet of rag paper and caught sight of Ayndra. 'What do you want? Go away, I will write no letters for you.'

'I do not want them written. I wish to know an you send letters outside the Empire.'

'Outside the Empire? Wherever might that be?'

'Suthine,' said Ayndra, gazing into the chest. 'Ho!' he said, and snatched something out of it. 'Surely you know a ship captain who trades with Suthine!'

'What have you got there? Give it to me!'

Ayndra sniffed what he held in his hand. 'Mountain sticks! I'll give you a half a sol for these.'

'Give me those!' The clerk tried to snatch the sticks back, but Ayndra dodged out of his way. 'I'll give you a silver sol, then,' he said.

'Then give it to me, and be gone!'

Ayndra flipped a shiny coin, stuffed the sticks in the front of his overtunic and went on towards the tents of the officers and court functionaries surrounding the canvas mansions of the lords. There were fewer people around, many of them liveried servants who gave evil looks to the idle wanderer; he had a look at the king's tent, where two guards leant on sarissas by the canopied porch. A couple of richly dressed men approached, one blond and very handsome in scarlet and purple, the other grey-headed and extremely tall. Ayndra said to a servant who was glaring at him, 'Who are they?'

'Who are they? Why, do you not know Lord Polem and Lord Golaron?'

'Who is Lord Polem?' Ayndra said.

'What are you doing here?' asked the servant. 'Are you –'

'Making my way home,' he said, and headed back towards the commoners' camp; a trumpet call, three short blasts and a long, echoed over the tents, and a number of other men in bright clothes or officers' scarlet hurried past him in his former direction. As he crossed the river, he saw a large group of Yiakarai with banners on the wall above the city gate. But it was growing dark, and from the other side of the river not much could be seen.

'Where have you been?' said Garget. 'Ogo's gone to the council.

15

Left me to wait for you.' He pushed his face up to Ayndra's and sniffed suspiciously at his breath. 'Get along, now! The Leader'll curse you.'

Torches illuminated a gathering of men outside Saripion's tent. The Leader stood on a box and spoke to the crowd.

'Lord Ailixond sent to the Yakkas, the usual terms: should they surrender peacefully to him, they would be received into the New Empire and allowed to govern themselves under our protection. But only this hour the vile barbarians have rejected our terms in the most abominable manner – they have cast down from their walls the heads of our heralds, wrapped in the very banner of peace they came with, and for this we are sworn to destroy them. I shall give you orders now for the conduct of the siege – who is that?' He craned his neck to see who had arrived.

'It is I, Garget, sir Leader, I was ordered to wait for the, the new man, Ali – Allerzanda.'

'Yes?' said Saripion. 'Master Ogo! See that your subordinates attend when I order them to from now on – where was I?'

'Order of siege,' said Purmo.

'Firstly, there is a guard to be kept. No Yakkas are to escape the city, but should they come from without they are to be sent in to it. If they come out, catch them and slay them if they fight, or send them back.'

'Why not kill them?'

'The more mouths they have to feed in the city, the sooner will they all starve and surrender.'

'A bad time of year to start starving them, they have their harvest in there.'

'Pray silence for the Leader!' called Purmo. 'Listen!'

'As I said. The catapultmen will keep guard on the river. Also sentry-go around the camp.'

'Sentry-go? Let that wait – what are we to eat?'

'The nightwatch. Two watches, dusk to midnight and midnight to dawn – the first watch this night, Vafro, Poriat, Cadi and Guldan; the second watch, Ogo, Al – er – his second man, Dieldo and Nain; for the other nights, Purmo will draw up –'

'Meanwhile, are we to starve before the Yiakarai?'

'A ploy to reduce the wages, perhaps,' said Aleizon Ailix Ayndra. Saripion gave up. 'Quartermaster,' he said. Hartir the quartermaster got to his feet. 'We will send out forage parties to find what they can, but foragers who go out alone will be disciplined. There will be a twice-daily dole of bread, bacon and whatever else can be found. Each crew to send one man to collect

16

the rations. Those who do not come get nothing. Sixth hour of morning and fifth hour of evening. The draught beasts have been found pastures and will be fed there.'

'What are we to drink?'

'Water,' said Hartir. He nodded to Saripion and sat down again.

'Now, men,' said the Leader. 'The conduct of the siege itself. We are to bombard chiefly the fortifications, not so much the dwellings. The engineers will bring wagonloads of stones for this purpose. The bolt-throwers are to be used to aim at enemy who show themselves on the wall. Hurdles and straw for pavises will be provided this night – it were best that you built them before dawn, lest the enemy start firing then. Further, the rules of a war camp stand – no women to be brought into the camp . . . any man drunk in pursuance of his duty to be fined a week's wages . . . now, Quartermaster, this evening's rations . . .' As he spoke, a couple of carts loaded with the material for pavises rolled up; he dismissed all the men except those who were to collect rations to go with them and start building the fences of straw-padded hurdles that protected the catapults from enemy arrows and slingstones. It was a long heavy job, by the uncertain light of torches and a cold wind blowing; Garget, sent to get rations for Ogo's crew, returned after an hour with a chunk of salt meat and three miserable lumps of hard-tack. It was eighth hour before the shields were up to Ogo's satisfaction and they could crouch round a tiny fire with Varro and his crew, gnawing on stringy meat and biscuits soft with damp, washed down with river water.

'Saripion, Saripion,' muttered Ogo. 'Three years ago, I was his second man, then old Leader Turmil died and he was made Leader – his name was Sarip then, but he got his red cloak and thought he was made a lord so needs must have a lordly name . . . and now for spite we're put on the midnight watch . . . ah, Saripion!' He said to Aleizon Ailix Ayndra, 'What for did you join this army, then?'

'Advancement,' said Ayndra distantly.

'Advancement? Ha! There's little enough of that! See me? Seven years I've been in the army, three years a catapultmaster, like to die a catapultmaster I should think unless Saripion should fall dead and some kind spirit make me Summoner, or Leader – ha! vain chance! Even should he come close enough to a fight to scratch hi'self, I've no friends in high places who'd secure me advancement . . . na . . .'

'Perhaps,' said Ayndra.

17

'Ha! Every boy who goes for a soldier thinks he'll be captain of the Companions some day – every common fool. I've never seen it.'

'Saripion made Leader, did he not?'

'Ah, but what's that? Leads fifteen catapult crews . . . and he's a fool . . .'

'Well then,' said Ayndra. 'But Ogo said 'Nonsense, nonsense, nonsense . . .'

From the records of the war kept by the clerk of the artillery and Summoner Purmo:

14:IV:461 Battering of the walls of Yiakarak began this day, and each day forward, all hours of daylight.

30:IV:461 Poriat, catapultmaster, dead of wounds received from arrows of the Yakkas. Our second death of this siege, but, by gods' grace, the enemy fire on us but little.

33:IV:461 This day the enemy on the walls in great numbers, and loosing fire arrows, set afire much of the pavise, the flames reaching the catapult of Master Lorlen.

34:IV:461 First breach opened in the walls by the catapult of Master Ogo. Many buildings within also much damaged with twenty days' attack.

1:V:461 In the night, when we cannot fire on them, the Yakkas come and shore up the wall, though each day most of their work is destroyed again. Still, the breach does not open wider.

5:V:461 Another man lost, the fifth to die, Barrin, catapultman of the second class, receiving a bolt in his chest when his catapult misfired. Snow falling thickly in the night. The enemy appear but rarely on the walls, still they show no signs of surrender. The catapults moved closer all to the breach, hoping to force the enemy to action.

8:V:461 First hour of morning: Varro and Parnir, on watch, captured a man fleeing from the city . . .

'Stand up,' said Varro, slowly and clearly, 'we shall do you no harm. Only get back to your city, and give us your weapon.'

'No! No!' exclaimed the foreigner, who lay prostrate before them. 'I am friend. I will see for your king.'

'No. We send you back there,' said Varro.

'No! I've ver' important message.'

'What is it, then?'

'I must see your lord.'

'O indeed? Why, think you, should we take you to see a lord?' Parnir said. To Varro he added, 'Who commands the guard this night?'

'O, no, no! I plead with you, take me to noble lord.'

'Lord Polem,' said Varro. 'But if we leave watch . . .'

'Arno and Yailen will cover for us – we should take him to the lord.'

'We've not seen his message,' objected Varro. 'What if we take him to the lord and it all turns out a pack of lies?' He nudged the foreigner with his boot. 'Aye. Where's your message, then? Give it to us.'

'I am not to say, to the king only.'

'You must say. Else how do we know that you have a message at all? Who has sent you? How are you called?'

'Kolparri, sirs, Kolparri, priest of the second road of righteousness, and I come . . . I come to tell you how the lord of Safi may enter Yiakarak.'

'O indeed?' Parnir said again.

'O yes, yes!'

'Let us take him to Lord Polem, Varro.'

'Find Arno and Yailen . . .'

The commander's tent stood by the bridge, a yellow canvas beacon in the winter night; inside it, shadows moved across the lamplight. The three men approaching heard a high-pitched giggle from within, a man's deep laughter, and voices whispering; there was no one guarding the door. Parnir paused, uncertain how to announce his entry.

'Go in, then, go in,' said Varro, holding Kolparri by one arm, falchion in his other hand.

'The Blessed One will –' began the prisoner.

'Hush!' said Parnir. There was another giggle from within. Parnir cleared his throat and lifted the door-flap.

Two oil-lamps burnt on the table in the middle of the tent. Lord Polem sat – or sprawled – in a large folding chair behind it; a young woman sat on his knee. She was unlacing his shirt for him while he pressed his face into her open bodice. Parnir's words stuck in his throat. Varro, outside, hissed, 'What do you wait for? Is the lord not there?'

'No –' Parnir began. The girl must have heard him. She looked round and with a squeal pulled her bodice closed.

'My lord, I'm, um, ah, I'm . . .' mumbled Parnir, and stepped outside again. He heard Lord Polem exclaim, 'Get out! – get you to bed, Thio, it's, ah, it's very cold . . .'

19

'O Polli!' said the woman. 'Will you not come with me? It's far too cold in that big bed all on my –'

'Don't call me that name!' roared Polem. 'Go! Go!'

'What?' said Varro. The door opened; a small person in an overlarge cloak pushed past them and ran away, stumbling as the trailing cloak encumbered her legs. Polem called severely, 'Enter!' Parnir seized Kolparri's free arm, and they frog-marched him into the tent.

Lord Polem was standing behind the table, his overtunic hastily belted over his open shirt. 'What do you want of me?' he said icily.

'My lord,' Parnir began again. 'We are catapultmen, Catapultmaster Varro and –'

'I care not what your rank may be. What do you here? Who is that?' He stabbed a ring-loaded finger at Kolparri, who wormed free of his captors, cast himself to the floor, wriggled under the table and kissed Polem's butter-soft red leather boots. 'My lord king!'

Polem bent over and peered under the table. 'What are you doing?'

'My lord king! I come from Yiakarak –'

'I am not the king.' Polem stood up again. 'Who is this?'

'My lord, he came from Yiakarak, he has a message for the king –'

'– he says he can let us into the city,' Varro interrupted Parnir.

'O?' exclaimed Polem. 'Get up, you – what is this? Have you come to surrender? Why are there not more of you?'

Kolparri knelt up. 'I will see the king,' he said. 'I will speak the king.'

'I am a lord of Safi. You may consider that what is said to me is said to the king,' Polem told him.

'I will speak the king,' Kolparri repeated.

Polem scratched his head, frowning; then he picked up a cloak draped over the table. 'We shall go to Lord Ailixond. Seize his arms again, and follow –' Then he realised that the cloak was about two feet too short for him, and embellished with feminine flounces. He dropped it again. 'Damnation! – let us go, then.' He wrapped his arms round himself, and plunged out into the snowy darkness.

The guards at the porch of the royal tent crossed their pikes over the entrance as they saw a party approaching over the patchy, glimmering snow. 'Who goes there?' said one offhandedly.

'Me, you fools, let me pass.' Polem knocked the pikes aside and dashed into the tent. The other three shuffled after him, found themselves in a dark airy space inadequately lit by one guttering lamp in front of some swaying curtains; Lord Polem was not in sight. They halted just inside the door, tightening their hold on the prisoner; one of the guards stepped inside after them. 'What is this?' he whispered.

'A prisoner —' Varro began; just then, the curtains swayed again, and the guard ducked out. Lord Polem came out from behind them, followed by a barefoot man in a crumpled shirt and white breeches, long dark hair falling over his face; he picked up the lamp and carried it up to the visitors, blinking sleep-sore eyes as he raised it to look at them. 'Good day,' he said pleasantly. 'Is this the traitor?'

Varro and Parnir both let go of Kolparri, stepped back, bowed as deeply as they knew how. 'My lord!' Kolparri dropped to the ground again, and kissed the king's bare feet. Lord Ailixond looked faintly amused. 'You're artillerymen, are you not? From Leader Saripion's division? How did you find this?' He shook the foot which Kolparri was clutching.

'We were on watch, my lord . . . he came, from the city . . .'

'He says he can let us into Yiakarak,' Varro said again.

'So I am told. Would you ask one of my guards to summon the head of the nightwatch and four of his men? And tell the captain your names, so I can send to you when I've discovered what this man wants. But meanwhile you were better to return to your watch. I'll send someone to tell you what happens.' He favoured them with a wide smile, tossing the sleep-ruffled hair out of his eyes; not tall, and small-boned, in his untidy clothes he looked like a boy. The two artillerymen bowed again, moving out. 'And thank you,' he said as they went out of the door.

'Get up,' Ailixond said peremptorily to Kolparri. 'Polem, come and take hold of him.' He took the lamp over to a stand of four hanging lamps, and lit them from it; replaced it on the table, and reached under it. Pulling out a pair of snow-stained white leather boots, he sat down on a stool and pushed his bare feet into them. 'You have searched him?'

'Ah. No . . .' Polem pinned Kolparri's arms behind his back and fumbled vaguely around his waist and under his arms. 'Where are your weapons?' he said.

'O no no no! No weapon!'

The king laced up his boots and stood up. 'Now, sir, who are you?'

'Most august lord, I am Kolparri, priest of the second road of righteousness.'

21

'And what message do you bear, sneaking out to me like a thief in the night? – stand up, address me to my face, not to the floor.'

'O great king! When many days ago your coming is heard to us, the Archpriest says you are sent by the Accursed One and in the Korhorn will all die surely, and so our army goes out to battle, but there is no victory and we must shut in the city while you siege it, but each day the Archpriest foretells your death, and yet it comes not and the walls fall and the people begin to starve and sicken and it is said the Accursed One punish us for we've not defend the land.'

'So you tell me I am the emissary of the Accursed One?' said Ailixond, with a faint ironic twitch of his eyebrows.

'No no, gracious lord! We have seen the falsehoods of the Archpriest for the Accursed One misleads him. The Blessed One sends you to cleanse Yiakarak of false counsellors and evil men, as is shown by your victory and now you will take the city, as God's will we open the gates to you.'

Ailixond's distant eyes warmed slightly. 'Open the gates? When? Are there many of you?'

'Among the priests fifty, we have many of the gate-guards and the Guards of God also, and seven days from this night we have all the guard our men, on that night the gates will open, the night when the moon fulls –'

The door curtains swished apart, spurred boots clicked on the boarded floor. 'My lord Sulakon,' said Ailixond.

'My lord. What calls me here at this hour?'

'We have captured a Yiakarai traitor. He offers to open the gates to us. But how', Ailixond fixed Kolparri with his gaze, 'am I to know that you are not lying? A fine way to lead us into a trap, opening the gates in the dark . . .'

'Or else he is a spy sent to survey our defences,' said Lord Sulakon. 'And I cannot think it wise to trust a man who has betrayed his nation.'

'But we need hardly trust him,' said Ailixond; he started to turn a heavy ring round and round on his left hand. 'Master Kolparri. What proof have you of your good faith? You are in our hands,' he said, as the guards and the captain he had summoned trooped quietly in behind Lord Sulakon. 'We may keep you here until your gates open . . .'

'Gracious lord!' Kolparri grovelled again. 'I must return to the city to carry to them your word.'

'Surely not! You must have some signal prepared in the event that we restrain you.'

22

'Lord king! I must return.'

'It is not possible,' said Ailixond distantly. 'You will be free when we have the city. By what means might you convey to your friends that we shall attack when they open to us? – and be warned, if it should turn out a trap, you'll be dead before your comrades have finished with my people.'

'A flag, a red flag,' Kolparri said. 'On your great tent. And they will show a red flag on the wall on the day before the full moon, and when the moon shines the gates will open. Show next day a red flag, lord. And I will stay until you have the city safe.'

'Indeed,' said the king lazily. 'We shall see about this. But till morning, sir priest, I shall see you safely kept. And then we shall speak more, and you can describe to me how many friends you have in the city, how many friends of the Archpriest, how the gates are guarded and the city lies.'

'My lord! Ask whatever I can tell.'

'I will,' Ailixond said. 'Captain. Take this man and put him in the prison-cart. You need not chain him, but guard him all night. I will give you audience next morning, sir priest, but until then, sleep sweetly.' He snapped his fingers at the guards, who surrounded Kolparri and led him away.

'The man's mad,' said Polem. 'He took me for the king, first.'

'Are they not devil worshippers in this land?' Sulakon asked.

'Devils? Gods? Let them hold what superstition they like. I wonder if there are many who think as he does? A pity he has not come with more companions.'

'I would not trust him,' Sulakon said. 'Is he not deranged – if not devil-touched?'

'It hardly matters. Even should they intend to trap us – as soon as the gate is open, we can block it so that they'll never close again, and we outnumber them, they'll never succeed – I have not wished to sit here much longer, it grows cold and it were better to be under roofs . . . next day at eighth hour, Sulakon, we shall question him in full, and bring it before the Council . . .'

'My lord. I must return to the watch.' Sulakon bowed out.

'And I, I . . .' Polem yawned and blinked. 'Is there wine here?' he said. 'It's well cold outside.'

'Under the table,' said Ailixond, who was pacing up and down. Polem knelt down and fished out a leather bottle, which he up-ended to his mouth. 'Aah!' he said. Ailixond halted just behind him. 'You've been with that woman again,' he said.

'Eh?' Polem turned to face him.

23

'Thio.'

'O,' said Polem, shamefaced. 'Well, I . . . how do you know?' They were hardly a foot apart; Ailixond, a span shorter, had to tip his head back to look the other in the eye. 'I can smell her on you.'

Polem hung his head.

'You know the rules. If I find you with her when you are on duty once more, I shall have her shipped home, which will be your fault and none of hers.'

'She's gone to bed now,' said Polem.

'And you'll not follow her, this night. You should go back now.'

'Can I take this?' Polem raised the wine bottle. 'She took my cloak,' he said. 'It's damnably cold.'

'Take it. I will see you at the Council.'

'Good night, then.'

'Good night.'

Varro's second man, Gemmat, set up an iron tripod over the bonfire, and Varro poured some wine into a scoured cooking pot to warm. When it was steaming, he ladled into the outheld bowls, and started the round of toasting with luck to Lord Ailixond. The moon rose in a blue haze over the eastern peaks as they toasted the expected victory, Varro's good fortune in capturing the enemy traitor, the king for rewarding with the wine, the siege for being about to come to an end, the gods for having preserved them all unharmed to the end of it . . . it was almost last hour when Aleizon Ailix Ayndra appeared.

'Where've you been?'

'Out,' he said, and sat down rather suddenly in the warm ashes at the fire's edges. 'O, what's this?'

'Mulled wine . . . find a bowl.'

'O, no, no, give me none.'

'No, no, you must drink,' said Ogo. 'Garget, find a bowl – Varro? My turn I think . . .' He tottered to his feet. 'I pledge the parents of my lord the king, without who, who, we're in a warm house in Safi 'stead of freezing in a ditchgot field!' He drained his bowl and held it out for more. Aleizon Ailix Ayndra gave a high-pitched giggle. 'A moment,' he said, and slipped away into the dark again. Ogo kicked Garget. 'Go, fetch'm a cup.'

'He goes to get it,' said Garget. 'Gemmat, have you heard about Mantissa?'

'Who she?'

Garget began upon an involved story. Aleizon Ailix Ayndra

24

reappeared, by now notably unsteady on his feet and giggling. He dropped to his knees beside Ogo, reeking of some smoky, herbal scent. 'Where've you been?' Ogo said.

'O, nowhere.' He looked up at the sky. The moon had flooded the vault of heaven with light, and the new snows on the eastern mountains gleamed. 'I saw them waiting,' he said, 'all in silence . . . look at the city, you'd think it floated in this light.'

'Who was waiting?' said Ogo. 'Get your bowl.' He reached for the ladle.

'O, no, no.'

'No, have this then.' Ogo put his own cup into Ayndra's hands. 'Must drink. The king sent Varro a skinful.'

'The king's tent was full of lights,' he said.

'Have you been in the king's camp?' said Yailen.

'I walked about.' Ayndra looked up again, the firelight catching his eyes.

'Do you never take off your hat?' asked Yailen.

'Only when I sleep,' he said, 'and not always then.' He tipped Ogo's cup back so far that wine spilled and trickled down his chin, and tossed it down empty. 'My thanks. I must go.' As he got up, metal showed between the folds of his cloak.

'Where will you go?' said Ogo.

'Over there.' He gestured toward the river. 'O! Ho!' said Garget. Ayndra giggled again, and made off.

'He's got's mail coat on,' said Garget. 'Do'need that for a brothel.'

'Some brothel' you do,' said Varro, and laughed aloud as he reached for the wineskin to fill the pot again.

The frost made the ground shine in the moonlight, isolating the men creeping across it until they disappeared in the inky shadows under the wall. A couple of torches gutterd over the gate, but there was no one to be seen patrolling the wall walk; the distant noise of the market camp carried up to the silent city. The battered metal of the great gates remained immobile in the gloom.

'If we've been fooled –' began Polem.

'Hush,' said Ailixond softly. 'Where's my trumpeter?'

Someone whispered for the trumpeter, who came and stood there ignored, silver instrument tucked under one arm while he blew on his frozen fingers. A thousand little sounds of creaking leather, scrape of metal, rasping coughs echoed under the wall.

'What if we –' began Polem again.

'Hush,' said Ailixond. Something struck loud and heavy behind

25

the gate, and a dog barked; there was a rattle of footsteps and a great groan of stiff hinges as a black line opened down the face of the gate. Ailixond struck the trumpeter on the shoulder. 'Sound! Advance!'

The soldiers burst past him as he blew and blew, the gates clanged back against the wall, and the Silver Shields poured into the city.

A dozen armed men were ranged before the untidy facade of the temple palace of Yiakarak, with more only half-clad, even half-awake, crowding out behind them as the first Safeen came running up the street at them. They had not time to raise a concerted warcry before they were swamped. A few torches shed yellow light over the wide high corridor within; black mouths opened off its sides, the air smelt of pine smoke and blood. Ailixond shouted, 'First company, with me! Second and third, go down the side ways –' Kolparri thrust past him, arms raised, shouting in his own language. Lakkannar leapt forward, sword drawn, but Ailixond seized his arm. 'Follow him!' The great corridor debouched down a worn flight of steps into the hall of the palace, where moonlight filtered through high windows; Kolparri ran straight across into the dark at the other side and up a flight of steps to a door, which was secured from the inside. Ailixond pulled him back while Lakkannar and a couple of soldiers attacked it and charged over the splintered planks into sudden light and warmth. Against the far wall was a wide bed, and an old man struggling to sit up, reaching under the heaped pillows behind him; but Kolparri was quicker. Before anyone else knew, he had thrust his hand in among the linen and then straight at the old man's throat. Blood sprayed over the sheets and the old man fell back with a bubbling shriek, his hands flailing at his throat; Kolparri stood over him with a foot-long blade shining dark in his hand. Ailixond stepped up to the bed and used his sword like an executioner. All the noise and struggle stopped instantly. The king drew his sword out of the bed and leant over it. He put his left hand through the old man's hair and turned the face to look at him, then glanced up at Kolparri. The priest had not moved; the knife in his hand was shaking. Ailixond flung the severed head straight at him, like a ball. Kolparri had caught it before he was able to scream. The king jammed his sword back into its sheath and strode out of the room. His voice echoed shouting orders in the hall.

Aleizon Ailix Ayndra stood in the doorway, moon at his back, looking at the corpses lying against the wall. There was a shuffle to his left. He jumped, and someone jumped back; he stepped after them, and they started to run. There were three of them, one in a nightshirt that fluttered like a shroud of a nightwalker. Ayndra caught up with them at the head of some stairs and one of them turned with a kitchen knife in his hand. Ayndra raised his sword and brought it down in a clumsy swashing blow, and the Yiakara lunged with his knife; Ayndra twisted aside and brought the sword down on his arm. The man screamed, the knife clattered on the floor, Ayndra dealt him a second blow and knocked him over the edge of the stair. Whether he was dead or unconscious, he tumbled to the foot of the steps and lay sprawled there quite still. Ayndra grabbed up the knife and charged on.

In a courtyard covered in frost-brittle grass he caught another man; he chopped him from behind between neck and shoulder and he fell down immediately. A door slammed on the far side of the court, then swung open again in a long squeal of hinges. Ayndra moved toward it, and there was a sudden flash of movement up the stairs inside – a narrow stair, twisting upwards, he would have tried to slash the other's feet if it had not been so cramped, but then they were in a room and it was suddenly quiet, a patch of moonlight like water on the floor – and the floor creaked. He swung round, and the Yiakara, leaping a moment too late, found a ready blade.

Ayndra let the sword drop, and stood there swaying; then he held the blade in the light, and saw that it was covered in blood. There was a bed a few feet away. He reached for a blanket. Someone screamed and burst forth from the bedclothes and he himself shrieked and thrust the sword at it with all his weight behind it. The body folded up over the weapon and he found himself lying over it. Long hair, scented like roses, tangled under his hands. He jerked upright and pulled the sword out. The dead girl lolled face down on the bed. He pulled off a heap of covers and threw one over her; he sank down under the others, on the floor.

By dawn a light snow had begun to fall; it powdered the corpses whom no one had yet bothered to clear from the streets. Some dozen men of the Silver Shields marched out of the temple palace, headed by an officer with a torch. Aleizon Ailix Ayndra hid in a doorway until they had passed. When he reached the river it was grey morning. He crouched at the water's edge to wash.

Ogo woke late, with a throbbing head. He kicked Garget out of bed to light a fire and they both squatted next to it.

27

'Food?' mumbled Ogo.

'No,' said Garget painfully. After a while he added, 'I wonder where he is.'

'Who?'

'Him. Aliz . . .'

'In some whore's bed, no doubt.'

'Gone whoring himself, I should think.'

'No,' said Ogo. He got up to go and relieve himself away from the wagon. When he came back, he said, 'There's Lord Ailixond's flag over the gate now.'

'Ah. Will we get a house, think you?'

'Who knows?'

The plain white banner over the gate stirred lazily; the snowclouds were clearing for a pale sunlight. Garget gazed blearily over the whitish landscape. 'Here he comes.'

'Who?'

'Aleizon Ailix Ayndra.'

As he came nearer. it was clear that he had slept badly. His face was chalk-white, there were purple marks under his eyes, and he was shivering. He crouched by the tiny fire and held out his hands over it. ' 's cold.'

'Where did you sleep?' asked Garget.

'Outside.'

'Where? Why have you got your sword?' Garget reached out and twitched at his cloak. 'Have you been in the river? Why have you your mail shirt on?'

Ayndra yanked the cloak out of his hand. 'Leave me!' he snarled.

'Where have you been?'

'Where I wanted to be!'

'Garget! Go and see if there's any food to be had. I shall make us a porridge,' said Ogo. 'Get honey if you can. Go!' He winced as he stood up. Garget made an insulting sign at him and shuffled away.

'Thank you,' said Ayndra thinly.

'No matter.' Ogo pulled his cloak up to shield his eyes from the sun. 'You see we have the victory.'

'O aye,' said Ayndra, 'victory . . .'

The snows of Fifth Month covered the scarred ground and the rubbish-heaps where the camp had stood; but before Midwinter's Day a second camp had grown up round the city, crowded with all the men and material who could not be lodged within the

28

walls. Cavalcades crossed the Korhorn, trains of food and merchandise, fine horsemen and ladies in horse-litters, droves of cattle, strings of horses; all the machinery of government followed the king, the Justiciar and the Treasurer and their retinues of clerks, envoys from provincial governors and lands as yet beyond the Empire, and, at the end of Fifth Month, Lady Othanë, Queen of Safi, all her attendants, and a dozen other wives of great lords, all with households to be given food and lodgings. And the traders followed the trumpets. By Sixth Month, the market in front of the gate was as busy as the quays of Safi.

The artillerymen filled the short dark days and long snowy nights with sleeping, gossiping, walking the slushy streets and staring at merchandise they could not afford to purchase, and playing interminable games of dice. They were called up by turns for half-month tours of service on the new road which the king had ordered to be built across the north pass out of Yiakarak, so that by the spring any vehicle he liked could be sent that way. They shared a warehouse in the traders' quarter, converted into barracks, with a company of archers; cramped and quarrelling through the tedious days, it was almost a relief to be sent off to the pass.

Varro sat on the sill of the window at the end of their dormitory. At his feet, Ogo sat crosslegged, darning a pair of stockings. Garget lay on a straw mattress by the wall. Gemmat wandered to and fro across the room, while Yailen, Varro's third man, idly watched the progress of his feet.

Gemmat paused in his pacing and picked up a leather cup of dice. He rattled them under Yailen's nose. 'Le's have a game.'

'Not I. Name of God, you've won next year's pay off me three times over.'

'Aye, and you've won it back again, and more.'

Ogo licked the end of his wool yarn, held the needle up to thread it. Varro shifted his body across the window. 'In my light,' grunted Ogo. Varro got down from the sill. 'Where's your second man? Never see him. Reckon he sleeps in the streets?'

'Sleeps?' said Garget. 'Ho!'

'God knows,' said Ogo.

'Yes,' said Gemmat, 'do you not suspect that he's . . .' he took a few mincing steps across the room, patting his tangled hair with one hand. 'No,' said Ogo. 'I am told he goes out and walks for miles.'

'Goes out spending!' said Garget. 'Owes me one sol four samisols and seven quarits, he does.'

29

'Strange fellow,' said Yailen.

'I believe him a runaway clerk,' said Garget. 'He'll be found out some day.'

'Not an offence for clerks to join the army,' said Ogo.

'Clerk or not, he's quite mad,' said Yailen. 'I spoke to him the other day, I said, "What for you in the army," and he said, "Fame," and I said, "What?" and he said "O I'll be as famed as Lord Ailixond I will." '

'Would you not be mad, named Aleizon Ailix Ayndra?' said Gemmat.

'Sounds like a woman's name almost. No wonder he's . . . that way inclined.'

'He should sell his mail shirt,' said Garget, 'and pay me.'

'So long's he keeps his hands to himself – and I've never known him do otherwise – he can do as he likes,' Ogo said. 'He works as well as any, and –' he looked at Garget '– better than some.'

Garget huffed, and rolled over, turning his face to the wall. Yailen succumbed to the lure of the dice cup; the rattle of the bones and the curses of the players punctuated the quiet air. The door below rattled, and the rickety steps to the first floor creaked loudly. 'O! Here he is,' said Gemmat.

Aleizon Ailix Ayndra stepped into the lull in conversation as if he were an actor coming before the crowd. 'Good day, friends,' he said, taking off his hat and running fingers through his ragged hair. 'How goes the day?' He squatted against the wall and ran his glance around them.

'As it ever does,' said Ogo.

'But not for long now. Leader Saripion spoke with me. He tells us that we go up to the pass in two days' time. On the ninth.'

'I thought it was not till the eighteenth.'

'No. We're to go for a halfmonth and nine days now. It seems that work goes not as fast as the king would have it. And we shall not have a wagon even to the foot of the pass, we must march all the way . . . you are dismayed?' He smiled at Yailen, opening his eyes very wide. Yailen looked away. Ayndra raised his eyebrows in a questioning flick, and crawled to the corner where his belongings lay, started sorting through the heap. Gemmat rattled the dice again. It was some several moments before talk resumed.

The wind cast ragged curtains of snow across the ground, ripping dark rents in them and closing them with spinning veils, tearing words from their speakers' mouths and tossing them over the precipices; it howled over the pinnacles of the quarry and sent weak icy breezes even into sheltered leeward spaces. A big roof of canvas covered the most windless corner of the quarry, open on the calmest side where a big bonfire burnt day and night, always with a twothree pots of barley stew and spiced watered wine heating over it. The men released from duty crowded round it, warming their hands on bowls of food; a huddle of tents weighted down with rocks and lean-to shacks spread out around it, where they slept in heaps of damp blankets and musty furs, close-packed as piglets fighting for the sow's teats. The places at the end of the row were not much sought after.

Garget sat complaining of his pains. 'Blisters all down my back from heaving great baskets of rubble . . . and Sheharn struck my fingers with a hammer . . . have you fur gloves? That you've no need for?'

'Felt mittens,' said Ogo.

'Let me wear them – see these? Like a cheese! Yester evening it was an hour before I moved my hands at all, and then they were burning – have you them now?'

'In the tent.'

'Where in the tent?'

'O hush you! I'll fetch them to you if you'll only cease your whining.'

'O, I will, when I –'

Ogo pulled the hood of his cloak up over his padded gambeson and went stumbling over the litter of broken stones. It was fifth hour and nearly dark, too dark to work in safety at stonebreaking, or carrying stones on manback to the head of the road where wagons could not yet go, or tamping down the new road surface as it unwound up the steep valley side. He pushed under the leather tent-flap and knelt, waiting till he could see in the rank gloom. Someone else was moving about on the far side, unfolding clothes or blankets; then a scrape and a spit of sparks, and a tiny oil-lamp flickered into light. Giant shadows bounded across the canvas, the dim light caught in fronds of blond hair; Aleizon Ailix Ayndra, shivering, half-naked, was kneeling among greasy sheepskins, searching for some dry underthings. Ribs showed sharp under his milkwhite skin. Ogo coughed, and he turned with a start –'

'Good God!' exclaimed Ogo.

Ayndra snatched up his discarded cloak and threw it across him – her –

'Shumar!' said Ogo weakly. 'Eh – what –'

'What?' snapped Ayndra defensively.

31

'You're a woman', said Ogo.

Ayndra spat, 'Ha!' and then started laughing. She turned her back on him again, and pulled an undertunic over her head. Through the wool she said, 'And what of it?'

'I . . . I thought you were a boy.'

'I never told you so.'

'No, but . . . I thought . . . there's a rule of no women in the camp.'

'No women in the camp. Is there a rule of no women in the army?'

'I never heard of −'

'Of any such rule.' She stood up, and stepped into her breeches. The lamplight formed vivid shadows on the white skin of her thighs. 'I am not here as a woman. I am a catapultman of the second class. And a sound worker, do you not think? I've heard you say that you've not had a second man as good as I.'

'No, but . . .'

'Then what difference if I turn out to be not a man, eh?' She struggled into a second overlarge undertunic. Ogo shook his head. Finally he said, 'I'd not have cared if you were a sodomite . . .'

'So why do you care if I am a woman?'

'I've never heard of a woman . . .'

'There are many things, master, of which you never have heard, − which is not to say that they never go on.'

'How is it that you are in the army?'

She pulled out a black overtunic and pushed her arms into it, fastened her leather belt over it, then smiled at him, wickedly bright. 'I have friends.'

'What − did they −'

'You know nothing, master, you need say nothing − is that not clear?' Picking up Parrek's old leather shirt, she put that on and stood up, head brushing the roof, transformed into a youth again; she was after all narrow-hipped and flat-chested, and the baggy clothes hid the shallow curve of her breasts.

'I suppose − mistress −'

'I'd be pleased if you still call me Master Aleizon Ailix Ayndra, and we shall live as brothers and friends − you understand?'

'Yes,' said Ogo.

'Good, good!' She bent over to wrap footcloths over her feet before she put her boots on. 'What is it that you look for here?'

'My felt mittens − Garget's gloves . . .'

'I think I've seen them − over here?'

32

Garget, for his sour temper, was made to sleep at the back of the tent where the rock wall made it damp and icy; Aleizon Ailix Ayndra chose the least sought-after place of all, next to the door. Even when the wind screamed with snow, she would still go out after supper for half an hour or more, and come back after all the others had fallen asleep – Ogo would doze off with her place empty, and wake at dawn to her back pressed against his side. But they'd been twenty days on the pass now, and before long would go back to the city; and this was the night he had decided to lie awake till she came in.

A gust of night-wind over his face signalled her entrance, and another breath of air as she flung her cloak down; he felt it settling slowly, half over him, as she pulled her boots off and crawled into the covers. He heard her say, 'Hfaaa! Faaa!', shuddering with the chill. 'Ayndra?' he murmured. She said nothing. He raised himself on one elbow. 'Ayndra?'

He felt her turn over. 'What?' she muttered. 'Bloody cold.'

'It . . . it need not be. Quite so cold.'

'What?'

He rolled towards her, and slipped his arm round her shoulders. She lay still; he felt her muscles tense, but she said nothing. Emboldened, he slid one hand inside her undertunic. To his work-hardened hands, her skin felt like silk. 'Ayndra?' he whispered again. She shifted in his embrace, turned, and was suddenly half on top of him; something warm and sharp pressed into the base of his throat. She whispered in his ear, 'Nobody touches me unless I say so. Nobody.' The blade pushed against his windpipe. 'Now you take your hands off me.'

Ogo pulled his arms away. She sat up, still keeping the knife at his neck. 'Next time I'll not hesitate, so if you wish to die throat-slit in my bed, you know what's to be done . . . recall. I am your second man. And I'm no man's doxy.' The blade jabbed deeper. 'Do you understand it?'

'Yes,' he said, his voice deprived of all sound by the rigid spasm of his throat.

'Good,' she said softly. The blade left his neck, and he felt her lie down again. Her voice said, 'And I sleep lightly. Most of all when I am touched.'

He lay stiff in the dark, listening to her breathing smooth into the regular pattern of sleep; it was a long time before his followed it.

From the records of the clerk to the artillery and Summoner Purmo:

33

1:VII:461 Kolparri proclaimed Archpriest and free to govern as he wishes within the borders of Yiakarak. To preserve the city's liberties, Lord Irailond to assume the office of Protector and commander of our garrison, and counsel the Archpriest on matters affecting the security of the state.

33:VII:461 This day departed from the city of Yiakarak, leaving 300 men to garrison the city and its outlying lands.

36:VII:461 Entering the marches of the kingdom of Haramin. Exceedingly poor roads. Two months it will take, it is said, to the city of Raq'min where lives the king of Haramin.

12:VIII:461 In a region of hills where the snow is thawing. Roads deep in mud. Our wagons travel with great hardship so that we lie two days' journey behind the vanguard of the army. There are no towns in this country, and the peasants exceedingly poor and barbarous.

18:VIII:461 We are told that the hobilars have captured some soldiers of the king of Haramin, who claim that his army is but ten days' journey away from us.

19:VIII:461 The king has ordered a division of the army. Lord Golaron to lead a strong force some three days' march north and occupy the principal road where it passes through hills. Lord Ailixond with the Companions, the Silver Shields and the phalanx to march east. Lord Casik remains with us, guarding the baggage train. It seems that we shall see nothing of the great battle to come. The roads are poor still, and we have lost several wagons axle-broken or bogged in the mud. We move toward the town called Kurs, where King Yourcen of Haraminharn is encamped.

25:VIII:461 We are told that Lord Ailixond is gone fifty miles in two days to meet Lord Golaron, and they move toward the king of Haramin. But we hear little news of what has befallen them.

26:VIII:461 Now it is said that Lord Yourcen is not after all in Kurs, but is gone in pursuit of Lord Ailixond with all his army. Meanwhile we follow the king, but some days behind, it is said to the shores of a great lake which they name Diroga. Much of our guards are gone away to the king's forces, and still we travel heavy and slow. Leader Saripion is much in fear of attack.

28:VIII:461 This day we hear that Lord Yourcen's army has come down across the road, lying between our train and the king. Lord Casik received the king's messenger at midnight, and we are ordered to move now, before the sun is even risen, in two days to meet the king by some route not the road. They say that the lights of the enemy camp at night are brighter and more numerous than the lights of a city. We are all in much fear of attack with our guards most of them gone away.

Purmo beat on the side of the wagon with his staff. 'Up! Up! Move!' he bellowed. 'Lord Ailixond's own orders! Wake up!'

'What? So Lord Ailixond has taken to ordering you in person?'

Purmo recognised the voice of Ogo's peculiar second man. 'No, Master Liz-landra, he does not, but I give orders to you, and I'll have no talking back. Now up with you.'

The other crawled out from under the wagon. 'My name,' she said snappishly, 'is Aleizon Ailix Ayndra.'

'You are all to get up, harness your oxen, and in a half hour when you hear the trumpets we march on.'

'What, now, all in the pitchy dark?'

'On the thirtieth day of this month we are to be by the shores of the Diroga.'

'Know you what that means?'

'The king, and the enemy —'

'I mean, what distance and over what country we must go.'

'It is a long march, Master Liz-landra, and so you must rouse yourselves.'

'I know it to be long! I have travelled in Haramin before, you —'

'Enough of this insolence! Else I will have you reported to the Leader — where is your master? We must face a great battle!'

'O ho! A battle?'

'Yes, master, and we like to lose it! Now, do you get on, I have work to do!' He ran off, and struck the wheels of the next wagon. 'Awake! Awake . . .'

'Devil take him.' Ogo crawled out and stood shaking his sleep-dazed head. 'Devil take all of them.' He shuffled over to the fire, banked with turves from the evening, and peeled one of them upward; a red eye peeped out under it. He picked up a few twigs and started feeding them to it. Under the wagon, the others were stirring: Garget, Varro, Yailen and Gemmat. Since, a halfmonth back, their wagon had tumbled over into a pothole and broken its back axle, they and all their goods had travelled in Ogo's wagon; there was no room to sleep inside it now, they lay all on the cold ground.

Varro sat coughing by the fire. 'What news, then?'

'To go to join the king,' said Ogo.

35

'Forced marches,' said Aleizon Ailix Ayndra, who was standing by the fire hopping from foot to foot, 'all the day, all the night, no resting, two days' journey maybe over poor country – ha! a good thing we've not to fight when we come there. Hehe!'

'You'll not laugh when we see the battle,' said Varro.

'Surely not! I shall be in fear and trembling . . . two days is a little time to go such a distance, for sure . . .'

'How is it that you know so much about it?'

'I have no understanding of where we stand,' complained Yailen. 'For all I know the enemy king may come upon us today – for all the lords know, either . . . all this time wandering through foreign lands and what is it but hardship and cold, hardship and cold, never a roof over our heads . . .'

'O hush!' said Varro irritably, and was started on a coughing fit.

'Up! Up!' Purmo came trotting back up. 'Where is your harness? Go fetch your draught oxen! Up! Move!'

'Devil take him,' said Ogo again.

The wagon rocked and staggered up the slope, as if its motion were invested with the heavy vertiginous poison of lack of sleep, squealing over wet grass to a halt below the hill's crest, where a haggard rider pushed in front of them – the drivers were too dazed to comprehend such a word as 'stop'. Ogo dropped the reins into his lap and slumped over them. 'Where have we come?'

'They're over the hill,' said the rider dully, and pushed off into the gloom, evening come an hour early with the heaviness of the rain.

'What's over the hill?' Ayndra shook Ogo's shoulder. 'Come, let's look at them.'

'Ah! I've not the . . . not the strength to . . . I want to lie down and sleep.'

'No, fifty yards . . . come . . .' She slid to the ground, and tugged the hem of his cloak. He tumbled after her. 'Ah! How can you run . . . witch! sor –'

'Hush!' She whipped off her hat and slapped his face with it. He staggered, but tottered after her to the hill's crest. On the far side lay the slopes down to the narrow plain on the shores of the Little Sea; near at hand, scattered with dim forms of tents, a few fires and torches, riders and footmen moving about; then a stretch of plain, divided by a dark thread that must be a river; then, far away in the rain, a glow of light, a gathering of fireflies, a city of lights – the camp of Haraminharn. Ogo shook his head and

36

groaned faintly; he turned, and stumbled downhill again. She yelled hoarsely, 'Do you not want to survey the battlefield?'

'I care nothing for the battlefield,' he said. The grass under the wagon was long, rank and wet; he heaved himself up on the wheel, and reached in for a swag of greased-wool cloth, used to cover the catapults in the wet; cast it over the ground, half-rolled himself in it, and lay face down. In fifty heartbeats he was snoring. From the driver's seat, Garget watched her dim figure; she stood on the skyline some time, and then came down whistling softly.

'How does it look?' said Varro's voice, in the rear darknesses of the wagon-tilt.

'Poor,' she said, 'o, very poor.'

'For them?'

'There's a great many of them!'

'Will they fight next day?'

'Who knows? They may not. I go to sleep.' She dragged out another length of greased cloth, and curled up in it, hat over her face. Varro coughed again, and clambered out of the wagon to go to the patient oxen and release them from the yoke they still stood under. He glanced at the two sleepers under the wagon. 'Ah!' he said. 'Ogo, do you not think that he has an evil spirit? But are you not bewitched by it too much to see? Ach . . .' He stood wheezing for some moments, 'Ach, this cough! You, have you ill-wished me? For it's sure that I've wished you no evil . . .' He nodded towards one of the still forms.

'There are no spirits,' her voice said. He started. 'No, none at all,' she said. 'The fates we make are all our own. Go you to sleep.'

Varro stood with the yoke in his hands; his skin was cold inside his clothes. It might have been the chill of waking suddenly from a doze out of doors. He said, 'His crew – and mine – are much different since . . . you came.'

'O, I'm sure not! You are well settled in your habits. What difference have I made?'

'Ah,' he said, 'there are . . .' he shook his head. 'I'll not talk to one whose face I can't see!'

'Then have your way. I'll sleep.'

'While you may,' he said, coughing; another night on the wet ground . . . he slapped the oxen to make them move away – they never wandered far – and shuffled down the hill to talk Purmo into letting him shelter in his tent.

It was midday when Ailixond began deployment into line of battle.

The river called Surani divided the plain between the two armies; it was shallow, fast-flowing, fordable all along its length. The Haraminharn had put up wooden palisades where the crossings were easiest. Encamped beyond the river, they straddled the mile-wide stretch between the sea and the hillsides. If they so much as fought Ailixond to a standstill – not even defeated him soundly – the Safeen would be forced into retreat, able only to go deeper into enemy land. The Haraminharn outnumbered them – now that they could all be seen and counted at once – by perhaps a fourth as much again. Lord Casik drew up the wagons of the siege train in a rough crescent, on the first rise at the edge of the plain; from that vantage, the whole was spread out as clear as a diagram. The rain had gone, and left clear air behind it; some light horse of Haramin had crossed the river, and cantered back and forth like idle racers, watching Lord Ailixond's men. Beyond the stream, the enemy footmen were assembling in two vast long blocks, and marching slowly forward: the first block kept their lines dressed, but the second rapidly went ragged and undulating. Archers, their bows like toys with distance, guarded the wings; the cavalry massed at the far right, by the lake.

The Safic infantry also took their places first, the Silver Shields on the right and the phalanx battalions in the front line, the mercenaries and the levies from the conquered territories as a reserve behind. As they began to advance, at an easy pace, the Haraminharn horsemen withdrew to the other side of the river; Lord Ailixond saw them join the force poised to strike at his own left, and sent the Thaless cavalry over to face them, on Lord Golaron's side. He himself took up station with the Companion Cavalry on the right, and the battle-line rolled forward; it was second hour after noon. Within the wagons, which would act as a wall of defence if it came to retreat, the men got out their weapons and put on steel caps and gambesons. Ogo and Aleizon Ailix Ayndra sat on the catapult timbers to watch the spectacle. The feet of armies raised no dust on this damp ground, and the flags and shining weapons were as bright as a mosaic picture.

'Pretty,' said Aleizon Ailix Ayndra.

'Not for long,' said Ogo. 'Look there.'

The soldiers in the middle of the enemy line were crowding to either side, to open a lane for a chariot pulled by four horses; it glittered in the sun, with gilded sides, ridden by a man in gorgeous vestments. The ranks closed around it, as if setting a jewel in dull metal. On the other side, the Safeen had halted just out of

38

bowshot; a rider all in white cut away from the front rank of the Companions, and cantered along the line, white helmet plumes tossing; a ripple of flourished arms and faint cheers followed him. 'There's Lord Ailixond!' said Ogo.

Aleizon Ailix Ayndra drew her sword from its sheath and laid it across her knees; her smile showed her teeth. 'Fa!' said Ogo. 'I'd not wish to be down there. Scared witless for hours and ending with a flesh-rotten wound, or else your leg taken off and a gift of a begging-pitch on some street corner in Safi – a fine fate!' She did not listen to him, she said, 'They're moving!' The war-trumpets howled in concert, and the two armies rolled forward, despatching hissing flights of arrows, some to stud the no-man's-land, others felling the toy figures; but the ranks closed seamlessly where they fell. Light flashed across the right wing of the Safi army as the Companions raised their steel-pointed lances, and the king's white flag went up in the Royal Squadron; the body of two thousand horsemen lengthed their pace from a walk into a trot, a canter, to full gallop – a steel-pointed wedge aimed direct at the Haraminharn, tipped by one white and silver horseman, Ailixond. The hooves of the first horses struck the river's waters in sheets of spray, like glass wings sun-gilt gold; they poured across the shallows and up the bank with hardly a check in pace.

The archers of Haraminharn stood valiantly forth on the bare ground, keeping up their fire as the dreaded Safic horsemen charged down on them; but short bows and light arrows took small toll of armoured men, and they turned and ran for the safety of their own lines, shedding bows and quivers; but the footmen had closed ranks and raised shields to resist the charge, and would not give way to the archers; they were struggling frantically with their own men when the Companions' charge struck home.

Their line buckled like wax under the impact. For moments, the ordered wedges of the cavalry squadrons showed clear as they drove into the ranked infantry, before they disintegrated into a turmoil of groups standing and fighting and retreating, lances stabbing and long swords slashing, iron-shod hooves trampling, all pushing the Haraminharn back onto their own centre.

As the Companions moved, the Silver Shields went with them, at fast march through the knee-deep river and up the sandy bank, to hammer into the collapsing enemy infantry. The battalions of phalanx that were the spine of the Safic army, lowering their twelve-foot pikes into attack position, rolled after them; the line extended diagonally across the field. The Haraminharn cavalry on the far left gathered themselves and launched a charge across the sandbanks of the rivermouth to meet the Thaless horse; vicious fighting followed, the two sides surging back and forth over churned ground. The companies of phalanx nearest them swung to engage with the cavalry to their left, so opening a widening gap between themselves and the battalions struggling through the river where the enemy had put up stakes; it was in clear view of the Haraminharn centre, where Yourcen had put his Household Guard and mercenaries from the south, from lands once free but now vassals of the New Empire; they ran forward into the unprotected sides of the phalanx. Unable to get the long pikes round in time to bear on the enemy, the Safeen were mowed down like corn; the fiercest fighting of the whole battle went over the river shallows, tainting the water with blood as men fell into it and drowned. Away to the right, the Haraminharn left had crumpled before the Companions, who were fighting steadily toward the centre, while the Silver Shields rolled up the remnants of the infantry; when they saw the phalanx embroiled at the river, they swung round and came up on the mercenaries' third side, forcing them onto the defensive; the ragged phalanx began to fight back.

King Yourcen in his chariot and jewelled robes was prominent as a lamp in the dark; his great enemy was only fifty yards away now; the Companions having cut through to the fringe of his bodyguard, he could see the riders' faces. He struck his charioteer on the shoulder; the heavy vehicle slewed round and began to trundle away. Men fell over in haste to get out of its way; the retreat acknowledged defeat: Yourcen had made the rout of his army certain. The infantry who were still struggling against the phalanx, whose sarissas poked through their ranks and spitted men like chickens, saw their figurehead running away, and gave up the unequal battle. What was left of the ranks dissolved, and they fled every man for himself; the cavalry of the right pulled back from the river and galloped after them. The Thalessi pursued them, jubilant; the fleeing footmen were beaten down as often by their own men as by the enemy riders. The rest of the Safeen poured across the river, yelling and brandishing their weapons, running for the enemy camp and the promise of looting. The artillerymen were pounding the sides of wagons and chanting 'Victory! Victory!' A horseman shot past them, yelling 'After them!' Aleizon Ailix Ayndra leapt to her feet and slashed the air with her sword. 'Plunder! Plunder!' she shrieked. 'We have the victory! Destroy them!' In two leaps she was on the ground, and running downhill, with a mile or more to go to the enemy camp.

Ogo snatched up his falchion and ran after her. In a moment the wagons were deserted, all gone to help in the rout. It was the fourth hour of the afternoon.

The Companions returned at seventh hour, with Yourcen's chariot; they had found it miles from the battlefield, standing empty, horses cut loose from the traces and Yourcen's splendid robes draped over the side, their wearer gone without trace. Lord Arpalond drove it now, a makeshift team of two horses drawing it; the rest of the lords clustered around it, light-headed and exultant; they did not care to rob the forsaken camp for discarded knives and bits of clothing. A red-cloaked phalanx officer ran up to them, seeking Lord Ailixond. The king had taken off his helmet and slung it at his knee; above the line of its brim, his forehead was clean, the rest of his face sweaty and black with dirt; his white cloak, piebald with mudsplashes, had had a long strip torn from one side, and his left arm was bound up with it. He was laughing loudly.

'My lord? My lord?'

The king turned, and smiled brilliantly. 'What do you want of me?'

'The mercenaries, lord. They threw down their weapons when the rest ran away — we've at least three hundred of them. What should we do with them, lord?'

Ailixond's eyebrows lifted, further brightening the blue eyes that gleamed in his grimy face: 'Kill them,' he said.

'But, lord, they laid down their arms . . .'

'Kill them.' Ailixond leant over, intense and frightening. 'I care not if they surrendered when they saw that they were like to lose their skins. They are traitors, they rebelled against the New Empire. Therefore they die.' He relented a little: 'Do you find any Haraminharn among them, take them prisoner. But all those that come out of my Empire, they die now.' He opened his eyes very wide, gazing at the phalanx officer, 'You'll see that done?'

The officer was grey-headed; the dirty young man on the tired horse could have been his son. He quailed before him. 'Yes, Lord.'

'Now,' said Ailixond coldly. 'Where are they?' He walked his horse beside the phalanxman, to the huddled mob of mercenaries, standing or sitting inside a ring of phalanx guards. A heap of weapons lay not far from them. Some of them cheered when they saw the king. Ailixond smiled faintly; they cheered more. He said quietly, 'Have the native-born removed. Then line them up with two of our men to each of the traitors . . .' He watched the sorting, and the remaining mercenaries being assigned to pairs of

41

phalanxmen; they went willingly, desirous of gaining favour with their captors. Then he raised his sword, held it a moment, and let it swish down through the air. When the prisoners saw it, some struggled, a few producing hidden weapons, but all of them very soon fell to the ground, like wineskins slowly emptying of dark liquor. He smiled his white smile again and rode away.

Ogo woke to a sheet of torn canvas waving over his face, dazzling the sun in and out of his eyes; he lay for a while before he could recall where he was with sufficient confidence to sit up. The Haraminharn army had left their supplies behind them − bread only a few days off fresh, butter, honey, rough wine in tarred barrels . . . he sat up, groaning with the stiffness of a night spent on bare ground and the pain of cheap wine in his head.

'Not dead, but merely drunken.'

'What?'

'Drunken, I said. You look worse than the dead.'

'O, hush you.' He got to his knees. Aleizon Ailix Ayndra was sitting outside the half-collapsed tent. 'I've seen you with those smokesticks of yours. At least wine's good wholesome stuff.'

'Not the wine which you drank so greedily last evening, if your face is any key to it.'

He snorted, and crawled under the folds of the tent to find a bundle wrapped in fine, if muddy, silk; looking askance at her, he carefully unrolled it. Inside was a gold cup and an embroidered silk purse.

'It's all there,' she said. 'Besides, the cup's only gilt bronze.'

'An it please you, Master Ayndra, I would not have you poking among my possessions while I sleep,' said Ogo stiffly. He picked up the cup and examined it. 'Only gilt, you say.'

'Yes. See where the base has been scratched − but you'll most likely find some ass who'll take it for gold, if you don't make the price too high.'

'Ay well.' He got to his feet. 'What have you there?' She sat on one bulging sack, and was holding on to another. He untied the neck of it, and plunged his hand in; but felt only something resembling sand. He pulled out a handful of coarse yellow powder. 'What's this?'

'They dig it from the ground in S'Thurrulass,' she said, 'where they name it sulphur.'

'What use has it?'

'In Raq'min they burn it to the gods . . . I think their gods have weak noses.'

42

'Is that what you will do with it?'

'O, it has other uses.' She had put the sacks in a rough wooden box, with a string at one end, by means of which she towed them across the grass. The plain of battle was darkened by the smoke from the pyres by the lake where they were burning the dead of Safi; men were already at work digging pits to receive the enemy dead. Three or four ox-carts moved across the field of combat, putting an end to dying men who were too weak to be saved, stripping the bodies – if they were not Safeen – of clothes and valuables, and tumbling them into the wagon to be taken to burial. The Safeen were more respectfully treated. Camp-women also wandered among the corpses; they were said to be most vicious of all in the deaths they meted out to the men they robbed, and even more vicious when they did not bother to kill, only to incapacitate. Some of them as they worked were singing.

> 'Kissed he me a thousandfold –
> See! my red lips are not yet cold . . .'

The city of Raq'min lay in the angle between two rivers, in the midst of soft green limestone hills, whose grass fed the sheep whose wool founded the wealth of the city; ranks upon ranks of thatched and tiled roofs marched up behind the massive walls, to the whitewashed fortifications of the citadel, the palace and the nation's heart, White Walls. No enemy had ever taken Raq'min. After his shame at the river Surani, Yourcen had fled there directly, and shut the gates. The land he left open to the Safeen. It was fortunate for his people that Lord Ailixond came to rule, not to ravage; only his quartermasters were allowed to take anything, and some of their seizures they even paid for; there was no plundering. But he who had been called the Sacker of Cities could not resist the prize of Raq'min; there could be no doubt but that the Grand Army would sit down before the walls for months, and, long before they had starved the city into submission, Yourcen would have summoned the northern provinces to his defence. On the twentieth day of Ninth Month, the vanguard of the army advanced to the stone bridge over the river Shar; by the twenty-second day, the siege lines were established.

The circuit of the walls measured more than five miles, too long to ring it all round; the siege artillery were placed opposite the gates and their flanking towers, the weakest points, and vulnerable protruding angles of wall, while the main camp was at the north foot of the city, where the main road ran up to it.

Masters Ogo and Varro were sent to the west side, against the Blue Gate, where the waters of the Shar, still running high with spring, flowed right beneath the walls. The brown and white stones, mottled and patched and weed-green at the foot, rose sheer out of the river, their reflections streaming and blurring over its surface. The Blue Gate showed a blank face to the world; heavy doors of black metal, scratched and rust-streaked, locked and triple-barred on the inside. The first span of a stone bridge extended over the stream, ending in broken blocks; another damaged arch stood on the near bank, and between them the Shar flowed round broken pillars. The middle of the bridge had been timber, which had been burnt and the supports smashed before the approach of the enemy. The bridge to the north, by the Dinarn gate, had also been ruined; the third gate, the East Gate, faced on to land. The catapults were set up on the far side of the river, and sighted on the towers, the most vulnerable part. There was plenty of rough stone for the taking in the hills; all day long, the air resounded with the groans and thumps of machines firing, crashes as missiles struck home and founting splashes as they fell short; a strangely pleasant symphony in mild summer weather.

After twelve days' bombardment, the masonry was crumbling, and the gate entrance was piled with rubble. 'Surely it cannot take long!' said Aleizon Ailix Ayndra.

'It will take two months at the least,' said Ogo. 'I proclaim the noon rest.' It had turned suddenly hot, and the men worked in undertunics, or stripped to the waist, all except Aleizon Ailix Ayndra, who forsook neither overtunic nor black hat. Now they squatted in the shade of the machine, and Ogo got out a leather flask. 'So long?' she said.

'O aye. We'd have to raze half the walls of the town before they'd show us white banners.'

'But as we go, in a month there'll be little enough left of that gate.'

'O, most likely. But if your men'll fight, you can hold a rubble-heap as well as a high-standing wall. Stonebreaking as we do now is to teach them the folly of resistance, not to knock down the walls. But I think this lot'll not submit until their walls are knocked down . . . two months, or three.'

'Ha . . . can you lend me a sol?'

'A sol? Milk of Heaven! Do you never leave off borrowing money? You must owe me ten sols now.'

'Seven and a half.'

'And four sols four samisols and three quarits to me,' put in Garget.

44

'O, give me a sol.'

'Tell me what you do with these monies!'

'I must buy a pestle and mortar – and a sack of charcoal – and some cheap dishes.'

'O yes? What purpose will they serve? Will you start a cookshop?'

'No, I shall not . . . I shall rest now . . .' She pulled her hat over her face. Ogo shook his head. Garget spat. Purmo came up to them. 'Hola! On your feet! Put your backs into it, else we'll all be here next year!'

'Devil take you,' said Ogo. He took a pull from his flask. 'To work,' he said, 'but we need not hurry.'

The catapults fell quiet every evening at sixth hour, and the men were free to go where they would. They had no guard duties in this siege; the army had swollen to a point where there were guards enough for all. Aleizon Ailix Ayndra sat talking to Ogo, while he drank from his flask, until she had talked a sol out of his purse and into her hands, and then disappeared down toward the market at the Stone Bridge, not to come back when they were gone to sleep; in the morning, when Ogo woke, he saw only Garget lying near him. It was quiet outside, untainted by the day's activities as yet; a high pure voice was singing:

> 'O welcome morning!
> O welcome new day!
> Who knows what fortune
> May yet come my way . . .'

Outside in the clear low sunlight, Aleizon Ailix Ayndra was kneeling by the ashes of Varro's fire of last night, scooping up white and black flakes. 'That's a fine voice you have,' he said. 'Though not much suited to a second man . . .'

'O, did you not know? I sing counter-tenor. But many misunderstand when they hear me, forcing me to prove my manhood by violent means, so ordinarily I keep silent,' she said laughing. 'I need a good deal more ash than this. I shall have to go round all the fires.'

'You'll be called a sorcerer,' he said.

'Will I? But that's not the worst. I must go to the stables and dig out the earth from below a midden there.'

'Indeed? Whatever for?'

'For . . . I cannot say clearly in Safic; I think there are only

45

words in S'Thurrulan ... I have to make a, a powder from ashes and the midden-earth, and powdered charcoal and sulphur mixed with it, and then ... then you'll see something the like of which you've not seen before!'

'And what is that?'

'I suppose in Safic it would be named powderfire.'

'But what purpose does it serve?'

'In S'Thurrulass, very little save the astonishment of children and fools ... I shall see what I do with it. But question me no more. In S'Thurrulass the communication of the recipe to others not of that land is a treasonable act.'

'Indeed?' said Ogo. But then he heard Varro coughing as he woke up. Ayndra leapt up and returned to their own fireplace, refusing to speak more.

The ten stone-throwing catapults opposing the Blue Gate had the range to a yard; the steady battering scarred the walls, but wrapped the men who served the machines in a stupefying tedium of load and fire and load and fire. Occasionally the bolt-throwing catapults let fly a skein of iron darts to keep the walls clear of enemy archers, but the hiss of a few dozen black arrows across the sky was scarcely a ripple on the lake of dust and sweat, buzzing with insects and the growing stench of the rubbish that collected around the camp; and up here on the hill it was sweeter than by the Stone Bridge. In the long blue evenings of Ninth Month, they lit fires to keep away the midges and sat in the eye-watering smoke watching the sun fade from the yellow walls of Raq'min and the dusk roll over the ranks of roofs.

'By year's end we'll have cast so much at that place that we'll be able to walk across the water dryshod.'

'Aye, and see them down the hill get to work at last ... we sweat all day, and when I've been down there you see 'em sitting polishing their swords ... and by night they're with the women – you know Valsta? With a cavalryman ... too damn tired to ...'

'And what's with your second man? ... all the campfires ... boils it up with mud and water ...'

'Dam'me if I know!'

'Would'a used the cookpot if I'd not got it off him.'

'Always a little touched, I thought he was – you should not have set him over Garget like that.'

'Garget a lazy good-for-nothing.'

'I do not doubt it wi'another put over him like that – he should be second if you'd still have that Aleizon with you.'

'You say so? I'll thank you not to say so to him! I'd not

presume to tell you what you should do with Gemmat drunk three nights in five!'

'Would you not? Yet you've put a pretty-boy over a man who's older in years and been long in the army – what do you think of?'

'Saripion ordered it –'

'Since when have you slaved after Saripion?'

'I'll thank you not to –'

'Quiet there!'

'Damn you –'

'Here he comes now.'

'Then act your place!'

'What do you call me? Do you say that I –'

'Son of a whore! Why do you persist in a quarrel each time we speak?'

'I? Persist in a quarrel? Damn you! You began it, saying my second man's a drunkard!'

'I began? You ponce's get! –!'

'Hush you! Hush you! Master! We'll have no blows here!'

Aleizon Ailix Ayndra came back when Garget was, officiously, cleaning Ogo's bleeding brow with a pad dipped in wine. She squatted across from him in silence for some time, then said, 'I dislike hot weather.' He grunted. 'It makes men short-tempered,' she said, very straight. Garget looked at her; she ignored him, sat staring at the fire a while longer, then got up and left again. Garget spat on the ground, and made a last, painful poke into Ogo's wound. Ogo tensed, but restrained his arm.

Aleizon Ailix Ayndra decanted the hot liquor from the cauldron, where she had boiled a mixture of wood-ash and the limey soil excavated from beneath a manure-heap, strained it through a coarse cloth into flat clay dishes and left it out where it would catch the sun and dry, leaving a crust of crystals which she scraped up and stored. And while the mixture boiled, she sat patiently grinding first charcoal and then sulphur in a mortar; and all this in between carrying stones, fetching water, greasing the engine's turning joints, receiving occasional instruction in how to aim and adjust it, and cooking meals with too much spice in them. The sunny weather disappeared; in its place came a season of downpours, turning the worn grassy path downhill to the Stone Bridge into a morass of mud. Ayndra put away the dishes and measured out the powders: five parts charcoal, five of sulphur, seven of the crystals *kaienno*. She obtained some flimsy wooden boxes and a great length of taper, and filled the boxes with the mixed powder, sealed each one with a length of taper pushed

47

through a small hole so that part of its length was inside the box and part outside – the box being lined with a closely woven cloth to stop it leaking – and stored them, completed, in the driest part of the wagon; until the twenty-eighth day of Tenth Month, when it seemed that the time had come.

By noon, the sun had come up, making the damp ground steam in the heat. Aleizon Ailix Ayndra picked a way across the rutted mud around the machine and put one of her boxes in the spoon. It looked foolishly small after the rough boulders that were the usual load. 'We shall fire this next.' She touched the burning taper in her other hand to the end of the box's wick. 'A shorter range, it's very light.'

'What is it?' said Ogo.

'The new weapon, powderfire.'

'So what does it do?' He started to reduce the tension in the ropes.

'Quick, quick, I don't want it going up here!'

'All right, all right . . . let it go now!'

The little box sailed up into the heavens, and arced down, landing among the rubble heaps in the mouth of the Blue Gate. 'So what does it do?' Garget said, and then there was a boom like a thunderclap and a cloud of smoke and fragments bloomed under the arch of the gate. Ayndra yelped in triumph; the others jumped in fright. 'It works! It goes!'

'What is it? It's witchcraft!'

'Another one!' Ayndra ran back to the wagon. Varro came up; others further away were turning towards them. 'What was it? What?'

'It was his makings,' Ogo said, 'the thing called powderfire.'

'I knew it was he! But what –'

'Another! Another!' called Ayndra, emerging with three boxes in her arms. 'I swear it's a vile sorcery,' said Garget.

'But what are they?'

'Let me see them,' said Varro.

'You'll see it in the air. Let me by.'

'I wish to know,' Ogo began, 'what it is – before –'

'A fine day to choose!'

'Let me by with it.'

'How are they made? What's in there?'

'Is that a taper?'

'No, let me put it on – then you –'

'How did you make that thunderclap? It was as if a lightning bolt struck without light!'

48

'Why a fine day?'

'Saripion and a party of lords come to inspect.'

'Ay! You've blown out my taper.'

'Do you need a lit one? Our fire –'

'Put it to the end there.'

'What? Inspect us?'

'Maybe even the king.'

'What to inspect for?'

'I thank you. Be ready to let it go when I say.'

'O, I know not – what do they see but a row of false faces, to be sure? I'd not dare speak my mind on all this with the king there.'

'It's burning!'

'Yes . . . wait now . . . Go!'

'That's they, there.'

'What? Shumar! And you chose this day for your nonsense!'

'What?'

'Look there! The lords and the king!'

'What? O, look –' Aleizon Ailix Ayndra did not follow Ogo's finger, pointing to the procession coming up the muddy path, bright blues and reds and greens of expensive dyed clothes at the head and one white-clad figure among them; her eyes tracked the thunderbolt box in the heavens. Ogo seized her shoulders. 'Look you!' he snarled. 'Never again –' and a roar and a blast swept over them. The air filled with bitter smoke; Ayndra jerked free of his hands. They lay trembling in the mud.

'God damn it!' she said as soon as she could speak. 'A fuse too short.'

Ogo got to his knees. 'You're more of a danger than the enemy! Will you kill me? Or have me sent to the pits for treason – if I'm not blown into the next world? And after I allowed – O, I –' He grabbed hold of her and shook her. She exclaimed, 'Don't touch me!' so viciously that he let go of her. They crouched, drawing breath for the next round. Garget had been further back; the crowd had scattered as rapidly as it had swelled. 'They come over here!' The royal party were only a couple of hundred yards away. Garget scuttled up and poked his head between them. 'What? What to do?' he squealed.

'They, if they saw it –'

'They'd be deaf, blind and stupid an they did not!' Ayndra snatched her hat – upside-down in a rut – and jammed it back on her head. Varro was hastening back to his own catapult, where Gemmat and Yailen stood gawping, calling 'To work! To work!'

Ogo said, 'To work. Yes . . . stand up . . .' but then the party of

49

lords and officers turned from the path to come straight toward them. The three stood up straight and rigid, and stayed so.

At Lord Ailixond's right, Leader Saripion, fawning on his every word; to his left, Leader Pardic, and behind, Lord Golaron, Lord Arpalond, half a dozen high officers, Purmo, the quartermaster, clerks, attendants, and numerous other assistants, summoners, place-seekers, and sycophants. Ailixond turned to Saripion. 'This is the one,' he said.

Saripion was clearly in a quandary of responsibility; the king was most polite and noncommittal. The Leader tried to strike a balance. 'As ever, my lord, you speak correctly – if I may – Master Ogo? The catapultmaster, my lord.' He swept out his hand.

Ogo made a clumsy bow. 'Ah, my lord, ah . . .'

'O, stand up. I've not come to hear you stammer honorifics, I've come to watch my artillery. What have you to show us? I've seen a smoke like thunder in the air – what have you done here?'

Ogo managed to point behind him. 'My lord, my, my second man –'

'My lord. Master Aleizon Ailix Ayndra.' She bowed, shading her face with her hat. 'You wish for an account of the mode of operation?'

'If you can give it,' said the king. He stood easily in the centre of the group, arms folded; he was shorter than most of the men around him, with a heavy wing of dark hair falling across his face. His eyes gazed lazily underneath it.

'The box is lined with cloth and stuffed with powderfire, which has the curious property that, when it's touched by a spark or a flame, it ignites as you've seen, with a great noise and tremendous force – the more effective when it's contained before the light is put to it, as you see here. I set light to the taper, and then we fire it in the manner of any other projectile.'

Ailixond walked up to the catapult. His retinue flowed after him and gathered round it. 'What stuff is powderfire? Sorcery I do not believe.'

'A mixture of – various substances. They make it in S'Thurrulass.'

'And they use it in war?'

'I've never heard of it. They use it to make bangs, and showers of coloured sparks in the night.'

'So what is this – you devised these fireboxes?' Ailixond got up on the frame of the catapult, gaining the advantage of its height. 'Let me see another one – how many of them have you?'

'O, a few dozen.'

'And they're easily made? Who assisted you?'

'No one. It's lengthy, but not so hard to make them. If many were set at it . . .'

'One could make a large number in a short time? But let me see one fired again.'

Ayndra put a box in the spoon, held down for her by several willing hands. Someone else helpfully put a light to it. Ailixond stood on the catapult, head tilted back, surveying the scene. 'My lord,' she said.

'Never let all these people disturb you,' he said. 'Do as you would if we were not here.'

'It's not possible,' she said.

'Why not?'

'If you will stand on the machine, my lord, we cannot fire it.'

Ogo, at the back of the group now, turned up his eyes to heaven. The faces turned to Ailixond like flowers waiting for the sun to signal blooming time. He overlooked them, blinking slowly; his eyelashes were as long as a girl's. Then he smiled fractionally. 'I am most sorry.' He jumped down beside Aleizon Ailix Ayndra. 'Move back!' he said to his people. The taper was sputtering close to the wood now. Ayndra leapt forward and released it. The machine crashed, it sprang into the air; she screwed up her face to follow it, then seized Lord Ailixond's arm, cried 'Get down!' and cast herself, pulling him with her, to the ground. Ogo's knees delivered him to the earth. The more determined sycophants imitated the king. Some two dozen pairs of eyes tracked the box down the sky. It flew, intact, over the walls and landed on the thatched roof of a large building. Ailixond shook Ayndra's hand from his arm and started to get up, attendants following; then there was a roar, distant but still such that several of them threw themselves down again. Smoke billowed up, lumps of thatch and roof-struts flew through the air; as the wind took away the smut, flames licked up round the blackened hole in the roof. The other catapults had stopped firing, their crews watching the spectacle; in the peace, an alarm bell in the city began to toll.

Ailixond got slowly to his feet. The snowy cloth of his overtunic and breeches was stained with grass and mud. The others stood there waiting. He amused himself picking a few stalks from his sleeve, then addressed them generally. 'A most interesting discovery,' he said. 'When time permits, we shall study it further. It reflects credit upon the catapultmaster and upon Leader Saripion, although while we conduct our studies I suggest that

51

they return to more traditional forms of ammunition. Meanwhile, Master Aleizon . . .' he turned to face her; their eyes were exactly level. She looked straight at him, and met a bright blue direct gaze. 'No one knocks Lord Ailixond to the ground and escapes with nothing,' he said. Her face froze but she did not lower her glance. 'Accompany me,' he said.

'Willingly, my lord.'

'Excellent,' he said. 'My lords, gentlemen. Recommence firing at the battery. Leader Saripion, we shall walk round among the rest of the machines and return to the camp. Master Aleizon, collect what you deem necessary and return to the camp with us. Catapultmaster, I thank you for your services.' He nodded to Ogo as he tried again to bow, and strode away. His retinue fell in behind him, establishing precedence again.

'O sweet Luamis! O Takar save me! O heaven! Shumar! God!' said Ogo, standing still where he had been when Saripion first pointed him out. Aleizon Ailix Ayndra ran to the wagon and got out her black cloak and a few other items tied up in a square of cloth. 'Goodbye, friends!' she said. Ogo shook his head. 'What have you done?' he said at last.

'Who knows?' She tossed her cloak over one shoulder, put her hands either side of his head and kissed him full on the mouth.

He was dumbstruck; he passed his hand across his mouth and looked at it, as if there would be some visible scar. She laughed. 'You should never wash again!' And ran off to join the tail of the procession.

'You'll be beheaded for a sodomite!' Garget exclaimed.

Ogo walked back to the wagon and sat down. 'I shall be cashiered for keeping a woman in the camp as well as trying to kill the king,' he said. 'God help me.'

'What?' said Garget.

'God help us everyone,' said Ogo. 'When I first found her out . . . I should have said to her then . . .' Garget was too amazed to speak. The other catapults were firing at a furious rate, filling the air with the groans of machinery. Garget said, 'And how long did you keep her to yourself? How long? No wonder, that you favoured him – that you favoured her –'

'What? O, no,' Ogo shook his head. 'I think she goes with women,' he said. Garget was choked with fury and disgust. He spun round and headed away to Varro's machine. Ogo crawled inside the wagon and pulled a blanket over his head.

When the procession reached the royal tent, it had shrunk to Lord

Ailixond, Lord Arpalond, Leaders Saripion and Pardic, and, ten yards behind them, Aleizon Ailix Ayndra. The king said a few words to Saripion and Pardic, sent them away with Lord Arpalond, and disappeared within; but before the door-flap fell, a voice said, 'Await me, Master Aleizon.' So she stood by the door, and waited, and waited and waited. Some of the passers-by stared at her, but none found her odd enough to question her. She squatted on her heels with her back to the tent and tipped her hat over her eyes. About fifth hour it began to rain. Water slid down the canvas and poured from the scalloped edges of the roof; it dripped off her hat and soaked the shoulders of her cloak. She endured it for almost an hour, but then got up; there were no guards in the vestibule. She lifted the door-curtain. It was dim inside, though there were lights and voices further in. She sat down again in the gloomiest corner, covered her face and fell into a doze.

'Hoy! Wake up! Ye cannot sleep here! – out! This is no vagabonds' house!'

She sat up. An armed man leant over her.

'I am not sleeping. I wait to see the king.'

'The king sees no vagabonds. Up! Out with ye!'

'I am no vagabond. I am Master Aleizon Ailix Ayndra, artilleryman of the second class, and Lord Ailixond has told me to wait for him here.'

'Indeed?'

'Indeed! He told me so himself.'

'Ha . . . come here.' He led her up to the curtain dividing the inner tent from the public room, and left her to wait again. She heard voices – 'His name? A right odd name – Aliz Alizinder, or some such . . . artillery . . . I'll call Firumin.'

Footsteps; other voices too far to overhear; more footsteps:

'Did he say his name was Aleizon Ailix Ayndra?'

'That was it.'

'Ai! You heard that the king went to the battery at Blue Gate this noon?'

'Aye.'

'This one that's waiting threw him over in the mud.'

'Threw the king?'

'Aye! They were watching a catapult. And some piece of sorcery, this man had made it – Firumin says to bring him in.'

The guard emerged from behind the curtain. 'Follow,' he said officiously. Through that curtain, to a long canvas-walled room, a table at the far end of it where a small soft man sat writing with a sheaf of papers before him. 'Master Aleizon Ailix Ayndra? I am Master Firumin, Steward of the Royal Household. You will please to follow me,' he said, standing. Ayndra draped her cloak over one arm while he peered between another pair of curtains. 'My lord? – go in, Master Aleizon, my lord awaits you.' The guard and a liveried servingman nudged up behind her as she walked in, swept off her hat and bowed. 'My lord . . .'

The first thing to come to a lowered gaze was a broad plain desk of polished pale wood, littered with book-rolls, pots of quills, penknives, inkwells, sand, letters and sheets of fresh paper. Two men were behind it, one standing and one seated. The scarlet tunic and sky-blue breeches of the one standing flamed against the neutral canvas; his blond hair was beginning to recede, but he had a charming smile. Ailixond was sitting in a folding chair, sliding a goose-quill idly between his hands. He laid it down as he looked up at her, and pushed his thick fringe back from his face. There was a white scar from a sword-cut on one cheek. His eyes were extraordinary. 'Well, Master Aleizon –'

'Ayndra, an it please you, lord,' said the – as it seemed – grimy-faced youth; waving rough-cut hair that would have been blond if it had not been dark with grease, a sallow skin, thin-lipped red mouth and strong features marred by an overlong nose. Ill-fitting overtunic and baggy breeches made her body shapeless to view. 'Ayndra, then,' he said. 'What have you to say for yourself? Explain, and if you think fit, excuse your actions of this noontime. And why you saw fit to interrupt me so rapidly.'

She took a deep breath. 'In the first place, my lord, I acted out of concern for you. It might have been that the firebox went off too soon – too close – and it's safe on the ground. And as for interrupting, my lord, no one calls me Aleizon, not no – not ever.'

The subsequent pause seemed to stretch out. She caught her lower lip in her teeth. Ailixond suddenly leaned forward, put his quill pen back in the inkwell. 'A fair answer. From this day on, you will be Captain, and Royal Advisor on matters concerning the artillery – for a period of two months, after which time, if you have shown yourself suitable for that position, I will confirm you in it.'

Ayndra's mask cracked. She said 'O what?' and her mouth opened wide in a laugh. 'How should I – I thank you, my lord – if I –'

'Thanks are not necessary. You have only to act, and I'll see what ensues – call Firumin,' he said to Polem, who went slowly to the door. 'Firumin!' he bellowed.

The steward bounded in, looking somewhat rattled, as if he had been far too close to need shouting for. 'Yes, lord?'

'Since I have just raised Master Ayndra to the rank of captain, he –'

'– she –'

'–'ll require the trappings of the rank. So if you would accompany him –'

'– her –'

'– to the Treasury, and take out an advance on his –'

'– her –'

'– next month's pay, I'll write out a note of –' he stopped, and looked at Ayndra. 'Her?'

'Yes,' she said.

'Is that – do you have a wife? If so –'

'No, I've no wife.'

'?'

'Myself,' she said.

'What?' said Ailixond.

'Do you mean to say,' said Polem, 'that you're a woman?'

She nodded.

'O! O! What?' exclaimed Polem. Ailixond stood up. 'Master – Mistress Ayndra – if you . . . I cannot have a woman in my army!'

'You mean to say "I think I should not have a woman in my army." That you *can*, I stand here proof. Perhaps there are more.'

'What? – does Saripion know of this? Pardic?'

'No one . . . except my catapultmaster.'

'You don't look like a woman,' said Polem.

'I look like a soldier,' she said, 'which is what I am.'

Ailixond looked hard at her. She met his eyes with a wide direct gaze. He raised his eyebrows a little, and then nodded. 'Your insolence is refreshing,' he said. 'But I advise you to keep a check on it in the future. You've two months to prove yourself. Now take this, and go with Firumin.' He scrawled a few lines on a scrap of paper, finished with an enormous flourishing signature. 'This for the Treasury clerks. Attend the meeting of the Outer Council at eighth hour of morning tomorrow. Firumin will give you a bed for the night.' He pushed the paper across the desk to her, and extended his left hand. On the middle finger he wore an immense uncut diamond set in gold; the Royal Ring of Safi, more essential sign of sovereignty than the crown. She took his fingertips and bent to brush the stone with her lips. 'Good day, Captain,' he said, 'and good fortune.'

55

'Good day, my lord, and thank you.' She walked radiant out of the room.

'Hooo!' said Polem, sitting down on the edge of the desk. Ailixond dropped back into his chair and threw his arms wide, arching his back. 'Something new,' he said.

'What did she do this noontime?'

'You remember, I decided to go up and view the artillery – Leader Saripion – do you know him? A bootlicker of the most determined kind – tried to pretend that he knew all about these fireboxes – one of the catapults was firing off little boxes that disappeared in a thunderclap and a great cloud of smoke, and fire – when it was clear that he knew less than I did. He handed it to the catapultmaster, who was too dazed by the presence of so much nobility to be able to speak, and then comes this – I thought – beardless boy, who speaks like a Great Market sophist and it seems is the only one who knows anything of what goes on. Then I displayed my ignorance by getting up on the catapult, and only she dares tell me to get down, and then cast me down in the mud for fear that the box would blow us both to pieces . . . I thought then, an unusual soldier.'

'But not as unusual as she turned out! – how did she ever come to be in the army?'

'By passing herself off as a boy, I don't doubt. It's happened in the past, from time to time . . . if she doesn't suit the rank of captain, I may set her Leader of the artillery in place of Saripion – that man, did I proclaim the sky green, he'd swear he saw emerald clouds in it.'

'But a woman! How will the men ever obey her?'

'Because I have made her captain, and if I make a woman captain, then captain she will be. I am the king.'

Polem shrugged. 'You are the king.'

'Give me that paper. I shall write out her commission.'

'No! Let the secretaries do it.'

'They take too long. There's a copy in the document chest. Give it here.'

'Pha! I'm a lord of Safi, I'm not an errand boy . . . the secretaries should do this also . . .'

'O, hush. Thank you.'

The Outer Council, the assembly of the officers and lords of the army, met in the public chamber of the king's tent; a table for the recording clerks and documents, chairs for the nobles, and facing them, rows of benches for the commoners. The lords Polem and

Lakkannar were already there; they watched the slaves arranging the seats, and the rest of the council filing in.

'What's this rumour that some woman's been made a captain?' said Lakkannar. 'Surely it's not true.'

'O no! As I stand here, I saw it done,' said Polem. 'Did you not hear that he was thrown in the mud by some commoner up at the Blue Gate catapults, when he went out to see them? And gets them down here and gets insults to boot, and then it turns out it's a woman and still he makes her captain – I was there.'

'Indeed? What sort of woman is she?'

'Walks like a man, dresses like a man . . . she'll be in here before long . . . I'm sure she'll not last five months, if she's not dead of camp-fever, or exhausted, or killed in her first little skirmish, she'll be with child and packed off to Safi to bear her bastard – there she is.'

'What, that one with the hat?' Lakkannar whistled. 'No beauty she! You don't think . . . he wants to bed her?'

'Ailixond? O, not in a thousand years . . .'

'Call her over. Let's see her close.'

'Captain Ayndra!' Polem gestured to her. She put her head up, but came no nearer. 'My lord?'

'Come over here.'

She stepped over the benches. Lakkannar stood up. 'I believe we've not met before, Mistress –'

'Aleizon Ailix Ayndra – if you would prefer to call me sir, my lord.'

'O, excuse me. I don't recall . . . of course, you are new to this rank . . .'

'We have met, my lord, but you would not remember.' She was watching a group of clerks, who were bent over a large, ornately sealed piece of foreign script. 'That's Haraminharn writing,' she said.

'I am sure I would,' said Lakkannar.

'O no you would not, my lord.'

'How do you know that I would not?'

'Because when we did, my lord, you almost rode me down. I was fording the river in Yiakarak and you rode the other way.'

'My apologies, I am sure!' exclaimed Lakkannar.

'Not at all, my lord.'

'What's Haraminharn script?' said Polem.

'That letter they have there . . . it's got the royal seal, too . . .'

'Indeed? – well, Captain Aleizon Ailix Ayndra, how do you like your new rank?'

'Well enough, my lord Polem.'

57

'O! You know me already, then.'

'I know what they say of you – my lord. But I should go and –'

'No, no! What do they say?'

'O, not a thing, my lord, merely that you're a great lord and a friend of . . . of the king, and a great many women.'

'Yes?' said Polem, interested. Ayndra was emboldened by his response. 'Yes. They say that you've known more maidens than Lord Ailixond's conquered leagues of land, and as for those who were not maidens, the sands of the sea . . .'

'O?' Polem stared at her.

'I must go, my lords.' She bowed, and dashed to a place at the end of a crowded bench. Lakkannar snorted. 'So this is the king's latest folly,' he said. 'She'll trip over her own tongue before she trips over anything bigger, I swear.'

'Do they really say that about me?' said Polem.

'They say much worse than that! I've heard it said that –'

A guard's pike thumped three times, the inner curtains parted and Ailixond strode in. 'Good day, my lords, gentlemen – are all here? We have some important business before we come to matters of every day.' He scanned four or five score officers, and eighteen lords. 'Excellent! Now yesternight I received, very late, a party of envoys from the city, come bearing a letter from King Yourcen.' He snapped his fingers at the clerks, who held up the text for display. 'He asks for an answer within two days. I have not yet considered in full what we should do. I would that you listened to his words first.' He snapped his fingers again; one clerk began to read from another scroll.

'The Most August Lord Yourcen, son of Yourcen, King of Haramin, Overlord of the North, the Puissant, the Valiant, the Ever-Victorious, Lord of the Seaward Plains and Dominant of the Mountains, greets his enemy, Lord Ailixond, son of Parakison, King of Safi.

'Be it known that you invaded our land of Haramin, which had offered you no provocation, and seized our towns, our crops, our people and our beasts of the field, even unto the gates of our city Raq'min. Be it known further that the people of Haramin have no quarrel with the people of Safi and wish no more than to live in peace under their own lords, nor will they submit to the tyranny of a foreign overlord imposed by force of arms. Accordingly, we make this offer to the men of Safi: take down your tents and return beyond the borders of Haramin, and you will meet with no resistance, nor will we harass you as you march through our land. And so long as you remain within the bounds of what is yours, we shall not trespass into your lands, and our peoples may remain forever at peace with one another. But if you do not accept this, and persist in sieging Raq'min, be it known that Raq'min has fallen to no invader, and the swords of our friends are sharpening in the mountains of the North. An you will stay before our gates, they will fall upon you, and harass you each step of the way as you retreat to your own lands. Nor will your land and people be safe from our armies, and if you keep any part of the earth of Haramin, it will be the five feet of clay that you are laid in.

'We await your answer.'

'Is is true, the army in the North?' said someone.

'It seems so,' said Ailixond. 'Our scouts have not progressed deep into the mountains, but sound rumours tell us that they are preparing to attempt the relief of Raq'min, although it is not likely that they will come until the hay-harvest is in, that is, in Second Month or later. With so long to assemble, also, the force may be very large, although one cannot tell how many of Haramin's provinces will wish to aid the king, or how many will stand back hoping that he and I will exhaust one another and leave them with no overlord at all.'

'It seems a poor return to us for relieving him,' Lord Sulakon said.

Lord Daiaron stood up. 'Perhaps so – but what return may we expect from this siege in any case? Already we have sat here for months. We may sit here for months more. Even if no army descends from the north and we are crushed between the enemy without and the enemy within, we will without doubt lose many men in the capture of the city. And we cannot hold the city unless we go on to subdue the north, a task which will take us years. Yet we have already been eight years away from our homes. I suggest that we send to Yourcen demanding some better return than free passage – some payment from his treasury, to defray the vast cost of this siege, at least! – in return for our departure, and return to the south. What benefit has the ever-grosser distension of the New Empire for our own home of Safi? Leave the barbarian territories to themselves. I am for home.'

'Payment? Shame on you!' exclaimed Sulakon. 'Are we a pack of mercenaries, to be satisfied by a few brass coins?'

'Make we an escalade, we will not have to fight hard,' said Lakkannar. 'We saw these men at the river Surani – weak as water, and their king an arrant coward.'

'They may not be so weak when their homes are threatened,' Lord Arpalond said.

'Ah! Still one Safin is worth ten of them.'

'I foresee trouble in the southlands an we accept such easy terms here! How can the Grand Army strike camp merely because some overblown barbarian asks us to?'

'I do not say that,' said Daiaron. 'We should bargain with them – after all, we hold the power. But all the same –'

'It would help an we knew if this army in the north will come – or when it will come, and how many.'

'I do not think he knows more. Swords are sharpening, indeed.'

'How can he? We've let no one out of the city for months.'

'We do not *know* that we've let anyone out.'

'No! Why should we give up? They must be short of food there by now – I say we should escalade, before this army of theirs gets here.'

'Nevertheless, Lord Daiaron – we do not consider only Raq'min. I do not think we could hold Raq'min unless we hold the north, and the north –'

'O, the north will come to us when we have taken their capital!'

As each of the lords or high officers spoke, factions among the mass of offiers spoke up in support of them. Ailixond had said nothing since his introduction; he watched the debate, noting who spoke and what they said, and very occasionally putting in a few words. Now he said, 'Raq'min conquered the north many years ago, but it remains divided into provinces that used to be little kingdoms, all at each others' throats. I am not sure that they will like to send an army to the relief of their overlord. But they will not collapse if he is beaten, nor submit gladly to our yoke – but each alone is small, and not so formidable.'

'A pity we do not know,' said Lord Almarem.

'Ah, no one ever knows,' said Polem, 'all the time we guess.'

'We should demand reward – money, and goods –'

'No! Rewards fit any army of merchants.'

'A shame to bargain at all.'

'We have the power. Yourcen goes in fear of us. It's for him to offer us gifts, offer us his submission.'

'They are too proud for that. We would have to fight hard to crush them – and for what?'

'Haramin is a rich land.'

'We have rich lands already. Let us ask them to come out and debate terms –'

'No! We should assault them as soon as may be.'

The debate was turning into clamour. Two parties were defined: those who wanted to make terms, and leave, led by Lord Daiaron and Lord Almarem; those who wanted to preserve Safic honour – or to garner the profits of conquest rather than agreement – led by Lords Sulakon, Golaron, Lakkannar. Ailixond banged on the table. 'Peace, peace!' he shouted. 'Enough chatter. Either we send to them asking for further parley – and leave off our battering of their walls – or we reject their terms altogether, unless some of you favour accepting what is said here. What says the Council?'

'We've cut them to pieces once – cut them to pieces again!' said Lakkannar. Lord Daiaron rose again and cried, 'Parley with them!' but the acclaim given Lakkannar silenced him. 'Fight! Fight!'

Polem looking at the waving fists, and saw Aleizon Ailix Ayndra standing to one side, saying nothing; she was gazing fixedly forward. He looked where her eyes led, and saw Ailixond, smiling to himself with his eyes very wide open. Polem raised his hands and shouted, 'Peace, peace now! We have your answer.'

The shouting died down; the assembly returned to their seats.

Ailixond said, 'While such men as you follow me / Indeed we'll never defeated be . . . tell me what you think to this.' He picked up a sheet of paper, and made as if to read from it, though he knew the words by heart. 'Ailixond, Most Serene Lord and King of Safi, greets the lord Yourcen. You offer me safety, and peace, if I abandon my siege of your city. Know that I have no need of your safety. Where I go, I impose my own peace. You say that I have invaded your land. It is yours no longer. In your craven flight from the battle at the river Surani, you forfeited all right to speak for the land and its people. Think not to hold Raq'min against me. I reject all safe conducts. And if you seek to address me again, let it be as King of Haramin.' He turned to the crowd again. 'You approve this answer? Speak.'

'Yes! Yes!'

'And you, my lords?'

Some answered loudly; some softly, and some said nothing; Ailixond picked out the hangers-back. 'If you have doubts, speak out now. Letters under royal seal speak for all of us here.'

Almarem looked away. 'I . . . o, send it.'

'Your words are not . . . conciliatory,' said Daiaron, 'my lord.'

'We do not speak of conciliation,' said Ailixond.

'Still, I . . .'

'What would you? The Council has spoken against parleying.'

'Then I suppose I must accept the verdict of the Council.' Daiaron glanced at them through slitted eyes. Ailixond tossed his letter to the clerks. 'See it sealed and sent under flag of truce to the East Gate.' While they were preparing the wax and tying the

61

ribbons round it, he brought up one by one those to speak of the minor, perpetual matters of conducting the siege and maintaining so large an army – supplies, new horses, discipline, reports from Safi and the other provinces of the New Empire – pausing only to stamp the royal seal deep into the pendent cake of wax. When the Council was dismissed, the lords who wished came to add their personal seals round the edges of the letter. Ailixond wished them all good day and went back into his own apartments. Polem wandered idly up to the table and picked up Yourcen's letter. 'Ha! It's all in foreign . . . can't read it. Who rendered it into Safic?' The clerks present shook their heads.

'I can read Haraminharn tongue,' said a voice behind him. He turned; Captain Ayndra was by the door, about to put her hat on. 'Come then, and look at this.'

'You understand, my lord, that, unlike you, I am not altogether at home with the high-flown niceties of stately language.'

'It surprises me that you are familiar with it at all, let alone that you can read it.'

'O, I can blaspheme in five languages and converse courteously in three, my lord.'

'None of which is Safic, it seems! Read it to me.'

'Ha . . . the most, most honourable Lord Yourcen . . . o, much nonsense of that kind . . . Lord Ailixond, having invaded our land despite no given-out cause of war, having taken our towns, having . . .'

'O, leave out all that! Does it say any different?'

'Different from what?' She frowned at the close script.

'O – different from – o, go on and see if it says anything interesting.'

'As you will, my lord . . . babble, babble . . . ha! . . . for sake of peace we will offer of our outer lands the part between Biit-Yiakarak and the Little Sea, easterly bounded by the sea, westerly, the – the name of some place, I do not know it – and in bond of friendship, to wive any you choose of my daughters with dowry of ten thousand poino – that's a silver coin – if you will give up siege . . . the rest, it's as they read out.'

'Sweet Lady Luamis! The crafty –' Polem began, and then recalled that he spoke before commoners. 'I thank you, Captain – you know, of course, that since you've been shown the correspondence of kings you do not speak of it?'

'O, of course,' she said, holding her mouth straight.

'O, yes – you saw that Daiaron and Almarem did not favour the siege . . .'

'Did you favour it, my lord?'

'I? O, Ailixond said we – what? Of course I favoured it! What am I at, saying this to you?'

'I inspire confidences, my lord, and I also keep them.' She cast the letter on the table and slipped out. Polem stood scratching his head. By now the clerks had all packed up and left. Eventually he began to look cheerily purposeful instead of puzzled, and went behind the curtains in search of Ailixond.

'Sir Leader, it's not possible that two men can do the work of three. Since my second man was lost to us, third man and I work as hard as we can, but if I had a new second man –'

'Master Ogo, you will have to work three times as hard if you are to expunge the shame you've brought on us here by the acts of your second man! To allow him to do such a thing to the Most Serene Lord and King? We might all have been given a month's bonus if it had not been for him! You should thank me that you've been spared punishment – and have you any news of him?'

'Gone for good, sir,' said Garget.

'We cannot tell,' said Ogo, 'we hear nothing.'

'I will obtain for you a new man as soon as I can. Until then, I shall not expect your rate of fire to be less than that of any other engine, not if it kills you to make it so.' Saripion departed, nose in air, Purmo scuttling after him. Ogo spat juicily. 'Pfa! A sad day for all of us.'

'It's all the fault of that bitch Ayndra!' exclaimed Garget. 'A woman in the army – it's brought the gods' curse on all of us! The rope on Gottir's machine snapped yesterday. And you – I do not doubt that she made it worth your while to keep her secret, I –'

'I told you!' said Ogo angrily. 'God's teeth! You slept in the same wagon for half a year! If we –'

'So you say! – a woman wearing man's clothes, anyway, no doubt she went after women herself, cursed of the gods . . .'

'O, Mother Maishis! There's an officer coming this way.'

'Ho! No doubt to take us off to the king's prison! I'll tell them that I never took any part in your filthy games!'

'You'll tell them nothing of the sort! You'll stand still and speak when I tell you to!' Ogo cuffed Garget round the head. 'O, faithless bitch!' he said. 'May she eat shit in the next life!'

'So! You curse her! But if I – I'm sure that you –'

'I said, silence!' He hit him again. Garget shut up; his nose started to bleed. He looked at the red-cloaked officer riding

63

toward them. 'Good God,' he said, 'does it not . . .'

'It looks like . . .' said Ogo.

'It is! It is!' squealed Garget. 'It's that damn whore all got up like a lord!'

Aleizon Ailix Ayndra wheeled wide round the catapult and pulled up in a swirl of scarlet. 'Catapultmaster Ogo!'

'You!' said Ogo weakly.

'Captain Aleizon Ailix Ayndra, if you please – Royal Advisor on matters concerning the artillery.'

'What? How on earth –?' said Ogo. Garget stood with his mouth open and an expression of outrage on his face.

'O, easily, easily!' She threw a leg over the horse's neck and slid to the ground. Clean hair made a gold halo round her head; she wore a rich, plain overtunic and breeches in fine blue-grey wool, high black boots and a blood-red cloak fastened by a gold brooch. A white linen shirt showed at neck and wrists. 'Did I not say I'd find advancement? I'm over my head in debt for all this, but in time – I speak of debt. I believe I owe you something.' She opened the gleaming purse bound to her new belt, and took out two new gold sols. 'Consider the extra a gift in return for the help you've given me. And Garget, hold out your hand.'

Into his reluctant palm she counted four sols, four samisols and three quarits. 'And by the authority vested in me, I name you second man here, which position I know you have long wanted. A new third man, his name is Tirran, will come next day.'

'Thank you – sir,' said Garget unwillingly, and felt for a rag to mop up his nosebleed.

'Captain?' exclaimed Ogo. 'I thought you were dead!'

'O, far from it! I have spoken with the king, and Lord Polem, and he gave me the rank of captain; I am included in the councils of the great – I shall do great things!'

'I cannot believe it,' said Ogo.

'I am sure Lord Ailixond will regret it when he finds himself thrown in the mud by every ambitious commoner he meets, but still . . .'

'And I made sure he would have you thrown in gaol, at the very least.'

'O no, he's a great man! He knows true merit when he sees it.'

'Does he know you're, well, you're – not a man?'

'O yes. I told him so.'

'And he still made you captain?'

'He did indeed! Though I think some would have told him not to.'

'Sir?' said a voice behind; Saripion had come running back. She turned, and held out her hand. 'Captain Aleizon Ailix Ayndra, sir.'

Saripion held out his hand, then snatched it back. 'You're Ogo's second man!'

'I was, sir.'

'Master Liz-landra! It is a grave offence to impersonate an officer! Where did you get that cloak? And the horse –'

'They are mine, sir.' She reached inside her tunic and brought out a scroll of paper. 'Written by the king's own hand – read it. If you can.' Saripion saw that it was writing, and gave it to Purmo.

'It says, I, Ailixond Most Serene Lord and King, and so on, do invest Aleizon Ailix Ayndra . . . it's a captain's commission, sir.'

'O – excuse me, sir, I am most sorry! A tragic error! I was not aware – I am most glad –'

'O, no need,' she said carelessly. 'I have raised Master Garget to the position of second man here, and arranged for a new third man to be sent up. I have merely come to collect a few of my goods, as I shall be residing near the Stone Bridge from now on – if you would like to help me?'

The catapults almost ceased firing as their men gathered to watch Saripion holding a sack while Aleizon Ailix Ayndra climbed in and out of the wagon, bringing out her sword and mail coat and a few boxes of powderfire and putting them in it. 'A man will come for the rest later – if you would assist me to mount?' Saripion took her spurred boot in his hands and lifted her up. She had slung the sack over her shoulders. 'Good day, Ogo! Good day, sir Leader!' The horse threw up its head and took off at a gallop; mud thrown up by its hooves spattered the onlookers. They could not see her clinging to the mane and straining desperately to bring it to a halt.

'The age of miracles is not past,' said Ogo piously.

'Remember your place! Keep your mouth shut!' Saripion snarled, and made off. Ogo stood there laughing.

'Captain Ayndra! Captain, sir!'

Aleizon Ailix Ayndra was exercising her horse on the cavalry drill ground, walk, trot, canter and gallop, wearing her dirty common soldier's clothes and a grimly dedicated expression.

'Captain, sir, Lord Ailixond requests your presence at dinner in his tent this night. At seventh hour.'

'What, to dine with the king?'

'Yes, sir.'

'O! I think you for the invitation ... please convey my acceptance to my lord.'

'It's not considered that you would refuse,' said the messenger. 'My lord has all the officers to dine with him at one time or another. At seventh hour. Good day!'

At half past the sixth hour she sat on the floor in the middle of her own tent; it was square and made out of white canvas and extremely bare. A curtain divided off the rear half, concealing a narrow bed which would fold up for travelling. There was a plain wooden box with clothes in it, and her mail coat hanging up on the post, and one folding stool. The floor was grass and earth. She took the last gold sol from her belt pouch and looked at the picture on the obverse for a while. She took out a bone comb and raked it through her hair, and shook out the cuffs of her shirt; there were sauce-stains on the front of her new tunic, and the breeches were greasy all down the thighs where she rubbed her hands on them. She looked at the coin-portrait again, then stuffed it back in her purse and threw the comb back into the box, picked up her red cloak and went out.

The hall of the royal pavilion was yellow with lamplight; Firumin met her there, and took her through to the king's own dining room, where a table for eight was prepared. Lords Polem, Arpalond, Lakkannar, Sulakon and Golaron were already there, with another officer whose face she did not know. 'Captain Ayndra!' said Lord Polem. 'A pleasure to see you here.'

'And you, my lord,' she replied, looking round the room. Lakkannar looked craftily back at her; Sulakon looked haughty and ignored her; the others nodded and returned to their conversations. Polem came and stood very close to her. 'Since you've had a halfmonth in your new position, how do you like it?'

'I've not had much to do so far,' she said.

'Indeed? – I must say, you look very well in scarlet. Although I had hoped that you might be in your proper dress this night.'

'What proper dress, my lord?'

'O, a gown, I mean – women's dress.'

She stared up at him. 'A gown? I haven't a single gown!'

'You have not? – would you like one?'

'O! No! – I prefer men's clothes, my lord, one can't walk properly in a trailing gown.'

'Ah, well, there's not an officer in the army who looks better in them,' Polem said. His brown eyes gazed warmly at her; she stepped back from him. 'The king!' said Firumin.

'Good day, my lords, gentlemen.' Ailixond took the head of the table. Firumin sat Ayndra on his right and the other officer on his left; Polem was her other neighbour. The wine-pourer came forward to fill their goblets, and the servers appeared with fresh bread and thick slices of roast meat. Ailixond greeted Ayndra, and fell into talk with the other officer, who turned out to command the Silver Shields; they discussed a recent Haraminharn foray through the Dinarn Gate. 'A strange sally . . . almost as if it were put on for show . . . to distract us . . .' Aleizon Ailix Ayndra fell upon the meat.

'Have you eaten nothing all day?' said Polem.

'Not enough,' she said with her mouth full.

'You are not drinking your wine – would you like some other kind? There's Thaless, Lysmalish – this is from Purrllum –'

'Never drink wine,' she said indistinctly. 'Water?'

'Of course.' He had a jug of it fetched for her. She seized another piece of bread and wiped her plate with it. He said, 'Have you been starving?'

'Early poverty. Eat when it's there, or starve when it's gone.'

'But you're not starving now?'

'Not presently, lord.' She bit into the bread; there was grease all over her chin. Just then Ailixond detached himself from the Silver Shield. 'Captain Ayndra?'

She choked down a mouthful of bread. 'My lord?'

'What have you done since last I saw you?'

'Practised riding, and, ah . . .'

'No matter, I am sorry to have left you idle for so long. I meant before now to ask you about this powderfire. Is it an invention of your own?'

'O, no, my lord, it's from S'Thurrulass, I mean, they make it there. The name I made up, I know not if it has a proper name in Safic – in S'Thurrulass they say it's death to give the secret of its making to foreigners, they call it purrius'th – I learnt it from someone there, but I know not if they'd punish me for it – if you find that someone has strangled me in the night, it will be them, but . . .'

'Do they use it in war?'

'No, they do nothing, they make displays of coloured fires with it and make loud bangs in the street at festivals, but when I saw it, I swore it must have better uses than amazing children and fools. I think that firing it from a catapult's not the best way – the last sixdays I've been thinking about it, and I thought, those fireboxes, it's a waste to use a catapult for them, and against the wall they do less damage than a stone, and fire-arrows set alight to buildings almost as well – if one mined the walls and filled the tunnel with powderfire, and lit it, it would go POUM! and the whole wall would fall down, though one would have to go to a safe distance, one would have to lay a trail of powder to the entrance of the mine or some such or else be blasted to the next world with it . . .'

'But we cannot mine here,' said Ailixond, 'There is too much water in the ground by the walls. And up by the citadel where it is dry one hits rock within a few feet –'

'But one could make a sort of, well, a pretence mine – it would be best against a gate. If one had lots of powder in sacks, and laid them close against the gate, and piled rocks over all, and then again had some means of lighting it from a distance, then I swear it'd be good as a ram, it would split the gate in two, I'll be bound – and one could use it against, say, Blue Gate, where it's hard to bring up a ram.'

'And one need only build a footbridge to get to the gate, instead of a structure sound enough to bear a ram,' said Ailixond. 'Except it would be a dangerous business crossing it – but I am sure that volunteers . . . would you do it?'

'O yes! Hold a shield over my head – but it would require a large quantity of powder . . . I made some . . .'

'What do you need for it?'

'Fine pure charcoal – hazel, or willow perhaps – and . . . have you seen the yellow stuff the Haraminharn use for purifying fires in temples? The S'Thurrulan name for it is sulphur – that, and then, I'd need to collect plenty of wood-ash, and dig out the earth from beneath middens – it's the right kind of earth here for that, it's lime one must have – then one mixes the ash and the earth and boils them up together, and strains that to make crystals, they're called *kaienno*, and then grind them all up and mix five parts of sulphur and five charcoal with seven *kaienno*.'

'Ah! All those can be obtained for you – would you accept the appointment to make a sufficient quantity of powderfire, and attack the Blue Gate in the way you've just described?'

'Certainly!' she said, edging her chair back; Polem was peering over her shoulder, uncomfortably close to her. Ailixond said, 'Of course, I could not give you sole charge . . .'

'Might I apply to assist with this enterprise?' said Polem.

Ailixond looked faintly surprised. 'Do you wish to?'

'You've said a hundred times that I should have some command.'

'Then . . . you may have it. You've met Lord Polem, Captain?'

'I have,' she said.

'Being a noble lord, he can commandeer anything which you have need of, and suppress Leader Saripion, whom I think you know . . . I'll give you some slaves to make powder for you also – but this can be arranged next day. Enough of the siege for now. How did you come to learn this about S'Thurrulass?'

'I was – I lived there for a while. For a few years.'

'Not only there,' said Polem. 'I believe the captain has been in Haramin before as well.' Ailixond looked at her. 'That was some years ago now,' she said. 'But I can speak the tongue still.'

'And read it too!' said Polem.

'Polem!' said Ailixond sharply. Polem looked sheepish, and turned away. Ailixond said, 'Were you born in the north?'

'I was born in Safi, my lord.'

'But your name . . .'

'I am not sure how I got my name,' she said, 'I was too young to remember! – it's a mixed name. Aleizon is a Haramin word, my mother said it means lightning. The rest I don't know.'

'Your mother was a northerner?'

'She came from Haramin, I think. But my father was Safin.'

'Yes? – I wondered how it was that one so young could be so well acquainted with foreign lands. I've not been north of Raq'min, and I've never seen S'Thurrulass – it's true, is it not, that women rule there?'

'Not exactly,' she said. 'Women and men rule both. But the women do all kinds of things which they're not permitted in Safi – well, which most are not permitted; they govern and they fight in the army and carry on all kinds of trade.'

'And you read and write as well?'

'I can read and write in three tongues! – though not so well in S'Thurrulan, for I was older when I learnt it. I'm not so young, my lord, as I pass for as a man.'

'Perhaps not,' he said, looking closely at her face in the lamplight. 'But let me introduce you to the lords here.' The servants were bringing round a dessert of fruits preserved in honey, and the best wine, for the lords to spend an evening in drink and conversation. Lord Lakkannar's coarse-grained handsome features took on a cast of private amusement as he said he was already . . . familiar . . . with Captain Ayndra; Lord Sulakon, the king's cousin, was haughtily correct and evidently disapproving; Lord Golaron was gruff, a generation older than the others there, serving Lord Ailixond as he had served his father Lord Parakison; Lord Arpalond, mousey-brown and unexceptional, peered at her through watery myopic eyes and offered her his hand. He showed

69

more interest than the others in her few words on the new weapon powderfire, and wished her good luck and the gods' blessing. The captain of the Silver Shields got up to leave, which she understood as a sign for her to go; she looked once over her shoulder as she was leaving. Polem was pursuing the wine-pourer with a demand for some red Thaless; but Ailixond was lounging at the head of the table, with empty chairs either side of him, and he was looking straight at her. The lamplight outlined his straight nose and gleamed on his long mouth; appearing not to have noticed her, he half-closed his eyes and tipped his chair back, starting to stretch, slow and luxurious like a cat. Someone might notice if she stood there. She dropped the curtains behind her and ran out.

The rebuilding of the bridge at Blue Gate began on the tenth day of First Month. The Haraminharn seemed not to appreciate the courtesy of this repair to their much-damaged city; they cast slingstones at the artillerymen and engineers when they approached behind large portable shields; they shot fire-arrows at the alley of stockading and the wooden shelter erected at the bridgehead to protect the labourers, although these failed to catch in the roof of uncured hides – which stank so vilely that several remarked that they'd rather risk burning. They tried to fire the new wooden struts that poked out over the stone-strewn water to link the ruined pillars of the old bridge, but were defeated by soakings of water, rain and more uncured hides; they resorted to throwing blocks of stone down in an attempt to smash the timbers. The artillery were still at work, though at reduced strength; they had the range so pat that the bridge workers were in no danger, and the bolt-throwing catapults swept the walls and made the enemy archers keep their heads down. Up at the battery, a party of slaves, supervised by Captain Ayndra, brewed up *kaienno*, ground sulphur (seized from Haraminharn temples) and charcoal, and stored it out of reach of damp. On the twenty-third, the Haraminharn brought up a small catapult of their own; although it was only cobbled together, when they put it on the wall-walk it was able to smash the shelter, kill one man and break the leg of another before the Safic catapults put it out of action. Captain Ayndra resolved to construct the rest of the bridge in wooden sections on land, and drop them into place when the time came; meanwhile they built a sort of open ladder-grid across the water; fire-arrows glanced off it and stone fell through it, and only three men fell off it and none of them drowned. The enemy seemed to lose heart, and contented themselves with shoring up

70

the gate from within, expecting a battering ram or even a helepolis. When the wooden struts reached the ruinous city end of the bridge, they either feared incursion too much, or had blocked the gate with so much material that they could not open it, to sally out and break the bridge; the Safeen guarded it night and day, and the Haraminharn did nothing except throw more rocks, whose ravages were repaired – and 'After all, they do but break down their own city for our benefit . . .' A battering ram was indeed being prepared, but for use on the East Gate, over land; Ailixond announced that the assault of the city would begin on the fourteenth day of Second Month. The Haraminharn had sent no more offers of peace, and seemed determined to fight to the last; and after the harvest, the men of the north would be free to fight. Aleizon Ailix Ayndra had had the powderfire mixed and put into small sacks; she said that it should be placed on the thirteenth. On the twelfth, under a hail of metal bolts shrieking overhead, they laid the floor of the bridge. At dawn on the thirteenth, Lord Polem and Captain Ayndra were down by the gate, the overfamiliar view bathed in the insubstantial clarity of sunrise; the wooden slats bore a few fresh, gaping splintered holes, but stood firm for footmen to run over.

'We shall have to go up to the gate,' she said, 'and lay the powder against its foot, or even under it if we can – but we'll be safe under the arch, they cannot touch us there.'

'Unless they open up and . . .' mumbled Polem, rubbing his pouched eyes.

'O! They'll not open up. As likely as the keystone falling out of the arch and crushing us all to death – Targo, go and tell the bastards up the hill to get on with firing, sweep the walls. I'm damned if we're to be shot full of arrows to give them a few winks' more sleep. Mallen, where are the sacks you brought down yesterday? In a dry place?' She was shown the 'dry place', while Polem nursed his head in the corner. 'God's teeth!' she cried, ruining his peace. 'A dry place, this? Lucky for you we've had no rain – good god!' Sacks were hauled out, and men crowded in with more. 'How many could one run with, Mallen?'

'Well, sir . . . three?'

'Three? Do you not think four would be better – like so, to balance?'

'If you say so, sir –'

'O damn you, never agree with me just to say yes! If you think three, tell me so.'

'No, sir, four, sir, I'm sure.'

'Very well. Let us tie them in pairs, so one can sling them over the shoulders either side – see?'

'Yes, sir.' The first bolt whined overhead. Blue Gate itself stood within an arch so deep it was almost a tunnel, bathed in shadow at this hour of the day; the long shadows of the walls fell cold over the water. 'I shall need two dozen valiant men to assist me laying this 'gainst the gate – who will come? Mallen? Who else? One, two ... thirty, thirty-one, thirty-two. That should be enough.'

Polem stood up. 'I shall be the thirty-third.'

'My lord. You need not risk your noble self.'

'Nonsense, sir, you have no power to dissuade me. Beside, thirty-three is a lucky number.'

'As you will, my lord ... how many sacks have we? Each of you take four ... send for more if need be ... my lord, you'll need take off that cloak, you might as well wear a sign reading Shoot Here.'

'Why so?' croaked Polem.

'None but a lord would wear anything so vivid.'

'O ... you are generous, to have such a concern ...' Polem undid the offending article, poison-green with silver embroidery in a two-foot deep band at the hem, and cast it into a dark recess. He sat down to put on his red-crested helmet. Aleizon Ailix Ayndra picked up a pair of sacks, fastened at the neck by thick cords whose trailing ends were fastened in a loop, and slung them over one shoulder. She took a few steps back and forth, then thrust one arm and her head through the loop so that the sacks hung across her, one before and one behind. 'Where is my helmet? Give me my helmet.' It was found, and passed to her; a broad-brimmed steel hat, without a crest, polished like a mirror. She already had on Parrek's leather shirt and her coat of mail. 'Give me your cloak, my lord.'

'But you said –'

'Yes, I know, let me have it.'

'Here you are, then.'

She snatched up a spade which was propped against the wall, wrapped the cloak round its blade, thrust it out of the narrow window and waved it up and down. A couple of arrows whizzed over; one thumped into the roof overhead. She pulled it back. 'We shall have to run!'

Polem retrieved the cloak and untangled it from the spade, knocking mud from its folds. 'Unbolt the door!' said Ayndra shrilly. 'Two more sacks, here – who will follow me? The important thing is to run . . .' As the wooden bolts rattled back, she felt a hand on her shoulder, a clean, cultivated, rose-scented hand. 'Captain,' said Polem, 'I cannot permit you to endanger yourself by going out first.'

'O, nonsense.' She shook it off her and signed to the man at the door, who dragged it open; earth steps led in a couple of strides to the bridge foot. 'Would you so besmirch my honour?'

'Would you so besmirch mine? – to allow a lady –'

'Ha! Lady!' She spat on the floor.

'Then let us go together.'

'As you will, my lord. Yailen, give Lord Polem a burden.'

Polem imitated her mode of slinging the sacks over his engraved coat of scale mail. They stepped into the doorway, and crouched in the trench below the bridge. A heavy bolt whistled over them, and someone on the wall shouted out. 'Now!' said Ayndra, and leapt upward. Her wooden-heeled boots drummed briefly on stone, and rang hollow on the planking. Polem was lost for a moment; he passed out of shadow into dazzling sunlight, and then ran. They were halfway across the bridge before the archers on the wall loosed their first flight of arrows – splashing into river, thrumming stuck in wood, one lodging in the powdersack bouncing on Polem's back. He found gaping at his feet a jagged hole, water glinting a long way below; he froze, seeing with entire and instant clarity the water running glassy over a great smooth stone, how blue the depths were – his balance started to go. A hand snatched his arm and jerked him sideways. He stumbled, and they were running into the long shadow of the wall. Ayndra let go his hand to scramble on all fours like an ape up the hills of rubble and fallen masonry, and dropped gasping under the arch, a few feet from the face of the gate. She stayed on her knees for five or six pants, enough to shuck off the sacks of powder, and jumped to her feet, waving her arms at the dark slit under the hide-roofed shelter. Three more men were running towards them.

It took almost an hour for the entire contingent to cross over. One man arrived with a ragged gash where an arrow had scraped his hand; one lay face down on the bridge, a shaft sticking up from his back. He might be dead, he might be feigning; the enemy did not think it worth wasting more ammunition on him. His friends would try to pick him up when they went back. Leaving the first few over to receive the others, Ayndra clambered up to the face of the gate itself. She stood up on a rubble-heap, and flattened herself against the blue-black metal of its face; even stretching her arms to full length, her fingertips were at least four

73

feet from its top. She slid down in a cascade of gravel, and knelt down by the crack where the two leaves met; peered through, but saw nothing, darkness. Something obscured the light that would else have been streaming through. 'I think we are in no danger – so securely are we shut out, they are entirely shut in . . . here's the place.'

'What do you here?' asked Polem.

'Here. For the powder. Hola! Mallen!'

Polem leant against the gate. 'Should you shout? They may hear us.'

'I should think it hardly matters, since we did not come here unobserved – but still. As you say. Mallen? We should clear all this away – in half a circle, o, five feet wide, down to the roadway.' They pushed away the debris, until the cobbles of the road were bare. The years had rutted them until they dipped well beneath the gate's foot; in places a dog, or even a small child, might have squeezed beneath. Ayndra lay down and pushed her arm under. She discovered an extensive cave, with wooden beams above. 'O very good! Push the sacks under here.' There were more than six score of them, in weight almost a thousand pounds of the stuff. They packed the gap under the gates, and piled them around the doors, rising to a flattened peak in the centre. 'Now lay these stones over them – bury them altogether. The biggest rocks first.' Polem leant still against the gate, watching them sweating and heaving. 'I can hear our friends on the other side,' he said.

'What do they say?' Ayndra said, puffing.

'I cannot tell . . . what if they open?'

'Then I set light to the powder, and all run like the devil away. They would be fools to open now.'

'They are fools to resist Lord Ailixond in the first place,' Polem pronounced. She looked at him, and returned to the rock she was trundling.

One gap was left at the side, with a trail of sacks laid end to end in it; this would be the fuse. It took till midday to entomb the powder to her satisfaction; 'Very good!' she said. 'Now we shall run the gauntlet again, and sit there and pray for a dry night . . . that's Danno out there, is it not? Who will pick him up?'

The lord and the captain watched them race the arrows over the sunny crown of the bridge, and drop out of sight into safety. Mailed backs this time offered no targets to the enemy; they themselves crossed without mishap. The Blue Gate looked little different – more stones against it, maybe, was all.

Ayndra told the men that they could all go away now, except

74

those on the duty roster. She sat down inside the shelter, and took off her helmet. 'A pity the Council has not more trust in our enterprise. For sure we'll gain entry here far easier than at East Gate, yet we've to sit and wait until we hear how it goes with the ram ... we should assault here first thing!'

'But you will not want any part in that in any case,' Polem said.

'What? Of course I will!'

'Well – you will see to the powder, of course, but then –'

'Then I shall go into the city!' she exclaimed.

'And fight hand to hand? You cannot mean it! That is no place for a woman!'

'God's teeth! Do you think – I will not be forbidden it!'

'But it is, it is most dangerous –'

'My lord. Do you think I know not what it is to kill a man? I have done it more than a few times!'

'What? But it – it is not womanly!'

'Then this for womanly!' She gobbed on his feet. He made a shuddering exclamation, and scrubbed his boot against the floor.

'Sir! I must ask you – I will not tolerate this vulgarity!'

'So am I vulgar!' she said defiantly. 'I will not – it's my place to fight if I wish!'

'It is not your place to spit upon a lord of Safi!'

'Then I apologise for it – but I shall do what I want next day!'

'Then all I have to say is, you had better remember your place then, or things may go badly for you! Good day!' He seized his green cloak and swept out. She spat again, and thrust herself back against the wall, knees drawn up, glaring furiously after him; she put the edge of her hand in her mouth and sat there biting at it, rocking to and fro.

'Four miles to East Gate,' said Polem. 'Bound to take some time to come.'

'O, I know,' said Ayndra. She held a tinderbox between her fingers, turning it over and over, twitching now and then at the scarlet cloak pinned to flow back from her shoulders. Polem had exchanged his plain helmet for one inlaid with a design of soldiers in battle, gold armour and silver flesh, whose red horsehair crest brushed the roof of the hut. The pommel of his long sword was a single, flawless piece of rock crystal. Perfume rose from him every time he moved. They had been waiting since dawn for news from the other side of the city, where Lord Ailixond was leading the attack with the ram.

'It's the true state of war,' Polem said, 'one never knows what it is that's going on.'

'I though it true only of common soldiers.'

'O, no, I can never tell what happens, not till later when Ailixond says . . . an they were in some trouble, they would have sent.'

The dug-out behind them was packed with volunteers from the artillery and the phalanx regiments; the main force of phalanxmen waited up on the hill. The Silver Shields were with Lord Ailixond at East Gate. For three hours and more they had sat waiting to enter the fight; the hut stank of sweat and fear, and the reek of fresh urine where nervous men had relieved themselves against the wall. Ayndra said, 'If only we had some riders, to see what has happened . . . we could send runners.'

'No, I am sure – to hear nothing is to hear good things. With Ailixond in command, nothing will fail.'

'I thought you hypocritical when first I heard you say things like that.'

'Your pardon?'

'But in truth, you're altogether sincere – are you not? My lord?'

'What? O – Lord Ailixond is a great man. If you come to know him better, Captain, you will see.'

Ayndra's lips curled in some secret amusement. 'I hope so, my lord.'

'My lord! My lord! A message!'

A commotion greeted the man who tumbled into the shelter, and held out a dirty scrap of paper. Polem tore it open; Ayndra poked her head under his arm to read it. 'Fierce resistance. They've fired the ram housing and destroyed a number of ladders. Force the Blue Gate immediately and draw them off. If you cannot, come round to join us. A.' Polem cleared his throat: 'A message from Lord Ailixond! He tells us to attack now.'

Ayndra thrust through to the door. 'I go to fire the powder – open up, open up!' To Polem she said, 'And alone, my lord – but watch me now!' She wormed through the half-open door; crouched to take a few deep slow breaths, and ran. This time the archers concentrated all their strength on her; the air sang like a thousand crows, and she threw herself into the shelter of the gateway with a head ringing from those that had glanced off her helmet and two like weird plumes wagging in her cloak. The watchers on the other side could see her cloak like a patch of blood as she knelt in the shadows, and dropped her burden of another sack of powder and the tinderbox. She tore open the sack and spilled a thick trail up to and around the fuse-line of sacks, opened the box and tried to knock flint and steel together. Her hands shook so much that the first few times she missed; twice more before she got a spark at all; three times, and the powder began to sputter. She backed away from it on all fours, watching it with her mouth open as it crept over the dusty ground and reached into the rough tunnel, the mouth of the first sack – she leapt up and fled, her legs pivoting limply, almost tripping her up in a hail of arrows, she found the end of the bridge and fell into the door; and Polem caught her in his arms. 'Are you scathed?'

'Listen! Listen!' she said. There were faint spitting bangs from under the gate. The men on the walls were still shooting a few arrows at the roof. 'O, will it –'

POUM!

'Yaah!' She threw herself at the window. A great cloud of smoke and stone fragments flew out of the gateway; the shelter shuddered, and a wave of bitter smoke burst through the slit window; they coughed, shouted, swore – Ayndra shrieked aloud like a lunatic. 'It's happened? Has it done it? Look there, look there! O, it works, it works!' Gravel was raining down above them; smoke billowed from under the arch, and people were screaming and running on the wall-walk. The wind over the river took the smoke, and, as it cleared, light showed through; light, and orange flames. The leaves of the gate had split from the base, like a flower torn in half; the wooden beams behind them had been cast up and away, and now lay strewn all over the road, splintered and broken and some burning. Through the smoke, one could see movement on the far side. Polem took hold of his sword. 'Let us go forth!' he said. Aleizon Ailix Ayndra fell from the window, pushed past him, yelling 'Go! Go! Go!' They charged out into the sunlight.

Over the bridge, bounding over the rubble in the gateway, gasping in the smoke, and into a line of Haraminharn, led by Polem with his lord's long sword; it gleamed like a mirror, inviting opponents to partner him in a dance of death; he cut them away like cobwebs, none could come near him. The enemy were hardly organised to receive them, they were still milling about in confusion at the tame thunderclap that had burst their gate; they broke and fled in all directions and left the gate empty, except for the Safeen running across the bridge. The rest of the assault force was pouring down the hill from the battery. 'East Gate,' gasped Polem, 'which is the way to East Gate?'

'Up on the walls,' panted Ayndra, 'we must see.' She turned and ran back to the gate tower, and dashed in through the dark

77

doorway. 'No!' said Polem. 'Wait! There may be –' From within
came a yell of surprise, a clatter, a long fierce wordless yell; he ran
in, to a gloomy spiral staircase, up it three steps at a time and
came upon Ayndra, leaning against the wall, a long knife on the
steps beside her. 'No matter,' she said, 'he was more affrighted
than I,' caught up the knife, and hurried on up. They emerged
breathless and cautious on to the wall-walk. As far as they could
see, there was no one there; the walk, wide enough for six men to
walk abreast, was littered with discarded arrows, bows and pieces
of gear. There was a fine view over the city roofs, columns of
smoke rising from hearth fires; to the south, the citadel of White
Walls, and to the east . . .

'Look, there they are! They're over!' Polem pointed to an
antlike swarming on the walls; impossible to distinguish more
than that there was fighting going on there. More feet beat on the
stone stairs: it was the captain of phalanx and a score or so of his
men. 'My lord! I have never seen anything – the whole gate –'

'O, later, later! Look. The enemy are over at East Gate, but as
soon as they know that we've entered – lord, I believe we're to
direct ourselves toward the citadel and White Gate? I think we
should divide into two, one to go by the walls, and to hold this
gate, and one to go by the streets.'

'The walls, yes,' said Polem. 'But the streets . . . they are very
narrow . . .'

'I know the streets, for years I lived here!' Aleizon Ailix Ayndra
waved her bloodied sword, like a child with a willow switch. 'We
should go down *there*, and –'

'Then you can lead with me, in the streets, and we shall go to
East Gate,' Polem said. 'Captain, can you set some men to guard
this gate, and clear the walls? There's a tower there – and that
tower to the south, and . . . o, I do not doubt you know as well as
I what you should do. Captain, which way?'

'O, and clear the gateway, Captain, put the fires out! This way!'
She ran down the stairs again. Polem received the captain's salute,
and followed.

He caught up with her in the street leading from the gate. At
least two hundred men were already gathered there, and more
were marching across the bridge. 'You must go slower!' he said.
'Leave off running into buildings when we do not know who is
hiding there. Now we are doing what I know how to do.' He
raised his voice. 'Men! First, third and fifth companies, and so on,
follow me, also the artillerymen. We shall advance in loose order,
and watch all the sidestreets. And you are not to go running after

loot, no matter what you see. We shall have plenty of treasure when we have won the town. We go now to join the king at East Gate! Forward!'

The houses had been shuttered and barred and the streets were deserted; they heard sounds of folk around them, but saw none of them. The road rarely ran more than twenty yards in a straight line, and there were dozens of side-turnings into courts and alleyways. They came to a small open space where the road forked.

'This way,' said Polem, pointing to the southerly fork.

'No, I think it's the other,' said Ayndra.

'No, see there? A bar across it. They'd not have put up a bar were it not an important road.'

'O, no, perhaps they intend to mislead us, or it is just some timorous householder –'

'You see craft where there is none. Let us take the barricade.'

'O, as you will – nothing worse than to stand here bickering –'

'Look up! On the roof!' yelled a man behind, just as the main body of the enemy force rose up from behind the empty-seeming barricade, and their archers on the housetops loosed a flight of arrows. Aleizon Ailix Ayndra screamed like canvas tearing, and ran straight for the barrier, snatching the knife she had taken at the gate tower from her belt. The Safeen, reeling from the suddenness of the ambuscade, ran after, and she reached the line of overturned tables and doors with half a hundred men at her back. They overwhelmed the makeshift, and the two sides fell into a melee; the archers could not tell friend from enemy, lowered their bows and made off over the roofs. Polem had run for safety under the overhanging eaves of a house; he moved along the wall, and found a pair of wooden doors barring the entrance to a yard. Over them, he could see a ladder leaning against the gable of the house. He beckoned to the nearest soldier. 'You, can you climb that gate?'

'Well, lord, if . . .'

'Give me your foot.' Polem made a stirrup of his hands, took the other's foot and heaved; the man got one leg over, then the other, and dropped down on the far side. Polem hissed, 'Open up!' and waved to every man within view to come to him. The gates creaked open, and they slipped in. A door opened on the far side of the yard, and a woman with a heavy bucket walked out; she had come several steps before she saw them. The bucket fell to the ground, the slops in it running over her feet; she put her hands to her face, and opened her mouth to scream. 'Stop her!' Polem snapped. A man seized her from behind, clapping his hand over her mouth. She struggled, the white cloth falling from her head and her hair coming loose; in desperation, he struck her face with his mailed glove. At the third blow she collapsed, and he dropped her; her head hit the ground with a crunch, and she lay still. Polem tried the ladder for stability, and climbed up it. He saw in front of him several enemy archers, clinging to the roof-ridge and watching the fighting in the street; he came up behind them as quietly as he could, his sword whispering from its sheath; breath hissed as he inhaled, and then the walls rang with his shout: 'Safi! Safi! Death to Raq'min!' In a clatter of breaking tiles, he threw himself on the enemy; two of them he was able to shove over the edge, and he lodged one foot in the deep stone channel of the guttering to fence with the third; it took him three strokes to spit him like a sucking-pig, and roll him over the edge. He climbed up the roof and scrambled along until he was behind the barricade. Aleizon Ailix Ayndra was duelling with a man in the street; she fought energetically, but not skilfully, her blows wasting energy and rarely striking well home, and he was driving her backward. Polem picked up a large ridge-tile, tested its weight, and lobbed it at him. It hit him on the shoulder and knocked him off guard; she ducked in under his arm and stabbed him in the stomach. He dropped his sword to clutch at his bowels, and fell forward; they rolled together in the dirty water of the kennel, until she lodged one foot on his thigh and heaved her sword free. A rush of blood followed it, and he slumped face down in the gutter. She sat up, breathing heavily. Not far away, a few knots of men were still fighting, but as she got her breath the Haraminharn were melting away into the back streets where the enemy would not follow them. Polem raised his sword and yelled, 'Victory!' She looked up, and her face split wide open in a grin. 'Not yet!' she shouted. 'Not yet!'

They paused in that street for a while, long enough to send the walking wounded back to the gate, leave a few to look after those who could not walk, gather up the rest and add ten score fresh troops to their numbers; they said that the phalanxmen held the wall from the citadel (which could not be entered from the lower city save through its gate) almost down to Dinarn Gate, but the citadel itself was heavily defended, with catapults being set up on the rooftops there. Then they advanced again; a few skirmishes, more citizens put to flight; and came up to a broad avenue, running up the hill from the marketplace near Dinarn Gate to the White Gate of the citadel. The din of combat was audible in the eastern quarter of the city; occasionally, between house-tops, they saw the wall, and sometimes men fighting on it.

Aleizon Ailix Ayndra pointed to a massive ornate building near the gate. 'That is where we should go to. But I think we should cross here as we like, in no order and at any place, for then they on the gate will hardly tell us from their own people – see all those running about below? – and gather at that hall.'

'But then they may pick us off on the way –'

'Ah, we can deal with them! Let's not delay!'

'But what can we do? We would need siege ladders – or more powder –'

'Ah, do you want to get to East Gate or not? Go now, gentlemen, run as you will, but we shall gather behind that hall there – you see it? Go!' She ran out into the sunshine. 'Come on! Come!'

The hall stood less than a bowshot from the White Gate; in time of peace the merchants of Haramin held their convocations there, but it was all sealed up now, and anyone who looked around the corner nearest the citadel was met by a hail of missiles. Almost two hundred Safeen were resting on its far side, more arriving all the time; drinking from flasks or buckets drawn from the public fountains, binding up wounds, cleaning weapons. Aleizon Ailix Ayndra was squatting near the gate side, supping water in a dipper from a bucket at her side, as Polem came up. 'I think I was mistaken that this is the best place to be,' she said, 'still, we can make ready to advance to East Gate – I cannot hear so loud the noise from there – is that good? We cannot approach the gate from here, that's for sure . . .'

'We should go to East Gate,' Polem said, 'but not till we have a greater . . . what's that? Down there.' She stood up, but he saw them before she could. 'It's Ailixond!' He shouted, 'Safi! Safi!' The cry echoed, and was repeated, all down the street; out of the shadows came a white banner, and then a white flag with the double row of stylised waves zigzagging across it, a figure in a white-plumed helmet walking beneath them. 'It's the king! The king!'

Lord Golaron stove in the doors of the merchants' hall with a few blows of his battleaxe, and the lords and officers went inside. Within, it was gloomy with shuttered windows, redolent of beeswax and dust – there had not been much business in the markets of Raq'min lately. Ailixond went naturally to the raised plinth at the end, and climbed on it, leaving the others to laugh

81

and shout. 'Call Polem to me ... Polem, came you from Blue Gate?'

'As soon as I heard – the powder! You should have seen it! The whole gate torn in half like rotten canvas, and the enemy frightened out of their wits! – they ran like rabbits! We came here with only half our force, we left the others to take the walls, the last I heard they were almost to Dinarn Gate ... I imagine they sent all their forces against you, we had such an easy time of it.'

'Yes,' said Ailixond, 'yes ... they had boiling water, and flaming oil, and the ladders – we were three hours back and forth in the gateway, once the ram had broken in ... open the window, Polem, I would see out.' Polem ran to fetch a long pike, and pulled open the shutter with it; the high window was covered by an iron grid, cutting up the view of the walls of the citadel, and White Walls itself beyond. Ailixond moved closer, the squares of sunlight illuminating his uplifted face; he stood still, with his eyes fixed on the afternoon clouds piling in the cream-blue sky. 'We shall take the citadel by escalade. If that should fail, next day we'll bring up the ram again.' Men passed in and out, giving and receiving orders; occasionally a question was passed up to him, and he answered it briefly, lost in his thoughts. Outside, companies thronged in the streets surrounding the hall, while others scoured the walls, and searched the main streets for parties of Haraminharn in arms.

'Lord? – the siege ladders are here, my lord.'

'They are? Then it is time.' Ailixond faced back into the hall, and signed for his helmet to be returned to him. 'Come, gentlemen, my lords – Blades blooded once shall drink again / And before night we shall hold all / Gate, walls and city, house and hall.'

The ladders were great unwieldy things, made from bulky spars lashed at foot-deep intervals between strong narrow tree-trunks, fifteen or twenty feet long; two men could stand abreast on them. They were carried by teams of four men, who wore wide-brimmed helmets with long neck-guards and studded leather coverings on arms and legs, for they had to go under heavy fire and get the ladders in place for the others to rush up them. Ailixond looked over them, and signed to his standard bearers. Both flags dipped, and the teams dashed forward. They lodged the feet of the ladders among the stones, and swung them up, crashing on the walls' crest; soldiers streamed after them, jumping on to the lower rungs to weight them so that the defenders could not push them over. Stones and arrows rained down; the first men at the tops of the ladders leant over the wall, slashing at the enemy, pushed over on to the cobbles, struggling over the parapet where they fought like demons; then the Haraminharn unleashed their catapults. They were mounted on the roofs of the palace, at such an angle that the heavy metal darts they fired fell almost vertically on to the Safeen – and on to the Haraminharn who crouched behind the battlements. A bolt struck the leading officer on the crown of his helm and passed straight through, shattering his skull; he fell back dead, and his men paused. The enemy pushed at the ladder where he had stood, and sent it flying backward; the crowd at the ladders' feet halted, or turned back, searching for shelter. Ailixond pushed the men surrounding him out of his way and ran into their midst. He caught hold of the man nearest him and swung him around. 'Back! Follow me! No turning back!' He ran straight into the hail of missiles, grasping at men as he went and dragging them after him; he seized hold of a fallen ladder and together they wrestled it upright. Ailixond was first up it, his white cloak shining; the tide turned, and flooded after him. He was eight or ten feet above the ground, with men pushing to follow him, when he lost his grip on the rungs and slid to one side. He called out 'Go on!' and tumbled over, landing like a dead seabird on the stones. Someone said, 'He's dead!'

'He's dead! The king's dead!'

Lakkannar leapt out and bellowed, 'Revenge! Revenge! A vengeance!'

'We will avenge! Go up!'

The ladders surged and bucked and the wall was beaded with struggling groups. Lord Lakkannar was up now, swinging a two-handed sword, and Lord Golaron's axe flashed red and silver. Under the ladder, Polem and Arpalond bent over Lord Ailixond; he was breathing, stunned by the fall, though his helmet had protected his head; a foot-long bolt stood like a nail upright in his right foot. Blood had filled his boot and ran out over the pavement. Polem lifted him in his arms, Arpalond held a shield over him; they staggered into shelter behind a house, and laid him on a mound of rubbish against the wall. 'Call a surgeon!' said Polem. 'A surgeon! – water! – wine, someone, bring wine!' Arpalond unbuckled the king's helmet and gently laid his head on a pad of rags. 'The bleeding's all over the place!' Polem exclaimed. 'Should we not cut the bolt out?'

'Wait till a surgeon comes –'

'Name of god, where are they? Where –'

'Pull it out!' said a cold tense voice; the king's eyes were open.

He looked, not at them, but fixedly at the sky. 'Pull it out, I say!'

'But Ailixond – if it makes it worse –' Polem began.

'Arpalond! Pull it out. Then bind it up as tightly as you can and make a tourniquet on my leg. The rest can be done later. It's not so grave – pull it out!'

Arpalond braced Ailixond's leg across his own lap, grasped the flanged end of the bolt and jerked it sharply upward. He felt it grate on bone as it came free. Ailixond stared blindly upward and inhaled sharply, panting like a wounded animal. Polem was tearing strips from his embroidered cloak. Arpalond looked at the bloody thing in his hands; fortunately it was not barbed. 'It's a clean wound,' he said, and tossed it away. Polem began to wind strips of wool around the ragged hole. Someone pushed through the onlookers and took hold of his hand. 'My lord, excuse me.' He began deftly to undo Polem's work, and wind a linen bandage round instead; it was the surgeon. 'Let me sit up!' said Ailixond; lifting him, Polem saw that he had bitten his lips to bleeding. 'Leave me,' he said, 'go back to the citadel, it's there that you are needed, not with me. Now go!' Three surgeons and their boys were there, and they drove the lords and officers away.

Aleizon Ailix Ayndra gripped the bare, splintering wood of the ladder, her face against the back of the man before, the one behind pressing against her legs. The ladder swayed, as if it were about to break beneath the weight it bore. She was above the heads of the mob now, upturned faces half seen below her, the battlements black in a painfully brilliant sky, a bolt falling out of it straight for her – she flinched, the stump of a stripped branch scraping her cheek. The man above gave a bubbling scream and let go the ladder to clutch at his face – he had committed the prime unwisdom under fire of looking up whence came his death; a bolt protruded from his eye-socket. He was falling on her – she pushed him aside, and scrambled up to the sloping base of the embrasure where the ladder rested. A man swung a short sword at her head. She leapt at him, mailed belly scraping on stone and feet scrabbling for purchase on the topmost rung; the blade swept harmlessly over her, struck the parapet and was knocked from its wielder's grasp as she crashed into his chest. They fell entangled on the wall-walk; the breath was knocked out of him just long enough for her to get out her sword and stab at him as he tried to get out from under her. Afterwards she could hardly remember what she did, except that he tried to shield himself with his hands, but she got up and pushed the sword at his face and kicked him in the chest and he fell over the inner edge of the walk. She found herself on her knees at the brink, shaking. Someone behind her yelled 'O bravely done!' Two or three Safeen had climbed after her, and more were struggling over. There was a knot of Haraminharn ten yards away; the two groups stared at each other, each unwilling to move first. Another bolt clattered harmlessly on the stone. Aleizon Ailix Ayndra began to move toward a well-armed youth on the other side. They went cautiously closer, breath hissing. He put his sword in the guard position, and his lips started to open, but she beat him to it.

'Safi!' She laid into him as if she was flailing corn. A man rushed past her to engage with the enemy, and another, and another. He landed a blow on her shoulder, but it slid off her mail and the edge gashed the back of her hand. She screamed with more rage than pain and lunged at him; he dropped to his knees and made to clutch her legs. By good fortune she stood with her feet braced wide, so that she did not fall at first; he heaved again, and she let herself tumble in such a way that she fell on his sword and covered it with her body. He rolled over on top of her; she seized her own sword at either end of the blade, ignoring the damage it did her hands, and drove it at his throat as if it was a wire cutting cheese. The edge went in, and blood poured out; he collapsed in her lap. She said, 'My god!' and dragged herself back against the wall.

'Captain! Come follow me! To the gate!' shouted a great bass voice behind her. She looked up and saw Lord Golaron towering above her, double-bladed axe in hand. He swung it effortlessly upward to point the direction, and took two strides forward as he continued the swing; the honed edge half severed the neck of one of the enemy swaying hand to hand with an artilleryman, who gawped to see his opponent vanquished by what at first seemed divine intervention. Golaron bellowed, 'Follow!' and charged onward. An unrailed stair led down the inside of the wall; he thundered down it. The party of men about to ascend quailed before him. Aleizon Ailix Ayndra jumped five steps to the ground, fell over, picked herself up; to the left, a wide road going up to the palace; to the left, the White Gate, closed with a massive bar and three bolts none less than three inches thick. There were a dozen men falling back onto it. Lord Golaron roared like a bear and charged at them, knocked down two and was standing with his back to the gate, still swinging his axe. 'Unbar the gate! We can hold them off.' She tried to reach the uppermost bolt; too high. Someone said, 'Stand up on my back!' and dropped to all fours in front of her. She got straight up on him and grasped the heavy knob; the bolt emitted a grating shriek as she dragged on it. A thrown knife hit the gate near her head. She heaved with both hands and the bolt shot back, and she shot with it, losing her stand; she fell on her back on the ground, winded. A couple of others were worrying at the lower bolts. She struggled to her feet and started pushing at the bar; a flight of arrows struck the gate and fell spent around her. Five or six pairs of hands joined hers; the bar jerked out of its sockets, and they jumped back and dropped it, then threw themselves at the gate. Well-oiled and almost soundless, it swung outward and a cheer went up outside. As soon as it was six inches open, hands grabbed it from without and hauled it wider, and men started to pour through. The few Haraminharn who were still fighting gave up the conflict and fled.

Polem was one of the first through, running uphill toward the gilded double doors of White Walls; but before he got there, they opened to reveal a group of men richly clad, and mostly unarmed, waving an assortment of blue flags and green branches; the leader recognised him by his dress as a person of the better sort, and addressed him in an incomprehensible gabble. Polem halted and spread his arms wide. 'Stop! Stop!' he yelled. 'They surrender! Stop!'

'Na! Get them!'

'No! They mean peace!' Polem half turned and menaced his own men. 'Stop, I tell you! Stop!' He brandished his sword at the Safeen, then turned and lowered it in the face of the Haraminharn, stepped forward and offered the leader his hand. The men nearest him paused, backing up the flood of Safeen behind; the relief of the men of the palace was plain to see. They grinned at one another, having no language in common.

'Make way! Make way!' yelled voices down the road.

'Interpreter! Who speaks foreign?' shouted Polem. The Haraminar went on nodding his head and mouthing what were undoubtedly assurances of undying friendship.

'Make way! Make way for the king!'

The soldiers were shuffling to either side, and a procession came up between them: at the head, four men were carrying broomhandles on their shoulders, lashed to the legs of a high-backed dining chair; sitting in it, without a cloak and without a helmet and with one leg tied up with bloodstained cloths, looking pale and serene, was Ailixond. 'Good day, my lords, gentlemen,' he said.

The notables of Haramin bowed before him; the leader made a

86

rapid speech. 'Bring an interpreter!' said Polem.

'O, no need.' Ailixond lifted his hands and pointed at the Haraminharn leader; then at the palace, then made a gesture encompassing everything around them; then indicated a circlet with his hands, lifted it up, put it on his head, pointed at the leader again and, gazing intensely at his face, raised his hands in a questioning gesture. The man paused, then spoke again, stabbing his finger in the direction of the palace doors, at Ailixond, and inside the palace once more, bowing his head again and again as he did so. 'Follow him!' said Ailixond. 'Raq'min is ours!' He pointed back at the tower by the gate, where there was a flagstaff; the flag of Haramin had disappeared, and a white banner was climbing, flapping sluggishly in the stiff breeze . . . its border gleamed gold . . . the soldiers cheered. 'Into the palace!' said Ailixond to his bearers. The Haraminar trotted at his side, still speaking and waving his hands. Polem went after them. 'Interpreter! Interpreter . . . hola! Captain!' He seized Aleizon Ailix Ayndra in the midst of the mob pursuing the king, and turned her to face him. Her eyes stared like pebbles and her mouth was open. She said 'Aaa!'

'Come with me!' He dragged her with him. Within the gold doors was an octagonal vestibule, with double doors on three sides; the pair in front of them slammed back; Ailixond passed swaying in his chair between lines of bowing and scraping Haraminharn, into a long hall. There were signs that fighting had been recently going on there; bodies were hastily dragged out of his way. Ailixond said, 'I did not know that we had penetrated thus far – sir. Did we . . .' He paused; it did not go well into hand-language.

'Here!' Polem pushed Ayndra forward. 'Make interpretation.'

'O, aah . . .' she squeaked and clicked; the Haraminar squeaked back. 'Traitors,' she said. They went through a door at the side of the hall, across a corridor, and into another antechamber; through a doorless portal, and into the throne room.

It lay at right-angles to the antechamber, so that one had to turn to face the throne. The floor was chequered in black and white marble. A dais of six broad black marble steps stood at the end. Scarlet and purple curtains draped the walls. Sunlight fell through clerestory windows. A square-framed chair, without ornament, but covered in gold leaf, stood on the dais. The bearers put Ailixond's chair down on the lowest step. Polem offered his arm; Ailixond pushed it away, put both feet to the ground, and hobbled, hissing between closed teeth, five steps up; he put his hands on the arms on the throne, and sat down facing them.

Sulakon drew his long sword. 'Lord Ailixond! I proclaim you king of Haramin by right of conquest!'

'Ailixond! Ailixond! King of Haramin!' The Haraminharn joined the acclaim. 'Ellizon! Ellizon!' Their leader jumped forward and made an impassioned speech; as the clamour died down, Ayndra spoke above it, a hoarse thin voice: 'He says, Lord Yourcen deserted them months ago, he ran away to the north, and by reason of this vile cowardice forfeited all right to the throne ... he says you, my lord, as conqueror ... he begs you to accept, this, this ...' Two of the entourage lugged a small heavy box to the steps; their leader opened it, and took out a golden case, knelt before the throne and proffered it to Ailixond. The king dipped his hands into it and withdrew a gleaming circle, shooting light in all directions – a wreath of golden leaves. He lifted it, and placed it on his head.

'Hail to the king!'

'All hail! All hail!'

The gold leaves reflected a rich glow onto Ailixond's face, into his wide-open blue eyes, drowning, ecstatic; his lips moved softly. Only Polem was near enough to hear him. He looked at the shouting crowd, and his fingers tightened on the arms of the chair. 'Mine,' he said, 'all ... mine!'

Seven days after the capture of the city, the twenty-first day of Second Month, the spoils of the captured city were auctioned in a field outside the walls; on the first day, the human spoil; on the second day, the goods and weapons.

The auctioneers, and the merchandise up for consideration, stood on a wooden scaffold. To the left were clerks of the royal counting house with money-chests and bead-frames; to the right, wattle pens with armed guards around them. At the foot of the scaffold, waited on as they reclined in padded chairs, were the rich dealers, agents of the brothels in Safi, the mines and the galleys; behind them, Safic officers or lords' servants, common soldiers and onlookers; and at the back, the main reason for the armed guards – common people of the city, with every coin they could scrape up, come to look for and if possible buy back men who had been captured, women who had been taken by the soldiers, anyone who had been found wandering the streets during the curfew of the first three nights after the Safeen had taken the city, and anyone else who had offended the military governors. They were brought up for sale one after another, with rings round their necks or iron hand-cuffs or wooden clamps fixing their arms behind their backs, made to flex their muscles or show their teeth; practised bidders made a purchase in a score or so heartbeats; before long there was a group of wailing relatives round the pen where the sold goods were put, jeered at by the guards –

'Wan'a go south, do you? Wan'a free trip?'

'Gi'ye a set of chains an'all!'

The young men went first, then the older ones and the damaged goods, one likely to recover from his wounds paired with one like to die, to get him off the slavemasters' hands at a nominal price; then the women, most presentable coming up first. Squatting in rows in the pens, they endeavoured to straighten their clothes and clean their faces with rags dipped in spit, handing a comb along the row –

'Here, girl, put your hair in place! And leave off snivelling, you'll ruin your chances, and mine an'all!'

She sniffled up the steps, fists to her eyes. The keeper jerked her hands down, pulled her headcloth straight, and, as she came into the public view, turned her right profile to the crowd to conceal the red birthmark on the left side of her face. The auctioneer began. 'A young maiden –'

'Maiden! Ha! An that's a maiden, I'm King of Heaven!'

'– a young maiden, not well-favoured, it's true, but amenable to schooling as a lady's maid, a seamstress, a kitchen maid, or . . . in any other trade . . .' He winked at a certain notorious dealer. The young maiden started to cry.

'Or even better – to water your garden!' interjected the wit.

'Shall we say . . . ten sols?' Any price to be rid of this fountain of tears.

'Eleven,' said a voice.

'Eleven? . . . any advance on eleven sols? . . . young, and quick-witted . . . a simple mind and a soft body, to mould to any shape you choose – do I hear twelve?' Silence. Reluctantly, he jerked the bell-rope; it clanged harshly, and the keeper pushed the girl to the other side. The buyer was paying the clerks; a wooden clamp was put on the girl's wrists, and a rope tied to it to lead her by. She stood there, unable to wipe the tears and snot from her face, while sealing-wax sizzled in a candle-flame and dropped on to the slip of paper stamped with the seal of purchase. The rope tugged at her wrists. She wailed out loud, and stumbled after the red cloak of her new owner.

The buildings by the Dinarn Gate had suffered from catapult missiles during the siege, and their own people had left them; so

89

they were suitable for billeting common soldiers and officers of the less aristocratic type. Ayndra was lodged on the second floor of a ramshackle house, above a company of phalanx and a score of artillerymen, who whistled and clapped when they saw what she led in.

'Hoo! Hoo! See what's come home from market!'

'Got'self a piece of skirt then, sir?'

'I have, gentlemen, and all for myself,' said Ayndra. 'If I find any of you so much as laying a finger on her, then – zzt!' she drew a finger across her throat, and went up the rickety wooden stairs to a tiny landing. She unlocked the ill-fitting door and pushed the girl first into the room. A small window to the west let in streams of sunlight; sagging canvas half-filled the room – Ayndra's tent, put to use as a roof-lining. She shut the door and leant against it. 'Sit down,' she said in Haraminharn tongue. 'Tell me your name.'

The girl squatted on the bare boards and blinked up at her, astonished by the sound of her own language. 'Master? I'm named Yunnil.'

Ayndra pulled a large handkerchief out of her sleeve and squatted beside her, reaching out to wipe the mess from her face. She flinched from her. Ayndra caught hold of her hands. 'Don't fear! I'm not a man, and I'll not let any man force himself upon you – I'll not let them touch you. Now, I'm Captain Aleizon Ailix Ayndra, and you should call me sir – not mistress, I'm not to be called mistress – and you're to be my maidservant. I'll ask you to wash my clothes and attend to the place where I live, and cook for me if I'm not dining at the royal kitchens – I'm a captain in the Safic army . . .'

Yunnil sniffed noisily. 'Then you are a traitor to our people – what do you here?'

'No, I'm Safic born, though my mother was a woman of Haramin – did they brand you in the pens? Show me your arm . . . o, your hands . . .' She undid the wooden clasp, and held Yunnil by one wrist, rolling up her sleeve. On her left upper arm, red and weeping, were the stylised waves of Safi. 'Were you seized . . . in the siege?'

'When your soldiers came – my mother, she went out, and they caught her, and crushed her . . . she's dead! And I went out, and a soldier, he threatened me with a sword if I would not . . . and I've not seen my father – he'd not speak to me, I'm ruined! No one would have me now!'

'O, leave off weeping – leave off! Please! Hush, hush, menami . . .' Yunnil opened her mouth and howled. Ayndra embraced her and pulled her close, rocking back and forth – 'Hush! hush you, hush . . . I'll give you all you need, and no one will harm you, I'll keep the men away from you . . . I'll teach you care of weapons, all sort of skills – but leave off crying, it does not help you nor anyone! Hush now!' She went on rocking her and talking and wiping her tears with the handkerchief until she calmed down, and collapsed in a quiet heap with her head in Ayndra's lap; from where she lifted her head to a pillow, covered her with a blanket and left her to sleep.

In the morning, when Ayndra woke up, Yunnil was sitting on the far side of the room, watching her.

'So you've not run off in the night?'

'No . . . sir.'

'A good thing. If a runaway slave is caught, they put them to death, or sell them into the mines . . . have you thought? I'll find someone to buy you if you'll not stay with me.'

'I have thought . . . sir, I'll serve you.'

'A good thing.'

'Whatever, sir, I have no other choice – will you beat me?'

'Only if you steal from me, or tell others my affairs. Come with me now, and I'll give you breakfast.'

The Outer Council, on the twenty-fourth day of Second Month, met around the throne; Ailixond would sit there, the lords on the steps, and the commoners on benches at the foot. Lord Polem, on the right of the chair, stood up and waved to Aleizon Ailix Ayndra. 'Captain! It's many days since last I saw you.'

'It is, my lord.'

'A pleasant city, do you not think, now that all the rebels are out of it?'

'If one has money, I do not doubt it.'

'Ah, but surely you have now.'

'I have debts, my lord.'

'Perhaps I might help . . .'

'My lord, you might lend me thirty sols.'

Polem's smile fixed. 'Thirty?' he said.

'I would be most grateful, my lord.'

'Gold or silver?'

'I had thought silver, my lord, but if you . . .'

'I will send you thirty silver sols by evening – indeed, I will send it to you as a gift.'

'O, no, my lord, I could not take it. I'll accept a loan, but not such a gift.'

'O, it is hardly a gift – a tribute!'

'I could not take it, my lord. I do not mean to disparage your generosity, but on no account . . .'

'Then I will make you a loan with no fixed date by which you should repay it – how is that, sir?'

'Thank you, my lord.' She bowed, and went on to a place on the far side of the room.

'Well, well,' said Lakkannar. 'What are you at with our little soldier-bitch?'

'She is a fine soldier,' said Polem. 'Although I would not complain at a little more of the bitch.'

'What, her? She's skinny and flat as a boy. Are you –'

'Stand for my lord the king! All stand!'

Ailixond grasped his long staff and hobbled up between the benches. 'Gentlemen, my lords, good day! Excuse me if I do not stand to address you – and excuse also the lapse between the convocation of this Council and the last meeting. We have been somewhat occupied . . .' He described the arrangements for the pacification and governance of the state of Haramin, and summoned clerks to give reports on the state of the Treasury, the treasures captured in the city, and on affairs in the other provinces of the Empire, before he went on to the question of the provinces north of Haramin, formerly under the dominion of Raq'min. 'You will recall that near New Year's night, we had a skirmish with the besieged at Dinarn Gate. It appears now that Yourcen who called himself king was making his escape from a postern gate in the citadel, and had sent his lieutenant Heshen to distract our forces while he ran away. His flight caused a rift among those left in the city. Some said that they should submit to Safi as soon as he was gone, since he had abandoned them. Others said that they should hold the city until he returned with an army from the north. The latter faction prevailed until we had stormed White Gate, when the peace party overcame the leaders of the loyal faction, and Master Heshen surrendered the crown to me. Yourcen, when he departed, promised to raise a new army among his vassals in the north. He has now had two months in which to do it, and we have no news of how far he has succeeded, although by now he must know that the city has fallen to us, which will not strengthen his claim on their aid. Now one may say that we should sit here and await his coming, being sure of crushing him if he appears – and if not, he will be lost and powerless in the north, and we may forget him. But to my mind, this would leave us perpetually exposed to any upstart who chose to present himself as the lost king and march against us; so I propose that we refortify the city and leave a strong garrison here – so that, if he should return, we can hold it against him – while I shall lead the rest of the army northaway and begin the reduction of the citadels of the northern vassals.'

Lord Arpalond said, 'But that may drive them to assist Yourcen when they would not otherwise have done so – do you not think?'

'I believe', said Ailixond, 'that they will hold back as long as possible, in hopes that Yourcen and myself will destroy one another and leave them free, or at least weaken the victor so greatly that he cannot enforce his rule on them. Certainly, we can offer them good terms if they will give Yourcen up to us.'

'A vile trick,' said Sulakon, 'and an evil precedent, to bribe men to revolt against their lawful overlord.'

'If Yourcen still deserves that name – but it is a vile trick. We know too little about the north to say with any sureness what they will choose to do. Nevertheless I think it clear that we cannot leave them to threaten us. I think that, with a little strategy and statecraft, we can keep Yourcen wandering through the winter, and if we must bring him to battle – having failed to bring him down by any other means – let it be when I choose, not when he likes. We must defeat him once and for all; but we should not sit waiting for him, nor, I believe, must we defeat him straightaway. It will be a winter of hard work, and hard weather – but I think, do you not, that we can bear it. If I may be permitted a trope, in this city we have our foot upon the neck of the kingdom of Haramin. Our winter's task is merely to hack through its thick neck . . .'

The army of Safi marched out of Blue Gate on the fifth day of Third Month, a bright windy day in the last of the summer. Six days later, it began raining.

Twelve days later, it was still raining. The infantry plodded through a sea of mud; horsemen soaked cloaked and hooded aback their mounts. The food was cold, because dry wood could not be found for fires: everyone was damp, because there were no fires to dry clothes with, and the wet got into everything. The road curved around a rain-pocked lake; in many places, water had risen to cover it, forcing wide detours.

The lords rode at the head of the column, where the road was not quite reduced to porridge, swathed in raincloaks of oiled wool; coats splashed with mud, their fine horses stumbled along with lowered heads. Lord Ailixond and Lord Polem rode side by side, the king marked out by the pale blur of his unbleached woolcloak among the others' blacks and browns, deep hood completely concealing his face.

He said suddenly, 'Speak to me.'

Polem was taken by surprise. 'Eh?'

'Speak to me. Make some conversation.'

'Conversation?'

'I realise that these conditions are no burden to those with no mind to lose, but I'm like to go out of my mind with boredom – say something!'

'O,' said Polem, 'o . . . is not this weather a dreadful thing? It never rains like this in Safi. What I would not give to see a river all dried up in summer again! Do you know, yesterday I opened a clothes-chest to get out a dry tunic, and there was mould on it! I said to my valet, I said –'

'Can you think of nothing apart from the weather? I shall be forced to string you up by the roadside! At least it will provide a spectacle.'

'O . . . I had a letter yesterday from Yiakarak. It was from Thio – you recall Thio? A little girl – well, perhaps not – but anyway, she writes that her child was born on the twentieth of Second, only it was not one child, but two! Twin sons! So that's six sons I have now, and five daughters – my oldest, he lives with his mother in Safi, and –'

Ailixond sighed. 'Ah, fetch me someone else to talk to.'

Polem turned his horse to the side and rode slowly down the column, muttering, 'I should not have to, I am not an errand boy . . .' The men he passed did not bother to look up. Over the rows of bowed heads, he saw another rider, wrapped in a black cloak topped by a broad-brimmed hat. He sat up and spurred his horse on. 'Captain Ayndra?'

'What is it?' She lifted her head, tipping a sheet of water from her hat-brim.

'Lord Ailixond wishes to see you.'

'Now, my lord? – whatever for?'

'Come with me, and I'll tell you . . . he wishes to speak with you, that is, he wishes to speak with someone, and I have no conversation, I cannot . . . you seem to have wide knowledge . . .'

'I do not know what I should say to a king!'

'O, say anything! – Only, do not speak about the weather, or your children –'

'Children?'

'O, no matter – and no foul language, he will not have foul

94

language, but anything will do.'

They passed the Companion Cavalry, and came up with the lords. Polem directed Ayndra to take up station on one side of the king, while he went to the other. The three horses fell easily into step.

The off-white hood turned toward Ayndra. 'Good day, sir?'

'A companion for you,' said Polem, 'Captain Aleizon Ailix Ayndra.'

'Good day, my lord.'

'Polem – have you said to the captain . . .?'

'I said you wanted someone to talk to.'

'A strange request,' said Ailixond. He sounded as if he were smiling. 'Are you fond of story-telling?'

'I can do it, lord, if you . . .'

'You might tell me more of S'Thurrulass. I've not known many Safeen who have been there, save merchants and they only know what goods one may buy there.'

'It's a long journey, and by land one can hardly pass, it would be a year or so even if there were a road, which there is not – and by ship . . . you know that our ships raided their land in the past?'

'I do. But nothing came of it.'

'No, but they remember, and they've no love for Safi, they say we are barbarians and keep our women shut up – I hardly know where I should start, lord, it's a land as rich as we are and with as much history – more, indeed, Suthine is years older than Safi, no one knows when their kingdom began . . . I did meet one Safin living there, his name was Scarlattin –'

'Scarlattin? An astronomer?'

'Yes, he was –'

'The king my father banished him in the four hundred and fiftieth year of the city, at the instigation of the College of Priests, who said that his teachings on the heavens were heretical. I had not known that he went to Suthine. His books were burnt in Safi.'

'O, no, he lives in Suthine still, or did a few years ago, and he has his book, Concerning the Motions of the Planets.'

'In which he teaches that the planets are not divine, but lumps of rock much like Sard, and turn around the sun, not around Sard – also that Sard has the form of a round fruit, and hangs in nothingness, instead of resting in the waters of the Eternal Ocean – night and day coming from the rotation of the fruit, not from the dipping of the sun into the ocean's waters each night . . .'

'He said that all his teachings had been forgotten in Safi, since

95

the priests forbade them to be taught – and if his books were burnt . . .?'

'All sorts of books come into the palace library that are not permitted elsewhere. The king has to know all that goes on in his kingdom, after all . . . when I studied the writings of the astronomers, though, and saw his book, I thought this. If the earth turns from west to east, and an archer shoots eastward, then an arrow from his bow should travel further than one fired to the west. Yet that's not so – so how can the earth turn?'

'Ha,' said Ayndra. 'I am sure there is an answer to that one – he said that no one had yet formed an argument against him – and I saw, a few years ago, the star of Maishis passing across the face of the sun, and it appeared as a round black speck . . .'

Polem took the opportunity to sketch a salute, and drop back between Lord Lakkannar and Lord Iadagon, where he could hear some more amusing talk. Lakkannar said, 'What does he want with your little she-soldier?'

'He wanted someone to talk to,' said Polem. 'But he liked nothing I said, and sent me to get someone, and I thought, she talks so . . . now they speak about the motion of the heavens, or some such! I do not understand it. Nor why Ailixond should care about such nonsense.'

'Ay well! I am sure he does not care for her face.'

'At least I am not made to listen, as when he has one of his tame philosophers to address us . . . do you know, I had a letter from Thio?'

'Who is that?'

'Thio – she was with me in Yiakarak –'

'What, was that the fourth or fifth last?'

'No! I only had to leave her because she was with child –'

'O indeed. And then there was, what was her name, with the mole between her breasts, and then –'

'How do you know about the mole?'

'Think you you were the first man she sold herself to?'

'Sold herself! She said she . . .'

'And asked you for new gowns, and gold bracelets, and . . .'

'Well! I wished to give her gifts, so . . . but as I said, Thio wrote and said that she had born me a son – twin sons! So now . . .'

From the Secret Chronicle of Firumin, High Steward of the Household of Ailixond VIII, Most Serene Lord and King of Safi, King of Haramin, Lord of Lysmal, Lord of Purrllum, and so forth and so forth:

20:III:462 The dismal hills of this country are full of bandits. They have taken care to keep clear of the army, but other travellers are commonly molested by them, and they live by tributes levied on the roads. No one dares travel here except in large armed caravans. My lord cannot endure this state of affairs, and departs with the Companions and the Silver Shields to clear the hills, leaving Lord Golaron in charge of the army. Among my lord's companions is now the woman (I do not think that she should be honoured with the name lady) called Aleizon Ailix Ayndra, who is very thick with Lord Polem. They say she is not yet his mistress, but no doubt that is what it will come to, despite her habit of wearing the clothes of a man and using words which would shame a common soldier. I cannot approve of this habit my lord has of raising commoners who take his eye to high rank. Aino was the last such, and he died in battle, and before that there was Pittirin who was sent off to some remote and inferior province when my lord tired of him. Not that any province could be more remote and inferior than that where we presently find ourselves.

24:III:462 Encamped before the so-called city of Benhanna'ram, a cluster of miserable hovels which the inhabitants share with their cattle, to siege it while we await my lord's return. Meanwhile I must attempt to support the Household in this miserable land, and they berate me forever about how hard they must labour and how poor the food they are given. I can hardly endure many months more in these barbarian wildernesses.

34:III:462 My lord returned this day, victorious of course. The robbers in the hills gave in easily, amazed at the speed of his movement. I hear a dramatic tale of how they came upon the robbers' castle while they were feasting, and my lord slew their chief with his own hand. Lord Polem swears that he put an end to six of them. The woman Ayndra is reputed to have fought valiantly. My lord announced this night at dinner that he would have her attend him as a member of the Household. She hardly left off stuffing herself long enough to reply. Lord Sulakon was displeased. I heard him later telling Golaron that it was neither right nor natural. Polem of course was delighted.

35:III:462 My lord brought back with him the second-in-command of the robbers. This day the villain went up to the citadel with a truce flag and Captain Carmago, and pleaded with the inhabitants to surrender. A number gathered to listen, but seemed not to be impressed, though hard to tell at a distance. He also brought back a quantity of greasy mutton, very poor stuff, and barley meal. How they expect me to make good meals from such filth I cannot tell. In Safi I would not feed the slaves on such muck.

36:III:462 This day the self-appointed king of Benhanna'ram surrendered to my lord. My lord was most gracious, restoring him to the lordship of his miserable lands after he had sworn fealty to the New Empire. They exchanged gifts, and all seemed content, except those like myself who must pack up the Household and go off on roads which worsen everyday . . .

18:IV:462 Encamped before yet another of these hill-towns, though one greater in size and more formidable than those we have taken so far. Six have fallen to us now in not a month and a half of campaigning. At least a siege will provide us with a rest. It begins to snow on the hilltops. How we shall travel, if, as it seems, we must, when the roads are covered I cannot begin to imagine . . .'

Polem and Aleizon Ailix Ayndra and a party of six soldiers, two of them mountain-born, sat up on the hillside high above the camp. Now and then the wind brought its faint noise up to them, but mostly they heard only the wind and the birds calling, and endless running water. The men were chaffing one another and pointing out their own tents, the horse-lines, the royal pavilion; the lord and the captain sat higher up the hill. Polem drank from a flask and offered it to Ayndra, but she refused. He stood up and clapped his hands. 'Let us go on! We have no time to waste.'

The way got steadily harder as they went higher, and they began to use hands as well as feet. The hill-citadel lay in the lee of a tall crag; Polem, uncharacteristically, had suggested that they send someone up there to get a good overview of the fortifications, and had named the party he offered to lead up there. They described a wide circle among the rocks and scree slopes, until, directed by the local men, they emerged on a level, grassy meadow directly above the town. A path of sorts led down about fifty feet, to a ledge on the face of the crag itself.

'I and the captain will go down and make a record of what we see,' Polem said. 'You may rest up here, and keep watch for anyone who might threaten us, in case we have been tracked – otherwise, do as you like, you need not bother us.'

'Would it not help to have more observers?' said Ayndra.

'I am farsighted,' said Polem, 'and the ledge is narrow, we should not crowd it.' Officers should not quarrel in front of the lower ranks; she submitted, and they picked their way down the steep slope.

'She don' wan'a be lef' alone wi'm,' said one of the guards.

'Would you?'

'There's not many women I know would not!'

'Ah, that's a funny woman . . . but she can look after herself.'

Ayndra scrambled diagonally across the slope to the foot of a rock pinnacle at the end of a sheer rock face. She gripped it with both hands, and swung round it on to a ledge of rock perhaps seven feet broad; two more steps, and she was looking over the very edge. She gasped at the view; the guides had led them very well. It seemed that if she were to leap from the cliff she would die on the cobbles of the market square, or crash through one of the tiny thatched roofs. Minute stonewalled fields covered the ground where the river had cast up fertile soil; water flashed white where it ran through rocky rapids. She saw roofs, pinprick smokeholes, the chieftain's dwelling – a larger area of equally grimy thatch, smeared with black in the direction of the prevailing wind; the irregular polygon of the walls and the midden-heaps outside, the Safic camp further up the valley; all as exact and pristine as a picture-map.

A small sound beside her woke her from contemplation of the scene: Polem clutched at her sleeve. He rocked back from the edge of the abyss. 'Such heights make me dizzy,' he said, and pulled her closer to him.

'Do they, my lord?'

'Yes!' He closed his eyes and threw his arms round her. She said, 'An you can face a mob of screaming savages set on having your blood, a harmless cliff should not frighten you – when it does not affront a mere woman, and a common woman at that?'

He was taken aback; while he tried to think up a telling reply, she snapped his arms from around her and knelt down. From the front of her overtunic she took a roll of paper, a portable inkwell and a couple of new quill pens, weighted the paper with a couple of stones and set to drawing a careful plan of the town, its walls and as many of the twisting streets as she could discern. Polem sat down some way back from the brink. She asked if he had recovered from his dizziness.

'Entirely,' he said. 'It was only a momentary thing.'

The quill pen scratched across the paper. Polem took from the pouch slung over his shoulder a white napkin, and began fastidiously to eat the cold roast mutton and bread which it contained, watching her as she drew, unaware of his scrutiny.

'Interesting,' he said. 'It does not look very formidable from here.'

'I talked with Amurret recently – you know him, my lord, the Chief Engineer – and he said that the walls here are ideally suited to undermining. They're footed on gravelly soil, not rock, and stand far enough from the river that we should get no water in the diggings.'

'You must be lonely, here in the camp, with so few other women about you, and those that there are are hardly of the type which you would wish to befriend.'

'He told me that the classic method of detecting a mine is by placing large bowls of water on the ground near the place where one believes it to be.'

'It would be possible for you to be introduced to the ladies who have travelled with the army – Lord Sulakon's wife, both of them that is, Lady Ailissa and the other, and Lord Arpalond's wife, and his lesser-wife too . . .'

'The water is supposed to show up by its motion the shaking of the ground where the excavation is.'

'But then I think you'd not agree very well. The ladies are not at all like you.'

'I am not sure that it would work. I would think that there would be too much shaking from other sources, and too little from the digging – although I suppose if the digging was near the surface, and the bowls right above it, and if it were that close, one would be as good as done for anyway.'

'I've never met any woman that was like you,' said Polem, growing desperate.

'Of course, I had the idea of a mine filled with powderfire . . .'

'Will you talk of nothing but bloody fortifications?' exclaimed Polem. Ayndra pushed away the stones, waved the plan to dry it and snapped shut the inkwell before she said, 'It would seem, my lord, that you need talking to on the subject of fortifications; it is, after all, the purpose that brings us up here.'

'God damn you!' cried Polem. 'It is only through my good offices that you are not still in the artillery, left back in Raq'min!'

'My lord, I never asked you to do me any service, although I'm most grateful for the help you have given me.'

'And you'd do well to remember it!' He made off along the ledge in a swirl of furred cloak. Ayndra looked after him, amused and a little rueful; she made sure the plan was safe in her bosom, and went after him.

The plan, rubbed clean of mud and fingermarks, was displayed on a board for the Council to study it. Polem stood beside it to hold forth, while Ayndra waited behind it, hands folded, impassive. The town was massively fortified, with walls made of stones set in a timber lattice, with the timber fired afterwards, in many places fusing the stones into a vitreous mass, and the other side faced with large irregular boulders, jigsawed together into a smooth face. The single gate opened on a narrow passage that turned a hairpin bend in the thickness of the wall before it led into the street.

'It appears to be blocked with rubble,' Polem said, 'but even if it were not, we would do no good attacking it with a ram . . .'

'It would take half a decade to reduce those walls by bombardment.'

'Starvation? . . . ah, too slow, we cannot waste a whole winter on this.'

Ailixond stood up. So far he had let them mumble over the problem without the benefit of his aid, and they had got nowhere. 'We shall mine the walls,' he said. 'Here is the place. Leader Amurret has tried the soil as near as he could get to the wall, and could not find rock even at nine feet down. And once the mine has reached under the wall, we shall fill it with powderfire and blast it. It will not take more than a couple of sixdays. Captain Ayndra, with Leader Amurret, will oversee it.' He nodded to the captain. She favoured him with one of her extraordinarily rare, genuine smiles; it transfigured her plain bitter features. Polem looked deeply disappointed.

Amurret had a corps of fifty miners; the engineers put up a large wooden shelter a safe distance from the wall, and they went into it and started digging, while another identical hut was put up on the other side of the town, to distract the enemy. The spoil was stored in the hut, and taken out under cover of darkness, so that they could not tell which was the real mine, if either was a mine at all. The tunnel went down twelve feet vertically, and then struck out underground; it was no more than four or five feet high, the roof propped by timber, with earth pillars left at intervals. The miners worked on their knees, stripped to leather breeches, wearing stiff-brimmed hats with candles set on them to light the work. In eight days, they were at the foot of the wall; then they had to work more quietly, and only by day, lest they alert the defenders as they hollowed out a long thin chamber in its base. Amurret took Aleizon Ailix Ayndra down to survey it for the placing of the powder. He gave her a miner's hat, its brim caked with tallow, and led her down into the damp hole, thick and warm with the smoke of tallow-dips. The earth floor sloped gently down toward the wall; it was not far to go. Hanging down out of the roof was an immense brown stone, the marks of the tools that had shaped it centuries ago still clear. They had to go on all fours to get beneath it, and emerge into a chamber perhaps ten feet long and six broad, forested with pit-props. A couple of miners were burrowing away at one end; once inside the wall's face, they had only to clear out loose-packed rubble. 'Chief danger's the roof falling before it's ready,' said Amurret. He had been a director of the silver mines in the south of Thaless, under Lord Parakison, before he had joined Lord Ailixond's military engineers. Ayndra looked around her. 'Is it much like this in a real iron mine, or a silver mine or whatever?'

'No,' said Amurret succinctly. 'Shumar's teeth! This is th'ome of the gods to compare. You high-noses, you've not seen it.'

'You take me for a high-nose?' she said.

'You're all high-noses. You not so much as some, sir, but a high-nose all the same. Now what will you do with this powder of yours?'

'Is it dry here?'

'As can be expected – feel it.'

'Ah . . . I have it. We'll sling nets from the ceiling and stuff them with bags of powder. We'll need a good bit to shift this – and I'll lay a fuse, and then we can stuff up the entrance with earth save for a little culvert with the fuse, set light to it, and run like the devil, and all will fall like a paper castle.'

'O aye? Your powder'll do it?'

'Did you not see what it did to the Blue Gate in Raq'min?'

'I was working on the roads in the south of Haramin while you were playing with your machines up there.'

'Then you must wait and see.'

'And who's to risk's life setting light to the thing?'

'O, I shall do that. If anyone's to be crushed, it should be I.'

Amurret nodded, looking slightly less angry.

'I've seen all I need for now. Let me back to the light.' She dropped to all fours and crawled under the stone.

She spent a day with a team of miners filling the underground chamber with sacks of powder – some brought from Raq'min, more made in haste in the last few days – and then, on the thirtieth day of Fourth Month, when it was snowing in the valley, they were ready to fire. She sent everyone else out of the tunnel; Amurret and his miner captains waited for her in the hut, while the king and the lords gathered on the edge of the camp to watch.

102

All the tallow dips had been extinguished; the single candle on her hat threw monstrous shadows as she shuffled bent double up to the wall that now blocked the chamber entrance. An inverted piece of clay guttering protruded from it, with an oil-soaked cord made of lamp-wicks running into it, passing down into the chamber and a heap of tinder and powder, under the bulging nets hanging silent from the ceiling. She took off her hat and tipped it forward so that the candle met the end of the fuse. It sputtered and caught; she waited till it burnt out of sight, and leapt up and ran. The only sounds were her feet and her breathing, laboured with anxiety, not exertion; the grey light of the entrance came into sight, and she bounded onto the ladder. A ring of faces surrounded the hole. She leapt upward, and then the first whisper of sound reached her; hands seized her arms, jerked her out and onto her feet. Then the roar started, as if a great beast was bellowing under the earth. The ground rippled, and a great gust of contaminated air blew out of the tunnel's mouth; one heard it through bones as much as ears – 'But look at that!' said Ayndra, pointing out of the slit window at the front of the hut. A crack was spreading up the face of the wall, like a tree sprouting between the blocks, and with vast dignity it began to slump into the collapsing earth, bursting forward in a cascade of rubble and dust as the ground sagged inwards. Smoke issued from the ground, and dust of stone and mortar rose in clouds. 'O beautiful!' said Ayndra. 'O, is that not beautiful?'

'I never thought – how can it be done? It's witchcraft!' said Amurret. She said, 'O no! O no! O no!' and started laughing.

'I swear you have a demon!' he said. She went on laughing. 'Let us go to the king! We shall go and receive the surrender of the men of Yollan! Go!' She ran out into the snow.

The lords had a canopy to shield them from the weather; under it, most of them had not yet thought of anything to say about the spectacle of the snow-capped wall sliding half into the ground and the ground itself giving in like an egg trodden by a boot heel, as the white earth fumed groaning – 'Is it not wondrous?' Polem exclaimed. 'You should have seen the Blue Gate! But this is far more – as if we've tamed the earthquake! Miraculous!'

Sulakon said, 'What power is this?'

Ailixond shook his head; his eyes gleamed.

'Here she comes,' Lakkannar dug Polem in the ribs. Ayndra stumbled to a halt, hatless, flushed, breathing hard. 'There it is!' she gasped; looked from side to side, and straightened up. Her face set in response to the hard glances around her. 'My lords? Should we not – that is, should we not – are we ready to advance . . .

'I have seen nothing like it!' said Golaron.

Ailixond clapped his hands and cried, 'The Silver Shields! Banners! Trumpeters! To me! My lords, we shall go forth into Yollan. I do not think we shall have much to do.' Ayndra stood, hat in hand, her expression verging on dismay as lords went past her and Ailixond turned his back to instruct the messengers waiting behind him. Polem, next to the king, tried to catch her eye and give her a cheerful smile, but she did not respond. 'What is this?' she exclaimed.

'Everyone's astonished, they don't know – I've never seen . . .' Polem started; then Aixilond spun round, stepped forward and clapped her on the shoulders. 'Miraculous!' he said. 'Come with me, Polem – follow!' He strode away from the canopy; a clutch of standard bearers and trumpeters and Captain Carmago of the Silver Shields came running to meet him. He ordered them to go up on the ruined wall – 'And the heralds. Call the king of Yollan, and offer him to surrender and we shall wreak no more havoc upon him.' He turned to Ayndra again, looking like a mountain cat that had smelt blood. 'I think you have frightened the wits out of most of my lords. I tell you, even though I saw what you had left of Blue Gate, I never believed that you'd do such as that! We can devastate half the north – they'll all submit as soon as we threaten them! – have I confirmed your commission?'

'No, my lord, I –'

'I'll have you to advise me in perpetuity! We could have taken Raq'min in half a month. Why did you not tell me earlier?'

'I did not know. I've never seen it done either.'

'Then the gods must have inspired you! – Carmago? Go up with them, I will follow as soon as their lords have come out. Where is my armour bearer? Go fetch your arms, Captain, and come up with me and I'll have the king of this place kiss your feet. Where's Agriano? Agriano! Send a company of slingers up on the walls. Send for my armour bearer! Trumpeter! Go up with Carmago and blow fanfares. Send the banners of Safi up there also. My banner to follow me . . .'

Ayndra looked utterly dazzled as he turned his attention on her; but as he was distracted, she started to grin as well; and then to laugh; and she was roaring so much that she could hardly run, to go and fetch her arms to take the surrender of Yollan.

On the sixteenth day of Fifth Month, the army of Safi descended into the valley of the river Hassa, now frozen and silent beneath the ice, and came to the large town of Hassalh (large for these parts, at least). The prince of Hassalh had already announced his faithfulness to the New Empire, his devotion to Lord Ailixond and his hatred of the vile Yourcen. The weather in the hills had turned bitter, and for the last three days the army had marched through unending drifts and blizzards; Ailixond suggested that the prince offer them hospitality for the harshest part of the winter.

The whole town was one vast, rambling, thick-walled house, with only the main roads open to the sky, all the rest layered with undulating thatch, beneath which the inhabitants pursued a warm, dark, stuffy existence during the snowy months. The people of Hassalh were of a different race and language from the natives of Haramin proper, and, since these foreign overlords were led by a king who was rumoured to be weapon-proof and a mighty warlock, they welcomed them into the rushlit streets and broke out their winter's barley stores to feed them, while the snow drifted high against the walls.

'Lady, sir, someone come to visit you while you were out.'

'What?' Ayndra was lying on her bed beside a brazier full of charcoal; she was lighting a stick of resin in it. 'Someone came to visit.' She was teaching Yunnil to speak Safic.

'Lord Polem, he said.'

'O indeed? Did he give you money?'

'Well, sir, he say . . .'

'How much money did he give you?'

'A silver sol, sir.'

'O did he . . . keep it, then. What did he say?'

'If you would . . . he said that he would like for you to dine with him.'

'O, would he?'

'Sir, he is . . . sir, they're saying to me that he's the best man in the army – o, and he said, next day the Companion Cavalry are, o, they go out, I cannot remember all, sir – he did say, sixth hour. If is no snow again – but then he say, you should come dine, this night.'

'With the king?'

'With him he say.'

'O indeed . . . now if I had a manservant I could send him with a letter saying Lord Polem do not attempt to bribe my servants . . . and if I had more pay I could pay him the money I owe him . . . on the other hand, i could go and ask him to lend me, o, what do I need, at least ten gold sols . . .' She took several greedy sniffs of smoke, and giggled.

105

'Sir, he is – most handsome man they said, in the army . . . sir, I do think him very fine . . .' Yunnil reached out for the proffered stick of resin. There was a pall of bluish smoke a yard thick under the low ceiling.

'I though you did not like men.'

'I don't like – but he's not same, sir, he's . . .'

'Whatever, he's not the most handsome man in the army. O no.'

'Who is, then, sir?'

'Give me that back.'

'Who is, sir?'

'What? The best man in the army? O, I should have thought it clear . . . shan't tell you.'

'O, sir.'

'Never know who you might go talking to after all.'

'O sir! I never tell. As you tell me the first day I serve you.'

'There's always a first time . . . god! So I am supposed to go out with the Companions next day? I cannot do it. I shall be thrown if I do not fall off. O, good god, what do I here?'

'He did say dinner this night, sir.'

'O, I shall not go, I cannot . . .' She fell on the bed giggling again, and dropped the stick of resin on the floor. Yunnil immediately seized it. 'Ha! Ha! Greedy beast!' said Ayndra.

'You the worst, sir.'

'O, be quiet, you uppity slave! . . . why do you not put on my hat and go to Lord Polem?'

'O, I could not sir, I could not.'

'No, put it on.' Ayndra fished under the bed, pulled out her black hat and dropped it on Yunnil's head over her headcloth. 'O! Ho! O, look, see yourself in this . . .' She held up a polished pewter plate. Yunnil stared at her reflection. The hat, much too large, seemed to fall down almost to her nose. They both collapsed in hysterics. Several loud knocks sounded on the door. 'Quiet!' Ayndra exclaimed. They froze. The knocks came again.

'Is anyone there?' came Polem's voice. 'Captain Ayndra? Are you there?'

Ayndra rolled over on to the floor. 'Yunnil!' she hissed. 'I shall hide. Open and say I am gone to, to the library, and I shall not be back till past midnight.' She squirmed under the bed, and pulled the blanket down to conceal her. Yunnil got to her feet, and staggered to the door. Polem knocked again. 'Are you there?' he said plaintively.

The door opened a crack; a gust of warm air, reeking of a

106

musky-sweet herbal scent, swept across him. Polem tried to push inside, but the entrance was blocked; Captain Ayndra seemed to have grown shorter, her hat barely came up to the middle of his chest – 'Is that you?' he said.

'My lord?' The hat tipped up; it was the Haraminharn slave. 'What are you doing?' Polem said. 'Why are you – is your mistress here?'

Yunnil shook her head; the hat slipped over her eyes, and she pushed it back. 'My lord,' she said, and stuck, deserted by Safic. Polem looked over her head; the room was filled with the sweet smoke, illuminated only by the glow of the brazier. 'Where is Captain Ayndra? Why have you got her hat on? Let me come in.'

Yunnil stepped back. 'No! No!' she squealed, pushing at the door.

'Where has she gone?' Polem said. 'Answer me! I order you.'

Yunnil gabbled at him in Haraminharn tongue. He struck the door jamb with a clenched fist. 'I will not be put off like this! Answer me!' There was movement within; he craned his neck, and saw Ayndra roll out from under the bed. 'What!'

She stood up. 'My lord? I . . . I dropped a coin, and had to go search for it. My lord, I would ask you not to terrify my servants, nor attempt to bribe them either.'

'I have made no such attempt! I came, sir, to deliver a message –'

'Since when did you run around with your own messages?'

'Captain! – I have not come here to argue with you –'

'Then what have you come for?'

'Captain – Ayndra – let me come in –'

Yunnil stretched her head round and wailed something in her own tongue. Ayndra strode to the door. 'My lord. Let me step outside and we may talk. Yunnil, sit in here and wait till I call you.' She snatched the hat from her maidservant and pushed her back into the room, stepped into the passage outside and closed the door, leaning against it. Polem smelt of wine and expensive perfumes. She folded her arms over her hat and looked up at him, in the glimmering light of the single torch set over the junction of passageways a few yards away. His soft brown eyes were as wide and gentle as a dog's; the fair regular features, flushed with wine and feeling. 'My lord,' she said.

'You do not have to call me that now.'

She said, 'What do you want of me?'

'I sent to you to ask if you wish to dine with me this evening –'

'And also to tell me of exercises for the Companions, next day, at sixth hour –'

107

'Please! Leave off talking of such matters when you know that that is not what I have come here for.'

'You have not said what you have come here for.'

'It must be clear to you —'

'My lord. I am an officer in the Grand Army —'

'And you're a woman,' he said, 'and I've met no woman like you. Ayndra, you do not know — I should be married by now, but I cannot marry unless I marry a noble lady, and noble ladies, they've never been outside of the House of Women and they're taught to hold stiff when a man kisses them, not like the women of pleasure, but I cannot marry a woman of pleasure — but you —'

'My lord. Some also would say that I should be married by now.'

'And you are not? But then —'

'And I am not. Nor do I intend to be. I will not sell myself into slavery of some man in becoming his wife —'

'But I would not —'

'My lord!' she said. 'You hardly know me! How many times have I spoken to you? You don't know — o anything!'

'We know enough!' said Polem. 'I know you well enough to know — Ayndra, Ayndra, I can't —' he pressed closer to her, so close that she could smell the brassy reek of male sweat under his perfumes. He said, 'Sometimes I want you — o, so much, I can't do anything, I —'

She lodged her back against the wall, fighting with the door latch. 'My lord Polem! You are overwrought, and I, I am not altogether in my right mind — when you have cooled — I will not speak to you any longer at present!' She got the door open and got half inside. Polem took hold of it. 'Ayndra!' he said.

'I'll slam the door on your fingers!' she exclaimed. Her lips drew back and her teeth showed like an animal; her eyes were enormously dilated even for the night. 'Leave me!' She heaved at the door, Polem got his fingers out of the way just in time. He heard the bolts on the inside slamming into place.

Ayndra slid down the inside of the door. 'Aah!' she said. 'Even here! Even now! O, sweet heaven . . .' She lay down on the floor. Outside the door, the sound of metal-studded boots on the stony floor receded. Ayndra sat up, and ran her hands over herself. There had been two gloves thrust under her belt; now, she found only one. 'I've dropped my glove! — o, I shall find it in the morning, I shall not open the door again, Yunnil, not even if Lord Ailixond — o, Lord Ailixond . . .' She lay face down again.

'Sir? Sir, morning is here, sir, time to rise up . . . sir, I have found your glove, sir . . .'

'Where was it?'

'Outside the door, but it was . . . see it . . .'

Yunnil handed Ayndra a well-worn black leather glove, but it was swollen and heavy. She up-ended it over the bed, and a river of coins poured out. 'Good God!' she said. 'Did you find it so?'

'It lay outside the door, all full up, so – and look, there is this.' Yunnil picked out a silver ring. It had a plain bezel, engraved with Safic characters. Ayndra squinted at it. 'It says, Polem son of Dalar. I shall send it back.'

'What of the money?'

'I shall send it back with a note promising to repay . . . how much is it . . . god's teeth! Thirty silver sols. I shall write, I thank you for this loan – but now. Where's my leather shirt? my gambeson? my woollen undershirt? my sword . . .'

The troopers of the Companions were all men of good family, who could afford to maintain at least two horses and purchase the expensive panoply. The lords rode in the Royal Squadron, and officers of bodies of men who would not usually be engaged elsewhere in the line of battle had the right of riding with them, though not all chose to exercise it. When they rode into battle, they carried two javelins and a sword; they had no shields, but they wore helmets, mail or plated corselets, and high leather boots, with breeches plated with metal or horn to protect the thighs. Exercising now on the level windswept meadows of the snow-covered Hassa valley, they carried swords but no javelins, and wore the leather shirts and padded gambesons which usually went under mail, for warmth in the icy weather, under layered winter cloaks and furs and scarves. Right wheel, left wheel, advance, walk, trot, canter, gallop, form squares, form squadron wedges, all in response to the trumpet calls which would deliver signals to them above the din of battle; they had to be perfectly responsive to command, for they waited in battle to deliver the hammer blow to the enemy line, at that ideal moment the selection of which was Ailixond's peculiar art; and when it came, they charged in unison exactly as he directed, headed by the Royal Squadron. Ailixond on this day was riding his warhorse Harago, a grey stallion almost as old as he was, who was now kept only for major occasions – small battles he would use one of his other chargers for. When he had worn out the Companions to his heart's content, and criticised squadron leaders and individual riders and described what they should practise in future drills, he turned Harago along the river bank to ride for some distance in the bright cold sun, followed by the lords, his friends and various members of the Household.

Lakkannar pointed at Aleizon Ailix Ayndra. 'You never told me how you got on with her.'

'I cannot tell,' said Polem. 'She has not said . . . I do not know . . .'

'She seemed civil enough two days ago.'

'But that was before . . . besides, she was only admiring my sword.'

'Your what?'

'My sword – you know it, do you not? It is four feet long and made of steel, it is a very fine –' He was interrupted by Lakkannar's guffaws. 'No wonder the women chase you, eh?'

Polem spurred his horse away over the snow. Lakkannar laughed louder. 'Poor fool!' he said.

Ailixond rode side by side with Arpalond.

'A desolate land,' said Arpalond. 'I am well sick of this cold. I've been ill and shivering for months on end – I'd give much to see warm climes again . . .'

'Ah, will you also start complaining that you pine for home? I have had enough of this endless moping for Safi.'

'But do you never wish you were home again? Eight years since we left there – some of the men left their wives and families there and have not seen them since.'

'It is possible to take leave to go home if one wishes. I have sent whole regiments home on occasion, when they can be spared –'

'Which is rarely enough, lately.'

'True – but when we have found Yourcen, then we may . . .'

'What will you do when we find Yourcen – if he is still alive to be found?'

'O, he is alive. I had a message from the head of a caravan coming from the north that he's said to be holed up in one of the cities of the Seaward Plains, though they were not clear which, and said to be trying to raise an army . . . I think it's sure we'll not meet him till late spring, or midsummer, and we shall have to go some way north and west of here.'

'Further north? How much further can one go?'

'O, quite some way – but as one nears the sea, and leaves the mountains, the weather's less harsh – the mariners say that warm seas wash up the coast well into the icy regions, and moderate the climate. Have you not seen the map we're making in the

Chancellery, with the aid of maps we found in Haramin and our own surveys?'

'I shall go and look at it. O, but you think we'll be travelling north at least till year's end?'

'O, perhaps,' said Ailixond, 'I cannot say now, who knows what will happen . . .'

'You know one thing at least that may happen. Have you spoken lately with Lord Daiaron?'

'He does not visit, and I shall not volunteer to receive him. I have too much to do now without wasting my time drinking with tedious and antiquated noble lords who persist in believing that Safi is the navel of the universe,' Ailixond said irritably.

'If you'll permit me to say it, you have become somewhat cut off of late from the currents of opinion in the camp . . .'

'Do you mean that I am unaware of the mouthings of that fool Almarem? I know what he says. I do not think anyone takes note of it. He should take himself back to Safi if he desires it so much.'

'But it is somewhat tedious sitting here in this snow-covered warren . . .'

'Are you trying to advise me of something? I wish you would say it straightly if you are.'

'I cannot say much straightly,' Arpalond said, 'because I do not see it straightly – but I talk to many people, and I listen to many more, and I tell you, I do not think that the army will stand for marching ever and ever onward until we reach the land of the setting sun.'

'Are you saying that I should think now about turning around? I cannot begin to consider it. When we have done away with Yourcen and completed our dominion of the lands that used to be the Empire of Haramin, then I can think of it – but I do not know where we may find ourselves when that happens, and as for now – do you know, this is the first day I have had out of the offices of the Chancellery since we settled in Hassalh?'

'I can well believe it,' said Arpalond. 'You've not yet learnt how to leave government to others.'

'Others do not know how to do it!' said Ailixond. 'Where's Polem? – but have you become of the home party, Arpalond?'

'I have no party,' said Arpalond, 'as you know . . . but I can tell you all the parties that there are.'

'And I thank you greatly when you do.'

'Polem went some time ago. I think he's not happy at present.'

'No? He is bored, I think . . . Captain Ayndra? You've come through without falling off as you threatened.'

'Only because this horse knows the trumpet calls better than I do.' Aleizon Ailix Ayndra kicked her chestnut stallion up beside the lords. Ailixond said, 'Have you seen Polem?'

'O . . . he went off somewhere, my lord. I didn't see where.' She pulled her black scarf up over her face. 'Ai! Gods, it's cold.'

'Get a fur cloak,' said Arpalond.

'I would, if I had the – aah!' The forefeet of her horse had gone through a crust of snow resting on the tall grass filling a hollow in the ground; he snorted and jumped, and she was tossed over in a great billow of black wrappings, landing on her back in the snow. The horse, who was middle-aged and tame and well-trained by his previous owner, a trooper of the Companions who had died of fever outside Raq'min, got out of the hole and stood there waiting for her to mount again. She lay there laughing. 'Hehe! I knew it would come in the end.'

Ailixond nudged Harago round, and took her horse's reins. 'Get up!'

She climbed to her feet, and stood there still laughing, beating the snow off her hat. The sun gleamed on her uncovered hair. 'You're not harmed?' he said.

'Only in my pride. I'll have to get much more practice before I dare go near a battle.'

'O, you ride well enough, if only you can learn to be ready for sudden shocks – I watched you earlier . . .' He handed her the reins. Arpalond was close enough to see that their gloved fingers met, and bounced apart as if either burnt the other. The chestnut bent his legs to allow her to mount again; Ailixond turned Harago round. 'Let us go back!' He touched him with his long spurs; they took off after him, streaming across the blue-shadowed snow in the air bitter and beautiful as a splash of sea-spray.

It snowed on and off throughout Fifth Month, but never hard or long enough to block the endless stream of messengers from the other provinces of the New Empire – news of a good harvest in North Lysmal, a rebellion in Purrllum, a governor imprisoned for embezzlement in Thaless, letters asking for money, advice, commands, warrants . . . now and then, Lord Ailixond had time to go out exercising his troops, or riding in the hills, with the Prince of Hassalh and his friends, that was the lords and, increasingly, Aleizon Ailix Ayndra. Polem pursued her on every such occasion, and plied her with sweet words; she was formal, and very cold. he was too preoccupied with his own desires to notice where her look was warmer.

Late in the month, Polem and Lakkannar were drinking in a

112

tavern near to their lodgings in Hassalh. A fire roared in the private room they had taken, and the shutters were stuffed with rags against the cold. Polem found the atmosphere conducive to drinking; by eighth hour, he wanted to confide all his thoughts, sprawled in a high-backed chair, long legs extended to the blaze. 'Do'know why I bother,' he said, gazing into his cup. 'Vile stuff! Might as well drink horse piss! – still, there's li'l else to do in this godforsaken hole . . . pit . . .'

Lakkannar leered at him. 'Why don' we ge' some girls in? Two? Three? Four even? I tell you, the girls here, got no skills but when you show 'em a gol' sol . . .' he tittered alcoholically.

'I don' wan' 'em,' said Polem. He set down his cup and reached for the wine jar. 'God's blood! 's empty.'

'Plen'y more where that came from.' Lakkannar lurched to the door and bellowed, 'More wine! More wine here!' A middle-aged woman – the host would not trust one of his girls – scuttled in, deposited two overslopping jugs on the table, and ran out again. Lakkannar filled Polem's cup, and his own. 'O'course, 's not wine,' he explained, ' 's barley spirit. Or whatever they make here. But's good 'nough once used to it. Drink up!' He downed his share in one gulp, and bent over to pour some more. 'Le's have girls before I'm too drunk to do anything to'm.'

Polem shook his head. 'See, Lak. It's that woman. She won't have me.'

Lakkannar did not need to ask which woman. 'She still re-resh-resh-isht your advances?'

'I wen' to her room and she was . . . she try to shut my hand in the door. An' I sent her a gift of, twenty sols, I don' remember, an' my ring! I sent her my ring! An' she send it back with a note saying I thank you for the loan which I will repay when I . . . ah, an' won' even speak to me – said she'd not marry, after she said she'd no husband . . .'

'I tell you what you done wrong,' Lakkannar said. 'She thinks you're soft.'

'Soft?'

'Soft. All this mouthing silly words an' gifsh. She needs a man harder'n she is so's can respec'm. You've done nothing to respec' you. No good persuadin' 'er. Y'ought to go out and force her.'

'Do you really think so?' said Polem. 'I've never . . . I mean, usually when I . . . I mean, they come of their own accord . . .'

'All women want it,' Lakkannar said positively. 'It's nature.'

'Are you sure?'

'Ha! I can see why she thinks you're soft! How d'you think to get women ever except with money? I'd not think you could manage any other way!'

Polem slammed his cup down. 'I'll not have you say that.'

'Get out'n show different, then!' Lakkannar said.

'I will! I will! I shall go now!' He dragged the door open and stood wavering on the threshold. 'You'll see me – in the morning, I'll . . .' He reeled out. Lakkannar gathered the jugs of drink to him, and kicked the door shut. 'Do'know wha' sees in her. Skinny little bitch,' he said, and took another swig.

Ailixond's library was kept in an annex to the Treasury; which might mean anything from a light pleasant room to a musty cupboard to a locked-up chest, depending on where his Treasury found itself. Polem, walking along the dark alleyway past the room where the clerks laboured daylong, saw a crack of light under one of the doors, and pushed it open; a little cubbyhole of a room, hot with lampsmoke and stuffy air, with books in leather cases and wooden boxes scenting its air with mildew and damp. There was one table pushed against the wall, and on it sat Aleizon Ailix Ayndra, bent over a half-unrolled book with tattered edges and spotted paper. She looked up instantly, and her eyebrows wrinkled her forehead. 'How did you know that I was here – my lord?'

'I ashk' your maid,' Polem said heavily. He gazed in puzzlement around the room. 'What d'you here? I never know why for we carry around all these, for he never reads them now and no one else . . .'

'I read them!' she said. 'I've never seen so many books! Why, I . . . but I suppose, it is late and I . . . I shall be going.' She started to roll up her reading. 'Is there aught you want here?'

'Is late,' said Polem. 'I shall walk with you.'

'I assure you, I can protect myself against marauders.'

'Still, 's dark, an' . . . permit me to accompany you.'

'If you will, my lord.' She stretched up to blow out the lamp hanging from the ceiling, plunging the room into darkness, and slipped past Polem; she was several yards away down the corridor before he got after her. The roofed-over lanes of the town were very dark; occasional flambeaux smoked at intersections, casting thick shadows, though it seemed that they were the only people out. 'A bitter night,' said Polem. She said nothing. 'Too bitter to sleep alone,' he said.

'I think not. I keep myself warm,' she said.

'I'll keep you warmer.' He swept one arm round her shoulders;

114

she stiffened. 'I'll warm your bed and your body, your sweet body
. . .' He had her pinned against the wall. She began to struggle, but
with his six feet to her scant five and a half, he could trap her like
a butterfly on a nail. He breathed barley-brew into her face, and
nuzzled his rough cheek against her neck. 'You do' know how
much I want you, ever since the firs' day I saw you . . .' He jerked
her overtunic open and thrust a hand inside her shirt; practised
fingers squeezed her breast.

'No!' she said, and then, more shrilly, 'No! Polem – my lord –
no! Take your hands off me!'

He lifted his head a moment. She put up her hands and tried to
push him away. He gripped her more tightly. In the flickering
light, his handsome features were grossly distorted by drink and
passion. 'Is 'at your game?' he said indistinctly. 'Is 'at your trick?'

'Please, my lord,' she said coldly. 'Let me go.'

'Let you go? Bitch! Do you not think I seen you looking at me?
You take my money, you do, you take all favours I do for you and
then when you got'a do in return, it's o no my lord no no – you'll
not play frightened virgin now! I will have you and begod you'll
love it! You'll beg for me!' He crushed her breast so that she
gasped; the fabric of her shirt tore as he attempted to pull her
clothes open. She raised her hands within his encircling grasp, as if
she went to embrace him, and something warm and very sharp
pressed against the base of his neck, right against the windpipe; it
ran like a line of fire across above his collarbone. Polem froze. She
leant a little harder on the knife, warm as it was from close
contact with her body. 'Beg for it?' she said. 'I'll kill you for it!'
She looked at him with half-lidded eyes and mouth pouting as if
ready for a kiss. Polem let his arms fall to his sides. 'Back,' she
said. He stepped three paces away. They stood staring at one
another; left hand on her hip, right pointing the knife at him. She
did not bother to pull her clothes together; flesh gleamed between
the ragged edges. Polem stood transfixed.

'Nobody touches me except I say so. Nobody, Polem, not even
you.' She flicked her wrist so that the knife spun up into the air,
caught it again and held it before his eyes a moment, then turned
and walked away. Polem put one hand to his face, then slid it
along his neck; it felt a stickiness, and he hissed at the pain. A
long gash lay right across his neck. A half-inch deeper . . .

It was the second day of Sixth Month, the sun bright enough to
melt the uppermost crust of snow where it lay out of shadow; the
night would freeze it to an ankle-risking sheet of ice. Aleizon Ailix

115

Ayndra sat as usual alone in the library. She wore black wool gloves with the fingers cut off them, and blew often on her fingers to keep out the cold. On the table stood a round book-box, its lid removed to show a jumble of assorted scrolls. Silverfish fell out when she unrolled them. Through the half-open door one could hear the buzz of the Treasury at work: voices mumbling as they wrote or speaking loudly for dictation, pens scratching, bead-frames clicking. She perched on the edge of the table, crosslegged, the book draped over her lap and her fingers bent up by her mouth, bundled in her old black cloak. The chatter in the next room fell quiet, and there was some conversation between a few voices, before it started up again, but she ignored it. Then a voice right in her ear said, 'Captain?'

She leapt off the table; the book fell from her lap over the floor, unrolling as it went, and she went after it, then in the corner of her eye saw white boots and white breeches and pulled back to her knees, from which it was impossible to bow – 'Good day, my lord,' she said. Ailixond picked up the end of the book nearest him. 'Let me help you . . . what do you here? What book is this . . . A History of Thaless? Are you reading it?'

'You gave me permission some time ago to make any use of your library I wished,' she said, rolling up the other end of the book.

'I did; but I . . . do you spend much time sitting here reading?'

'Days and days when there's nothing else to do.

'Well! . . . it must be years since half these have been so much as looked at. Some of them I inherited from Ailixond sixth, even.'

'Which is just how they appear – what did you think I would make use of the library for?'

'I think I never thought about it at all – you can take books somewhere else, you know, if it's cold here – it's damnably cold! Get the clerks to give you one of their braziers, at least. Here you are.' He handed her the end of the book. They were kneeling face to face on the floor. She said, 'So, what do you here, my lord – if I may ask what you do in your own library?'

Ailixond looked at her, then away, bringing his hand up to brush the hair out of his eyes. 'To speak truly, I am running away from my duties! – I was listening to an excessively tedious report from the Governor of the Needle's Eye, relating how he had dealt with the rebellion there, and asking me to advise him on what he should do with the rebels he has captured – not but that they are very likely dead from being herded in the bowels of Purrllum all the while it takes the message to get here, and, if they are not, they will be by the time it returns – and how he should govern in the future to pacify the people and keep the road there clear and open and the corn harvest going to feed Safi – and I said, I must consult a book on the laws and customs of the Needle's Eye – have you seen it? I think it was written by one Caredden – and departed to fetch it . . .'

'Why did you not send a servant?'

'God's sake, will you say that too? Everyone seems to believe that if I could get a servant to pick my teeth for me, I should have one do it! – beside, then I would have to sit further talking to Lord Cahilar's oldest son, and he is such a fool, I wonder indeed how he managed to ride all the way from Purrllum without falling off his horse –'

'It's not only fools who fall off their horses, though!'

'Ah, true, but still – what hour is it? I cannot wait long, I have to answer the letters from Safi after noon, and give out the month's edicts to the Justiciar. I am well pleased to find someone looking at these books, I had thought that we ought to leave them in Raq'min since no one reads them and I have not the time, but I always think, well, it may be that there will be . . . I have read two-thirds of them at least, but now I never . . . have you seen Caredden's book?'

'It's in this box – why do you never read them?'

'Because now I am the Lord of the New Empire, which I never used to be – ah, thank you! Perhaps I should employ you to put them all in order again.'

'I would be –'

'But there would hardly be time, since it's several month's labour and we shall be leaving here before long – I want to move on a good way before the thaw, because then we shall have to sit still a halfmonth with the roads not fit to go anywhere.'

'I'll start it in any case –'

'Write down what you do and you'll be rewarded. Captain, I hope to talk to you longer at some time when I am not so pressed – be assured, I should far rather stay here than go and worry about the affairs of Purrllum, but – good day!' He paused in the doorway and looked at her. She was still sitting on the floor; when she left off her usual grim expression, she did not look plain at all. 'You should smile more often,' he said, and swept away.

Aleizon Ailix Ayndra sat still on the floor; she put up her hand and pushed the edge into her mouth, raising and lowering her eyebrows and widening her eyes as if she was highly excited; it was some time before she opened the book on Thaless again.

On the tenth day of Sixth Month, the vanguard of the army of Safi crossed the Hassa on a wooden lane laid over the ice, and began to climb up into the hills. By midday, they were well up above the town. Aleizon Ailix Ayndra, whose duty it was that day to ride back and forth watching for stragglers at the sides of the column, halted her horse on the skyline for a last look at the view. Snowy slopes, the long grey and brown column of footmen, heads down, suffering the necessary blisters and aching muscles of the first few days back on the march, before their feet and legs got hardened to it again; the red cloaks of officers, outriders like herself, the heavy lumbering line of wagons; far away the tiny silver-pointed squadron of cavalry bringing up the rear; the trail snaking down the dull frozen river and, in the grey distance, the little town, one of the thousand provincial towns which the army had passed through and left with its debris, like the drift-stuff cast up as a wave breaks and retreats, deserters, bastards, broken hearts and broken windows, daughters ruined and sons run away; passions that in thirty years would be old grandparents' tales and in sixty years passed into the utter oblivion that had already engulfed a hundred generations before them. Five months from now the army would have forgotten Hassalh. She kicked her horse on. She had a message to take down to the rearguard.

The rearguard leader's scarlet cloak shone like a lamp in the monochrome landscape, topped by bright gold hair. She avoided Polem's face with her eyes as she delivered the message; but noted that he had a scarf round his neck so that one could not see any part of it. He sent four of his men off to look after the overturned wagon which she had reported, and she made to leave with them.

'No, sir,' said Polem, 'stay here.'

'An it please you, my lord, I should go back to my watch.'

'The watch can wait, I have a few words to say to you.'

She made a gesture of resignation, and went on side by side with him. Polem took a deep breath. 'I would apologise for what I did to you, sir.' She said nothing. 'I was not altogether myself, that night, sir, and indeed I should thank you for preventing me from carrying out a course of action that would have demeaned the both of us, and myself most of all.' Still she said nothing. 'I am very sorry,' said Polem, 'and I shall never do such a thing again.' He reached for her hand, and then thought better of it. 'And, sir, I should like to enjoy your companionship still, as friends, not in the way of man and woman – you may trust me, sir, not to attempt anything like that again –'

118

'May I?' she said.

'Yes! Here, my hand on it.'

He reached out again; she took hold of him. 'Very well, my lord, here's to friendship.'

'Tell me one thing,' he said, emboldened, 'would you really have cut my throat?'

'O yes,' she said. 'You know what they say, my lord – death before dishonour!'

'Ay? – it's your death they mean, not mine!'

'What, kill myself? – what sort of a fool do you think I am?' They laughed together. 'Now let me go, I must ride on,' she said, and waved as she spurred her horse on up the line.

It happened that Lord Polem received the messages from Safi, but he said that he had other things to do, and gave the canvas-wrapped package to Captain Ayndra to deliver to the king. The guards outside the tent knew her well enough by now to admit her without query; within, it was deserted, although the notes of a flattanharp sounded behind the curtain; she stood still, hearing the shower of grace-notes falling from the unseen strings. But very likely the musician would know where the king was. She lifted the curtain, and saw Ailixond standing with his back half-turned to her, the flattanharp on the desk before him, his face, gazing down at his fingers flickering over the strings, as distant and abstracted as a coin-portrait. He had not seen her; she let the curtain softly fall, and stood there watching him, admiring the clean lines of his profile and the skill as he played. It was at least an hourtenth before he sensed that someone was there, turned his head enough to glimpse them and lost the thread of the music; the tune dissolved into discord, and he ceased. She swept off her hat. 'My lord – my apologies for entering without announcement –'

'There's no need,' he said.

'Lord Polem sent me with these – letters new come from Safi.' She held out the fat packet, sewn up in canvas and fastened with half a dozen different seals, and he stepped forward to take it; his fingers slid over hers. A shudder ran up her arm from the contact. She said, 'If that is all, my lord, I should go back . . .'

'Have you duties that are so urgent?' he said.

She looked severe, then gave it up. 'I suppose not!'

'How long were you there before I noticed you?'

'O, I could not tell – I was listening to the music – I took it to be a musician playing when I came in. I was not aware that you played.'

119

'I was brought up to practise the arts of peace as well as war – I used also to play the upright harp, but that was years ago, before I was the king, and I've little enough time for even this one nowadays – look at me, is the floor so very fascinating?'

She brought her head up. 'You are used, are you not, to having people act toward you just as you wish them to?'

'Only in the ways that do not really matter. The others one cannot force,' he said.

'I have seen that you do well enough in forcing them too.'

'Then you have not seen clearly, for I do not force them, only I convince them that that is how they wish to act – do you play music?'

'But poorly, and in the mode of Lysmal.'

'Play something for me, then.' He moved the flattanharp, so that it lay between them on the table; it was a thirty-string piece, in fine-grained wood inlaid with shell. 'You must excuse my ineptitude, it must be more than a year since I last touched a string.' She retuned some of the end strings, and ran off a few scales, then started into a melody; when she had repeated it a few times, she looked up, and in a voice of startling purity, began to sing.

'How many leagues to Themisson?
None, I say, and all;
The slender towers have fallen now
And roofless stands the hall.
The black ships of the blue-wav'd flag
Came out of the eastern sea,
And robbed, and burned, and raped, and slew,
Wading in blood to the knee.
My sister fell on Aethar quay,
My brother at S'Thaudorr;
Ask not of me where I dwell now,
Themisson is no more.'

The last chords fell like stones into a spreading sea of quiet. This time it was Ailixond who would not look her in the face. He said almost in a whisper, 'What song is that?'

'It's an old song from S'Thurrulass, it's about the time when Safi destroyed their city of Themisson . . .'

'Parakison fifth's expedition oversea,' Ailixond said, 'while the lords rebelled and set up Ailixond sixth in his absence . . . did you put the words into Safic?'

'More or less . . . I had to change them a little . . .'. They were

120

standing so close now that the exact equivalence of their heights was plain. She could smell a faint lemon scent on the clean linen that he wore, and under it the warmer musk of his skin, along with the smell of mud and leather and sweat from her own clothes. She raised a hand to her throat and took a step backward. 'I don't –' Ailixond said, 'Do you mean to –'

'– my lord?' quavered a voice from the doorway. Aleizon Ailix Ayndra spun to face it; Ailixond, more practised in dissembling, turned casually to face Firumin, who was clutching at the curtain with eyes like an owl's. 'What is it?' he said calmly.

'Excuse me, my lord, but . . . it's fourth hour . . . the Chancellor . . .'

'You may show him in – but one moment, Firumin. The watch my attendants keep has become slovenly in the extreme. Not only was Ayndra unable to find anyone to show her in, but she came in here unannounced and unnoticed, and had she been an assassin, I should most surely be dead by now – and your head, Firumin, the first to roll. Which is not to say that I distrust the Captain, but, Firumin . . .'

'Yes, my lord, I'll see to it . . .'

'Do so. Now you may show in the Chancellor.' As the curtain fell back for a moment, he turned back to Ayndra, who had moved well away. 'You'll get your wish of leaving now.'

'Did I say I wished that?' She made as if to go, but halted, suspended; he held out his left hand. She bent to kiss the Royal Ring. Her hair fell softly over his hand, and his fingers tightened, and let go; and she slipped out as the clerks made their bows and the Chancellor came in behind.

On the twelfth day of Seventh Month, Ailixond's outriders (as he called them) or spies (as they were generally known) sent back the first sure news of Yourcen; which was that he had wintered somewhere far away between the mountains and Great Droagon Sea, and was at the moment some way north of the Grand Army, moving south and west with a force rumoured to be very large, some said as many as fifty thousand men. The spies said that, according to their sources, he intended to go round the army, to retake Raq'min and then deal with them at his leisure; this information was contained in a letter from a northern prince, whose attachment to Yourcen had not prevented Ailixond from annexing his lands. He stated his devotion to the Safic cause, and prayed that, when the vile Yourcen was defeated, he would be allowed to resume governance of his lands as vassal of the New Empire.

'But is he trustworthy?'

'Since his self-interest is favoured by the course he adopts, I should say yes,' said Ailixond. 'Otherwise, if Yourcen were defeated, he would stand to lose all, unless he has already made himself out to be a loyal friend of Safi.'

'But what if Yourcen were victorious?'

'Should Yourcen be victorious, no one will care any more – but Yourcen will not be victorious. I shall bring him to a pitched battle, in Eighth Month, or Ninth perhaps, I make sure of it.'

'But it seems that they outnumber us already. No matter. His army cannot consist of other than a pack of mismatched levies, half of them at feud with one another and none having been under arms for longer than eight months.'

'While we have been in arms, in foreign lands, for eight years – close on nine,' put in Daiaron.

'A long time,' Almarem chimed in.

'Best-trained army in the world!' boomed Golaron.

'Practice and discipline will overcome a rabble of twice their number,' said Ailixond. 'We shall turn west – he must not be allowed to return to Raq'min. If we can force him westward, eventually he will see that he has to fight a battle or else wander off into the grass plains for ever . . .' The discussion ran on, but Ailixond took less and less part in it; he gazed into space, smiling to himself, and finally dismissed the Council.

'He has been in a strange mood lately,' said Polem to Arpalond. 'Distant . . .'

'He is always that,' Arpalond said.

'No, but even at times when he used not to be – perhaps I should have said distracted, he seems to have found something to think about which pleases him, but says not what it is.'

'Ah, most likely it is the ever-spreading area of his dominion that so affects him,' Arpalond said. 'Or perhaps he dreams of battle – I feel that he intends this coming one to be a masterpiece of his art.'

'Ah! We shall see,' Polem said glumly, 'fifty thousand!'

'Most likely there are more like twenty, and a deal of baggage,' said Arpalond, 'you are coming to sound like Daiaron.'

As the spring grew warm, the army of Safi turned westward, into a region of stony moors, away from the flatter ground leading into the seaward plains; they progressed slowly, often halting to spend time in drill and weapon-practice, and foraging in the countryside; the hunting was good there, and the lords as well as the commoners spent much time in pursuit of the wild goats and sheep of the hills, and the deer in the valleys.

Two days before the end of Seventh Month, when the trees were showing a green haze of leaf, Aleizon Ailix Ayndra was lying on a flat rock in the sunshine, hands behind her head, eyes closed; she had forgotten to secure her horse, who wandered away toward the stream in the middle of the valley, reins trailing in the grass, while she dozed under the pale caress of the sun; until a shadow fell across her. She opened her eyes and rolled them upward; a dark human shape cut across the light. She pushed herself up onto her left arm, to bound onto her feet, while her left arm dipped into the bosom of her shirt; then, feet spaced and knees slightly flexed, she faced the intruder with a knife in her right hand. But then she laughed, and tossed it up to hold it reversed. 'Good day, my lord, I should have guessed . . .'

'– she says, since one does not say Not you my lord! again!'

'How have you found me? I thought I was well out of the way?'

'What, when you left a trail a blind man could have followed? And lie out here as exposed as a bean on a meat platter? And when certain sources, discreetly questioned, indicated that you had left, and in approximately this direction.'

'O for the days of freedom lately lost! When I was a common soldier, no one marked where and when I went,' she said.

Ailixond sat down on the rock, and signed that she should do likewise. 'Then what do you think it is like for me?'

'Worse.'

'Impossible, impossible.'

'Then how is it that you are out here quite alone – or is there an army of guards just over the hill?'

'It is still possible to tell Firumin that for a few hours no one is to disturb me, and then disappear, if I put on a dark cloak and ride a horse from the stables . . .' He gestured at the undistinguished hack with a bundle of brown wool flung over the saddle cloth, pegged a dozen yards from the rock. If the massed forces of Yourcen appear round the bend of the road and they come rushing into my tent, they will find me gone, but otherwise . . .'

'You will not be missed?'

'I think not.'

'So . . .' She slipped the knife back into its hiding-place, and sat crosslegged with her hands loose in her lap. 'Then, if I may ask the question – my lord – why?'

'Do you need to ask?' he said.

'One almost never needs to ask – except for questions where no one knows the answer – but I want, I want to hear the spoken answer.'

Ailixond turned his face away from her, and took a deep breath; then languorously tossed his head to flick the hair out of his face, and in so doing glanced at her under his lashes, and away again – 'Where did you learn to do that?' she said.

'Do what?'

'The way you tossed your hair back just then – the way, the way you move all the time, the things you do when you're speaking to a crowd – I've never seen a man do like it, it's like a woman almost but it's not a man who's a lover of men, either – but you know that they're all half in love with you, all the ones that don't hate you? And I know why because – because sometimes I think I am too, and then I think, is it not that you are doing it to me the same way that you do to them? And then you've drawn me into your company where I'm hardly at home after all the day spent helping the common soldiers to haul stuck wagons out of the mud, and then all these noble lords, and – I don't know what you're doing! And now you've come off here in secret – for what reason, for what?'

Ailixond took a deep breath as if he were about to start on a speech, and then held it. He looked at her, his face was slightly dipped so that he looked up at her – 'I'm not at all sure, myself, what I am doing,' he said, 'I thought that if at last I could see you where no one else is and no one to come in on me, then you would tell me – for I can't tell what it is that you want, you say nothing at all –'

'About what? For there's a many things that I feel it's not my place to comment on –'

'No, not that – about whether you – you know that I – do you know,' he said, lifting his face open into the clear light, 'I cannot even say it now, I cannot even say it to myself – I want to ask you –'

'Yes,' she said, and seized hold of his hands. Ailixond stared at her, astonished. She said, 'God's teeth! You're shaking –' and he snapped his hands free, threw his arms round her and cast her down on the rock. His breath was hot on her neck. She wrestled furiously, without speaking; she heaved at him, she twisted out from under him and jerked back; they crouched facing one another, disturbed, breathing heavily. 'What's this?' said Ailixond. Aleizon Ailix Ayndra shot up her eyebrows so that her eyes

124

glinted with white, and burst out laughing. 'What!' said Ailixond. She said, 'O, what foolishness this is! O, o, o!', buried her face in her hands, rocked back and forth; Ailixond watched her. He said, 'I cannot understand you!'

She got back her breath, and looked up again. 'But why – why? You're the king and I, I have nothing –'

'Ah! But now you're lying to me! You speak directly, you don't give fog and flattery – you've spoken the truth to me –'

'You mean, I've spoken the same things as those which you believe to be true.'

'It is not true', he said, 'that I expect you to come to me because I am the king.'

'I know it – but it lies like a sword between us –'

'Only if you let it lie there! I've come out here without the crown, guards, servants . . .' he tossed his hair back. 'You're doing it again,' she said.

'Doing what?'

'Putting the hair out of your eyes, like . . . like this . . .'

'I don't know that I do it! How else am I to see what's before me?'

'Have your hair cut!' She burst out laughing again. Ailixond started to laugh as well, a thin frustrated ripple. She stared at him with a hand over her mouth. 'Now I've not seen you do that before – you're laughing!'

'I can hardly help it! Are you mad? Why won't you answer me?'

'Because you've asked me no question!'

'I thought I had –'

'What?'

'Ah! do you know, you fascinate me?' she said. 'Even your duplicity is as natural as rain! I hardly know you – how can I say that I want to stay with you? I've got thus far with no man's aid that I got using my womanhood with him, and I'd still go on so, but I never saw – I never saw anyone as beautiful as you!'

Ailixond looked at her with eyes as vividly surprised as a child's. 'Ay?' he said. She said, 'O, good god!' and wound her hands in his long hair, jerked his head back and fastened her lips on his, forcing his teeth apart and scooping deep into his mouth. They rolled together onto the ground. Ailixond pushed his face into the hollow of her neck; she could feel his heart hammering within the cage of ribs. They lay like that for some time; she brought her hands up and ran her fingers through his hair: black, and clean and soft as silk. When he at last lifted his face, she said, 'When?'

'Not presently –'
'I did not think so.'
'I shall make some occasion.'
'We shall make some occasion,' she said.

It was the ninth day of Eighth Month when a party of outriders came in with the news that they had themselves come upon Yourcen's army, they had hidden behind a crag and watched it march past them, and it had taken hours and hours to pass – 'A vast body! Greater than ours, it is – what, perhaps fifty thousand foot, twenty thousand horsemen? Hard to tell, they weren't in order, they march anyhow, all jumbled up with their women and children and wagons and all . . .' They related as much as they could remember of the soldiers they had spotted: well-armed guards from Raq'min, archers on shaggy ponies from the grass plains, footmen in all kinds of armour with every conceivable weapon, pikes, halberds, billhooks, axes, glaives, partisans, slingers, heavy-armed and light-armed horsemen, even a party of two-horse chariots – and all lumbering southward at a distance of two days' and two nights' riding from the Grand Army, with a range of hills between them. Four messengers were sent post-haste to Raq'min, with a message in Ailixond's own hand as the final sign of urgency, to send every man that could be spared to join the army in the field, and prepare the city for defence meanwhile. It turned out that the two armies were marching almost parallel, separated by forty or fifty miles of moor, forest and river. Yourcen seemed to have no scouts, spies or advance troops; most likely he relied upon the knowledge of natives in his army to guide him. So far he seemed ignorant of the presence of the Safeen. They hoped that he would continue in that state. The army continued to march southward, waiting for the right time, moving slowly to leave time for drilling every day; the lords, too, went out riding in the hills to exercise their warhorses.

Captain Ayndra purchased a new horse, one young and not tame and battle-seasoned like her first mount; he kept up better with the lords' own stallions, but she had a hard time restraining him. She was fighting him, and swearing at him, now, when in a group of six they were gathered on the crest of a hill between mist-filled valleys, about to turn back before evening came on – 'What hour is it?' said Polem.

'Dinner hour!' said Lakkannar. 'Let us go!' He kicked his horse, who reared half up; Aleizon Ailix Ayndra's mount appeared to take fright, for he jumped up and bounded over the hilltop like a rocking horse, she hauling furiously on the reins, then half reared and bolted away, she hanging on for dear life; then Ailixond's Harago took off in pursuit. The others were for some moments too surprised to follow, and by then the pair were out of sight, the deadened thunder of hooves on the thick grass rapidly fading –

'Ha!' said Lakkannar. 'We should never have brought that woman along, unless it were on a leading rein.'

Sulakon began to descend the slope. 'We should go after my lord the king,' he said.

Arpalond looked doubtfully at Polem, who shrugged. Lakkannar said, 'But surely they can see to themselves?'

'We should go together,' said Sulakon. 'You remarked, Arpalond, that it is easy to get lost in this mist.'

'Who knows where they are now?' said Lakkannar. 'Night's coming on. They'll find their own way back before we find them.'

'Yes,' said Arpalond. 'I think it will do no good to search.'

'But Ailixond,' said Polem.

'He's no child! He'll get back safe – and even if he sleeps the night under a bush . . . ah, god damn women . . .' Lakkannar turned back toward the camp; the other two followed, and Sulakon, reluctantly, last.

Some way away, though not much later, Aleizon Ailix Ayndra pulled up her horse beside a clump of scrubby thorn trees and slid down to the lank yellow-green grass. The mist enwrapped her; she stood with her head up, listening. The horse tossed his head, and she took hold of the bridle to quiet him. 'Ssh, sshh.' A jingle of harness sounded further away, then the faint clump of hooves on the muffling sod. A white cloak and a grey horse loomed out of the mist. She took a picket peg out of her tunic front and started hammering it into the ground, then uncoiled a thin rope from the saddlecloth and tethered the horse with it. Ailixond came up behind her, but she went on as if she had not noticed. Only when she had finished the task did she look round. He had thrown a coarse piece of felt on the ground and was sitting on it, hands in his lap.

'Well, here I am,' he said.

The lords, when the king had not returned by eighth hour, resolved that if he had not shown by next morning they would go out with the Companions to scour the hills for him, in case some accident had befallen him. They waited through the night, unsure whether they should give the army orders to march on next day; finally they decided to let them go on at a slow pace while they

searched. They sent for the troop leaders of the Companions, and
then fell to arguing again over the best way to carry out a search
in rough country; in which debate they were interrupted by the
arrival of Lord Ailixond. He looked somewhat damp and creased,
but unperturbed: 'Why have you not moved on?' he said. 'It is
eighth hour already! To your places, gentlemen, my lords.'

'We intended to go out searching for you,' Sulakon said.

'Indeed? You are kind – but you need not have worried. I
decided it better to sleep out there and return this morning, rather
than go on and very likely lose myself in the mist. Let us get on
the march! We have no time to waste.'

Polem said, 'Captain Ayndra . . . have you . . .'

'I believe she is safe,' Ailixond said.

'O . . . did you see her?'

'She has gone to her station. Let us get moving! To places, all of
you!' He nudged Harago on. Polem looked puzzled. 'Did she
come back last night?' he said.

'Did you see her?' said Arpalond.

'No. But then . . . o, I suppose I had better go – am I not
supposed to do rearguard duty this day? Or is it next day? Have
you seen the list? . . .'

The reinforcements from Raq'min began to straggle in on the
eighteenth of Eighth Month, and continued to arrive over the next
four or five days, those that had been mounted, though the
footmen would take some days more to come.

Ogo groaned aloud as he got down from his commandeered
farm pony. 'Owwh! Whyever I listened to them, I shall never
know – come to the aid of the king against Yourcen, riches and
glory to be had indeed! Come to saddle sores and bandy legs, it
should have been . . . I wish I had gone sick in Raq'min.'

'Much aid you'll be to Lord Ailixond!' Garget sniffed. 'Could
not harm a fly on a pudding skin, let alone a Haramin.'

'Look you! You may be Summoner now, but still you do not
speak so to me.'

'Ah!' said Gemmat. 'I shall never go anywhere save in a wagon
again.'

'Nay! There's no more glory I shall see than the glory of the
bruises on my arse!'

Saripion, at the head of their party, called out to Garget, who
cried, 'This way! This way! Leader Saripion directs us to our rest.'

'To our final rest,' said Gemmat.

'May that upstart Garget rot in hell!' muttered Ogo. 'And

Saripion too, damn him, putting my second man over me ...'

'Lord Ailixond did it to the one you used to have,' said Gemmat, hoping to curtail a speech he had heard a hundred times before.

'Not the same!' said Ogo. 'And beside –'

'O hush! Let us get on and rest!'

'I heard tell that this Yourcen's got a pack of black witches out of the north, who call down plagues in the wind.'

'Na! Who told you that? A pack of nonsense.'

'But sure it is that his army's much greater than ours.'

'Is it so? Peasants and barbarians, they cannot count for much. Beside, who says that it is larger? Captured men of theirs?'

'No, it is our own spies, who have seen it ... and did you not hear? This is no rumour, but when Lord Arpalond in the vanguard came upon the river, yesterday, he met a great number of their horse, as many as we have even though this was but a part of their body, on the far side; and they fled only when they saw that he had the whole army coming up behind, after they had stood some time defying him to cross, and are gone to fetch up their king. And so we march along this river waiting for them to come up on us.'

'Aye, well, for what else did we come up here but for to be come upon by them?'

'Aye, but I never thought I would have to fight – are we to be put into battle?'

'I know not ... I should hope, well to the rear! ...'

It was the twenty-fourth when Ailixond's scouts succeeded in capturing one of Yourcen's outriders, from whom they succeeded in extracting a clear account of his master's movements, and found that they were racing Yourcen southwards; after which Ailixond turned cross-country to meet him, until Arpalond was met at the ford of the river Setarh by a detachment of cavalry, whose size rapidly became magnified in rumour to many times its true dimensions, and which did no more than yell abuse at him and then gallop away. The army of Safi followed the Setarh for three days, and then Ailixond suddenly ordered them to halt and make a fortified camp, with a ditch and palisade. A ridge rose up, blocking the view of the country before them, and it was sure now that Yourcen was behind it. A hundred, a hundred and fifty, two hundred thousand men, said all sorts of voices; but all they saw were a few horsemen on the skyline. In the dark with a quarter moon, the king and his horsemen went out in front of an army drawn up for combat, until they came out on the hilltop over what, by Yourcen's choice, would be the appointed field, and saw the campfires like a dozen cities in the night. The lords stopped there; behind them still came on all the men and horses of the battle-line, with the new forces left behind to guard the baggage in the camp, but all awake with weapons.

'And so are they awake,' said Golaron.

'Like an ant-hill, it is!' said Lakkannar. 'And I had not believed that they said, but still, they are . . . very many of them . . .'

'Pass back the word to halt,' said Ailixond.

'My lord.'

'Halt: for since we have come up on the crest of the hill, we shall halt here, settle, light fires, what-you-will, and attempt to refuse any attempts to draw us out next day — we shall wait to fight the day after next, after we shall have surveyed the ground. Go, tell them that.' He rode back and forth, staring at the brightlit spectacle of the plain, for much of the night while the army settled down, as far as was possible on the ground, behind him; speaking very little to anyone who chose to ride beside him for a time. One could see parties of men with bows or spears moving about among the multifarious fires of the enemy camp, in a midgelike vibration among the distant flares, in which the farsighted could pick out weapons carried on shoulders, sticking up in regimented lines. As the dawn came up with the curiously chilling clarity of summer sunrises, other formations appeared; much of the plain had been smoothed out for the chariots to run over it, but the front of Yourcen's line had been protected by stakes and pits; about seventh hour, in full light of midmorning, Ailixond led the Royal Squadron down to gallop across the front of Yourcen's army, so fast come and gone that it was not until they had almost completed the circuit back to their own side that the enemy realised that they were not more of their own and got a few arrows off towards them. It was clearer then that much of the bustle 'down there' was preparation for rather than direct incitement to battle, and his troops, though just as numerous as rumoured, were a very diverse grouping, and many of them hardly seemed to know how to hold a sword — but the groups at the front of the line were well-trained. The rest of the day was given over to resting.

Aleizon Ailix Ayndra woke before anything thinner than a blue gloom could be seen under canvas; she sat up on the edge of her bed, running her hands up and down her legs and shivering, until

Yunnil awoke at true dawn, and went out to fetch fresh water. Officers had been able to have their tents brought up, while the soldiers slept under their cloaks. She drenched her head and face in river-water, and began dressing, with a fine linen shirt and under-breeches, and strong but flexible leather breeches reaching to the knee, fitting into the top of high spurred boots. Then a padded woollen gambeson, with leather and metal studs strengthening it on the sleeves, and over that the stiff and clashing mail shirt itself; she stood very still for Yunnil to do up the fastenings, and silent all the while, until Yunnil made a granny knot of the thongs on the mail, bent close to undo it, and burst into tears. Ayndra jumped. 'O what? – don't do that! Don't weep on my mail, either, you'll make it wet and rust it . . . what's the matter?'

'O, I cannot do't . . . I can' do the knot . . .'

'No, it doesn't matter then, leave it – o, leave off crying!'

'O, but, sir – what shall I do if you're killed, and I all alone in the middle of nowhere?'

'I shall not be killed – look, get me the belt with my sword, I'll fetch my knife. You've no need to worry. If I die, all this will belong to you – I owe about a hundred sols to Lord Polem, if you go to him he will sell things or whatever, and – and if you go to the king, well, not to the king, go to Master Firumin, do you hear? and say you belonged to me, and could you speak to the king? – but leave off crying! I shall not die, you'll not be so easily rid of me. It's in the box there. Thank you.' She stood still again while Yunnil buckled it round her waist, but she held her hands up in front of her, clasped together and flexing again and again. Yunnil snivelled. 'You have breakfast?'

'No, I . . . but I wonder if it would be better if . . . no, I should be sick – but then – o, can you go and get a lamp lit or a fire brand or some such? Go now!'

Yunnil shuffled out. Ayndra knelt by her bed and pulled the pillow off it, fumbled inside it; she brought out first a knife, which she put in the empty sheath on the right side of her swordbelt, and then a cloth packet, which, unwrapped, revealed several resin sticks. She took out one; the rest were hidden when Yunnil came back with a burning oil lamp. 'Ah, give it here!' She stuck the stick in its flame, and sucked on its smoke like a baby offered the breast; then handed it to Yunnil. They sat together, giving it back and forth, until it was reduced to a stub. 'Ha!' said Ayndra, sitting back. 'Now, I shall have the flimsy red cloak and the gilt brooches . . .'

By full light, she was in the horse-lines, which were abuzz with troopers leading out horses, checking their paces, dressing them in ornate harnesses or fastening leather shields to protect their chests and faces, while the lords' servants led out their mounts, usually two of them, a quiet horse for the preliminaries and the warhorse for the charge itself. The animals were as nervous as the riders; they pranced and threw up their heads, waiting. Those riders up and ready milled about between the campground and the top of the hill, going up to where they could clearly see the enemy: long blocks of footmen were slowly massing out there in the plain, behind the blocks of stakes. The Safic infantry were lining up out of enemy sight; the lords' servants were taking down their tents, and carrying them back toward the camp in the valley, followed by all the others who were not intending and ready to fight, armourers, farriers, hawkers of food and water, women, those whose officers that morning judged them unfit. It was very sunny. The sun was well up in the sky when a white and gold rider on a black horse came out from the bustle where the lords had camped, and signalled that the phalanx regiments were to begin to advance to positions.

They were the backbone of the Safic line. Lord Sulakon and Lord Golaron took the Thaless horse out to the left wing, with the Safic horse and provincial levies armed with long spears like those of the phalangites out to the far left, reaching backward in case Yourcen's far longer line should attempt an encirclement. The Silver Shields stood to the right of the phalanx, between them and the Companions, with another backward-reaching wing beyond – squadrons of mercenary cavalry and, concealed within their ranks, heavy-armed footmen. Parties of skirmishers, slingers, archers and javelin-men were put out in front of the line, most of all at the vulnerable corners; and the rest of the infantry waited in a long block, in reserve, behind. It was intended that, if Yourcen did try to encircle the Safeen, they would face about and the extreme wings would move back so that the army formed an armoured square.

Yourcen's army was extended below them. The whole front line was massed cavalry squadrons, and, in front of them, chariots with scythes glittering on their wheels – a hundred of them, two hundred? Yourcen, in a chariot, could just be picked out in the middle, with, on either side, ranks on ranks on ranks of infantry in enormous packed squares. Ailixond commanded seven thousand cavalry and about forty thousand footmen, including those guarding the camp and those left behind in Raq'min and elsewhere; the enemy cavalry he estimated at thirty thousand and the infantry, numberless – 'a hundred thousand?'

He said to Arpalond, 'He must have some loyalty still among his people, to raise that number of them . . . I suppose a good few of the men who ran off from the mountain provinces during the winter must have gone to join him.'

'I do not think that all those footmen will do much,' Arpalond said.

'I should hope that you are right; but all those horsemen . . . and they breed good horses out here, larger than ours . . . go and call the chief priest, and the allied princes, and any of the lords who are to hand. I wish to make a tour of the lines before we start.' He looked up into the sky: clear, promising heat and dust. The ground below, cleared by Yourcen's minions for his chariots, would be like a smoke-bowl. 'I hope,' he said, 'that we all know well the trumpet signals.'

The priest of Takar wore a gold wreath, the allied princes all their gold and fur, despite the heat; the soldiers stamped and cheered as they passed. Ailixond dipped his lance in salute, but said nothing; he looked up into the sky, and then suddenly pointed up; eyes followed, and saw a black speck, descending, growing, wings spreading – it was an eagle, stooping out of the sun with, just in front of it, a fat and terrified partridge. It struck some twenty feet above their heads; the eagle screamed, and flew away grasping the decapitated body of the partridge, while soft feathers rained down on the heads of the watchers. Ailixond kicked the priest. 'It is an omen!' he hissed. 'We are the eagle, and they are the partridge – tell it!'

The priest raised his hand, and kicked his horse out to face the army. 'My people!' he bellowed. 'You have seen the sign of the gods! The victorious eagle signifies that we shall surely slay the partridge of Haramin . . .'

'Good, good!' said Ailixond, and flourished his lance once more, dug his spurs in and galloped back to his place at the head of the Companions. He had lost the fixity of his hieratic pose; his eyes glittered, and his teeth showed. 'Advance!' he said clearly. 'Forward, to the right.'

Aleizon Ailix Ayndra rode well to the back of the Royal Squadron, mailed backs all around her, the air reeking of horses, oiled mail, urine, dust. She could see little of what went on on the outside; but now, at least, before they were in the thick of it, men on the outside called out what went on for those further back to hear. 'Our right's going out . . . and he's moving to meet them –

133

and the scythe chariots, here they come!'

'Are we moving?'

'No, wait, wait . . . aiee! That's our javelins! See, they got one of them, he's crashed into his neighbour – lots of them! . . . but some of them – ah, see that! The phalanx, they've opened up for them, they're running right between! Canna' do a thing!'

'What'll they do now?'

'The infantry behind are going to get them – can you see much below? So much dust . . .'

'Going to be a thick day . . .'

'Their left wing's all going over rightwards – are we moving?'

'No, keep still.'

'The king's sent for his Harago.'

'Keep back, now, no moving till the order!'

'Dress ranks there.'

'Form wedge! Prepare to charge!'

'Watch for the king now.'

'Wait for the trumpets.'

Lances lifted, reins shortened, horses sidestepped into line. Noise and disturbance was clear to be heard, downhill and to the right of the Companions, as well as the yells where the infantry were pulling down the scythe chariots and murdering their riders. Then the trumpets blasted right at hand, and hundreds of deep voices yelled, 'Safi! Safi! Saaafi!' Ayndra thrust her feet down, gripped with her knees, one hand clenched around the shaft of her lance and the other tight on the reins. She threw back her head and screamed the warcry as she felt the horse beneath her extend from the walk into the trot, then the change of pace as his feet began to stride out in pairs in the canter, and lengthening and speeding up until they were in a flat gallop, down the slight slope over the hard ground, a mad kaleidoscope of speed, the rush of air, concerted hooves hammering, the ground if she glanced down a blur, grey-brown dust, the sun, the helmet pressing on her brow and her palms wet inside her gloves and heart like a hammer and the shouting and the speed, like flying, ecstasy, a fear so fierce that it lifted one up out of the sense of terror into a plane where each moment, because it might be the last, was seen in a light so clear and complete that it was as much like the confusion of ordinary life as waking was like sleep – 'Safi! Safi! Victory!' And then the horsemen before her burst out in all directions, and her mount charged on; she saw a distorted screaming face with a black beard and thrust down with her lance, and the face fell away, pulling the lance from her hand and she snatched her sword out and screamed aloud. Then the world was a ten-yard circle of choking, roiling dust and struggling figures, the horse pushing forward into it; slashing, thrusting, striking, fighting, no sensation of time or its passage. When they talked of the battle afterward, all she could summon was a succession of precise, disjointed, affecting images: a hand clasping her foot, and the exquisite founting of fear as she brought her sword down on its wrist, a grating sensation through the blade and a scream and the hand fell away; someone shrieking 'Save me! Save me!'; her blade shearing a shoulder and, it must have been reaching an artery, releasing a spurt of blood like urine in the sun; and her horse jumped forward and all of a sudden she was out and gasping in a space, she could look around, she saw that there was blood all over her and perhaps it was her own but if it was she could not feel a thing – 'O bravely fought!' someone shouted. She tried to reply, and croaked; her throat was raw, she must have been screaming and shouting all the while – 'What?' – then saw that it was Lord Arpalond. He spurred his horse past her, shouting, 'Follow me!' She went after him into the cloud ahead, and temporary lucidity dissolved into bloody chaos again.

Then out of the dirt loomed bright colours, shining metal – she had come through somehow to the fore of the fight, where the leaders of the Companions were cutting into Yourcen's household troops, the men who had escaped with him from Raq'min, and among them she saw the white sign of Ailixond, and pushed on up behind him, until she could see that he was all over smeared with blood and filth. He lifted his head and cried in a furious carrying voice, 'A lance! A lance!' Looking, where he pointed, was the chariot of the enemy king, red and gold fringes, and a pale staring face next to a man bent over, dragging on the reins – 'A lance!' cried Ailixond again, and someone pushed one into his hand and he cast it at Yourcen, who was standing like a bird before a snake; but it seemed to burst the invisible bonds that held him, struck him on the shoulder as he recoiled, and fell out of sight behind the gold fringes. The charioteer whipped the horses frenziedly, and they pulled away, the surrounding footmen surging behind so that the Companions scattered after them, all over the field, cutting them down indiscriminately.

In the Safic camp, the women huddled together in the middle, while the guards patrolled the ditch and tried not to show how anxious they were. Ogo and Garget were trailing unaccustomed pikes around, followed by Thaleken and Carlat, Ogo's new second and third men.

135

'I wonder how it goes over there?' Carlat said for the dozenth time.

'O, we shall find out soon enough,' said Ogo.

'Did you not hear that there were even more of them than had been thought? More of their horsemen than we have in all our army, let alone the footmen!'

'Lord Ailixond has never been defeated,' said Garget.

Thaleken said, 'There's a first time for all things.'

'There's riders coming over the hill,' said Ogo. 'Hundreds of 'em.'

'We must have won!'

'To the gate!' shouted Garget. 'To the gate, to welcome them!' He shouldered his pike and ran off. The others followed; men from all over the camp, and women too, started toward the wooden gate. The horsemen were still some way off, their badges not discernible. Ogo got up on the palisade to get a better view.

'Where are they from? Can you tell?'

'Open the gate!'

'Not the Companions, that's for sure ... the Thaless horse have blue cloaks, do they not? Then it's not them ... I do not think the mercenary cavalry ... can you hear them shouting? I do not think they're any of ours! It's the enemy!' He jumped down. 'Hola! Come back! The enemy are coming!'

'Shut the gate!'

'What is it? Are we defeated?'

'No, they are our men, are they not? – we can't be defeated!' The gateway was jammed with people running every which way, some trying to pull the barrier back into place, others running back, or just standing still trying to tell what went on; the sick and wounded who had been left behind had grabbed up weapons and come forward to add to the disturbance. Saripion stood in the middle of the gateway bellowing, 'Get into line! Form phalanx!' and some tried to obey him; others went to shield the women, or to protect their own baggage, or to man the palisade. A ragged line formed across the opening, while some tried to shut the gate, and then the enemy were on them.

A battalion of phalanx, with its pikes pointing outward, was impenetrable to cavalry, but this ragged front of mismatched spears in untrained hands was no more than an irritation; the Haraminharn mowed down the centre of the line like grass, and dashed on into the camp, disregarding the men at the side for sake of plunder. Ogo clutched his spear in both hands and swung it at the nearest rider, catching him on the side of the head and unbalancing him; as he swayed, Ogo dropped the spear, seized his leg and pulled him to the ground. They wrestled in the trampled grass. Ogo dragged out his falchion as the horseman got his hands round his throat; as the pressure increased, he stabbed upward, and the grip suddenly slackened. Ogo pushed the weight off him, and pulled out his short sword; a rush of blood followed, and the man went limp and still. The fight had moved on into the camp, where the booty was; Ogo got to his feet among a mess of discarded weapons and trampled bodies. A great pool of scarlet attracted his eye – an officer's cloak, lying in the gateway. He saw no one around; he slipped out into the open and saw that it was Saripion's. His one-time catapultmaster lay dead at his feet, face down, hoof-marks all over his cloak of office. Ogo knelt down and pulled the cloak over his head; to do so, he had to undo a brooch studded with semi-precious stones. He looked at it, then stuffed it up his sleeve and undid its partner.

'Ogo!' rasped a voice behind him. He shoved the second brooch out of sight. 'Ogo!' He looked round, saw only bodies, started to get up; one of the bodies moved; it was Garget. 'What is it?'

'Help me!'

'All right! We must get away before they come back!' One could hear fighting among the tents, and glimpse people running between them. Ogo reached for Garget's arm and pulled upward. Garget screamed aloud. His right arm was a pulp of blood, almost severed at the elbow and then trampled. Ogo stared at it. 'God in heaven!' Garget's eyes rolled whitely. 'Is it broken?' he said.

'No,' said Ogo, 'no, come up, come away, get you to the physician, you'll be fine – up now, don't mind the pain.' He lifted Garget to his feet, his good arm over his own shoulders, and they stumbled away among the wagons parked near the palisade. Ogo saw a large wagon with provisions in it; he pulled Garget under it and made him lie down, with a cloak folded up for a pillow, then looked in the wagon and found a skin of wine. He had just pulled it out when he heard hooves, and threw himself flat behind a wheel; two riders went by, one with a screaming, struggling woman over the horse's neck in front of him. They did not seem to be looking out for Safeen to fight. He crawled back to Garget and put the neck of the skin to his mouth. 'Here, drink.' Garget spluttered and swallowed; wine ran over his face. Ogo sat beside him, listening to the racket from the middle of the camp where the women and the lords' tents were; after some time, he heard a sound of galloping and, peering out, saw a rush of riders making for the gate. Not long after that, the massed pikes of a phalanx appeared, and entered the camp.

'What's that?' said Garget. 'Is that more of them? Will they kill us? We should get up, we should go . . .'

'I think they are our men,' said Ogo, 'they are phalanx. I shall go and ask them . . .'

'No! Don't leave! Don't leave me alone!' Garget took hold of him onehanded, and would not let him go, so Ogo sat with him until he saw a group of phalanxmen marching nearby. 'Hola!' he called. 'Safi! Safi!' They turned. 'Under here!' he called.

'Who are you?'

'Ogo, catapultmaster, with a wounded man . . .'

They came over, and peered under the wagon. 'What has happened?' he said.

'Were you in the fight here?'

'Aye, and my friend . . . how did they come here? Are we defeated?'

'No, we have a great victory – Lord Ailixond's killed their king! Your friend, what's with him? Wounded by the vine, by the smell of it!'

'No,' said Ogo, 'see his arm?'

'O, aye? Ah! . . . he got that fighting here?'

'He met them in the gateway – who were they?'

'There was a gap opened between third and fourth phalanx regiments, and they went for it – we closed up before the footmen got out, but a many of their riders got through, and came here – but we've mashed them utterly! Nothing left! Aye, and you should have seen them this morning, an army like I've never seen . . .'

The Companions were rampaging over the battlefield, cutting up the remnants of Yourcen's guards who were trying to cover his retreat, when a filthy and exhausted Thaless cavalryman came panting on a winded horse up to Lord Ailixond. 'My lord! Lord Sulakon! Says you must to the left wing, enormous numbers, we can hardly hold them, my lord, you must . . .'

'Where are they?' said Ailixond. The messenger pointed; in a great turmoil of dust on the far side of the plain, one could see phalanx spears and the vague outlines of ranked footmen over against them. 'Now, my lord, now!' gasped the messenger.

'Where is the trumpeter?' said Ailixond.

'I saw him fall from his horse when we first hit them,' said Polem.

'You must come, lord!'

'O, I come,' said Ailixond tranquilly. 'Lakkannar, can you

138

shout for the recall? My lords, go round and summon all you can
– we shall charge again, over there, and fast!' Lakkannar inflated
his lungs and shouted, 'Recall! To me! To me!' beckoning with his
bloodied sword. Those within earshot turned back, and called to
others further away; within an hourtenth, they had perhaps half
the Companions around the king, the rest having run away who
knew where – 'Form wedge,' said Ailixond, and watched the
dirty, sweatsoaked, bloodmarked riders shuffle into place. He
coughed, spat, and raised his own sword. 'When I give the signal
. . . charge! Safi!' The Companions launched themselves forward
again, this time in silence; they plunged through the scattered
groups of enemy infantry running hither and thither on the plain,
going headlong for the place where the leftmost phalanx regiments
were locked in combat, the spiked butts of their twelve- and
fifteen-foot spears driven into the hard ground to make a fence
against the enemy; somehow they saw them coming, and raised a
dust-hoarse roar – 'Safi! Safi! Ailixond!' The phalanx commanders
gave the signal Forward, and the men heaved the spears out of the
ground and began to power forward into the enemy, all the pikes
swinging and thrusting in time to the chant of 'Safi! Safi! Safi!' The
Companions took up the chant as they hammered into the allies of
Haramin; hand to hand against other horsemen, the hardest
fighting they'd had yet, the air scorching and stinking in the heat
of the day and reeking like iron with blood, dizzy and half-blind
with sweat and exhaustion and still they came on and still from
some further spring of energy which one never knew one had one
lifted leadlike arms against them – Aleizon Ailix Ayndra was right
behind the king when they burst out between two parties of the
enemy and found that there was a hedge of spears in front of them,
still swishing side to side with foot-long blades smeared and
festooned with all kinds of rags of clothes and blood and – but
they swung to either side, parting before them, and revealed men
behind them, grinning like monkeys under wide-brimmed helmets,
sticking pikes into the ground and waving their fists, shouting
'Victory!' Ailixond pulled Harago to a stop, and shoved his sword
back into its sheath. His face was streaked grey with dust, in
which sweat had made sticky rivers, and his white finery was a
stained mess; he opened lips which flashed bright red in the grime,
and laughed out loud. 'Victory!' he yelled. The pikes, further
down the line, were going up to make way for a party of riders –
Lord Sulakon at the head of the leading troop of the Thaless
horse. Ailixond pulled off his helmet, and shook out his hair,
hanging in black rats'-tails with sweat; he held up his hand, and

Sulakon pushed his horse on to come up beside him. 'My lord!'

'My cousin!' exclaimed Ailixond, and threw one arm round him, kissed him; then turned to the phalanx and the cavalry gathering round him, and threw up his hand for quiet. He got it almost instantly, though they knew what he would say; they hung on the clear, carrying voice as if a god spoke to them.

He said, 'We are victorious. The enemy have fled!' They bellowed in reply, stamped, beat on shields; he still held his hand up, until they were quiet again, and pointed out over the trampled field. 'That way lies the enemy camp,' he said, 'and everything in it is yours.' There was a pause; he let it hang a moment, and then cried, 'Go! Take it! You have conquered, take what you will!' He threw out his hands as if he was scattering the wealth of Haramin before them; there was a great roar, and the ranks dissolved. Ailixond picked up the tail of his cloak and wiped some of the grime from his face; his blue eyes shone like cornflowers. The lords and officers gathered round him; he surveyed them. Arpalond was bleeding from the shoulder, Hasmon had a cut on his face ... 'You, Arpalond, back to the camp, call out the physicians and the wagons for the wounded – and you, Hasmon, and Ellakon ...' He picked out the wounded or clearly exhausted, giving them reasons to retire without shame; the rest he gathered round him. 'Now, as you heard, I've given the camp over to looting,' he said, still laughing: 'Which means, of course, that we have as much right to loot it as any; and there's one part which I should like to get first to and claim, and that is, the treasury ... who will come with me? Let us go!'

The Silver Shields were first among the enemy tents, running wild and jubilant, slashing at guy-ropes so that pavilions collapsed in billows of canvas, rummaging through abandoned belongings, snatching one thing only to cast it aside as soon as they saw something that took their fancy more, breaking, smashing, casting things in all directions, not even bothering to chase the few camp-followers who had not already run away – unless of course they were women, whom there were better things to do with than killing.

Two of them were loping along between tents whose trimmings marked them out as abodes of the rich and noble, when the flash of gold caught their eyes: a chariot rammed half into a tent and left there, one horse still in the traces but the other places slashed and empty; but that one had gold on its bridle. 'Look here! Hey, hey!' They grabbed at the reins, and tried to get the horse to draw the chariot out so that they could get into it; from its body came a groan, and a hand in a purple sleeve hooked itself over the edge. A man dragged himself upright, one hand pressed to his left side where his rich robe was sodden with blood; he croaked something at them. They started, touched with fear; he was equally startled at what he saw around him, and cast about for assistance. But they were the only ones to hear him, and they did not understand his words. 'Kill him!' exclaimed one. His partner drew his sword, and leapt up on the yoke to swing at the occupant. He, too dazed and sick to dodge, let it take him in the side of the neck, and as he crumpled, the soldier finished him with a stab that severed the jugular. Blood flowed over the leather floor, welling over the gold torque around the ruined neck. The killer climbed into the chariot and stuck his hands into the blood to pull the torque away. The other held back. 'You know who it is?' he said.

'A rich one!'

'No – more than that – do you not think, it is their king?'

'Who?'

'Lord Ailixond did not kill him. You have.'

'Gods!' said he with the torque. 'What shall I do? Do you think . . . I mean, would not the king want to finish him hi'self, and . . .'

'Get away quick, that's what we should do! None'll know it was us.'

'What about this?' he held up the torque.

'Ah, keep it! If they give out reward for this, we can show it as proof, and if not, we'll find some merchant . . .' So they grabbed up what they had stolen, and fled, leaving Yourcen to stiffen in a welter of his own blood.

On the other side of the rambling assembly of tents and shacks and bivouacs, twenty or so of the Companions charged into the camp. A man leapt up at their approach and ran – 'After him!' shouted Ailixond. There was a shrill yell as Aleizon Ailix Ayndra kicked her horse after him, and snatched at his head. He dodged to one side; 'Yaah!' she shrieked, and fell sideways from horseback on top of him. The impact of her mailed body knocked him to the ground, and, before he had recovered his wits or his breath, she was sitting astride him with her knife alongside his neck. 'Well done!' Polem shouted.

'Ask him, where is the treasury,' said Ailixond. 'Or the king's tent, if he does not know the treasury.' She bent her head over her victim's and whispered in his ear; he answered, muffled in the grass, and she climbed off his back and let him stand up. She

141

looked back, and saw that someone had captured her horse. 'If you would follow us, my lords?' She kicked the cowed man of Haramin. 'The treasury!' and they set off at a trot, passing other Safeen, who would bow and make way for them, until they came to a square tent, sagging where in one corner its pegs had been pulled; Ailixond swung down, and almost fell before his legs regained the habit of standing; he pulled apart the unlaced flaps of the door, and stepped cautiously inside, one hand on his sword hilt. His feet slipped and grated on a carpet of coin. Someone must have been forced to flee in the midst of looting; coffers had been flung open, money scattered on the floor, even a couple of half-filled bags had been left behind; not that their contents would have made much impression on what was there. Here were at least half the contents of the treasury of Haramin, wealth collected over centuries, and, it would seem, more that had been gathered recently. He recognised gold and silver sols from Safi, Haramin's own gold poino, the ring-shaped thesh from Suthine, a score of lesser mintings – the wealth of nations. And every last debased worn-out clipped copper of it his. He snatched up one of the half-filled bags and up-ended it; gold poured out like rain. He started laughing again – 'O, look at this!' – spun round and met Aleizon Ailix Ayndra. 'What!' she said, and dropped to her knees, started scooping coins into her helmet. 'O, my lord, I . . .' she looked up at him, shaking her head, 'My lord, Ailixond . . .'

'Don't kneel to me!' he said, and seized her hand; she leapt up, and fell against him, and they tasted blood on one another's lips. 'O, but look at all this!' she said. 'Is it all money?'

'It's my money!' said Ailixond. She bent down again, and threw double handfuls of coin up into the air. The rest of the lords were crowding in behind; tearing the front of the tent open and letting the sun in – box on box on box of it, most of them still locked . . . and Ailixond and Aleizon Ailix Ayndra skidding about on the slippery coins, laughing like hysterical children . . .

Firumin stood to the fore of a great crowd of attendants in front of the royal pavilion, flanked by slaves with bowls of scented water, cloths and towels. The ravages of the enemy raid had mostly been cleared from the camp; it was seventh hour, and, all the way from the battlefield to the pavilion, the army and its hangers-on flanked the route by which Lord Ailixond returned in triumph. They heard the noise of the crowd long before the head of the procession came into their sight: Ailixond, bareheaded but still armed, surrounded by the banner bearers of the army, followed by those lords who were still with him and officers, and running after a great melee of soldiers and horsemen and women and followers, half those who had lined the route earlier having fallen in behind, waving kerchiefs and captured flags and weapons and shouting and singing. In line directly behind the king came a file of men of the Silver Shields carrying bags and boxes stuffed with the treasury of Haramin; they shed loose coins all along the way, which were greedily seized upon by the crowd, and had phalanxmen to guard them to either side in case anyone should feel that avarice was stronger than loyalty. As Ailixond came up to the space in front of the tent, he ordered his companions to the side so that the money bearers could come through, and dump their burdens on the ground there. 'Behold Yourcen's riches!' he said. 'Go, call the Treasurer and his clerks, and have them sit here and count it, with guards around them. Next day I'll give out shares of it in gift to all of you.' He slid down from Harago, and plunged his face into the bowl of water which Firumin brought up to him; then stood still while servants came and carried away his cloak and sword and helmet, took off his mail shirt and the spurs from his boots, and all the while men were still depositing money-chests on the heap of booty, while the crowd increased around them; he ordered a double rank of phalanx to stand around it, and went inside.

In the midst of the turmoil, Firumin's cohorts had carried on their labours, and brought forth a feast remarkable for its quantity if not any acme of culinary excellence; laid before the lords and high officers, most of whom had not eaten since sunrise, it was attacked as if by a swarm of locusts, and wine flowed like water. Ailixond was at the head of the table, discovering what had gone on in the parts of the field which he had not been able to observe; drawing in chalk on the table top, calling people from all over the tent to come and fill in parts of it and then talking so fast when they came that they could not get a word in: 'Ah, the same as at Surani, it's the rigidity of the phalanx line, that's a danger, if we were to meet someone who could exploit it . . . but the footmen in among the horse, that was good – what's that out there?'

'They're shouting for you.'

'I shall go out and speak to them . . .' He dashed out of the tent; the cheering doubled. The feasters in the tent went on toasting one another and slapping each other on the back and relating feats of arms they'd seen or performed themselves that day. Aleizon Ailix Ayndra sat on a bench at the back of the tent with a large cup of water. When she put it to her mouth, her hands shook so hard

143

that it knocked against her teeth; when she stiffened her muscles, she only trembled more. She put the cup down and shivered.

'Good evening, Captain,' said a slurred voice. 'Who?' she said. Lord Arpalond dropped down beside her on the bench. 'How is it with you?' he said pleasantly. 'You're not scathed?'

'I'm surprised I'm alive!' she said.

'Na, you should not be . . . I saw you, you were a demon!'

'I know not what I was.' She picked up the cup, but her hands were still shaking. 'I know not why I am like this! I was in a fine way not an hour ago – o, I don't know what I've done – I want smoke . . .'

'Drink some of this.' He made to pour some wine from his cup into hers. 'No!' she said. 'I cannot . . . you've hurt your shoulder?'

'Ah, a flesh wound, bruise it is mostly – you should drink something.' She shook her head, and sucked up some water. 'Let me fetch you some food,' said Arpalond.

'I should be sick.'

'No, you must.' He got up and reeled back into the crowd. She got up and moved back behind the curtains where the servants' door was.

Ailixond came back into the tent for half an hour; the crowd was still milling about outside, with cooks from the royal kitchens and all sorts of hawkers going about among them with food and drink; several bonfires had been lit, and people were playing music and dancing; before very long, the king went out to speak to them again. Arpalond eventually made his way to the back of the tent again; the bench there was empty, but by this point he was past caring about anything. Firumin had already sent to several lords' households to come and carry away their masters; the king's own men took away officers who had not their own establishments of slaves. By midnight, the company had thinned, leaving a litter of spilt wine, broken crocks, bones, breadcrusts, among which the most lively and determined were still moving; and Aleizon Ailix Ayndra came into sight again. She sat at the foot of the table, head fallen forward onto her folded arms, pale strands of hair trailing in the debris on her plate. At about first hour of morning, Firumin came out to clear up, and asked those still present if they would leave. Polem went up to her and put his hand on her shoulder. She did not respond. There was a ripple of applause outside; the door flapped, and Ailixond came in, looking dazed and ecstatic. 'Ah, gods above!' he said. 'Ah, Polem – have they all gone now? But who's that with you . . .'

Polem was well-nigh asleep on his feet. 'Poor thing,' he said indistinctly. 'Dead asleep. Shall I . . . shall I see her home? Have you been out there all this time?'

'I have,' said Ailixond; he grinned, and shook his head like a dog coming out of the water. 'Polem, have you ever known a day like it? What next shall I do? Have you seen them? I could do whatever I like with them now, if I said walk on water they'd run out on the sea – this morning, when I saw the enemy I thought, this is the end of it, but no! And now – I can do anything! Anything!'

Polem blinked at him. 'I know you can,' he said dully. 'But I should take her home now.' He patted Ayndra on the shoulder.

'It's you who need taking home,' Ailixond said, 'you'll fall over any moment. Go, get yourself to bed – I see to all that needs doing.' He looked up; blue eyes met brown, while she lay between them. Polem saw the king's face swim in and out of focus. 'Yes,' he said, 'yes, you're right. You're always right. Goonight . . . slee'well.' He put one hand to his head, and staggered toward the door. Ailixond stretched out his hands and laid them either side of Ayndra's head, and slid his fingers round inside her shirt. He suddenly bent over and kissed the back of her neck. She stirred, turned her head to the side and opened one eye up at him; then reached out one arm, wrapped it round him and dragged him close to her.

'Come away,' he said, 'come with me.'

Polem was sitting on a chair outside his tent, wearing a hat pulled down over his eyes and drinking from a bowl of warm milk, while a slave polished his boots. He frowned at the guard who approached him. 'What is it? – do not shout, man, do not shout.'

'My lord, they've found Yourcen.'

'Who? – o, their king? Where is he?'

'In their camp.'

'What! Have you got him prisoner?'

'No, my lord, he's dead.'

'You slew him? Why, the king –'

'No, my lord, it looks as though his own side killed him, his throat was slit. Some time yesterday by the look of it.'

'So! Have you done anything . . . that is, the body . . .'

'No, my lord, we thought it best to leave him until we had orders.'

'Aaah.' Polem yawned and rubbed his eyes. 'I will go and tell Lord Ailixond. Come after me, then.' He got up, and went leisurely toward the king's tent; the two sleepy guards at the door acknowledged him but, 'Lord Ailixond's not risen,' they said.

'What? It's past midday.'

'Yes, but he's not up yet, lord, at least, there are no orders.'

'Ah, let me in. I shall see him – wait here, sir, I will be back.' The guards reluctantly let him pass; he was, after all, the king's best friend, who was allowed to come and go freely as he liked.

Polem walked through into Ailixond's apartments, and crept into the bedchamber; the foot of the high blackwood bed, carved with the waves of Safi, was toward him; the air was static and slightly sour, articles of clothing strewn all over the floor. Polem picked his way between them, and looked over the foot of the bed. Aleizon Ailix Ayndra was sitting among the pillows, wrapped up in a sheet with her knees drawn up to her chin. Ailixond was sprawled across the bed, his face pressed against her thigh and one arm passed up between her legs. He was still sleeping, but she was looking straight at him, as directly as if they met in the street. Polem opened his mouth and said nothing. She grinned wickedly, and then buried her face to the eyes in the sheet, snorting with laughter. Ailixond coughed, and started to turn over. Polem took a deep breath and fled.

'Did someone come in then?'

'Yes.'

'Who was it?'

'It was – hehe! – it was Polem.'

'Ha! – did he say anything?'

'No, he . . . I think he was a bit, a bit surprised . . .'

'It'll be all over the camp by evening – what are you laughing at?'

'He looked, he looked funny – o, poor Polem!'

'Why poor Polem?'

'O, I think he suffered a shock – it is funny, do you not think? You should have seen him! He went like this . . .' She knelt up on the bed and imitated Polem staring over the foot of it. Ailixond sat up. 'Leave off. I must get up.'

Ogo sat in the back of the quartermaster's wagon, looking out at the hills. Sometimes he picked up his spare pair of boots and buffed them idly with the rag he held; mostly, he just sat. Carlat said, 'Are we to get any of this money that Lord Ailixond's giving out?'

'Who knows? We've got no officer now. I know not if we'll follow the army or be sent on garrison duty, or . . . who knows? If

146

we had a Leader, he could go and get the money, perhaps, but most likely they'll give it to those who were in the battle . . .'

'But we fought too.'

'But not in the battle. Most likely the king never even heard of it.'

'But we must hear –'

'O, hush you! Go and ask others if you have such a passion to know.' Ogo tossed the rag back into the wagon and sat with his hands limp between his knees. 'Eight years ago, four of us came out from Safi. Now there's only I here, and for what? Out in the middle of barbarian land . . . ah, to hell with all of them!'

'I shall go.' Carlat jumped down, and loped off toward the centre of the camp. Ogo still sat glumly staring out.

'Master Ogo! A visitor.'

'O, indeed? Tell 'em to come round here.'

'But master – an officer . . .'

'I care not who it is! Tell 'em to come round here.'

'He says to go round to him. In the back there. Sir.'

'Ogo!' exclaimed a bright voice. He looked up. 'O! – Master Aleizon – sir?'

She jumped up on the wheel and scrambled into the wagon. 'Ogo! I have something to give you.' It was a package wrapped in cheap cloth and fastened with the royal seal. Ogo goggled at her. She was wearing a shirt and tunic the like of which he had only seen on lords, fountains of lace on it, high boots shining like mirrors. 'How should I address you?' he said.

'Call me sir, if you like. Call me Master Ayndra, if you mislike to call me sir.'

'Are you become rich now?' he said. 'You are still captain?'

'I am that – open this thing.'

'What is it?'

'Open it, fool! Can you not guess?'

'Is that not the king's seal on it?'

'It is. Open it! Else I shall do it.'

'As you say . . .' He fished out his eating knife to slit the strings. As he cut the seal off, he recalled what he had heard round the fire last evening. 'Master Ayndra – is it not true that you . . . I heard a story that . . . I wondered if it was you that . . .'

'I am still Royal Adviser on matters concerning the artillery,' she said, 'although we have not seen much of that lately. Get on with it!'

He pulled the canvas open, and saw a folded paper lying on top of scarlet wool. 'What is this? You know I cannot read.'

147

'Ah, have you lost your wits over the winter? See here, can you spell out your name? It says that you are leader of the artillery in Saripion's place, wittol! Shake out the package, and put it on.'

It was an officer's red cloak. He said, 'Have I to thank you for this?'

'If any should be thanked, Lord Ailixond is the one. But the artillerymen here are in disorder since their officer was lost, so you are ordered to go get yourself a summoner – or take Saripion's summoner – Purmo?'

'Purmo got the fever with bad water last autumn, and Saripion chose Garget – but Garget, he's had to have's arm taken off since in the attack it was broken and smashed, I saw him in the hospital and he'll have to go home, I know not what'll become of him . . . I suppose he could keep a market stall or – but what am I ordered?'

'To take yourself a summoner, and make a list of all the artillerymen here, go then to the Treasury and tell the clerks – they will give you the share of the captured money which is due to you, and tell you what's to be done next. We leave here on the thirteenth. We'll need you to come with us, for I think there's siege work to come this summer, though if you are set on garrison posting that can be secured for you.'

'By asking of you?' he said.

'No, merely by making out that all the men here are tired, or some such. You're the leader of our section of the artillery now, you should go to the next meeting of the Council, you'll have to confer – well, confer with me, in truth, for I suppose I have charge of that part of the army – what story did you hear that you thought was me?'

'That you . . . that you and Lord Ailixond . . .'

'That I am the king's mistress? Well, it is true, but it makes no difference to any other thing. Put your cloak on, and get about your work, sir Leader. I shall see you in the Council.' She jumped down from the wagon and was gone. Ogo spread out the cloak, new and bright as fresh blood; then fastened it with Saripion's brooches, and went to show himself to his friends.

The hospital was set up outside the camp: an expanse of ground covered by a canvas roof, divided up within into long alleys where the wounded lay on rough mattresses or heaps of straw or grass covered by blankets, shielded from light and wind which were known to engender the flesh-rot and a variety of other diseases, with a physician always in attendance at the end of each ward, to see to the dressing of wounds and urgent cases; it was usually the

148

business of the woman, or the friends, of a wounded man, to see that he was fed and kept clean, though one who had no one to care for him would be looked after in some fashion by the hospital slaves. The main business of the physicians was to ease the deaths of those who could not be saved, patch up the men who would recover and go on with the army, and get the ones who would have to be invalided out into a state in which they could take themselves off in the caravan southward; the rest was left up to other people, so there was always a great business of people about the hospital, looking for news, fetching and carrying food, paying for physic, taking away dead bodies to be burned ... Aleizon Ailix Ayndra joined the queue waiting to speak to the clerk in charge of records.

'Do you have a man named Garget, Summoner to the late Leader Saripion, in your care?'

'Garget, Garget ...'

'I think he has had his arm taken off, and is to be sent back to Safi.'

'Ah, yes! Garget. Says here, well enough to go in a few days – you wish to speak to him?'

'No. Only see that someone gives him this.' A bag heavy with coins was plumped on the table. The clerk looked excited. 'I will be able to discover whether or not he has received it,' she said. 'An he does not, I shall take steps to discover where it went. You should tell him that it is a gift from someone who wishes him as lucky a future as may be.'

'From what person is it come?' said the clerk, staring up under the black hat: a pale face, long dandyish fair hair, rich clothes.

'It matters not. Only see that it goes to Master Garget. Good day!' She turned, to get out of the sick-stinking gloom. The rest of the line twittered after her – 'Who is it? Who for? What was that ...'

The clerk took the bag and put it in the fee-box at his feet. 'Next please,' he said.

'By the end of the summer, so, we shall have come to the shores of Great Droagon Sea. Our fleet by then will have sailed northward to meet us. Then we've only the Seaward Plains to quell, this land north of the mountains going up to the sea, and then the New Empire will stretch from end to end of the lands we know, from Southern Ocean to Great Droagon Sea, and from Shessar Ocean to the Sea of Safi ...'

'Lead us! Lead us! Victory!'

149

Amid the acclaim, Lord Almarem got to his feet. 'My lord,' he said loudly. 'I question the wisdom of your words.'

Ailixond turned on him. 'Indeed?'

'My lord. Your justification all last winter was that you could not leave the king of Haramin still at large, and perhaps so. But now that he's destroyed, what reason have you for going on? What threat do you concoct to the north?'

'Do you claim that the threats I have spoken of are imagined?' said Ailixond.

'O, not, I do not, but since we now have . . . you have the victory you wanted – can you not decide that it is enough? Nine years since most of us saw our home! What reason can there be . . .' Almarem's impetus began to fail as the Council quietened, and Ailixond glared. The king put his hands in his belt and stepped away from the table. 'Almarem,' he began, pleasantly enough. 'No doubt you recall our session before Raq'min in which we received the late Yourcen's offer of safe passage out of what he still called his lands, and secure borders thereafter, in exchange for abandoning the siege of the city. We rejected that offer, and you all know what followed, although there were some who would have accepted Yourcen's offer of that which we already held, and that which many of our men had died in the waters of the river Surani to win. Correct me if I am wrong, but I believe you were one of those, although you did afterward submit to the majority, lacking even the courage of your dubious convictions – but you would then have had us abandon all that we have since gained, in return for a safe journey out of the lands we had already captured. And now you would have us halt here. So we leave the lands before us, the Seaward Plains, where it is reported that there are many towns and rich cornlands running to the sea, and do not progress to the Stream of Ocean, where we could unite the whole of the Empire into one sea-girt realm. Instead we leave a weak and indeterminate frontier among these unpopulated hills, open to the ravages of the tribes of the western plains and the ambitions of the native princes. Perhaps we should build some forts to protect it? – but then we would have to leave Safeen to garrison them, which I am sure you will agree is not a fate we should wish upon any one. So let us leave it, and depart southaway, to Raq'min – but then, Raq'min is also a long way north; perhaps we should fix our furthest outpost in Yiakarak? But it is a barbarous land – perhaps we were better to withdraw to the Safic side of the mountains, but that leaves us still with Lysmal . . . I wish, my lord, that you would favour us with your solution to these problems of the territorial disposition of the realm, and your arguments for abandoning what we have fought so long and hard to come by. What is it that you mislike in travelling further? You mutter, my lord, about returning home. If you have such a passion to see Great Market again, you know that you can always request to go home for a while, or indeed to be released from military service altogether – would that suit you better? We all know that it is a strenuous and fearful life. Would you prefer it if I put you in charge of the caravan of the men honourably discharged to go home? Tell me, and I will see it done if it is within my power,' he said, stepping up to arm's reach of Almarem, looking up at him with vulpine sincerity. Almarem stepped back from him. 'It is not for myself I ask it!' he said.

'Then for whom?' said Ailixond; sweet vitriol.

'For all of us,' said Almarem.

'O, is it so? It is not good of us all then to leave you as sole spokesman – is there any one who will aid you.' Ailixond looked round at the Council; his eyes lingered on Lord Daiaron. Almarem said, 'We have to stop somewhere!'

'Undoubtedly true,' said Ailixond. 'I say again: you are free to put forward any reasoned plan which you have . . .' he paused, looking questioning. Almarem had reddened, his hands clenched: he took two rapid breaths and burst out, 'Leave off this playing!'

'What playing?' Ailixond said lightly.

'This! – you know what you're doing! How much longer will you reason your ambition as if it were causes of state? When last did you allow any voice but yours to speak?' He stopped, with his mouth open, panting. Ailixond looked at him, narrowing his eyes slightly. 'Only just now,' he said. Almarem's lip trembled. Ailixond put his head on one side and smiled at him. He said quietly, 'You can state your case.' Almarem hit the table with his fist. The clerks' inkwells jumped. He said, 'Liar!'

Ailixond's eyes widened so that a ring of white showed all round the iris. He said softly, 'Get out of my sight.'

Almarem shuddered, once, all through his body, and turned and ran for the door. Ailixond rocked on his heel, and stretched out his arms a little, breathing in like one who comes out of stale air into fresh. 'I think we have answered all the questions that require a full Council to see to them,' he said. 'If you have further queries, come to me as usual. We shall march on the thirteenth. Good day!' He nodded to the assembly, and passed behind the inner curtains. The Council sighed as if they'd all laid down a heavy burden, and rose in a soft hubbub of gossip to leave.

151

'Psst! Psst! Psst!'

'What?' The slave dozing by the servants' door of the king's tent sat up. 'Who's there?' He lifted up a corner of the curtain. Aleizon Ailix Ayndra put her head through the gap and showed her teeth at him. He hastily pulled it up for her to come through, said tremulously, 'My lord . . . I think my lord retired . . .'

'Pouff!' She faffed her hand at him, and shot on into the tent. He sat down on his stool again.

Except for the watch-lights by the doors, the only lamps lit in the tent were in Ailixond's bedroom; she opened the curtains silently. He was sitting half-undressed by the bed, his bare feet propped up on it, rocking back and forth in a tilted chair; he was reading a thin sheaf of papers. She whistled softly; he glanced over his shoulder, and hooked one foot under the bed so that he could turn over the chair-back to see her.

'I thought you would not come.'

'I came in by the back door.'

'Where went you after the Council?'

'Out into the country. Is that a letter you have there?'

'From my mother.' He folded it in half and pushed it under his seat on the chair; reached one arm over the back of it, indicating that she should come closer, but she still stood by the curtains. She said, 'You should not have done that to him.'

'Done what?'

'Lord Almarem.'

'What did I do? He was struck down by his own stupidity.'

'He spoke truly when he said that what you did was unfair.'

'O indeed?'

'And you know it!'

'Will you tell me that I know not how to run my own councils?'

'O no! You know how to run them very well.'

'Then what are you saying to me?'

'That you should not be so vain and vicious.'

'What?' The chair rocked back onto four feet again. Aleizon Ailix Ayndra giggled. Ailixond sat up straight. He said, 'Almarem made me exceedingly angry.'

'After you had cruelly humiliated him in front of his peers.'

Ailixond smacked the side of the chair. 'Do you think that you can now keep my conscience? – stop laughing!'

She shook her head. 'O no – but I lie when I say you should not, you know, for I was most impressed – you truly were playing with them! Poor fools . . .' She had come round to the other side

152

of the bed from him; suddenly dropped to her knees, and leant on the edge of it. Ailixond had his hands in his lap, looking at her with the slight edge that forbade any further foolishness. The lamplight made a web of shadows through his ruffled hair and around the unlaced collar of his shirt. She said, 'Shall I stay here this night?'

He steepled his hands in front of him, then opened them out to show her the palms. 'That's for you to decide,' he said.

'Ay?' she said.

'If you do not come of your own free will, then it's worth nothing to me. I cannot force you to do what I want you to.'

There was a silence. He started to brush the hair back from his face. 'And what's that?' she said. He dropped his hand again, and spoke in a suffocated whisper, 'Stay with me.'

She stood up; she might have been laughing, she might have been crying. 'You've answered the oracular question', she said, 'rightly; so you win the reward . . .'

'And what's that?'

'It's whatever you want it to be,' she said, and she was laughing after all. 'Come over here.'

'At least, you cannot say that they have not been discreet.'

'Discreet! – what would you count as indiscreet?'

'For instance – embracing in the sight of others . . . exchanging words of love in the midst of public councils . . . I do not think I need to state what I mean,' Arpalond said.

'He keeps her here, in public,' said Sulakon.

'I do not know what you mean by keeps her. As far as I can tell, she performs her duties just as before, and is paid for them as is suitable to her rank in the army. I have it on the best authority that he has not given her so much as a brass quarit in gift, nor any presents in kind.'

'I have not said that he is wasting the substance of the state on gifts to his paramour. I am saying that I do not consider it right or proper that the king of Safi should live in open concubinage, or as it were better called, since he has not seen fit to get any blessing for it, common-law marriage – like a vagabond in the slums – with a woman who practises heaven only knows what perversions, wearing men's clothing and mimicking men in all her activities being only the surface of it, I am sure, even if the rumours that she practises witchcraft are false, and, furthermore, abandons his lady wife for her sake.'

Polem said, 'He has not abandoned Othanë.'

153

'I do not think it can be called anything else, when he has not seen her for a year and a half. She is still in Raq'min, and he has not sent for her to come out to him.'

'He has left her behind for months before,' Polem said, 'we all know that . . . well, he never chose her, it was the work of his mother, and . . . he has not made any attempt to repudiate her. I do not think he would do it, unless she asked for it.'

'Which she would have all reason to do, when she hears of this shameful state of affairs,' Sulakon said.

'Have you said any of this to Ailixond?' Polem asked.

'Not presently.'

'Then why do you not . . .'

'I thought it better to discuss with my lords my peers, and attempt to determine how things stand before I speak to him. It is after all a delicate matter.'

'For which reason, I cannot see what objection can be made,' said Arpalond. 'I have never seen, or read, of a king who took a mistress with less scandal accompanying it. Do you expect that he should live celibate all his life? He has never even had a concubine besides Othanë until now.'

'He has not presently so much as a concubine! It is nothing but whoredom.'

'Do you suggest that he marries her?'

'It would be better —'

'She'd not agree to it,' said Polem.

'What? Do you know if he —'

'I do not think that it has been at issue,' said Polem, 'but I do not think that she would want to marry. I am sure she would not be a concubine, either.'

'I am sure you are wrong,' said Sulakon.

'I don't think so,' said Polem. 'Although I've not asked them, so . . .'

'You say she'd refuse?' asked Arpalond. Polem nodded.

'Concubinage would be most appropriate,' said Sulakon. 'If he will not agree to that, then he should take her as his full wife, although a poorer candidate for King's Wife it would be hard to conceive of — best of all would be if he cast her off entirely, and out of the army altogether! Her whole demeanour is an affront to the gods and to nature.'

'It is not necessary,' said Arpalond. 'If you worry about the succession, then, if she were got with child, I do not doubt that marriage would follow. Until then, what need to worry? I do not doubt, either, that it will not add to Lady Othanë's happiness, but that is in the lap of the gods, no business of ours. If you wish, Sulakon, to present to the king an argument that he should enter into some kind of contractual union or put her away altogether, I shall not go with you.'

Sulakon looked at Polem, who sheepishly shook his head. He mumbled, 'I do not think that I can talk about marriage in any case.'

'Quite so,' said Sulakon. 'I shall make it my business to speak out alone, then, if I must.'

'Have you spoken to her at all?' said Polem.

'I have not.'

'You should!' he said, and, when Sulakon glared, hung his head and mumbled again, 'for the sake of fairness, at least . . .'

'No matter,' said Sulakon. 'I thank you for your patience. Good day, my lords.'

Polem sat up as soon as he had gone. 'Cantankerous naught-wit! . . . do many think like him?'

'He will find more than a few to support him,' said Arpalond, 'not that it will impress Ailixond at all . . . only it will make life harder for her – and since I think I have come to see what Ailixond finds in her . . .'

'He's no concern for Ailixond either,' said Polem sullenly. 'If he'd but watched when . . . it's years since I saw him laughing, and now, well, he laughs all the time.'

'You know her well, do you not?'

'Well . . .'

'You ought to tell her, though, not to be so confident, at least not openly. It does her no good.'

'I will do it. But I think you'll not impress her either.'

After the winter in the mountains of Pirramin, the army had travelled westaway, into the little-habited moorlands that led in the far west into the grass plains, that went on so far to the west that no one had ever come to Safi with news of what was at the other side of them, though S'Thurrulass was known to lie some way south and west; but they did not pursue that route any further after the battle of Palagar (the name of the range of hills behind the battlefield). North of Pirramin, running to Great Droagon Sea, lay flat lands with many towns in them, which had been ruled by the kings of Haramin, though they had lost them some time ago; they marched east until they came upon the main road north into the Seaward Plains, and followed it. In the north, the summer of 462 and 463 would be known not only as the summer of the Safic conquest, but as the year of the drought. It left off raining in Eighth Month, and from then on the sun shone without interruption. The corn shrivelled in the fields; the grass on the hillsides turned brown and white, and rivers ran down to brown thick trickles between banks of mud and stones, in a land where in an ordinary year it would have rained twice in a sixday, even in the midst of summer. The people abandoned their broad fields, and deepened wells to feed the garden plants. The army laboured past them like a vast dark grimy animal trampling along the road, swathed in dust and flies. They halted outside the gate of each brick-walled town, and asked for submission; sometimes they got it. If not, they fetched up the battering-ram which had been made after Palagar, a single tree-trunk with an iron cap to it, slung under a stout wheeled housing, and stove in the gates; if the town did not give in when faced with the ram advancing and the massed troops of Safi behind, they would go over the walls with ladders as well. Ailixond always led the assault, as he had done ever since the army set out; and he had always used to fight with Polem at his side, to cover his back. Polem still accompanied, but the one now who fought as the king's shield bearer was Aleizon Ailix Ayndra. And, like Lord Polem, she was allowed to go in and out of the king's tent as if it were her own; but she did not go to live in his Household, and continued to order the artillery who travelled with the army and fulfil the duties of a captain at watch and supervision. Many evenings she did not even dine with the king, unless it was with some few of the lords who did not refuse to recognise her any further than the rules of conduct to officers of the army required. It became known that Lord Sulakon had had an interview alone with Ailixond in which he had made representations concerning her, but no one knew exactly what had passed between them, only that Sulakon had been seen leaving in a furious temper, and had not since dined with Lord Ailixond or accompanied him anywhere outside excursions of duty.

In the last days of First Month of 463, the army reached the sea.

The Seaward Road turned east a few miles before the shore, and ran over a rough stone causeway round the mudflats of a broad estuary, before it reached its final end in the port of Pomoan. Centuries ago it had been an independent city, the chief port for the plains; then Haramin had taken it, turned it into a provincial capital, and built up the harbour with good stone quays, to provide anchorage for the fleet. But since the Seaward Plains were

156

lost, at the end of the last century by Safic reckoning, and allowed to disintegrate into a welter of tiny independent city-states, Pomoan had gone into a long slow decline; the harbour had not been dredged in fifty years, and it was a generation since the merchant ships had come up from the east to meet the land trains coming with fur and leather out of the grass plains, and the grain shipments from the cities of the plain. The 'palace' of Pomoan was a muddle of buildings that had been splendid five generations ago, but presently mouldered in the remains of decoration eighty years out of style; grey stone floors and stone walls to a height of four feet, then smoke-blackened wood up to heavy carved ceilings, the principal rooms draped with faded tapestries. Ailixond took a set of rooms which looked out through small iron-grated windows onto the harbour and Great Droagon Sea; from where he sat at his desk, he could see lines of men bearing baskets of gravel, sands and stones to the sea-wall, and carting away the loads of sludge that cranes mounted on quayside or steady boat dredged out of the harbour, while he read over the despatches from all over the Empire: reports half a year old from the distant sun-scorched hills of Lysmal; treasury returns from Purrllum and the Needle's Eye; accounts of the internal divisions among the tribes of the Merkits; Irailond's tales from Yiakarak of the Archpriest Kolparri worshipping before a picture of Ailixond which he had placed in the temple; the veterans discharged after Palagar had reached Raq'min, and many of them had decided to settle in the north; Lady Othanë greets her beloved lord, and wishes that she may soon come to join him, she hopes he is well and sends him a present of twelve shirts embroidered by her own hands and a tapestry which she and Lady Pittea have been half a year in the weaving of, a picture of the battle of Surani; Lady Sumakas greets her son, Ailixond, I like not the pretensions of my lord Governor of Safi Meraptar, you many think him innocent but I tell you he thinks already that you will never come back from up there and is all but ready to order his coronation robes, besides he did not tell about the recent troubles in Thaless for fear of revealing his incompetence in putting them down; Lord Meraptar greets his lord the king, and if I may presume, my lord, your lady mother obstructs me in the pursuit of my duty and raises factions against me in the city and in the palace, and lately has gone about relating a whole pack of falsehoods about my campaigns in Thaless, perhaps you could request her . . . someone came whistling along the passage and pushed open the door without knocking. 'Ailix, can you . . .?' Ailixond turned to look round; the man standing by

157

the window with paper and charcoal in hand clicked his tongue in irritation. He said, 'Good day, my lady.'

Aleizon Ailix Ayndra glared at him. 'Sir,' she said. He nodded. She looked fiercer. 'Good day, sir.'

'O! – good day . . . sir?'

'Good day.'

She nodded, and wandered up to Ailixond's desk, where she began to go through the papers. Ailixond arranged himself again. The artist kept glancing from his profile to the other side of the room and back again; Ayndra found a document which interested her and sat down on the floor with it. Ailixond said, 'Are you finished?'

'A moment more . . . ah, there it is. I should hope to have a die prepared within a sixday.'

'Come and show it to me then.'

'Thank you, my lord.'

'Thank you.' Ailixond remained still until the door had closed; then jumped up from his seat. She looked up. 'Lend my fifty sols.'

'What? God's sake, I am not a moneylender.'

'I mislike borrowing from moneylenders, they are all villains, and they give bad terms beside. And when you fail to pay them back, they come with club-men and remove your possessions, unless you have upped and run away before they arrive.'

'It was only at month's end that you borrowed twenty sols from Polem.'

'O indeed? Do you keep his purse-strings?'

'He does not keep his own counsel.'

'I was in need of it.'

'How? I do not know what you do with money, it runs through your hands like water.'

'No more do I, for if I knew I should not do it, it is a very poor state of affairs, whatever it is.'

'You lie when you say that. I cannot believe that you do not know.'

'True. But I shall not leave off while I still have rich men to lend me money on terms of no interest and repayment at distant future date.'

'You may have fifty sols advance on your pay.'

'Ha! Ha! When you have Shumar only knows how many millions piled up in boxes all over the Empire?'

'It's not mine to give. Our family estate is very poor. Polem has far more than I have. The rest of the money belongs to the state.'

'And who is the state?'

158

'Well . . . it is true that the state is not too far separate from me, but . . .'

'Ah! I know you cannot give it. Give me a note for an advance. If I were not your mistress, I could hold a sinecure and receive vast sums of money . . .'

'Well then. You know what to do.'

She laughed. 'Yes. Borrow!'

Ailixond scribbled on a scrap of paper and handed it to her. She stuck it inside her tunic. 'You kow,' he said, as she looked up to take the note, 'I could swear – have I said this to you? – that you have the family eyes.'

'You have not. What eyes are they? They are bloodshot perhaps . . . they have eyelids that sag round them . . .'

'You've seen them. Blue, with a black rim to the iris. Sulakon has them . . . Ailissa . . . my father . . . o, for a long way back. All our family have them.'

'Sulakon?'

'He is my cousin. Also my sister is his wife.'

'I thought that when you called him cousin it was only a courtesy.'

'I should call him brother. Though I think he'd not welcome it presently.'

'Two days ago I met him on the stair, and I said Good day and he said nothing.'

'I know.'

'What was it he said to you when we were outside Tengam?'

'Among other things, that if I wished to have you as my companion I should at least take you as a concubine. He said that he did not favour full marriage in this case.' Ayndra put down the letter she was reading and sat crosslegged, gazing up at his face, dark against the sunlight that reflected off the sea outside. 'One thing that I – I have never asked you anything about your wife. About Othanë.'

'I have never said anything to you about her.' Ailixond's hands met, and the right started to turn the Royal Ring round and around. He glanced at Ayndra. 'If you . . . I would explain it all to you, if – when I can . . . it's not a thing I can easily talk about,' he said. She nodded mutely, and stood up; went over to the window, and rested her arms on the high narrow sill. Ailixond said, 'She has sent me a letter, asking if she can join me . . . I've not seen her since we left Raq'min. I cannot easily put her off much longer.'

'No . . .' said Ayndra very softly. She pushed one arm between the bars of the grating and dangled it over the sun-warmed wall.

'Does she know?'

'I cannot tell – if you mean, have I told her . . . I'd not know how to say it.'

She turned back into the room. The diffuse sea-light shone full upon his face; in the summerdark skin the blue eyes were lambent, artificeless, drowning. She shivered as if cold fingers touched her hair. Ailixond said in a soft raised voice, 'What is it?' She shook her head, and walked round behind his chair; he tipped his head back to follow her. She knelt down, and laid her cheek against his hair; he leant back against her. She slid her right hand under his chin and, very delicately, ran her fingertips over his face: chin, cheekbone, nose, the hollow of the eye, feeling the beginnings of wrinkles, the smooth flesh wearing down onto the bones. He had gone entirely limp and passive; even his hands were still. She shivered again, and passed her fingers over his mouth. He brushed them with his lips; then suddenly seized them. His eyes snapped open, wide, he stared at her like a clown or a child, two inches away over the back of her hand. She butted him with her head, and giggled. He let go of her. She stood up, sighing, '– ah! Tell me, then, tell me – where shall we go next? After how long staying here?'

'I sent down to Annarun some time ago, for Parhannon to bring the fleet, and they'll be here within the halfmonth – then we'll march east along the coast, and reduce the sea-holds . . . overwinter some way to the east . . . I cannot talk about all that!' He tossed the quill he had picked up over the desk, toward her.

'It's not your common state, is it?'

'It is not,' he said.

'No . . . you know that in a halfyear, perhaps, we'll hate one another.' He looked questioning. 'It all depends how the madness leaves,' she said.

Ailixond shook his head.

She said, 'And then, we might be companions for ever . . . I do not think it very likely.'

'Do you not?'

'There are too many obstacles . . . and beside, did you ever expect a long life?'

'What? Do you think I'm about to die?'

'Not in particular – it's as likely that I will, after all.'

'True,' he said, 'I never thought that I would live much beyond thirty.'

'So what do you say now?'

'Well . . . I say I'll not live beyond forty unless by gods' grace. I mislike to give myself less than a year before I must die, or be too

160

old for any thing. But even then, the last six kings of Safi have not died peacefully in their beds, at least not without foul play being at least a possibility . . . ah, but I never think about duration.'

'No; that's for fools who think that there's no meter beyond the notches on the sundial . . .'

'What obstacles do you speak of?'

'For one,' she said, 'I do not wish to be married.'

'What? Have you –?'

'Don't speak of it!' she said vehemently. 'And then . . . o, but you know what I speak of.'

'I did not think that you were concerned . . .'

'O, they chatter like talking-birds, and with as much sense, but still . . .' She perched on the vacant secretary's desk on the far side of the room. 'You see, it is not possible for you to leave any of this, but I . . .'

'Where would you go?'

'Any number of places.'

'S'Thurrulass?'

'Any number – I don't say that I will, or even that I think of it, but only that – it's a thing I could do.'

'Where are your family?'

'Ha! You'll find no net for me there. No, but they are scattered. My father took my mother in a respectable marriage, but when he died, when I was a suckling infant, his first wife put her out of the house, and she would never speak of him without cursing him for giving her no settlement in his will.'

'Yes?'

'I could not even tell you what part of the city it was that they dwelt in. And my mother I have not seen for many years, I do not know even if she still lives, nor have I any known sisters, or brothers . . . I carry my family with me, and home's where I lie down to sleep.'

'I carry my family with me,' said Ailixond, 'except for the roots of the vine, which lie still in Safi . . . my mother boasts that she has never gone more than thirty miles as the crow flies from Great Market.'

'Arpalond said that he did not think that there was a door in the city which would not open to her, if she was given a month's grace to do it in.'

Ailixond looked away. 'It's very many years since I left the House of Women,' he said. 'One might say of Arpalond that there's hardly a secret in the army that might not be laid bare to him, if he were given a month to seek it in.'

161

'He told me some things which I was most surprised to hear; I cannot imagine how he came to know them.'

'His discretion saves him. I have never known him say any thing where it would be better left secret, nor heard any report that he had done so. There is no one that he does not speak with.'

'Why?'

'It's his pleasure. He doesn't like to do things in himself. I have told him that if there should be a history, he should write it.'

'If there should be a history –!'

'O! As you will. When there is a history . . .'

'What have you told him to call it?'

'Ah. Now I said that it would be well called The Acts of Lord Ailixond Ever-Victorious, or if that should fail, why then, plain Acts of Lord Ailixond, but he said he was set on calling it The Path of the Hero King . . .'

'Ha! Has he written any of it?'

'He tells me from time to time that he has collected some papers with records of sayings on them, which he says are most hard to remember, but the rest he carries in his head, which I am sure he will not lose. I have never seen these papers, but I do not doubt that they are there . . . I shall have him to read me excerpts from it when I am burning in the tyrants' pit of hell. Where also I shall be with my family . . .'

'But why should Arpalond be there?'

'Because he will go all throughout hell, observing it. Thus being punished, as he has lived, by proxy.'

'And see Lakkannar in the pit of drunkards . . . Polem among the lechers –'

'– among those betrayed by weak-willedness –'

'– and Golaron for . . . for faithfully serving tyrants – and Sulakon in the pit reserved for the self-righteous – I do not think you will be among the tyrants, you know, I think you will be among the utterly incurably vain self-indulgents –'

'– and you will be in a pit such that it utterly suits you, and you can affront no one in it!'

'And I shall be infinitely joyous there!'

'You will not; it will be full of people just like you.'

'I should find fine friends there, in that case.'

'You would not. If you met someone like you, in half an hour you would try to scratch one another's eyes out!'

'Nonsense. We should unite against the world and become incurably villainous. All my life I have wanted to find . . . to find the other Ailix.'

162

'But then – do you suppose you have?'

'I cannot think that I would find one better,' she said.

'And within half an hour we were fighting.'

'Ha! This time I must let you have it.'

'Indeed. Let us go out now. I said I would go down to the drill ground . . . and then to the Treasury – I shall remint most of the money I took at Palagar, it's for that I was having a new picture . . .'

The four months' drought broke on the day that the Grand Army and the Fleet of Safi departed from Pomoan; the lords mounted horse or gangplank swathed in raincloaks, sheets of grey water drenched the limp banners, and the people danced bareheaded in the streets astream with mud. The dead white grasses of the hills revived and covered everthing in a mist of delicate green blades, a mistimed spring in autumn; as the army marched east along the coast, and the fleet followed them as closely as the vagaries of road and shoal and river allowed them, the journey took on the aspect of a festival.

Lord Sulakon rode at the head of the army, with Lord Golaron, who hated ships; Casik, Lakkannar, Hasmon, Daiaron, Almarem went with them. In the flagship of Lord Admiral Parhannon travelled the king, Lord Polem, Lord Arpalond, and Aleizon Ailix Ayndra. Late in Second Month, Ailixond went ashore for a while to receive the surrender of the petty state east next to Pomoan, and then they sailed on; the seas were getting steeper now that autumn was well along, the short northern summer dead. The festival lasted till the tenth day of Third Month, when a dark mass appeared on the horizon, north of the low cliffs of the coast: a rocky island, crowned by the stubby tile-roofed towers of a town. The fleet sailed around it, just out of arrow-shot: the sea-gates were closed, and the harbour shut off with chains. They anchored in the sheltered waters of a bay a few miles back, and the flagship went up to the sea-gate with all its banners flying. The trumpets shrieked in the shadows of the cliffs, resounding from rock and black water; sails slack in the lee of the island, the ship glided past the deserted quay and the wide shallow stair leading up to the gate itself. No one answered the herald's challenge. Finally Ailixond ordered them back to the moorings. That night all the talk was siege machines, asault by land and sea, starvation, fire: the soldiers were back to the war.

163

From the Secret Chronicle of Firumin:

11:III:463 The army on the land arrived on the shore this day. It turns out that there is a causeway, uncovered at low tide, some way across the straits, but it ends going down in a good depth some way before the Island. They were used to have a bridge there, but have of course taken it up. My lord has decided to build up the causeway till it stand above high tide, and put back the bridge, and also to try bombarding the city meanwhile with machines on ships. In charge of this is need I say who? Also a man Ogo who it is rumoured was her lover before when she was a common soldier. I do not know what my lord thinks of this.

14:III:463 I hear much complaint from the cavalry who are made to work on this causeway. The footmen of course are used to it but the others think they are of too good a class for labouring. I too am not best pleased since my lord wishes me to help with the making of wicker hurdles to build up the roadway. As if I had not enough to do. Furthermore the weather is bitter cold. At least with the woman on the ships my lord has unbroken sleep at nights.

16:III:463 My lord afflicted with a rheum, I swear from staying out at all hours on the causeway. He will catch his death soon, I swear it.

17:III:463 A gale so severe that the ships ride at anchor and can do nothing. Accordingly the woman came ashore in a rowing boat to see my lord. The boat well-nigh overturned as it came in to the shore. My lord who was there watching it would I am sure have leapt in to save her had she gone in. As it is I paid the priest to sacrifice for an abatement of the storm. In the night the spray blowing from the sea freezes all over the tent ropes. We ought to be within walls in such conditions. I pray that we may take the Island soon and put the barbarians out of their houses, bound as they are to be damp and verminous.

18:III:463 I suppose it is some benefit that my lord stays in his tent with the woman all day long. Still I pity the men who must go on digging and carrying for the causeway . . .

25:III:463 A great misfortune befell us in the night. The enemy set fireships among our fleet where they were at anchor, and we were all got out of bed at first hour of morning, with people running all ways in pitch-black dark, until we came to the sea and saw the flagship afire in the middle of the waters and Lord Parhannon gone in another boat to save it. It looked like the floating candles in the summer festival; however when I said this my lord did not take it well, while we stood there close on an hour until a rowing boat came, and the woman leapt out of it all wet. It appeared that she had stayed on the burning ship until she had to leap into the sea to escape it. I believe she has the protection of the devil, to come through unmarked by fire or water. I was made to give up my bed for her maidservant to sleep in it. Then she has lost all her clothes and money in the fire and went begging it off anyone who would lend it to her. I found her maidservant another place to sleep. Still, the causeway progresses at a great rate.

35:III:463 The causeway is well enough finished and a wooden bridge ready to be brought up for the assault.

36:III:463 Lord Sulakon went with a large force and a battering ram along the causeway, while my lord took ship with the Silver Shields and came down on the harbour where the catapults had breached the wall, went in and released the chains so that all our fleet entered the harbour, and fought a mighty battle to go through and open the gate to Lord Sulakon. He had suffered much from a devilish invention of the Island men, a device which threw hot sand through the air, to penetrate the gaps in armour and burn men's eyes and faces – the army was most furious and as soon as the gate opened they went out to rape and pillage as my lord would not usually permit, but this day he did. If I look out now I can see fires on the Island and I swear I can hear the noise of its destruction . . .

'Those who will can go burning and raiding,' said Ailixond. 'I do not choose to take part in it. It is only that in this case I did not think that I could have denied it.'

'It is expected,' said Lord Hasmon. 'But for a long time they've gone without . . .'

'I do not like to see a town with its people subject to rampage,' said Ailixond. The victory banquet was small this time, and quiet; the greater part of the high officers and lords were on the Island still.

Polem leant over and murmured, 'Is she . . .?'

'I do not know,' said Ailixond.

'But were you not together?'

'Until we reached the gate. Then she went up on the walls, and I've not seen her since . . . I do not think she is dead, I would have heard of that.' He tapped his goblet on the table, and the wine-pourer ran forward. Hasmon went on, 'The men will be happy, at

least, to have this . . . it's been a hard task, building that sea-road
. . .' Ailixond did not bother to feign interest. Hasmon's talk ran
out like water soaking into sand. Polem looked oppressed and
stuck his nose into his wine cup. Ailixond gazed rigidly at the
doorway; then lifted his head as the curtains parted. Sulakon
strode in: fully armed, except for his helmet which he carried
under his arm, and deposited with a clang on the table.
'The Island is quiet!' he said. 'The fires are under watch, and no
one any longer walks the streets except our patrols.' He looked at
Ailixond. 'I have seen to it all, my lord.'
Ailixond's fixed expression did not change, but he rose, and
held out his hand to Sulakon, who bent to kiss the Royal Ring.
Ailixond gazed over his bowed shoulders, and said, 'Ha!' The
company followed his glance, even Sulakon turning as he
straightened. Aleizon Ailix Ayndra stood in the entrance, white-
faced and stony-eyed, wet ragged hair straying over her forehead
and the collar of her black cloak; under it she clearly had her right
hand pressed to her left shoulder. Her eyes flicked over the ring of
staring faces; she nodded, said hoarsely, 'Good day,' and dashed
over to the side of the room. There was a pause before
conversation resumed. Ailixond questioned Sulakon about the
disposition of the guards on the Island, but kept half looking over
to the side, not quite far enough to beckon her with his eyes. She
had sat down on a bench and was asking a slave for something.
Firumin emerged from behind the curtains, and whispered to her;
she answered curtly, and sat with her head down until a servant
bought her a hot steaming bowl. She sipped it for a while, and
then brought out a resin stick, lit it in the nearest lamp and bent
over to suck at the smoke. A flowery sweetness stole through the
odours of sweat and wine, the greasy smells of congealing food
and lampsmoke. Sulakon shot a glare in her direction. She stared
sullenly back at him, and blew a plume of smoke from her
nostrils.
'Le's sing song!' exclaimed Lakkannar.
'Wha', victory song?' said Polem.
'Na! Goddam' boring. Na, like, o – four an' twenty virgins took
a journey to Thaless! An' when they came, back home again –'
Ailixond sat up. 'Enough!' he said harshly. Lakkannar halted,
mouth open, his face belligerent.
'An you will sing these wineshop chants, go find a wineshop to
sing them in.'
'O? . . . as you will, my lord,' said Lakkannar with abominable
grace. He addressed himself once more to his winecup. Ailixond

finally caught Aleizon Ailix Ayndra's eye, and indicated that she should come over. She got up, slowly, and shuffled round behind his table. One of the servants ran up with a chair, and she squeezed in between him and Polem; they put their heads together and started chattering in low voices, while Polem gazed at them with a beatific drunken grin. Sulakon raised his voice: 'It is good,' he said, 'that my lord cousin does not tolerate the singing of impure songs in this our victory celebration. It is a pity that he does not purify . . . other things in the same way.'

Ailixond was as drunk by then as he ever got; his movements a little slurred, and his arrogance increased till it was impressive by its completeness; he looked at Sulakon as if he were a tiresome parasite yet too insignificant to be crushed by a finger nail. Aleizon Ailix Ayndra, however, looked like a wolf that smelt blood. Her lips narrowed and her face seemed to become pointed. She said, 'What do you mean?'

Sulakon said, 'I mean that it is not meet to allow any of our – our people to flaunt the god-given natural habits which lay down the proper conduct of men and women, both in their dress and activity – and toward each other –'

Ayndra spat explosively. 'God-given! Pfah!'

'In their justice and wisdom they have decreed that the proper habit of women is chastity, and their concern the care of our homes and of our children – that they should not usurp the clothing and concerns of men, nor should they seek them out in lust, nor venture to kill them in war –'

Ayndra said in a high clear voice, 'But submit to rape and murder if by some ill fortune they should find themselves on the losing side of their men's war? What for their chastity then? And is lust and violence the proper pursuit of men?'

'It is not,' said Sulakon.

'Then I think that you should tell that to more than a few of the gentlemen gathered here this night – not that those are god-given laws any more than the so-called laws you have just called down upon my head. I tell you this, Lord Sulakon, if your gods are so powerful and I offend them so greatly, then why do I stand here now? – why did this sword that I took in my shoulder this afternoon not go through my heart? And why have the soldiers of Safi been permitted to despoil the chastity of so many of what you call good women on the Island this day? I do not think that much can be said for your gods, at least not lately – are they sleeping? Or gone on a journey? Are they even perhaps dead? I tell you, Lord Sulakon, if you had not been born noble and –'

Ailixond had risen up beside her, and laid his hands gently on her shoulders; now he pressed down. He hissed in her ear, 'Sit!' Sulakon exclaimed, 'Blasphemer!' She shrieked, 'Deluded hypocrite!'

Ailixond pulled at her left arm. 'Sit down!' She gave a strangled cry and collapsed into her chair, hunched over her wounded shoulder. Ailixond said, 'I think, gentlemen, my lords, that it is time for us to retire.' Sulakon was red-faced and puffing like a bull. He said, 'I will not –' The tent was in uproar.

Ailixond brought his fist down with a crash on the table and bellowed, 'Silence!' in the voice that carried above the roar of battle. The dishes leapt on the board; the voices died. He said, 'I will not allow quarrels at my table. It shames all of us that such insults can be exchanged between officers of my army. I shall ask you now all to leave me.'

Sulakon bowed curtly, and was first out of the door. Ailixond stood quite still, watching them push to file out; Polem smiled anxiously, and when it was not returned, offered his arm to Lakkannar and tottered out with him. Ayndra was still hunched over, moaning; she glanced up at them and muttered, 'The halt leading the blind.'

Ailixond sat down beside her, as the servants crept out to start clearing; she did not look at him. He said, 'That was neither amusing, nor necessary.' She made slit eyes at him, her mouth as sulky as a child's. 'Beside,' he said, 'you have made an enemy.'

She sucked in a breath. 'He – ah! – he hates me anyway.'

'True. But now he cannot even be civil to you. He cannot now recognise you at all, even when he should, unless it be to challenge you.'

She said, 'You ought to have pulled my other arm.'

'It was necessary to silence you.'

She sat up. 'What! – do you say that Sulakon has been shamed so much? What think you have I been? Hauled back to my seat like your puppet!'

'I did not do so!'

'You did! Why did you not slap your hand over Sulakon's mouth? You would not treat him so – and not only because he's taller than you and you could not!'

'I could indeed!' said Ailixond.

'O yes? – but should I sit still to be insulted in front of half the officers in the army? I will not!'

'You do not have to repay in the same coin.'

'And then have you pull my arm half out of its socket – ooh, ah,

168

sweet Luamis – I've been made a fool of –'

'It was your own doing.'

'It was not! My own doing that since I'm a woman I'm called unnatural and god-cursed and a whore for doing what all of you do all the time? And since it is unjust I suppose I should sit rejoicing in the benefit my submission to it does my soul? – and are you going to talk to me now of peace and civility? and then to be assaulted by you to silence me! An I wish to quarrel with Lord Sulakon, I will, and it's no business of yours!'

'Everything that goes on here is my business.'

'It is not! You've not bought me – I'm not one of your chattels!' She sprang up. Ailixond reached for her hand, but she shook it loose from his grasp. He said, 'I did not mean –'

'Then you should not do what you don't mean!' She flung away from him to the door. He called, 'Stop! Come back!'

'I won't!'

'No – don't – I tell you –'

'I don't care!' she threw back over her shoulder. 'Yes, and you, Firumin, you can come out of your corner! Don't think you are not observed!' She ran out; the curtains flopped down behind her. Ailixond slowly turned. 'Firumin?' he said softly.

Firumin stepped shakily out of the shadows. 'Well,' said Ailixond.

'My lord?' quavered Firumin.

'I have told you a hundred times not to skulk behind me to overhear my private conversations. Explain to me the reason for your arrant disobedience.'

'If you, if you had needed anything, lord, I –'

'If I had needed anything, I could have called. Give me a better reason.'

'Lord, I, I do not know, I meant no intrusion –'

'You know not why? Then I shall tell you. You revel in sweeping up every morsel of scandal, filth and gossip, so that you may go and spread it among your painted friends, making much of your access to the private lives of the great – so now it will be, o, my dear! my lord had a fight with the woman, and do you know what they said?'

'My lord, I do not ever –'

'Do you not? But know this, Firumin, should I catch you listening in corners again, I shall have you flogged till you cannot stand. Now get out!'

Firumin made a bob that passed for a bow, and ran. Ailixond was left alone in the half-cleared hall, among the guttering lamps

169

and the cold food. Black smuts and twists of smoke sailed up above the orange flames, to smirch the canvas roof and blacken the edges of the smokehole. He brushed the fall of hair from his eyes, and turned back to his bedchamber.

'Captain Ayndra,' said Arpalond. 'You've been assigned command of the harbour garrison on the Island, with effect from next day. You were best to go this day to carry your things into the harbourmaster's office.'

'Indeed,' she said, without joy or sorrow. 'And for how long?'

'I am told that it is while we repair and order the Island for our garrison. After that, I have no orders.'

She nodded glumly. 'I thank you, my lord.' And went walking across the causeway through the weeping smoke that drifted from the Safic funeral pyres on the beach, followed by Yunnil and two men pulling a handcart filled with her possessions, or rather such as she had replaced after the fire on the ship. She took up residence in the squat grey stone building next the breach in the walls which she had directed the making of; the walls of the room where she and Yunnil slept glistened with damp, which froze glibly in the night cold. In the day, the men worked at repairing the damage their own attack had made, and in refurbishing the harbour so that the fleet could anchor there; she shuffled about with them, still crooked by the stifness of her healing shoulder, head wrapped in an interminable black woollen scarf against the ravages of the sea gales. In the halls up on the rocky crest of the Island, Lord Ailixond received its rulers, the Council of Five, accepted their allegiance and reinstituted them, as a Council of Six – the sixth being a Safic delegate, who would command the small garrison and the naval station, as well as ordering the surfacing of the causeway with stone, and other civil and military projects . . . it was announced that the army would depart on the midday of Fourth Month. It was cold enough now that the spray froze in icicles on the eaves of seaside buildings. Aleizon Ailix Ayndra came back with nose and eyes astream from her day's work, and found Yunnil huddling outside the door of her room. 'What is it?' she said. 'Have you cooked my supper? God's teeth! my hands are too stiff to take my gloves off . . . for what do you wait?'

'Sir, someone to see you.'

'Where are they, then?'

'Inside, sir.'

'What! You should not have let them go in.'

'I had to, sir . . . will you, he said, sir, go in . . .'

170

'Of course! I live here,' she kicked the door open, fumbling in her sleeve for a rag on which to blow her nose. 'What is it, then? – ay!' Ailixond was sitting among the heap of rough blankets on her bed. 'Good day,' she said.

'Good day.'

'I . . . my lord. I did not expect to find you here.'

'Have you been living in this place all this time? I'm surprised you're not as mould-ridden as the walls.'

'I've lived in worse places,' she said, and blew her nose noisily into the cloth. 'But, well, what –?' Ailixond tilted his head toward the door. She pushed it to. 'Arpalond told me to go live here!' she said.

'I had not seen what it was like. You should have asked for another.'

'I never thought of it. After all . . .'

'I've not seen you for twelve days,' he said. She shrugged, unwinding the scarf from her face; around her eyes and nose the skin was red with wind-chap, and she had a cold sore by her mouth. 'Why did you not come?' he asked.

'I was sent here . . . you did not ask me to.'

'I did not think that – yes, I know. So I've come to you now.'

She wiped her nose again and said in a strained whisper, 'Am I going to stay on here when the army leaves?'

Ailixond shook his head; he gestured to her to come. She dropped her scarf and cloak on the floor and stepped over them.

Yunnil squatted outside the door, blowing on her fingers, for a while after she heard no more conversation; when she grew tired of waiting for fresh instructions, she gently slid the door open until she could see inside. Aleizon Ailix Ayndra had her back to her; she was sitting on the floor by the bed, leaning between Ailixond's knees. He was bent right over her, hair falling over her shoulders. Yunnil inched the door shut again, and went off to the guardhouse kitchen.

'What have you done to your face?'

'The cold did it. The sea winds are terrible . . . and the spray, everything gets covered with salt, all sticky . . . you consigned me to it, too . . .'

'I thought it better – you understand, I am in a corner. I must not create factions among my subjects, so what was I to do?'

'Send Sulakon away somewhere.'

'He could not do a duty like this, it's not . . .'

'Suitable to his dignity.'

171

'No. And the same when there are quarrels . . . I cannot quarrel with any of them except when it's favoured by reasons of state . . .'

'Reasons of state? Are they distinct from reasons of your own best interest?'

'Not any longer, I think . . .'

'Tell me. What is it like to be the king?'

'Tell you? I do not know how I can. It's my life, I think it has eaten up my soul.'

'But don't you remember before? – how old were you, when . . .'

'Twenty, I was twenty when my father died – but do you know, I was never intended to be the king? That was my elder brother, the other Ailixond. He was eight years older than I and a foot taller, and his mother was Lady Amia – he always rode in front of me in processions, he was married and had a son before I even got my lord's bracelets, and then I overheard the slaves calling me the little Lord Ailixond, and my mother was not noble born, it was clear that my father married her in a fit of lust and lived to regret it. They said I'd have second commands all my life, and be watched all the time in case I offered any threats to his throne, that was why I was sent so much to school in the hopes that I'd satisfy myself with study and want no part in politicking, until he started to sicken, the year before my father died, and I got a few of the commands that would have been his. But he was still the heir presumptive. And then – I can see it now – I was walking across Great Court with my father, and he stopped all of a sudden and clutched at his chest and fell to the ground, and he was dead. Like a bolt from the blue. And the other Ailixond took to his bed on the next day, and before my father was even burnt, let alone the full Council of Lords convened to elect the next king, he was dead too. And ten days later, I was chosen king, and my mother – my mother always said I should be king, and she called me to her room and took out a full set of coronation robes, she'd had them all made ready . . . and I went out, after the coronation, to ask the acclaim of the people, and they roared my name . . .' He brought his left hand out from under the blankets, and held it up, the fingers splayed, the huge uncut diamond like a lump of scoured ice on his middle finger. 'It's said that once you have on the Royal Ring, you never take it off – it's cut off, or dragged off, but never willingly taken.' He closed his fingers and laid his other hand over them. 'And never mind what I say at other times, I'd not take it off now.'

'No matter how much trouble it causes to other people.'

'No!'

Aleizon Ailix Ayndra started to laugh. 'And that's why you understand that you cannot stop me . . .'

'Only put you in a place where you will cause the least destruction . . .'

'Ha! Least destruction! Let you talk about destruction! How many deaths are you the cause of?'

'O, any number . . . I cannot tell . . . what's this on your arm?' He ran his finger down the long ridge leading from armpit to elbow on the smooth underside of her upper arm. 'It's a knife scar,' she said. 'I got that before I learnt to fight properly – years and years ago. It was in a wineshop off Yellow Temple Square . . . it was with a man who called me a whore's bastard. He got away, for that time – it was just after I . . . began to live on my own. Before I went to S'Thurrulass. But I've no wish to talk about it. Are you going to make us march off in this hellish weather?'

'It's not so bad. The sea moderates the cold here; Parhannon says that warm waters come up from the Shessar Ocean so that it's not so harsh as in the mountains – the grass plains are far colder in winter. Much further north it is where the seas freeze.'

'O, I know, we sailed up there once . . .'

'What, up where the seas freeze?'

'Yes! I saw ice floating on the seas, and once a white bear on an island of ice – we'd gone up there to get furs from the tribes who live up there – they come down on to the ice in winter, in the summer they go inland . . .'

'When did you go there?'

'O, years ago, when I was a child – it was in Pomoan that my mother found a broken-down old priest whom she enlisted to teach me to read, for the price of a skin bottle of wine for each lesson – she thought I would catch a better husband if I could read and figure, some young merchant who could use me as his clerk as well as cook and housekeeper.'

'Is there any place in the Empire where you have not been?'

'O, I've hardly travelled inland – although we did go by land down to Haramin, to Raq'min, until my mother's husband there died and she decided to go back to Safi and set up a shop with the money he had left her – she'd almost forgotten by then that she was Haraminharn born, and she said that there was more money in Safi. She used to sell herbs and medicines, and she had a back room where she took some customers, where I was forbidden to touch the bottles; I believe she used to sell poisons there.'

173

'Where did she keep the shop?'

'The third street on the left going down Fish Street from Great Market, down an alley going off past a wineshop called the Brown Bull.'

'Indeed? – and what was her name?'

'Mistress Cattiraen.'

'I know it!' said Ailixond.

'What, surely you never went there?'

'I recall hearing my mother tell slaves to go there to buy medicines for her.'

'Indeed? – we used to have many servants from great houses coming to us, though I'd not have known which were of the palace.'

'My mother had many servants of her own who'd not wear palace livery. Her family had lived in Safi for a long time, and many of their slaves served her after she married.'

'Well! Well!' said Ayndra. Ailixond grinned. 'I should have let her send me out.'

'Why?'

'I would perhaps have seen you.'

'You'd not have had any reason to speak to me if you had; you would only have seen me climbing up to get jars down from high shelves, while my mother charged you double because of the richness of your clothes. Besides, most of the time she would not let me in the shop because my ill-manneredness would offend the customers. And then I'd not have dared speak to such an august person as yourself.'

'Does your mother not still keep a shop?'

'No – I think she perhaps offended someone august herself, or something . . . perhaps she merely fell over and split her head in the street; it was after a great festival with a great deal of wine drunk, it was my sixteenth birthday, and she said Well! Aleizon, you're a woman now, and all this is yours! and walked out. And I've not seen her since . . . a merchant offered to buy the shop from me a sixday later, and I agreed. I think now it was a very poor price, but I knew nothing. I did not want a shop, I wanted . . .'

'What?'

'To be a hero. With a sword.'

'And is that what you've been pursuing?'

'Ah, no, I've pursued nothing save the way of a vagabond. I'll not ever be a hero . . . you're a hero, you are . . .'

'I am not. I'm the king of Safi . . . the best who ever lived! All

174

the other kings of Safi are nothing to me!'
'O, be quiet! – ya!'

The army laboured eastward under the lash of marine gales and
snow-spattered winds, through short dark days and long nights
filled with a diamond dust of polar stars; pausing in filthy
seashore settlements, detouring into the hinterland to visit farming
villages, obtaining their allegiance and what food they had to
spare, sometimes, if they were very short, giving them of the
biscuit and salt meat that the ships brought up from the south, out
of the steel-green seas. So came a fishing smack, on the first day of
Fifth Month, carrying a messenger to the king, who was then at
the head of the army moving along the road; but as soon as he
opened the letter, he said, 'Halt! Immediately! Everyone – and
summon the Council to come up here.'

'What, on the road?' said Polem. 'Why not this evening, if –'

'No! Now!' said Ailixond. 'Go!' He turned to the messenger.
'How long since you left Pomoan?'

'We've been sailing for fifteen days, my lord; we were the last
out before they closed the harbour – and that was six days after
the siege began.'

'Siege?' exclaimed Polem. Ailixond waved him down. 'How
long did Haligon think he could hold out?'

'There was food for a couple of months – but if they assault –'

'I see. And if Haligon has shown himself so incompetent already
– and in so doing has thrown away the useful myth that a Safic
army is invincible –'

'It's you, my lord, that's invincible,' said the messenger.

'Not so,' said Ailixond. 'Only, my luck is better . . .' In the dusk
behind, the column was coming to a noisy and chaotic halt, while
the officers galloped up to the king. Within half an hour, they had
assembled round him; he was a pale, faceless figure wrapped in a
white bearskin, but his voice was clear as glass in the gathering
dark. 'Haligon, Lord Governor of the Cities of the Plain, is
besieged in Pomoan by a rebel army, and blockaded there by a
fleet of rebel boats. Some time in Second Month, it seems, the
people of Tengam rose up in the plains and murdered our garrison
there, only two of them escaping to win through to Pomoan, and
when Haligon sent what he describes as a small force to suppress
them, he discovered that half the other Cities of the Plain were
rising in rebellion. They cut our force to pieces, and the next thing
Haligon knew, he was besieged in Pomoan – since early in Fourth
Month. He begs assistance as soon as may be – that is, if Pomoan

175

has not already fallen, for he writes that the rebels are numerous and determined.' There was a silence.

'A disaster indeed,' said Sulakon.

'I do not like to do it,' said Ailixond, 'but the army must be divided. It is not possible that we should all return to Pomoan, but we must send a large force to put down the rebels as soon as may be. And the best part of the fleet, also – if they can break the blockade before the land army arrives . . .'

'God knows where it may have spread to by now,' said the messenger.

'The worst of this is, it's clear that the plains had been rotten with dissent for months – and what had Haligon done? What had he found out? Though this must have been brewing even while I was in Pomoan . . . Sulakon, Golaron, I shall send you back westward, and Parhannon with the fleet and as many men as we may cram into his ships. The Silver Shields must go. I shall stay here . . .'

'When is this to happen?'

'You'll leave next morning.'

By noon the next day, two ships rocked at anchor where the whole fleet had assembled, and a much reduced cavalcade went on to the east; already stripped of most of its followers, who had stayed in Pomoan to escape the rigours of winter, they had lost almost half their numbers to the relieving force. They marched east for three days, to Dompadde, the nearest thing to a town that the region possessed, and encamped there to wait for news from the west, meanwhile setting in order all the lands within reach, while rapidly exhausting the few entertainments offered in four or five miserable booths passing for taverns, and living off dried fish and an execrable barley beer; marching about on guard duty, exercising when the weather was fit, and being sent off in parties led by one of the few lords remaining to show the banner of Safi in nearby villages. By the tenth day of Fifth Month, it already seemed as if they had been sinking into the slush-and-ice-ways of the camp for a year.

Two guards stood, as usual, outside the king's tent, wrapped up in furs and woollens till they looked more like small bears than men. Just before last hour, their reliefs wandered up, managing to march the last ten paces and exchange a sketchy salute – 'Ah! Thought you'd not come.'

'Never wanted to.'

'Ay well, I wish you a fine time of it . . .'

'They still up in there?'

176

'He might be . . . there's none else there, though.'

'Is she . . .?'

'She went.'

'Ay, well then . . . goo' night.'

'Goo' night.'

They took up the vacated places under the porch, and stood there warming their hands over the brazier provided for night duty for perhaps half an hour; the camp was well-nigh silent, and they saw no one moving in any direction. Then one said, 'No one there.'

'Go, then.'

'If anyone comes . . .'

'I'll not let them enter till I've been inside.'

'Good.'

'Go, then.'

One of them looked to either side, and slipped within. The other stepped closer to the brazier and started rubbing his hands together over it, whistling, and looking around, although the camp was deserted, the stars rockhard with frost.

In Ailixond's bedchamber it was hardly warmer, and no lighter, than outside; he slept lightly with the cold, turning again and again under the piled furs and quilts on the bed. There was a small thump at the bed's foot; just enough to open his eyes. He lay still, breathing as if he yet slept; the darkness lay over his vision like a cloth, generating only the fictional prickles and patches of colour in blindness. The faint, very faint, whistle and rub he heard could have been the amplified pulse of his own blood; he sighed as if dreaming, and turned over, burrowing beneath the pillows until his left hand grasped the object that lay there, and relaxed among the blankets. For a long time there was quiet; then a clank, cloth sliding on cloth, and the soft press of a leather sole on the canvas-covered floor; then another footstep, and another. Someone was standing by the bed. A metallic hiss – a blade drawing out of its scabbard. Ailixond started to slide his left hand out from under the pillows.

'Shumar guide me!' whispered the other, and Ailixond threw himself over to the side. Someone loomed over him, and the sword intended for his heart went into his shoulder. The attacker made a strangled exclamation; the king pulled out the long knife that was hidden in his pillows, and lunged for him. He carried him over onto the floor, and they struggled there, one naked and the other muffled in cloak and boots. Ailixond got the knife up against his throat. 'Be still!' he hissed. The man gripped his wrist in gloved

177

hands. Ailixond twisted over and ground his knee into the other's groin; he grunted, and his grip slackened. In a fury of desperation, Ailixond drove the knife straight up beneath his chin, and pulled it out, and stabbed it in, again and again; a burning fluid ran over his hands, the body under him flailed and grew still. He rocked back on his heels, and the pain of the wound in his shoulder washed over him; hot blood trickled over his ribs. He hauled a cover off the bed and pulled it round his shoulders, got up and groped his way to the curtains. 'Firumin!' There was no reply. 'Firumin!' he shouted. 'Firumin!'

'Whaat?' murmured a sleepy voice.

Ailixond took hold of the tent pole by the door. 'Firumin!'

A bobbing glow appeared in the depths of the tent. 'I come, I come . . .' A few moments later, Firumin staggered out of the back room, wrapped in a long nightshirt and clutching an oil-lamp. 'My lord . . .?' he mumbled, then looked up and gave a shriek. Blood had soaked through the blanket over Ailixond's shoulder; his hands were covered in it, and his feet had left dark prints on the floor. 'Gods!' yelped Firumin. 'O gods! O what? My lord! Help!'

'Come here,' said Ailixond. Firumin ran after him, and looked into his room. The lamp displayed a guard lying on the floor, blood all over him, a bloody sword lying in the bed, more blood all over the sheets . . . 'Murder!' he wailed. 'Treason! Help!' Ailixond stepped over the corpse and sat down on the edge of the bed. Firumin wrung his hands and gibbered.

'Go now,' said Ailixond, 'go quietly – summon the guards – no, go quietly to Lord Polem, and Lord Arpalond, and tell them to come here but one first to go to Captain Patto and tell him to go and apprehend my lords Daiaron and Almarem, and the other guard outside my tent, and the captain of the watch for this night, and whoever it is who devised the order of guards this month. And leave off wailing. And call the Physician also. Go now!' Firumin stared at him. 'But, my lord, if I leave –'

'I think I am safe now,' Ailixon said. 'Go!' Firumin scuttled out. Ailixond laid his elbows on his knees, and put his head in his hands.

It was so that Polem found him sitting when he rushed in half-dressed and frantic; he did not move when he entered, only lifted his head when Polem put a hand on his shoulder. His skin was clammy to the touch. Polem knelt beside him, pulled up a sheet, and rolled the blanket down from his shoulder. Ailixond looked into his eyes, but said nothing; Polem put his arm round his good shoulder, and started to wipe away blood from the other.

178

Ailixond said, 'It was the door-guard . . . they must catch the other. If he's not already fled.'

'I came in by Firumin's door, I did not see. Arpalond went to get Patto's men out, he'll not get far.'

'And Almarem, and Daiaron. A trial in especial – high treason . . .'

'Yes indeed . . . be still, now.' Polem tore a strip off the sheet, folded it into a pad, and began to bind it over the wound. Ailixond shivered. 'What's that?' Voices yelled outside, and feet thundered; there were the sounds of a scuffle, a short scream, thumps. The door-curtain billowed, and half-a-dozen armed men burst in; Captain Patto pushed between them. 'My lord! What happened?' Ailixond pointed with his chin at the body. 'This attempted to murder me. I want you to go straightway to Almarem's tent, and arrest him on suspicion of conspiracy and high treason. The same with Lord Daiaron – and have you the other door-guard? And whoever ordered the guards this night – and all this month – arraign them all, on suspicion of conspiracy, swear I'll release them as soon as they've proved their innocence, but let them not communicate with any one at all, wives, mothers, friends, no one at all. Go now!' As Patto bowed, and made to leave, another mob came pushing into the tent, crying, 'We have him! Kill the traitors!' Arpalond led them, followed by a near-hysterical Firumin and pursued by what seemed to be half a battalion of phalanx in all stages of disarray, bearing along with them, half-paralysed with terror, the second guard. They threw him to the floor beside the corpse of his confederate, where he grovelled. Ailixond, a torn sheet kilted round his loins, stood over him. He tried to kiss the king's bare foot, but it was jerked away from him. 'You did well to take him alive. We shall no doubt learn much from him.'

'No!' said the prisoner. 'I'll tell you – I only had to wait – I did not know –'

'O, be silent,' said Ailixond. 'Speak when you are questioned. Take him away from me.' The prisoner was hauled out of sight. 'Gentlemen, I thank you. If you would offer further aid in searching for conspirators, offer your services to Captain Patto, whose task it is to see which of the other suspects we may trap. You should search for anyone making to flee, and apprehend them, enchain them and keep them under guard. I thank you again – and, presently, wish you good night.' The mob crowded out; Ailixond gave a sigh, and dropped back among the tainted sheets as the Royal Physician came in, trailed by four assistants

179

with rolls of bandage, jars of hot water, clean rags and pots of
salve; the king had to remove to his chair, where he endured the
cleansing of the deep hole under his collarbone with boiled water,
wine and salt and stinging salves, while servants crept in and out,
removing the body, putting fresh linen on the bed, clearing as
much of the blood as they could. Polem leant against the bed's
foot and tried to divert Ailixond, who was grey-faced and silent.

'Let me in!' demanded someone outside. Firumin remonstrated:
'No, no, sir, you cannot.'

'Why not? . . . o, is that all? Look, Firumin, if I have seen a
naked man before, then it does not matter, and if not, why then I
am sure that it is time I did.' The curtains billowed, and Aleizon
Ailix Ayndra rushed in. 'Hoo!' she said. 'It looks like wedding
preparations in a slaughterhouse.' Ailixond gave a thin smile. 'My
felicitations, my lord, on evading your murderers.'

'They are not murderers,' he said. 'Should they attempt your
life, that's a murder. My life, it is treason. High treason.' The
Physician offered him a cup of thick steaming liquid. 'Only drink
this, my lord, and all's well.' Ailixond sipped it. 'Ugh! What is it?'

'It's a decoction of herbs that promote the thickening of the
blood.'

'And also the turning of the stomach, I should think. Still, I
thank you.' The Physician bowed, and shooed his apprentices out.
Ayndra sat down on the floor by the bed. Polem said, 'Did you
not throw the knife that brought down the guard as he fled?'

'Pure luck! Even I cannot aim for, and be sure to hit, the legs of
a running man, in the dark, at twenty or thirty paces.' She looked
to Ailixond, who was grimacing over his potion. 'I thought you
were dead!' she said. 'No one knew what had happened – it was
the rebels, it was a rebellion in the camp, it was a murder – excuse
me, a treason or whatever – I could not get in here for the crowd
all running around without shouting . . .'

'You'll not be rid of me so easily,' he said.

'You're shivering,' Polem said, 'shall I bring you a cloak?'

'No. I'll return to my bed.' He swallowed the last of the vile
brew and went to turn back the covers. Polem said, 'Sleep well!'
and made to leave; Ailixond caught hold of his hand, and
embraced him. Polem impulsively kissed him. 'Thank god!'

'There'll be no trouble now,' said Ailixond. 'Go now, and rest –
we'll seek them, tomorrow . . .'

On the outskirts of Dompadde, a canvas and wooden courtroom
grew up on the snow: a dais with three sides, judge and jury in the

centre, prosecution on one side and defence on the other, with banks of seats for onlookers on the fourth side of the sunken square where the participants would stand to speak. Arpalond and Ailixond stood on the prosecution dais, while Polem strolled to and fro in the pit; the carpenters were hard at work on the benches for the audience, while others carried in tables and chairs for the jury.

'But you have not ten nobles for the jury,' said Arpalond. 'You cannot try him without a jury. You must wait until they come back from Pomoan.'

'What? – have we not ten?'

'Not unless you wish to include Daiaron when you try Almarem, and vice versa.'

'But we have myself, yourself, Polem, Hasmon, Casik, Ellakon, Haresond, Sargond, Issaron . . . ah! Nine, indeed.'

'Na, you can try him!' said Polem. 'He's a traitor, we all know it.'

'No. It's been said often enough that I'm imposing my own vagaries of desire on the state – if I take justice into my own hands . . . I cannot flout the law.'

'Then try him with nine lords. He's fortunate to get a trial at all. Your father would have straightway lopped his head off.'

'I cannot do it! If it's not a legal trial, I might as well lop off his head without bothering with justice. I will not do it.'

'Then you must imprison them until the others return,' said Arpalond. 'We can try the commoners, at least.'

'But we would have still to keep them, figureheads for whatever other discontent might arise – what if Sulakon came back defeated, and we had all to go back to Pomoan to suppress it? We could hardly carry prisoners with us then . . . and if we have to wait here long, the men mislike it . . . no, I want them dealt with.'

'It's that, or give them a fraudulent trial,' Arpalond said again.

'Indeed . . .' Ailixond took a few steps across the platform; then lifted his hand. 'I know what I shall do!' he said.

'Lop their heads off?' said Polem. 'Can't they have a posthumous trial?'

'No, no, no! Look you – I can create lords whenever I wish, can I not?'

'Yes, but – none of the young lords are here –'

'Young lords? It need not be a noble's son.'

'A commoner? O, you – o,' said Polem, 'you cannot!'

The king smiled wickedly. 'To quote a mutual friend – you may think I should not, but I can, Polem, I can!' He swung round to

181

go. 'Tell them all, Arpalond, to convene the court, here, at sixth hour of morning next day. Almarem to be tried first,' and dashed out.

'O no!' said Polem. 'You know what he will do?'

'Create a lord?' said Arpalond.

'Yes! And who do you think . . .?'

'O ho!'

'Yes . . .'

'Well! Not an ill choice, if he must . . .'

'But think! When Sulakon returns . . .'

Arpalond was standing in front of the row of ten chairs, before which the Vice-Justiciar and his clerks had their tables; the elderly Lord Haresond had taken the floor, while the seats were filling up with a noisy crowd of soldiers.

'. . . but, an I count rightly, there are but nine lords here, that is there will be when my lord the king arrives, which means, my lords, that we cannot rightly try Lord Almarem and Lord Daiaron, for, no matter what crimes they may have committed –'

'All stand! All stand for the king!'

The courtroom rose to its feet as Ailixond walked in. He stood at the edge of the dais, and acknowledged them; as they were sitting down again, he said to Haresond, 'You were saying?'

'I was saying, my lord, that we cannot try the noble lords, since we are not able to make up a jury of ten of their peers, and so we must surely postpone their trial until we have a tenth lord –'

'As you have now!' Aleizon Ailix Ayndra bounded out onto the prosecution platform. Haresond frowned at her. 'Young sir! You have no right to interrupt me in that way – but where is this tenth lord?'

'Here,' she said, and theatrically raised her arms to let her full sleeves slide back. The lord's bracelets were shiny and unmistakable on her wrists; the crowd gasped. She turned from side to side to make sure that all had seen them, then lowered her hands and strolled past the other lords to the tenth chair of the row.

'Let the trial commence,' said Ailixond, and went to the first chair. 'Bring in Lord Almarem.' Pikes clashed in salute, and six phalanxmen marched in with Almarem, bareheaded and with his wrists linked by a foot of heavy chain, in their midst. They ranged themselves behind him as he took his seat on the dais of defence. The Vice-Justiciar rose to read the schedule of charges.

A strange trial: most of the witnesses could not appear in person, but gave evidence through written accounts of the

182

revelations that five days' questioning had drawn from them, since they were chained up awaiting their trials later, while the principal witness was also judge and juror. The tales began more than a year ago, relating how various dissenters from the king's career of contest, in voicing their dissent, had found one another out and been found out by the lords, who had insinuated them into the duty lists for guarding the king, letting them go on becoming trusted and known in their places, until with the division of the army they decided that the time had come, and they had only to wait for a night when they knew the king slept alone. The same story was repeated with slight variation until the hour's recess at midday; when the court gathered again, it was the turn of the defence. A law-clerk stood up to speak.

'My lords, gentlemen, we are gathered here this day –'

'Silence!' said a high-pitched voice. Almarem jumped to his feet, chained hands held in front of him. The lawyer paused. 'Silence!' he said. 'I will speak for myself.' He looked across at Ailixond.

'It is your right,' said the king.

Almarem jerked his head up and stepped down onto the floor. 'Yes,' he said, 'yes! I am charged with high treason – and what I say is, if it is treason to put an end to a tyrant who has lost all sense and reason, who drives men to death and destruction in foreign lands and will ruin Safi if it is necessary to further his ever-growing folly of conquest, in pursuit of his own glory, then yes, I am a traitor!' His lawyer plucked at his sleeve. 'My lord! If you say –'

'Leave me! You have made up your mind days ago that I am to die, this trial is no more than a farce to dignify your revenge, so I'll say what I will! Yes, I tried to kill you, Ailixond, most unjust lord and king, and all I regret is that I failed, but you'd better watch out, watch closely now! for it was only ill luck that we failed, and someone else will do better and it'll not be long, else you change your cursed arrogant ways –' By now the court was in uproar; Almarem went on shouting above it. 'With your Council that you say decides, but does nothing but say yes to what you tell it – and your talk of necessities of state, ha! necessities to satisfy your pride – and now you'll have me slain because I argued against you, and you hope thereby to frighten all your rivals for however long you may – murderer! Witch's son! And your sorceress whore that now you'll have everyone to call lord, I thank god I shall not –'

Aleizon Ailix Ayndra put her hand inside her tunic and slipped out of her seat; she shuffled along the dais, slowly withdrawing her hand. Arpalond jumped up and ran along behind her; just as she whipped out her hand with the knife, he seized her wrist in both hands. They wrestled, while the spectators stood up and yelled and Almarem went on pouring abuse at them and Ailixond – 'Slaves! Lackeys! Arse-lickers!' he shrieked. 'And you, you're besotted with her, you and that wine-sodden bed-presser Polem and all the rest of –'

'Silence him,' said Ailixond coldly to the nearest guards. They leapt down and cast themselves on Almarem, stopped his mouth with gloved hands and hauled him back to his seat; despite his frenzy, his born lord's dignity prevented him engaging in an unseemly struggle with them. The cries of 'Traitor! Death! Stop his mouth!' subsided. Ailixond stood up. 'My lords. I think we have witnessed enough. I request of you your verdict.' Arpalond and Ayndra had left off their fight and returned to their places. Ailixond looked at Polem.

'Death,' he said, and the rest of the lords added their voices – 'Death! Death!' The crowd joined in the cry as the Vice-Justiciar stood down to speak. 'The judgement of this court is this: Almarem, Lord of Safi and the Land Gates, you are guilty of high treason, and will suffer the penalty of death. It is your privilege, my lord,' he said to Ailixond, 'to pronounce on the place and manner of the execution of the sentence.'

'The manner: beheading. The place: here and now.' Ailixond scanned the court; they hardly knew whether to believe him. 'You have heard me,' he said. 'The sentence has been pronounced in due form. Let justice be done.'

'Justice?' screamed Almarem, and was gagged again.

'Now,' said Ailixond. There was a clash of arms as the guards stood to attention, then lifted Almarem up and marched him out into the snowy central space, where they forced him to his knees. Two black-clad men stepped down from the dais where they had sat behind the clerks. One took out a scarf and offered it mutely to Almarem, to cover his eyes; he shook his head. The other drew his long sword.

'My lord. Will you forgive me this deed?' he said.

'I forgive you,' Almarem said shrilly. The executioner took up stance to his left; the guards moved away. Almarem turned his head to the right, and looked directly at Ailixond; the king met his gaze. The executioner swung his sword back and froze; the courtroom had gone silent; a faint whine, a scythe of light, and a thump as the honed edge bit into the back of Almarem's neck. His body twitched, and began to pitch forward. Ailixond jerked forward as if he would have leapt after it, as if something picked him up and shook him, once; he thrust his right hand against his mouth. The executioner swung again, and Almarem's head tumbled with his untenanted body into the snow, in a great spout of arterial blood. A universal groan rose from the watchers. Ailixond was standing with his eyes half closed, breathing rapidly. The executioner drove his sword point into the ground and stood to attention. 'It is finished,' he said. Ailixond turned his back. 'Take it away,' he said.

A slow buzz of talk began to rise as slaves in royal livery came out with a stretcher, picked up the body and the head and laid them on it, covered with a heavy cloth; others scattered sand over the blood. Ailixond said, 'Send for Lord Daiaron.' He stood still with his hands behind his back; the right was turning the Royal Ring round and round on the left. The court waited in almost silence. Eventually, a party of guards entered; the first two with pikes reversed, and, after them, four others carrying another stretcher covered with an identical cloth. They stopped in front of the king's chair. 'My lord?' said one. Ailixond spun round; his eyes widened as he saw their burden. 'What?' he said. 'What is this?'

'My lord ... Lord Daiaron.' They had laid down the stretcher; one pulled back the cover. Daiaron lay face up, his face pale, his features screwed up in a grimace. His arms had been folded on his chest; there was a spreading patch of red around them. His lord's bracelets lay unclasped in the blood on his chest.

'Haaa!' said Ailixond. 'How came this about?'

'He asked for a glass of wine. His guards thought, no harm in it – he smashed the glass under a cloth, no one heard it, and when they came to find him – as you see.'

'What!' said Ailixond again.

'Proof of guilt,' said Lord Hasmon.

'Proceedings are suspended!' said Ailixond. 'Leave me! All of you. Go! Depart!' He strode toward the door; Polem caught up with him as he reached it. All heard him say, 'Leave me, I said! An I want you, I shall call you!' He swept on by, leaving Polem standing dismayed; no one else dared follow. The Vice-Justiciar got up, and announced the court closed until such time as the commoners would be tried; the lords left, the crowd streamed out; Polem remained standing there, until Aleizon Ailix Ayndra came up beside him, sliding her hands up and down her wrists, checking on her new lord's bracelets as if, an she did not feel them, they would disappear. 'Let us go,' she said.

185

'He won't let me help!' said Polem.

'He'll let no one help. Come, let us go.'

'Where? Shall we –'

'Let us go to your tent, and you can drink hot spiced wine, and I'll drink herb tea.'

Polem's tent had a wooden floor raised up on supports to keep it out of the mud; inside, it glowed with braziers, and the walls were hung with bright wools to hide the canvas. Furs covered the floor of the room where he spent his days.

'So you are a lord now,' he said. 'I've not had time to congratulate you . . . if these were ordinary days, I'd make sure that there was a feast given for you, as there ought to be, but . . .'

'No matter,' she said. 'I think I hardly want to make anything of it – I'm not a lord! I cannot be a lord! I've not the least idea . . .'

'O, no, I am sure you will do very well. You've twice the wits of most of the lords there are, for a start.'

'But such a trifling ritual . . . It's not usually so, of course. Ailixond and I, and he called in Firumin to witness it – he put the crown on – I'd never seen it before! I never thought that he'd carry it in a box at the bottom of his document chest, as if it were a spare set of harness buckles! – and then took it off afterwards . . .'

'When I was made a lord, by King Parakison, the king wore his coronation robes, and half the nobility of Safi were there.'

'Ha! Well, I'm only a makeshift lord, I deserve no more than a makeshift ceremony. But I had not known that it was so easy – that even I could be a lord of Safi.'

'We don't like to let the commoners know that! It might cause them to lose respect for us – but you are not the only not noble born, you know; Golaron was plain Golar when I was a boy and my father first took me out with the army to see them drilling, and Casik. And there are four or five women lords in Safi – though I never heard of a woman not noble born who was made lord, it's true, it's rare anyway unless a lord has no sons . . . I mean, since one does not wish to have too great a number of lords . . . do you not think we should go and see him?'

'I do not,' said Ayndra. Polem got up and started to wander round and round her chair. 'Gods! It was so fortunate . . . if he had not waked . . .'

'There's no purpose in fearing what might have been, but was not,' she said.

186

'But most of all now, with the army divided! – what could we have done? If we had stayed here, we would have had to send to Sulakon and the rest, and then, should they go on, or come back –'

'If we had any sense, I think, we would have kept it secret as long as we could. Even counterfeited his departure to join Sulakon! – someone wearing his white bearskin gets on a ship and sails away – leaving us as secure as we might be, here, and wait till the rest of the army returns – always assuming that they are not cut to pieces in Pomoan, which of course they might well be . . .'

'How have you thought about it so much?' he exclaimed.

Ayndra grinned to herself. 'I think about a good many things,' she said. 'Is it true that we would have to go back to Safi to crown a new king?'

'The full Council of Lords – that's every lord that there is – has to gather and elect a king from among their number. It's never been done out of Safi – I do not know if . . .'

'Perhaps Ailixond should write in his will that it can be held in Raq'min, or anywhere, if he has not already . . . do you know what is in his will?'

'No one knows what is in it,' Polem said. 'I know I've never seen it.'

'Then I am sure that no one else has. Still . . . it was fortunate that he had a knife under the pillow.'

'He has always – it's not the first time someone has tried to kill him, though it was never before while he was sleeping. But he has had a knife like that – I know from when, it was the time when the other Ailixond, I mean his elder brother, died.'

'The other Ailixond? He told me about him.'

'O, what did he say?'

'That the other was expected to become king when Lord Parakison died, but when the old king died all of a sudden, the other died just after, and they chose Ailixond.'

'Ah . . . did he say anything more?'

'What more? Only that the other was always foremost, until he started to sicken about a year before his death.'

'O, is that what he said? I wonder if . . .?'

'What do you wonder?'

Polem came to a stop, putting his hands on the back of her chair. She looked up. 'You will swear never to tell anyone if I tell you this now?' he said.

'It's hard to swear that when I know not what it is,' she said.

'No, you will see when you hear – do you swear?'

'I swear – I'll swear on my lord's bracelets,' she giggled, displaying them. 'This is very serious!' Polem said.

'O, of course, of course. I swear.'

'Well, you see, I never knew if Ailixond knew – perhaps he does, but he did not say, but then . . .'

'I think he'd not lie to me.'

'No more do I – but, if he knows, how the other Ailixond died. I mean he did sicken, but, well – the truth is, Lady Sumakas poisoned him. Ailixond's mother. She started giving him poison well over a year before the end; it was intended to be very slow so that it would seem to be a natural wasting disease and it would not be tasted in the food or any thing, but then Lord Parakison was struck down – for all that I know, that was the work of the gods – and she finished the, the task in a much shorter time than she had intended – you will not tell to anyone that you know it, though, will you?'

'How is it that you know, if, as you say, Ailixond does not?'

'Well . . . Lady Sumakas had three or four of her slaves, who were charged with going into the palace kitchens and . . . and I, well, one of the slaves – it was when I was very young, it was not long after Ailixond married . . . and after that, I could tell, because she had told me the signs of it. His hair fell out, and his fingernails, before he died.'

'How many others know of this?' said Ayndra, still grinning.

'I do not know! I think I've told no one but you, and that's only because, well, because . . . Arpalond knows it, I think he found it out from the women somehow. But I'd not dare mention it in Safi, for if Lady Sumakas found out . . .'

'Indeed, I have heard mention of her poisonings. She is said to have poisoned very many people, in truth, far many more than she has, I do not doubt. I've heard the tales about her sorcery also.'

'Ailixond will not have any of that,' Polem said. 'I think it was that – when Almarem called him, witch's son – they used to call him that when we were boys.'

'People say of me that I am a witch.'

'Well, they should be made to stop – now that you are a lord –'

'Now that I'm a lord, they'll say it five times more often, being convinced that I must have bewitched Ailixond. Let them say it, I say – it only shows them for the fools they are! And besides it makes them frightened of me, and so they should be!' She laughed.

'These things are not funny,' said Polem. She shook her head.

'Perhaps I am a witch, in the way they understand witchcraft.'

'Don't say such things! It's not to be jested about.'

She shrugged. Polem paced around the tent some more. 'I still think about it, though! If they had not missed . . .'

'O, drink some more wine! and leave off such thoughts – unless you will arrive at a reasonable conclusion to them; after all, such an accident could befall him at any time.'

'I know, I know! And then what would become of us?'

'O, hush, hush, hush! It has not yet befallen us. The conspirators have been done away with, unless any went with Sulakon, who will no doubt deal with them as they deserve if they should rise up.'

'But why did he tell me to go away?'

'I cannot tell,' she said. 'But one thing I would ask you – why do we go on in the way we do? I mean travelling on and on into other lands . . .'

Polem turned round and looked at her. 'Because Ailixond wants to,' he said. 'And, well, for me . . . I like it well enough, and . . .', he looked sheepish, 'I do what Ailixond wants to, that's what I want.'

'But what is it that he wants?'

Polem said, 'I thought that you would know that, if anyone does.'

'I know one thing,' she said. 'And that's that the road must come to an end, somewhere – there comes a time when you find that you have to turn back. And it's better to choose it than to have it chosen for you. But I know not if he ever thinks that.' She gathered up her cloak and rose. 'But don't worry. And I'll not tell a soul that which you told to me.'

Arpalond, Casik, Hasmon and the Vice-Justiciar supervised the trials in ordinary, before a jury of ten officers of the army, the next day and into the day after, thirty-six men in all and all found guilty; they were strangled and thrown into a mass grave, since traitors did not deserve to be burnt. Ailixond did not emerge from his tent, nor even send out any messages. Polem went there on the evening of the first day, but saw only Firumin, who said, 'I have orders not to admit anyone until my lord tells me.'

'Then go and say that I am here.'

'No, he said not to go in, he would ask if he wanted anything.'

'Then I shall –'

'No, my lord, please. I shall be flogged if I let you in!'

'Why will he see no one?' said Polem.

189

'I cannot tell, my lord, I only know my orders.'

'O . . . well, then . . .' Polem went away.

In the small hours of the next morning, one lamp burned beside a pile of household accounts on Firumin's table; Lord Ayndra sat facing him, tossing a set of ivory dice. Piles of coins lay before each of them; hers was much the larger. 'Pay up!' she said, 'Pay up!'

'My lord, you will bankrupt me.'

'O, nonsense.'

'No, my lord, really . . .'

'Do you know, I've had my captain's pay cut off? Since I'm a lord now, I cannot expect to be paid.'

'But have you not lands?'

'How should I have lands? I have not a thing, Firumin, not a quarit – I am over my head in debt, I know not how I shall live!'

'You will be given some honorary office that gives you revenue but requires no labours, my lord.'

'Perhaps, but I have not got such a thing yet – pay up!'

'You'll have the over-governorship of Raq'min. Of Haramin province, that is.'

'In truth, my lord, I do believe –'

'I do not cheat, if that is what you imply!'

'Did you say the over-governorship, my lord?'

'The what?'

'I said the over-governorship,' said a hoarse voice behind them. Firumin leapt up. 'My lord!' he squealed. Ailixond stepped forward into the light. 'Fetch me something to eat,' he said. 'Some bread . . . cheese, if you have it . . .' Firumin bobbed, and dashed out of sight. Ayndra stood up. Ailixond blinked at her: he had been sleeping in his clothes, unshaven for two days, with his hair all over his face.

'What have you been doing?' she said.

'Thinking, for the most part . . . did you hear? I'll award you the over-governorship of Haramin province, so that you get a share of the revenues . . .' He rubbed his eyes. 'I slept for most of the last day.'

'You thought about more than that.'

'I did . . . is it all over with?'

'It's finished.'

He nodded. 'How do you like being a lord?'

'No one remembers to call me it yet, and I hate to have to tell them. But they'll learn.'

'They will.' He reached out for the nearest tent pole; 'Lean on

190

me,' she said. He put his hands on her shoulders. She said, 'What's this over-governorship?'

'A sinecure. You'll get the gate revenues, the ship tax, and a share of the road tolls. I think you'll never have to go there unless, of course, you wish to . . . have you been sitting here all this time?'

'Only this night. Polem came last night, but Firumin sent him out.'

'He should not have worried.' Just then, Firumin came in with a platter piled with bread, dried fruit, and a cloth-bound local cheese. Ailixond never said any other thing about the conspiracy of Almarem and Daiaron; if he ever said what he had thought in two days' seclusion, he never said that that was when he thought it.

Sent 16:V:463, outside Dompadde.

Ailixond greets Lord Sulakon, Lord Golaron, Lord Parhannon. I am greatly pleased to hear of my lord Admiral's victory outside Pomoan. Hearing of the prospective success of the army in raising the siege, I am resolved to wait here no longer, but continue the advance along the coast until we meet the mountains, and turn into them to meet with the tribes there. When you have relieved Pomoan, leave there a suitable force, and the fleet, to hold the town and complete the pacification of the plains. Lead the rest of the army southeast to rejoin me as soon as you may.

The only item of news which you should know of here is not good: on the tenth day of this month, one of my guards attempted to murder me as I slept. He succeeded in wounding me, but I afterward slew him, and the whole was discovered to be the work of my lords Almarem and Daiaron. The former has been tried and executed, the latter killed himself before he was brought to trial, and thirty-six accomplices were put to death afterward. I urge you to make this known and seek out any who may have been part of the plot, especially any who have been known to associate with Daiaron and Almarem over the last year, and arraign them for trial.

Received 23:V:463, on the Coast Road.

Lady Othanë, King's Wife of Safi, greets Ailixond Lord and King. Dear husband, it is so long a time since I last saw you, a year, and I have been in Raq'min for so long and very cold and lonely. I think of you all the time. I thought then that I cannot bear to be away from you any more, that was the first day of Third Month, the day of our marriage thirteen years ago now, and I thought, I shall set off for the north to be with you. In the last letter you said you were by the sea in a place called Pomoan so we shall start on the sea road but please write to say where you have gone to if you are not there now. We shall not go very fast of course but I shall surely be with you by Seventh Month. I pray daily that you are safe and well and then when we are reunited the gods will at last bless our union. Your loving wife salutes you once again and wishes you all good fortune.

Received 12:VI:463, in the citadel of Keparr Todo.
Lord Sulakon greets his lord and cousin Ailixond, Most Serene Lord and King of Safi.
My lord, I have received word of your lady wife Othanë in the city of Pomoan: she is at the edge of the Seaward Plains. I have sent a troop of cavalry to assist her escort in guiding her eastward to the Coast Road without approaching the rebel cities, a danger of which she seems as unaware as she is of your whereabouts. She asks if you are well. I have not told her of the attempt on your life. I pray that you will soon send messengers to assist her in her journey through these barbarian lands, and assuage her fears for your welfare.

Keparr Todo was a castle set on a mountain: in the middle of Sixth Month, it was cut off from the outside world by a sudden heavy fall of snow, and the lords of the army marooned within it. The chief of Todo gave up his large chamber to Lord Ailixond, while the lords, if they did not want to venture setting up tent in the castle yard, lived in the vast, littered, man and dogcrowded hall, the core of a world of yard-thick stone walls, tiny shuttered windows, kitchens deep in the earth with fireplaces with yard-wide inglenooks cut into them. Lord Ayndra lived neither in the hall, nor in one of the improvised dwellings where the soldiers who could not be squeezed within walls shivered; Ailixond left the communal meals early, and was never to be seen outside of her company. They had the big bed upstairs that would usually have been shared by the chief of Todo, his wife, his mother, and his two unmarried daughters; on top of the piled blankets they spread Ailixond's white bearskin cloak, the fur so deep one could plunge hands into it up to the wrist. Polem was left with no one to talk to, after Arpalond had gone off to chat with another of his myriad acquaintances; he left the hall when the smoke got too much and wandered out into the fetid corridors – the mountain people cleaned their floors, once a year, in spring, and then let the muck accumulate to make it worth their while to do it again next spring.

He stepped fastidiously over a pile of foul straw, to a little window in the wall, overlooking a small open space with a flight of stairs on the far side. He looked out at the square of light the window threw on the peeling plaster of the far wall, and saw Ailixond move into it; Polem was about to lean out and wave, when a blond head came into the torch light. Ailixond closed his eyes, precise, beautiful features relaxing; she turned her head to kiss him. Polem turned his back on the window and went back to the noisy hall.

In the mornings, the king's room flooded with glassy winter sunlight; it got dark early, but then they filled it with braziers and lamps. It was hardly possible to go out; for six or seven days in midmonth the keep was swathed in a howling blizzard; it hardly mattered, one could lie in bed all day, the messages of government were banned by the exigencies of the weather, they were snowbound.

But nothing lasts for ever, and the snow on the roads was already thinning.

Lord Sulakon sacked Tengam, the chief town of the rebels in the Seaward Plains, and put it to fire and sword. The men were killed. Two thousand rebel slaves, from Tengam and elsewhere, women and young boys and children of both sexes, were sent south on foot, in the snow; if they should die, what matter? they were rebels. He rode into Ailixond's camp at the head of a tired but triumphant army, in the early days of Seventh Month. He was leaving Ailixond's tent when he discovered Aleizon Ailix Ayndra in his way.

'Good day, Captain.'

'Not quite, my lord.' She cast back her sleeves and held up bright gold bracelets in front of him. He stared. 'My lord,' she said again.

'What is this?' he said.

'Since Almarem's trial.'

'What? – a lord?'

'Good day, my lord.' She bowed, and walked away. Sulakon puffed a few times, and turned back into the king's tent. Ailixond was alone; he turned wearily. 'What is it?'

Sulakon bowed. 'My lord, is it the case that you have created the woman Aleizon Ailix Ayndra a lord of Safi?'

'I have.'

'Then, my lord, I must protest! She is not at all fit –'

'How not? Tell me.'

'I – her life is not – that is, my lord –'

'Sulakon. I am well aware that you and my lord Ayndra are not friends. But it requires more than personal feeling to ban her from the lordship.'

'Then – is she of Safic birth? The child of a full marriage?'

'So I believe.'

'You have had written proof?'

'I have not.'

'Then what –?'

'I have her word.'

'– her word!'

'And I trust it,' said Ailixond. 'The creation of lords is my business. I carry it out as I like. I note your protest. If you should find firm evidence for it, I shall listen, but until then, Sulakon, I have nothing to say to you on the matter.'

'Then all I have to say, my lord cousin, is that if you will promote her into the nobility and thus license her to meddle in state affairs, it is the concern of all of us who guard the Safic state, and I believe that I speak for most of them when I say – either marry her, or send her back to where she belongs. Good day, my lord.'

'Good day!' said Ailixond. He resumed writing, one hand with its quill crossing the page from left to right, the other returning from right to left;* the Governor of Purrllum, a month later, was puzzled by the way in which my lord's handwriting, which had been thin and even, suddenly changed into thick black letters scored into the page.

The main body of the army wound slowly through the hills; meanwhile the king led selected bodies of men away from it to rampage at speed among the strongholds of local rulers, running for four or eight days away and returning at the head of what looked like a mob of vagabonds, filthy with days of fighting and sleeping rough, hostages and new vassals in their wake; while the snow thawed in the valleys and winter retreated from the hills, and wagons lumbered like cripples through the pestilential mud of the unmade roads, carrying supplies and reinforcements; and other things; not all as welcome as some were.

The lately returned officers were celebrating in Lord Polem's tent; for some reason, Ailixond had not received them in his as

*Note Safic characters are written *boustrophedon*, that is, first left to right, then right to left, then left to right, etc.

was usual. When Aleizon Ailix Ayndra returned from the latrines, she sought out Polem – 'Where has Ailixond gone?'

'O,' said Polem, 'he has gone to, to wash, and put fresh clothes on . . .'

'To what end?' she said, and then her face changed. 'What! Is she here already?'

'Who?'

'You know who I mean. I heard that she was coming – is it she?'

'O, well,' said Polem, 'the message only came half an hour ago . . . we had not thought that a cavalcade with ladies would travel so fast, when the roads are so bad . . .'

'Should not we then all dress up for the welcoming parade?'

'He said, not unless we wanted to,' Polem confessed.

'What! so how long has this been expected?'

'O, no, I told you, we thought, it would be next day, or the day after –'

'Ha! That is more than I was led to expect!'

'I would not worry about it were I you, truly I would not. She comes of her own accord, he never even sent for her.'

'Even so – it will make things no easier.'

'You will not find her any rival, I swear it.'

'Rival? – Ha! Rival!' She laughed harshly, and ran out.

Mounted guards with pennoned lances rode first into the camp; then horse-litters crowded with slave women, then two more ornate litters bearing the waiting ladies, and then a large one draped in white weatherstained silk, blazoned with the blue waves of Safi; and then strings of pack horses loaded with baggage, before the guard bringing up the rear. The procession moved on until the queen's litter was brought before the royal tent, where a crowd of onlookers had gathered, and a number of the older lords, clustered about Sulakon. A servant ran up and placed a set of wooden steps in front of the litter; the curtains twitched, but no one emerged. The crowd chattered, and looked from side to side; eventually a group of guards pushed out of the royal tent, laying wooden duckboards from its door over the mud to the litter, and followed by a trumpeter. He stood by the door, lifted his instrument and blew a solitary fanfare; the tent-curtains were pulled aside, and Ailixond, newly shaven and washed, and dressed in white silk and a cloak with a gold hem, stepped out alone. He walked up to the litter, and lifted the curtains aside; a small, plump hand with rings on each finger and painted nails reached out and took hold of his fingers. He bowed to kiss it, saying,

'Welcome, my lady!' The two waiting-women who rode in the litter appeared in the opening, assisting their lady to the steps; she tottered down them, and fell into Ailixond's arms; a bundle of soft woollen travelling robes, only hands and a round face with tears running down in streaks of eyepaint showed, and silk-slippered feet under the full skirts as she lifted her mouth up to Ailixond. His face was set in its regal mould; he planted a chaste kiss on the painted lips, and the crowd cheered. Othanë burst into tears, and pressed her face against his shoulder.

'Put your arms around my neck,' he said dispassionately. She whimpered. 'Do it!' he said. 'I will carry you.' As she obeyed, he swung her up into his arms and carried her into the tent. The crowd cheered frenziedly.

An hour later, the lords were formally invited to deliver their compliments to the queen; cleaned and combed, they filed into the king's dining room, where Othanë stood beside Ailixond. She had retouched the paint on her eyelids and mouth, dressed her hair with gold nets, and put on a red silk dress; she looked up at Ailixond every five heartbeats. He held her hand and did not look at her. 'O Ailixond!' she said breathlessly. The lords filed in and bowed, one after the other, over her hand – 'Good day, lady, you are prettier than ever . . . welcome to the army . . . it is good to see you once more at your lord's side . . .' Othanë bobbed in courtesy to them, and kissed those who were long known, or related by blood or marriage, to her; and then appeared one she did not know, a person with dirty blond hair, a grimy face, white teeth and eyes as blue as Ailixond's. 'Good day, my lady, you will not know me.'

'No, I do not – my lord?'

Ailixond sucked in a breath. 'Lord Aleizon Ailix Ayndra.'

'O, I am pleased to meet you, Lord – Alaiz nailizainer?'

'Aleizon Ailix Ayndra. At your service, lady.' The eyes glinted at her. 'What kind of name is that?' said Othanë.

'It's my name!' said the strange lord, and laughed.

'O! – are you from Safi?'

'I am, lady, though not for a while.'

'Pardon?'

'My lord has been living in foreign parts for some time,' said Ailixond. He caught Ayndra's eye. She stood straight, and they looked at one another; his expression was fixed, but she twitched her mouth up in a sarcastic grimace. Othanë looked from one to the other. Ayndra gave a smothered laugh. 'Well, well! I think I have some business to attend to. Excuse me, my lord.' She sketched a bow, and dashed out. Arpalond stepped forward. 'My lady Othanë! How long is it since I last saw you?'

'O, a very long time, Lord Arpalond, to be sure – tell me, Ailixond, has that Lord Allersanner been a lord for long?'

'Lord Aleizon Ailix Ayndra?' said Arpalond. 'But very recently, lady – it was a consequence of the plot carried on by Lord Daiaron and Lord Almarem against your lord husband –'

'Plot! What plot! O, Ailixond, what is this?'

'Don't let it distress you,' said Ailixond, 'it is all over – let me explain.' He nodded to Arpalond, who smiled, and slid away again.

With the relaxing of the rigours of winter, several other ladies were already travelling with their husbands; until Othanë's arrival, the premiere had been Lady Ailissa, Ailixond's sister and Lord Sulakon's first wife; she, with her co-wife, Lady Noma, Arpalond's wife Ditarris, Hasmon's wife Pomoea, Arillis, wife to Lord Casik, and a flock of lesser-wives, gathered to welcome the King's Wife. They had hung up Othanë's tapestry of the battle of the river Surani, and laid out trays of what sweetmeats could be obtained in such a poor spring; and, after they had greeted the queen, sent away the concubines, leaving only the ladies well enough beloved of their husbands that they would rather have them following the trumpets than leave them in a safe place and keep mistresses to sit down and tell Othanë a year's freight of gossip.

'And Lord Golaron is not at all changed! I do not know how he goes on so from year to year and never looks older.'

' 'tis because his hair went grey before he was thirty and he has not changed since.'

'A pity that the same cannot be said of Polem! A sad sight, the way he has to comb his hair to hide where it has fallen out.'

'He spends five or ten sols every month on some new potion to combat baldness, I have it on surest authority.'

'But no effect from any!'

'You know what it is that causes it!'

'O indeed?'

'O yes! Celibate priests rarely go bald.'

'O, nonsense, nonsense!'

'Lord Aleiz Nailizainner,' said Othanë. 'Who is he? Has he a wife?'

There was a sudden pause.

'He – that is, if you mean Lord Aleizon Ailix Ayndra?' said Ailissa.

197

'That is the name.'

'That's no man ... she is a woman ... have you not heard about her?'

'No,' said Othanë. 'Except Ailixond said she was a lord because of the plot ...'

'O, is that what he said?' exclaimed Pomoea.

'My brother has been extraordinarily close-mouthed in the matter,' said Ailissa to the rest of the ladies. They exchanged snide looks. 'Should we ...?' said Ditarris.

'I did not think he had such craft in him! So much for royal honour!' said Noma. Ailissa glared at her. 'Do not you presume to infringe my brother's honour!' Othanë looked distressed. 'What is this?'

'I think we should ... it is sure to come out ...' said Ditarris. 'Were it not better to leave it up to Ailixond?'

'I do not think he will do anything – did he not even tell you that she was a woman?'

'I believed that she was a man,' said Othanë, 'and no one told me any different, until now – what do you talk about? What has Ailixond done?'

'I fear that I must take it upon myself,' said Ailissa, 'as your sister, Othanë – this is not a pleasant thing to say, but that woman, Othanë, she is only lately a lord; not long ago she was merely a common soldier, but also – not to put too fine a point on it, Othanë, she is Ailixond's mistress.'

Othanë let a piece of marzipan fall from her mouth. 'Ay – pardon?'

'Since Ninth Month,' said Ditarris. 'Sulakon believes that he should marry her, but he will not – Arpalond said that –'

'Marry her!' squealed Othanë. 'So he did not ask me to come! He will put me away! He will divorce me as a barren woman! O Maishis! O Luamis! What shall I do?' She covered her face and stumbled from the chamber, wailing.

'See what you have done now!' said Pomoea. Arillis asked, 'Is that true? – that he means to divorce her?'

'I have heard nothing of it,' said Ailissa. 'In any case, Othanë would be the last to know if he did.'

'Lady Othanë wants to see me? In God's name, whatever for? God's teeth! I have no desire ... o, devil take her! Yunnil! Where's my best shirt?'

The House of Women, in the army camp, was a cluster of tents pitched together on the edge of the baggage camp, well out of the way of the soldiery, with the queen's tent in the middle of them. The ladies gathered there well in advance of fourth hour of afternoon, while the servants brought in the indispensable sweets and spiced fruit wines.

'They say she's very ugly.'

'She was with them in the last campaign in the hills.'

'And with Lord Polem, they say, and with all the men when she was a captain, and before that with the common soldiers . . .'

'Hush! She comes.'

Lady Othanë came titupping in, crushing a lace kerchief in one hand, nodding as the ladies acknowledged her; she sat down on the chair in the middle of their semicircle. A slavewoman followed her. 'My lady. Your visitor is here.'

'Then invite her in,' said Othanë, and put the kerchief in her mouth. The rest of the women fell quiet. Military boots clumped on the floor; the curtains flew apart, and Aleizon Ailix Ayndra burst in in a waft of fresh air, halted before them, posing arrogantly with one hand on her hip and her black hat in the other. 'My ladies. Good day!'

'Good, good day – will you not sit down?' said Othanë.

'O, surely.' She dropped to crossed legs next the table with the sweetmeats. They stared at her cavalry boots, her shirt with vast heavy-cuffed sleeves, her breeches which fit as tightly as a second skin. She said, 'Myself I think you know already – may I ask who you are?' The black-haired woman, far gone in pregnancy, on Othanë's right, fixed her with bright blue eyes. 'Lady Ailissa,' she said. 'Sister to Lord Ailixond. Sulakon is my husband. Also the husband of this, Lady Noma. You see here also Lady Ditarris, Lady Pomoea, Lady Arillis, and, as you know, your hostess, Lady Othanë.'

'Good day to you all.' Ayndra picked out two preserved apricots and stuffed them in her mouth.

'You are welcome, lord,' said Othanë. 'But, may I ask you . . .'

'Ask what you will. I reserve the right to answer it.'

'Why is it that you wear men's clothes?'

'Because I would look a fool an I tried to lead an assault in a gown.'

'But you are not leading an assault now,' said Ailissa.

'No, but one never knows . . . I like men's clothes, besides.' She stood up again, and wiped her hands on her thighs; began to pace around the room, making sure that they stared at her legs.

'So you lead assaults?' said Ailissa.

'I do. My position is Royal Adviser on matters pertaining to the artillery. Also Over-Governor of Haramin province.' She grinned. 'And other positions without title, of course,' she said. 'I have served more than two years in the Grand Army now, from a common soldier in the artillery to . . .'

'I have never heard of a woman in the army before,' Othanë said, 'how ever did you come to join it?'

'The usual way, lady, how else? One approaches an officer and says I wish to go for a soldier! and he says, in what division, and if one says, why, the artillery! then he receives one as it were a long-lost brother, for no one in their right minds ever joins the artillery, since it is not heroic − not that any other part of the army is heroic, but one finds that out later . . .' She was behind them now; they craned their necks to look at her. She stopped behind Othanë's chair. Ailixond's neglected spouse would have been pretty if she had not been so fat; her hands were long and delicate, but the lines of her face were hidden in cushions of plumpness. The eyes under the painted lids rolled round to fix on Ayndra with pleading jealousy. She said, 'Have you been in the battles?'

'I saw the battle of the river Surani. I rode in the battle of Palagar, in the Royal Squadron of the Companions.'

'O! so you know what it was like? You see, I am beginning a tapestry of it, to match the one you see there, that is the river Surani.'

'Dusty,' said Ayndra.

'Your pardon?'

'It was dusty. Very dusty. Positively choking.' There was a pause. She said, 'What have you brought me here for? What can I tell you? What game should I play for you? Tell me what you believe me to be − then shall I act it, or shall I play someone else entirely? What do you want of me?'

Othanë stuffed the handkerchief up to her mouth again. She said, 'Are you − that is, do you − Ailixond −'

'I am not looking to usurp your place, if that is what you fear − I've no desire to be King's Wife of Safi. But then − is that what you fear?'

Othanë clenched her hands, said in a high voice, 'I do not fear you − only I − can you not see! I envy you − you've that which I've so long wanted! So long!'

Ayndra said, 'I know it − but it is not in my gift!'

'Is it not? − I wish that no one had it, if I·cannot! No one! And you − thee never was anyone, till you −'

'That was never in my thought,' Ayndra said.

'But if it is now –'

'But even if it had been, I would have done no other than I did. Nor will I do other now. Look,' she said, 'you have your place, and the things belonging to it, and I have mine – and if you like it not, it's your place to leave, or do some other thing. But I will not. Do you see? I bear you no malice. Nor will I be brought here as a butt for your tedium. I owe you nothing. Let me go!'

'Go then! Go!' Othanë shrieked, and burst into tears. Ayndra gave a brief stiff bow, and swept out as she had come. Othanë cast herself full length on the floor and screamed. The other ladies jumped up to cluster round and comfort her, except Ailissa; who sat still, immobilised by her swollen body, but gazing after her with intrigued blue eyes.

Ailixond was still writing, an hour past midnight; he did not notice Aleizon Ailix Ayndra, entering unannounced. She slipped around the walls and stood behind his chair, like a ghost in a black cloak, and stood looking around at the austere elegance of the furniture: very plain, sound, expensive; nothing of the pleasures of the flesh, or the pleasure in display; it was made for pleasures more subtly corrupting. In front of her he sat, writing with his usual two-handed trick, a quill in either hand and an inkwell at each elbow, going back and forth across the page. His hair fell forward like black raw silk. She stretched out her right hand and, very gently, slid her index finger down the soft track of hair on the back of his neck, under the collar of his shirt. Ailixond dropped his pens and started upright, then twisted round as quick as a fish and snatched her hand.

'What are you writing?' she said.

'You'll see.' He flicked the letter over.

'To whom?'

'My mother.'

'Ah, your mother.'

'Yes.'

She said vaguely, 'I'd most likely write to my mother an I knew where she was.' He drew her arm down into his lap so that she was forced to come up beside his chair, but said nothing; he pushed up her shirtsleeve and ran his hand up and down her arm. She shivered as his fingers ran over the sensitive skin under the upper arm. Ailixond leant his head against her and closed his eyes. She said, 'Did not your mother choose your wife for you?'

His head snapped upright, eyes wide. 'Why do you say that?'

'I wondered – how it came about, that . . .'

201

'That I have a wife who . . . who's nothing to me?'

'She's not nothing. You ought not to say that.'

'She's nothing to you.'

She looked down at him. 'You know better than that! Don't – don't try to put me off with soft words.'

He gripped her harder. 'I was married to her when I was eighteen – she was fifteen, she comes from a very old family, she – she had not got fat then, she . . . I had no choice in the matter.'

'No. It's not usual for noble men to marry so young, is it?'

'It's not. I would have refused if I had understood things better, but I . . . the other Ailixond had a wife already.'

'And so you had to have one to set yourself up as a proper rival to him. I understand.'

'Do you?'

'I don't know. I went to see her this day.'

'What?'

'To the House of Women . . . she invited me. Your sister was there. And Arpalond's wife, and some others.'

'I knew nothing of it!'

'Are you surprised? She can act without your orders, as she has shown . . .'

'She acts against my order.'

'Would you not then wish us to meet?'

'I cannot think what you would have to say to one another!'

'Very little, indeed . . . she said that she was envious of me.'

There was a heavy silence. Ailixond slipped out of his chair and stood up; he took her two hands. Ayndra looked straight in his eyes. 'She said – she said, you have that which I have so long wanted . . .'

'And you – there's something which I have long wanted to ask you –'

'What is it?'

Ailixond gripped her hands again. 'Marry me.'

Ayndra leapt with surprise. 'What!'

'I know it's sudden – but present events – I've thought about it, and, I did not know how else –'

She broke her hands free and stepped back. 'What!' she exclaimed again, and started to laugh.

'I have had enough of sly looks and whispers,' said Ailixond, 'I've had enough of winks and sniggers if ever I mention your name, Ailix, I – Ailix, what is it?'

'I can't do it,' she said. 'You have a wife!'

'But what obstacle is that? I can divorce her –'

202

'And then she said – she said, you've that which I have so long wanted, and I said, you have your place and I have mine, and I will not take yours – I don't want to be King's Wife of Safi! I don't want to be any man's wife! How could I be queen of Safi?'

'I care nothing for what you may have been – Ailix, please –'

'Listen to me!' she cried. 'Do you know what marriage is? Do you know that I'd never again have a thing I could call my own, that you could not take whenever you wanted? Do you know that you could beat or kill me and I'd have no right of redress? That I could not go any place unless you gave me permission? That you could convey me into a prison or a mad-house whenever you wished it? Have you thought of that?'

'But I would not –'

'And do you not remember that I said, I'll stay with you so long as I can go whenever I wish?'

'I would not constrain you! – do not you wish it?'

'To be married? I do not!' Ailixond looked betrayed, resentful. She said, 'How can you ask me that?'

'What? – do you not realise? I'm not offering a sop, I'm – gods' sake! you could be King's Wife of Safi –'

'But do I want to be King's Wife of Safi? The present one, after all, seems not to love it so much –'

Ailixond brought his hands down in a chopping gesture. 'And you think it's not good enough for you? If you care for nothing, do you think others are so free? – and beside, have you never thought, if you have a child –'

'Ho! A child! It's not possible!'

'What? Not possible? Do you –'

'Never!' she yelled. Ailixond made a wordless sound of fury and struck wildly at her. His fist caught her on the temple, and threw her off balance; she stumbled, slipped, and fell over so that her head struck the corner of his desk. She howled and fell to the ground. Ailixond stood over her, fists clenched, gasping as if he had been running. The Royal Ring had cut into her forehead on one side; the desk had made a scrape down the other side of her face, just beginning to bleed. She put a hand up to cover it. 'Well, my lord,' she said, and clutched the side of the table to pull herself to her feet. 'I know not how you think to control an empire when it's plain that you cannot even control yourself.' Ailixond moved forward. She said, 'O no! Not me!' and made a dash for the door. He did not follow her.

The whining sounded like a wounded animal, a large one;

Arpalond came up behind it slowly, until he saw the hunched shoulders in the moonlight and knew it for a man – or, as he saw when he got a good view of the head, a woman. She was sitting on a stone by the bare trees dipping over the river, bent double, rocking to and fro with a cloth pressed to her head. He coughed. She looked up instantly. 'Who is it?'

'Arpalond.'

'O? – o, what do you . . . you can leave me, I am not ill.'

'Are you not?' He stepped down the bank. 'What have you done to your head?'

'Nothing.'

'That's not the truth.'

'It is a part of the truth, near enough to it, and when can we ever achieve more than a part of truth in this imperfect world?'

'What, will you chop logic now?'

'I'll chop logic when I want to, and neither you, my lord, nor any other, shall stop me. I thank you for your concern, but I go now to sleep.' She got up and went stumbling away in the direction of the camp. Arpalond followed her, a short way behind; far enough to see that it was her own dark tent that she went into.

Ailixond turned over his half-written letter. '. . . and by the time you read this, we will be married . . .' He held it up and rent it in two, top to bottom, then in quarters, eighths, again and again, frantically, shreds falling to left and right, until it was beyond tearing up like that; he opened his hands and let the bits flutter groundward, like a flight of dying butterflies.

'This king that we're going to see,' said Polem. 'There's a story that his daughter is the most beautiful woman in the whole of old Haramin – well, they say in the Empire, but they cannot mean our Empire . . .'

'O, so you think to find a wife at last?' said Lakkannar.

'Ho! I am sure she would not have me. They say she's as proud as Orgullo, she is eighteen now and still not married because every man that's asked for her she will not have, saying he's not great enough – most likely she'll die an old maid, they say.'

'She must be a shrewish piece, if it's so. Maybe her father is so besotted of her he will not let her go – have you not heard that they practise that all the time in these back hills?'

'It's not so,' said Aleizon Ailix Ayndra sourly. She was wearing a white bandage, bound over her forehead with hair half covering it, for the last several days.

'What, about this daughter? I am sure she –'

'No. They never practise incest here. I've heard of the daughter also. She is very beautiful, I believe.'

'O, indeed? – most likely she is fat already, and shines her face with bear-grease, and stinks like a vixen.'

'Is your head better?' said Polem. 'You must have fallen heavily.'

'I did. It aches a great deal. Especially when I am addressed.'

'O, all right, then . . .'

'And another of their vile ill-cooked feasts that we must all go to,' complained Lakkannar. 'And not a good skin of wine in the hall . . .'

'But we will see this famous lady,' Polem said.

But the chair next to the king of the town and his wife remained empty until after the first course had been loaded onto the tables. Ailixond sat in the middle of the dais, the king Poressen and his dignitaries at one side, and upwards of a thousand people crammed into the body of the hall, the ones packed by the walls without even space to sit down, while an ox roasted over the fire in the middle of the hall and the air grew thick as soup with smoke and sweat and the reek of burning fat. Ailixond's cup bearer stood behind his chair with the skin of wine that saved the lords from barley beer. Ailixond sat swirling his cup around and around and looking thunderous and majestic. Polem looked miserably at the immense joints of undercooked meat being laid before them. 'I suppose I should eat some,' he said. Ailixond said nothing. 'I wish Lord Ayndra were here,' said Polem. 'I wonder what she did to her head?' Ailixond said nothing. 'What's that over there?' said Polem. 'Coming to sit next to Por-what-sin.' Ailixond put down his wine-cup. A figure clothed in a drifting cloud of rose silk veils glided up behind Poressen; he turned to smile as she threw back her head-veil, slipping it back from a wreath of orchard blossoms and a heart-shaped face more delicate than the flower petals. 'That must be her! The famous beauty,' said Polem. 'Well! She is . . . Lakkannar, will you say now that she is fat and covered in goose-grease?' Someone offered a glistening side of beef to Ailixond, with a vast carving knife; he ignored it. Polem took the knife, smiled apologetically at the server, a noble of Poressen's kingdom, sweating like a cheese under a bearskin cloak, and began to carve. Poressen's daughter slowly lifted her face until she was looking straight at the foreign king. He raised his wine-cup, bowed his head a little toward her, and drank from it. She dipped her head, then looked up again, gave a very brief, enchanting smile, and turned, pulling her veil across her face, to her mother. 'Would you like some of this, Ailixond?' Polem asked.

'What?'

'This.' Polem speared a dripping slice of beef.

'O, put it down – you have seen her? Polem, I want you to find out her name.'

'Who? – the beauty?'

'I shall marry her,' said Ailixond.

Behind the other high table, Setha Poressen's daughter whispered behind her veil. 'You have seen their king? The one in white, is he not? I shall be his queen. I am going to marry him.'

Poressen's wife made a sign to avert bad luck. 'Do not say such things! How can you know it? He has a wife already, and his mistress is a sorceress!'

'It matters not at all,' Setha said serenely. 'He will marry me. I can see it in his face.'

As soon as the wedding was announced, the whole of Poressen's town dissolved like an ant-heap stirred with a stick. Guests and traders poured in from every point of the compass; everyone had to have new clothes; the daylong celebrations had to be planned, staffed and provisioned; by the end of Eighth Month, it was like living in a dream of delirium shared with ten thousand other fevered. Ailixond disappeared under a sea of priests, new relatives, allies, envoys and tailors; Polem suffered alone, until he could bear the chaos no longer, and went to discover what had happened to Aleizon Ailix Ayndra. He walked incautiously through the door of Poressen's house and ran slap into a heap of white linen. Clean sheets fell everywhere, wailing aloud; Polem dropped to his knees to help ramass them, and found Firumin. 'O! see what you have done! Look at all this – all to be done again!'

Polem handed him a pile of crumpled napkins. 'Where is Lord Ayndra?'

'In the kitchens. O, however am I to do all this? Why must I do it all? Not a servant they have here who knows so much as the correct way to fold a bed cover –'

'In the kitchen? Whatever is she doing in the kitchen?'

'She has charge of the wedding feast. There is far too much for any one man. However shall I find beds for all these people? They shall sleep on floors and I shall be punished for it. It is too much!'

'Charge of the feast? I had not heard –'

'O, I shall go mad! It is too much!' Firumin bundled up his load all any-old-how and rushed away. Polem made off to the kitchen.

A blast of hot air rushed out as he opened the door; the view within was like the punishment of the damned if it took place in a market held in a public washhouse. Fires roared on every side, cauldrons boiled, dough was mixed, ovens clanged open and shut, scullions bore animals alive, dead and dismembered, live geese, bundles of vegetables, pats of butter, sacks of flour – Polem seized a boy who ran past him. 'Where is Lord Aleizon Ailix Ayndra?' The brat looked blank. Polem repeated the question loud and slow; the boy gabbled in a foreign tongue and pointed off into the depths. Polem thanked him, and pushed on, while the cooks and greasy-aproned scullions stared at his blue silk tunic. He came to a row of steaming pots; Aleizon Ailix Ayndra was spooning a sample from the end one, with Yunnil, a napkin over one arm, standing at her side with a bowl. Ayndra took a mouthful of soup, swilled it around in her mouth, and signed to Yunnil, who held out the bowl; she spat into it, and turned to salute him, before turning to the next pot. 'More pepper here!'

'Must you . . . spit?' said Polem.

Ayndra whipped the napkin from Yunnil's arm and wiped her mouth. 'Spit? For god's sake! I'd be bloated as a farrow sow if I swallowed every time I tasted.' A potboy ran up with a pepperpot, which she shook into the pot, and tasted again. 'Ah! Much improved. But it is time to attend to the brideloaf.' She marched off into the confusion; Polem caught up with her again beside a large scrubbed table, on which two servitors dumped a basket-load of saffron-coloured dough. Ayndra unbuckled her belt, threw off her overtunic, rolled up her sleeves and pushed her fists into the dough. She began to thump it and beat it up and down on the table.

'Should you do that to it?' asked Polem.

'Do (thump) what?'

'Hit it as you do.'

'God's teeth! Have you never seen bread kneaded before?'

'What do you take me for, a woman? or a potboy?'

'Name of god!' She tossed her sweat-stranded hair back from her shining face. Where she had worn the bandage, there were fresh pink scars on her forehead. 'Why are you doing this?' asked Polem.

'Because my lord the king ordered it.'

'Ordered you to do this?'

'He ordered me to oversee the wedding feast. Two thousand are to be fed, as well as food given out in the camp.'

'But must you cook it all?'

207

'I am not cooking it all . . . only the parts that you and I will eat, and for the . . . bridal pair.' She paused; Polem saw that no one was watching. He reached out to stroke the new-healed marks.

'I know how you got that.'

'I told you how I got it. I fell.'

'He never should have.'

'Who never should have done what?'

'Look – let me tell you – I am sure that he never meant it! And all this – it will not last, I swear it! You must not let it come between you –'

'Come between us? There is nothing between us.' She pummelled the brideloaf. 'How can you say that –!' Polem caught at her arm; she jerked it free. 'Easily,' she said, 'since it is true –'

'O, it is not – it is political for him to have a wife who –'

'Do you think I care?' she retorted.

'Yes!' Polem said. She slammed the dough on the table. 'Look you. I have quarrelled with Ailixond. But that gives you no entitlement to come without his or my asking it and attempt to matchmake again –'

'I am not doing any such! I only – I've not seen you for days –'

'And neither does it mean that I come weeping to you saying O Polem, Polem I recognise my folly! I regret nothing that I have done, though others may – so if you can do naught but stand there mouthing at me, out of my way, I have work to do! Leave me!'

Polem gulped, bowed sharply and set off through the crowd. He looked back once; she was bent over the brideloaf, beating it as if it were living and she set on hammering it to death.

A red and white striped pavilion without walls hung like a monstrous inverted flower over the high dais facing the gate of Poressen's town; between those seats and the gate was a flattened, sanded arena, banked seats all around it, and a platform jutting out under the roof where the marriage itself would be solemnised. Later, they would serve the wedding feast there; a vast field kitchen had been two days in putting up some way behind. The tents for the robing of celebrants stood between it and the wedding place. In the central one, the groomsmen were robing Ailixond in his full-length, full-skirted ceremonial robe, heavy white silk with gold sleeve-linings; the pointed cuffs of the full sleeves turned back to the elbow and the points laced to gold cords on the shoulders. Polem, still in everyday dress, sat on the clothes-chest and pushed Ailixond's long sword in and out of its sheath. 'You must be looking forward to this night!' he said.

'You might say that,' Ailixond replied. 'I would prefer it an you did not.'

'I think you are mad.'

'Your pardon? I am aware that —'

'No, no, I do not mean Lady Setha. I mean to put Lord Ayndra in charge of the wedding feast.'

'I would rather you did not mention that name here,' said Ailixond.

'We shall all get pepper poisoning!'

'O, Polem, an you have nothing to say, can you not be silent? Have you my sword?'

'Here . . . you ought not to be nervous, you have done it before.'

'Either be silent, or leave me!'

'Ah well . . . I suppose I ought to go and put my robe on. I shall be back.' Polem stood up, and sauntered out. Soldiers, camp-people, and citizens of the land of Haridt were starting to crowd onto the benches near the gate; the dignitaries at the high tables would come out later. The kitchen was smoking like a volcano; food prepared in the last several days was being ferried to it to be fried up, heated, put in pies or cakes, drowned in sauces, spiced and decorated. Up in Poressen's hall, the bride, dressed from head to foot in scarlet silk and gold, sat on a throne surrounded by the mountain of gifts, while her family came to wish her farewell and good luck, and the bridal litter was prepared in the courtyard. The bridal procession, with the bridesmaids and musicians, gathered outside; the representatives of the lords of the provinces, of allied nations and of Safi itself, were announced by Ailixond's heralds and seated under the pavilion. The common people filled the sides of the arena and packed the road from the hall to the gate. At midday, Ailixond came out, and stood on the high platform, three lords of Safi in their brilliant robes to either side of him; at the same time, Setha was lifted into the red-draped litter, and the musicians led the way out of her father's hall. Ailixond stood like a statue, the skirts of his robe and gold-bordered cloak stirring a little in the wind. Guards with sarissas cleared everyone out of the central space and formed a cordon at its edge; the high priest of Shumar, followed by twelve other priests and a dozen acolytes with incense, walked out to the foot of the steps to the platform. The choir high up behind the pavilion began to chant; in the arena, one could hear the horns and drums of the procession of Haridt. A cheer went up as the first of them came to the gateway – the musicians first, then twenty bridesmaids, chosen from the noblest families in Haridt and all in white with flowers in their uncovered hair, and then – a greater cheer rising as it came under the arch and out into the sunlight - the bridal litter. The procession divided into two, going to either side; the litter came on alone, the bearers set it down, threw back the curtains, and stepped behind it. Setha stepped out, alone; one hand raised to her shoulder, as if she still wished to veil herself. Ailixond stepped forward, and walked down the steps; his groomsmen followed in echelon, a few paces behind. The silk flowed like water over his limbs and reflected light up into his face; Setha stood with her gaze lowered, until a shadow fell across her, and she looked up. Her lips parted, and she seemed transfigured as she looked at Ailixond's face. A mingled gasp and sigh ran across the crowd. He took her right hand, and, as her bridesmaids came up behind his attendants, led her up the steps, which the priest of Shumar and his procession had climbed meanwhile; the priest stood at the top, flanked by four priests with a silver bowl and censers of sweet incense. He made the sign of blessing as the bride and groom turned to face the crowd, and he stood between and just behind them; they loosed hold of each other, and he began to recite the words of the marriage vows; they repeated them after him, Ailixond clear as a deep-voiced bell, Setha inflectionless and stiff except for her singsong accent as she repeated words she had been drilled in in a language she did not understand.

'I, Setha Poressen's daughter, vow myself in marriage to Ailixond Parakison's son, my lord, my husband. I will obey him in all he asks of me. I give to him my body as I now give him my hand –' The priest joined their hands, and another knelt before them with the silver bowl of holy water; the priest dipped their hands in it. '– in token of my gift and obedience, in a sign that in body and goods and in our children we are become one, for ever and ever, to the end of my life. To this I swear.' The priest flicked drops of water over either, then jerked the linked hands out of it and signed; the bearer tossed the water out over the steps in a glittering arc. 'And as it may be impossible to bring back these waters, so is it impossible to fracture this union!' he cried, and took their other hands and joined all four in the clasp of his own; and the war-trumpets screamed aloud in a storm of fanfares, and the horns of Haridt blew, and the crowd yelled themselves hoarse and the soldiers beat on their shields. Ailixond pulled Setha to him, and kissed her, and the stands shook. Up in the ladies' gallery, Othanë began to cry.

Aleizon Ailix Ayndra stood at the door of the field kitchen. She wore a sky-blue robe with saffron sleeve-linings, her sword, and a large greasy cook's apron; she stood like a drug-dazed statue of Justice with a ladle in one hand and the pepperpot in the other. It was almost sixth hour after noon; after hours of choirs singing celebratory hymns and odes, gifts and tributes and oaths, the wedding feast was to be served. A slave in the royal livery came up to her with a gold-handled bowl. 'Let me taste that.' She dipped the ladle in it, and sucked a noisy mouthful of soup. 'Agh! Tasteless. No flavour at all.' She shook the pepperpot liberally over it, and the pierced lid tumbled off; all its contents cascaded into the soup. 'Lord!' wailed the servant.

'Ah, no matter.' She fished out the lid, stirred the soup some more, took another mouthful and snapped her fingers. 'O, exquisite! Take it up.'

The king and queen had gold bowls, and pearl-handled spoons; but they hardly noticed the soup poured out for them. Ailixond left off gazing at Setha for long enough to nod, and indicate that she should sip first. She raised a spoonful to her lips, swallowed, and coughed; her eyes watered, she dropped the spoon and choked. She pointed to the soup and spluttered. 'Why, what is it?' said Ailixond, and took an incautious mouthful; then it was his turn to choke and cough. Setha coud not help herself; she began to giggle. Ailixond wiped his brimming eyes. 'Firumin!'

The steward materialised, harassed and flapping. 'My lord?'

'Deliver this message to Lord Ayndra. This is a wedding feast, and so you should endeavour to provide food which is pleasant and acceptable to all, no matter what your own tastes may be. See to it.'

'Is that all, my lord?'

'Go and tell it to her!'

Aleizon Ailix Ayndra, still in greasy apron, was sitting crosslegged on the largest kitchen table. Yunnil, in her best gown, was passing her a burning smokestick; they were both laughing foolishly. 'What do you want, Firumin?' she yelled. 'All goes well! Fish is on its way!' She and Yunnil fell to laughing again.

'My lord, I bring a message from Lord Ailixond.'

'O indeed? Spit it out, then – spit on me! Ha ha!'

'My lord says, this is a wedding feast –'

'O no –'

'My lord – this is a wedding feast, and the feast should be

211

pleasant and acceptable to all. No matter what you may wish for it. See to it.'

'Is that all?'

'It is.'

'Did he ask for an answer?'

'No, my lord, but . . .'

'Then tell him this. Hot spices inflame the passions – you have it?'

'Yes, my lord.'

'Off you go, off you go!' Her maniacal laughter pursued him all the way to the royal table.

'At half past the sixth hour, more liveried slaves brought out the plaited, seed-studded brideloaf on its flowerdecked platter. Lord Ayndra leapt down from the table, threw off her apron and tossed it into a corner. 'I thank you, kind friends, for your labours, but I shall go now and join the celebration.' She bowed to the kitchen slaves, and strode away, the full skirts of her robe swirling. Just as the brideloaf was placed on the royal table, she slipped into an empty place at the end of the lords' long table, grabbed up a goblet and shouted, 'Wine here!' She was very soon answered.

Ailixond stood up as the loaf was put before him, put his hand to his swordhilt and in one movement, continuous and graceful as a breaking wave, drew it, swung it flashing over his head, and clove the loaf in two; he stayed the fall of the blade just as it came down to the board, and withdrew it hardly blunted, sheathed it, and broke a piece from either side of the loaf, handed one to Setha and bit into the other himself. The crowd cheered. He looped one arm round her and lifted her out of her seat, and they took another bite of each other's pieces of bread; he swallowed his and kissed her, again and again. The crowd went into a near frenzy. Aleizon Ailix Ayndra drained her wine-cup and called for more.

After the soup, the fish, the game, the pies and the roast, Ailixond's flattanharp was brought up to the table, for the lords to play and sing the Wedding Song, a verse each: it had been tuned and set in the correct mode, so that they had no more to do than stumble through the chords and sing as best they could, depending on original skill and amount of wine taken; it passed irregularly up and down the table, as one after the other decided that it was time to get it over with and signalled for it to be brought to him. Aleizon Ailix Ayndra's signals were ignored; finally, when it was going to Lord Ellakon on her right, she leapt up and snatched it. Ellakon looked affronted. 'You shall have it later!' she said, and struck a few notes, then set to rapidly retuning it, into the mode

212

appropriate to narrative and edifying compositions; and then began to play, deftly, and not the Wedding Song. Silence spread around her as people began to listen. Then she began to sing. Setha looked up on the instant, as she heard the soaring voice after the gruff tenors and basses, and Ayndra caught her eye.

'If thou beest born to strange sights
Things invisible to see
Ride ten thousand days and nights
Till age snow white haires on thee.
Thou, when thou retorn'st, wilt tell me
All strange wonders that befell thee
And swear
No where
Lives a woman, both true, and fair.

She bowed; and sat down. No one applauded; a rustle of comment ran through the assembly. Nor did anyone take the flattanharp, till a servant noticed Lord Polem's gestures and brought it to him. He stood up to play, ignoring the need to retune it, and sang lustily:

'What mean'st thou, Bride, this company to keep?
To sit up, till thou fain wouldst sleep?
Thou mayest not, when thou art laid, do so;
Thyself must to him a new banquet grow,
And you must entertain,
And do all this day's dances o'er again.
Know that, if Sun and Moon together do
Rise in one point, they do not set so too;
Therefore, thou mayest, fair Bride, to bed depart.
Thou are not gone, being gone; where'e'er thou art
Thou leav'st in him thy watchful eyes, in him thy loving heart.'

Setha could not understand his words, but the greeting the audience gave was unmistakable. Her bridesmaids left their places, and the litter was brought to the foot of the steps; Ailixond ceremoniously handed her up, while people shouted the usual pleasantries, and she was borne away, shut up in darkness of lemon-scented curtains, to the chamber in the hall of Haridt where Ailixond's black carved bed had been placed, draped with scarlet and surrounded by lamps, to be undressed, clad in a transparent silk shift, and propped in bed to wait for him.

The bridegroom processed to the marriage bed on foot,

213

preceded and followed by a long train of riotous revellers, waving torches in mad arabesques, roaring obscene and predictable jests. Even Ailixond, walking between Polem and Sulakon, was only half sober, and he the steadiest of the lot. Half of them never made it as far as the hall, but some two dozen climbed the stairs and crowded into the antechamber, with someone blowing blasts on a small horn, while they sang the last verse of the Wedding Song:

> 'As he that sees a star fall, runs apace
> And finds a jewel in its place
> So doth the Bridegroom haste as much
> Being told this star is fallen, and finds her such.
> And as friends may look strange,
> Through a new fashion, or apparel's change,
> Their souls, though long acquainted they had been
> These clothes, their bodies, never yet had seen
> Therefore at first she modestly might start
> But must forthwith surrender every part
> As freely as each to each before gave either eye or heart.'

Under cover of the noise, Ailixond stripped, and put his arms into the sleeves of the long nightrobe which Polem held out for him. Polem paused with his hands on his shoulders. 'You are happy,' he said, not quite a question.

'I am,' said Ailixond.

'You hardly know her.'

Ailixond shook his head. 'I have seen her.'

'Then – so long as you are happy.' He slapped him on the back. 'Good fortune. May you be blessed with sons.'

'Then do this for me.' Ailixond slipped something heavy into Polem's hand, loosened his hold and slipped away. The door to the bedchamber was pushed open; Setha could be seen within, sitting up in bed with her eyes modestly cast down. Polem, finding in his hand the iron key of the bedroom door, looked up, and saw, just behind him and grinning all over her face, Aleizon Ailix Ayndra. He exclaimed, 'What are you doing here?'

'I am the spectre at the feast,' she said.

'You are that!'

Ailixond was being sent through the door; he turned, and closed it carefully behind him, shutting out the wellwishers, who started to stagger downstairs to get back to the drinking. Polem held up the key, with one hand, to show why he stayed, and held

214

on to Lord Ayndra, though she struggled, with the other. When they were alone, he put it into her hand. 'Then you can do this,' he said triumphantly.

'Do what?'

'Lock the door on them,' said Polem, 'it's traditional. Bridegroom's best friend.' He pushed her at the door, and reeled out to the stairs. She stood in the middle of the empty room. One torch sputtered in a wall sconce; Ailixond's discarded clothes were draped over a chest beneath it. She walked like a cat up to the door; there was the keyhole, and a bar, too, ready to be dropped. She reached up for it, her face against the wood, and froze; a voice came faintly through.

'Lady, lady – do you understand a word I say to you? I've never seen . . . I've never seen one so beautiful as you . . .'

The bar crashed home, the key rattled in the lock, but neither of them heard it.

By midnight, all the good wine had gone, and they were well into the mediocre; by dawn, any who still remained would be swilling down something better suited for pickling than inebriating. Polem, Arpalond, and Lakkannar, with several other young lords, were huddled near the vacant thrones, with Golaron a little further down; Sulakon had left after the procession to bed, and all the ladies had gone just after the bride's departure. At the far end of the high table, Aleizon Ailix Ayndra lay with her head on the board.

' 'a shink Ailison's fool to ge' married,' said Lakkannar. 'You ha'n' go' married. Wish I'd not.'

'I would'a go' married if a could fin' woman I wanted to marry,' complained Polem. 'See, wha' the trouble is, I wan'a marry dance girl an' I can', but I don't wan'a marry a lady but if I do I mus' marry a lady . . . so I don't.'

'Ha! I still say 's a fool to marry that foreign bitch,' said Lakkannar. 'And wha'bout her?' He gestured largely in Ayndra's direction. She opened a bleary eye. 'Wha's he going to do with her now? Keep 'em all together? But I don' think that one'll stand for it, the foreign bitch won' . . . bu' then I s'pose he might get a son on her, no hope o' tha' from her . . . you know wha' they say about her sort – no grass grows on a public highway!' There was a crash, and a shriek; Ayndra leapt up on the table, dragging out her sword, and threw herself toward Lakkannar, howling like a wildcat. Lakkannar heaved himself up, and pulled at his sword. Golaron bounded forward and seized Ayndra round the waist; Polem grabbed Lakkannar's arm, and Arpalond clung to his other side. Ayndra thrashed in Golaron's grip as he pulled her off the table and set her feet on the floor. 'Lakkannar! I'll kill you!'

'And you, you bitch!' rejoined Lakkannar.

'I'll murder you! Bastard!'

'Whore!'

She screamed; Golaron clapped a hand over her mouth. Half a dozen lords in concert forced Lakkannar down in his chair. 'Quiet,' said Polem, 'quiet, 're all drunk.' Golaron swore, and whipped his hand away – 'Bit me!' he barked, and swung at Ayndra's head, but she ducked. 'Not so drunk as I'll let you say such things about me! Lakkannar! I challenge you to single combat!'

'No!' said Arpalond.

'I will!' she yelled. 'You'll not stop me – Lakkannar, do you hear?'

'But duelling is forbidden between members of the army –'

'I accept!' roared Lakkannar. 'Weapon?'

'Knives.'

'When?'

'Dawn! This dawn! In the square in the town.'

'Done! I accept!'

'Golaron,' she said, 'will you be arbiter? Let me go, I shall fight no more presently.' He reluctantly let go of her, still shaking his bitten hand, looking at her as if she were an animal of a kind he had not seen before. 'If my lord Lakkannar will accept me,' he said.

'Very well. At dawn, my lords.' She bowed, and ran out down the back steps.

'Good gods,' said Golaron.

'Farewell, Lord Ayndra,' said Polem.

The just-risen sun cast long cold shadows, painful half-congealed stretches of light; four rebellious and sleepy servants were marking out with posts and ropes the duelling square, in the main marketplace of Haridt. A contingent of all-night drinkers had straggled up from the gate, shivering in the fresh wind, to see the sight; Lakkannar arrived with them, accompanied by Ellakon and Golaron. Polem rolled up a short time later, carrying a leather flask under his cloak; he passed it furtively around. 'My own,' he explained.

'Is she going to come?' said Ellakon. 'Be damned if we're here for no reason!'

'She'll come,' said Polem. 'Here, give that bottle to me . . .' A

216

figure wrapped in black, alone, appeared on the other side of the square. The watchers turned and stared at her. 'She's done for!'

'Not a hope!'

'You have your weapons, Lakkannar?'

'I have.' Lakkannar patted his hip under his cloak. Perhaps a hundred people, Safeen and Haridan and subjects of the Empire, had gathered round the roped-off square; they were somewhat rowdy.

'Good day, gentlemen,' said Ayndra. 'My lords.'

'Goo' day,' said Polem.

'Drunk at this hour.'

' 'm not drunk! I jus' haven' go' sober yet.'

'Let us commence.' She slipped under the ropes, swept off her cloak, unlaced her overtunic and dropped it in the corner. Lakkannar followed more slowly. The drunken spectators clapped and cheered.

Up in the tower of the hall of Haridt, the sun crept in through the cracks in the shutters and striped the pillows of the bed; Ailixond lay still, not wishing to wake Setha, who slept on. He could hear the noise outside, but not to distinguish what it was that they shouted about, until Golaron's familiar bellow rose above it.

'My lords! You are sworn to fight with knives, within this space, neither leaving it nor lowering weapon until one of you shall die, or give submission to the other?' A high hoarse voice yelled, 'I swear!' and a deeper one repeated it. Ailixond threw off the covers, hastily wrapped himself in the nightrobe thrown over the bedhead, and slammed back the shutters. Ayndra had shut her eyes, leaning back against the ropes with a smile of unreadable joy on her face. 'Turn your backs!' Golaron called, and the duelllists obeyed. 'Ready! . . . Fight!' He stamped three times, and the combatants sprang to face one another. Lakkannar brandished a knife more like a short sword, and let out a great war-yell. Ayndra crossed her hands, slipped them inside either sleeve, and jerked them out, flashed up and out; Lakkannar screamed aloud and skidded over, crashed to the ground and lay there, moaning; one thin-bladed throwing knife protruded from the muscle of his shoulder, and another stood in his groin. Ayndra folded her arms and stood still.

'What happened?'

'What did she do?'

'Is he dead?'

'O, he's alive,' said Ayndra calmly. She stepped up to

Lakkannar. He scrabbled for her foot, but she skipped over him and snatched at the knife in his shoulder. He screamed again as it came free; she danced out of his reach. 'Shall you let me get the other?'

'Goddamn bitch!' he roared.

'Say no more, else I shall be obliged to plunge it in your throat.' She bent over and grabbed at his groin. He tried to defend himself, but she snatched hold of the knife hilt and heaved; it came free in a rush of blood, and Lakkannar collapsed, writhing, groaning through set teeth. Ayndra held up the bloody blades. Then she turned, and saw the white figure leaning out of the high window. She took both knives in her right hand, gripped her right upper arm just above the elbow, and jerked the clenched fist upward. The figure in the window disappeared. Ayndra wiped the knives on her breeches, put them back in their hiding places, and picked up her discarded clothes. 'Polem!' she called. He turned to her from the group bent over Lakkannar. She tossed something at him, cast her cloak over her shoulder, and danced away. He saw that she had given him the key to the bridal chamber.

Shortly after sixth hour, Firumin was behind the banked seats of the arena, directing the slaves in clearing up the ruins of last night, the removal of insensible revellers and the installation of fresh cloths, cups and crockery for that day's entertainment, when he saw Aleizon Ailix Ayndra stalking through the debris, dressed all in black with her hat pulled down over her eyes. She demanded, 'How long will all this go on for?'

'All what, my lord?'

'This . . . junketing.'

'Three days.'

'Ha. Good day, sir.' She almost knocked him flying as she strode past him. He spluttered in annoyance, but he had more important things to do than bother about insults; he called to the slaves again.

In the mid-morning of the fifth day of Ninth Month, Aleizon Ailix Ayndra let herself into her tent, which stood outside the town; 'Yunnil?' she said, 'Yunnil?' She went through into the bedroom. Her bed was a mess of rumpled blankets, and Yunnil was asleep in the middle of it. She breathed deeply, and shouted, 'Out! Up you get! Out of my bed!' The maid lifted her head, then sprang out of her nest as if she had discovered that wasps shared it with her; she landed on her knees at her mistress' feet. 'My lord! . . . what happened? I thought, my lord – I feared that you were dead!

218

I heard that Lord Lakkannar . . .'

'He is not dead, I take it?'

'No, my lord, but . . . my lord, what has happened?'

'I have been away. Yunnil, I need a bath. The Council meets at midday – go fetch some hot water.' Yunnil pulled on her gown and mantle, and scuttled away. Ayndra sat down on her bed, resting her elbows on her knees; she took off her hat and laid her head in her hands, running her hands into her greasy hair. Then she stood up, and began to strip off her grimy clothes in preparation for the bath.

Oppressed by the burden of almost four days' continual drinking, eating and merrymaking, the Council began to stumble into the royal pavilion at approximately noon. Lakkannar came in, limping delicately and leaning on a stick; his shoulder was bandaged. They were all gathered, waiting for Ailixond, when Aleizon Ailix Ayndra walked in; there was some consternation. She smiled at everyone, reserving an especially wolflike grin for Lakkannar, and sat next to Polem.

'Where have you been?' he said. 'I've not seen you for days!'

'O, around,' she said.

'You have made a number of enemies, you know –'

'O, I know . . . how was it when you let Ailixond out of the bridal chamber?' She sniggered.

'I only tell you –'

'I do what I will. If others dislike it, that's for them to suffer.'

'You ought –' Polem was interrupted by Ailixond's entrance. He looked tired.

The king announced that every man in the army would be given a present of three silver sols, in commemoration of the wedding, and a new series of gold sols bearing his portrait and Lady Setha's would be issued. Furthermore, in three days' time they would march east from Haridt; he gave an account of the territories they would pass through; the Chancellor gave a report on finances, and on affairs in the other provinces, including the death of the governor of Haramin, who would have to be replaced. 'And now,' Ailixond said, 'a disciplinary issue. Stand up, Lord Lakkannar, and Lord Aleizon Ailix Ayndra, if she be here.'

'I am,' she said, rising.

'I would prefer not to stand, my lord,' grunted Lakkannar.

'I will permit it in your case. But, my lords, as all are well aware, you fought a duel a few days ago, in contravention of the edict banning duels between members of the army of Safi. It is fortunate that neither of you died. Considering that there were no fatalities, neither of you will be imprisoned, nor dismissed the service altogether. I regard my lord Lakkannar's wounds, and his being defeated, a sufficient punishment. My lord Ayndra, you hold the post of over-governor of Haramin province, and you have heard that my lord Governor of Haramin is lately dead. Since you have shown yourself, in my view, lacking in restraint to such a degree as to unfit you for further service with the army, you will, as soon as you are able to pack, depart to Raq'min and take up the governorship there.'

Ayndra looked surprised, but then brightened her face. 'I thank you, my lord,' she said, and sat down.

'Council dismissed,' said Ailixond, and disappeared behind the curtains. Ayndra put her hand in her mouth and strode out of the door before anyone could speak to her.

It took five days, in fact, for the army to get ready to move on from Haridt, while Lord Ayndra assembled a party of fifty horsemen, some of whom would go on home from Raq'min, and filled four light wagons with their baggage and her own. They travelled with the army for half a day, until they reached the point where the road they followed crossed the track leading south into Haramin. She had said farewell to anyone she wished to say it to on the previous evening; she had turned away from the main column, when Polem, who was commanding the rearguard that day, came galloping up. 'My lord! Wait for a moment.'

'What is it?'

'I . . . well, Arpalond sends his good wishes, and I, I want to say – I do not know when I will see you again, so . . .'

'Perhaps sooner than you think! Do you expect highwaymen to murder me, then, or my subjects to rebel?'

'I am sorry that you go – the court will be a sadder place, now.'

'Will it? I am sure it did well enough before I came along.'

'But we have grown used to you.'

'And I to you,' she said distantly. Polem took her hand.

'I wish you good luck in Haramin.'

'It will not be so bad – I know the country, after all.'

'But it is – there's no powers laid down for a governor, you know; you have all the power you are able to get, and when you come there, they'll have been left for half a month and more with no one in command, and –'

'Do you say that I know nothing of government? It's true that I've never practised it until now. But I think I know how to do it.' She gave him a lopsided, vinegary smile. 'Imitate Ailixond.'

'You are very like him,' said Polem.

'Do you think so?'

'O, yes, yes – do you know, all this, I do not know what has come over him, I cannot talk to him, no one has talked to him for sixdays on end, I think he must have gone mad – I am convinced that he is mad, to send you away like this! I am sure as soon as he recovers he will see what folly it is –'

'But by the time he does that, I will be far away – and does he ever admit that his past actions were folly? I think not.' She glanced at her retinue, who were chafing to be off, and waved to them. 'I come!'

'Not in so many words, it's true,' said Polem, 'but he does –'

'It is time I went. Farewell, Polem, and good luck.'

'And to you, and – do nothing too outrageous!' Polem said plaintively.

'O, I shall not – after all, I'm being dismissed the court at the price of one of the finest provinces of the Empire. I may have lost a king, but I have gained a kingdom . . . I'll not forget you. Good day!' She nodded to him, and spurred her horse away, galloped to the head of her followers, who moved off after her down the green rutted track of the Haramin Road. Polem stayed watching until he could no longer pick out the black hat at their head; in all that time, she never once glanced back.

A voice whispered: I regret nothing that I ever do.

He patted his horse's neck, and turned back to the army.

Ayndra ordered her entourage to halt just on the other side of the last hill before the ride down to Blue Gate, and put up the banner of Safi, form up in ten rows of five, and then walk orderly up to the gate. The Shar was as clear as it had always been, but the gate showed patches of bright new stone that had not yet weathered to the soft shades of the old, and the doors of the gate, which stood half open, were new and painted sky-blue. A number of Haraminharn were gathered on the wall-walk and within the gate, fronted by a quartet of gate-guards.

'All hail to the Governor! Lord Aleizon Ailix Ayndra!' cried the flag bearer. Several other guards appeared, and a red-cloaked captain; they came to a ragged attention, looking around for the Governor. She sat her horse just behind the banner, bareheaded, dressed in rusty black and brown.

'Good day, sirs,' said the captain. 'We welcome my lady Governor – is she . . .'

'Who?' said Ayndra ingenuously. 'Lady Governor?'

'It is a woman, is it not, sir?' said the captain. 'We heard of her, that she . . .'

'O, what did you hear?'

'Well, sir . . .' he became conspiratorial. 'That she was Lord Ailixond's mistress, but now that he is married he has cast her off, and sent her, gods save us, here to be governor.'

'Is that what you were told?' said Ayndra.

'Is it not so, then?'

'It is true that she was his mistress.'

'Indeed? Do you bear her with you? What sort of government will it be, then — all silks and perfumes and female fuss?'

'We don't see much of that,' said Ayndra.

'No? But I cannot stand here for ever — do you bear her with you? Where is she?'

Aleizon Ailix Ayndra shed her wittol's act. 'You speak with her now.'

'What?' The captain did not understand.

'I am she,' she said.

He blanched, and seemed to shrink. 'Lady!' he gulped.

'You will call me my lord, an it please you.' He opened his mouth to speak, but she shushed him. 'I can see,' she announced, 'that there is much to be done in Haramin. Pray, Captain, conduct me to White Walls.'

The news went out with the fastest post-riders to every city in the realm, from the army lumbering westward toward the grass plains: Lady Setha, King's Wife of Safi, expected the birth of an heir some time in Tenth Month, setting off a cascade of obscene cracks among the Safic garrisons wherever it was received, and the lodgement of numerous bets on the child's sex; many of which were confounded when, even faster, the riders came out to announce that on the twentieth day of Tenth Month, Lady Setha had been delivered of a son, well-formed and healthy and named Parakison. In Safi, they rang bells and lit bonfires; all around the Empire, they found it a sound excuse to lie drunk in the gutters outside the wineshops. The Governor of Haramin read out the announcement from the wall above White Gate, but ordered no official celebrations. The army, having spent a year wandering around the mountains and the sea coast and the western moors, was reported to have finally pacified all those regions, and was now preparing to venture out into the grass plains proper, those wild and mysterious regions where the land trains going to trade for furs, or bring goods between the north of the old

222

Haraminharn empire and S'Thurrulass were piloted like fleets of ships over the trackless seas of grass; but in the provinces, things went on from day to day, and, even if there were some changes in the administration, they made little foundation for stories. Roads were repaired and markets ordered, goods transported and taxed, monies collected and the surplus, with the accounts for the whole province, sent off to the court; retired veterans from the Grand Army were received, and contingents of volunteer recruits, new horses and military supplies sent off.

'I assure you, sir, I am sent here on the authority of Lord Ailixond himself! – have you not heard of Lord Polem?'

'If you will wait, sir –'

'Shumar! Do you know nothing?'

'My lord – we will send to the Governor –'

'Damn your sending! I have know Lord Ayndra for years. I will not stand here waiting while you pass foolish messages from one to the other and back again. Parro, Haldin, come with me – no, as I think, wait here. I shall not be long.'

'But sir – my lord –'

'Out of my way! Damned foreigner!' Polem shouldered the Haraminharn officer aside and forged on into the palace of White Walls. He recalled from his sojourn there in 462 the approximate location of the king's private apartments, which, he was moderately sure, would be used by the Governor in the king's absence; he found the door to them unlocked, and dashed in, before any of the servants could stop him. He found himself in a stark, bright, white sunlit corridor, with glazed windows looking out onto a courtyard full of autumn colours; the door of a room near the end was open, and a woman was speaking loudly within. 'You will! And you will, three times – I see you in black, it is mourning . . . and in black again but armed – ah! an avenging angel –' A laugh began, but the voice went on, 'and a third time, in scarlet, scarlet and gold –'

'Haha! What is that then, my wedding?' exclaimed a familiar speaker. Polem broke into a run. 'No,' said the first voice, 'not quite a wedding – I could swear – no, I'm losing it –' Polem threw the door wide. 'Ayndra!' he said.

'God's teeth!' said Aleizon Ailix Ayndra. 'How is it that you are here?'

She was sitting in a high-backed chair, tilted back at a dangerous angle, with one leg hooked over the arm and the other holding the chair from falling backward by its traction on the

223

table-leg. A spectacular red-headed woman with long loose hair and a half-unlaced bodice was sprawled in an upholstered low chair on her left, sucking at the vapour of a piece of burning resin; the room stank of sweetsmoke. Aleizon Ailix Ayndra jerked her chair back to the vertical. 'Polem!'

'I come here – well, I come here to visit, but, that is, Ailixond sent me, to, well, to observe the affairs of the province – I am most glad to see you, truly I am,' said Polem, 'but your servants! Your officer was some foreign fool who, I swear, did not even know my name, and he would not let me in, but I pushed past him, and, well, here I am!' He held out his hand, and Ayndra took it and stood up. He clutched her other hand and kissed her roundly on both cheeks. She stood still, looking faintly, sarcastically, amused. 'What do you mean, observe the affairs of the province?'

'I am not quite sure,' Polem confessed. 'He showed me some accounts, but I cannot recall . . .'

'What! Were the accounts not in balance?'

'No . . . there were some items that seemed odd – lime plaster, I recall, and whitewash, and artists' pigments –'

'Did you not see White Walls as you were coming in? And did you not remember how it used to be grey?'

'I did, and I thought, there is the plaster and the whitewash, but then, your officer . . .'

'I have very many Haraminharn in my government. You cannot expect them all to know the lords' list of Safi. It was exceedingly sloppy on his part to let you go in without assuring himself that you were who you claimed to be.'

'I left my boys with him.'

'Boys? What boys?'

'O, Parro – he's my oldest, and Haldin, he's my next. I had them brought up to court from their mothers' houses, a few months ago, to go into the army and learn how to be men.'

'Then I had better go with you and speak for you, and you can be given rooms in the guest wing – Diamoon,' she said to the redhead, who had followed their conversation with attention, 'stay here if you wish. I know not how long I shall be.'

'Ah! I think I shall go then, and cast your fortune in proper form.'

'You waste your time.'

'You waste your time if you take no account of what I say,' said Diamoon. She heaved herself up from her chair and stretched. Polem realised that he was staring at her breasts, and pulled his eyes away. Diamoon grinned, feline, and made a curtsey; she was surprisingly graceful for her bulk. Ayndra nodded at her. 'Mistress Diamoon, a – prophetess –'

'Witch and soothsayer, my lord,' said Diamoon. Ayndra spat like an angry cat. 'I have told you not to say that! Introduce yourself in that manner once more and I'll dismiss you my service.'

'But my lord Polem is not one of those who will be affrighted by it,' Diamoon said.

'Perhaps not – but you do not know –'

'I always know, my lord.'

'O, get away with you!' Ayndra flapped her hands at Diamoon, who bowed her head to Polem and glided out of the room, leaving a draught of musk from the wide skirts of her red gown.

'Who is she?' he said.

'I employ her – she is listed under the clerks of the library – but you will no doubt come to know her well if you wish – as I can see that you do. She calls herself a witch, a fire witch, but I give it no credit – she does tricks and gives out ambiguous prophecies. You will see.' She led the way into the corridor; it was some distance to the door at the end, but Diamoon was nowhere to be seen.

The officer of the guard, several of his subordinates, half a dozen Safic cavalry troopers, and a score of palace servants were gathered at the side door of the palace, with two boys in their midst, who called out as soon as they saw Polem, and, as Ayndra called out to their captors, were allowed to go through to him. The older was like a copy of Polem, but fifteen years younger and grown too recently tall to know what to do with his long legs and oversized hands; his half-brother must have taken entirely after his mother, for he was brown-haired and round-faced and looked younger than he was; fourteen, with Parro the elder sixteen. Ayndra said to him, 'Have you eaten yet this day?'

'No!' he said.

'Not properly,' said Parro.

She sent them off to the kitchens in the care of one of the cooks, to be brought to the guest wing when they had had enough. The troopers were sent to the barracks; the baggage bearers, with their pack horses, ordered to follow her and Lord Polem to the suite which would be his. It became clear that the entire east wing of the palace was given over to guests of many kinds; officials from all over Haramin, from the mountains, merchants contracted to supply the government, nobles of subject regions come to visit the

225

capital, craftsmen, clerks, Safic officers journeying to or from the army or provinces further north, and most of these accompanied by secretaries, servants, guards, dogs, and families; the corridors were like thoroughfares aclamour with half a dozen languages. Ayndra deposited Polem in a large room which appeared to have been very recently vacated by more than a few people, and, saying that she had to go and sit in judgement, left before he had had time to say another word to her. He sat down on the bed while baggage was carried in, fresh linen brought (and he pushed into a chair while the bed was remade), beds for Parro and Haldin carried through into the adjacent dressing room, a tray with a flask of wine and a set of goblets brought, several servants presented themselves at his disposal, and Parro and Haldin returned chattering of the delicacies they had devoured, while people ran up and down and shouted in foreign tongues outside and a party of women entered and, without so much as a by-your-leave, began to hang brightly coloured tapestries round the walls of the room; and all this when he had not even got round to asking for a cup of wine for himself. Parro said, 'What think you of this place, then – is it well governed?'

Polem looked at the woman nearest him. She smiled, curtsied and replied in foreign. He shook his head.

'It is worse than the Grand Army,' he said. 'I have not the least idea what is going on.'

It became clear before very long that the affairs of the Governor's court were conducted indifferently in Safic and Haraminharn tongue; she switched between them without warning, and most of her attendants did the same, but it was confusing for those who lacked her facility. She offered to take Polem with her when she sat in judgement in the courts, when she went to visit the gate-guards and tollkeepers, when she sat (in a blackwood chair next to the dais with the empty gold throne) in the throne room to receive a prince from the mountains, when she rode out to the iron foundries in the next valley where they were making weapons for the Grand Army, when she consulted with the clerks of the provincial treasury, when she sat at dinner with the aldermen of Raq'min or the officers of her guard or her treasurer and justiciar; but if it had not been for Mistress Diamoon, who offered herself as interpreter, he would not have understood one half of what he saw. Haldin and Parro were given freedom of the Governor's stables, and amused themselves riding half-broken horses and receiving instruction from the Haraminharn weapon-masters attached to the court, who took them in the evenings down into unsavoury parts of the town. Their father might have disapproved if he had not been so well entertained by Diamoon. He had been six days in Raq'min, and had not since the day he arrived managed to speak alone to Aleizon Ailix Ayndra; as soon as he had eaten the breakfast brought to his room, he went out to look for her before she could go off on further business; but the maze of corridors past the kitchens were too much for him, and he went to the front doors, which they had not so far passed through, nor entered the great hall. They were unwatched, and, when he pushed them, unlocked. He stepped inside, and his foot knocked over something; a pot, which rolled across the floor in a spreading lake of blue paint. 'Shumar –' he began, but then his attention was caught by the upper walls and the ceiling: a blue expanse of sky, a few sculptural clouds and, directly overhead, a vast eagle, beak agape and yellow eyes blazing as it hooked its talons, just about to sink into a terrified partridge, fleeing under the shadow of its wings. It was cleverly done; the ceiling seemed to open up overhead. The ladders and pots of paint and the half-drawn forms on the walls explained why the hall was not in use; he could hear voices within, and the sounds of activity. he pushed the door open a little, and peered in. Several people were at work on the left-hand wall, and others were drawing on the fresh plaster behind the dais; the right-hand wall was complete, showing a cavalry regiment – by its banners, the Companions – going into action, and, in the next panel, phalanx advancing, and then a complex and dust-clouded scene of battle. The painters talked to each other in Haraminharn tongue. He was about to walk out, not least to have a better view of the paintings, when someone spoke in Safic:

'I think that he has no clear reason. Lord Ailixond seems not to have been forthcoming with one; except to discover what – as he puts it – you had been up to ... Polem suspects he may have had other motives, though.'

'O, such as?' said Aleizon Ailix Ayndra's voice. Polem ducked back out of sight, and found that there was a long gap between door and door jamb through which he could survey much of the hall unseen. He bent down, and saw Lord Ayndra and Diamoon, strolling down the hall together.

'He thinks,' said Diamoon, '– mark you, these are his words, and none of mine – that Ailixond has not forgotten you, indeed, that he still thinks ... warmly ... of you – and it's said, in the army, that since the heir of Empire was born, my lady Setha wants no more children, and is become somewhat cold ...'

227

'Ha!' said Ayndra, and spat on the floor. 'I do not believe a word of it. More than likely I am suspected of embezzling the taxes – and, being cleverer than most governors, at the same time having the wit to suborn my treasurer and send in false accounts – or else setting up on my own to declare an independent kingdom here as soon as he is far enough away.' She sat down on a paint-spattered bench, and fished in the front of her tunic. 'Polem does not think so,' said Diamoon.

'Ah, Polem . . . where is a light?' She produced a stick of resin.

'Give it to me . . . you said he knows Ailixond very well, though, did you not?' Diamoon turned her back, briefly, and produced the stick alight.

'Ailixond does not confide in him as regards matters of state.'

'Is this a matter of state?'

'Of course it is. Give that to me.'

'Do you ever wish to go back to court?' said Diamoon.

'It is none of your business.' Ayndra sucked a deep breath of smoke, motioned to one of the painters, and blew it out again through her nostrils; she addressed the artist, as he approached her, in Haraminharn. Polem stepped back from the door, and heard a crash; he looked round, and saw that he had overturned a vat of earth-colour, which had joined the blue streaks on his boots and was about to join the blue puddle on the floor. Ayndra said, 'What was that?' He heard boots coming closer, and retreated, into the spilt paint. The door creaked open. 'Good god!' she said.

'Good day,' said Polem.

She called over her shoulder, and a boy in a paint-covered apron ran up with a handful of rags. 'Here,' she said, 'clean your boots, before I let you walk any further on my floors. What are you up to – were you in truth sent here to spy on me?'

'I did not mean to spy on you,' Polem said. 'I came to look for you.'

'I would have sent for you in any case.'

'Sent for me!' he said, mopping at his stained feet. 'There you are – sent for me . . .'

'O, is that it? Come through, then, come through.' She nevertheless paused to give lengthy instructions to the painters, and explained to him that the hall would represent the entire battle of Palagar, with Ailixond's triumphal victory procession behind the dais, before she sat him down in front of the sheet-draped high table, and crouched at his feet. 'We may talk now. I am not immediately busy.'

He looked around. 'Where is Diamoon?'

'Diamoon is never where she is not apporprite, at least, if such absence does not conflict with an overwhelming desire of her own. Have you not had much pleasure from your time here, then?'

'O no, I did not mean . . . you are very much the governor.'

'Does it surprise you?' She sucked at the lump of sweetsmoke, and extinguished it, hiding the remnant in her purse.

'You are much different,' said Polem.

'Do you think so? – o, of course I am much different, my position here is entirely other than what it was before! You can tell me how it goes at court, besides, I have not asked – it is true, is it not, that he intends now to forge out into the grass plains? And has he all the army behind him in it?'

'Yes, and no,' said Polem. 'The lords are all on our side ever since . . . but the soldiers – they grow tired, I think, indeed we all . . . only Ailixond . . . Ailixond never changes.' He looked shrewdly at her. 'Now I shall tell you something I had from Arpalond. He told me that Ditarris says that Lady Setha – beside proving most arrogant, and having nothing to do with the other ladies – resolved after Parakison was born to have no more children, and furthermore, that she was always cold and used to complain that . . . anyway, he has left her behind. Saying that with a small infant it is not possible to follow the army.'

'Ah, come, come – surely you are not reduced to following Arpalond to gain knowledge of these things?'

Polem's shrewdness changed to dismay. 'I am,' he said. 'He never speaks to me of . . . not since, after he was married to Othanë.'

'But you think that I will care to know it,' she said, and fixed him with her blue eyes. Polem could not say a word. She stood up, put her hands behind her back, and began to pace, or rather strut, along the edge of the dais. She said, 'As you say, I am very much the governor here – do you not like the form of address, Governor? It saves me from endlessly correcting oafs who would call me my lady – indeed, I have a well-ordered place, I have things to do, and it is known who I am and how to speak to me and the respect that is proper when one does – and whatever I do, it's plain that I do it because I can and I wish to and not – it's said, as you know, that a governor has what power he can get, no more, nor less, unless of course he should grow so proud that he is restrained by the king . . . do you follow my meaning?'

'I am not sure,' said Polem.

'And most of these things were lacking when I was at court.'

'But Diamoon says . . .'

229

'What does she say?' She turned.

'That you . . . she says it is not your most favoured occupation, sitting in judgement and taking taxes, and . . .'

'And what?'

'That you would like to be travelling again,' Polem said.

Ayndra stretched up, looking severe; then fell into a grin, let her arms go, and took a few dancing steps along the edge of the platform. 'Ah! I cannot deny it,' she said. 'But when I shall be able to do so . . . I would not like to have to do this for the rest of my life.' Polem shrugged. 'If I am still here in five years' time,' she said, 'I shall at least apply to be sent as ambassador to S'Thurrulass. And if I should be still here in ten years, why then I shall dress up in old clothes and run away under another name. But then, I suppose my presence here even in the next year depends on your report – does it not?'

'You said yourself that he never discusses matter of state with me,' Polem retorted. She laughed, 'I shall, I am sure, give a very good report,' he said. 'I have never seen such a government – I cannot follow it all, there is so much – but then, I never could follow government, it is all I can do to read a romance let alone a book of laws. I do not know why I was sent here, indeed –'

'If it was a report on the government that was desired,' she said, still dancing.

'But I would have liked to come and see you, in any case,' he said.

'Ah! You are so kind, my lord.' She pranced behind his chair. Polem stamped his foot. 'Leave off leaping around like a, like a – a demented grasshopper!' he said. She came to a halt with her hands on the chair-back, either side of his head, and paused; he twisted round to look up at her. She was looking grave again. 'It's hard when you have not seen a friend for some time,' she said. 'How long do you intend to stay here?'

'O . . . half a month? I do not know.'

'Then we have plenty of time. But you must excuse me a little while I do that for which I came here, that is, instruct the artists – and then, we shall go out riding. And you may introduce me properly to your sons, and tell me about them, and about affairs at court . . .' She leapt off the dais and bounced down to the other end of the hall, and started chattering in foreign again. Polem gazed down at his painted boots, then at the murals; shook his head. 'Ah, you are not so different after all,' he said aloud, 'I still cannot understand you.'

230

Polem greets Ailixond. As you see I do not write this myself so at least you can read what I say. It is written by Mistress Diamoon a member of Lord Ayndra's household, that is I was going to put servant but she says that she is not. I have been here for twelve days now, and I wish you had said more to me of what good or bad government in province is, but from what I see here it seems in good order although I suppose that there are some expenditures that could have been done away with like the murals in the hall but on the other hand they are very fine and show your victory at Palagar so I suppose it is all right. Apart from that, everything is done in Safic and Haraminharn tongue which causes there to be more clerks than there would be if not but it seems to make the people happy, indeed I am told that they think themselves better governed than they were with their own king. There are a great many people here from all over Haramin and in the mountains too. I must say since I do not follow their tongue I do not understand the half of what I have seen in the courts and so on but it all seems very orderly and I see no evidence of bad practices or of money being stolen or the people suffering extortion by officers or any other things that might go on so I am sure that it is all in good order although the court appears not to be so due to the very large number of people running about at all times and the servants who are not very servile, I think this is because most of them are not slaves but freemen and women, and it is safe to go about in the town at night and there are not many thieves. The roads of the province too are safe. The Governor, Lord Ayndra, intends to go to the port of Shgal'min on the east coast at the start of Second Month and I will leave then to rejoin the army. Have you gone far since I left you? Have you won many victories? I await all the news and send best wishes to you and the little prince and everyone else who knows me. Gods bless and keep you all in safety. You may ask me all that you wish to know when I return. I go now to see some device Lord Ayndra has made to propel balls of stone through the air by means of a charge of powderfire, so farewell.

'He has asked me to come away with him.'
'What, to go to the Grand Army?'
'Yes. I said that I must ask you if I could be released from your service before I gave him an answer.'
'O, indeed? As if you would not leave tomorrow if you wished to.'
'No, lord! I would ask you – you've rewarded me well, after all . . .'

231

'Well, I would not keep you here if you wished to go – I cannot imagine that service unwillingly given is worth having. But will you go?'

'Ah, no! It is nothing but lust; it would be over in a month – not like his affection for you.'

'What?' said Ayndra, as if surprised into anger.

'He has deep respect for you,' said Diamoon. 'I think there is only Lord Ailixond that he thinks better of.'

'Ah, well, no one could replace Lord Ailixond . . . I am sure that Polem has not married because he knows that his true vocation is to be Lord Ailixond's wife, but since he is not a woman he cannot do it.'

'He believes that you must be pining for Lord Ailixond, you know.'

'O, does he?' said Ayndra. 'So you will not go – what will you tell him, that I forbade it?'

'No, that I have things to do . . . and that I have a husband.'

'Who is at present you know not where.'

'O, he will come back.'

'Indeed?' Ayndra rocked her chair back and forth, biting her thumbnail. Then she said, 'I am not sure I could stand even five years of sitting in one place governing it, even this place . . . perhaps the mountaineers will be good enough to rebel, and give me an excuse to go running around there at the head of my own army.'

'Would you not go back to the court?'

'I suppose it is possible,' she said. 'But not unless I am requested to do so. I have not many friends there, though perhaps in time they will forget my offences . . . I doubt it, though; the lords of Safi have long memories for insults to their honour. Perhaps if I had been more circumspect . . . ah, damn it! Circumspection never brought me here. Let us give Polem a state banquet to send him on his way, Diamoon, and you can appear in public with him.'

'Hah! think you that I wish to be known as a scarlet woman?'

'Ah, you may leave off playing the respectable wife! – and it will put paid to the silly tales that he has come here because he is my lover; do you know, they say now that Parro is my child?'

'What? Is that even possible?'

'Scarcely, Diamoon, I assure you, and even that includes I think a good deal of divine blessing and good luck – no, it is not possible. Although from what Yunnil tells me, I think Polem may be a grandfather before next year is out, which will put him to much embarrassment . . .'

The wagons of the Grand Army appeared like sail-less ships on an axle-deep sea of yellowed, seeding grass, a terrestrial sea that stretched out north and west further than map or legend, with water-holes taking the place of islands and the land trains which crossed them steering by the stars. Occasional trees and clusters of huts pocked the outer plains, but in the deep plains there were neither roads nor houses, and the wild horsemen, who owned no land save that beneath their villages of tents and the hooves of their horses and had not yet bowed to the lord of any of the settled lands, the stonewall people.

Polem deposited his sons with those members of his household who had been left to care for his possessions in his absence, and galloped up to the head of the army, where the other lords shouted out in welcome. Ailixond was riding alone, some way ahead, though behind the fringe of advance troops and archers who led the column now that they were in dubiously friendly country. The king did not respond to the shouting, and only turned when Polem pulled up beside him; he showed a sombre face, but it lightened when he saw who it was. 'You travelled fast,' he said, 'did you not say you would leave Raq'min at the beginning of this month? And it's not yet the midday.'

'Ah, there were not many of us – and the boys have new horses; indeed, they were given them by the Governor –'

'By whom?'

'By Lord Ayndra. The Governor, that's what they call her.'

'Ah, yes.' Ailixond frowned slightly, then said, 'How is she? Is she . . . well?'

'O, very well!' said Polem. 'A thousand things are afoot in Raq'min, and do you know, she is very noble, one would not think that she had not been born to it, although she does not stand on ceremony – but you have come far since I left you, have you met any enemies yet? Have you met the grass plains people?'

'We are not yet in the territory of the horse people,' Ailixond said, 'but we come close, and they move eastward at this time of the year . . . I am pleased to see you back, Polem, I am become short lately of people to – talk to . . .' He looked off into the distant sky again. 'But tell me about Haramin, for you'll hear what has gone on here soon enough, and then hear it again.'

'Well, then . . . but how is the little prince?'

'He is in Pomoan, and his mother. It's not reasonable for an

233

infant to be trailed after an army, with winter coming on, and a harsh winter too – and the horse-archers to face . . . no, tell me about the south.'

'What? I have not been south.'

'You have been some way south of where we have been lately. What are these murals you write of? and these devices with powderfire? Ah, good god, I have had no one but Arpalond that I speak with lately, and he listens, but you know how it is with him, he will have no particular friends . . .'

'Is that what he says?' said Arpalond, and leant forward. 'Then for once, Polem, I will give an opinion, and it is this: firstly, I pray that we meet with these horse-archers as soon as may be, and that they give lip-service to the New Empire, and, secondly, that Ailixond contents himself with that, and does not insist on going further – it is my view, indeed, that Almarem's witlessness was one of the worst things that befell us, for if he had not thought to resort to assassination, then there might have been a peaceful halt, and a turning home, some time ago, but no! he must strike, and force all opposition into silence, until now, when . . .'

'When what?' asked Polem. 'Do you mean that there's unrest in the army?'

'I mean that they most certainly will not stand for going any further away from Safi after this winter,' Arpalond said.

'Ailixond seems not to be very happy, either.'

'He is isolated. After he married – well, you know how it was; and now – while he was away in Lady Setha's apartments, the thoughts of the army moved on apace, and now . . . it is a good thing that you have come back. You should talk to him.'

Polem looked unhappy. 'I cannot get him to do anything that he does not want to do anyway,' he said, 'nor have I ever been able to.'

'But you can still talk to him . . . you saw Lord Ayndra in Raq'min?'

'I did.'

Arpalond frowned slightly. Then he said, 'It was a bad day when he dismissed her.'

'So I thought also. I wondered if he . . . that is, since he sent me there to . . . although he said nothing – and she did not seem very willing to come back to the court. Indeed, she had her own court there – seemed better off than the rest of us, in truth . . . I hope that we do turn soon. I have had enough of living in a tent in miserable climates and eating vile northern food and the wine all ruined by travelling.'

It loomed out of the grassy sea long before they came up to it: an earth mound beside the trail, perhaps twelve feet high and piled with whitish rocks, crowned by half a dozen black cross-shafted poles: the standards of the nomads whose territories they were entering. A land train would wait beside it until they met with messengers from the tribal lords, who, on receipt of appropriate gifts, would hand over such a standard as safe-conduct through the plains. Coming closer, one could see that the cross-shafts were hung with streamers of stuff resembling black and brown horsehair and strips of leather; and then, as they came abreast of it, the whitish rocks could clearly be seen to be skulls. The tallest standard was topped by a horse's head, crow-picked but not above a sixday old. Ailixond ordered the guards to ride all in armour, doubled the outriders, and recommended those camp-followers who were still with them to move into the middle of the column and arm themselves if they could.

'Noble king,' said the chief of the land pilots, 'surely it were wise – that is, we would wait here for a safe-conduct . . .'

Ailixond looked down at him. 'A safe-conduct, sir? Unlike your merchant employers, I come here neither in search of money profit, nor for the sake of my health – and what safe-conduct could be better than the Army of Safi?'

But for two days, they saw nothing but the grass and the sky; the only human things in these plains, it seemed, were the ghost voices in the wind . . . 'What's that, there, those things? . . . nothing, birds, deer, I know not . . . no, it comes closer, I swear it . . . look, those black poles . . . attack! attack! The enemy!' The cry echoed down the column, and was joined by shouts of, 'Halt! Draw up the wagons! Form a circle!' The baggage train drew up, and began to move into a closed circle; the infantry marched back to move inside its defensive wall, while the cavalry pulled on helmets and laced up leather shirts as they broke away from the column to form a screen between the approaching enemy and the rest of the army. Now they could hear the barbarians screaming and chanting, and soon see them clearly: small shaggy horses, garments of fur and leather, streaming hair, short bows, yammering and yowling as they came on – and then they turned as smoothly as a flock of birds in flight, and galloped broadside on, sending a flight of arrows whistling at Ailixond's stationary army; a horse screamed and tumbled with flailing hooves, arrows thudded into mail, the natives yelled derision at the stonewall dwellers who were too stupid even to fight back; they wheeled, and came pouring back again. 'Now,' said Ailixond, and the trumpets sounded, and the Safic cavalry charged. They took the horse-archers unawares; their bows were useless at close quarter, and their crude knives useless against long swords and armour; they lacked, also, any conception of the honour of resistance, for almost immediately they turned and fled, like a shoal of fish in whose midst a stone is cast. Behind the cavalry, the wagons and the footmen had just about completed their defensive manoeuvres. The enemy had left fifteen dead; the Safeen had lost one man and two horses, and a few superficial wounds. Ailixond was much complimented – the horse-archers were notorious for the number of stonewall armies which they had shot to pieces, even shooting backward as they fled from those who pursued them – but waved them all away. 'We'll not take them with that trick again,' he said, 'they will not let us get close like that – I think, now, we'll see them only in the distance, at least until we are far into their lands, and they have drawn up a great body of riders, enough, they think, to cut us all to shreds . . .'

'And what then, my lord?'

'Then we defeat them,' he said; 'it should not be so hard – they have but one idea in tactics, after all . . .'

As usual, he turned out to be right.

Like flies on the horizon, like the buzzing multitudes that signal a fainting fit, the tribesmen followed the army ahead, and at a distance; standing on a wagon at night, one could see their campfires. As Third Month wore on, they grew bolder, and began to gallop past the column by day, yelling, and even loosing a few arrows; but Ailixond did nothing, except to order no one, whatever the circumstances, to leave the column to chase after them.

On the twenty-fifth of the month, they came to a wide, shallow brown river, fringed by trees, and prepared ropes to guide the crossing. As soon as the footmen began to wade into the water, horsemen appeared on the far bank, watching. The cavalry detached themselves from the main body, and went, among the trees, half a mile up or downstream, but they crossed unobserved, the watchers being fascinated by the paraphernalia of the main army. The Silver Shields were first to go across, shields slung at their backs; as soon as they were all over, they put on the arms which they had carried on their shoulders, out of the wet, and formed up into a solid rectangular formation, linked shields and headed out into the face of the enemy.

At first the nomads fell back, but when they saw the metal-coated footmen marching onward, and remaining only a group of footmen, such as they had defeated many times before, and separated from the rest of their people who were down by the river still, they started to move closer; and then set up the war-yell, and rushed forward into a mad whirl around the precise lines of infantry, who raised their shields over their heads and went on marching until the horsemen closed the circle and they had to stop. The nomads had only to ride round and round, discharging arrows into the close ranks, and enjoy the long-drawn-out festival of massacre. The Silver Shields received the barrage with complete stoicism, holding up their shields and aiding as best they could those who were wounded. The horsemen revelled in an ecstasy of bloodlust; while, on either side, the Safic cavalry came up out of the valley and skirted round them, and then, without trumpets or banners, charged. When the nomads finally heard the thunder of ironshod hooves, they were trapped between Safeen on the inside and outside; the Silver Shields gave up passive resistance, whipped out their swords and slashed their way into the packed, trapped riders; the whole melted into a clangorous melee. Steppe ponies, disembowelled, tangled their feet in their own guts; archers were dragged from the saddle and their throats slit, or thrown down to be trampled by the hundreds of hooves. The noise of battle was audible down by the river, but they had orders to continue crossing in an orderly manner, and leave the battle to itself – even though it might be that the best of the army was being murdered hardly a mile away. They climbed out of the shallows, and waited; they saw nothing.

And then a single horseman appeared on the lip of the valley, and careered down to them, hauled his blood- and foam-spattered mount to a halt and roared, 'Get me that coward of a land pilot! Now! Go!' They recognised then the king's white cloak, and several ran off on his errand, while others crowded as close as they dared to Harago's rolling eyes. Someone dared to murmur, 'My lord – have we –?'

Ailixond slammed his fist down on his thigh. 'Of course we have won!' he shouted; they fell back; he lowered his voice. 'The barbarians have been crushed. We are victorious.' More riders came up on the skyline, and then the Silver Shields, re-formed and marching as disciplined as ever. Ailixond unbuckled his helmet and shook out his long hair, looking away still as if the cheering spreading through the army was a hundred miles away. The land pilot was led up to him; he stopped at a good distance, torn by uncertainty. Ailixond looked down, and beckoned him closer.

He quavered, 'What do you want, my lord?'

Ailixond let him suffer a few moments before he smiled beatifically. 'What,' he asked, 'does one do when one wishes to parley with these barbarians?'

The Lord of the New Empire and the Old Man of the Grebenyi met three days later, half a day's journey from the river Snarda, on a cold grey day of rain fast turning to sleet. Ailixond's tent had been hung within with tapestries, and furnished with the best the lords between them could summon, for they mostly lived far more richly than did he. The tent was ringed by sentries in mirror-bright armour, holding their pikes vertical against the gale. The chiefs of the Grebenyi advanced at a proper pace – very slowly – while their herald bellowed the glories of their genealogies in a voice like an iron saw on slate. The lower orders dismounted first, helped their superiors down, and they proceeded into the tent, to face the lords of Safi arrayed like peacocks around Ailixond in his plain chair. The Old Man, who could not have been more than thirty-five, surveyed the seat which he was offered, and looked at the Safeen with puzzlement; finally he lowered himself down on the edge of it, and sat there fidgeting. His escort squatted on the floor. The standard bearers remained by the door. Ailixond asked what they carried on their poles, relayed through an interpreter; 'The hairs of my defeated enemies,' came the reply.

'Indeed,' said Ailixond. 'It is not the custom of my people to do so. We prefer to enter into union with those whom we have defeated.' The Old Man nodded. 'I believe that you are at feud with other tribes who ride these lands.'

'They are subject! They are abject thieves, footsloggers, they use their horses as women and their women are whores, they are cowards one and all – I spit upon them,' said the Old Man.

'Then you will no doubt wish to reaffirm your ascendancy,' said Ailixond. He signalled to the guards at the door of the tent, who had collected the weapons of both sides as they entered and laid them on a table, to bring his sword and the Old Man's and lay them before them. Polem walked up, and produced a third sword, which he laid between them: two long straight blades in shining twice-forged tempered steel, and a poor, dull-coloured, one-edged overgrown knife. Ailixond told the Old Man to examine the middle sword; Polem held it out to him. He took it, ran his thumb down the edge and blinked at the line of blood that followed it; pulled a hair from his head, and laid it over the edge. It fell in two.

He clicked his tongue appreciatively.

'It is a good sword.'

'You may have that sword, and twelve more like it, and more if you will give furs or whatever else of value you have in payment, if you agree to certain conditions. The first: you swear that you, your tribe and your heirs, will become and remain vassals of the New Empire. The second condition: you will fight with us when we go to subjugate the tribe whose lands run with yours – the Gilangi, I am told their name is. Do not answer yet – there is a third condition: the surrender of sufficient of your grazing lands along the banks of the Snarda to allow us to build a city, and plant sufficient fields to feed it. You must take all three pledges, or none, and if none, then we return immediately to a state of war. Immediately, as we stand here.'

The Old Man looked around him, then up at the canvas roof. He scratched in his matted hair, trapped something, and cracked it between his fingernails. Ailixond affected not to notice. The Old Man looked at the swords. 'We get swords, and the Gilangi not?'

'Vassals of the Empire may be provided with swords,' Ailixond said, 'but not my enemies.'

'Then I join the tribe Em Pyer.'

Ailixond smiled. 'My lord. I welcome you to the realm of Safi.'

'. . . grindingly poor, they are; in a hard winter they expect that half their children will die and even if the weather is mild they hardly make it through, and they use the pieces of iron the traders give them until they are worn away, and yet they have until now held their own against armies a dozen times better equipped and trained. Were they united and disciplined, I think they could hold their own against us even – but, of course, they are not . . . the key is to give the Grebenyi the ascendancy over the others, and then keep hold of the Grebenyi. And it is here that the city comes in. I suggest that we give the Old Man a place in it where he may pitch his tent – if he will not accept a house – and a share of the revenues, the food that the farmers grow to help them through the winter. And then we will build a road, and, what with the river and the road, the merchants will come here, and the fur traders from the north – furs, leathers, hides, grain – I swear that one could make grain to grow here the like of which has never been seen . . .' Ailixond paced up and down the tent, talking for hours at a time; the lords of the Inner Council watched him, and listened, but they did not say much.

Polem asked, 'What name will you give this city, then?'

239

'I had not thought of it – what would you say?'

'New Safi?' Polem suggested.

'Hardly,' said Sulakon.

'Ailixondia?' said Arpalond.

'That would be tempting fate,' pronounced Sulakon.

'A little clumsy,' said Ailixond. 'I know; we shall call it New Hope, for so it is in these desolate lands. If we go to work felling trees, and send to Pomoan for the fleet to bring supplies up the river to us, we can have wooden walls built before the snowfall is settled – and the ships can bring up building stone. And colonists – five years free of taxes for anyone who settles here . . .'

Polem said to Arpalond, 'It still works.'

'What is that?'

'Why said you that he should call it Ailixondia?'

'Ah,' said Arpalond, 'I was, as you may say, testing.'

Polem sighed. 'What I meant was, although hardly anyone wants this plains thing, still he has us all following him, but – it is getting hard – o, for god's sake! If he throws it all away for the sake of some land not even worth having – and I,' he said plaintively, 'I cannot do anything.'

'I think you could avert it, if any of us can,' Arpalond said.

'O, but how? Have you ever seen him do anything that was not because he wanted to do it? And have everyone else do it too, and he feeds on them, all the people he has to worship him . . . I fear, though, that if they get beyond that, if they will not do what they don't want, and he cannot make them – I cannot think what he might do.'

'Think you that it would destroy him?'

'O, no,' said Polem seriously, 'only he will do that – not that he will I mean, I pray that he will not – but it would change him, and I do not know what into . . .'

Polem glanced at a few of the plans which Ailixond showed him, but it required more effort than he was used to giving to bits of paper to make sense of them; he soon dropped them, and wandered round the room, poked idly at the brazier and finally halted behind Ailixond's chair.

'This new city,' he said.

'Yes – what of it?' Ailixond slit open a grimy canvas packet; several letters tumbled out.

'Well . . . you must have seen – I mean – you must have seen that, well, not everyone, that is – what do you plan to do next?'

'We shall winter here, to complete the foundation of the city.'

'But what then?'

'Why, then . . . for a start, it depends on what has befallen us this winter, on how things have gone with the tribes.'

'Yes? Well . . . of course, these Grebenyi are our friends now, but, well – you must have noticed that we, I mean, the lords, though Arpalond says the common soldiers as well . . .'

'Good god!' said Ailixond. 'Listen to this, Polem. "The mountain tribes have risen . . . we believed it to be a small thing and sent fifty of our people and three hundred of our subjects to quiet them, but they did not return and, within a sixday of their leaving, the garrison of Prallash were all slain and five only escaping came to us . . . since the midday of Third Month they are outside our walls, and we do not know how far this cancer has spread, and there are so many here now that we may last a month only with the food which we have, if they do not come upon us earlier. Noble lord, we plead for assistance as soon as it may be sent." It is from Geranno, who commands in Hassalh.' Ailixond threw the letter across his desk. 'The north-east again! What is it that is so bad there? Why does he plead with me rather than with Haramin?'

'It may be that he has – and beside, Lord Ayndra has gone far away into the east of Haramin,' Polem said.

'Perhaps, perhaps – still, I cannot refuse this now it has come. I shall send . . . now, to spare . . . Polem! It is time that you had a command of your own, now that I have sent you already as my king's eye. Every upstart has a city, these days, while you have not commanded so much as a troop of horse.'

'What! – I do not want so much as a troop of horse!' Polem exclaimed.

'Then I think that you should – and do you not like the prospect of yourself as Saviour of Hassalh?'

'What if I do not succeed in saving Hassalh? I know nothing about command, Ailixond, god's teeth –!'

'You will save Hassalh, and the honour of Safi, if I send you, for you have seen enough of war that you cannot be ignorant as you claim, and I shall send a couple of captains with you who will tell you the directions you should give out, while you will merely have to preside over the men and ride about in your abominable orange cloak and look pretty.'

'But –'

'I will have no buts!' Ailixond said. 'How long will it take you to pack up your things? Two days? You can have no more than a pack horse –'

'I do not want to go to Hassalh!' said Polem. 'I want to stay here with you.'

'O, nonsense! To do that which one dislikes is good for the soul. The day after next. Now, to go with you . . .'

Lord Polem, with one thousand cavalry, and eight hundred mounted infantry, arrived outside Hassalh in deep snow on the twenty-third day of Fourth Month, and drove off a force of besiegers who outnumbered them by at least two to one; the victory had been directed by a trio of experienced officers, but Lord Polem led the conquering army in to the ecstatic welcome of the besieged, and discovered unexpected pleasure in so doing. He had been through these mountains before, and in winter; they had, after all, only to drive a few bandits out of their eyries, burn a few hovels and take a few hostages. He dismissed his advisors to see to the reconstruction of Hassalh and its environs, and took the cavalry and infantry off into the mountains; handicapped by his rank and his royal connections, they had to let him go. For several days, despatches arived, invariably stating that the enemy had fallen back and were fleeing before the army of Safi, until, in Fifth Month, one came that said, 'We have discovered the leader of this revolt, and where his castle lies, far into the mountains, and are accordingly gone there to root out the weed of corruption at its roots. I do not doubt that we shall soon return.' But no letters came after that; snow and silence closed around Lord Polem, leaving his attendants able only to guard the roads and hope.

The Governor of Haramin and her entourage moved on from the east coast into the mountains as winter drew in, trudging along snowy tracks under grey fluffy skies and through white storms, showing the banners of Safi in the remote outposts; crowding for a few days into straw-thatched castles or stubby fieldstone towers, and then struggling on through the bitter cold. They were camping in a cramped two-storeyed fortress on the border of Benhanna'ram when a tired and distraught rider arrived out of a stormy night, and demanded to be taken to the Governor – when he heard that it was her men whom he had encountered – although it was almost midnight; he said that he carried an urgent message from Lord Polem, upon which he was taken up to the first floor, into a torchlit room stuffy with snoring humanity, with a wooden door to the private room of the tower's lord. It creaked open, showing a pokey smoke-stained closet, holding only a large rumpled bed, a cold brazier and a wooden chest, on which sat the

242

Governor of Haramin, half wrapped in a cloak over a dirty grey undertunic that had clearly been slept in, and with her hair sticking out every which way. She stood up, rubbing her eyes.

'Good day, lady,' said the messenger, and almost overbalanced.

'God's curse! Let him sit down on the bed. You're near dead – whatever message from Lord Polem is this? I thought he was with the Grand Army –'

'Not since Fourth Month . . . the king, he sent us to, to put down the rebels –'

'Sent who? Sent Polem?'

'Yes, lady.'

'Luamis! My title is lord! – what, was he drunk at the time?'

'Pardon, my lord?'

'O, nothing, nothing – Shirren, can you not fetch us a fire? It's cold as a corpse's kiss in here – I chatter as a bird. Carry on, deliver me your message.'

'Lord, I have . . . from Lord Polem.' He fished in his tunic and eventually brought out a creased, sweaty scrap of paper. She held it up to the sputtering flambeaux. 'Ah, heaven bless me! this is not writing, this is the path of a spider – can you tell me briefly? I shall read this in daylight, perhaps.'

'Well, my lord, we, we chase the barbarians, into the mountains, in the end even to the castle of their leader, but then they came up behind us and we got into the castle but they all ran away, and . . .'

'Appeared later, and shut up Lord Polem in their castle? From which, I expect, they had farsightedly removed all the foodstuff.' She sighed. The messenger nodded groggily. 'Ah! So I must go rescue him, I suppose . . . how long did it take you to reach here?'

'Four days, going night and day as long as I could.'

'And how long can they hold out? – a sixday? Two?'

'I know not, but, lady, they have not much to eat.'

'Lord, if you please! – what hour is it?' She went to the narrow window, and pushed open one of the rag-stuffed shutters. 'Shumar! Impossible to tell. Nothing but snow, snow, snow.'

'It's passing midnight, my lord!' called someone at the door.

'Ah, no time at all! – look you, lie down here, rest while you may, and we'll have started back to Lord Polem before dawn.' She dropped to her knees, pulled her boots from under the bed, and sat on the floor to pull them on, while three men carried in a pot of hot coals and a shovel with which they removed the dead coals from her brazier to put in the fresh ones; a number of other people poked their heads round the door, and Lord Ayndra

243

started yelling in foreign, while pulling on several tunics one over the other and wrapping her head in a scarf, before running out into the tower room and kicking sleeping guardsmen – 'Up, sons of bitches, up!' The messenger closed his eyes, and tumbled off the cliff of consciousness.

Someone shook him, and slapped his face; he opened his eyes on a lamplit blur, and could not for a little remember where he was, but 'Sixth hour,' said a light sarcastic voice, 'we left you as long as we could – drink this, now,' and someone gave him a steaming cup of wine, flavoured with something bitter and hot spices. It burnt in his stomach, lifted him up and down the steps into a torchlit, slushy yard, milling with men and horses, and Lord Ayndra, on a splendid grey stallion, in the middle of it; he was hoisted onto an unfamiliar horse by her side, and they were off under the grey streaky clouds of winter dawn.

Four days later, they came to a place where the bridle-path – much broadened recently, it was clear even under the fresh crust of snow, by a large number of riders – they followed entered a narrow defile, passing between two steep cliffs barely ten yards apart. The messenger, who was presently strapped, limp as a rag doll, on a led horse, had told them before he succumbed to exhaustion that it would run on so, not always so narrow but always constrained, for about an hour's ride at walking pace, until it debouched into a deep valley mostly taken up by a frozen lake, with the castle and Lord Polem on its far side. As they gathered outside the cliffs, none of the enemy were in sight, 'but,' said Lord Ayndra, 'as soon as we are too far in to turn back they will appear as if by magic, I do not doubt.'

'They are here now,' said Gerrin, her captain of horse. 'Have you not been watching the hillsides? – rocks that move, and strange showings on the skyline . . .'

'Listen to this. A third part of our number remains here, to keep open the pass, while the rest enter it, and meanwhile someone goes on ahead to go through to the castle, and speak to our people there, to urge them to come forth as soon as we come through the pass, and join with us so that we all retreat together, as, doing so, we shall no doubt be severely harassed – thus breaking the siege with as little loss of life as possible.'

'Who do you mean to send on?' Gerrin said.

'I would send our friend there, since Polem's people will know him, but since he is . . . no, there is one person most likely to have the gates opened on sight, bar Lord Ailixond of course, and that is myself. I shall go. Think you that the lake ice will bear?'

244

'Perhaps, but you were better to avoid it,' said Gerrin.

'Indeed. You will command the men who go through the pass — give me a little start, an hour or more, and mill around here and shout and attract them; it is possible that they will not miss just one rider.'

'But ought you not to take a troop, or —'

'Ah, no! I will do better alone, I am sure of it.'

Gerrin shook his head, but she tossed hers; 'Good luck, then, my lord,' he said.

'I thank you, I shall be gone.' She flicked the reins, and the big grey dappled horse was off like a bird.

Among the rocks the sun did not reach, and it was silent, blue and cold; looking up, one could see the long snowy slopes, crowned by black teeth of rock, their long shadows mauve and indigo. There was a sudden rattle; she glanced all round her, but saw nothing. 'Come, come, we must move on,' she said to the horse, Anagar, and nudged him into a fast walk. Above her, another shower of stones pattered down. She tipped her head back: nothing. She went on. The way was narrowing again; she was coming to cliffs perhaps twenty feet high, ragged edges slicing up the sky. There was a strange round stone up there, the wind had carved it so that it looked ... almost human, but ... it moved, it disappeared. Stones grated together, distant and clear in the still air, and there was a pluck, as of an arrow being nocked. She brushed Anagar's sides with her spurs, and he leapt forward; something whizzed past her head, and then another rattled almost under his feet — a black-feathered arrow. Anagar threw up his head and bolted. She crouched down as low as she could and clung to his mane; then something thumped her between the shoulderblades, throwing her forward on his neck, she lost the reins, had to grab at the mane; a voice howled like a wolf above her. She got hold of the reins again, and felt something dragging at her back — it must be an arrow that had stuck in her cloak and the mail underneath it, but she had no time to wonder at her escape, for Anagar thundered between the last pillars of rock and out into the sunlight.

Half a mile away, the castle crouched — a grey wall, snowy roofs — no banners flying, and its gates shut, but a lichen of tents and huts around it; waiting until starvation drove the Safeen out into their arms, they had not bothered to ring it, only set up their shacks on the most advantageous neighbouring knoll. Should she go right, or left? But before she decided, they decided for her, as, half way between her and her objective, a troop of riders emerged on a long fan of scree, and turned toward her. She spurred Anagar on again, round the other side of the lake. Distant voices shouted; she urged him to a gallop, careless of the treacherous ground, and seeing in the corner of her eye that they too had broken into a gallop – how many of them, twenty, thirty? Now they were rounding the edge of the lake. A rock spur thrust out before her, and she turned down to the beach of the lake, and up again, and –

'Yiha! Yiha! Yihaaa!'

Anagar pulled up short and half reared; another score of horsemen were pounding out of a concealed valley, swords drawn. She did not pause to think; she dragged him around, and struck out onto the lake ice. It rang sound; she looked back, and saw them milling about on the beach, shouting; she slowed Anagar, and laughed at them. A loud report rang out; she looked for the source; they saw it before she did, the hairlines of darkness like forked lightning, netting the bubble-clouded, wind-scoured ice. A great shudder went through the horse's limbs, and he sprang forward; she pulled him away from the land – the enemy were there! – and headed him toward the castle, racing the cracks, as they exploded like charges of powderfire, and behind began to gape into black mouths. Someone on the walls yelled, 'Go! Go! Go!' She threw up her hand in salute, and Anagar's hind foot went through the ice. Frantic, she ploughed his sides with her spurs; water bubbled up over the sagging edge; he struggled, heaved and carried on. The Safeen on the walls bellowed encouragement, and the gate began to swing open. The ice rang differently, they were over shallow water now, ten strides, five, two, and they were on solid ground again, twenty yards and they were inside and they slammed the gate to behind her, and Anagar came to a halt, sides heaving; a stream of men poured round her.

'Shumar! I made sure you were dead!'

'Where do you come from? – are you Safin?'

'I have never seen such luck!'

'Are you come from Lord 'lez'nailix Ayndra?'

She let out the last of the deep breaths which she had drawn to try and quell her racing heart. 'Do I come from Lord Aleizon Ailix Ayndra? – do I! I am –'

'Aleizon Ailix Ayndra!' In a bright orange cloak, coming down the rampart steps three at a time, the soldiers fell back before him; Ayndra slid to the ground, where she found that her legs would not support her, but by then Polem had caught hold of her and enthusiastically kissed her. There was cheering. She regained her feet, and slipped from his embrace. 'Good day, my lord,' she said.

'O Ayndra! O, sweet Luamis – o, heaven's blessings! A thousand praises! I thought – are you alone? Have you –'

'My army will come through the pass in an hour or so,' she said.

'What – your army? You have left them?'

'I have. And went on alone, to warn you of our coming.'

'Good god! An you had been attacked –'

'I was attacked – do you not see?' She felt at her back; the arrow dangled now, snagged in her cloak.

'What, that too? But – o, sweet heaven! When you went through – I made sure that you were dead!'

'Did you?' she said, taking off her hat – 'Did you? Why, then . . . so did I!' Touched by the hysteria of release, they laughed; 'Come,' she said, 'and I will tell you what to do.'

'Come with me here, we may talk in private.' He led her up a flight of steps on the outside of the castle's squat tower and into a room on the first floor, out of which a large number of people had evidently been lately cleared; straw strewed the floor, and at one end a fire without a chimney filled the rank air with smoke. She saw a rickety chair, and dropped into it, taking off her hat. 'Well, Polem, a pretty knot you are tied in – how ever do you come to be here?'

'Ailixond sent me,' said Polem, wishing for a place to sit down, but unwilling to take a sooty hearthstone.

'What? O well! only the gods never err.'

'Your pardon? Do you mean . . . until we came here, we had won a heap of victories, we chased them all the way here from Hassalh.'

'Ah, they let you follow them – and so you did, into a bag's end. Now, as I said, in an hour or so my army will come through the pass, and I have said that, when they show, we shall sally forth to meet them, and retreat together once we have broken through the enemy, who will no doubt attempt to chase us all up here to deal the death blow when we have been weakened by starvation and confinement. So you may convey this to your men, and have them all pack up and gather in the yard. They should carry nothing they cannot run with, and given each a share of whatever food there is, so that we need not bother about distributing it on the march.'

The enemy observed their activity, and began to gather closer to the castle, with more coming down out of the hills, while the sky darkened, swelling with coming snow. The lords stood up on the walls, watching the light fading over the lake.

247

'All my men are mounted,' Ayndra said. 'We should put your footmen in between a front- and a rearguard of cavalry, some of yours and some of mine in each group.'

'And one of us at the front and one at the back,' Polem agreed. 'It would seem suitable.'

'Then, since the rear is the position of honour in retiring –'

'– you must take it.'

'O, no, no, you deserve it more than I, I have disgraced myself.'

'Nonsense. You are the senior.'

'But I am sure that I should defer to your prowess.'

'Exactly. I shall let you have this honour in order that you may salvage the ruin of your military reputation, lest it be obvious to all that you are not fit to command a soup kitchen.'

'I what? – if I remember rightly, you were not so successful when you had charge of a soup kitchen.'

'O indeed? At least I –'

'My lord! Look, look!'

Ayndra looked, and gave an ignoble whoop. 'Gerrin! Let us go.'

'One moment – we shall decide this by tossing a coin.'

'A good idea! Let me see, have I –'

'No matter, I've a gold sol here. Which side?'

'Waves.'

'Then . . . waves, you win, heads, I win the choice.' He brought out a large gold coin, and tossed it to her; she slapped it down flat on the back of her glove, then looked at it. 'God curse it! Heads.'

'I shall take the van – give it to me.'

'No!' She held it away from him. 'I shall keep this, at least.'

'No, let me have it.'

'We must go.' She jumped down the steps, on the way turned over the coin – Polem!' she shrieked. 'You bastard! This coin has two heads!' He gave her an ironic bow. 'Ha! For such a forethought device, you almost deserve the vanguard!' she exclaimed, and splashed down into the slushy yard.

The enemy were still hanging back, as the Safeen divided to go either side of the lake; but from the castle one could see a large party descending the snow slopes to come down behind them. 'Open the gates! We must go now!' The gates swung back, and Polem's lurid cloak burst forth at the head of his cavalry. The enemy yammered like wolves, and came running down from their camp to meet the footmen following him. But the cavalry spread out to form a screen behind which they could march out and round, to go along the other side of the lake from the barbarian ambush, while the Safeen from the pass stood and held them off –

they hoped! – until they had met up, and could all turn back together, but at the same time allowing the barbarians to unite and follow them. The Safeen who fell victim to pursuers or arrows, they had to leave lying if they could not stagger on; it started to snow, raining great clots of whiteness among the arrows.

Gerrin struggled through the press at the mouth of the pass, until he found his lord, but she ordered him to get back to the front and join Lord Polem, and move on, not stopping for nightfall or anything, else they would all surely be cut to pieces. She cursed him when he did not leave immediately. The barbarians were firing nearly blind now, but as the Safeen packed together entering the pass, they must hit somewhere, and the black and white wind wailed over the rocks. 'It will get worse,' she said, 'much worse – go, now, and get on!'

The vanguard, when they arrived at the castle guarded by a tiny detachment of the army of Haramin, had been two days without word of the people who had been in the latter half of retreat, after three hundred barbarians had charged out of the hills – three days after the night march through the pass – and cut a swathe through the middle of the exhausted column. They rested, and ate, and packed together round fires, and three days went by; then, on the fourth, a slow-moving, shaky but still compact column of footmen and horsemen appeared over the nearest hill, and dragged up to the gate; they plodded into the yard, dropped their packs or even themselves into the slush and ordure, fell asleep on their feet or on the first piece of floor they were allowed to lie on. Polem recognised the big grey stallion at a distance, and leapt on his horse to go and meet it; the rider, as he approached, he saw to be slumped, swaying, held in place by tethering belts while a tall man in a ruined officer's cloak led Anagar by the bridle. He pulled up beside them. 'Ayndra! – Ayndra!' The sagging figure lifted its head, and stared at him with bleared eyes out of a wilderness of stubble. 'My lord . . .' it mumbled through cracked lips. Polem gaped. 'Shumar help me! Is she –' he began, when a loud cracked voice said 'Have you gone blind?' He looked around frantically; 'Behind, behind!' shrieked the voice, and a hand tugged at his leg. He looked down, and there she was, among a group tramping, bowed like turtles, at the horse's tail, lank strands of hair straggled over her face; her eyes were sunken in discoloured sockets, and her lips cracked by cold. 'O! – come up behind me, here!' he said.

'Can't . . . too tired to jump up,' she said, 'go on, and I shall hang on to your foot . . . do you see? More than a hundred lost, I think, I cannot say, many went off into the dark, or we'd find them cold as the snow and all covered with it in the morning . . . we picked up all those who could not keep up with you, you see. Dropped quite a few of them, though.' She giggled, and leant her head against his leg. 'All your fault, too, you know . . . ah, I thought I'd never make it, do you know, I have not slept for, I do not know, nights and . . . nights . . .' She closed her eyes; her face was chiselled with fatigue lines under the dirt. Polem leant over to put his arm round her shoulders; she must have been exhausted, in that she did not shrug it off until they had dragged into the castle yard, where she pulled away and went to stand in an open space, taking off her hat and unwinding the scarf under it from her head and neck. 'Well, gentlemen,' she said in a penetrating voice, 'I am returned from the jaws of death . . . go, look after yourselves, unless some fascinating and important event shall have befallen any part of my dominions since I was last here, in which case . . .'

Polem came up behind her. 'This came,' he said uncertainly.

'What, what?' This was a letter bearing the royal seal. She grasped it, and spent some time looking out her knife to slit the binding. 'O, and here . . . since you've given me a letter, Polem, let me give you . . . knife, knife . . .' She gave him a creased, dog-eared packet; he unfolded it – 'But this is my letter! The one I sent you . . .'

'I know. You may as well have it, for I could not read a word of it.' She slashed open her letter and pulled out the heavy cream paper inside. Polem attempted to peer round at it. She raised her left arm and pushed at his face with her open hand. Forced to withdraw, he asked, 'What does it say?'

'It is Ailixond,' she said. 'He says . . . he says he wants me to come back to the court . . . he doesn't mention any reason why, except Lord Garadon will be the new governor, and I, I go back to the army . . .'

The river Snarda had frozen so hard that a road of planks and straw had been laid across it, saving the building of a bridge until the thaw came; on the other side, gap-toothed wooden walls reared on the lip of the valley, ringed by tents and enclosing half-built houses and halls. Polem, when his men had recovered, had set off for the plains immediately, while Aleizon Ailix Ayndra went back to Raq'min to receive the new governor, hand over the

250

instruments of power, and pack up her possessions to leave; it was the end of Sixth Month before she reached New Hope. She sent messengers, before she crossed the river, to announce her arrival; they were directed to the king's tent pitched within the shell of New Hope. Ailixond was standing in the snowy space in front of it, talking to his architect and the heads of the engineers, the artillery and the miners, who had all been pressed into service as builders; it was some time before he bothered to turn to the dismounted riders waiting behind him. 'What do you want of me?'

'My lord . . . the Governor of Haramin announces her approach to the camp of the Grand Army, and the city of New Hope.'

'The Governor of Haramin? – I take it you mean Lord Aleizon Ailix Ayndra, the former governor. How near is she?'

'On the far side of the river, lord.'

'Indeed . . . go fetch Lord Polem, and Lord Arpalond – the rest of the Inner Council may attend if they wish. And the duty company of the Silver Shields, summon them to form an honour guard here, in front of the tent. You of Haramin may wait here – Master Firumin will see to you. So let us settle this rapidly, gentlemen, the ground here . . .' When he had finished with them, they left, and he stood there in the bright cold sunlight, while the Silver Shields formed lines on either side, and the other lords came up to the tent; he stamped his feet occasionally, to warm them in the biting cold. Another aisle of men formed beyond the Silver Shields; he recognised many of them as artillerymen, recruits from Haramin, men who had been sent on Polem's expedition – all who had had some touch on Lord Ayndra in the past. Then one heard the sound of many people approaching, and they came into view: a motley crowd trotting around the horsemen, and the first of the horsemen on a great splendid grey horse, but picked out by black cloak and wide hat; the onlookers, some of them, waved and shouted, and she waved back, she took off her hat and her hair gleamed in the sun. The runners halted where the honour guard began, and she got down from her horse – which, he noted, several competed to hold – and came on on foot, hat in hand, head very high. She squinted in the brightness of the light thrown off the snow, and put her head on one side to open her eyes wide; she looked inquisitive. 'My lord,' she said, 'good day!' and made to bow deeply, but her left foot was on an icy patch, and she slipped and fell to all fours and started to laugh. 'O ho!' she said as she stood up, 'so long I have bowed to no one, I cannot recall how it's done!' and stilled, facing him. Ailixond tossed his heavy

251

fringe from his face and said, 'You will have to learn again, then, now that you are returned from your kingdom.'

'It was never my kingdom,' she said. The hard light drenched his face, contracting the pupils so that blue eyes glowed in the snow-dark skin; a web of lines had hardened his mouth and confined his eyes; he looked his age. The beautiful features had become static, the man, the conqueror, king; the ambiguous, burning youth had disappeared altogether. She said the first thing that came into her head. 'How are you building a city, here, where the ground must be too hard to dig? How can you make foundations?'

'All that you see now is only temporary,' he said, 'wooden shells. When the thaw comes, and the ships can bring stone, then we'll make foundation for the true buildings, that'll go up next year. But come inside, and we shall talk.' He favoured her with a smile, and swung round in a drift of white furs. His face might show its thirty-odd years, but he walked as gracefully as ever. She stuck her hand in her mouth; then took it out to greet Polem and Arpalond, as they went into the tent.

The Council, as had usually been their habit, stared at her. It had usually been her habit to ignore them; now she stared back. She beckoned to Polem.

'What is it?'

'I forgot to tell you this earlier – but in a very few months' time, you will be a grandfather.'

'What! – how ever –'

'Did you ever meet the young woman from the stillroom who was Parro's companion in Raq'min?'

'What young woman? – what, is she – was she –'

'As I said. You will be a grandfather.'

'O! Luamis! Did Parro give her – any money, or –'

'I did not see it, if he did.'

'O, then – if I give you some, will you see that it's sent? And I'll speak to Parro –'

'Hush, hush,' she said, 'Ailixond.'

Most of the business was to do with the building of New Hope, and the sendings being prepared for building materials from all the neighbouring provinces, to be sent as soon as the winter broke; there was a proclamation, too, to be read out in the squares of the towns in every part of the Empire, promising free lands and five years' exemption from all taxes to anyone who cared to come out and settle in the new city. Then there was a

252

report from the Grebenyi, who were encamped for the winter a few miles downstream from the city, but who came to its markets with furs and hides in greater numbers every month: their trappers, who ranged for months over the snowy plains, had met outriders of their neighbours, their enemies, the Gilangi. The grazing lands of the two tribes had a long border, but in their wanderings they might meet once in every one or two years, and would then fight, and attempt to carry off as much of the breeding stock and work animals of the other side as possible, both horses and women. Conditions were hard in the deep plains and the Gilangi were moving further east than usual, since they had heard that there was raiding to be had there. The Old Man of the Grebenyi wanted to attack them immediately, but Ailixond said that he would first send ambassadors, as a prelude to enslaving them. The Grebenyi would send two of their men who understood Gilangi speech, and he wished to send two lords to accompany them; he asked for names. He was asked what his choice would be. He paused, and then said, 'I would name first, Lord Aleizon Ailix Ayndra.'

Sulakon stood up. 'I believe, my lords, that Lord Thaskeldar would be willing to undertake this duty.' The man he signalled to stood up also: one of Sulakon's generation, the decade before Ailixond, who had grown up under old Lord Parakison. 'I would, my lord,' he said.

'I will do it!' called Ayndra from the chairs on the left of the king; she did not bother to stand up. 'Then we have our embassy,' said Ailixond. 'Four men of ours, and four Grebenyi, will go with you, so that you are protected, but never appear like a war party. It will be two days' ride at least, out from New Hope – some more of the Grebenyi will be guides . . .'

The tents of the Gilangi sat like cobwebby button mushrooms in a waste of snow. The Gilangi horsemen crowded like a herd of rough animals around the ambassadors, hunched, dung-smelling, unspeaking, raising a fume of breath and stink around them. They were asked to dismount outside a squat tent with a clump of standards in front of it.

'This Old Man tent,' said the Grebenyi interpreter.

'I do not see how we are to conduct this, if all we have is this incompetent to put their speech into Safic,' said Thaskeldar.

'Ah, we will understand . . .' Aleizon Ailix Ayndra looked sharply at the tribesmen who were leading away Anagar; fortunately, they seemed somewhat in awe of a creature which

253

looked to be of an entirely different world than the shaggy ponies they rode. But the front of the tent had opened, and they were crowded inside. It was thick and gloomy inside; by the time that they could see where they were, they were standing in the middle separated both from the Grebenyi and from their own men. Gilangi ringed them round; in front was a heap of skins and cushions, many squatting around it, and a bulky figure sitting atop of it. When he spoke, they could not help starting: deep and vibrant, speaking Safic and with hardly a trace of accent. 'My lords. Allow me to hear your message.'

Lord Thaskeldar coughed, and brought out a piece of paper. The light was hardly strong enough for reading, but he knew it by heart in any case. He spoke slowly and sonorously, coming gradually through the fence of salutations to the message proper: '. . . you will be welcomed into the New Empire an you only swear allegiance to Lord Ailixond and his heirs. But if you refuse this, then be assured that you will be attacked and subdued, as surely as I subdued the Grebenyi, for –'

The Old Man spat noisily. 'Tcha! I know it all. Your little king says, surrender to me or be slain. Benefits of the Empire? O aye, sweets given to a slave they are, sweets to bind the chains tighter. We have all that we need here.' He stood up; he was tall and very broad. 'Little Ailixond may think that he can deal with us as with the Grebenyi – ha! A woman could defeat them, cravens that they are. He may attack us if he wishes.' He laughed, strolling toward the ambassadors.

'Do you reject the terms of peace?' Lord Thaskeldar asked stiffly.

The Old Man halted within arm's length of him. 'Yes.'

'Then we shall depart,' Lord Ayndra said pleasantly. 'We may well meet again, sir, but until then . . .' She made a mocking half-bow and turned to leave. The Old Man hissed: 'No, no, no!' Hands seized her arms; a whole wall of Gilangi had crept across the doorway. They turned her to face him again.

'Sir! I pray you, permit us to leave,' said Thaskeldar.

'Permit you? Ah, but arrogance has always been a fault in the lords of Safi; I think you will regret it in a while, now.' He reached out, and took Ayndra's hand in a vise-like grip. 'May I remind you – we are ambassadors, and inviolate?' she said.

'In civilised lands, may be; but you are with the barbarians now.' He regarded her with eyes hooded by fat. 'So what have we here? A man on the verge of old age, and a mere youth, yet to hear them, you would think they were chosen of heaven . . . you

254

will be disillusioned, I think.' He said to Thaskeldar, 'For you, I know how . . . make the most of your sight, for you'll not have it much longer.' Four or five men surrounded him, and stopped his mouth with a cloth; they pulled him backward, but Lord Ayndra was pinned down by the Old Man's hold. 'And what shall we do with you, pretty boy?' he said, and twined his fingers in her hair. 'What long locks . . . it would look fine on my standard, so fair, so fair . . .' His hand glided across her cheek. 'So Ailixond sends beardless boys on his missions now? Smooth as a woman . . .' The large fingers slid down her neck, into her shirt – then jerked back, as if burned. She lifted her head; her eyes glared, her mouth was like a box. 'Ye gods!' he said. 'You are a woman – and such lovely blue eyes! They are indeed short of men in Safi.' He barked a command, and the Gilangi surged forward; some started to pull at her clothes, but the Old Man barked again, and they desisted; she stood there with one shoulder bared, rigid with desperation. A thin voice creaked behind the Old Man, and a claw of a hand twitched at his sleeve; a bent, filthy old man, his white hair yellow with smoke and grime, spoke in a voice like a child's. The Old Man blinked at him, then grinned. 'Ah! It seems that we cannot do to you as we will to your companion, lest the grass die when the Earth Mother forsakes us for blinding a woman – but we will find something for you, do not fear . . .' His lackeys closed in and hustled her out of the tent, through daylight to a low leather structure; a flap was lifted, and she was thrown into an ill-smelling darkness, landing on hands and knees in rough straw. The light from the door disappeared; voices chittered for a while, and receded. She crawled forward until her head ran into a leather wall; then felt her way around it, until she had satisfied herself that she was imprisoned in a vast leather bag. She sat back for a while; then fished inside her tunic. The Gilangi must have trusted the Safeen to observe the convention that ambassadors went unarmed. She took out her knife, and set to work on the thongs which laced up the door-flap. It was a slow job; the knife had not been razor-sharp, and grew rapidly blunter. Sometimes horses passed, or people talking, and she had to wait till they were gone. She had been at it for perhaps two hours when a large group approached, came very close, halted; she stuffed the knife back in its hiding place, and crawled back in the darkness. Someone began to pull at the thongs, got halfway down and stopped with an exclamation: they had found the cut. The flap was hauled up, but bodies blocked the light. She pressed back against the back wall. Someone bawled an incomprehensible summons; then stertorous breathing came closer, and great hands seized her, though she struggled, and hauled her out.

It was afternoon. The frozen, trampled snow was treacherous, slick with the heat of the sun. The Gilangi past whom she was dragged jeered at her as she slithered to the edge of the camp, where a tall wooden post stood in the snow, thongs dangling from the top of it. The Old Man stood in a crowd of attendants not far away; she could not see Thaskeldar anywhere.

'Bind her up,' said the Old Man. One of her captors fumbled at the clasp of her cloak. She pushed him off. 'I will do it.' It was her best scarlet; it looked like blood already when they threw it down. They indicated that she should also take off her overtunic; she hesitated, and they pulled it open. Her knife tumbled out. The Old Man hooted with pleasure. 'Ha! The kitten has claws,' he said. 'You will wish you had used it to cut your throat – but come on, my pretty little lord, the sooner you strip, the sooner it will be over with.' Ayndra looked round at the grinning faces, anticipant eyes; she returned their glances with a sullen glare, and slid her arms from the tunic sleeves. The chill struck her immediately; she stepped up to the post, and began to unlace her heavy linen shirt. Hands took hold of it behind her, and pulled it down over her shoulders; she folded her arms over her breasts, until another pair of Gilangi seized her hands, pulled them up and bound her wrists to the thongs at the top of the post. Her face was thrust against the stained wood, her back arched: she had to stand on her toes if she was not to hang from her hands.

'Begin,' said the Old Man.

There was a whistle, a whine, and a line of fire snapped from shoulders to waist – crack! and the other diagonal was drawn. Crack! right across, the whip's slender tip curling round her ribs. Crack! and she could not help stiffening under each blow, her back felt as if it had been set alight, she bit her lip, impotent hands fisting in their bonds, the crowd blurred and ran, the wood scarred her face –

'Enough.'

She waited for the next blow, but it did not come. Instead a finger intruded itself below her chin, forcing up her slumped head.

'How did you like it, then, my lord? You did not find it pleasant? Have you lost your tongue? Come, speak to me – do you never say a word?'

'Not to you,' she said.

'O, the proud one! You'll not be so proud next day, when the whip takes off the fresh scabs. Twenty or thirty strokes each day

. . . by the fifth, unless you are stronger than you look, they'll have to carry you here, and by the eighth – have you no answer?' His hand strayed down, over her ribs, and thumbed the hard nipple of one breast. 'Ah, but still . . . if you were to agree to join my household, then you need suffer no more, so long as you do . . .' She lifted her head, and spat full in his face. He inhaled; and dealt her a back-handed blow across the face, slamming her head against the post, and turned away. The thongs at her wrists were loosed; as soon as the tension went, she fell to her knees in the bespattered snow, but they yanked the clothes up over her back, heaved her up by her raw shoulders, and hustled her back to the prison tent, cast her into the straw. She lay there face down, breathing shallowly and listening to the thump of the blood in her ears. Then a hand touched her arm.

She started up and lashed out wildly; the other scrabbled at her, and moaned. She reached out, and knocked against a heavy bandage. 'What is it?' she said.

'Who are you – who –'

'Lord Thaskeldar?'

'Lord – Aleizon Ailix Ayndra?'

'Shumar! – what have they done to you?'

'I – I cannot see, nothing, it's all gone! I'm blind! They held a hot iron, very close, can't shut your eyes even if you do, it's red and it all went black and I can't see anything, anything, god in heaven, it hurts –' His voice broke, he struggled against sobs.

'It's very dark in here,' she said. 'I cannot see a thing.' Blind as he in the stuffy blackness, she reached out for his hand; he jerked it away from her. She sat on in the blackness while he wept on the other side of the tent.

In the evening, a pitcher of cold water and a pan of greasy soup was pushed in, but he would have none of either. The night was very cold, and she woke up every time she fell asleep. About midday they came and took her away again. It was the same as the day before, except that, when they pulled her shirt off, all the soft scabs which had stuck to it came away with it, and the Old Man, though he watched, did not speak to her. Thaskeldar did not ask where she had been, and she did not offer to tell him.

On the third day, when they had tossed her in – they had had to put her on her feet to get her to walk, she was like a drunkard – he crawled over and said, 'Where do you go to?'

'Nowhere,' she said, and hid her face in the straw.

On the next day, when they cut her down afterward, she fell down in the slushy snow and lay there; a gaoler splashed icewater over her until she revived, and they could get her back to the prison on her feet – just. The evening and the night and the next dawn blurred into a haze of sick dreams. She heard people shouting some of the time, but then at other times she thought that people far away were there in the tent with her, or that she was somewhere else entirely. 'Do you hear anything?' she said to Thaskeldar.

'I do not know,' he replied. He was hostile; it seemed that he both feared and despised her. She lay down, and dropped back into the dreams. The leather floor started to rock and sway; spears of light poked her head; she covered it with her cloak. Hallucinatory voices called to her; she tried to curl up, but her back was too stiff and sore. Then someone took hold of her arm, and loud Safic voices called her – people had opened up the tent, and were trying to get her to come out. She took hold of Thaskeldar's hand, and, blinking like a daystruck owl, staggered out; he followed with his bandaged head thrown back, straining to hear what went on around him. As they emerged, there was a concerted sigh; among the tents were half the lords of the Companion Cavalry, on foot now, and the Silver Shields; they all carried weapons, and were fully armed, except Ailixond who stood in the middle of them with his helmet off. Someone took Thaskeldar's hand away from her, and they were all shouting and exclaiming, except Ailixond, who said nothing at all. She went on walking toward him, because the ground was swaying so much that if she tried to stand still she would fall down. Polem was waving his hands, but she could not tell what he said. Thaskeldar was speaking. 'Hot irons,' he said, 'blind!' Blind, blind, blind went the voices in her head. She saw that Ailixond was looking at her. A swarm of bees was encroaching on the outskirts of her vision. Someone said, 'And how is it that Lord Ayndra escaped punishment?' The bees were all over everything, except for Ailixond. 'But I did not,' she said, and pitched forward into the buzzing blackness. Still Ailixond did not move.

Arpalond leapt forward, and slipped an arm round her; she was white as a sheet, with a livid purple bruise on one cheek. Her back felt somehow pulpy, like a bruised apple; he peeled back the red cloak, and gasped. The once-grey overtunic was sodden with blood and pus, caked black and brown all over, with thick bars of crimson soaking through.

'Thaskeldar!' said Ailixond. 'What has befallen her?'

'What? What? I do not know! Every day she used to go off with them, traitor –'

'No traitor,' said the king. 'I think she has been flayed alive.'

'Flayed? But I knew nothing of it, nothing –'

In Arpalond's arms, Ayndra rolled over and opened her eyes. 'What's this?' she said thinly.

'What have they done to you?' cried Polem.

'Flogged me,' she said dreamily, 'every day – four days now. Have you driven them off? Did you take the Old Man?'

'He has escaped,' said Ailixond.

'Will you pursue him?'

'Of course.'

'Then will you . . . will you promise me – one thing –'

'What is it?' he said. She blinked at him, and almost laughed. 'O, not much,' she whispered, 'but when . . . you catch him . . . let me kill him . . .'

'It's your gift,' said Ailixond. But she had fainted again.

It was a bad time of year to go on a chase over the plains: the snow was melting, and the ice on the Snarda groaned and thundered as it broke up and moved on down to the sea. The Grebenyi volunteered to go after the Gilangi; after reinforcing them with his own light horse and mounted slingers, and supplying them with weapons, Ailixond let them go. He had extracted a blood oath from the Old Man of the Grebenyi that he would bring back the Old Man of the Gilangi alive. It was Seventh Month before they returned; and he was in their midst, his feet tied together under the belly of his horse, deprived of his weapons – his captors showed a fine Safic sword, but of a pattern twenty years old – and appearing not in the least affrighted.

'Well, well,' he said, when he was brought to the royal tent, 'if it is not the little king and his would-be female man!'

Ailixond ignored the remark. 'You know my terms.'

'And you know that I have rejected them.'

'Then you know what your fate will be.'

'To be taken about in chains to prove your manhood, no doubt, little one.'

'I need no such proofs,' said Ailixond dispassionately. 'You will die here, and very soon.'

'At my hand,' Aleizon Ailix Ayndra stepped forward. The Old Man smiled. 'Is your back yet healed? Well enough to press a mattress with your noble lovers again? What, are you –' Polem gagged him with a gloved hand. Ayndra drew her knife.

'Wait,' said Ailixond. 'You are not of this land. Tell me your name.'

259

'What interest has it for you?'

'I wish to know it,' said Ailixond. 'I shall write it in the Chronicle. Although I do not intend to ask you how it is that a Safin came to be Old Man of a tribe in the grass plains.'

'Have it, then! They used to call me Gamarro.'

Ayndra opened her eyes. 'Wait,' she said. 'Did you not use to command Thaless Gate? In Safi?'

The Old Man, for the first time, looked surprised. 'You know that, do you?'

'You were dismissed on a charge of gross immorality – but do you not remember me?'

'I cannot imagine how one so fine as you slipped my mind, o lady-lord, but I cannot . . .'

'It was a long time ago.' She moved closer to him. 'Do you not recall Aleizon Ailix Ayndra?'

'No, I . . . haa! Ah, but surely not! A lord of Safi? No! Was it your baseborn sister, perhaps?'

'I have no sister,' she said.

'What? O, I cannot believe it! And you a lord of Safi? And I can guess how! So it's true that it sets them all on the path to –' Then she stuck the knife in his throat, and he stopped laughing, she jerked it out, thrust it in, again and again – dark blood soaked his furs, and he sagged like a punctured wineskin. She stood over him, breathing heavily. 'There,' she said.

Ailixond, behind her, asked, 'What was the meaning of that?'

'I thought that I had met him before,' she said, 'and I had . . . I never thought that I would receive such a chance for vengeance – but that it should be him again, o . . .'

'We must see to the rest of them,' he said, dismissing the incident.

The Outer Council met on the twenty-third day of Seventh Month. The winter had left them, the grass was fresh, the trees leafing; the Gilangi were finished, and they and the Grebenyi had been so organised as to keep one another in check, while colonists were on the road already now that spring had come, and ploughing had started (though the deep tangled sod was proving unexpectedly resistant, and it might be that a new, heavier iron plough would have to be made for these plains) and the fleet had loaded up with building supplies . . . 'and it is a new campaigning season,' Ailixond said. He looked around, and, in chairs, on benches, limbs stiffened and spines straightened. 'We have no more than chewed the edge of the grass plains,' he said. 'And there

260

is our ancient foe of S'Thurrulass, lying south and west, and unknown lands lying beyond that, all the way to the encircling ocean – the world is at our feet now! Any part, we have but to reach out . . .' He saw that the audience did not like his speech, and paused. There was a rustle among the officers' benches, and a man stood up. 'My lord.'

'Captain Carmago? Be pleased to speak.'

'Yes. My lord . . .' Carmago took a deep breath. 'My lord – I would have you know, first, that I do not speak for myself but for many others, my own phalanxmen, and the Silver Shields, and horsemen, and the auxiliaries, and I know not how many more, and this is what I have to say – you can say what you will about new worlds, lord, and you can go and conquer where you like, lord, that is your right. You are the king. Only, lord, if you will go on further you will have to get a new army, for if you will go on away from Safi, lord, we will not follow you.'

Ailixond's hands fell slack at his sides. 'You,' he said clearly, 'you are saying that you refuse any longer to follow me.'

'That's it, my lord,' said Carmago.

Sulakon exclaimed, 'Mutiny!'

Ailixond stared at Carmago; he spoke slowly, as if his attention were elsewhere. 'You realise that this is treason, and may be punished as such – death, or imprisonment for life.'

'I know it, lord, and you can put me to trial if you will, but lord, you can't hardly execute the whole army, nor imprison them neither.'

'The whole army?' Ailixond said bleakly.

'Yes, my lord. It's been twelve years, you see, there's a lot of us that have been twelve years on the road, even got wives and families back home we've not seen in all that time, our children grown up and our wives most like off with some other man, and all these new lands – we've had our fill of them, lord. We won't go any further. We want to go home.'

'We. You say you speak for a great number – how many of you here? How many? Stand up! You need not fear. Show yourselves.'

He waited; another captain got to his feet, then the man next to him, then a whole bench, then twelve, twenty . . . more than three-fourths of the army's officers revealed themselves, mutineers. Ailixond's eyes fixed on the space in front of him. He said, 'Indeed, gentlemen, I thank you, for such a civil mutiny I've never seen.'

Someone at the back said, 'It's for you've always been civil to us, lord, we couldn't ask for no more than you've given us – it's just, well, lord, we won't go on any more.'

'And the men?' said Ailixond. 'They too?'

'More than us, my lord.'

'Then I . . . I would speak with all these thousands, that you carry with you. It's eighth hour now – the first hour after noon, at the gates of New Hope. Assemble there, and prepare your demands. There'll be no treachery on my part, I promise, I'll have no guards ready to slaughter your leaders, or any other – come, then, and we shall talk. And see what follows – but go, now! Go!' He stood with his hands folded and his face calm and set, until all the commoners, and the lords who were not close to him, had left; then he spun round, and his face lit up. 'How many of you knew of this?' he demanded.

'My lord! How could you let them go? They're traitors!'

'O, hush, Sulakon! What else was there to do? But how many of you knew?'

Polem stood up, cleared his throat. 'I knew.' He hung his head, and began to babble. 'I knew that Carmago – I knew that something – I mean, not this, I couldn't have said, but it's true that –' Ailixond made a dismissive gesture, and he dried, stood there looking utterly dismayed.

'I, similarly,' said Arpalond. Half a dozen other voices agreed.

'And I suppose you all thought that if you said nothing, then it would all go away? – or is it that you agreed with them? You too wish to go home to Safi, home, to where you can sit and cultivate a vineyard and go once a year to Thaless, and for that you'd exchange – o, anything, have you not thought? All the lands to the west – but no, you'd rather rot in Safi –'

'Better in Safi than in some godforsaken barbarian land,' said Hasmon.

'I think we should go back,' said Lakkannar. 'I've had my fill of all this – one land the same as another, after a while, and no wine, and the people, all dirty and foreign . . .'

'You have done enough for two lifetimes,' said Golaron. 'Can you not go to Safi now, with your family – watch your son grow up, get more sons, secure the provinces – you've twenty years in front of you, perhaps . . . let the men rest, and in a few years you'll have a fresh crop who'll let you take them wherever you wish, over the sea – but let us have a few years of peace, in the meanwhile.'

'Peace,' said Ailixond, 'peace! Are there none of you who do not desire stagnation?'

'I do not,' said Aleizon Ailix Ayndra. Every eye in the room

262

swivelled to her face. She looked up. 'I'll go to any place,' she said, 'for what I am worth.' It was not clear in what degree she spoke sincerely. Ailixond looked at her, then tossed his head. 'Thank you. Any of you who choose to attend at first hour may do so. Good day.' The curtains stirred and rippled in the draught of his passage, and he was gone.

Polem put his head in his hands. Sulakon and Golaron made tête-à-tête; Aleizon Ailix Ayndra sat still, blank-faced.

'Thank god that's out at last!' Lakkannar said jubilantly. 'A year from now, we'll sit in the Hall of Stars —'

'Are you so sure?' said Arpalond. 'Five gets you fifty . . .' he jabbed his thumb at the curtains '. . . gets a compromise that's at least two-thirds his own way.'

'But this meeting with the mutineers — rankest folly, I call it!' Sulakon was saying, his voice rising. 'An he thinks he can sway them — more likely they will —' He was interrupted by a minor explosion; it was Lord Ayndra spitting on the floor. She grinned at him, and went out.

Ailixond emerged from his self-imposed seclusion only an hourtenth before the time of the meeting. He found that most of the lords were waiting in the front hall of his tent.

'A bodyguard awaits you without,' said Sulakon.

'Send it away.'

'But what an —'

'But what nothing! Tyrants who go in fear of their subjects need bodyguards, perhaps.' He blew past them like a white whirlwind; they followed him like scraps of paper caught in the wind's wake. The tents and half-built houses were empty, only a few women and children peering out, but there was the rumble of a large crowd from the place where the gate would be. They had not gone far toward it, when they found the way blocked; it seemed that the whole army of Safi were there. The lords halted, gathering round Ailixond.

'We should perhaps — if we could get round —' Polem began.

'Nonsense!' said Ailixond. 'We shall go through.' He strode up to the nearest knot of soldiers; when they turned round, they melted like ice in an oven. 'Excuse me, gentlemen,' Ailixond said, and walked on. He did not need to speak again; a path opened like magic through the middle of the crowd, breasting ahead of him as if he carried a glass shield. He walked undefended through his mutinous army, unobstructed and untouched; faces pressed in around his train of lords, but the lord of empire chose his path at

263

liberty. They flattened themselves against the wall as he climbed the steps to the mason's platform over the gateway; as he arrived there, the dark crowd turned pale in a slow wave of faces lifting to the sky, and the packed mass gave a deep sigh.

Ailixond stepped to the edge of the platform and raised his hand. 'Gentlemen,' he said. 'My comrades of so many battles – I cannot speak to you each one. Have you any of your number who will take it upon them to speak for their brothers?'

There was a stir near the platform; climbing on some hidden eminence, or lifted by his comrades, a man appeared head and shoulders above the crowd: a face wrinkled, scarred and blackened by years of war, above a matted squirrel-fur collar and a grimy frieze gambeson.

'I know you,' said Ailixond. 'Cabbo, file leader in the second battalion of phalanx.'

'Tha's me.'

'Speak: I listen.'

Cabbo nodded his head up and down a few times, cleared his throat, and began. 'My lord king. We've heard tell that now the winter's done, you want go on into the grass plains, and we've all come here to tell you, if that's what you want, we'll not do it.'

'No! We'll not go! We've had enough!'

'– we'll go no further. And we don't want no more of barbarian lands – and barbarians coming into government, we want to go back to Safi, my lord king. We want to go home.'

'Home! Home!' More and more voices started to clamour. Fists beat on the walls and the struts of the platform. 'Barbarians out! Foreigners out! Home! Home! Safi!' Cabbo bellowed, 'Shut up!' Ailixond waited, poised, for the racket to wear itself out. He looked around; the crowd in places seemed ready to work itself up into a riot. He took a deep breath, and yelled at the full pitch of his lungs – 'SILENCE!' A shocked quiet fell like a curtain in his vicinity; others on its edge found themselves shouting in quiet, and subsided; still more heeded their captain's cries; peace spread outward like waves from a stone in water. Ailixond caught Cabbo's eye. 'Continue, sir,' he said.

'An' we've seen half the army come to be made up of barbarians, and there's some say that Safi's not even to be the capital any more, but some other place, and barbarians for officers and a barbarian for queen – when it's us of Safi that's been left dead all over the battles we won for you lord, we fought for this Empire, and now, we want to keep it. We want what's ours and we want to go home!' He ceased and the shouting began again.

Ailixond held up his hand; the noise lessened.

'So,' he said. 'You want the Empire, and yet you want a life of ease and comfort, and no more travelling and fighting – but do you think that we can have one without the other? How many of you remember what Safi was like thirty years ago? A struggling city, controlling a few miles of land, forever at war with the Lysmalish and the Thaless, raided by pirates and S'Thurrulass – that was when a fox-skin cloak was riches! But the king my father saw that we need not live so hard. He began to train the Silver Shields, and the phalanx, and captured Thaless, and when I succeeded him, thirteen years ago, I saw that we, ourselves, were a weapon which could conquer the world. You, the army of Safi, you have trampled the armies of Lysmal, of the Needle's Eye, of the Land-beyond-the-Mountains, Haramin, the Seaward Plains – even these grass plains which were said to be unconquerable by an army out of the citied lands, even them we have made our own. Thirteen years I have led you to victory – thirteen years, and not one of you has been killed in flight. I have not flinched from shedding my own blood, in the same ranks as the rest – and if I have won an empire, how many of you have ranks and riches now that you would not have dreamt of when first we set out? My father found you in rags. If you but let me, I will leave you in silk and gold and jewels! We stand at the brink, at the brink of conquests such as no one has ever dreamed of, let alone achieved – lands compared to which that which we hold now are no more than children's playfields, and waiting to be taken! Think what you hold now. You can have ten, fifteen, twenty times as much – or,' he paused, 'you can go home. Leave it all. Go, and sit still, like old men past working, living on the memories of past glories – you can go home and rot! The choice lies with you.'

There was, at first, silence; then the rumble of voices began.

'No! No! Home! We want to go home!'

'Safi! Safi! Safi!'

Ailixond lowered his hands. 'So,' he said, so quiet that only those on the platform heard him, 'rot, then, and may you live long to regret it!' He leapt down the stairs. Polem ran after him. Sulakon stepped out to face the crowd. 'Gentlemen!' he shouted. 'Gentlemen! I beg you, cease this noise, and disperse! Lord Ailixond is answered. I assure you that we shall all set out on the road to Safi – to the capital of the World Empire!' Cheers greeted his speech, fists, hats thrown in the air, stamping, shouting – 'We go home! Home!'

265

The full moon floated over the wide waters of the Snarda; the trees at the side of the river tottered on eroded black webs of roots, strange lumps of earth, tufts of grass and bushes nesting among them; some had fallen over, and lay half in the water, the river singing through the net of branches. The cool air was filled with the green smell of water. In the direction of New Hope, a faint glow dimmed the stars, and the sound of rejoicing banished sleep; but it was quiet by the river. Ailixond walked cat-silent through the trees, picking a way through the bars of light and shadow, foreign stars like splinters in the sky. Something landed with a heavy splash in the water; he stopped, and looked for its source. There was a second splash; he scanned the water's edge. There was a strange excrescence on the bank there, almost . . . ah, it moved, it threw another stone. He walked up to the tree by which the other sat, and leant against the ridged bark. 'Good evening,' he said.

The pebble-thrower gave a strangled shriek. 'Ha! God's teeth, what are you at, you son of a whore? Will you make me fall in?'

'You should curb your language,' Ailixond said.

'What? – o, god's teeth! Good evening, my lord, if I had known – still if you will creep up unobserved . . .'

'Still you were better not to express yourself in a stream of imprecations.'

'O, I try not to. I do not succeed, but I try . . .'

'What are you at, besides, my lord? Sitting out here when all the camp is so festive.'

'Festive? I want none of their festivity.'

'Do you not? You could ride in triumph down the Street of Dreams.'

'Perhaps I could. There are other things in life than those found in the Street of Dreams.'

He did not reply for a while. An owl screamed in the wood.

'If you wish to go back to Haramin –'

'Have I said that I do? Unless, of course, you wish that I –'

There was another pause. He said finally, 'I did send for you to come back here.'

'You did . . . I'm not ungrateful. I began to think already, there, I have been too long in one place.'

'Well. You are threatened now with being even longer in one place.'

'You are wrong in that.'

'How am I wrong?'

'Because, even an we do all return to Safi, and I too, I need not

266

stay there, I can go on an embassy to Suthine, I can go back to Raq'min, I can go live in the country . . .'

'But I cannot do that.'

'No,' she said. Then she said, 'But can you even do it now?'

'Do what?'

'Go further – look, I have seen what it is to administer the lands you hold now – how much more can you do? O, yes, if you had good governors, but those that you have now are not all so good, so you watch over them, and going on and on will not make them any better, only if you sit down for a while and teach them, then you could go to other places, but now . . . you've conquered all these lands, and I do not say that it was easy, or that any other could have done it, but it's over and gone, and then, to hold the conquered lands – now that is the test. Do you not think?'

His head turned toward her. The moonlight caught his eyes, slid irregularly over his features; his teeth showed. 'What are you saying? That what they have done is all for my own good?'

'I'm no judge of good,' she said. 'I only judge what can be done, or done best, not how good or evil it is.'

'But you say that I overreach myself?'

'The Empire's a half year's journey end to end already,' she said.

'Ah, but with attention to the seas, and the navigable rivers, and the roads built up –'

'Which take time, and money, that's not to be had if the court is off in distant fastnesses –'

'Aaah,' he said, a long sigh of frustration; he beat his hands on the tree-trunk. She fell silent. The river chuckled and slopped, reeking of spring.

Ailixond said softly, 'The worst of it is, if I had known earlier – Arpalond, Polem – for how long have they known that these things went on? And the others – whether they went in fear of me, or whether they had a part in it, or whether, even, they did not care –'

'You slander Polem if you say he does not care.'

'O yes? Then what was he at?'

'I think – I cannot speak for him, but I think that he . . . he wanted to protect you.'

'Protect me!' exclaimed Ailixond with shuddering ferocity. 'What, to keep me safe from the harsh truth? I swear, hiding the truth is as great a deceit as lying straight on –'

'As you should know!' she responded.

'What?'

'There has been more than one occasion when you did not tell the Council the whole, or even the better part, of what you knew to be going on, in order to sway their decision —'

'O indeed? When was this?'

'Well, for once, outside Raq'min, when you got a letter from Yourcen, and the translation you gave of it — well, it was not honest —'

'And how should you know?'

'Well — I was a new captain, then, and Polem wanted someone to read Haraminharn tongue, and I — he swore me to secrecy, then —'

'Polem, eh?' Ailixond said bitterly.

'You ought not to criticise him,' she said.

'Ought I not? Why are you so much in favour of him?'

'You have no more loyal servant than Polem — no more loyal friend. And if you hate anyone over this, it should not be him.'

'Indeed? And who are you to tell me what my friendships are, or should be?'

She turned to face him, but her face was in the moonshadow. 'You know who I am,' she said.

'Do I?'

'Do you not? Then if you do not, Ailixond, I shall not tell you.' She leapt down from the tree-root, on to the narrow beach of river sand, and dashed along it; in a few moments she was out of sight. Ailixond stood still for some time; when he moved at last, it was to drop down where she had been sitting, and stay there, with his head resting in his hands.

Like iron needles to a lodestone, the lords gravitated, after they had been out riding in the early morning, to the king's tent; they muttered in groups, or lay down and dozed, or sat saying nothing, and looked out at intervals and saw that the crowd of commoners outside had grown still larger. It was a quiet crowd; they did not shout, or brandish weapons; they were waiting. No one needed to ask what they waited for; the lords were waiting for the same.

'Sit down,' said Arpalond to Polem, 'or go elsewhere.' Polem sat down for perhaps an hourtenth, but got up and started pacing again.

'You will wear a groove in the floor,' said Lord Ayndra.

Arpalond wandered over to the door. 'More of them than ever . . . listen, they've started calling.'

'What do they say?'

'That they want to see the king . . . they want him to come out and speak to them.'

'He must come out,' said Golaron. He looked at Sulakon, who got up. 'I will go and ask him to come out.' He headed for the curtains, but Polem got in his way. 'Excuse me,' said Sulakon.

'I will go,' said Polem.

'No. I think it better that I —'

'No, I will go.'

'My lord. I think it better if a blood relative goes.'

'But —' said Polem.

'And someone who holds some prestige in the army,' Hasmon said. Polem's jaw dropped. 'What!' he said; but Sulakon had passed him, and gone behind the curtains. 'What do you mean, prestige?' said Polem; no one answered him. Silence fell; the muttering of the crowd outside could be heard clearly. Some distant faction had started to chant, 'We want the king! Where is the king?' They waited. Sulakon's raised voice came clearly through: 'You cannot sulk in here any longer, my lord! It is your duty to the state!'

'I am the state! Speak not to me of duty!' The curtains swirled, and Ailixond strode through. Some of the lords rose, some bowed; he waved a careless hand. 'Open the door! And fetch me something to stand on.' There was a sort of cheer from outside as the flaps were pulled back, and someone came up with a footstool, which they carried out and put down in the entrance; when Ailixond went out and stood up on it, the field of faces outside gave a great roar. He waited until they had quietened down. Then he said, 'What have you come to ask me?' The roaring began again; eventually it clarified into one coherent chant — 'Going home! — Where are we going? Going home?' Ailixond shouted, 'You ask, where are we going?' and waited again, until the shouting had died down. Then he said, 'We will go no further! But listen — we'll not turn back — we'll go southaway, due south into the plains, that we may come to Safi as directly as we may, without retracing all our journeys through the north. It will still be long, but — a year perhaps, and we will be in Safi. We're going home!' His last words were lost in a frenzy of jubilation. The massed crowd leapt up and down and shouted, clapped, stamped; and Ailixond stood there, smiling. They all thought he laughed with them.

It took a long time to pack up the winter camp, decide on who should be left to maintain New Hope and receive the colonists, prepare wagons for the road and replace animals lost in

269

the winter; tents and shacks came down, markets packed up, scarred ground and heaps of rubbish were revealed, people carrying strange burdens ran all over; Ailixond drifted through it all, smiling faintly, seeming quite at peace; the rest of the world might be harassed beyond toleration; not he. Ten days later, the first part of the army (almost half – mostly provincial regiments – would wait for another halfmonth until the residents of New Hope began to arrive) was ready to move off; he stood in the wet grass, watching the off-white canvas of his tent billow and sink and be bundled up, leaving a sea of mud and darksickened grass, while the lords' horses stamped and shifted behind him. The king-pole of the tent tilted from the vertical and slid groundward in a great sigh of canvas – 'Psst,' said a voice behind him. He looked round; Aleizon Ailix Ayndra was making her wide-eyed maniacal face at him. 'What is it?' he said.

'I have obtained a map from the land pilot,' she said.

'A map? Surely not.' He looked at the tent. 'I assure you, it will be most inaccurate, if it exists at all. I am well aware that the land pilots do not use maps.'

'I know that they do not, but I still happened to – well, to obtain a map before they went out of use, shall we say?'

'Went out of use? I am sure that I do not understand you.'

'We go away today, southward?'

'That is correct.'

'And it is true that Safi is south of us – well, a little east of south, but we cannot expect to steer directly for Safi at this distance, especially, if we go south and not east, with so many obstacles in the way, like S'Thurrulass, for a start . . .'

Ailixond abandoned his study of the collapsing tent and looked round at her. She was grinning wickedly. He started to smile as well.

'Most soldiers,' he said, 'are ignorant of geography. And most lords similarly. And ignorance is a blessed state.'

'Of course it is! O, S'Thurrulass – I would far rather ride in triumph down the avenues of Suthine!'

'In which case you should keep such far-fetched fantasies to yourself, at least for the time being.'

'O, I will, I will!' She started to laugh. 'S'Thurrulass, hurra!'

'Ay well – you told me it was such a fine place, I could not but . . .' Ailixond lifted his hand to conceal his face, but his shoulders shook with suppressed amusement. The servants were folding up the canvas, and dismantling the poles. 'Come,' he said, 'we should be on our way – for I have promises to keep – all these people, they rely on me to take them home – o, fools that they are!'

'Fools that most of them are,' she said.

'Most of all the ones that do not keep their mouths shut,' he said, and turned to join the rest of the lords.

Lord Ayndra's household had been left in Raq'min for the winter, to travel on when the roads were clear; they set out in late Sixth Month, and, at the end of Seventh Month, she received news that, when they were on the Seaward Road, they had met a cavalcade from Pomoan, bearing the queens of Safi and the little prince, and were travelling with them for mutual protection into the grass plains. From New Hope, they followed the unmistakable swathe of the army through the grass; and, in Eighth Month, they caught up with them. The king received the queen in state; Lord Ayndra excused herself from the ceremony, and rode out to collect her own people alone.

Two days later, she was knee-deep in mud, howling at the team of a dozen men trying to rescue a wagon gone axle-deep into a concealed pothole, when a voice piped, 'My lady, please?'

'God's teeth, pull! – do you not know by now, I am not to be called lady? Go away, till you've learnt to address me.'

'But my lady, my lord, my lady says –'

Ayndra turned her head, and found that a woman in a rose-pink mantle was teetering on high pattens between two escorting archers. 'Which lady?' she said.

'My lady Setha, King's Wife of Safi, mother of his heir,' said the woman fastidiously.

'I hardly thought she was the mother of his mattress. What has she to say to me?'

'My lady, my lord, requests you to visit her, in her coach, at seventh hour this evening. She will be pleased to receive you and any escort you choose to bring.'

'What, again? What is this attraction I have for the House of Women? – pull together, damn you! One, two – pull!' The lady fluttered, the soldiers blasphemed. 'O, tell her I'll come! and I wish her joy of it. Good day.' She stamped off to go to the back of the wagon. 'Let us try and put something under the wheel here . . .' The lady sniffed, and minced off in the opposite direction.

The interior of the queen's coach was a long tunnel of silk curtains, shaded lamps, cushions, heavy perfumed vapours, delicate gilt furnishings; and, at the far end, feet raised on a velvet stool, Lady Setha. She extended a white hand to the raffish figure in heavy boots and mudspattered cloak. 'Good day, my lord. I believe that we have not met before.'

271

'Not properly, no.' The scarecrow swept off its hat and bowed with a courtier's extravagance. 'My pleasure to meet you, lady.'

'Please to be seated, my lord.' A slavewoman brought out another little gilt chair; it creaked dangerously as Ayndra dropped into it. Setha smiled sweetly. 'My lord, Aleizon – may I call you Aleizon?'

'No, you may not. Call me Ayndra, if you will, or else the jawbreaking whole.'

'My lord Ayndra, then – I am delighted to speak with you at last. I have hear much about you.'

'I am sure that you have, but I would tell you to believe none of it, except that I do not know exactly what you have hear, as you say.' Another slavewoman had glided up with a loaded tray. 'Are these to eat?' said Ayndra.

'Please to help yourself, my lord. You were until lately Governor of Haramin?'

'I was.'

'But you decided to return here?'

'Not exactly.' Ayndra grabbed a handful of almond paste figures and stuffed them in her mouth.

'Then you . . . requested it?'

'I was requested,' she said with her mouth full.

'By my lord my husband?'

'In his own hand.'

'Indeed?' Setha said. Ayndra laughed. 'O ho! There speaks the man himself. Did he teach you Safic?'

Setha drew herself up. 'You were tired of Haramin perhaps?'

'You want to know why I came back here? I hoped that you could tell me that, lady. Some say that I was too popular with the people; some that they hated me so much that I had to be removed before they rebelled; some, that I had pretensions to the kingship of Haramin, and intended to rebel; some, that my life in Raq'min was such a scandal to the name of Safi that I must be replaced; some, that I was with child by Lord Polem; some others still, that I had been conducting necromantic rituals in the cellars of White Walls; others, that I had a house of male concubines for my own use; others, that Ailixond had become so lonely without me that he had to recall me . . . o, the list has no end to it.'

'But surely you know which of these . . .'

'I assure you, lady, I do not.' Ayndra finished the last almond paste sweet, and started on the nut cakes. 'Let me look at you,' said Setha.

'What?'

'Please to sit up.'

Ayndra straightened from her lazy slump, but went on munching. 'I do not look very well presently – you should see me in my ceremonial robe, or in armour . . . ah well, some of us have beauty and some of us have wit, and few of us have both, indeed.'

'You should not wear the grey,' said Setha, 'it makes your face the more yellow.'

'Perhaps, but it saves washing. If my face were my fortune, I'd be still in penury.' She bent forward and tested the hem of Setha's gown between her sticky fingers. 'Best silk of Lysmal, fifteen sols the yard. How much gold leaf in a month do you use on your fingernails? O, to have married into money!'

My lord!' said the queen shakily.

'And why have you eaten none of these honeyed delights yourself? Come, you must try one, else you will surely be accused of poisoning me if I should fall ill any time in the next year.'

'Rumour has it,' said Setha, 'that you are my husband's mistress.'

'Rumour says many things. Not all of them are true.'

'But this?'

'Ah, so we come to the heart of the matter – had you prepared a more subtle introduction to the question? I am sorry if I spoilt it for you. Do you wish to tell me to stop if it I am, start it if I am not, or merely to watch my step?'

'Answer!' said Setha, flushing.

'Could you ask me again? I like to be sure what it is that I am replying to.'

Setha's voice rose to a shriek: 'Answer! Are you my 'usband whore?'

Ayndra examined her dirty fingernails. 'Do you mean to say, am I his bedmate, or do you wish to know if I was reimbursed in money for opening my legs?'

Setha was struck dumb by horror and indignation. She spat a few syllables in her native tongue; they did not sound complimentary.

'Then here's your answer,' said Aleizon Ailix Ayndra, picking up her hat. 'I was,' she stood up, 'I am not,' she put the hat on, 'and I will not be. It's done with. Good day, lady.' She swept out in a flail of tattered cloak. Setha clenched her hands into fists, and sputtered after her in the mountain language – 'I will kill you! I hate you! Bitch! Bitch!'

273

It was the nineteenth day of Eighth Month, and already hot
enough for midsummer; although they were no further south than
the north of Haramin, the heat built up early this far in the
interior. By midday, the heat haze shimmered over the distance,
and the feet of the army sent up mouth-clogging clouds of dust;
on the watery horizon, black dots and dashes seemed to move
along it, to swarm and swell into antlike figures, sunlight glinting,
the drumming of hooves underlying them . . .

'More tribesmen?'

'Armed!'

'It's an attack! Attack, alarm, attack!'

'An attack! O, bless them!' Lord Ayndra, hatless and tunicless,
rocketed down the line, and ploughed to a halt by the side of
Yunnil's wagon; she looped the reins over the side and clambered
aboard. 'Yunnil! Yunnil, drat you! Where's my sword?'

Yunnil was sitting in a stupour of heat and boredom in the
driver's seat, the reins slack in her lap, the oxen mindlessly
following the wagon in front of them; waking, she almost tumbled
back into the body of the wagon, and was met by a flurry of shirts
and tunics being tossed out of a chest – 'Ha!' Ayndra dragged out
her sword, sheathed and complete with belt and knife, and knelt
up to buckle it on. 'Yunnil, you are supposed to drive . . . the
night's for sleeping! It would be better if you took yourself now
into the middle of the column, unless you wish to defend yourself
against marauding tribesmen.'

'Your pardon?'

'We are under attack.'

'What? – attack! My lord! Is there –'

'O, as I say, move to the middle of the column, and keep your
head down. You'll be in no danger unless they overwhelm us, in
which case there's no remedy.' She slid over the side of the cart,
back to her horse, and was off like an arrow.

'Attack, attack! Alarm!' The cries disturbed the column as if it
were an ants' nest doused with boiling water; frantic searches for
weapons, sections halting while others marched on or turned
round to look for the assault; but Ailixond said only, 'So – an end
to peace at last! And ourselves caught in column of march, o, my
. . .' His mood snapped out of laziness. 'Get the cavalry to spread
out, flanking the column and all the wagons with those who
cannot fight to the middle of the column, prepared to halt
immediately if ordered, but till then move on and do not break
up! Get a cordon around the baggage, and hand out weapons, but
prevent any wild rush for them . . .' Cheering, jeering, the enemy

274

horsemen rushed up on the army and swerved suddenly to gallop along parallel, rejoicing in the disorder they had created; some had small bows, and arrows arched into the packed ranks; the footmen slowed down, fell out of step, halted, the first wagons ran into the troops in front of them, stop, forward, go back, help! 'A sword! Who has a sword?' cried Ailixond. 'We must head them off – let not them go round to the other side –' he urged his horse forward, the other lords closing round him. They had not had time to get the arms out of the baggage, and they had not been in battle for an age, months and months – 'Has no one a sword?' he yelled.

'Here, my lord!' Aleizon Ailix Ayndra tore up and sprang her sword out in front of him, then tossed it, and he just caught it. 'Bless you!' he said. 'Forward! Charge them, we can beat them back by our weight alone – let not them stay out in bowshot – Safi! To me!' With hunting swords, knives, weapons snatched from marching footmen, the Companions crashed into the attackers. Ayndra was left behind, like a rock when the wave flows away; she raked them with her glance, and kicked her horse back to where the Thaless cavalry rode, or, rather, were milling about – 'This way!' she shrieked. 'Follow me!'

'What is it? What is happening?'

'Lord Ailixond's engaged the enemy – can you not see? They're almost weaponless, they cannot hold out, but if we charge them –'

'But how can we? We're not half armed –'

'No matter! We wait here and they'll all be killed! Just hammer into them!'

'We must –? Who are you, anyway?'

'I'm Lord Aleizon Ailix Ayndra – come on, you god damned cowards! The king needs you!' Her horse reared up and danced round on its hind feet; she spurred it viciously, and it bounded away. Half a dozen Thaless broke away in pursuit, then the rest of the regiment followed, and threw themselves in her wake into the flank of the tribesmen. Ayndra whipped out her knife and drove it into the wool-wrapped back of the first to pass her; he looked round with an expression of surprise and she stabbed him in the neck. He tumbled off his horse, his head striking her thigh as he fell. She laughed hysterically, and drove on. Safeen and plainsmen intermingled in a bloody potpourri, neither side armed with much more than knives; but Ayndra met one swinging a scimitar. She managed to slash his wrist, and he dropped it, but clutched hold of her hand, and they wrestled; he was forcing her arm down to pull the knife from her hand, then he had it free and – she threw

275

herself from her horse at him, and they slid over his pony and struck the ground in a forest of hooves. She fell uppermost, and brought up her knee, jabbed it into his groin. He groaned aloud, but he still held her knife out of reach. A horse gathered itself and leapt over the two of them; he, looking upward, flinched and froze, but she did not see the vast hooves and instead threw herself forward over his face and grabbed the knife. The horse galloped on, and she sat up astride of him and stuck it into his neck. He made a hideous gurgling sound, and his limbs flailed; she held on to him, and heard a great rumble in the air and the ground – glanced up to see god only knew how many horsemen bearing down on her. She shrieked then, terrified, and fell flat on the bloody carcass, arms wrapped round her head. The ground shook like an earthquake, and dark shadows and gusts of air and thundering hooves engulfed her. She lay paralysed, rigid; then, as suddenly as they had come they were gone. She raised herself on jelly arms and looked round. The battle had swirled away; god knew where her horse was, either; and here she was next to a corpse in a sea of trampled grass. There was the wagon train, half a mile away – and, o heaven, here they came again! She flopped down again, praying that the tales about the surefootedness of horses had some truth in them. She burrowed half under the corpse for greater protection, and lay like one dead herself, while they raged back and forth overhead. Voices screamed and shouted, blades clashed; with a scream and disorganised bundling of limbs a body fell to the ground; she shut her eyes and wrapped her arms tighter round her head. The racket ebbed and flowed, a patch of light, then back again, then hooves that beat up to her and halted. She stole a glimpse: ironshod hooves – Safeen, then, and not moving presently. She wriggled out from under the limp body and struggled to her feet; she craned her neck and saw a white tunic. She tried to shout, but it came out a cracked whisper; she coughed, and tried again. 'Ai-ailix!' The rider nearest her rose in a flash of panic, which was not much soothed by the apparition with dust-filled fair hair and blood-spattered clothing that had arisen at his side. The demon smiled, white teeth in a filthy face. 'Where is the king? Is that him there?' She waved, and jumped up. 'Ailixond!' He turned, but looked at rider's level. She ducked under a couple of horse's necks, and came up by his side – 'Here!' At last, he saw her, and it was his turn to jump. 'What have you – are you scathed?'

'No,' she said, 'no, I . . . I sort of fell off, and then – I've been on the ground, you see . . . You've still got my sword.'

'And I thank you for it.' He might have been for a brief gallop, no dustier than at the end of an ordinary day. 'Have we won?' she said.

'Completely routed. They like not to fight at close quarters. And after the Thaless horse came out – I shall reward their captain . . .'

'Will you?' she said. She ran her hands through her hair. Ailixond looked away. 'Is that your horse?'

'I cannot see it.'

'We must go back to the column – what do they there?' He spurred his horse away; the rest of them followed him, leaving her standing again, except for one rider leading another horse by the reins – it was her lost mount. 'I thank you,' she said dully, and struggled up on its back again. People had climbed on the wagons and were cheering to the cavalrymen, who waved to them; Ailixond, she saw, was heading toward the middle of the column where the queens rode. 'Ay well,' she said, and turned her own horse toward Yunnil's cart.

'We are in hostile country now. We should not have forgotten that we have left the lands of our allies the Grebenyi far behind. From now on we shall march behind a double screen of scouts, and the cavalry will ride armed at all times, with, if you can, mail and helmets where you can easily assume them . . .'

'Hostile country, he says . . . where are we? What lands do we have to pass through, if we are going back to Safi by this way? Where do we find a road? Do these plains go on for ever?'

'Where is a map?'

'Ask the land pilot, why do you not?'

'He has none, he says, they do not use them.'

'Where does he say that we go?'

'Southaway, he says. He says he has never been to Safi, he only knows the way he is told to steer – southaway . . .'

But the grass plains did come to an end, and an end as sudden and definite as a line on the unseen map; the hills rose up on the other side of a divide as clear as the cut of a knife, leading away as far as the eye could see to east and west, as if a dish of custard were laid flush with one of piled egg-whites whipped till stiff. The land pilots led them along this edge of a world until they came to a wide valley, with a recognisable track leading into it, the first road-like thing they had seen since they left New Hope; they passed down it, and the hills enfolded them, and the plains passed out of sight. It was two days before they came upon the first proper building they had seen for more than half a year; in the evening, a party of tipsy soldiers wandered across the valley to the walled, slit-windowed farm, and beat on the barred gate. 'Come out, you'n there! Come out! Welcome your returnin' heroesh!' No one answered; they beat harder. 'Come out, damn you!' A shrill voice gabbled on the other side of the gate; someone appeared on the roof that overlooked it, and shrieked in a foreign language. The soldiers argued, and suggested that they should beat their way in. They found a piece of wood and beat upon the gate with it. The people within yammered, and an arrow fell out of the dark and transfixed one of their number. They fled back to the camp, dragging the wounded man, gave him the rest of the drink and extracted the arrow –

'But I thought we was in Safi!'

'Well, mebbe we're not quite there yet – shut your mouth.' But next morning, on the march, their friend lagged behind, and had to be put on a wagon, and then the captain started to ask questions; he took their tale to Lord Golaron, who took it to the king, who summoned Lord Ayndra. They talked in secret for a while, and then she left by Firumin's door, while he sent for the lords of the Inner Council, to listen to Golaron speak.

When they had done fulminating, he said, 'The principal question is, where exactly do we find ourselves?'

'Have you not questioned the land pilot?' said Sulakon. 'Why, indeed, have we gone on so far if we did not know whither they were leading us?'

'Let us go arrest him now!' said Lakkannar. 'I'll do it.'

'And I,' said Polem. Sulakon went with them, and a party of guards. They had only just made a noisy departure when Aleizon Ailix Ayndra wandered in; she looked shifty. Golaron still stood in the middle of Ailixond's small travelling tent. 'But for how long have we not known where we are?' he said.

'It was quite clear: we were travelling through the plains,' Ailixond said. 'We should have hoped to reach the Girran marshes after we left them, but whether the land north of the Girran is inhabited, and by hostile peoples . . .'

'Would not any people be hostile if drunken soldiers come beating their door down in the middle of the night?' said Lord Ayndra.

'But if our path has wandered, where may they have brought us to?' asked Golaron.

'There is only one place, in truth,' she said, 'and that would be the northern marches of S'Thurrulass.'

278

'S'Thurrulass!' said Lord Hasmon.

Ayndra sat down on the bench at the side of the tent. 'It's the archers of S'Thurrulass one should watch out for,' she remarked. 'Long bows, most dangerous, they can pierce mail even, and that at a good range.'

'But what are we to do if we are in S'Thurrulass?' said Hasmon.

'Turn back.'

'Get some new guides.'

'From where? Growing in the trees perhaps?' she said.

'Surely all this is in vain until our present guides are brought here,' said Arpalond. Ayndra raised her eyebrows a little in Ailixond's direction, but he was rocking his chair back and forth and staring at the roof. Suspicious glances were traded round the gathering; silence fell; they listened. 'What is that noise?'

'My lord!' Lakkannar burst in. 'Fled! The pilots are all fled. Run off!' The rest of the arrest party bundled in after him – 'All gone! Aye, and it seems that their servants went yesterday, and took their baggage!'

'It seems we have uncovered a conspiracy!' declared Sulakon. The Council broke into a confusion of dismay.

'What are we to do now?'

'Are we not well and truly lost?'

'Go back!'

'Impossible! We should wander around in circles in the plains – and besides, ridiculous to retrace our steps –'

'We have been tricked!'

'How were they allowed to get away?'

'Why did we not question them sooner?'

'Because,' said Ailixond, 'nothing seemed amiss – we knew that we might have to pass through unsubdued lands to return home most directly, indeed, we knew it –'

'Did we?'

'Have we no maps?'

'For how long have we been wandering at the mercy of –'

Ailixond smacked the arm of his chair. 'Silence!' he exclaimed. 'Now let us consider. We do not know where we are; nevertheless, it is most likely that we are in the north of S'Thurrulass, having come down some way west of our preferred destination. Waste no time cursing those who are imagined to have tricked or misled us. I shall post rewards for their capture, and, otherwise, it is too late. But consider our next action.'

'And what should that be?'

'S'Thurrulass is full of witches –'

279

The king stood up. 'Silence!' he said furiously. 'It seems to me that, firstly, we shall continue for the time being the advance along the road on which we find ourselves, and, secondly, that we shall endeavour to question such inhabitants as we find, and, thirdly, that we shall proceed with more caution than we have lately been accustomed to employ – guards day and night, and no more excursions . . . and, finally, we shall not make it generally known that this misfortune has befallen us, since I think it unwise to spread alarm among the people. Nor shall we bicker among ourselves. Do you understand?'

They responded sullenly. He sat down again.

'I do not like this at all,' Sulakon said. 'How many other undiscovered traitors may we not have among us? I swear that the pilots had been warned, to run off as they did –'

'Ah, very likely they'd been planning it for months,' Lakkannar said.

'Nevertheless, to leave just as we came to apprehend them –'

'Enough of this!' Ailixond broke in. 'I see no further benefit in this gathering. It were better that we waited for morning, and move on, and in so doing discover more of the land where we find ourselves. Go now! We shall move on at dawn.'

There were more than a few sour glances as they left; but he stayed rocking in his chair, and took no notice. Only he said to Sulakon, 'Consider, my cousin, that this is not the worse – at least we have discovered their perfidy. I do not think that anyone planned that drunken soldiers should be shot at by the farmers of this land, whatever land it is.'

'Perhaps, my lord,' said Sulakon. 'But I may say, my lord, since you took it upon yourself to determine our path . . .'

'Do you accuse me of failing in my duty?' Ailixond said coldly.

'That is not for me to say,' responded Sulakon.

'Then I'll say only this: nothing will be helped by conducting a great witch-hunt for suspected traitors. Only, we shall move on, and no doubt determine our position in the same way as we have been used to in the past. Do you understand?'

'My lord,' Sulakon bowed curtly, and walked out.

Lord Ayndra sat on the table in the night commander's tent, swinging her feet and chewing the end of a battered quill, occasionally making notes on a crumpled sheet of paper. She did not look up as heavy boots tramped in the doorway. 'What is it, what is it? . . . twenty less seven, that is thirteen . . .'

'My lord! We have captured a spy!'

'What? A spy?' She woke into interest.

'Found him trying to sneak through the camp – here, you, get forward. Kneel down!'

The spy was short and skinny, in a tatterdemalion assortment of coloured rags and a grimy turban. 'We took's knife away, lord.'

'His! Gods, you're not worth your keep. That's a girl.' She spoke in a foreign language, and the prisoner bowed. 'Let her go,' said Ayndra, 'she will do no harm – how many of you have stayed to guard the camp? Let two of you wait here, and the rest get back to your duty. I'll send to you to tell you what comes of this – but if this is the first of a wave of enemy night fighters, you had better be on watch. Go now!' She switched to S'Thurrulan, and addressed the ragged suppliant: 'Do you know where you now are?'

'O, your honour, I did not know that our army was out here! I feared that foreign raiders – are the barbarians going to attack? I did not mean to go into the camp. –'

'You think that you are in the army of S'Thurrulass?'

'Your honour?'

'We are the barbarians. This is the army of Lord Ailixond of Safi.'

The girl's legs deposited her in a heap on the floor. She gibbered.

'No, no, no one will hurt you,' said Ayndra, 'what is that you say?'

'L-l-lord Alizhan? Alizhan the Terrible?'

'If that is your name for him, yes – why are you so distressed?'

'But your honour – Lord Alizhan – they say he, he –'

'O, go on! What do they say?'

'O, but he's a monster! He spits children on his sword, and roasts his enemies alive, and all his women he has to take by force, for he's not five feet tall, and black all over, and hairy like a beast –' She collapsed into silence, for Ayndra was doubled up with laughing. 'Black all over, eh? Well, you will see him next day. Meanwhile, tell me how you came to be in the camp.'

'I was – I was looking for someone . . .'

'At this hour of night?'

The girl shook her head mutely.

'You had better tell me,' said Ayndra, 'or the lords of Safi . . . I will protect you, but my powers are limited.'

'I looked for my family – have you seen them, your honour?'

'What are they? Travellers?'

'We – we go about to markets, we mend pots, and forge iron, and . . .'

281

'Wandering tinkers? I see. Whither were they bound?'

'Hallasila.'

'And how far had they to go when you lost them?'

'About six days in our wagon, your honour – the day before yesterday I was with them, but I went off with the, with a man, we were on a farm, and . . .'

'So you walk the Hallasila road hoping to catch up with them.'

'Yes, your honour.'

'Well, I can assure you that, if they saw us, they ran off and hid, for we have found the road clear – we are four days from Hallasila?'

'Yes, your honour,' said the girl, puzzled; why ask for anything so well known?

'Well, well . . . how would you like to enter the service of Lord Alizhan?'

'Your honour?'

'We cannot let you go, you know, and we'll need interpreters, and guides – you know the roads, I do not doubt? You'll be well paid, and I'll give you a place with my household . . . when did you last eat?' Almost as soon as she had come in, the girl's eyes had fixed on the plate with half a loaf of bread and a much hacked about cheese, sitting next to the lord on the table. Ayndra pushed it toward her. 'Finish that, then – what is your name?'

'Gobrian, your honour.' She tore up the bread and started pushing it into her mouth. Ayndra returned to her piece of paper; she looked dolefully at it. 'O, Shumar . . . I seem to have a gift for collecting female waifs of tender years. You two there, can you find my household among the baggage? Go and wake someone there, and tell them to come fetch a new member of my happy family. We'll take her to the king next morning.'

'Is my lord the king risen yet?'

Firumin peered sourly at Lord Ayndra and the dirty creature trailing behind her. She smiled brightly at him. 'Permit me to see him, then.'

'He is taking breakfast.'

'I have some important news.'

'Is it highly important, my lord?'

'It may be crucial to the war,' she said. Firumin remained unappeased. 'On the other hand, it may be crucial to the peace – does that please you better? I see not. O, for the days of yore, when things were . . .'

282

'Things were what?' Ailixond came white and elegant through the curtains of the door. 'Different,' said Ayndra, and bowed, saying to Gobrian, 'Yo shela Dissa Alizhan.' Gobrian fell to her knees.

'Do you know that you are five feet high and black and hairy all over?' said Ayndra to Ailixond. 'Your pardon?' he said. She said, 'I have found out where we are! And I have a guide for us.'

'Is that who this . . . person is?'

'Mistress Gobrian – she has no Safic, she is of a family of native tinkers. She left them to earn a little money of her own, and came back and found that they had gone on to Hallasila without her. We are four days' travel from Hallasila, the chief city of the northern marches, and she has a fair knowledge of the town itself . . .'

Ailixond glanced to either side, and saw that Firumin was out of earshot; then he smiled. 'The land pilots did very well, then,' he said.

'Did you doubt them?'

'I hope that we do not catch them.'

'I am sure that we will not.'

'Hallasila,' said Ailixond. 'Does not the Warden of the Marches live there? We cannot pass by and leave such a stronghold unreduced, to come down and destroy us . . . and besides, we are all out of practice, a hard siege would be a fine tonic – do you think she could make a plan of the town, if you pressed her?'

'I will try,' said Lord Ayndra. Gobrian was gawping openly at the king. 'She told me the S'Thurrulan picture of you,' said Ayndra, 'that you are five feet tall and black all over . . .'

'O, does she think so.'

'Not any longer.'

Ailixond nodded to Gobrian, and held out his hand; she shuffled forward and kissed his fingers, upon which he raised her graciously to her feet, and released her. 'I'll summon the Council, now, before we march,' said Ailixond.

They acquiesced sullenly; they had no choice but to agree to the siege. Next morning, they left the heavy baggage, the women and the camp-followers, with an armed escort, and marched off to invest Hallasila.

By midday, the heat rose like a wall off the windless sides of the ravine. The sides fell together rapidly, to form a deep narrow gorge, at the bottom of which a narrow tributary ran down to join the Siudni. On one side, the ridge rose up to perhaps six hundred

283

feet above the river, and sloped away into woodland; on the other side was the rock of Hallasila, standing at right-angles to the ridge, a complex of vertical faces, rock-falls, narrow fields carved out of the rock, and the low walls and terraces houses of the town, bordered on its north and east sides by massive cliffs falling sheer into the waters of the Siudni river. The top of the rock sloped gently to the south and west, planted with orchards and vegetable gardens, until it fell away in great slopes of scree. The road into Hallasila twisted up the southern slope, to the only gate; zig-zagging up the bare hillside, it could hardly have been more exposed and vulnerable. But the Silver Shields were encamped on the ridge overlooking the town, and they laboured with the engineers and the artillerymen on the dangerous slopes of the gorge, above the invisible, tree-hidden river; a gap of five hundred feet separated them from the town rock, but they were working hard to bridge it. They cut down trees, lowered them into place, lodged on rock ledges and built up into deceptively fragile webs, to support the platform that thrust out across the void, floored with branches and trampled earth. Ailixond was everywhere, under the struts of the causeway, down the mountain where the forest fell beneath the Safic axes, standing for hours at the top of the cliff to watch it all, leaving his companions pale and yawning in his wake; he never yawned, or complained or slept in, but the lines around his eyes and mouth were making his face grim even in repose.

The catapults were carried up the mountain on pack horses, and put together there. On the fifth day of building, all day and by torchlight at night, they went into action. There were three large catapults with crews of ten, constructed over the winter in Haramin and carried out to New Hope with Lord Ayndra's household; after lugging them – most said, pointlessly – all this way, they justified their existence now, as the only ones yet able to reach the town. The slingers and the army were set free to wander where they liked in search of vantage points, and fire at will to pick off defenders. But when the catapults went into action, the defenders began to retaliate: yard-long arrows appeared out of nowhere, in a man's back, pinning a hand to the timbers.

'What can we do?' said Sulakon. 'The closer we come, the worse it will be; we are as fish in a barrel to them.'

'But the closer we come, the heavier our bombardment, and the more stealthy they must be,' Ailixond said absently. His eyes were fixed on the activity below. Lord Ayndra was holding up a large wooden semicircle with a plumbline depending from it, sighting along its straight edge onto a tower of Hallasila; behind her, they were loading a stone into one of the oversized catapults. She drew a charcoal line where the plumbline fell, and went back to the catapult master. 'She should not expose herself,' he said, 'it's clear who she is – why they've not picked her off so far –'

'We cannot go on without protection. Why are none of them wearing armour? Can we not put up pavises?'

'Have you ever worked in armour – laboured?' They were altering the elevation of the catapult by levering up the front of the frame, and pushing woodblocks under it.

'We shall do what we can, but the forward part – it is not possible – and it will obstruct the artillery's line of sight –'

'The artillery! I do not think that that exercise is well conceived – indeed, I have always thought that the use of artillery is a great expense which could well be dispensed with –'

'Do you think so?' Ailixond said irritably. 'I cannot afford debates on theoretical tactics of that type – if you think we should have pavises, gather a company and put them up, but it is too late now to reconsider our entire art of war. You may write a book on that, when the siege is over.' The catapult groaned like a house in labour and heaved the stone into mid-air; it flew through the air, and crashed audibly down on the roof of the stubby thatched tower. The catapultmen cheered. Lord Ayndra waved her hat in the air and danced across the platform. 'We'll work at night,' said Ailixond, 'torchlight will very likely fox any but a cat-eyed archer, if we work by handheld lights –'

'And who is to hold them?' demanded Sulakon.

'The only men who need to be armed,' said the king carelessly, and leapt down from the pile of boulders they stood on, to the rough steps carved out and built up on the hillside, down to the causeway; on the way, his usual entourage of officers, messengers, attendants and favour-seekers appeared like fish caught in an invisible net which he trailed as he ran, until, when he reached the platform, he had a score of men following him; all of which he accepted with as much regard as he gave to the rays of sunshine. Sulakon folded his arms and remained standing on the skyline, watching the toiling figures below.

By the seventh night, when they were still working during daylight, but had the bolt-throwing catapults in action now, forcing the Hallasilan archers to keep their heads below the parapet, they were over half way, had thrown an arch across the twenty-foot cleft going down to the river, and were advancing on the far side; and the closer quarters of Hallasila were half ruined.

It was in the evening supperhour that a panting foot messenger came running up the mountain from the camp at its foot where Golaron guarded the road and river crossings. 'My lords! The embassy from the town, they're, down there, now with Lord Golaron – they want to make terms. Sue, for peace, my lord. Will you –'

'I most certainly will not come down!' said Ailixond. 'Send them up here. I will be ready to receive them.'

There were three of them, and each one laden with semiprecious stones, but all dressed in long loose tunics over trousers and high-heeled boots, although the middle one, who spoke, was a woman; she had a great deal of paint on her face, and the others only a little, and they deferred to her. They might have been performing animals for the sort of countenance the lords of Safi gave them. Furthermore, when they came into the tent, they looked around them and bowed to Lord Sulakon. Ailixond gazed at them as they did so, and then made a sign with his hand; when they turned to him, he rose, slowly, and offered his left hand, with the Royal Ring, to the woman. They bowed three times over as they realised their mistake.

Ailixond smiled unpleasantly. 'I presume that we have need of the services of an interpreter.'

'I have the Safic, my lord Allixhan,' said one of the men.

'Perhaps you have. But I think if my lord Aleizon Ailix Ayndra interprets, we will be spared misunderstanding.'

Upon which Ayndra stepped forward, made a half bow and a brief speech, to which the Hallasilan woman replied at length; they exchanged, after that, several sets of greetings, until Sulakon said, 'My lord, can you not curtail these pleasantries?' The ambassador smiled, seeming not to catch his meaning, and addressed herself to Ailixond, pausing to let Ayndra insert her translation.

'She is greatly honoured to meet you, my lord – that is, I am greatly honoured, she says, to meet a man so famous for his conquests, a man renowned the world over, and – I cannot say that!'

'You can,' said Ailixond.

'I, well . . .' Ayndra looked away. 'And – she says, she is also felicitous in encountering one so marvellous attractive in, ah, appearance; she says my lord, that you are – very beautiful –'

'What!' exclaimed the king. The lords' solemnity was marred by their guffaws. 'Ha! Ha! Beautiful! Will she compliment you on your fine eyes next, think you?'

286

'How,' said Ailixond, 'does one reply to that?'

Ayndra said, 'Think of all the times you have said it to, to your wife – how does she reply?'

'Do not you know?' Polem said to her.

'I? O, no,' Ayndra tapped her nose, 'I wouldn't know.' The ambassador spoke again. 'My lord, she asks if you are married.'

Ailixond's expression grew a little fixed. He said, 'Tell her yes, twice. And ask her why she and her companions have done us the favour of visiting us? You may add that we are, of course, at work on the causeway at all hours.'

When she heard this, the ambassador launched into an elaborate speech. 'My lord, we know that you will be at our gates in a few days, and, in truth, we know that we cannot hope to resist so great a captain as yourself, and that in so doing so much blood of Hallasila and Safi would be shed . . .' it went on; finally she said, 'So, my lord, if you will swear peace with us, we shall open our gates and you may enter the city as a guest of the Warden of the Marches.'

'I do not see why I should exchange an invitation to the city for possession of the city, if I can be sure of taking the latter, and within a very short time,' said Ailixond. 'What advantages has this offer for us? We should not like to see all our labours on the causeway in vain . . .'

'My lord. We cannot swear allegiance to you, for we are bound to the king and queen in Suthine and only they can release us. But we offer you our eternal friendship –'

'O, enough of that!' said Ailixond. 'My conditions are these: allegiance to the New Empire. A Safic garrison in the city, to control the road and the river. Safic troops to be permitted to go all over the region and take whatever supplies they need, so long as they pay for them – there would then be no ravaging. A detachment of their men to join the army, as a pledge of good faith and as hostages for those we leave behind. All these together, or nothing. Vague pledges of friendship will not satisfy me.'

'Ah . . . my lord, they ask to be allowed to go apart to confer for a while.'

'Let them go into the porch of the tent,' said Ailixond. The three Hallasilans retired there; the Safeen watched them twittering together. Lakkannar leant over and, reluctantly, tapped Lord Ayndra on the shoulder. 'What are they saying there?' he murmured. She said clearly, 'I cannot hear it.' Ailixond looked round at him then, and he retired sulkily. Ayndra stepped up beside the king's chair, and without looking at him, said quietly,

287

'What they say about Suthine is nonsense. S'Thurrulass is a mishmash of principalities that dip their banners to Suthine and go otherwise very much their own way – the king and queen lead in – I cannot think of the exact Safic word, it is like worship – but each province has its own laws, they throw over allegiance whenever they like –'

'Hush,' said Ailixond, 'they are returning.'

More flowery compliments to his valour; and then the man spoke in Safic. 'It is not able for us to swear allegiance to you as we are,' he said, 'only we offer peace, and the supplies, as you ask, if there is an end to attack.'

Ailixond looked blankly at him. 'It is not possible. You must give all that I have asked, or we continue at war. Perhaps you should reconsider the laws binding you to Suthine.'

The man spoke to the woman, who answered in S'Thurrulan. 'If that is so, my lord, we must return to Hallasila and debate with our lords. We are not empowered to offer more on our own.'

'As you will,' said Ailixond. 'My soldiers will escort you out of the siege lines.'

Lakkannar coughed. 'My lord! Are you letting them go back?'

Ailixond flashed a forbidding glance at him. 'My lord, they are envoys sent under flag of truce. We can do no other.'

'But after they have seen all over our camp –'

'It was hardly secret before. My lady, my lords, I wish you good luck in your debating, and I pray that the answer you decide upon is favourable to all of us.' He extended his hand, and the lady kissed his ring; then Golaron's soldiers took them out, to go back down the mountain and climb round to the road up to Hallasila. As soon as they had gone, he said, 'I do not trust any of them further than I could kick them.'

'Quite right too,' said Aleizon Ailix Ayndra. 'I'm damned if they were not lying in their teeth throughout – how do they think they can get a simple truce when we are about to overrun them? Ha!'

'Indeed? How can you say this on so slender a footing?' said Sulakon. Ailixond made a dismissive gesture. 'Put the men back to work. We'll continue with the siege, at least until they send another embassy.'

They built up the causeway on the far side of the incised valley, and began, behind the ridge, constructing a drawbridge to drop over the gap; it took three days to make it ready, and they still heard nothing from the city, except that the archers continued to shoot. Ailixond announced that they would assault the city by night. The older lords of the Inner Council demanded that he send

288

envoys to Hallasila to offer terms, before the final attack, but he refused: 'They know what I ask of them, and they have not replied; I take it that they have rejected us. When we go over the walls, an they mean peace they'll not find it hard then to tell us so. Full moon next night; we'll go then. No, I know that we'll be clearly seen, if they are looking, but better to see who we fight than slay our friends in the darkness – and I will not wait here for the moon's waning.'

'And I expect that they will up and surrender as soon as they see that we mean to fight,' said Lord Ayndra; she shrugged, and grinned at the hostile faces. But it turned out exactly as she said; they'd hardly got over the ruined walls before the lord of Hallasila and every notable of the town arrived, unarmed, ready to surrender and accept everything Ailixond asked, while the soldiers cheered and swaggered through the streets. It was all finished before the dawn came, a Safic garrison in the gatehouse and the towers – Lord Ayndra said to Lakkannar, 'Do you not feel something of a fool in all this armour, faced with this?'

'You do, perhaps,' he said, and turned his back on her.

It was from Hallasila, on the last day of Ninth Month, that Ailixond declared formal war on the kingdom of S'Thurrulass. The former ambassador, who turned out to be the lord's oldest daughter, told them that the government in Suthine maintained six thousand infantry and four thousand cavalry always under arms, usually near the capital, but could raise many more given a little time; she was silent when asked if they had known, if Suthine might know, that Ailixond was coming into their lands. That they knew now, there was little doubt, but it was important to the Safeen to know how long they had had the news for; and, for that, there was no answer forthcoming. Ailixond left the Thaless horse and the Lysmalish levy in Hallasila, with orders to tour the neighbouring regions and rout out any resistance that was not susceptible to the pleading of their new-found Hallasilan allies; while he marched with the rest of the army, off down the main road that led eventually to Suthine.

'I wonder how it is', said Lakkannar, 'that she knows so much about this country.'

'Yes,' said Lord Ellakon. 'Now – do you not remember, how, when we discovered that the land pilots had fled, she was absent, and returned only after you had gone with the others? I thought then . . .'

'What did you think?'

'That, if she had gone to warn them before we came, well, it would have been – I mean, her lateness, it would have been possible – and did you not say that they had only just fled?'

'She knows a great deal about this country,' Lakkannar repeated, 'a deal too much, in my view.'

'Have you an idea whyever she was brought back from Haramin?' Ellakon asked.

'No, how should I know? I no longer hear any of their secrets. I know nothing.'

'I did hear that she was involved in a plot there . . .'

'It might well be,' said Lakkannar, 'she was much in with the barbarians in that land, also, I recall . . . I heard tell that she practised sorcery there, also – I have thought sometimes that she has ensorcelled Ailixond, so that he listens to her counsel and not that of us who he has known since we were boys at the school, and in his father's army – ah, Safi is coming on bad times, ruled by women! It was an evil day when she was brought to him – Polem, that was, she ensorcelled him also, they say . . .'

'No woman need ensorcel Polem,' said Ellakon. 'But I think that we should watch her closely. We would all benefit if she were no longer whispering in Ailixond's ear.'

'This is not war,' said Ailixond resentfully, 'this is – it is like running a race with friends so sycophantic that they always allow one to win – ah! I am sick of it.'

Aleizon Ailix Ayndra giggled. 'The S'Thurrulans do not recognise war as an art,' she said.

'Do they not? Their weapons –'

'O, they fight if they must, if they are put to it, and they enjoy parades, but they have no idea that it is honourable to resist, and see no shame in surrender if it's clear that the fight would be costly and they like to lose it.'

'Indeed,' said Ailixond. 'Still, I . . . for heaven's sake! It is too easy. I feel that they'll revoke their allegiance the moment I am not here to enforce it.'

'Very likely they will,' said Lord Ayndra. Ailixond gave her a black look and strode away. She shrugged, 'God's teeth!' she said to Arpalond, 'he is not sweet-tempered lately.'

Arpalond merely shook his head, and sighed.

She said, 'He is right in a way . . . there's something – o, I do not know . . .'

'What do you mean?' said Arpalond.

'Well, things are not well in the court –'

290

'You need hardly tell me that.'

'And even though these people are falling like ninepins – do you not feel, sometimes – or maybe that I imagine it . . .'

'What?'

She grinned without mirth. 'Like the shadow of a bird far overhead . . . o, the scent of disaster, the sense of impending doom, the bird of desolation flying above us – do you not?'

'I would not put it so dramatically,' said Arpalond. 'But something must happen soon – though the gods know what it will be.'

'O aye. It may be that we'll meet the S'Thurrulan army, because they are bound to fight, you know, sooner or later – but that would be a good thing . . .'

'If we won,' said Arpalond.

'What, think you that we might not?'

'You know more than I about their forces – but you know that the spirit of the army has gone. Perhaps that is what you feel as the bird of desolation.'

'Perhaps,' she said, and walked away.

'It's clear, at least,' said Ailixond, 'why it was this city that they chose to stand in at last.' The cornfields by the river were yellow, and spangled with poppies; they ran up to the circular brick wall of Merultine, the outer wall, for there was a second ring inside, the citadel, high-towered and single-gated. 'Brick walls, they crumble perhaps, or we dent them, with the catapults, but it would be a year's labour to take them down, for we'd need to do so brick by brick . . .' He scuffed his feet restlessly in the grass, and rubbed his hands across his mouth.

'But look, the harvest, they've not even tried to take it in or –'

'Ah, we should sit down before them? I will not do it. That town's been built to withstand a year's siege – do you not doubt that they are well prepared? I suppose we sit here until their army of the field comes upon us. No, twelve days, I will not give it more – a battering ram, I do not think the gates are as strong as the rest . . .' He sent the engineers out into the wooded sides of the valley before the army had finished pitching camp; Arpalond carried the order. The chief engineer said that it seemed hurried – 'Hurried?' said Arpalond. 'Ah, he does not halt these days to breathe.'

It took two days to set up the siege lines – now that all the encumbrances that had been stripped away after the Battle of Palagar had been replaced, and in greater abundance – and only four days after that the ram was ready; the whole camp was infected with a hectic mood – 'but it's not,' said Arpalond, 'it's not the same everywhere – there's much dissent, among the footmen most of all; they want to move but it is not within the walls of Merultine – they've no desire to fight unless it be the price of removing an obstacle from their road, but, even then, there are more than a few who believe that it need not have been in their road in any case – ah, I cannot tell the half of it.'

'You are the same,' said Aleizon Ailix Ayndra.

'What do you say?'

'Up in one breath and down in the next, and you do not say always what you would like to mean. Your judgements lately are not so considered.' She bounded out of her chair, and stood fidgeting on the other side of the tent. 'Nor am I free of it,' she added; she stepped back and forward almost as if she would start dancing. 'Arpalond. When he calls them through the gate next day, might they refuse to follow?'

'You can surely answer that as well as I,' Arpalond, still, said.

'I think they will follow,' she said. 'But it may not be – too fast . . . ah! This is a bad time.'

'Your bad time has been slow in coming.'

'But it approaches, I swear it – where is he?'

Both knew who he was.

'Gone to see the queen, and the little prince.'

'Ha . . . have you seen the little prince?'

'Have you not?'

'I do not go, these days, to the House of Women,' she said, still shuffling to and fro.

'A very forward child,' Arpalond said.

'Is that so?'

'He is not left to nurses, or slaves, or older children . . . he's the image of his father.'

'They all come with the stamp of the mould on them, that family. You know Ailissa's children?'

'How do you, if –'

'I have seen them in the camp, now and then – the oldest boy – beside, they always have some liveried chattel with them . . . so do they teach him that he will be lord of the world when he's grown? – and when the present lord has ascended to new worlds to conquer?'

'I could not tell you,' said Arpalond, 'you would need to ask someone more privy to the queen's secrets than I. Even Ailissa seems not to know.'

'And Ailissa knows everything in the House of Women.'

'Most of all since she ceased to be able to command everything there.'

'Ah, but I know nothing of these intrigues.'

Arpalond watched her for a while; she noted it with her eyes, but went on as if she were unobserved. He said, 'You think poorly of other women?'

'I think poorly of a good many people,' she said. 'But not women more than men. Is it the noble ladies that you think I despise? No more than I do their husbands.' She spun to face him again. 'Do you think that they'll follow him?'

Arpalond said, 'I cannot tell.'

'We would be in a dangerous situation here an they did not, and the S'Thurrulans knew it – they could enslave us all, no doubt about it . . .'

'But do they see that?'

'He is quite right that things would change an their army in the field came upon us, and asked for battle . . . but perhaps they have too much sense for that.'

'Do you mean that they know how things are with us?'

'A good many S'Thurrulans have joined the baggage train. It would surprise me if none of them were spies of Suthine. More likely, half are spying for Suthine, and the other half spying on them, or each other, to see if various ladies and lords are treating with us, or making too much money out of selling things to us, or trying to direct us to waste the lands of their rivals.'

'What? You make it sound as if we are like a wild animal in a house, that knocks over ornaments and frightens the slaves and precipitates a quarrel over who let it in, and all unbeknownst to it which wishes only to escape.'

'Or to find some food,' she said, laughing. 'It's a wide and subtle land, S'Thurrulass; they were civilised people here when Safi was a huddle of mud huts, you know . . . you know, also, that I am suspected of spying for them?'

'So I have heard.'

'It is not true.'

'I never thought that it was.'

'Good . . . ah, I think things will go off well next day, after all! It's time for a fight – I wonder, only, why they chose this city for their stand.'

'It may be that we'll find out next day.'

'I doubt it,' she said.

The blunt black iron cap of the ram ruptured the leaves of the gate halfway through the morning of the next day, and was rammed on through to allow the Silver Shields to follow – into the arms of at least five hundred armed fighters, who bounded from alleyways and dropped from roofs and stabbed or shot and were gone before the Safeen had time to reply. Ailixond stood in the middle of the street with his shield held overhead, sword in hand, calling furiously to them to spread out, cover their heads and for gods' sake get up on the ramparts and put away the archers! while those archers showered him with arrows – there were three trailing in his cloak and two stuck like giant pins in his mail when Polem at last seized hold of him and dragged him out of the roadway and under the low eaves of an overhanging roof. As soon as his friend exerted his full strength, Ailixond gave up struggling, but his face lit with incandescent fury – 'Let me go! Gods' sake, what do you think –'

'Stay here!' exclaimed Polem. 'You must! – you've seen those arrows go straight through mail shirts –'

'Ah, what does it matter? I cannot hide – get on, get on! Where are the steps up to the walls? Where are – what –' The thatch bulged downward, and part of the eaves collapsed in a shower of straw as someone slid down it, crashed to the ground, rolled over and threw herself up against the wall, where she collapsed, laughing maniacally. 'O what?' said Aleizon Ailix Ayndra. Polem let go of Ailixond, but he no longer needed to restrain him; his whole manner had changed. 'Are you scathed?' he said.

'No, but I have made a very great fool of myself – why are you waiting? Let us go! Go!' She scrambled to her feet and bounded out into the sunlight, drawing her sword; she waved it at the Silver Shields clustering unwillingly around the ram and under the gate. 'Come on, damn you! Cowards! Filth! Will you let a woman beat you all? Come –' then an arrow whanged into the earth between her feet, and she danced back into shelter. 'I did not realise that thatch was so slippery, you see – at least this, it's an old roof I think –'

'Ah, you fool! You'll kill yourself one day,' said Ailixond.

'And so will you –'

'So let's do it in company – come on!' Ailixond waved to the reluctantly advancing Silver Shields again, and ran out into the open, and this time they came after him. 'To the walls!' he said.

'This way, I saw it!' yelled Ayndra, bouncing up and down like an eight-year old. 'This way, this way!' She grabbed Ailixond's arm and pulled him after her, laughing, and he was laughing as well, and a mob of men finally ran after them, and Polem at their back, but they were insanely light-footed for all their plate and mail, and he could scarcely keep up with them; it took all his breath, but even then they were both talking and laughing throughout. They ran up on the walls, and pushed several people over them, they ran through streets and squares and up and down steps and disappeared as if by magic into sudden narrow passages and burst out into the golden sunlight, running, running, until they were facing the blank wall of the citadel, upon which they dashed round to its gate and found a dozen Safeen hiding near it, picked them up and bore them over the arrow-studded gap to crouch in under the arch of the gateway, safe at least from an attack from above. 'Where are the ladders?' said Ailixond. 'Send for them, send for them!' The flash of life was dying out of his face again; the lack of passion in the men around him was palpable. He signalled to a group squatting in an arcaded porch on a nearby house, and a couple of them ran over to him; as they came closer, one of them was Arpalond. Ayndra said to him, 'How goes it?' but he only shook his head. 'Siege ladders!' said Ailixond. Ayndra said, 'I'll go and –'

'No,' he said, 'no, I – you're better here. Arpalond, can you . . . who here can run? To the gate?'

'No, look, they're coming now!' Ayndra pointed down a sidestreet. 'See, Golaron with them.' The ladder teams were scuttling up the road in the gutters, keeping as close to the walls as they could; the archers in the towers of the citadel had seen them, and were doing their best to pick off the bearers, so bringing down the ladder and tangling up the rest of the team so that they could shoot them too. The first one reached the arcade where Arpalond had sheltered, and threw themselves down there, not willing to chance the run to the wall when so few were there. Ailixond, when he saw them, dropped the shield from his arm and dashed out into the open, to where the ladder lay on the cobbles; he seized it and yelled, 'Come on!' He had it half across the street by his own effort before they were shamed into action, and, as he ordered them, swung it up against the parapet. Ailixond leapt up on it immediately and started to climb. 'Ya! Come on!' howled Ayndra, and elbowed her way to the ladder to get next up; arrows whistled past them. Arpalond caught up Ailixond's shield and jumped on to the first rung, calling, 'Come on, damn you, will you let your king die while you stand here? What are you at? Come on!' Ailixond was climbing over the parapet. Ayndra right at his back; Arpalond turned to go after them, and the guards at last surged up behind. Ayndra tumbled over, all fours on the wall-walk; they were on an open stretch between two towers, swept by fire from either side, and overhung on the town side by large trees. Arpalond clattered over, and pushed Ailixond's shield into her hands. 'Give it him!' Ailixond turned to his left. 'This way!' he called, and then there was a great splintering sound, and yells and screams – 'O lord!' wailed a soldier who had come over after them, 'the ladder's broke!' An arrow glanced off the wall beside him, he looked from side to side; the four of them were marooned – 'What can we do?' exclaimed Ayndra. 'This,' said Ailixond, stepped to the inner edge, crouched there, and jumped.

Ayndra threw up her hands. She screeched, 'You'll break your bloody neck!' and tilted out over the brink; her balance went, she screamed like a seagull as she jumped.

'Madness!' said Arpalond, slid over the edge, hung by his hands a moment and dropped. The soldier, utterly bewildered, picked up the king's shield which all the lords had forgotten, and, having nowhere else to go, jumped after them.

The grass under the trees was long and thick; Ailixond landed with his knees flexed, caught himself on his hands and was up with his sword ready, when Ayndra hit the ground, fell over on her face, scrambled up and ran to his side. There was a building on the other side of the garden, and three or four of the enemy looking out of a window; then their faces disappeared; a few moments, and the door flew open and several of them charged out. Ailixond seized her arm and thrust her back against the tree-trunk; she yelped in protest as Arpalond ran up on her other side, and met the first of the attackers, fencing grimly with him until Ailixond had dispatched his man and turned and stabbed the other in the neck; the rest of the assailants drew back, but more were barrelling out of the door and ringing them round, waiting – Ailixond looked up, at the sun dappling through the branches. 'They can't shoot us from above,' he said. Arpalond laughed weakly. 'Do they need to?' he said.

'They'll have another ladder over – we can fight till – but watch! They come –' There were six of the enemy advancing; they hesitated, and then came on all in a rush. The air was sweet with grass and flowers; gold coins of sunlight patterned arms and faces and mouths twisted with hate; the enemy drew off, and left three lying in the spattered grass, but there were fifteen or twenty of them now. Ailixond shifted his stance to look back at the wall, and suddenly gasped. He said, 'Help me!' just as they rushed forward again. Ayndra growled like a cat and showed all her teeth; she had her knife in one hand now, sword in the other, and

as Ailixond thrust weakly at the man coming at him, she cast
herself bodily in his face, and her knife flashed; he screamed and
crumpled, and she spun round to find Ailixond standing with his
head tipped back and the sword falling from his hand, the other
with outstretched fingers around the shaft of the arrow that stood,
through his mail, in his ribs. Brilliant blood striped the Royal
Ring. Ayndra hissed and dived for the shield, which the soldier
still held – 'Get it over him!' Ailixond nodded dizzily, and
slumped to the ground as if he fell asleep on the spot. Air and
blood had formed a bloody froth round the lips of the wound.
The soldier knelt and lifted the shield over him. A voice on the
wall shrieked, 'Is he dead? Is he?'

'No! He can't be dead!' There was a crash as a ladder, brought
over the wall, was dropped down inside; the S'Thurrulans looked
up, and fled. Polem was the first down the ladder; he fell on his
knees by Ailixond, white as linen. 'He's not dead! He's not dead!'
he gabbled.

'I don't know!' Ayndra unbuckled his helmet as familiarly as if
it were her own; hesitated, and then lifted his head into her lap,
but her hands hovered half round him, half away; he was
unconscious, greenish, pallid. The Silver Shields were pouring over
the wall now – 'Is he dead! The king's dead! They've killed him!
Dead!' They wrenched the gates open from within, and the rest of
the Safic army went rampaging into the mansions of the citadel,
slaying all whom they met there.

Polem seized Ailixond's hand and began chafing it, repeating
like a charm, 'He can't be dead! He can't be! O god! He can't be!'

'The Physician, where's a physician?'

'Bring that ladder over here!' shrieked Ayndra. 'Now!' She leapt
up, tore off her cloak and threw it over the ladder; then she
dropped to the ground and lifted Ailixond's head again. 'Lift him
up, lift him!' In a moment, the ladder was carpeted with all kinds
and conditions of garment, and fifty or sixty hands lifted it, and
lifted Ailixond on to it; as they laid him on the makeshift litter, his
eyelids fluttered, and then opened wide. Someone else cried,
'There's a bed, in here! In here!' Ailixond moved his head from
side to side, but he could not speak; they were bearing him into
the house. He sought out Ayndra, and fixed her with blank wide
eyes. 'Who's . . . the fighting?' he whispered.

'No one – I don't know –'

'Sulakon,' he breathed, and dropped his head back. She cried,
'Sulakon! Sulakon! Sulakon!' and, by some magic, there he was –
'What?' he said.

'Ailixond wants you to take charge of the siege – god knows what the men are doing now – and tell them, tell them he's not dead –'

'You need not tell me my duty,' Sulakon said, and was gone, as the soldiers lowered the ladder to the ground inside the wide bare room, and made a web of hands to lift Ailixond up onto the unmade bed. Arterial blood welled onto the white linen. Ashen, in a voice like dry leaves, he said, 'Cut the arrow out.'

'I've sent for the Physician –' Arpalond began, but Ailixond scrabbled at his hand. 'Cut it out now,' he said.

'But we know not – what damage –'

'Then I . . . myself . . .' He took hold of the shaft and made an attempt to break it; a fresh rush of blood came from the wound. 'No,' said Golaron, pushing through the press, drawing a long knife from his belt. Ailixond put his hands at his sides; his face was dewed with sweat. Golaron grasped the knife and drove it firmly into the wound. Ailixond threw his head back; his left arm slid over the edge of the bed, and met Aleizon Ailix Ayndra's hand. Golaron forced the lips of the wound apart, and grasped the revealed shaft; there was a splintering noise; Ailixond's fingers closed on Ayndra's like a vise. Golaron's hand came up with a jerk, and a viciously barbed arrow shot out of the king's side; a rush of dark blood vomited onto the bed. Ailixond's hand relaxed, and his whole body went limp. He had fainted dead away. Golaron threw the arrow on the floor; Ayndra pulled her hand free, nervously, by stages, and then stood up, massaging her crushed fingers. In the silence, tiny distant screams and the clash of blades resounded. At the foot of the bed, someone was trying not to sob; Polem had his cloak pulled up over his face. Ayndra put her hand in her mouth, then spun round and shoved her way through the crowd. 'Has anyone gone for the Physician?' said Arpalond.

'Is he dead?' shouted a voice from the doorway. Arpalond picked up Ailixond's wrist, pulled off the wide lord's bracelet and fumbled for the pulse; they waited; eventually he found it. 'No,' he said, 'he lives – go get the Physician, for god's sake!'

Aleizon Ailix Ayndra came back five hours later, when it was dark. The guards outside the room did not want to let her in, until Polem heard her cursing them, and called out to let her enter.

Clean linen, several chairs, and a table with the Physician's instruments had been brought, and a brazier over which water could be heated; Ailixond lay under clean sheets and blankets, quite still. His eyes were sunken in purple shadows, and his ribcage hardly moved with his breathing. The Physician stood at the bed's foot, rubbing his hands in a towel; a couple of his boys crouched by the box of drugs. Polem and Arpalond sat by the bed, but everyone else had been expelled from the sickroom; they formed a large crowd outside, now that the sack of the city was to all intents over.

'Where have you been?' asked Polem.

She knelt down by the bed and started to take off her helmet. 'I've been fighting ... there aren't many people left here, you know, of the people who used to live here, and our men – we are going to need to carry many bodies out in the morning –'

'Don't talk about that!' he said hastily. She shrugged, and looked up at the Physician. 'Well?'

'Three ribs broken, more fractured – it is hard to tell – even if it heals cleanly, he might never – that is, in wounds like this, the lung quite often sticks to the ribs on the inside, and restricts the use of that arm, not to mention breathing – and infection ... besides, at this time I cannot be sure, though it does not seem dirty –'

'O, yes, yes – but – will he live?'

The Physician shook his head; she started. 'O, no,' he said, 'I did not mean – I meant to say, only, I cannot tell – and then, even if he comes round now, a month, a year – I cannot tell.'

'Ah,' she said, shaking out her sweat-dark hair, 'you speak good news, indeed –'

'It's not my profession to lie,' he said.

'You have decided not to move him from here.'

'No, my lord, the less shaking about the better.'

'It does not matter. The citadel's been emptied after all, the court can move in –' she laughed without joy, and shook her head.

Polem was looking out of the window. 'There's a great cloud of smoke rising over the lower city.'

'They are still fighting there,' Ayndra said. 'How did you bring these things here? Are they – yes, I know them, I ...'

'Firumin brought them,' said Arpalond. 'He has gone for more things – he said nothing of the fighting.'

'He cannot have missed it. It's a bloodbath. They all think him dead still, and they go about killing anyone they meet who does not scream in Safic – o, god damn it all!' She picked up her helmet and flung it viciously at the wall. It rebounded with a clang and rolled noisily under the bed. Her dirty smoke-smutted face contrasted with the pale skin of her forehead where the helmet's brim had protected it. No one said anything. The Physician finished wiping his hands and tossed the towel to his boys.

'Polem,' said Ayndra, 'what are you going to do?'

'What? – o, stay here – I'll sit up, Physician, all night, I'll – whatever you need –'

'Good,' she said dispassionately. 'I go now, to rest, and eat, but – I'll come back.'

'There'll always be a place for you here,' he said. She nodded, and shuffled out, but paused in the doorway. 'O, and – you will send for me, if . . .?'

'Of course,' he said.

Polem lay stretched out in the fragile inlaid chair which Firumin had found in a neighbouring room; he had taken off his helmet and mail shirt, but still wore the padded shirt under it and heavy studded breeches. He breathed heavily, his mouth open, hands hanging slack. Ayndra stepped up behind him, then bent over and ran her hand through his thinning hair. He woke up with a start, and looked about him, dazed; the little chair creaked. 'Wha . . . wha . . . what hour is it?'

'Second hour of morning,' she said, 'and no one about at all, except our patrols, and rats in the burnt houses – go now, get you to bed.'

'But I can't – on your own –'

'O, begone! I can do perfectly well on my own. Moreover, there are six guards sitting just outside the door.'

'But – how can you have slept?'

'O, I've slept – as much as I am able to. Look you, go!'

Polem rubbed his bleared eyes, and staggered out, glad after all to go to a soft bed. The room was hot and stuffy; two lampstandards of four lamps burnt there, and the brazier, and a couple of S'Thurrulan lamps, with double alabaster shades painted on the inside of the outer shades with a scene of ducks swimming among waterlilies; she took off her black cloak and tossed it over the chair. Ailixond had been propped up on a heap of pillows, on his left side, to help drain fluids from his lung. His bare arms lay outside the covers, gold bracelets gleaming above the white stone of the Royal Ring and the wedding band next to it. Unconsciousness had washed all the strain lines out of his face, leaving the fine skin as flawless as a child's, except for the black shadow of beard; the eyelashes that had always been too long for a man lay like a drift of soot across his cheek. Her hands, clasped in front of her, closed on one another until the knuckles stood out like ivory knobs; then she reached out her right hand and lifted the fallen locks of hair back from his face. He lay as still as before, waxen, not seeming to breathe. She shook the hair away from her fingers and thrust her hand into her mouth, then suddenly folded her arms and strode away to the window, shoulders bowed and tense; she leant her forehead against the closed shutters, and shivered as if a cold gale disturbed the tallowthick air. The floor was laid with terracotta tiles, brown with a pattern of white slip flowers painted under the glaze; in places, the pattern had worn away to the rough red-brown clay beneath. She shut her eyes.

About sixth hour, a grey light began to creep through the slits in the shutters; birds had been singing in the garden for some time before. She took down the bar, and pushed the shutters back; it was a grey still day. A dead man lay face down in the grass under the window; ants were crawling over his back, and his hair was speckled with dew. She leant against the frame of the window, gazing without vision; someone coughed, dragging and painful. She looked about for some early walker; they coughed again, and then she knew that it was in the room, and turned. Ailixond had slid from his high pillows to the edge of the bed, where he lay with his head half off the mattress, coughing and coughing, deep, tearing, phlegmy coughs; then he spat a great gob of blood on to the floor, rolled over and saw her. He opened his mouth to speak, and started coughing again. She pulled a large crumpled handkerchief out of her sleeve, and ran to the bed, gave it to him; he put it over his face, hawked several times into it, then wiped his mouth and let his hands drop back. His eyes met hers, but it was a little time before he could speak. 'What day is it?' he said.

'It's tomorrow.'

'Ah . . . and we've taken it?' as he looked around the room.

'Yes, and everything in it – after you – they thought you were dead, they went rampaging everywhere. There's hardly a soul who lived here left alive, not dead or fled –' she halted, eyes fixed on his face, hands clasped again.

'Thought I was dead?' he said, faint and ironic like sand on steel. 'Scarcely surprising, for so did I – I can remember Golaron's knife going in, and then I thought, this is the end, and pha! blackness, the lights . . . went out . . .' he choked, and put the handkerchief over his mouth again, while he pinned his left arm to his side with the right, as if to hold the wound steady against the racking coughs; but it was clear that pressure on the site gave him great pain. She got up and ran to the door – 'Guards! Guards! Get the Physician! – get Lord Polem! The king's awake!' Her yells sparked off a great commotion; perhaps a score of people were dozing outside, and they all jerked awake at once and started babbling. She cried, 'The Physician – urgently!' and ducked back inside. Ailixond had turned as far as he was able, to see the door; it was ringed by faces, but Aleizon Ailix Ayndra shut it on them. 'Let the Physician come first!' Ailixond put his hands by his sides under the covers, and tried to sit up, or at least move further up the pillows, but the exertion started him coughing again, then seized up his throat so that he struggled to breathe. His face paled and his lips went blue; his right hand strayed over the cover, as if he wanted something to hold on to, and she caught it, but had no idea what else to do, whether he should lie down, or sit up, or try to clear his throat, or what he should do; he opened his eyes a couple of times, and nodded at her, but could not speak. The door crashed back, and people funnelled into the room; Polem's voice cried, 'O, you're awake! You're alive! O heaven! You're alive!' and a gaggle of lords swirled around the bed. Ailixond moved his head from side to side; his eyes rolled. Then the Physician pushed between them, shouting 'Out! Out! Everyone out! The king must have peace and quiet!' Polem turned round and started to bellow, 'Everyone out!' while the Physician's boys put down his box of drugs, opened it, fetched up bleeding bowls, towels, rolls of linen and bandages, all sorts of metal instruments, needles, threads, and made a wall around the bed with them, while everyone except the king's closest friends and relatives was expelled. They pulled back the covers, and started to strip off the bandages, heads together like witches in coven; no one else could see a thing, and the words in which they discussed what they saw were incomprehensible; heaps of linen fouled by blood and pus and scabs were carried out, and bizarre instruments disappeared into the coven; the lords sat around apprehensively. Finally, the Physician stood up. 'It seems clean,' he said. 'However, I think it must not be allowed to close too early, so that the fluids will drain – my lord must lie on his back for three days at least, no moving, no laughter or coughing if it can be helped. My lord, we have strapped up the broken ribs, and if you try to move you may find it hard, but it is better, I think, an you do not move at all.'

'Three days?' said Ailixond resentfully.

'Six would be preferable,' the Physician said. 'I will give Master Firumin further instructions concerning your food and housekeeping, my lord, and meanwhile, rest and quiet . . .' he looked around at the lords; most of the Inner Council had managed to sneak back in. Ailixond lifted his head. 'Polem,' he whispered, 'Arpalond . . . Lord Ayndra . . . the rest of you, go . . . I'll hold a Council later, meanwhile, Golaron and Sulakon, take charge.' The rest of them filed out, giving fulsome wishes for his health; Firumin and the Physician stood muttering together in the doorway.

'Vultures,' said Ailixond.

'What, all those . . .? No, I am sure not,' said Polem, 'you should have seen – everyone, when they thought you might be dead –'

'I do not mean the commoners – it's a penalty of the crown, there is no peaceful death, they stand round you to catch your last breath, name your heir, name your heir – and then, an one names him, most likely they all desert to him, and leave you to die like a beggar.'

'O, no, no!' said Polem. 'It will not be so – and do not speak of those things. No one could possibly want – I mean, if you were to – were to leave us, here, whatever would we do? Sweet heaven! we'd be utterly bewildered.'

Ailixond shook his head.

'It's true,' said Arpalond, from the window. 'You have not – that is, when you are able to hold a Council, will you instruct us in . . . that which we should do, if such a misfortune should befall us?'

'The papers which I call my will,' Ailixond said. 'It is all there, at least, all that can be said now, but that . . . I can do nothing about the greatest danger, that is, when the lords and governors abandon . . . abandon good government for the pursuit of personal advantage and civil strife, and it is that, which I cannot predict, nor prevent, that would tear the Empire apart.'

'O surely not!' said Polem again. 'Now that – with Parakison –'

'If I die now, Parakison will never come into his inheritance – if he ever would,' Ailixond said distantly. Polem said, 'Don't talk about that! Talk about, about . . .'

'Tell me what took place yesterday, then, after I fell.'

'What, the sack? Well, I – I mean, I was in here, all the time until in the middle of the night –' Ailixond shook his head, and signed with his eyes to Ayndra. She pulled her chair across the floor to the bed. 'Yes. After our ladder broke . . .'

No one disturbed them for almost an hour; then there was a scratching at the door. Ayndra ran up to it and pressed her face to the keyhole. 'You cannot come in! We will send out if –'

'Please, it is myself only.'

'Who is myself?'

'Firumi ı – let me come in, my lord.'

'O. Come in, then.' She unlocked the door; Firumin slithered in, carrying a steaming goblet. 'The Physician sent this.'

'Bring it in, then.'

Firumin crept up to the bed, and reverently offered the cup to Ailixond. 'The Physician said that you were to drink it all, my lord.'

'O indeed.' Ailixond took it in his right hand, and sipped. 'Firumin. This has been laced with poppy-syrup. I can taste nothing else.'

'My lord, the Physician said – if you do not –'

'The Physician no doubt said that I ought to be drugged insensible, otherwise I will be out of bed tomorrow and walking round the walls. Coughing every step of the way and leaning on you, Polem, but still out of bed.'

'I will take it away, lord, if you do not –'

'No, leave it. I trust his judgement. Of course, he may be poisoning me by slow degrees, but one must take some things on trust.'

'O, no my lord! I am sure that –'

'Firumin!'

Firumin's head bobbed like a cork on the ocean, and he retired to the wall, until Ailixond had drained the cup, which he ran away with. Polem began to chatter merrily about all kinds of inconsequentiality. Ailixond said less, and less, and then nothing at all; he was asleep. Ayndra went on gazing at his quiet hands, long hands much coarsened by war and hard riding, the fine artist's fingers thickened and calloused. Polem coughed slightly, and caught her eye. She said, 'I wish one could see these papers of his . . .'

'It's not that that distresses me! It's – do you know, I have been with Ailixond since we were sent to the palace school, and I think, sometimes, that I should have got a life of my own instead of trailing about always after him, but then – and he did try, when he sent me off to that rebellion, and, o, other things, but still . . . if he died, I don't know what I should do!'

'We'd all be cast adrift,' she said. 'He ought not to fear telling us his plans, they'd never replace him while he lives . . . you know that some say that you are his chosen for the next king?'

'What? O, impossible! I could no more govern the Empire than I could – chase some barbarians in the mountains, indeed. I think he would name Sulakon, because the Council of Lords would like him, though, I think, if he were left to himself, he would . . .'

'Name you, Aleizon Ailix Ayndra,' said Arpalond's voice, from where he had been sitting a long time in silence by the window.

'Ha!' she said, 'so that's how you find out half your secrets – but no, impossible that it might be me.'

'You think so? I tell you what would be the best solution. You two to marry, so that Polem could look splendid at festivals and impress the Council, while you told him what to do.'

'What? Ridiculous! An I were to have all the labour of the kingship, I should want the reward – I should go about in scarlet and gold like a ponce at the summer festival, and be grovelled to by commoners, I should!'

Polem looked from one of them to the other. 'Arpalond,' he said.

'Never. Are you not aware that I have sworn an oath never to do anything in government? And I have no desire to be grovelled to.'

'I do not follow all this,' Polem said.

'Nor should you. Be good, for you've no need to be clever,' said Ayndra. 'Ah, but I'm exhausted, Polem, I shall take myself at last to bed – good day, my lords, good day . . .' she went off yawning, only at the door she looked back, once; but no one saw her.

'He's dead! They lie to us!'

'Yes! Liars, liars!'

'They have him dead in there – they'll tell us he lives till one of them is chosen king, and then tell us he's newly dead!'

'We want to see the king!'

'The king!'

'The king! The king!'

Ailixond said for the third time, 'Firumin, fetch me my clothes. I have lain here long enough – can you not hear them?'

'But my lord, Lord Sulakon went out –'

'And they shouted him down – do you think I could not tell? Get me my clothes, I will go out to them.'

'If you will do this, my lord, I will not answer for the consequences,' interpolated the Physician.

'But you . . . can you not have them carry you?' said Firumin in desperation. 'Yes! I will get the lords to do it.'

'A fine idea!' said the Physician.

'Carry me, then! – but still, give me my clothes. I will not lie here any longer.'

305

The soldiers had gathered around the fire-scarred gateway of the citadel; some were up on the walls, and many more in the streets outside. A wave of noise met everyone who appeared from the large house where the court had moved in; this time, it was Lord Ayndra. She ran up onto the walls, and shouted, 'The king is coming! Clear a way!'

'Liar!' roared several voices.

'Where is he?'

'Traitors!'

'Peace!' she yelled. 'He comes presently – clear a way, a way! Look there,' she said to those nearest her on the walls, 'can you not see, where they are opening the doors . . .' A ripple of noise spread, as first a guard of Silver Shields pushed their way out, and then, borne up on a couch with poles tied to its legs, flinching every time the lords who carried him jolted the litter, and keeping his left arm pressed to his side, he was smiling brilliantly at the crowd pressing against the cordon of armed men and shouting themselves hoarse. She ran down the steps and joined the procession at the end, with the servants, as Ailixond swayed on out of the citadel and down the street toward the camp. People ran ahead with the message that he was coming, alive and well, and, by the time they reached the gate of the outer city, half the army seemed to have streamed out of the camp and gathered in the open space between, waving pieces of cloth and flags and banging swords on shields; a rose flew through the air, Ailixond caught it and raised it to his lips, provoking a fresh roar of applause. A forest of hands pushed around the guards, trying to reach him, touch him, while the lords sweated and struggled through the press.

'O, sweet heaven, the gods know what this will do!' the Physician complained.

'None at all,' said Lord Ayndra. 'Do you not see, this is better than a thousand rare medicines?'

'But look at them, they cannot even march in step – jolt and jerk all the way!'

'What else do you expect? They're noble lords. Only common footmen learn to march in step.'

'Yes, but – what do they now?' The couch had disappeared below the heads of the crowd. Ayndra leapt at the wall of backs, punching and kicking indiscriminately till she had won through, just in time to see Ailixond push away the assisting hands and, whitely triumphant, stand up. They were entering the camp now, and his big white tent was in sight; he hissed, 'Out of my way!' to the soldiers around him, and as they shuffled inside, he walked out into the crowd of his worshippers. They made way before him, but clustered round his sides, offering garlands and flowers and bits of tawdry jewellery, charms, good-luck pieces, healing talismen. His retinue struggled after him, obstructed by those who saw them as conspirators who would have kept their king from them. He appeared then on the steps of his tent, decorated with flowers and cheap ornaments like the statue of a god on his feast-day, and addressed the crowd. His voice was so weak that only the first few ranks could hear, but the rest cheered loyally all the same; he made the sign of blessing over them all, and stepped inside. The crowd surged up to the doorway, shouting, 'God bless! God save you!'

The lords who got in past the door-guards' fence of pikes found him propped up on the nearest of the great tent-poles, coughing and holding tightly to his left side. Polem exclaimed, 'Ailixond! You can't ever do that again – never! You'll kill yourself!'

'No matter,' gasped Ailixond, 'I cannot die, not now – did you not see? They're mine,' he said luminously, 'all mine! I can do whatever I will with them! They love me again.'

The army's euphoria lasted for days; enriched by the plunder of Merultine, some even demanded that they move on – as soon as the king was well – and sack the neighbouring cities. Meanwhile those people of Merultine who had been able to flee started to creep back, with country people who set up stalls in the burned and ruinous gateway, selling early fruits and vegetables, chickens, rabbits, loaves of bread . . . Golaron set Safeen to guard them, but more to keep off soldiers who might wish to rob them than to restrain the trade, and it was from the market that news came of the S'Thurrulan envoy, a royal envoy from Suthine. Lord Ayndra, Polem and half a dozen of the Companions were sent out to meet them and escort them to the king's reception. They rode southward down the valley for half a day, until they saw a cavalcade approaching the ford half a mile away, flying red flags with gold circles on them, and carrying green wreaths on poles. They moved on to a knoll overlooking the river, and paused there to watch the others cross. Polem unfurled the Safic banner and drove it into the ground beside him. There were forty or fifty people in the S'Thurrulan envoy's party, glinting with cloth of gold and rich dyed clothing; Lord Ayndra said that a rider dressed in purple, on a black horse, was the leader, and then fell quiet, craning her neck the better to scrutinise them. The armed

307

members of the party had crossed first, and clustered on the river bank, staring up at the Safic party; they had long javelins, and bows slung at their backs. 'Ought we not to display a truce flag?' said Polem.

'Those green wreaths. Those are their truce signs ... I'm sure I ... at this distance ...' Ayndra frowned, tapping her thumbnail on her teeth.

'What is it?'

'I think I recognise – no, I cannot be sure ... o, let's go down and meet them! Bring the flag!'

'But what if they –'

'O hush! They outnumber us, we cannot be a threat!' She dug in her spurs, and shot away. The S'Thurrulan guards lifted their javelins, and a few unslung their bows, but Polem saw her wave to them and shout out, upon which they lowered them again. He caught up with her as she was questioning them; they answered, and she exclaimed. Then the rider on the black horse, who was in the middle of the river, leapt forward in a sheet of spray and thundered up the bank. Aleizon Ailix Ayndra yelled 'Ylureen!' and the other shrieked 'Aleizon!' They both whirled out of their respective groups, tore off to a hundred yards' distance, halted, stared at one another, gabbled in S'Thurrulan, clasped hands, then embraced, and trotted back, laughing uproariously, to where the Safeen and S'Thurrulans were staring at each other, lacking introductions and, it would seem, interpreters too. 'What is it?' repeated Polem.

'My lord. May I present Lady Ylureen, Ambassador to the Court of Safi from the Court of Suthine?'

'Delighted, my lady, I am sure,' Polem said, and bowed from the waist. Now that he looked closer, he saw that the person he had taken for a man was a woman of middle years; he was confused by the way they all had here of wearing loose long tunics over trousers and winding bright coloured cloths round their heads, and then, both sexes, painting their faces and dying their hair all kinds of unnatural colour. This one was clearly noble; her clothes were heavy silk, and she wore three gold necklaces and a clashing line of bracelets. He nodded to her again, and said to Ayndra, 'Have you explained to her who we are? Are they coming to see Ailixond?'

'O, yes, yes,' said Ayndra carelessly, and set off chattering in S'Thurrulan again. '– Polem, join in with them, we'll all ride together to the camp.'

'Do you know her?' Polem asked.

308

'O yes! I – you know that I lived in this country? I was Lady Ylureen's bodyguard. I think it's something of a surprise to discover that I'm now one of the foremost in the New Empire.'

'Bodyguard?' said Polem reflectively; he observed how Lady Ylureen looked at Lord Ayndra. It was that which had first encouraged him to take her for a man. He rode beside them all the way back to Merultine, and concluded that they were retelling to one another all that each had done since they parted – however long ago that had been; he was more or less ignored, until they came in sight of the burnt ruins of Merultine, upon which the S'Thurrulans sent up wails of outrage. 'Polem,' said Ayndra, 'could you ride on, and say that we are here? And ask where we should take them. It's close to dusk – will Ailixond receive them this day, or next morning? And where should they camp? Thank you.'

'Thank you!' said Polem, but she was addressing the foreigners again. He grunted resentfully, and called two of the troopers to come with him.

The first question Ailixond asked him was, 'Where is Lord Ayndra?'

'With them. They're led by a lady, Lady – Illereen, or some such name, and Lord Ayndra is an old friend of hers, she says she used to be her bodyguard – and o! you have never heard such a chatter as they kept up, all the way here. No one said a word to me –'

'Where are they now?' said Ailixond. He was out of bed, but lay on a couch in his bedchamber still; the air reeked of medicinal herbs and incense from the High Priest's prayers.

'Outside the town, waiting to come into the camp – will you see them now?'

'I will see them next day. Go and find Golaron, and he'll give them a place to camp, and send Lord Ayndra to me. Ninth hour I will see them, tell them, next day – and set the Silver Shields to guard them, in case, you may say, our men mistake them . . .' He began to cough, and fell back; Polem reached out for him, but Ailixond waved him out of the room. Polem could hear him coughing all the way out of the tent.

A wooden dais of seven steps had been constructed to raise Ailixond's chair above the rest of the audience chamber; the lords were ranked either side of it, with rows of clerks and soldiers behind. Lord Ayndra sat on the steps; she would, as usual, interpret. Just before ninth hour, Ailixond walked out and, slowly, unassisted, climbed the steps and sat down. His eyes were vast and dark in a pale face, the whites tinged with yellow; he had got alarmingly thin, until his hands were like articulated bones covered with yellow parchment, and his clothes looked as if they had been made for a man twice his size. He snapped his thin fingers, and a gong boomed; the curtains over the door swung aside, and the S'Thurrulan envoys entered, led by Lady Ylureen.

She wore a gown of gold silk, the broad yoke cutting straight across below her shoulders, which were white with powder; her eyelids were gold, her lips carmine, her hair reddened artificially and dressed with gold wire and her hands aglitter with rings. She sailed down the hall like a ship in the sea of her skirts, and sank down in a billow of silk before the dais, giving out drifts of perfume. Lord Ayndra stood up, and addressed her. 'Ailixond, Most Serene Lord and King of Safi, of Thaless, of Lysmal, Lord of Purrllum, Overlord of the Land-beyond-the-Mountains, Lord of the Merkits, Protector of Biit-Yiakarak, King of Haramin, Conqueror of the North, Lord of the Seaward Plains and Master of the Seas of Grass, Lord of the South and High Admiral of Safi, Ailixond, eighth of that name and called the Ever-Victorious, bids you welcome,' she said.

'I accept his welcome, in my place as Ambassador to the Court of Safi from the Court of the Lord and Lady of Suthine and Cassirine, Glorious, Worshipful, Beloved King and Queen,' said Ylureen, and rose slowly to her feet; the lords were staring at her. She stared right back at them. Six men and women almost as gloriously dressed as she were gathered behind her; they were all frankly examining Ailixond. He gave no sign that he noticed their gaze. 'I am pleased to welcome my lady Ylureen,' he said. 'Lord Ayndra will interpret for us.'

'She has already told me so,' Ylureen replied. 'She and I are acquainted of old, my lord, for years since she was captain of my bodyguard, solace of my evenings and delight of my nights.' She smiled directly at Lord Ayndra, who met her eyes blankly, and said in Safic, 'Lady Ylureen is pleased to accept my service in that respect, since we are old friends. I was in her service in Suthine.'

'Excellent,' said Ailixond. 'Now. My lady will no doubt have witnessed the condition of Merultine, which not long ago was a flourishing and well-defended city.'

'So I have,' said Ylureen, 'you are not called the Monster without reason, o Ever-Victorious.'

'My lady has, and the sight of the ruins distresses her.'

'Then she will be aware of the threat which hangs now over all the other fair cities of S'Thurrulass. Nor will the men of Safi be

310

easily dissuaded from further ravage. What has she to say to us?'

Ylureen beckoned to a woman with apricot-coloured hair, who gave her two scrolls of papers tied with silk ribbons and weighted with dangling seals; she opened one of them. 'My lord. We did not ask for this war, nor for your invasion of our territories. Nor are we ashamed to say that we had thought our March-Warden's seat of Hallasila impregnable until you came by it. Our army waits outside Suthine, but we know that it would cost us much to face you in battle, and we believe that two nations as powerful and prestigious as Safi and S'Thurrulass do only waste their blood if they remain at odds; and so we come to ask you to lay down your arms, and travel as a friend through our fair lands. We will offer you the use and direction of our fleet, all sixty of our warships, and ten thousand gold thesh with them, to be put to use in whichever part of your Empire you shall see fit. Moreover, we will offer you a further five thousand thesh every year for ten years, if only you will remove your garrisons from those towns which you have seized, and return all prisoners of our nation. In return for this, we will carry your army at our expense down to Suthine, and allow you free passage through our lands to your preferred destination; also, we will sign with you a treaty of eternal friendship, alliance and devotion between our nations, promising to aid one another to the best of our abilities if ever either of us should be threatened by forces outside our realms, and to assist one another in trade and commerce. These papers, my lord, contain the details of these treaties, laid out by the King and Queen in Suthine, and the pledges and assurance which we offer in addition.' She held out the scrolls to Ayndra, who passed them to Ailixond; he snapped them open, glanced over the writing, and handed them back to his chief clerk who stood behind the throne. Ylureen folded her hands at her powdered bosom and stood, statuesque, waiting.

'My lord,' said Ailixond, 'what have you to say?'

Lakkannar said, 'What is a thesh?'

'A coin,' said Ayndra disdainfully.

'How much worth?'

'About four silver sols, by weight,' she said.

'Hmm . . . think you we could get more money out of them?' Lakkannar said.

'Let us not move from here until they have given us the payment,' said Golaron, 'or at least an instalment – for what other guarantee have we? These seem extraordinarily generous terms to be offered so freely.'

311

'Repeat that to my lady,' said Ailixond. 'How soon can we see all this? And what proof of sincerity has she?'

'We ourselves – that is, I and my retinue – will accompany you to Suthine,' Ylureen said. 'And you may take hostages to the borders of our land, if you wish.'

'But have you not observed that we are being deprived of all sovereignty over our conquered territories?' Sulakon said. 'What are we, a crowd of merchants, come looking for trade and money? I do not like this treaty.'

'This is true,' said Ailixond thinly. 'But consider, cousin – even an we can conquer all this land, can we hold it?'

'They have shown no sign of rising behind us, yet,' Sulakon said, 'a spineless race – you see, they even send a woman as their ambassador! Where are their men?'

'We are yet near at hand to visit retribution,' Ailixond said, 'but consider also – what of the willingness of our own men? It will not get easier if we move on into this land, where, as they say, their army awaits us.'

'You speak for terms!' Sulakon said, as if he accused the king of a crime.

'I speak,' said Ailixond, 'for the road to Safi – and do you not favour that path? Do you say that we should spend yet more years in trying to capture barbarians lands that, I cannot believe, we will ever hold? This land is neither ungoverned, like the grass plains, nor fragmented in government, like Lysmal, the Needle's Eye, the mountains of the north, nor ill governed by a coward, like Haramin – nor do its rulers slay themselves on our sword points, or send their young men to die . . . yes, my lords. I speak for the acceptance of this treaty, given that we can, as my lord Golaron has said, hold them to it. Do you stand against me?'

Sulakon stepped back. 'You are the king,' he said coldly. 'And I have heard the speech of my brother lords.'

'Yes,' said Ailixond. 'Then, my lady, we will accept your money, and your fleet, and the Grand Army of Safi will travel down to Suthine where we may cement our friendship with your king and queen. And I hope that there may indeed be perpetual friendship between your land and mine.' He held out his hand. Ylureen went up three steps and sank to her knees in a susurrus of skirts, bending her head to touch the diamond with her lips. 'Truly,' she said, 'I am honoured to meet so great a conqueror. Nor are you at all as rumour would have you. Merultine has seen your terrible face, it is clear, but you have also a smile to charm the moon down from the sky.'

'She says that you do not look like Alizhan the Monster,' Ayndra said.

'O?' said Ailixond. 'Then she disproves the slanders current in Safi that describe all ladies of S'Thurrulass as ranting, man-crazy, painted hags.'

Ayndra said to Ylureen, 'And he has heard that all women of S'Thurrulass are whores, but you do not look to be one.'

Just as Ailixond had, Ylureen looked suspicious, but she too was too well-bred to show a gross reaction; she stepped back from the throne, and bowed again.

'Excellent,' said Ailixond. 'I think we should put an end to this formal meeting; if you would like to retire for a short time, I will send for my clerks, and we can sit together and discuss the details of the treaty, and provide you with a written answer for your lord and lady.'

The lords were introduced to the lords and ladies of S'Thurrulass; wine and cakes were handed round; the two letters were read out, and translated, and discovered to be identical in text except that one came from the King and one from the Queen, but both had to be heard through and replied to – Ailixond dictated the answer, having by now gone through so many similar things he could give them out in his sleep – and all the lords put their seals to it; invitations to displays of martial skills by the Safic army, music and banquets were handed out, the last compliments exchanged, and, late in the afternoon, the Ambassador was bowed out. Firumin chased all the servants and clerks out of the way; Ailixond, who had not risen from his chair throughout, though he had conducted all the proceedings with infrangible grace, dropped forward onto the table with his head in his arms. In the silence that fell round him, the rattle and wheeze of his breath sounded. He said, 'Someone else must see to the phalanx display. And lead the Companions for me.'

'We will arrange it all,' said Arpalond. 'A chair by the parade ground . . .'

'And it's not the habit of their royalty to ride with their troops,' said Lord Ayndra.

'Ah, yes,' said Ailixond. 'One further matter . . .'

'Ought you not to go now and rest?' interposed Polem. 'I mean, if you intend to be at the banquet this evening . . .'

'No,' said Ailixond into the hollow of his arms, 'I should like to settle this first. We agreed to send a delegation in advance of the Grand Army to arrange the reception in Suthine. I should like to . . . select its leaders.'

Arpalond grinned. 'The first one is obvious,' he said.

'After this day's performance, I am not so sure,' Ailixond whispered.

'Pardon?' Polem said.

'I would never play such games if I were on my own and responsible for the whole enterprise,' Ayndra said.

'Would you not?' Ailixond turned his head on one side to fix her with a dilated, feverish eye.

'Send with me, as one might say, a lightweight of the traditional faction,' she said. 'Not Sulakon, for he would abominate Suthine. Polem would adore it, Arpalond would like it as much as he ever likes anything . . .'

'Sending you, the Council will want to send Sulakon.'

'Put forward a nothing like Hasmon,' she said, 'or Ellakon, even.'

'If you promise to be good.'

'I promise,' she said. 'And I should be delighted to return to Suthine as a lord – do you know, Ylureen believes that I must have been a lord all along, but concealed it? O, send me to Suthine!'

'I'll send you,' said Ailixond, and slowly sat up, coughed several times, and got to his feet. Polem tried to take his arm, but he pushed him away, and walked alone to the entrance of his own chambers. 'I will see you all at seventh hour,' he said, and shuffled out of sight.

The Council spent three days wrangling over the composition of the delegation to Suthine, while the S'Thurrulans were entertained by paradeground spectaculars, banquets of their own land's looted plenty, and Safic music and singing; in the end, while the rest of her party remained with the army, Lady Ylureen and her husband took upon themselves the duty of escorting the lords Aleizon Ailix Ayndra, Sulakon, Polem and Arpalond, with a train of servants, spare horses, clerks, messengers, banners and robes and clutter sufficient to maintain the state appropriate to a Safic royal embassy, through the as yet unravaged lands of S'Thurrulass to its capital by the sea. The rest of the Grand Army would wait by Merultine until the first instalment of the treaty had been paid, which would coincide with the arrival of the fleet to carry them downriver to the capital.

With Ylureen's royal authority, they never had to sleep rough once, nor pay in any way for their living; sometimes they put up in inns, sometimes were housed in the residences of local nobles or

314

the mayor of the town, and were welcomed as if they were kings themselves; S'Thurrulan hospitality proved more than lavish.

All the lords were formally equal, but the S'Thurrulans generally assumed Aleizon Ailix Ayndra to be the foremost; combined with Safic views on decency, this gave her always a room of her own, and often the best one in the house. Polem, by fair means or foul, was usually able to secure an individual chamber; Sulakon and Arpalond more often had to share.

She walked in carelessly, pulling off her clothes and shedding them as she crossed the floor. She was naked except for her shirt when she stopped dead: there was someone else's head on the pillow. They must have heard her, for they – he – sat up immediately; a young man, eighteen, perhaps twenty, altogether naked. She could smell from three yards' distance the musky perfume drenching his skin, as she turned back the covers.

'Lady,' he said, 'it's warm for you.'

She asked, 'Who sent you?'

'Lady Ylureen.'

'Are you one of her household?'

'Yes, lady.'

'You have somewhere else to sleep? You can sleep here if you wish. I'll take a blanket and sleep on the floor.'

'But, lady, I –'

'Did not come here to sleep. But I did. And I should not wish to tempt you.'

'Lady, I only come to give you pleasure.'

'I do not doubt it,' she said. 'But no. No! – you wonder why? O, I am sworn celibate, it is my time of the month, I am dedicated to the Goddess, I am happily married, I am tired, I am afflicted with the pox – take whichever reason you prefer. It's not for any unfitness in yourself. Give me a blanket, I shall sleep on the floor.' She tugged the embroidered coverlet from the bed, wrapped herself in it and lay down; she was soon asleep, for it was late and she had been riding all day, but the cold from the window awoke her before dawn; the lamps had gone out, and the whole house was silent. Swathed still in the cover, she got up and shuffled over to the bed; it was empty, the pillows as smooth as if a dream had inhabited them. She crawled in between the sheets; a faint musk still lingered there.

'You must . . . aah . . . excuse me, I cannot seem to keep my eyes open . . .'

315

'Splendid traditions of hospitality they have here,' said Arpalond.

'Yes,' said Polem, yawning again.

'And did you . . .?' Arpalond said to Ayndra.

'I', she said distantly, 'have cast off the foul yoke of sensual bondage.'

'Admirable,' said Arpalond. 'Perhaps you would like to share Sulakon's chamber.'

She spat, and spurred her horse away.

That night they dined in an inn, eating downstairs and sleeping above in rooms opening on to a gallery ringing the yard. Ayndra kicked the door open – not a quarter as spacious as last night's – sat down to pull her boots off – 'O no,' she said. 'Will you be punished if I send you away?'

The girl sat up. She wore a ribboned shift of linen so fine as to be translucent. 'Lady,' she whispered.

'Not now, do you hear? I will not, I am too tired.'

'But lady, I can –'

'I know what you can, and you can leave. Now. Do you hear me?'

'Yes, lady.' The girl got out of bed, picked up a mantle that lay folded at the foot, and left in silence.

When Ylureen emerged that morning from her room, she almost walked into Aleizon Ailix Ayndra, who was leaning on the rail of the gallery, hat shadowing her eyes.

'Good day,' said Ylureen.

'Send no more of your people to my room at night.'

'No?'

'No.'

'Have you a sickness? I know a –'

'Not that kind of sickness,' said Ayndra, gazing at her fingernails. Ylureen tried to capture her gaze, but she evaded her. 'It is someone else?' she said. Ayndra shook her head. 'The big blond one is most attached to you,' said Ylureen.

'Polem and I have never been lovers. I have nothing against your pretty children, and I thank you for your solicitude, but if I choose to relieve my solitude, I will choose the place and the partner.'

'As you will, then.'

'Thank you.'

Lord Aleizon Ailix Ayndra greets Ailixond, most serene Lord and

King of Safi and a great many other places.

Arpalond, Sulakon, Polem and your correspondent have all been installed in the Royal Palace in Suthine, with a deal of processing and speechyfying and overeating but as yet nothing of any import said nor councils taken on matters of state. It seems that they await your arrival for that. We have been greeted by cheering crowds – they pay them well for it, I am informed – and a banquet with fifteen courses, nine-tenths of which was taken away untouched and given out in the streets to the beggars. The great banquet hall was one wall all glass windows which they open to throw out scraps to the commoners. When times are hard the commoners have been known to climb in and steal the food before it has been picked over, and at times the plates and jewels and even unpopular diners, but at this time they are pleased with their rulers and do no more than shout for food and cheer when it arrives. They have been told that their skilled and clever ambassadors have saved them from Lord Alizhan who otherwise would now be burning their houses, eating their children, blaspheming in their temples and so forth. I do not know if their mood will change when they discover to what height they have to be taxed to pay Lord Alizhan not to burn their houses and so forth. Then the next day we had another procession to see the glories of the city. Descending the main steps to the harbour, suddenly a woman rushed out of the crowd and wrapped herself over Polem crying his name. This was one Diamoon, who was with me in Raq'min. She calls herself a witch and is taller than Polem and before he knew where he was she had his shirt undone. Polem blushed redder than her dress and tried to untangle himself, though not trying very hard. Sulakon went also scarlet, not I think from the same cause. I said to her Diamoon what are you doing and she said o my lord how does it seem what think you I am doing? Polem was half dead of shame and Sulakon two-thirds dead of apoplexy. The crowd meanwhile shouted many things too crude to commit to paper. I said to Diamoon I have not dismissed you my service I know not what you do here in Suthine but I will not permit you to continue in my employ unless you let go Lord Polem and follow us in a decent manner, in Haraminharn, which confused all save Diamoon who went to the rear of the procession. The crowd booed and shouted for more. She waved to them and pranced about in a most unseemly fashion; our tour of the harbour was less than peaceful thenafter. Arpalond, as soon as he found a place to conceal himself, laughed himself stupid over the affair. Sulakon remains perpetually affronted by the things which he witnesses daily here and hardly comes forth from his rooms. The nobility here have decided that he is a little odd and avoid him, though they have a great liking for Polem. Our lodging here is magnificent, Polem says that it is much greater than the palace in Safi, though I cannot say for I was never there, but gold and marble everywhere and I must remember not to stare like a yokel. We await eagerly the coming of the fleet. Polem and Arpalond join me in wishing you all a pleasant cruise, good health and fortune.

'Polem!'
　'What?'
　'Polem! The fleet's coming! Wake up! Ailixond's here! Polem, are you dead, or only drunk?'
　'Wait, wait . . . I come.' The lock rattled; Polem's door creaked open, and a crumpled head peered round it. 'You called me out of bed,' he croaked. 'Good god, you are all dressed up . . . what hour is it?'
　'Did you not hear? The fleet is half an hour from the quayside. The King and Queen are to receive Ailixond and we must all be there in full dress.'
　'Shumar,' said Polem blearily. 'Why did you not call me earlier?'
　'I believed that you must be up. It's last hour of morning. Shall I wait for you?'
　'No, you need not, I shall . . . o heaven . . .'
　'Do you know how to arrive at Haus'thorr Quay?'
　'Where?'
　'I shall wait for you. Go now and dress.'
　'And I?' said a voice within. Ayndra peered under Polem's arm, and saw Diamoon, wrapped only in a blanket. 'You may join the retinue,' she said.
　'Ceremonial dress?'
　'Of course.'
　'And jewels?'
　'If you wish.'
　'O very fine!' Diamoon hurried away, blanket unravelling as she went. Ayndra sat down on the doorstep and amused herself retying the shoulder cords on her robe and picking bits of fluff off the saffron sleeve-linings. From time to time she cried, 'Where are you?' and 'Will you run all the way?' There was an hourfifth to spare when Polem emerged. 'Do you like it?' he said.
　She moaned. 'Can you not see colours?'

'Of course I can,' he said, 'these dyes are very expensive.'
'So they should be, it should be an offence to wear them at all.'

The flagship was slowing to come alongside the quay; rows of figures lined the deck, with one in white alone in front of them, the windy sunlight catching the gold circlet on his head. Sailors in blue livery leapt ashore, roped uncoiling after them; the gate in the gunwale was pulled aside, and the gangway swung into place. Without exchanging so much as a glance, as if the same invisible master pulled their strings, the King and Queen rose. In the stern of the flagship, a dozen Safic trumpeters blasted a military fanfare across the crowd, and the rest of the nobility rose to their feet. Twelve phalanxmen with mirror-shiny pikes marched down the gangway and snapped to attention at its foot, sarissas inclined to cross blades in a steel arch; between the gleaming shafts, alone, came Ailixond. He wore the same white robe with gold sleeves at his wedding, though it hung loose from his shoulders, and his eyes glinted in a wind-burned face. A long way behind him came his wives, identically dressed in cloth of silver, with Parakison in a white smock embroidered with gold stumping short-legged between them. Golaron, Lakkannar and Ailissa led the lords of the Council, and their wives if they were with them, all in their brilliant and furiously clashing best. Reaching the principal platform, the queens and the retinue were gently halted and led to the chairs awaiting them. Ailixond went on alone. As he reached the royal dais, he held out a hand to each of them; first the Queen, then the King, leaned forward to kiss him on the cheek. He returned the gesture, and all three sat down as one. A woman crawled up the steps on her knees, kissed the hem of the King's robe, then the Queen's, then Ailixond's, while they ignored her. She sat back on her heels, eyes fixed on the floor, and said, 'Worshipful lord, permit my poor self to interpret between you the people of S'Thurrulass.'

'I permit you,' said Ailixond.

On the lower level, a man moved into the aisle and began to orate in S'Thurrulan. The woman translated in a low voice: 'Worshipful lords, worshipful lady, lords, ladies, we are honoured to be present at an occasion which will be marked in our histories for so long as records shall be preserved, the day when the far-famed Lord Alizhan brought an end to the enmity which for centuries has divided our great nations . . .' Ailixond, used to looking regal throughout tedious ceremonies, listened to that speech, and the three that followed, each longer and more

319

repetitious of the same platitudes, but the S'Thurrulan nobility seemed to recognise no such obligation, and chattered quietly from the start. The King and Queen never moved at all. Parakison, who was supposed to be beginning his education in the duties of a king, wriggled in Othanë's lap. 'Wan' go Dadda,' he said. Othanë's shushing was ineffective; she resorted to the box of sweets hanging from her belt, and closed his mouth with a sucket. Parakison munched it greedily and exclaimed, 'Gimme 'nother!' Othanë complied, and again, and again. The last speech dragged to a hyperbolic halt, and the interpreter whispered, 'Worshipful lord, go we now into the palace, the banquet and after you speak with the mighty ones yourselves.' She slithered down the steps; S'Thurrulan horns hooted from all sides. The King and Queen, still without speaking, stood up; the whole crowd imitated them. Othanë put Parakison, who was by now rather smeary about the face, on the ground. 'Be good now, and you'll go with your father.' Setha glided up and seized the child's hand. 'Come with me, Parakison, we go to the palace – o, look at your face!' She whipped out a wisp of lace, dabbed it in her mouth and scrubbed at his cheeks. 'Othanë, I must ask you not to feed him those things.'

'He likes them,' said Othanë.

'So he may, but that means not that they are good for him. Now, Parakison, walk straight like a lord.' She led him toward the aisle, S'Thurrulans falling in around her. Parakison tugged at her hand. 'Gimme swe-eet!'

'No, Parakison. We are to have a banquet soon, we shall eat then.'

'Don' wan'! Wan' swe-eet!'

'Be silent, now!'

Parakison raised his voice: 'Wan'a swe-ee-et!' Setha slapped him. He howled. The King and Queen were descending the steps in a slow march, like sleepwalkers, Ailixond a yard behind them. Setha shook her son. 'Do not you dare cry! Now be silent.' Parakison moderated his squalling to a snuffle as his father passed; Ailixond did not turn his head, but his eyes flicked to the side and caught Setha's gaze. She threw up her head and glared stonily. Parakison had his damp face in Othanë's skirt. Ailissa pushed past them. 'Come! We precede these foreigners.' Ylureen, Ayndra and Arpalond were first after Ailixond; behind them, Ailissa found herself next to a red-haired woman whose jewels and dress marked her out as a person of quality. They were trailing along the quayside now, with guards marching either side, keeping back the noisy and malodorous commoners. 'Good day,' she said, loud and clear so that the foreigner could understand. 'I am Lady Ailissa. May I ask who you are?'

'Lady Ailissa – sister to Lord Ailixond, wife to Lord Sulakon?'

'Yes,' said Ailissa, rather surprised. 'Are you . . . that is, do you come from . . .'

'Neither Suthine nor Safi. My name is Diamoon.'

'Diamoon? . . . o!'

'You know my name, lady?'

'Lord Aleizon Ailix Ayndra . . . mentioned you. In a letter.'

'Indeed? I did not know that she wrote to you.'

'She writes to my lord my brother.'

'And you were most disappointed that her letters contained no declarations of passionate desire for him, were you not?'

'What!' exclaimed Ailissa. 'How dare you!' Ayndra swung round and said something very sharply in a foreign tongue. Diamoon made a brief curtsey. 'Excuse me, my lady.' She slipped away toward the rear of the procession. Ailissa was red with indignation. 'By what right is that woman here?'

'No right at all,' said Ayndra.

'Then how . . .'

'She sailed onto the rostrum and asked for a place, and since she looked like a lady they gave her one. You were taken in by her jewels, were you not?'

'I did not know that Polem spent so much on his sluts.'

'They're no gift of Polem's. She claims that they are family heirlooms – for all I know, she comes from a noble family in her homeland. Wherever that is.' They were ascending another great flight of steps, up to the great double doors of the palace, flung wide to receive them. The guards turned into the wide aisles either side of the column-lined central corridor, carpeted in purple cloth thick with the dust of disuse; this corridor cut straight through the palace. It was the royal way, where one might walk only accompanied by the King or Queen. From time to time, footbridges crossed it, to allow passage to lesser mortals; people crowded their bannisters, and some dropped flowers. Polem caught a couple of roses thrown by young women, bowed extravagantly, kissed the petals and stowed them in his sleeve. The spectators cheered, and rained flowers on him. Up ahead horns hooted deafeningly under the roof, and there was a flood of light as another massive pair of doors at the side of the corridor were flung open. They turned into the Great Hall: the largest room in S'Thurrulass, more than a hundred feet long, and lit by a west wall that was all window. The sun was gloriously refracted through the varying thicknesses, the ice-greens and lemons of the leaded panes, and dappled across the stepped dais on the other side and the white cloths of the tables lining the gleaming floor, laid with pewter for the lesser orders and gold and silver at the high table. Servants were lined up along the wall; they led the nobility to their places, while doors in the other walls opened and a mob of other people poured in and struggled for seats on the floor of the hall. They were hardly settled before the first dishes of the feast were carried in, headed by a silver tureen whose bearer knelt before the King and Queen, who nodded fractionally but ignored the rich-smelling soup ladled from it into shallow gold bowls and laid before them. Ailixond was not unhappy to be free of obligation to eat, while another interpreter crawled up to them; when he had done kissing feet, the King and Queen spoke for the first time. The interpreter said, 'We extend to you our most loving welcome. We hope that you will encounter nothing but pleasure as you stay in Suthine. All things or persons that you should wish for your enjoyment ask only and we will send it. You must excuse that we have not spoken with you before now, but the skycaster instructs us that it is an illfortunate day for us should we speak or eat under the open sky.' He did not identify which of them had said what; as far as Ailixond could tell, they seemed to complete one another's sentences. 'If the hospitality I have received in journeying down the river is a fair taste of what is to come, then I am sure that I shall lack for nothing,' he said.

'How not, our brother? We shall not forget the honour of receiving in our house one who is without doubt the warrior of the age. And we do not believe that the lords of our two nations have ever before met. What may we not do with the joining of our varied excellences?'

'What indeed?' said Ailixond. 'We may march together out into the grass plains, and into the western lands even unto the stream of Ocean, for I believe that your navigators know of faraway lands where we of Safi have not even heard tell, let alone set foot.'

'Indeed, our brother, we shall send to you our most skilled captains if that is what you wish to learn of . . .' The soup was removed, another dish replaced it; they went on conversing. 'Eat should you wish, our brother,' they said. 'It is our custom never to eat before the people. Should you wish to join us, we will eat later when we have gone away.' So they were served with, and allowed to be taken away untouched, all of twenty courses; above the noise of the other banqueters could be heard the crowd in the square, who received the remains of each course tipped into great vats and carried out to them. Ailixond too took no food, but did not refuse the varied wines, all colours from straw-pale to oxblood, that came with it. From time to time he looked down on his followers. Parakison was asleep in Othanë's lap, smeared with half a dozen different delicacies; Ailissa and Arpalond exchanged idle gossip; Polem's red woman was seated next to him, he sliding further into her arms as he sank deeper into drunken repletion; Aleizon Ailix Ayndra sat with her chin on her hands, staring into space. Once he caught her looking up at him, but she only nodded deferentially and went back to daydreaming. The westering sunlight had thickened to syrup before the horns honked again, and the three rulers rose; the diners followed, some immediately and some only after prolonged shaking and kicking. Ailixond was led away down the royal corridor, while palace functionaries took the rest of the Safic nobility to be distributed through the extensive courts and passages and wintery garden rooms of the palace.

'I've no great liking for all this, in truth,' said Aleizon Ailix Ayndra, sitting crosslegged on the black bearskin spread in front of the eight-foot-wide fireplace. 'Look at it! If this were mine, in five years I'd have stripped off all the gilding and sold it, it would end up as White Walls, chill and underfurnished and painted in black and white.'

'But I think that you take pleasure in living among it, for a while,' said Ailixond.

'Indeed, it's very pretty. It makes me feel like a yokel from a village for the first time come into the city, who is forever stopping in his tracks and staring mouth agape at all the buildings and the dressed-up people.'

'They do dress up, these people.' Ailixond got up and stepped up to the fire, leant on the ledge of painted marble above it. They were in the dayroom of his suite: the sky-blue, gold-ribbed ceiling stood on gilded pillars, and the floor and walls were marble. The walls were lined with all kinds of chairs and small tables, inlaid and painted and decorated in fifteen different styles. He picked up one of the little statuettes that were lined above the fireplace. 'I am not sure that I am much in love with this land, but it fascinates me. It seems that they care first about the form of anything, before they think of the content. I had some trouble to understand why – for example – some liaisons outside marriage are censured, others tolerated, until I understood that.'

'Indeed. Style, comfort, sensuality, and talk. It's not possible for

323

any of the nobles who would have any standing in the land to stay more than a few months away from the court for fear of what's said in their absence, and then when they are at court they are all acting all the time.' She laughed. 'The lords of Safi are such simple people – or most of them, at least.'

'They are a far older nation than we.' Ailixond drummed his fingers along the mantelshelf. 'I feel that they still live in the world when there was no other power to match them. So they feel no shame at suffering one defeat after another by foreign invaders, then paying them off to escape further conflict and even then having to entertain them before they can induce them to leave their land; indeed I believe that they see what they have done as a triumph, for sooner or later we shall go and they've preserved the greater part of their land unravaged.' He looked down sideways, eyebrows lifting to brighten his eyes. 'Nor would I say that they are entirely mistaken in that view. But they are clever enough to fete us while we stay here, as it were giving beads to the barbarians. And how many of our people even bother to speak to S'Thurrulans, if not to command a slave?'

'Arpalond has taken an interpreter into his service for the whole of his stay within their borders . . . I found her for him, she'd been a merchant who used to trade with Safi when she was not running sweetsmoke for Lady Ylureen . . .'

'You used to be in Lady Ylureen's service, did you not?'

'Yes,' she said. Ailixond waited for her to say more, but it was not forthcoming. Instead she said, 'We see little of you these days.'

'In their world, royalty associate only with royalty. They thought that I must be entirely solitary – so they welcomed me so warmly – before they became used to my having friends among the lower orders, such as Polem, and you.' He shook his head. 'I thought that my place restricted me – I knew not what the world meant. Some days they cannot eat and speak outdoors, other days they cannot wash, or lie down between the hours of dawn and dusk, or name any animal, or touch a person not of the same sex – they were surprised to hear that we have no ritual days in Safi, but when I asked them why they had to do such things, the only reasons they had were that it had always been so, and some talk about the harmony of the kingdom. You know that we carried the day at Hallasila because someone let a stray dog into their rooms on the day preceding? And they have no names – they lost them when they were crowned, and they'll not have them back till they die and the new couple become the King and Queen. I understand now why they have S'Thiraidi as commander of the army, and not themselves. They travelled during their parents' lives, but now they live here, or in the Summer Palace on the West Shore, or travelling the one road between them which it's their custom to use, and they'll never go elsewhere again. If I had besieged this city, and taken it, they'd have stood here to die, or if I'd not slain them I think they'd have slain themselves, though they are too courteous to speak openly about the war between our nations.'

'And had you done away with them, think you that you'd have had to take on the ritual calendar – you and . . .'

'It appears that it would be hard to retain – or attempt to gain – the loyalty of the people if one did not follow it, since they say that the good fortune of the land depends on the King and Queen doing as it prescribes. Or so the nobility tell the people, so that they can use it to bind the King and Queen and restrain the life-and-death power they have over all their subjects – the price of their loyalty is to make oneself into a painted doll, honoured and obeyed and granted every luxury while your Lady Ylureen and her friends govern in accordance with their own interests.'

'And her enemies. Ylureen has plenty of enemies. You were at the funeral of Lord Borabine?'

'I was.'

'Then you know how he died.'

'A wasting disease,' Ailixond said innocently.

'O yes. The sort of wasting disease that comes out of a phial.'

'That's not unknown in Safi, either,' he said.

'But the lords need not have their food tasted and forever be testing the loyalty of their servants and have people with concealed weapons follow them everywhere in public to protect them from assassins.'

'Only now and then, at least. During the election of the next king, perhaps . . .'

'I'd not know about that,' she said.

'Yet,' said Ailixond half under his breath. She said, 'What?' He glanced out of the window at the angle of the light. 'What hour is it?'

'About ninth, I should think.'

'Then I shall go to fetch Parakison – you too?'

'If you like.' She followed him out into a passageway, through a door which he unlocked, into an arcaded walk with grassy lawns and fountains drained for the winter either side of the blue and white paving. It curved round, and at the end of it they saw a cluster of women dressed in soft bright colours. Ailixond lifted his

hand and waved to them; they came chattering toward him. He
called, 'Parri!'

'Dadda! Dadda!' A small figure detached itself from the group
and belted down the walk. Ailixond dropped to one knee and held
out his arms; Parakison landed in his embrace like a small solid
missile, and he swept him up laughing. A few steps behind him,
Aleizon Ailix Ayndra came to a sudden stop. Her hands closed on
one another and her mouth sharpened in a stubborn line.
Parakison planted a wet kiss on his father's cheek as Othanë and
his nurse and half a dozen ladies and their maids came rustling up;
they greeted him, and let him lead them back through the garden.
Aleizon Ailix Ayndra came behind, her hands consciously relaxed,
her face blank and sad in the white, gentle winter light.

Suthine was far enough south, and near enough the sea, that it
rarely snowed there in winter, but endless grey fogs rolled up out
of the ocean and swathed the city in raw damp cloaks, smirched
yellow and brown by myriads of cooking fires. The rare clear days
were glassy-pale and followed by bitter nights; next morning, the
trees and grasses were hoared with frost, and children slid and
tumbled on icy paths. Those who did not need to go out stayed
closed up in warm rooms, with furs on the floors and the windows
shuttered. The ritual of court life filled the time with feasts and
plays and sacred processions and weddings and funerals and
dances; almost two thousand people lived within the walls of the
palace, but so divided that each group might in its own eyes
almost have been the only community there – the S'Thurrulans'
slaves, the free servants, the secretaries of government, the
political nobles of Suthine, the Safic visitors, their own servants,
the royal families. Ailixond had grown up moving between the
three worlds of the palace in Safi – the Women's House where
children lived till, if they were boys, they were removed at age
seven to the men's rooms, and the public halls where the
petitioners and foreign visitors and government functionaries
moved. He knew of the fourth world, the kitchens and the
outhouses and cellars and side passages where the servants
worked, but never had occasion to go there. Here the men and
women lived with no distinction made between their places, the
servants were as servants everywhere, and the public rooms,
including as they did a variety of audience chambers for the nobles
who carried out the actual work of governing, halls for dancing
and music and the performance of plays, were far more extensive
than those in Safi; but, far more secret than the House of Women

326

because so narrowly select, and spreading its ways in the thickness of walls and high galleries and roofwalks and enclosed gardens far outside the bounds of the western wing where what everyone knew as the King and Queen's apartments were, was the fourth world of the royal rooms. One could walk for half a day through its age-stained corridors without crossing the same path twice. So he came to understand how the King and Queen had such wide and surprising knowledge of events in the palace though so few ever conversed with them, and why the political nobles were so circumspect in their dealings, since they never knew when they were observed – all the major public rooms had some concealed watching or listening post in them; also why the King and Queen worked so hard to maintain the centrality of Suthine in their realm, and to discourage any growth of power and independence in the provinces where they could not watch it. He saw, without needing them to tell him, how the Safeen made up their own Safi-in-exile within Suthine, ignored the invitations of their hosts except for state occasions and a few gatherings which courtesy demanded that they attend, and continued in the patterns which life in the travelling court had made habitual over the years. The only ones who escaped that enclosure were Polem, who was always with Diamoon and often taken by her to S'Thurrulan junketings or to low haunts in the city, and Lord Ayndra, who he caught sight of at odd times and in odd places in every reach of the palace; several times with Lady Ylureen, but on other days with rough-looking servile types or even slaves who seemed overly familiar with her. When he went to visit the Safeen, which was not often, she was never there, and public events were conducted in the manner of S'Thurrulass so that there was no chance to speak personally. When there was a banquet, he sat up high with the King and Queen and watched the others as if he were a spectator at a play.

Since this was no great occasion, the tables were kept to the edge of the hall, under the ranks of oil-lamps; the floor was open, for dancing, with musicians playing under the window. In Safi, only those trained and paid to danced, but here anyone who wished might get up, and the children of any half-decent family learnt a dozen different steps in their schools. S'Thurrulans would break off even in the middle of serving to go out and prance about the floor. The Safeen sat still and watched them, unless they were very drunk or reckless. Lady Ylureen was dancing now with her husband, who was shorter than she and had dyed his hair and beard bright blue. Setha, Othanë and Ailissa sat clustered under the dais. As usual, Ailissa was talking: '. . . the shamelessness, the utter shamelessness! Three times now I have come to the door of our rooms and discovered one of the creatures in the very act of propositioning my poor Sulakon – of course he dismisses them, and I am assured that he would never betray us with any of those . . .' Aleizon Ailix Ayndra sat behind her, watching the dancers. In the lamplight her hair was spun gold, gleaming like butter. Her still features wore a cast of pale-bitter melancholy, their natural habit whenever she was not enlivened by strong feeling, until someone dancing caught her eye; she raised her head, then shook it at them. Ailixond followed her eyes and saw Ylureen beckoning. Ayndra shook her head again. Ylureen came up to the dais and walked round to Ayndra's chair; she produced a small something from the neck of her dress and lit it in a lamp. The two of them bent over its smoke and nudged each other, giggling. Ailissa stared fiercely at them but they took no notice. He could hear that they were speaking S'Thurrulan, but he did not understand if halfway well enough to tell what it was that they spoke of. Ylureen stood up and ran down to the floor, waving. Ayndra rose to her feet, and Ailissa managed to catch her eye with an icy glare. 'Will you join in this undignified – this dancing?' she spat. Lord Ayndra gave a peel of laughter, kicked her chair backward and vaulted over the table. Ailissa shrieked, the other diners turned to stare, as Ayndra landed at the foot of the dais and bounded across the floor, crying, 'Yoolal! S'Thspaal yoolal!' The orchestra, which had been playing a slow tune, switched to a furious rhythm. Ayndra and Ylureen clapped each other's hands, linked arms, swung round and round, seized upon other dancers and pulled them into the swing. S'Thurrulans watching clapped in time with the drums and called, 'Yaay!' Some of them ran down to join in. Ailixond started to grin, then found Ailissa and Sulakon looking at him and restored his face to impassivity.

'Yoolal is a dance from the eastern forest,' observed the Queen, 'the province where my lady Ylureen's family holds its land.'

'Was not my Lord Ayndra formerly in the household of Lady Ylureen?' added the King. 'Ylureen's barbarian,' said the Queen. 'It seemed a strange thing to us, that one of your nobles should come here and work as one of common blood – do you often send your young lords out thus, to educate them?'

'That was before my lord Ayndra was elevated to the nobility,' Ailixond said. 'I had not the honour to know her in those days. I think I have explained that our noble lords need not be born of noble families.'

'But few of them are not.'

'True as it stands,' he said, 'but I think that within the Empire we may find good reason to admit many more who are not of our few old families.' Aleizon Ailix Ayndra was whirling like a whipping-top under the tiered lamps by the window, framed by a hundred fragmentary reflections in the leaded panes. She threw her arms wide, and Ylureen embraced her, they fell laughing on each other's necks. The musicians, equally breathless, were glad to pause, and the lines of twirling dancers broke up and filtered back to their seats. Ayndra and Ylureen moved towards the door which led to a garden, to the Fountain Court. 'My lord Ayndra,' said the Queen again. 'She is your lover.'

Ailixond had absorbed enough of S'Thurrulan customs not to be disturbed by such a remark. 'She was,' he said, 'but no, no longer.'

The kohl-rimmed eyes in the snowy-powdered mask regarded him closely, acute and amused. 'You should speak to her again,' said the Queen, 'there is no sense in suffering your separation because you are too proud to beg.'

Ailixond's eyes widened; he looked direct and hard at her, but said nothing. Her deep-red mouth curved in a smile. He gave a slight shrug. The music had changed, and different people were dancing. Ailissa's voice rose again: 'I see no sign of Polem – no doubt he is occupied with that red-headed slut. I think I shall speak to my lord brother about finding him a wife . . .' Ailixond excused himself, and slipped out into a royal corridor. There was a lamp hanging by a chain from a brass staff by the door, which he took with him to light the unfrequented passages that led by a roundabout route to a corridor which had spyholes into the Fountain Court.

Dark, peeling stuccoed columns bulked massive in the moonlight. Almost full, the colourless radiance drew vivid diagonals down the plastered walls, inkblack and white light like a metaphor of good and evil. They were standing on the border between the two, in the limit where categories dissolve. Ylureen was mostly in shadow, with her back to him, but Ayndra was leaning against the wall with the moon full in her face. The roof was low on the squat columns; in the velvet sky, the stars were hard enough to cut one's hands upon. She turned her face to the side and spoke, still in S'Thurrulan. Ylureen handed her a stick from which rose coiling smoke, and she cupped it to her face. He could not hear clearly enough to know what was their conversation. The stick passed back and forth. Ylureen moved

329

further into the light, shawl slipping from her wide powdered shoulders. The jewels in her hair glinted; her stance was insistent. Ayndra shook her head, twisting away, her fingers beating angrily on the wall. Ailixond caught a strong whiff of sweetsmoke. Ayndra turned her head away, her mouth slanting down in a slash of pain. Ylureen reached out and touched her cheek, then covered her entirely from view with her body. It was some minutes before Ayndra broke away, and then Ylureen stood at her back, stroking the hair back off her face. She spoke more clearly now: 'I will not lie to you,' she said. 'I'm no longer Ylureen's barbarian. Nor are you fighting for your councillor's chain or command of the business. I can give you nothing which you cannot get elsewhere.'

Ylureen said in a high voice, 'Do you never think of yourself? You speak as if you had no needs. Do you so condemn yourself to celibacy? Why?'

'Why?' said Ayndra distantly. 'Why? Because it's what I want to do. It would be a lie!'

'Lie!' repeated Ylureen, almost in a sob. Ayndra turned her head back over her shoulder, the deep eyes wide. 'What do you want from me, then?' she said. 'Pity?' For answer, Ylureen buried her face in her neck. Ayndra dropped back against the wall; now it was her turn to stroke the other woman's hair, her face fallen into calm melancholy again. They stood so for some while, until Ylureen stood up, and they exchanged some more quiet words. The older woman turned to leave. Ayndra kissed her briefly on the cheek, they brushed fingertips and she departed. Ayndra put her head back; then slid slowly down the wall until she was sitting on the frosted pavement, elbows resting on her drawn-up knees. She looked at the other side of the court, giving Ailixond the momentary illusion that she knew where the spyhole was, then up, it must be at the star-strewn sky, and whispered to herself, but in Safic this time, so that he could tell the words. 'And it won't be long,' she said, 'before summer comes . . .' She dropped her head, and her hair shaded her face. He could tell no more of what she said.

'It's early in the year to be leaving.'

'Think you so also?'

'It's what they say. Spring comes late here.' Aleizon Ailix Ayndra leant against the shelf over the fire and picked up one of the blue and white vases. 'Is this not the waves of Safi?' She turned it in her hands, studying the motif.

'It was a gift. They had the two of them made for me.'

'They're very skilled, the craftsmen here ... when shall we go, then?'

'We shall leave the eighteenth of Seventh Month. The footsoldiers and the baggage a day before, I think, for ease of traffic on the Coast Road.'

'Ah.' She frowned faintly at the vase. 'You are bored here?'

'I am.'

She looked up. He shot her a sharp glance. Both fell into a grin; she began laughing. 'You must have been.'

'Incredibly so. I would have left sooner, but as soon as we leave Suthine province the roads worsen, and north of Ukariss there's hardly a road at all, we cannot attempt the marshes unless in high summer ...'

'I want to go from here.'

'We're going.'

'You're leaving me.'

'I'm going away from here.'

'You have no need to.'

'You mean that you petitioned the King and Queen to request that I remain.'

'Ambassador to the Court of Suthine?'

Ayndra ignored Ylureen's question for the packet in her hands. 'You bring me a present.'

'In spite of everything.' Ylureen pushed it into her hands, went on talking while she untied the ribbons and wrappings. 'I had not heard that you'd rejected the request.'

'Not rejected. It was never so much as formally made.'

'Was it your Council of Lords that rejected it? Or does your little king not bother to seek its judgement on his appointments?'

'An you must know, he spoke to me as soon as asked as to whether I would stay before he put any name to the Council.'

'And you said no?'

'These are very beautiful,' she said distantly: long soft doeskin gloves dyed dove-grey. 'Though it's hardly the time of year for gloves.'

'Listen to me!'

Ayndra jerked her head up, though her hands did not leave off easing on the gloves. 'You're jealous of him? I cannot help it!'

Ylureen spat, explosively, dyed tresses snapping like cattails across her face. Ayndra yanked her gloves off, slapped them down on the balcony rail, and took the glowering face between her hands; she had to tip Ylureen's face down to hers to kiss her, hard; then released her, and went back to sliding the gloves on. Ylureen was like one dazed.

After a while she said, 'You're not as you were.'

'Nor are we any of us. Look down there, they're bringing the horses out, I must go.' She snatched up her hat and danced down the wide stairs in a clatter of military boots. The courtyard was filling up with the barbarian lords in their bright, rich, simple clothes, all jostling and sweaty like a crowd of animals. The big blond one stood almost below Ylureen, remonstrating with the red witchwoman who stood arms akimbo, insolent. It was plain what went on between them in spite of the foreign language.

'You're leaving me.'

'I am decided to stay here.'

'I'll buy you a carriage – you can have a bodyguard and six women servants –'

'I must practise my trade for a while. I will not live as a kept woman.'

'You can practise your trade with the army.'

'I dislike it. There's not so much trade there and there are lords who are forever cursing sorcerers and agitating for our expulsion, nor do I think your Ailixond favours us overmuch, while here –'

'What do you say, *my* Ailixond, as if he –'

'But there are parts of him that are yours as they're nobody else's,' Diamoon said, 'even if you've never –' she began gesturing with her hands. Polem roared. 'Brazen bitch! Why, I'll –' She shrieked with laughter and fled into the crowd. He was too possessed of dignity in new clothes to follow her, and, beside, they were lifting the trumpets to sound for the king.

Ylureen watched him from the balcony; she did not hear her husband until he touched her shoulder.

'Is she here?' he said.

'She's going.'

'With him?' He nodded down toward the centre of attention. Ylureen shrugged. 'They're like animals,' she said. 'Or children.'

'Indeed?' They stood in silence as the lords of Safi mounted their horses and got ready to ride away. They'd said lengthy ceremonial farewells to the King and Queen for the whole of the previous day, so that they'd have almost an entire day to start on the road. Ailixond raised his hand to the crowd, the Royal Ring flashing in spring sunlight like a star.

'If they are animals,' Lord Gishiin said, 'he is a greyhound among bulldogs. Or a peregrine amid goshawks. Is he crippled in the left arm?'

332

'I think not – why?'

'He uses it as though it were weaker than the right. See, he does not hold up that hand to wave. The horse obeys him through no more than the pressure of his knees – clear that it's a finely trained beast. He does not pull on the reins left-handed.'

'He was wounded in his left side at Merultine,' said Ylureen. 'When I went there he looked like a ghost, though they'd not say that they feared he was at death's door. They give out now that he's altogether cured . . .' She was drowned out by a final blaring of trumpets and the racket of iron horseshoes on the paving. Aleizon Ailix Ayndra was riding next to the king; they dashed away down the cleared highway in a sunny flutter of multi-coloured cloaks and blue and white banners. Ylureen looped an arm over Gishiin's shoulder. He gazed after the spectacle, unresponding. 'I said I would go to Chahalo's this night.'

'Go next day.' She embraced him closely. He leant back against her.

'I'll stay,' he said.

The harbour of S'Themiss was crowded with ships, come for the spring markets in furs, leather, glass and wood prepared over the winter; in return they brought wines, dried fruit, unpolished gems and minerals from the south, ebony, mahogany and spices, which were exchanged for gewgaws from the manufactories of the Eastern Shore. Ships from every trading port of the empire rocked on milky-glass waves, among others with unrecognisable flags or no flags at all. Ailixond asked the harbourmaster who guided them round the quays the origin of any vessel he could not himself place, and asked to meet the captains of one foreign squadron, from South Lysmal, the island that lay separated by a hundred-mile strait from his province of North Lysmal. In Safi the island was a mythical habitat of warlocks, demons and monstrous animals, and all who went there returned sorely changed, if they returned at all. The men from the ships were very dark of skin, brown-eyed and loaded with cheap clinking brassy jewellery, but otherwise acted like any other merchants and sailors. They knew of the kings of Safi, but preferred not to trade with them; S'Thurrulass better, they said, because so far away. They gave a picture of a wet green homeland, hot all year without winter or summer and clothed with forests that held, they said, the vastest trees in the world, especially in the far south where there were no cities, only barbarous wandering tribes, idolators and demon worshippers. It must be they who inspired the tales told of Lysmal in Safi, for their own city of Shullish was a small peaceful place

333

which intended only friendship toward the mighty Empire. They left before the banquet to which they were invited, saying that it was the Moon of Long Fasting and they could eat only plain food prepared according to the rules of their gods.

'They used to have forests like that in North Lysmal,' Ailixond said.

'Do they not still?' Aleizon Ailix Ayndra was cutting the canvas covers off the basket of exotic fruits the Shullishi had left as a gift to the king.

'In the eastern part. In the west, Safi's cut down many for ship timber, but they ravaged them long before that – all the desert hills were forests once . . . fuel for iron-forging . . .' As the wax-sealed cloth peeled away, sweet vapours pervaded the room. 'Even in the east they have no trees as tall and hard as the woods they bring here, and they only bring fragments for marquetry, and bits of furniture.'

She brought out a round, greenish-mauve fruit, wrinkled as if it had shrunk inside its skin. 'I wonder how one's supposed to eat this.'

'It would be a great source of riches for the Empire, to possess such a wealth of southern forest.'

She turned it round a couple of times, shrugged, and bit into it; spluttered as juice spilled over her chin and down her shirt. 'You don't listen,' said Ailixond.

' 's nice. What other ones have they got? Look at this one! As big round as your hand.' She produced a giant yellow egg smeared with red and green. 'How do they keep so long? I know what it is that you're saying, you must have said it fifty thousand times – the Empire needs this or that other thing. There must be five or six kinds in here and none I've ever seen before. What you mean to say is that I Ailixond would like to have South Lysmal too.'

'I think that is why they'll not trade with us. Suthine would never bother with a land so distant.'

'Suthine gets what it wants without methods so crude as conquest.'

'I have no interest in bits of furniture.'

'I, on the other hand, would not mind more of these fine fruits.'

'Take the basket. I'll not eat them.'

'I will leave you one or two. You might give them to Parakison.'

'They gave me another basket; I sent it to the House of Women.'

Ayndra perched on the edge of the table, curled round the fruit basket in her lap. 'Are we in truth going back to Safi?'

'Eventually,' he said. 'You know we have to make our own road after we reach the marshes. A year, perhaps, if we meet much fighting.'

'I think you have little desire to see the place again.'

He half smiled. 'I think I've not tried to feign any. There's South Lysmal, and I should like to come back to Suthine with the fleet – I'd like to sail to the far west where they say the land comes to an end, but there is only a narrow sea and another land beyond it . . .'

'And if one sailed always westward, one would come to its shore which is the far side of the ocean beyond the Land-beyond-the-Mountains.'

'It's possibly so. None of their sailors have made that journey. They don't cross the narrow sea now, they say there's no trade there – perhaps one day they'll send some dreamer to see if it is an island, or another great land.' He tilted his chair back, smiling at imagined landscapes.

'Sulakon thinks you will sit in Safi and govern.'

'I'll sit in Safi when I'm old. I know all these arguments.' His lord's bracelets rattled on the arms of his chair in anger, but he spoke coldly. 'I think that my presence is better used in parts of the Empire still in need of subjugation. I think it unlikely that I should be able to depart westward in the next several years. But I'll not sit in the palace and be . . . all that which I left behind me.'

'Ay,' she said softly, offering neither support nor criticism. 'I know not what I'll do, then.'

'Ambassador to Suthine?'

'Maybe. I think I'll take these to safety.' She went cradling the basket of fruit like a baby.

'A fine excuse for a spring.'

'It's a clear day. Often they have more rain at this time of year. Rainstorms, wet gales blowing in off the sea.'

'I can better bear cold than this dampness.'

'For why have you come down to tail with us at the stump-end, then?'

'Why is it you still do this tedious task? Up to your knees in slime half the day, riding into the night . . .'

'What should I do instead? Play sticktoss in a covered cart? I should rather see the rainstorm. What is it you do up there all day, in any case?'

'Precious little, to be sure. Those who have cares of state pursue them. Sulakon prepares documents for the Council, Polem bemoans the absence of his red woman . . . why do you not come in the evenings these days?'

'Too tired,' said Ayndra offhand. 'Fah!' said Arpalond. She shrugged. 'Things aren't as they were.'

'No. Ailixond is all day in a covered cart, scribbling, meeting with all manner of riffraff, petitioners . . .'

'Covered cart likely the best place,' she said curtly.

'Why? Do you . . .'

'You know more than I do, no doubt. The Physician says he's as well as he'll ever be.'

'It's not a subject which one is allowed to discuss. I make a daily offering for him. He may live another twenty years.'

'Or he could be dead in two . . . Shumar! why did he ever . . . I could have stopped him, I was there . . .'

'You could not have,' Arpalond said. 'No more than any will get him to admit himself an invalid, before he falls too sick to stand.'

'Aah . . .' They went on in silence; he watched her stiff profile, she stared at the road. He chattered over fragments of gossip: 'Ailissa has fallen out with Setha – she had heard that she had a paste of herbs to prevent conception, but when Ailissa requested the use of them she denied that she had any, then Ailissa's tirewoman found a seller of medicines who boasted that he'd supplied the queen with this and that and would also secure some for my lady – Ailissa says that she has provided Sulakon with a sufficient number of heirs, but Setha deprives Ailixond of sons merely because she fears to lose her looks . . . also she has plans for the education of Parakison which do not square with Ailixond's, but no one can say what they are for she spends all her time muttering with those twin slaves and never confides in the other ladies – she has asked Ailixond to send for a party of cousins and servants from her homeland, to assuage her loneliness among an alien people.'

'And has he sent for them?'

'He can hardly refuse. In any case they'll not be able to join us until we've passed the marshes.'

'I suppose not,' she said vaguely, looking up. Seabirds tossed like ashes in the updraught of the wind. 'What is it?' said Arpalond.

'What should it be? Things go as well as may be expected.' She shrugged, added, 'You are kind to come and talk with me. Do you never fear that your confidences will be passed on?'

'I would not speak to you in that way if I thought so.'

336

'Would you not?'

'No. Why should you go tell Ailixond why his wife has not fallen pregnant again? It would look suspiciously like female jealousy, and you would rather die than show anything resembling female jealousy.'

'O indeed?' She roused from her withdrawn stupor.

'And you have no desire to usurp Setha's place.'

'Although she believes that I have, and would give much to be rid of me.'

'She asked Ailixond, in Suthine, to send you back to Raq'min.' He paused; she failed to ask for more, but he went on anyway. 'He refused, she demanded an answer, he said that you were indispensable to his government, she shrieked and wailed and declared that to be a lie, that he cherished an adulterous passion for you . . . in the end she clawed his face and he struck her. He's not been with her since.'

'I suppose you found out before long about the royal passages in the walls of Suthine, and how to enter them unobserved,' she said drily.

'Only a few. One must not abuse a privilege.'

'If the King and Queen had come upon you they'd have thrown you in the sea . . . I'm not sure that Ailixond would not have, either.'

'Lady Setha would have demanded it.'

'And thus secured your salvation.'

'As may be,' he said. She gave him a very sly look. 'Damn you,' he said. She giggled. 'I must go patrol my constituency. My thanks for your company.'

'And for yours,' he said, 'you are welcome to visit –' But she had shot away down the line. He nudged his horse on, to rejoin the lords at the head of the column.

'There's a visitor come up behind us on the road to whom we ought to send an escort, the last day our march – send a troop of Thaless horse . . . will you wish to take them?'

'What visitor is it?'

'Master Serannin.' Ailixond saw that the name was a strange one. 'The painter,' he said.

'O?'

'Ha! some one dweller in Safi not known to you.'

'Really! I never claimed to have any wide acquaintance at all. And none in court circles.'

'Serannin is scarcely the court circle.'

337

'Nor artistic circles, neither painting nor the theatre and of the musicians, only the street singers . . . I have no education, you know.'

'O! how this unaccustomed garment becomes you.'

'Modesty, you mean?' They fell into conspiratorial giggles. 'No, but when should I go? Is he far away? How is he coming in any case?'

'They took ship from Safi to S'Themiss, and are coming in cavalcade up the road. They're perhaps two days behind us now. Leave next morning and bring them up the last day to me.'

'What for is he coming? What is there to be painted? I cannot see . . .'

'I shall have two pictures. One of the Inner Council and one of the Outer.'

'O! portrait painter.'

'What, did you think –'

'Well, I thought it could not be house painter, with us on the march, but . . .'

'You are astonishingly stupid tonight.'

'Yes, I'm a little confused.' She was bowed over the table in a fog of sweetsmoke and giggles. 'God's sake!' he said. 'I can hardly breathe.'

'Nonsense, you should breathe it, it relaxes the passages in the throat.'

'Where do you learn these lies?'

'In S'Thurrulass I learn them. Ask any of their physicians.'

'O nonsense . . . you will go tomorrow?'

'Did I not say so? Push the lamp over here.'

'What's that? I must have smoked a gold sol's worth merely by sitting in here with you.'

'And do you complain?'

'I must say, indeed I . . . I hardly think it can be the effect of that stuff, but again I cannot believe that your company has such an emollient effect . . .'

'What are you laughing at now?'

'You know.'

'I suppose I do.'

'Pass that over then.'

'What? . . . haahaha!' She leant back and cast an eye at the door-curtains. The gap where they should have met shivered slightly and closed to a hairline crack. She shrieked with laughter again and stood up to lean over Ailixond as if to catch the clouds of smoke escaping from his hands.

338

The Thaless horse were sent to escort Serannin to the king in parade uniforms, with the banners of Safi and two trumpeters to sound a fanfare as they entered the camp at evening; still their military glory was tarnished by the three wagons they accompanied, followed by two hired applecarts for surplus baggage and three dozen riders on mismatched rented nags from Themisson. At their head Lord Ayndra rode between a thin, long-nosed man on a pony so short that his feet hung almost to the ground, and a red-faced man stout as a barrel, a fringe of grey hair sticking out like a straw crown round his sunburnt pate. The latter was Master Serannin, the former his chief assistant Pazarin, heir apparent to the master's studio; they had brought with them a mob of background-painters, figure-painters, landscape artists, colour-grinders, canvas-stretchers, inkmen, papermen, frame makers, apprentices to all and any of the painters' trades, servants and hangers-on, above fifty people in all. The master and Pazarin were taken in to be presented to the king and any other of the lords who would meet him, although he and Ailixond were well known to each other since he had been portraitist to Lady Sumakas ever since the end of his apprenticeship.

'I trust that you had a smooth crossing,' said the king.

'Be it smooth as a millpond, my lord, yet I finish by offering up my guts to the sea-gods – nay, it was not so rough as might have been, the worm-ridden nutshell of a carrack broke not in half and we had two days' more biscuit in the hold coming into harbour . . .' Serannin snatched a cup from Firumin and tossed it down his throat in one gulp. 'Aaah! Lord king, you have the best taste in wine as in painters – always from Thaless . . .' He fished in the front of his grease-spotted green tunic. 'Your lady mother, when she heard that I was crossing the ocean, sent me this missive to convey to you.' In its canvas wrapping it looked thick enough for a book. Ailixond looked not overjoyed to receive it. 'My thanks for the service. Have you come all prepared to fulfil the commission I mentioned?'

'Have you more of this good wine? It will not be short in the doing, my lord, for how many of your valiant warriors do you wish portrayed?'

'In the Outer Council there will be perhaps two hundred to be shown.'

'O lord!' Serannin swigged his second cup as rapidly as the first. 'This is fine news, my lord; all the painters in Safi will be employed for the next year and the merchants will have to employ five hundred more of us to get their faces put up behind their counting houses. I shall of course do all the faces myself, Pazarin will assist with vestments and the like – do you wish also portraits of the noble lords?' Pazarin was watching Aleizon Ailix Ayndra, who wandered three times round the tent, paused behind Ailixond, took a knife out of her shirt, breathed on the blade and put one leg up on the table in order to polish the blade on her thigh. Serannin kicked him. 'We can begin the sittings next day,' he said. 'More wine? Perhaps I could take part payment in a shipment from the royal cellars.'

It was almost half a month before Lord Ailixond found time to attend for a first sitting. In the meanwhile, Serannin had begun on Lakkannar, Sulakon, Polem, Hasmon, Ellakon, Arpalond and Aleizon Ailix Ayndra, and had collected a vast fund of scandal and confessions in confidence, extracted by soft subtle questioning as his drawing pen scratched over fine rag paper. A fair amount of it had centred upon Ailixond, but, after asking if Serannin's food and travelling arrangements were to his liking, the king arranged himself so that the light fell across his face and stayed still and silent. A couple of strings had been rigged up in the top of the wagon's high-framed tilt, and Serannin's favourites of his works of the past days hung up there like washing, the best two or three of each subject. Discards lay in a heap in one corner. Ailixond's eyes flickered over the pictures, but his face remained still as a statue. When Serannin had done, he got up to look more closely at them, shuffled through the pile of rejects. 'Would you permit me to go away with one or two of these? I should like to have a piece from your hand, and I find these more immediate than the finished work – perhaps you could spare this one? Put your name on it for me.' He handed one over, picking it apparently at random. It was Lord Ayndra, pale hair wild, grinning sarcastically, head tilted so that her nose looked like a witch's beak; that was why Serannin had not thought it suitable. Still, if the king wanted it . . . he put his mark in the corner, and gave it to Ailixond, who tucked it in his tunic and went away.

The Coast Road came to an end at the town of Agasthine, outpost and bastion of S'Thurrulass in the north-east; it sat with its feet in the water and its back against the hills, marking the end of civilisation and the beginning of the barbarian lands. The road entered its west gate paved, and left the east gate as a muddy track scattered with sea-sand and gravel to keep it drier in the rain; as

340

far as Suthine was concerned, it had ended. The peace and protection so far afforded the Safeen would end similarly once they left bowshot of the walls. Ailixond decreed a halt of twelve days, to pack up and dispose of unneeded baggage and followers, drill and repair in readiness for hostile lands, and to collect the due payment of tribute from S'Thurrulass itself. The six S'Thurrulans who presented the great chest of gold thesh looked unhappy as it was unlocked before Ailixond, and his clerks began counting it and putting it into bags sealed with the waves of Safi.

'I think they'll not regret it when we are gone out of their land,' he said, 'so I intend to make use of their hospitality before we leave – I have suggested that there should be a farewell feast . . .'

'And I suppose they felt obligated to offer to provide the meat and drink for it.'

'I offered to provide the wines at the high table. It was their suggestion that they give free beer to all who wished it.'

'Beer is cheap here, after all – will they also give their firewater?'

'I should hope not. I have never seen Polem so drunk as at that feast where they served firewater in place of wine.'

'Still they say it's sovereign against the cold and damp.' She was sitting on the corner of his desk, eating honey-cake out of a leaf packet bought from a street stall. 'Have some of these. We should have them for a dessert. Here, try.'

Not wishing to refuse, he broke off a corner and ate it. 'Would it be possible for you to take charge of the cooking?'

'Whaat?'

'Firumin needs someone to help him.'

'Have you forgotten the last time?'

'We shall have no soup this time.'

'O! – I know how to make good soup. Only then, I meant to put in a little more seasoning, but the spice-pot fell open and all the pepper fell in the one bowl, I was too far away to think there was anything wrong . . .'

'It was like eating fire. I thought the roof of my mouth was burnt out, I could hardly see for tears – watch for the crumbs, you'll make sticky smears all over my papers. Who's that?'

Polem pushed the door open. 'Good day – Lord Ayndra, they said you were in here, there's someone come up with the tribute asking for you. Some old friend of yours, I was told. They wait in the garden.'

'Did they say who it was?'

'No. Some person from Suthine.'

341

'From Ylureen?'

'I know not, they did not say, not that I saw them in any case.'

'You'll excuse me, my lord?'

'Of course.'

She left the pile of cakes among the documents. Polem took one and munched it. 'Umm! – where did you get these?'

'She bought them in the street somewhere. She's forever trying to feed me sweets and suckets. Brings them here, eats them herself.'

'You should eat more. You're far too thin.'

'Ah, nonsense.'

'No, it's the truth.' Polem picked up Ailixond's hand and slid back the shirtsleeve, to show how he could encircle his forearm below the wrist with thumb and forefinger. 'Last year I could not have done that. And look at this.' He slid the lord's bracelet up and down. 'They're supposed to fit – well, I know they used to fit.'

'Leave off!' Ailixond shook his arm free. 'I am sick of being told what I should or should not do with myself.'

'You need to be told. You ought to take more care of yourself, for the sake of everyone else even if you will not do it for your own sake. No one will blame you for it.' Polem ducked his head to the side, trying to catch Ailixond's eye; when he did, he met a blue stare as sullen and insolent as a child of thirteen who has realised that *ought* does not mean *have to*. 'Sweet heaven!' he said, desperate. 'Sometimes I could hit you!' Ailixond said, 'It's too late for that.'

Polem blew like a restless horse; he cast himself away from the desk. Ailixond gave a faint shrug; his mouth had turned thin with resignation. 'I run up a flight of stairs and gasp like an asthmatic at the top,' he said. 'If I try swordfighting I must go sit down after a quarter-hour, when before I could go on for hours. Do you think I don't know? I do not wish to die prematurely and leave all that I've fought for to fall into rebellion and collapse. I may be struck down next day – as you may, or any of us. I will no longer do the things I lack the strength for, but I will not live like an invalid, I will go on as I have always done. Does that not content you?'

Polem beat his palm against the wooden windowframe. 'I wish I . . . I wish it had been me that was hurt. I wish I'd stood in front of you –'

'Good god, no! It's my place to go up on walls and be shot at.' Ailixond tipped his chair back, grinning. 'It is what they pay me for.'

342

'That's one of hers, isn't it?'

'What?'

'That's what they pay you for. Aleizon Ailix Ayndra says that.'

'She does . . . did I tell you that we're to have a farewell feast?'

'O, good news – when's it to be? Will it be their food?'

'No, ours. She's to have charge of it.'

'O, a pity – I like their food . . . perhaps she'll make some of it . . .'

There was a sort of garden in front of the governor's house of Agasthine, mostly grey stone paths with the beds full of windblown sand and only sea holly and tamarisk thriving there. The visitor, swathed in a fine red-mauve cloak, was lounging on a stone bench behind a windbreak wall. 'Good day,' said Lord Ayndra. The visitor stood up, removing her hood – 'Good day, my lord.'

'Diamoon!'

'Yes, my lord. I had business to finish in Suthine, so I could not leave when you did – and also . . .' She moved up very close, so that Ayndra had to put her head back to look in her face. 'I made a foretelling for you, my lord, and it said that, before next summer, I mean not the summer that we enter upon but in the next winter, something will change the course of the New Empire. I burnt a lock of your hair and spoke with my spirit familiars, and they told me that you will have something that you have long desired, and something that you have greatly feared – and they left a doggerel verse: the prophecy I gave you before –' her voice changed, becoming low and grating.

> 'Your rise began with powderfire.
> Through death and death you'll rise yet higher.
> Through many battles, unscathed in all
> Except the last; in blood you'll fall.'

'The battle in which we die is always that in which we are well bloodied,' Ayndra said. 'And how did you have a lock of my hair for necromantic conjuring with?'

'It was not necromancy! I can talk with the dead, but it is difficult and extremely costly – I could call the spirits for you to see if your mother is among them, or if she yet walks the earth –'

'O, nonsense. Is that all you came here for?'

'Well, my lord, with no laws against sorcery in Suthine, there

343

are witches and foreseers and magic women in every street, and they do not take kindly to a newcomer who only wishes to earn a small honest living. But in the army there is a deal of profit to be made with luck-charms and weapon-charms, love-potions and telling good fortunes and drinks to prevent conception, and . . .'

'It is true that I need someone to look after my accounts. I do not trust the clerks in the king's Treasury, either they cannot add up or they embezzle money.'

'Or, my lord, you spend more than you believe.'

'Well then, Diamoon, you may prove that to me and then recommend economies.' Diamoon had stepped backward and relaxed from her impressive prophetic pose; she even giggled. 'Get him to buy a box of smoke,' she muttered.

'What? You sound like a drunken chambermaid. Does Polem know you are here?'

'No, I thought it would be amusing to get him to take the message in ignorance. I knew he would hear that you were asked for and go in to the king. I knew you were with the king,' she added.

'Indeed? One wonders why you bothered to leave Suthine to come here and see us.'

'No, my lord, I wanted to come. But please keep silent until I have a good trade here, for I'll not be his kept woman.'

'As you will, then. Have you any baggage?'

'Of course, I have all my tools and the chest of drugs and —'

'Come and I'll find a porter to take it to my rooms.' They went into the governor's house. 'I tried a foretelling for Lord Ailixond,' said Diamoon. 'But I had nothing of his that the spirits might involve themselves in, and they would not speak much.' She waited to be asked what they had said, then carried on as if she had been. 'They said only, beware of the Summer Palace when it is not the time, and then, swans will fly southward.'

'They do that in every winter. If you imagine that I'll steal the shavings of his beard so that you may talk better with the spirits, I certainly shall not. The king warned me before that associating with you might bring trouble for me.'

'Well! My lord, if you —'

'But I said, nonsense, they are a pack of fools, half of them know I am in league with the devil already.'

'What! you are not —'

'O yes, did you not know? I signed a pact in my monthly blood, my soul to the devil for three sols' worth of wit.'

'A pact? Is it true then: I have read of it, but I never saw —'

344

'O Shumar, are you a naught-wit? It was a jest. There is no devil. The evils we make are all our own.'

'My lord, I would not be so sure of that,' Diamoon said seriously.

The land between the borders of S'Thurrulass and the great marsh at the head of the sea was mostly forest, scattered with fortified farms and occasionally a hamlet; the people were mostly criminals fleeing the justice of S'Thurrulass, or masterless men who had gone out into the ownerless land to take what they could till from the forest and pass it on to their descendants. All were suspicious and independent of mind; some of them came to the camp to sell food, fish or wild honey and fruits, accepting any currency so long as the metal was good or trading for bits of ironwork and weapons, and disappearing as soon as their business was done. The army lumbered slowly over the unmade track, improved by a few logs or bundles of brushwood thrown down where the potholes threatened to make it impassable; the unsprung carts jolted fit to shake one's teeth loose, so that all those who could ride took to horseback or even walked. At such a slow pace, there was ample time for those who took pleasure in it to ride off all day, or for several days, into the deep forests in search of game. Ailixond, though, no longer went with the other lords, and often spent the day travelling in one of the wagons of the House of Women, taking bundles of papers with him, though the clerks had to follow in separate vehicles. Lord Ayndra was even less to be seen, except as a raggedly clad rider hurtling up and down the column at the head of her corps of engineers, mechanics, wheelwrights and labourers, who came to the rescue of broken-down carts and impassably rutted patches of roadway. If she appeared at the shared suppers in the king's tent, it was only to gobble a double portion of food, tearing up bread with hands stained by axle-grease, make her excuses and go off to sleep; she had voluntarily assumed the task of giving reveille to the whole army every morning. She never had time to talk.

Serannin, Master Painter, greets his most honoured benefactress, Lady Sumakas the King's Mother of Safi.

Lady, I have been now close on a month in the army of your son, preparing studies for the pictures which he has asked of me, and with much opportunity to observe the truth of those matters which were spoken of when last I was honoured to be admitted to your presence. I must say, firstly, that the fears you have concerning your noble son's health are by no means excessive, although this is one matter on which rumour is almost silent, for I think no one dares to contemplate what may be clearly seen: that my lord king is in the grip of a wasting illness arising from the wound he received in S'Thurrulass, and which the physicians can do nothing to cure. It may be, of course, that they having been with him throughout do no notice the signs as one does who has not seen him for some while. He rarely rides all day and is not seen to go hunting nor to join in weapon practice as he used to (the lords Lakkannar, Sulakon and Golaron have charge of drilling the army now), and is grown so thin that he resembles an ascetic priest rather than a noble warrior. But all these are no more than appearances, and it may be that it reflects no more than the pressure of governance upon him, which forces the abandonment of the sword for the pen of the statesman. I have no access to the Royal Physician, who, I am told, is in any case invariably discreet (for which the king rewards him richly, so richly that no offers of gifts will influence him to any breach of trust).

But not all the news I bear is bad. The little prince Parakison, who I have seen several times in the company of his father, is a most bright and sturdy child, though small for his age. Nor does he fall too much under the influence of his foreign mother, spending much of his time in the company of Lady Ailissa's children. Indeed it seems that the king and the Lady Setha have had a falling-out, since he rarely visits her and then only to see the child. It seems that he favours Lady Othanë more than he has for many years. The woman Lord Aleizon Ailix Ayndra is no longer his mistress. She leads a corps of rude mechanics and dresses like a common soldier, as I am told she was when she first came to the army; she is hardly ever in the king's company, let alone with him solely. I suspect however that some feeling remains between them, indeed I am puzzled by their avoidance of each other, so much that either refuses to be drawn in conversation concerning the other. As for the other lords, I detect in them no signs of unseemly ambition. All are devoted to the king, and even though they may not agree with every policy he chooses, I have no doubt that all would be loyal to the death if his authority should ever be challenged. The army is in good order and I am well cared for here, wanting for nothing. I will write again concerning the other inquiries which you wish made. The gods bless and keep you safe. This letter given in my own hand, in confidence, as always.

'Do you see that shine on the horizon?'

'It must be the start of the marshes.'

'Yes. We'll be in among them in a sixday. Sooner.' Aleizon Ailix Ayndra shaded her eyes with her hand; the ground fell away suddenly from the hilltop where they had paused, into a sea of treetops fading silver green in the summer haze, shrinking into scrubland and the distant gleam of the marshes. Anagar stamped and snorted, shaking his head, but the flies that pestered him only fled for a few moments. She took her hat off and flicked it at them.

'He doesn't shy,' Ailixond said softly.

'No, he's used to it.' She leant over the horse's neck to scuffle her fingers through his forelock. Somewhere in the forest a woodpigeon called sleepily.

'How quiet it is here,' he said. 'I've not been out of the camp like this since we left Agasthine.'

'This is the end of the hills, here. From now on it'll be flat for miles . . . shall we go on?'

'If you like.'

She glanced briefly at him. 'You need not come with me if you don't want – I'm sure you'll find your way back –'

Ailixond began to deny it, shaking his head vigorously, but the speech got lost in a hacking cough, so fierce that it bent him almost double and made Harago shift nervously. He pulled a scrap of rag from his sleeve and spat into it, then cast it away in the long grass. When he finally looked forward again, she was staring at him with sharp curious eyes. 'Let's go, then,' he said, and stroked Harago's side with his spurs; he sprang away downslope, thundering through the flower-spangled grass into the green and sighing trees. He did not pull back to a walk until they were once more within sight and earshot of the column's stink and dust.

The wagon pulled up so suddenly that the ink slopped out of the secretary's inkwell and splashed across the halfwritten letter. He began to curse, then slapped his hand over his mouth – 'Saving your presence, my lord –'

'Ah, no matter. I'd not be able to send it off for days in any case.' Ailixond got up and went to stand on the box beside the driver. 'What is it this time?' He shaded his eyes to look ahead where the march was backing up, but the flat horizon swallowed the view in a dull heat haze. The air was as oppressive as a bathhouse. He looked around for a messenger. 'Send up ahead to ask what ails them,' he said irritably.

347

'As I can, my lord.' The runner went on foot; the path through the marshes was often so narrow that a man on horseback would never have pushed past the people already occupying it ahead of him. Those who were mounted frequently led their horses on account of the wet unstable ground, and no day went by without the whole tramping mass, stretching out over miles of scrubby wetland and reed beds drying dank in the sun, being entirely halted by some vehicle's collapse. It crumpled up like a ravaged concertina in a chorus of plaints and slaps at whining insects. Ailixond watched them stand and stamp, waiting for the ripple that would announce someone pushing through to him. He scuffed his feet restlessly on the boards. 'A chafing journey.' He put his head between the muslin screens at the front of the canopy. 'Have you recopied that spoilt page yet? Come up here to me when you have it. You need not hurry if you have no mind to.' He sat down beside the driver, swinging one foot over the edge of the wagon, swatted a fly on his neck; it crushed in a scarlet smear on the edge of his palm. 'Full fed,' he muttered.

'I think they're moving at front, lord,' said the driver. 'Are they?' Ailixond jumped up again. 'It seems so.' Whips cracked among voices exclaiming encouragement or cursing as they pulled themselves on to swollen feet again. The driver merely had to shake the reins of their ox-wagon to get the beasts moving again; they were a hundred yards on and Ailixond had turned his back on the path to return to dictation when there was a knock on the side of the wagon-box. 'Let me up there, then.' He snapped his fingers at the secretary to take a rest and ducked outside. 'Take my hands.' She swung her feet to the side as she jumped so that her bare feet scrambled up on the rising spokes of the front wheel and bounced her up over to his side. She dropped down on the box. 'Ah, Shumar! Have you something alight in there?'

'There's a firepot in the box with the water jar.'

'Haah!' She ducked inside on hands and feet like the tame monkey of the forests which the Lysmalish captain had shown him, dipping in her shirt for a loose stick, thrust it among the tiny red eyes of coal and puffed furiously on it. The secretary sat watching. She caught his silent eye and pushed the fuming stick at him; surprise made him slow to take it till she almost thrust it into his hand, and then he only managed a few half drags. She caught it back and went outside, where Ailixond sat in the sunshine, and dropped down with her back against the side. They passed the stick back and forth, saying nothing; the blue smoke fretted like slow rags in the dull breeze.

'We had only to throw a few bundles of brush down and the pothole was filled, they drove out of it. An easy one.'

'The fen people came again, to trade for food.'

'Did you get any of the things they brought?'

'Golaron bought these for me.' Ailixond reached under the driver's seat for a bundle wrapped in reed matting and tied with a grass string. 'Or rather, for my ladies . . .' It held three necklaces of carved bone beads and several bangles pieced together from some hard wood blackened by age. 'This is the bog-oak; they say it's lain in the marshes ever since a former time when all this was a great forest.'

'Pretty.' She pushed her hand through a bangle and rubbed her finger round and round its smoothness. 'I want to learn to paddle one of their skin boats.'

'The round ones?'

'Yes. I tried one two days ago but I could make it do nothing except spin in a circle, I know not what they do . . . I should perhaps try it with a tall pole . . .' She rested her head on her drawn-up knees; sun and wind had turned her hair bleached-blond and bushy as wheatstraw. In the dirt and sunburn of her face the blue eyes were like live pebbles; though she must have felt his gaze on her she gave no sign. 'When shall we stop today?'

'You must know as well as I do, you talk to the guides before I do even. I know nothing, closeted here in this cart –'

'O nonsense. I see your foot messengers everywhere. Here comes another now. I'll be bound he'll ask me to go see to some fool who's overturned a load of flour in a fishpond.'

'My lord? Lord Polem sends from the back party, he says could we please travel more slowly for the path is so churned up when they set upon it that they cannot go at half our speed and are likely to be left back behind an hour by the end of the day. Already they are detached from the main body and he sees some fen people on the lake in boats watching them.'

'Does he? I think you may assure him that they are unlikely to fall upon him, however much he should dawdle.'

'I could go back and impel him to greater speed,' said Lord Ayndra, 'I should be most unwilling to cause the main body to drag its heels for the sake of some stragglers.'

'You could give him that message, then –' Ailixond began addressing the runner, but she interrupted – 'I'll come with you presently, indeed now I'll come.' Ailixond said nothing until she had climbed down to the ground, and then he cancelled it before it was half done – 'Ah! You know as well as I do what's to be done.'

She shrugged. 'I suppose so –' and darted off after the runner, upstanding mop of hair bobbing among the dusty mud-streaked ranks of phalanx like a ball of foam on a river. Ailixond beckoned to his secretary. 'Come up to the front. I should prefer to sit out where the air's fresher . . . stay just inside the curtains, there the papers'll not blow away . . .'

The marshes steamed and stank in the hot darkness; the stars swam faintly in the obscured sky like specks of mould on leather. The air in the queens' tent was heavy with perfumes and medicinal vapours, the thin greasy smoke of the guttering oil-lamps by the door. The nurse Gilmis bent over the tiny flame with a flask of new oil, watched it dim and grow up again. Parakison whimpered and thrashed, trying to throw the sweaty sheets off his limbs, but as soon as he was free of them one of the maids tucked them over him again. The sour aura of sickness hung like a net over his cot.

'You should give him poppy-syrup,' whispered one of the women.

'We shall be awake all night.'

Gilmis hissed softly at them and crossed the tent to lay her hand on the child's forehead. 'His fever's not reduced,' she said.

'The Physician says it will last at least a day more before it breaks,' murmured a deeper voice. They looked up at Ailixond, where he stood by the curtained wall, out of the low circle of light. 'It's all through the camp,' he said. 'Infected water.'

'He won't sleep,' the maid said again. Ailixond came silently out of the shadows and dipped his hands into the twisted sheets. 'I'll walk with him a while.' Parakison, half delirious, twitched and moaned, squirming in his father's embrace; Ailixond bent over him, saying things too soft for the servants to hear. They went up and down, up and down, like a slow heart muffled by the carpets on the floor. A dog howled somewhere among the wagons, and every so often a horse whinnied in the picket-lines. The maid dropped dozing over the side of the cot; Gilmis nodded in her chair, falling in and out of sleep so that she lost all sense of time, until something woke her with a jerk. She looked at the lamp and saw that it was two-thirds empty again, and Ailixond was straightening the sheets in the cot. Parakison lay straight and still in bed, sleeping quietly. Gilmis rose blearily, laid her hand on his forehead and found it cooler.

'If I may leave you with him now,' said Ailixond.

'Of course, my lord, of course – you must have healing hands.'

'Perhaps,' he said. Gilmis looked at him, but the thick fall of

350

hair hid half his face. She began to thank him and curtsey, but, 'It is nothing,' he said, and was gone from the tent like a shred of cloud blowing off a mountain.

The sky was no longer perfectly dark outside. As he walked back to his own tent, a wash of deep blue was rushing out of the east to drown the stars, and the thundery heat had dissipated into cool, almost fresh. As he acknowledged the salutes of the sleepy guards, the sunrise horns began blowing, far away at the leading edge of the camp; it straggled over a mile long on a narrow spit of higher ground. It would be a half hour before Firumin came with breakfast and the tent was taken down. He went through to his bedroom and fished in the wooden box by the bed for a flat flask, which he drank deeply from, before lying down on the un-disturbed bed. Outside the daily tumult was already beginning.

It was Second Month and already the summer was dying, rotting like the rushes in the luke-warm rain. The Grand Army had still (the guides said) half a month before they would emerge from the Girran. The heavy wagons moved slower than walking pace and the sky wept endlessly on their passing.

'O god, o Shumar. O Luamis –' sgluck-suck, sgluck-suck '– o, god help us. Polem.'

'Yes?' Looking round, Polem saw Aleizon Ailix Ayndra, ankle-deep in mud and mired over the knees, peering up at him from under the dripping brim of her hat. 'Ailixond says to stop now, and make camp.'

'But it's only third hour after noon.'

'I know, I know, and it feels like the fiftieth. We are stopping.'

'O well then.' Polem pulled his horse up; it tossed its head and huffled at Ayndra. She snarled exhaustedly. 'Do we camp here?' he said.

'Yes.'

'But it's swimming in mud.'

'Everywhere swims in mud, Polem, an it's not already swimming in the water. Now get on and tell the rest to make camp.'

'Look, I do not think –'

'Ailixond's orders. Do not quarrel, Polem, I am in no state to tolerate quarrels. O yes, and Ailixond invites you to dine this night. Come at any time once we are halted.' She coughed harshly and spat into her hand, flicked the gob away in a sort of farewell gesture and tramped onward, huddled into her cloak like an old woman. When Polem wandered into the king's tent, three hours later, she was still coughing.

351

'Are you afflicted by the damp also?' Ellakon was saying to her.
'So it would seem.' She snuffled into an immense once-white handkerchief. Polem went and sat by her. 'Are you ill?'
'I can't recall the last time I was ill.'
'You're shivering.'
'O, nonsense.'
'I shall get Firumin to make you a posset.'
'A posset!' She swore foully and blew her nose like a trumpet. Then Firumin called them to the table. Polem found himself between her and the king; both of them picked at the food and sent it away; after a while he saw that both of them were similarly prone to coughing and wheezing. He was concerned. 'There's lung fever in these marshes, I am sure.'
'Why?' said Ailixond shortly. Polem took aback. 'Well, I thought, you, well . . .' He turned to Lord Ayndra. 'You seem as if you had it.'
'Lung fever? Seems as if I had a cold.' She stabbed a piece of meat with her knife, only to toss it across the plate. Firumin intervened with an offer of wine. Polem got up to relieve himself. When he returned, he glanced at them as he came through the door and saw Ailixond produce a flat metal bottle in a leather case and offer it to her. She sniffed at its open neck and rejected it scornfully, saying in a penetrating whisper, 'Have you been drinking that?'
'At times I find it pleasant,' Ailixond replied. She said, 'Phu! If you drink that you'll go blind.' 'What?' said Ailixond. Polem went to take his chair, while she muttered, 'Filth! Poison!' and Ailixond said, 'Nonsense.' 'What's that?' said Polem.
'Nothing,' said the king. 'What are you looking for? Do you want more to eat?'
'O, no, thank you.' Polem could not see what he had done with the bottle, and in any case Firumin was now pressing a cup of some steaming slop on Lord Ayndra. She sniffed sadly in the fumes of honey and cinnamon. Polem said to Ailixond, 'How much longer must we spend in these godforsaken mud holes?'
'Half a month, if the rain does not let up soon.'
'O Shumar – and do you not feel that it gets into your joints? I am sure I become arthritic . . . Firumin!' He leaned back to ask the steward for more wine; thus he missed Ayndra rapidly up-ending the bottle over her posset and shoving it back to Ailixond under the table. The other lords had mostly risen from the table and left, though Arpalond and Sulakon were chatting at the foot of the table. Occasionally Arpalond shot a glance at the three at the

352

head, though he gave every impression of deep attention to Sulakon's words. He caught Polem looking confused and gave him a brief sardonic grin; which confused him so much that he offered to go.

'Yes. I shall go also.' Ayndra drained her cup, stood up, swayed and tipped backwards. She would have struck the ground like a felled tree if Ailixond had not leapt out as he rose and caught her so as to break her fall. Her eyelids flickered almost as soon as he landed with her; he immediately laid down her head and moved back, rubbing his palms against his thighs.

'Why am I on the floor?' she said. 'And you too. What, did the earth shake?'

'No,' he said. 'You fainted.'

'Fainted? O, deplorable.' She began to pick herself up. 'Please excuse . . . it's all going round in circles. Buzzing.' She lay down again.

'Polem, have Firumin send for my lord's servants. Can you deny now that you're sick? You'll be carried home.'

'The faint will be the worst of it, it'll get better now,' she said plaintively. 'But I'll go home to bed. Walk home.' She rolled over and slowly got to all fours, then stood up carefully by holding the chair and the table. Ailixond looked up at her from the floor. 'You are stubborn beyond all reason.'

'It has its purposes,' she said, 'as you well know. Where's my cloak?'

Ailixond said to Firumin, 'Don't give it her.' To Ayndra he said, 'Not until Mistress Yunnil, or whoever will come, is here to walk with you.' He stood up to give his hand to Sulakon, who moved to leave, his lined face carefully blank. She sat down, propping head on hand. 'All right then.' Ailixond stood coughing into a square of rag, which he stuffed away in his sleeve.

'You're all mad here,' said Polem. 'What did you do with that bottle?'

'What bottle?' said Ailixond. The door-guard looked in to announce Yunnil, and Firumin came forward with cloak and hat. 'I'll walk with you,' said Polem.

'Thank you.' She waved ironically at Ailixond; he stood grinning secretively by the littered table. Arpalond offered his farewells and followed them.

Polem recognised the wagon by the motley crowd around it: some of the mob called the Rescuers who ran with her to accidents, artillerymen, assorted provincials, horsemen, servants, even a few painted camp-followers and the filthy army-bred urchins. He pushed through them to mount the steps of the small vehicle. Yunnil peered under a lifted flap, and opened it when she saw who he was. The crowd cried, 'Lord Ayndra!' and 'Is she worse?' and all manner of foreign exclamations. Yunnil chattered at them in Haraminharn tongue; Polem pushed on inside.

It was dark within, and close, though it was an hour before sunset; the Physician had evidently been imposing his views on the dangers of light and air to the sick. Only a lifted smoke-flap gave a feeble light. Ayndra lap propped up in bed at one side, and someone sat in the deeper gloom behind her head. She indicated a wooden stool; he pulled it up to the bed. She whispered something to him, but he could not distinguish the words. 'Pardon?' he said.

From the shadows a voice said, 'She has lost her voice.' He knew that voice; he almost toppled off the stool, leapt up, poked his head into the tilt, stood bent over – 'Diamoon!'

'O good lord,' wheezed Ayndra. 'I forgot that you had not met.' She was ignored, they were embracing over her. She croaked, and was not heard; reached up and tugged Polem's sleeve. 'Elsewhere. And elsewhen.' Diamoon let go of Polem, who stood waving his hands and exclaiming, 'O! – O! – I'm sorry, but I – I had no idea! How long have you been here?'

'A while,' said Diamoon.

'But what have you been doing – why did you not say she was in your service?'

'She's not in my service.'

'Well, then – but you must have known –'

'I did not want that we should meet till now,' said Diamoon airily. 'I will explain all to you later. I shall go and sit outside.'

'Go and see the man with the black star flag,' husked Ayndra.

'Must you?' said Diamoon. 'You are sick, my lord.'

'I've nothing else to do, lying in bed. Go and fetch it, it's paid for.'

'As you will, my lord.' She winked at Polem and pushed very closely past him leaving. Ayndra sagged back among the pillows. She was dressed in a very loose white nightshirt, tied at the neck with silk cords; within its folds she seemed small, as if sickness had shrunk her. 'And has the world fallen apart without me, then?' she whispered.

'We all want you to get well,' said Polem. 'And all those people outside – can you hear them? – they're all calling out . . .'

'I think that most of them are owed money.' She giggled feebly into the pillows.

'I'm sure not. Lots of your people are there . . . Ailixond is very concerned about you.'

'Well, you may tell him that it is not the lung-rot. The Physician says it is a marsh fever, which is to say it is a fever but he knows not which or whence, but it makes me cough and lose my voice and feel as if the entire corps of Companions had galloped over me. You talk. It hurts my throat to speak.'

'O, well, I, ah . . . Ailixond said he hopes it's not serious, indeed I saw him worried as I've rarely seen him, you know I . . .' Polem lost the thread of his exposition, lacking the confidence to speak of the delicate matters which he did not in any case perceive clearly.

'I was not unworried myself,' she said vaguely. Polem frowned. 'I think sometimes there's a conspiracy between the two of you,' he said.

'Between who? Myself and Ailixond?'

'Yes.'

'I don't think there is,' she said.

'I never get a straight answer when I talk to either of you!'

'Perhaps because you never ask the right questions,' she answered drily. He shook his hands in frustration. 'What were you doing with that bottle?'

'What bottle?'

'You had one last night. I distinctly saw it. I know not what he did with it after that, but he had it.'

'O, that bottle.'

'Yes.'

She turned her face into the pillows again. 'It has lifewater in it. They must have offered you lifewater in Suthine.'

'O. Yes.'

'But should you wish to know whether he drinks it all the time, or at all frequently or how much, I cannot tell you. I thought it was the kind they make in low taverns. Ylureen says you'll go blind if you drink much of it – but it was a very fine one, I'll say that, still I think it's all the same . . .'

'You've got him to smoking your stuff as well.'

'Not only I.' She shook her head. 'Many people get the taste of it in S'Thurrulass. I for one, indeed.' She looked at him, eyes like sloeberries on parchment. 'It's no bad thing, you know.'

'I'm not such a fool as you take me for,' Polem said in a low voice.

'I don't think you're a fool. Talk to me. Tell me a story. I am bored beyond endurance.'

355

'I hardly know any stories.'

'O, come, you must have some tale of someone I've not seen for a while.'

'O, well . . . I had a letter from Parro, you remember Parro? Well, after I took them to Raq'min when I came to see you, I got them into the service of Irailond, that was Haldin rather, Parro went to Purrllum – I'm sure I must have told you? No? Well, Parro wrote to me saying that he would like to marry, but the girl's parents, since he was a bastard, they were not willing even though he said he'd take her with no dowry, not that he'd ask me until all this had happened, but . . .' He chatted on until the light had faded so that it was quite dark inside the wagon, and Diamoon came in with a lit lamp. 'It is the dinner hour,' she announced. 'We shall not be serving a public supper.'

'I should go, then.'

'Thank you for your visit. Come again soon.' Ayndra closed her eyes. She heard Polem and Diamoon at the door, arranging a rendezvous later that night. The witch returned to the bedside rearranging the neck of her gown. 'What do you wish for supper? I could make you a clear soup –'

'I do not wish any soup. I shall go to sleep.'

Diamoon took the vacated stool. 'You were most patient with all his blather about his wayward sons.' Ayndra shrugged. 'And why not?' she whispered. Diamoon said, 'And why should he think that you are in a conspiracy with the king?'

'Tell me, Diamoon, tell me, since you always know these things better than I do.' She rolled away from the lamp. Diamoon sat watching her for a while, until she was sure that she slept, then laid her hands round her throat and held them there for a while, head lifted as if listening for something. Her face slowly adopted an unseasonal perturbation; she dropped her hands, and went to call Yunnil to bring a firepot and more blankets. A thin rain began to drum on the canvas tilt.

The fever raged on and off for five days. Ayndra had intervals of lucidity, mostly in the hours around dawn, when she lay still and only raised her dry-leaf voice to ask for something to drink, but mostly she swam deep in the sea of diseased dreams, husking fragmentary admonitions to nameless audiences. Diamoon abandoned Polem's bed to sit behind Lord Ayndra's, and brew aromatic herbal potions on a tiny charcoal stove to give to her when she was waking; she sent Yunnil round all the medicine men in the camp, looking for powdered roots and tree-barks with foreign names. Polem came every day. On the fourth day the rain built up into a torrential thunderstorm, halting the march at midday in a huddle of temporary shelters and vehicles packed with supernumerary passengers. In the middle of the afternoon, when Yunnil and Diamoon were sitting with a firepot between their feet peeling tubers for soup, the door-curtains burst apart with the entrance of a great rainsoaked swirl of white and grey, like a seabird blown in by the gale; the billows of raincloak settled as the wearer pulled his hood back and tossed a wet flick of hair out of his face. Yunnil tried to get up to curtsey but he waved at her to stay still. 'Don't bother, there's little enough room in here.' He cast his eyes up at the sagging roof, which only just escaped the top of his head.

'My lord,' said Diamoon.

'Mistress Diamoon, I take it.'

'Yes, my lord.' She looked disapproving, being somewhat surprised. 'We have not been introduced.'

'Do you think it matters?' Seeing that there were no chairs, he sank down on one knee by the foot of the bed, where the light caught his face as if he'd dropped into sunlit water. Diamoon warmed helplessly to the gleam of his eyes. She said, 'I am sure you are welcome wherever you go . . . my lord Ayndra is sleeping.'

'Is she?' He took notice of the bed as if for the first time since coming in. 'I shall not ask you to wake her.' Ayndra tossed her head, and her eyelids fluttered. She mumbled under her breath and turned to the side, pressing her face into the pillow. Diamoon took hold of her wrist and held it for some moments, then tucked it back under the covers and reached for a damp rag warming round the firepot, which she pressed against the invalid's chest, in the neck of her shirt. Greenly sweet vapours rose from it. 'She's quiet presently. She was waking most of the night, until dawn.'

Ailixond sat back on his heels. 'Will it disturb you if I remain here a while? Do not let me keep you from your work.'

'If you do not mind us making soup, lord –'

'Not in the least.'

Yunnil had squeezed behind Diamoon and heaved out Ayndra's travelling box, which she pushed mutely along the floor towards the king. He took it, thanking her as he sat down. Diamoon took up her vegetable knife again. They sat in silence under the steady beat of the rain. Ailixond was so quiet that one might almost have forgotten that he was there. Diamoon looked round at him once or twice, and found him always gazing at the bed. So used to being looked at, he gave away nothing of his thoughts, nor even

357

bothered what attention others might be paying him. The two women peeled and sliced vegetables, chopped herbs, set them in a stockpot to simmer. Diamoon got out her medicine chest and a small mortar and pestle, adding a sharp reek from the salve she began to grind to the smells of smoke and wet wool and cooking. Ayndra's sleep had grown less troubled and she lay still. Ailixond sat up suddenly, throwing off his meditative state like a servant tossing a dust sheet off a chair. He said, 'I take it that you are well provided for?'

'Not as well as we might be, my lord,' said Diamoon. He looked at her. 'Send to me, then, any bills you may incur for medicines or what-have-you . . . and, of course, you may call the Royal Physician whenever you need.' As he rose, he held out his hand. Diamoon did not comprehend the gesture until Yunnil took his finger-ends and brushed the great stone of the ring with her lips. Diamoon stayed in her place, not ready to leap up and bend over, but unsure if she had committed some solecism. Ailixond did not extend his hand further toward her. Accepting Yunnil's homage, he gave an almost sarcastic grin. 'Do not worry, Mistress. I do not demand it of those who are not my subjects. I wish you good day.' He swept out in another gust of swirling cloak. Yunnil crept to the door and peered through a slit after him. 'Toh kash! He has half a dozen people with him. All this time he left them to sit in the rain!'

'Well, he could hardly have hoped to bring them all in here,' responded Diamoon. She moved into the back of the cart, and stayed there murmuring over the medicines she was grinding. 'The fever's almost broken,' she said. 'I think she'll waken tomorrow.'

'What day is it?'

'The twentieth of Second Month.'

'Sweet heaven, it's the autumn already, when I'd hardly noticed that it was spring . . . it's a fine time to come out on to the dry land.'

'Indeed. The raiding season.'

Ayndra nodded. 'Months since I did any weapons training.'

'I saw you throw three knives into the gold of the same target only yesterday.'

'That's no weapons training, that's mountebank's foolery. I mean with a sword, with a shield . . . heaven, I've forgotten what day it is since I've been ill, I still can't shout, should I shout too much my voice gives out . . .'

'Is that altogether a bad thing?' said Polem.

358

'Ho! I see that Diamoon's infected you with her damned insolence.'

'Insolence! One thief calls the other a robber – besides, what entitlement have you, a mere newcomer, to be insolent to me?'

Ayndra made a gesture of blowing dust off her palm at him. She said to Ailixond, 'Think you that we will be fighting soon?'

'It is most probable,' he said distantly. 'Did you not hear what I said at the Council?'

'You know I can never listen to that sort of thing,' Polem said. He searched in his belt pouch. 'Look at these dice! All made out of amber – look at this one, it has a fly trapped inside it. Shall we have a game? – not you, Ailixond.'

'Thank you,' said Ailixond hoarsely. He brought a handkerchief to his mouth and attempted discreetly to cough into it. Lakkannar leant over. 'A dice game? Have you played in the mode of Suthine, Polem?'

'A lady there tried to teach me, but I never . . .'

'I know it. Come over, I can explain.'

'I could never follow the rule of three . . .' Polem followed Lakkannar's beckoning. Ailixond spat and thrust the handkerchief back into his sleeve. 'There is a town three days ahead. We shall halt there for two or three days while I drill the army, for I've no doubt that the hill people will attack us. They've been tollmasters on these roads all the time remembered.' He coughed again.

'Shall I ask Diamoon to send you some of her medicines?'

'You could do that.'

'You made a great impression on her when you came to my bed of sickness.'

He flicked his eyes at her and made an airy trivialising gesture. Ayndra laughed and lay forward on the table. 'Shumar, I am all the time so tired still . . . I think I shall go.'

'I', said Ailixond, 'shall go and work.' He snapped his fingers for Firumin and asked him to call the Treasurer and his two chief clerks. 'We have not finished calculating the revenues due from Tenth Month yet.' The dice rattled on the far side of the room. Lakkannar clapped his hands and Polem swore. He got up and went through to his bedroom without speaking to them.

There still remained a three months' march through the rough country between the marshes at the head of the Sea of Safi and the borders of Safi itself, from whence it would be no more than four sixdays on good roads to reach home. These crumpled lands had never been united under one master; loose federations, constantly shifting, bound together the towns of the valleys and the coastal plain, but the herdsmen in the high hills lived by levying tolls on all who passed by, robbing and enslaving those who would not pay. In the southerly parts of their domain, every king since Parakison II had campaigned against them, but never managed to suppress them for more than a few years, and the north lands the army entered now had always been independent. The marching order in hostile country was restored, with armed scouts and outriders, and wagons with women and children and valuable supplies in the middle of the column. The first three tiny city-states they passed through offered fealty, and a good part of their surplus harvest, after they heard that the king intended to suppress the raiders from the hills, but by the end of Second Month the army had turned away from the sea, into the wild lands. A couple of renegade tribesmen guided them towards the stronghold of the chief of Shinaltey, the oldest and grandest of their patriarchal clans. It was Ailixond's intention to separate the forces he would use for the assault from the rest of the army when the time came to enter the high valleys; everyone said that, faced with such a mass of opponents, the tribesmen would hide until they saw that they were directly threatened.

'No sign of anyone,' observed Arpalond. 'One would think all this land uninhabited.'

'No doubt they've all fled to their castle,' Lakkannar said.

'I think it's damn suspicious,' said Lord Ayndra.

'Do you, indeed?' said Lakkannar. They exchanged vicious looks. He checked that his sword was loose in the scabbard for the fifteenth time.

'There's a little house up there,' said Ayndra. 'And not a wisp of smoke from it, though they're surely living there; look, it has a cabbage patch and some fruit trees in the –'

'Listen!'

'What?'

'It's just some driver –'

'No! What's happening?' Ayndra kicked her horse to tear off the road, up the side of the hill to get a view round the curve of the road where the phalanx and the baggage were ascending; she careered round and came back down again, yelling, but not so fast as to forestall the message-rider who pulled his horse up almost into the king's party, incoherent with shock and breathlessness. Still he hardly needed words to make clear what had happened, and Aleizon Ailix Ayndra was on their backs two minutes later, shrieking, 'Attack attack attack!' The Companions swung round

360

to gallop back to their aid, but Ailixond had already gone. When the body of horsemen rounded the bend in the road, they saw a mob of riders on shaggy ponies entangled with the phalanx in the middle of the column, while the rest of the army knotted up behind them; they were slashing at the footmen, who dragged them down from horseback, stabbed mounts and riders, beat at them with anything to hand. The pony-men saw the cavalry coming, doubled their efforts and drove into the infantry, who marched in ranks of eight or nine; they easily broke out on the other side and galloped off between the hills. The Companions caught only a few stragglers, dismounted and wounded. Ailixond had reached the skirmish first of all of them, and alone among the lords had actually killed a tribesman. He sat astride his stamping warhorse with the bloody sword in his hand, his face unnaturally brilliant. 'Pick that one up –' he gestured with his sword at the man whose neck he had half severed, lying where his horse had thrown him '– and show him to the guides. They will know which his tribe-mark is. The same with the other dead men. Then we'll know where we're to go tomorrow. Whichever they are, we'll destroy their citadel. Polem, get back to the head of the column, they'll come round and attack us there if we leave it unguarded. Hasmon, tell them down there to get back in order, we'll be moving again as soon as we've gathered up our dead – and tell the outriders to double their watch from now on. How was it that we never knew they were coming? – what is he, then?'

The guide had uncovered tattoos on the dead man's forearms. 'Poltriy, lord. They are younger brothers to Shinaltey. Their chief dwells in the same valley.'

'Good,' said the king, breathing heavily. 'Two birds with – haugh! – one stone . . .'

Hasmon and Casik were left in charge of the column, with the Thaless horse to lead it, while the Companions and the Silver Shields went into the mountains: harsh country, marsh and moor and heather, with the sheep that were the tribes' only husbandry beyond their small spade-worked gardens running wild, guarded by shepherds who lived as rough as their animals most of the year. They marched for two days before they met any resistance, and then the barbarians bounded out from some eyrie in the crags, poured slingstones and arrows into the Safeen, and were away before the Silver Shields could catch up with them. After that, they slept without fires, and ate cold food. The guides knew a number of ways to Shinalt, which they said was perhaps a day and a half

361

away. Ailixond decided that their best hope of approaching relatively unremarked was to split up. He sent the veteran companies of the Silver Shields, and all the cavalry, along the best-known path, where they would have to take the worst of the attack and hope to convince the enemy that they were all there was; he lent Harago to one of the captains, along with his white cloak. The rest of them would go on foot, in three parties, each to go by a separate path and lay up a short distance from Shinalt until the king's own party had contacted them and arranged the details of the assault. It was a hard walk, in mail and carrying weapons, tramping over sucking mires of green moss, fording rock-strewn streams and slinking along mountainsides below the skyline. No living creatures save sheep and wild birds appeared among the rags of mist blowing over the wet grasses; it appeared that they had all gone to the citadel for safety, or were shooting at the supposed royal party on the main path. The men cursed and complained as the bogs soaked their feet and every hilltop was succeeded by another yet higher, but Ailixond, in full armour, walked all day behind the guides, and asked for no more rest than they did. He hardly spoke except when addressed, and his face looked like stone. The second evening after the attack brought them within reach of Shinalt valley. The soldiers were allowed to make a fireless camp around a black tarn in a stony socket of the mountains, while the king went up with the guides to overlook their target in the fading light.

The foam shone on the dark river in the heart of the deep-cleft valley, swirling out into a shallow pool that ran almost up to the walls of the castle, built on the shallowest slopes. One irregular tower overlooked a huddle of thatched roofs, stained black with soot in the direction of the prevailing wind, and surrounded by a heavy wall of roughly dressed stones. The only gate lay to the south; looking from the west, he could not assess its defences clearly. The sinking sun bathed the rough buildings in an artificial brassy glow; even from this distant vantage, one could hear the chatter of human and animal voices, and see people moving on the walls. 'Sir,' he said to the chief guide, 'I will ask you to lead twos and threes of our men to where the other captains lay – can you point out to me where their paths emerge?' One was on the same side, one directly opposite; they'd not all view the sunrise equally. It would have to be some given signal. 'We shall begin to advance as soon as the last star has disappeared, and when we have crossed over into the valley, then the trumpets will sound and the assault will begin . . .' It was nearly dark when he returned to the lakeside, to the small green lawn they'd chosen for their bivouacs. Someone was sitting on a boulder by it, bathing their feet in the lake water. 'God! My poor feet. God! I've not walked so far in years. How ever shall we attack when we're all worn out to death already?' Sliding down to wade in the cold water, she caught a shadow behind her. 'Who comes? O, have you – ayy!' Ailixond had dropped down on his back on the ground, as suddenly as if he had been knocked unconscious. She splashed out of the lake and fell on her knees beside him, but before she could speak she saw he was looking at her. She sat back, shuffling over crablike because the studs on her mail breeches would have bruised her bare legs kneeling.

'I thought you'd passed out,' she said shrilly.

Ailixond said, 'I knew I was about to, so I lay down before I fell down.'

'You know it's coming?'

'Yes, it's not the first time –' He stopped. She stilled, staring at him with eyes like hardboiled eggs stabbed by sooty pokers. Ailixond turned his cheek to the stones and sighed. In the quiet, Polem's voice came to them. 'This way . . . o, no one's here . . .' Boots thumped on peat. Ailixond's eyes slid in their direction, he raised his head and shook it fractionally. Ayndra nodded once and got on all fours to fetch her boots. When she turned round Ailixond was sitting up, and Polem was saying over him, 'What are you doing here?'

'Resting,' he said. 'They'll put the tent up without me. My help is never accepted when offered.' Polem was distracted already: 'Have you been bathing your feet? Think you that it helps?'

'I'm not at all sure,' she said. 'I've heard it said that it's better not to take one's boots off at all, to save the pain of putting them on again next morning.'

'Indeed. A hot bath is what is really needed . . .' He turned to Ailixond. 'Can we not have a fire in the tent tonight? – since this night we have a tent –'

'I am ashamed enough of the tent as it is,' said Ailixond. 'Most certainly I shall not have the sole campfire within it – even did I wish to be smoked like a mackerel . . .' He stood up with care. 'But go and find Dorin, he has our pack of food.' Polem's cloak dimmed like a lamp snuffed behind heather bushes. Ailixond leant against the boulder. Aleizon Ailix Ayndra sat at his feet. He watched her rolling down her breeches, lacing up the ankles, wrapping her feet and grunting as she pushed them into stiff boots. The sun was no more than a pale orange glow behind the

363

western ridge. She tipped her face up at him. 'Do you ever say what you really think?'

'Almost never,' he said. 'And then it's only by mistake.' She continued searching him with her eyes. 'But you can trust the things I've done,' he said, 'because I do nothing that's not what I —' his voice failed, wheezing.

'— really think,' she said, entranced by thought. He went on wheezing, shaking his head and feeling in the sleeve of his leather shirt, dragged out a lump of rag, burst out coughing into it and spat several times. 'Now it all comes out in the wash,' he remarked impersonally; caught her eye again, and flicked the rag open in her direction.

'It's too dark,' she said. 'I cannot see what's in it.'

'It's still clean,' he said, 'I think,' and tossed it into the roots of a cloudberry bush. 'Let us see what they have made of this tent.' She followed him in silence.

The heavy thatch of the eaves hung down almost to waist height over the mud-plastered walls and the curving buttresses that supported house corners; there was hardly room for two people to walk abreast in the middle of the troughs of waste and mud that threaded between the clumps of low buildings. Under the crumbling keep, the alleys opened into a cramped gravelly square, but the walls that cast it into damp shadow showed no more openings than a few arrow-slits. Polem peered cautiously round the edge of the buttress that they crouched behind. 'How are we to get in? Do we wait for the others?'

'We find the main door of the citadel, firstly,' said Ailixond, upon which Lord Ayndra sprang out and round the corner, to scuttle along the face of the next wall, sliding on the greasy ground between flung stones into a narrow alley. By good fortune there was no one there — all those who were not warriors were barred into their houses, and as for the rest she could hear a ferocious clangour still from the walls — until she was half way round the tower, and come suddenly upon a flight of stone steps, rising up between two houses and then ending in midair, six feet of space between the last tread and the door into the tower, set on its first floor. An arrow, falling from the parapet, bounced off her helmet, leaving her ears ringing. She turned and skidded back the way she had come. They were still arguing under the eaves, though Ailixond had sent some of the common soldiers off on an errand. She fell on her knees beside him. 'I've found the door.' He was leaning limply against the wall, and looked feverish. 'I do not

364

doubt that it's well above the ground.'

'There are steps that go up, but stop, and they've taken up the drawbridge.'

'No matter, we'll find one. Captain Peldir, go and tell Carmago to lead all his forces to the tower and take no regard for the walls, except as he needs to hold them off . . . tell him where he should go.'

'O, you'll find it easily enough . . .'

Ailixond found a deep doorway just by the steps where he could survey the entrance in relative safety; he craned his neck while Aleizon Ailix Ayndra tried to ram a broken iron bar through the latchhole to trip it from outside. 'I cannot do this.'

'Excuse me, then – Ailixond –' Polem made to throw himself at it. Ailixond, stepping aside, glanced down the street. 'Polem! Take the rest of us down there and – Garin! Stop them!' Polem gave a yell as the door caved way and was carried down beneath him; an abject chorus of screams came from within. The soldiers had fanned out across the street just in time to meet the Shinaltey who came shuffling up it, going cautiously so that they should present a united front. Ayndra seized Polem's arm and half hauled him to his feet, propelled him out of the door and cried, 'Get at them!' The women and small children in the dark room screamed even louder when she waved her sword and said, 'Sit quiet and we'll not hurt you!' as Ailixond came in behind her – 'Is that a fire there? Get kitchen rags, oil – firewood, straw –'

'What are you going to do?'

'The drawbridge is tied up in the doorway. Set fire to the base of it.'

'What about Polem?'

'He can do it as well as I can. You will have to watch my back – and carry – can you not get them to quiet?' She hissed at the two women, who were huddled with five or six children on a low bed in the back corner, while Ailixond ran through all the kitchen things, finding a pot of dripping, several rags, some oil-soaked splinters for use as torches. He knotted a couple of rags round pieces of firewood.

'But how will these little things make the door catch fire?'

'No matter, even if they are only disturbed by the smoke they will open it –'

'And if Carmago's not here, will you and I charge them solo? Do we not need a ladder, some wood –'

'As soon as the bridge lowers, it will be easy to leap it.'

'But what if Carmago's not come?'

365

'He'll come,' said Ailixond. 'Make some more of these . . . I shall try lighting them – did you not see, there is a broad sill underneath the door and if we toss them on to that –'

'They will shoot us to pieces while we are throwing them –'

'That's what mail is for. They have not S'Thurrulan arrows. Only throw the quicker, and never look up whence the arrows come.' He lit one of the kitchen torches, and waved it round his improvised dripping-soaked firelighter until it burst into rank yellow flames. They burst out of the door again, hands high, trailing black fat-smoke and spitting. She reached the top first and tossed her load with more panache than accuracy, swung round and stood half over Ailixond to look down the street where Polem and a dozen Silver Shields were pushing against at least a score of Shinaltey. 'I know not how much longer Polem can hold up, he is falling back already – it's only the narrowness of the street that keeps off their full number –' They dashed back into the doorway. Several wads of rag had fallen hissing into the mud, but enough had lodged at the base of the drawbridge to send up a column of stinking smoke. 'I think I can hear Carmago,' said Ailixond.

'Can you? I cannot distinguish a thing in all the racket.'

'No. There is more to warcries than shouting to pretend to false bravery, you know.' He leant out of the door and cried, 'Safi! Safi –!' and fell into harsh coughing. A great splash poured down from the roof of the tower, but the fire was protected by the arch of the door and continued to smoke. 'They are going to lower the bridge down over it,' said Ailixond, 'we must rush it as soon as –'

'Safi! Safi! Safi!'

'Carmago's here.' Ailixond stepped past her out of the door; now there were half a dozen Shinaltey trapped between Carmago's men and Polem's, all funnelling up the street towards them. The bridge had groaned half way down; they were pouring water over it in an attempt to put out the flames. A man leaned out over the edge with a rake and pulled the whole burning mass over into the muddy moat; the bridge halted, began to creak upward again. 'Right,' said Ailixond. 'I'm damned if you're going,' said Ayndra, and leapt up the steps. She cast herself at the rising bridge, got both arms and one leg over the edge and pulled out her sword as she rolled over. The men hauling on the ropes stood there staring. She whipped out her knife and tossed it at the one who stood nearest. He let go the rope to clutch at the blood running over his chest, and his companions dropped it to clutch at him. The bridge sagged sharply to one side, straining the other rope which began to slip out of hands that had not expected such a tug. She threw herself at them, swinging her sword like a scythe. They let go, and the bridge dropped down with a bone-jarring crunch. A stream of men yelling, 'Safi!' poured across it. She was carried on the crest of their wave, landed on the edge of an inner door which hands were trying to pull shut and jammed her boot over the sill. All the crowd in the passage pushed at her back, her ribs felt as if they'd been cracked by the buffet; she fought her way round the door and hands seized the edge to pull it open again. They were in a smoky, half-lit hall; logs were kicked from the central hearth in a scatter of sparks and men headed for the stone steps that would lead into the ground-floor weapons room and the cellars. The women would be there too, crouching among the casks of salt mutton, though others might be hiding upstairs. She ran for the ladder going to the top storey.

It did not take half an hour to clean out all resistance in the keep, though they might fight a little longer on the walls. She had managed to collect all the women together in the top room, and put guards at the ladder's foot to keep wandering soldiers out; but she could not stand the number of them who were weeping, and climbed up to the roof, where there was a narrow walk behind a wooden parapet. The men who had fought their way up to it with her had been dismissed below; she stepped over the body of a tribesman and leant over the rail. A dead man, one of the Silver Shields, lay face up in the mud of the moat, an arrow protruding from his chest. From three floors up she could not recognise his face. The ladder creaked under a climber, and she turned to peer down the trapdoor. Ailixond jumped up onto the roof, slammed the trap shut and sat down on it, gasping. He pulled his helmet off and shook out sweat-stranded hair. 'Hah! . . . a pleasant eyrie you have here. Make sure that none come up until I ask them.' He got up and moved away to the far side; she stood with one foot on the trapdoor. Ailixond leant against the steep smoke-blackened thatch of the roof and closed his eyes.

'Is it all finished?' she said.

'It's finished. Those who have not surrendered have run away. It does not seem that any who escaped were great leaders, though we have not identified all the dead or captured.' He shook his head. 'Is there any water up here?'

'It's not clean.' She pushed a wooden bucket toward him. 'It was for tipping over in defence.'

'It will do.' He knelt to lave his face and hands, then fished inside his mail shirt for the silver flask. 'But only to wash in,' he said, drinking, 'too dirty else.'

She sat down on the trapdoor. 'How long shall we stay here?'

'I should like to leave the day after next, but I think more likely after two days, or even three.' He hid the flask again. 'You were quite the hero of the piece.'

Her response was uncharacteristically shamefaced. 'Well, I . . . were you going to jump?'

'Think you I've lost my nerve?'

'No! But I do think –'

'You think that I'm not fit for it any longer.'

Her hands sprang out as if they'd been let from iron bonds. 'All right then! I don't think you're fit for it, I think that you were not wise to come on this march in your present state of health; it is not as if there was no one else who could have led it in your stead and if there is not then it's only because you'll let no one else lead, likewise your, your idiocy for throwing yourself away at the head of everything, I mean you know what it's led to before now, and it's not as if I am aiming to take over from you, I wouldn't want –'

'Take over, what do you mean? Take over?'

'You know what I mean! Starting to scheme to take over the Empire because you know you're going to d–'

She clapped her hand over her mouth, crouching, staring at him like a wild animal; she ducked; his fist caught her a blow on the side of the head. 'I'm not dead yet!' he hissed. She launched herself at him, bore him over on to the boards and banged his head against them. Ailixond twisted and heaved her over, punching her head to the ground as his right arm came free. She attempted to stab his eyes with stiff fingers, but he caught her wrist; while he was wrestling her hands down, though, she managed to kick him in one eye and then in the throat. He choked and fell forward; she had kicked him twice more – ineffectually, in his mailed groin – before she realised that he wasn't fighting any more. Her nose was streaming blood all down her face and neck; she crawled back, snuffling, and fumbled for her neckscarf to try and mop it up. Ailixond was on his knees, coughing into another bit of rag. There was blood all over his hands; at first she thought that some of it had stained the rag red. Ailixond tossed it over the parapet and leaned back. A bruise was rapidly forming where she had kicked his head. He spoke very softly, hoarsely. 'But an I gave up my idiocy of leading from the front, they would all take it as an admission that I was as well as dead in any case. So better I go on acting the part for as long as I can, and then ring the curtain down in one . . . you do understand? Don't you?'

368

She spoke muffled by the cloth pressed against her still-dribbling nose. 'I understand. Don't you see that I've been playing?'

The captains drew straws, and he who picked the short one was left with fifty men to guard Shinalt castle, while the king departed up country, his train swollen by Shinaltey prisoners and by renegades, younger sons, dispossessed heirs, and ambitious men of commoner clans, all prepared to betray other citadels in return for the rule of them as vassals of Safi. Now that the largest stronghold had fallen, they did not bother to approach stealthily, and in most cases those gates not opened by treachery gave way when the Safic troops and their new allies appeared before them; so, though the country was very wild, it was easier going, and the storerooms they raided were stuffed to overflowing. When they reached the Grand Army, on the fifteenth of Second Month, they had four carts loaded with furs and sheepskins, leather and berry preserves and wild honey. Ailixond would have disposed them himself, but before they were even within hailing distance of the column, he was summoned by a royal messenger to the queens' vehicles. It was two hours, and the army was preparing to camp, when he came back, and then Sulakon preceded him. 'My lord has asked that I make this announcement. The King's Great Wife of Safi, Lady Othanë, has made it known to him that she expects the birth of an heir. This is of course joyful news; nevertheless she has asked him to remind you that early judgements can be mistaken, and accordingly he wishes public congratulations to be kept until the birth.'

'May I ask one question?' said Arpalond.

'You may, though I cannot promise to answer it,' Sulakon replied.

'When is that to be?'

'At the end of Seventh Month, or early in Eighth Month. You see,' he added, 'why we may not yet be too secure.'

'Nevertheless, Lady Setha will not like it,' Arpalond observed. Sulakon drew himself up disdainfully. 'That is as may be,' he said, moving away. 'Master Firumin! The king asks you to summon the Chief Clerk of the Justiciary, and says that he will eat supper at his desk this night.'

'My lord Ayndra. This matter requires your attention.' Ailixond tossed her a water-stained sheet, covered with crabbed writing and heavily sealed.

'What is it? . . . o, it's Garadon, from Raq'min – tell me it in

369

brief, unless you want me to waste an hour's third reading it.'

'He complains of the difficulty of conducting affairs legal and fiscal in Safic and Haraminharn tongue, since he speaks not a word of the latter, and does not trust his interpreters, all of whom entered the service while you were governing there. Furthermore, whenever he attempts to, as he puts it, reform the Haraminharn sections of the imperial service, he meets stony resistance and "It is not the will of Lord Ayndra" at every turn – are you in communication with civil officials in Haramin, may I ask?'

'Does he mean to say that I maintain a government there? I do nothing of the sort! I –'

'I did not ask you that. Do you write to them?'

'I answer letters which I receive,' she said innocently.

'You are aware that for one lord to treat in matters of government of a province which another governs, whether it be by written note or in verbal consultation, without the full knowledge and connivance of the lord provincial and the royal authority, is, by the letter of the law, treason?'

'I was not until just now.' Aleizon Ailix Ayndra uncrossed her legs and spoke rapidly. 'I devised the form of government which now prevails in Haramin, since, when I arrived there, they had only the remnants of Yourcen's administration, almost inactive since most of the officials had run off and taken all of the money, and the imperial military governors whose civil powers are very limited. Consequently I am the principal fount of wisdom concerning its mode of operation, and various of the chief clerks have been accustomed to write to me asking my opinion on points of procedure, or to pronounce judgement in hard cases. Which letters I have answered to the best of my ability and without consulting any others, since I was not aware that I ought to have done so.'

'But you have been so informed.'

'I have.' She got up and strolled over to a lamp. 'I think, my lord, that you should refuse his request to promulgate a decree that the government of Haramin should be conducted in Safic only, unless it cover solely military affairs, in which I feel there is political reason to conduct them all in Safic.'

'And you will write to him relating the actual nature of your correspondence with his clerks, and agreeing to conduct it under open seal henceforward.'

'I will do that.' She stuck the end of a smokestick in the lamp flame and drew heavily on it. Sulakon glared. Ailixond looked at him to be quiet. 'Next matter, my lords. In the Land-beyond-the-

Mountains. The eldest son of the chief of the Mirkits has abducted the daughter of a minor chief of the Shaarikits, who is however the granddaughter of the paramount chief of the Shaarikits, and the two nations have fallen into bloodfeud that threatens to become war. Lord Polion has been forced to triple his garrisons, and patrol all the regions where Mirkit land borders Shaarikit, which has emptied his treasury, and he still fears that war may flare up at any moment.'

'Another grant in aid? The Treasury must be empty already. For god's sake, cannot these provinces raise enough in taxes to pay the cost of their governance?'

'I will send money from Safi, where the New Empire has brought such an influx of trade goods that they raise more than enough in taxes to garrison the rest of the Empire.'

'Yes, but what about this public bread dole he thinks will be necessary in Purrllum?'

'Why do we not ship this fine harvest they have had in New Hope south to the Land-beyond-the-Mountains? I'll be bound it would be cheaper than buying it in Lysmal.'

'You forget the cost of bringing it by land train to some port like Pomoan, where grain ships could load it,' said Ailixond, 'and they have a long winter in New Hope. I am sending some of the most loyal clerks in the Safic Treasury to study the grain markets in Lysmal and ensure that the Treasury purchases at fair prices.' The sweet grey pall of the drug-smoke gathered above the heads of the Inner Council; Ayndra was wandering back and forth behind their chairs. 'But what of this matter of the Mirkits?'

'Has he not tried a punitive expedition?' said Lakkannar.

'Summon them to court,' said Lord Ayndra.

'Summon them to court?' Lakkannar guffawed. 'Ha! – and will they then swear undying friendship? I'll be damned –'

'Summon this abductor son,' she said, 'and twenty others like him – fifty – all the chiefs' sons . . . and the same for the other tribe – say that they are to become officers of the Empire, that they'll receive rich weapons, and instruction, and gold, if they do not think it ignoble to receive money – offer them horses, whatever they give as gifts of honour, so that the chiefs cannot refuse to send them, and at the same time you may intimate, through whatever priests they have perhaps, that if they . . . behave badly . . . their boys will not return. And besides, you may thus remove all the young hotheads and corrupt them with civilisation.' She giggled.

'Very wise,' said Ailixond. 'These letters should be sent off this night – I excuse any of you who do not wish to stay and assist me with them.' Lord Ayndra skulked at the back of the tent until all except Arpalond had left; she came forward and slipped the smokestick discreetly into the king's hands. 'I should be pleased to have a copy of the decrees on provincial government.'

'You will have one when I have found time to dictate it to the clerks in the Justiciary – indeed, it's time it was done, as soon as I have called Meraptar from Safi . . .'

'You are calling him here? But we're only a few months away –' began Arpalond.

'You know how things are in Safi,' said Ailixond, cupping his hands over his face. 'As soon as I arrive there I will hear a dozen different tales of every story and there will be no discerning right from wrong. I wish to have one story told to me by one of the prime movers among them, alone, away from his own people . . . and my mother's.'

'One is never away from your mother's people.'

'But in my household she does no more than watch.' At that, Arpalond looked up, questioning, but Ailixond outstared him. 'I'm sorry. I'm sure you know best,' he said. Ailixond dipped his hands under the table again, and the smokestick reappeared between Lord Ayndra's fingers. 'But perhaps you'd like to write to Meraptar requesting his presence at court. It's not something I particularly like to give to a clerk.'

'Of course. Will you want to word it?'

'I think you know what to say.' He clapped his hands, and in a few moments a servant arrived with a portable writing-desk, which he offered to Arpalond. Lord Ayndra pulled up a chair to the end of the king's table. 'I shall write to Garadon.'

'Bring another inkwell. And a jug of spiced wine.'

'Of course, my lord.'

Ailixond pulled out several pieces of paper and took a quill in each hand; he fell to scribbling immediately, leaving the other two to chew on pens and exchange meaningful glances until they got bored and resorted to writing.

By midmonth a heavy frost fell every night and the long grass in the hills was bleached like bone. The low sun in the evening caught in it like a gold fur, streaked by the ravelling shadows of the camp-women and urchins, straggling over the hillsides stripping the laden berry bushes, as the first fires opened like eyes in the shadowed valley. The lords returned to the army at dusk, from pursuing the migrating wildfowl, or some mad errand devised by

372

Ailixond to visit a nearby hamlet or a cliff or a river; every day he was off somewhere different and then worked half the night. He generated so much work that half the clerks were prostrated with exhaustion, and Firumin was perpetually distracted. For the time being they met no more hostile tribes, instead moving into a more settled area where Safic ships had raided the coast, and imposed ephemeral tributes, more than a century ago. Ailixond took the Companions and most of the lords on a sixday's journey to the town of Gombollan, but it was a ceremonial, not a military, tour. The Lord of Gombollan hoped to win better terms by negotiation than by resistance, and spent a day feasting the king and his splendidly clad entourage, at the same time as protesting the poverty of his domains and their further impoverishment in order to provide such a spectacle. In the hall at dinner a small flattanharp was brought to the high table, and it became clear that young noblemen took turns to perform songs on it.

'Shumar save us,' said Lakkannar.

'I thought all Safic lords could play exquisitely upon the flat and the upright harp,' observed Lord Ayndra.

'Why do we not put forward one of us, as a, a representative?' Polem suggested. 'Yes, and let it be Lord Ayndra,' Lakkannar put in.

'As you will.' In half an hour the harp had found its way to the king's party. She stood up and spent some time retuning it ostentatiously to a minor key, though none of the Gombolloin took much notice until she began to sing. And then even some of the Safic lords sat up; but nothing to the brush-fire of amazement that ran through the barbarians. Ailixond leant over and whispered something in Arpalond's ear, but Polem did not realise what had happened until she passed the harp to the lord of Gombollan, and he said, 'God's teeth! m'lord, you've an unusual voice for a man.'

She said in a silken voice, 'But indeed, my lord, I thought that you knew.'

'I'd not think so.'

'What, you had not heard that in Safi ... youths with exceptionally fine voices, we ...' She waved her hand, smiling sweetly. The lord of Gombollan was thunderstruck. Eventually he said, 'Excuse me, young sir, but it must be an unfortunate state.'

'I wouldn't say so.' She went slinking back to her seat. Ailixond leant forward to trap the chief's attention. 'We have yet to discuss the matter of tribute,' he said.

While the second course was being cleared, Ayndra came to the back of Polem's chair and put her hand on his shoulder. 'What?' said he.

'We shall set in train some requests that will result in Ailixond leaving these festivities.'

'What? They'll be drinking most of the night, I'm sure – what are you doing?' Her hand had strayed over his chest.

'Misleading the Lord of Gombollan. Keep still and behave as you commonly would with me. The lady of this place clearly takes pleasure in your company. Ask her to show us whatever accommodation she has prepared, and say we will go to look at it now.'

The lady immediately departed to make ready the Lord's own chamber, and came back requesting their pleasure at midnight. Ailixond left most of his party to continue drinking, and, when they had eventually secured the departure of their hostess, sent all but Polem and Arpalond after her. He said to Aleizon Ailix Ayndra, 'Why did you tell such an absurd story to my lord of Gombollan?'

She scuffed her feet and burst out giggling behind her hand. 'He told himself the story in the first place.'

'Do you expect me to maintain the truth of it?'

'That's your choice, is it not?' He glared at her. She added, 'He'll never dare ask openly after the truth of it.'

'Oh, indeed. And I do not doubt that you've been in some barbarous nation where castrati are called *she*?'

She shrugged, laughing. 'Anything is possible.'

Ailixond sat down on the massive bed. 'Next time it will be a public apology.' 'Ha!' she said angrily. They glared at each other. Arpalond tugged quietly at Polem's sleeve; they left to rejoin the party. Ailixond lifted his travelling box up on the bed and fished in it until he found a bottle. 'I receive the distinct impression that my lady expects that all the lords, at least, will sleep in here.'

'How much of that vile brew do you drink in a day? A gallon?'

'Not as much as that.' He put the bottle under the heap of miscellaneous pillows. 'Will you rejoin the merriment below stairs?'

'Only if I must.'

'Then leave them it.' He lay down on the layered fur and wool coverlets. 'The old man is as slippery as carp in a stewpond. It will take me most of next day to pin him down . . . I could have done it this night, if I were not so tired . . .'

The Safic guests were to have spent a second day hunting in the hills around the Lord of Gombollan's old family castle, but a rainstorm cut short the excursion after midday; the party returned drenched to dank heat, idleness and quantities of mulled wine in his princely dwelling. More meat was brought, singed without and bloody within. At the varlets' end of the hall, Aleizon Ailix Ayndra was talking with a group of youths, using a falsely high-pitched voice and much limp-wristed display. Ailixond fixed the chieftain with his gaze. 'Let us see. What exactly was the sum of tribute which you used to pay to Safi?'

'Ah, well m'lord, not many of us remember those days, it was before my father's time even . . .'

'You do not recall? That is no obstacle. We may as well fix the value from records of recent years.'

'Records, m'lord?'

'Call your chief clerk to me.'

'Excuse us, m'lord, but we keep no clerks.'

'You do not? Who then keeps track of your monies? Is there any one among your retinue who can write and cypher? I will speak with them, no matter who they be.'

'Well, the wool merchants keep a clerk, and I believe the priest . . .'

'Call the priest, then, and the wool merchants' clerk. And the comptroller of your household.'

'Why, m'lord, 'tis only m'lady who has charge of that.'

'Summon her, then, also. I have no prejudice against women in government.' Shrieks of laughter from the far end of the hall; some demon in him added, 'nor, indeed, against eunuchs.'

'Eunuchs, m'lord?'

'Singing eunuchs. Now what is the annual value of the wool staple which you send to the coast?'

On first entering the king's tent, Polem saw only Aleizon Ailix Ayndra, crouching on the edge of his desk with a smokestick under her nose. 'What is that in Ailixond's chair? Is Firumin drying linen on it?' Then he saw the Physician hovering in the background, and two hands emerged from beneath the towel draped over the linen rack in Ailixond's chair, lifting it up like a bridal veil; a dark glance stooped from beneath it, and let it fall again. 'O, my apologies,' said Polem, 'I did not recognise you under that — good god! What have you under there, a chymist's furnace?'

'No so much less,' said the towel hoarsely. 'Herbal inhalations,' said Aleizon Ailix Ayndra, inhaling deeply. 'Do I see a packet of letters in your hand, Polem?'

375

'O, yes, the message-riders have just got in – one of them says that Lord Meraptar is come up to the Chiaral river and will be on us in two hours.'

'What, two hours?' The towel extended a hand and thumped the table. 'I made sure that he would not be here until Fourth Month! – has he ridden all the way with the post?'

'By return, it would seem. And Sandar with him.'

'O, fine news! Call Firumin, we must receive him in state – he already believes that I call him here solely to cashier him.'

'What, have we to ride out –'

'Better to hold state here, but I must send out someone to receive him presently.'

'I shall go,' volunteered Ayndra. The towel began to say, 'Only an you promise –' but she interrupted. 'I shall be the very model of courtesy, certain sure, neither shall I spit nor curse nor scratch nor utter false or inflammatory statements.'

'You will school Polem during the ride and he will speak.'

'Thank you,' said Polem, slightly affronted. He paused. 'Then go!' said the towel. 'How much longer?' The Physician consulted his small water clock. 'We are almost at the hour.'

Lord Meraptar was made Regent of Safi for the first time in 440, when the old Lord Parakison went on his first great campaign in Thaless. When Ailixond left Safi in 453, Meraptar had been left to rule in the king's stead, and had held court there for fourteen years since, each year more like to a king himself as Ailixond moved further afield, and news of his fresh conquests took longer to reach home; had he died in the grass plains, Safi would not have known for months. Meraptar governed Safi, regulated its courts and markets, put down rebellion in Thaless, received the growing flood of foreign tribute, prisoners, trade goods, merchants and envoys from the New Empire, and sent out annual detachments of Safic youths trained to the old king's exacting standards of drill and horsemanship; and endured fourteen years with the turbulent Lady Sumakas, who in his condition of widowerhood found no challenge to her paramountcy among the noble ladies, and who aspired to governorship among the noble lords. He had last seen Lord Ailixond when he was a youth hardly twenty-one years old, setting out afire with a ludicrous ambition to conquer the world. Now he was to meet with a man almost thirty-five, the undefeated master of the known regions of the world; when the summons came, he had wasted no time in answering it. With him he brought his eldest son, Sandar, in hopes that time might have mellowed his appreciation of the king, and besides, to leave his heir-apparent in Safi while he rode to the king might be construed as – well, the gods knew what poison pen of Sumakas' had drawn this peremptory and unexpected call; he should display no hint of disloyalty. He dipped his hands in the bowl of water offered him by Firumin at the door, splashed his face and wiped them; then, still in travelling clothes, strode into the lamplit tent.

While they rode toward the camp, the king's tent had been transformed. As if out of thin air, the stepped dais, the lords' chairs and the chair of state had appeared in a tent extended to four times its size, and the lords themselves brought in in court clothes. Meraptar halted in the middle of the room, with Sandar at his shoulder. The Governor's son regarded with small cold eyes the noble soldiers who had been his companions at the palace school, the weather marks and wrinkles, war scars and footprints of wine – and Ailixond, who still looked half-grown. Not a grey hair in his head; no doubt his mother sent him her raven dye – and the woman at his feet, like some pet dragon sprawled over the steps, Aleixon Ailix Ayndra his sorceress whore. She was smiling in a manner sweetly vacuous, but he was not taken in. Ailixond held out his hand, and Meraptar advanced to kiss the Royal Ring. Sandar had to follow him. The hand he took was hot, dry, and exceedingly thin; he felt the pressure of the witch's eyes upon him. As he stepped back, he caught her gaze, striking him like a splash of vinegar. Under the straw-coloured fringe, her eyes were the identical crazy blue as the maniac's who sat above her. He moved out of range as his father began speaking. 'My lord king, lords and councillors, I bear the heartfelt greetings of the citizens of Safi's land and city . . .'

Ayndra spoke without moving her lips. 'Has Lord Meraptar been in Suthine? It would appear that he has acquired their habits of oratory.'

'. . . and rich gifts in token of the honour in which they hold you, my lord; all of which promises will be reaffirmed by my son and heir.' He indicated Sandar, who nodded slightly. 'I will serve Safi as my ancestors have done these three centuries,' he said, his voice deep and soft as distant thunder, and the king's servants marched in with the first of the gifts.

Sandar dipped a finger into the bowl of soft soap and flicked it in disgust. 'Fit for a common bathhouse. Can he not even procure decent soap, after all the monies he has looted?' Meraptar was pouring hot water over his head; he did not answer. Sandar went on. 'He receives us without even allowing time to change our dress, accepts all your offerings and dismisses us shortly without so much as a word of explanation for calling us on this fool's errand.'

'It is his right,' said Meraptar.

'The king has no such right. He may have had all these foreigners kissing his feet for years, but that does not entitle him to treat lords of Safi like common petitioners.'

His father spoke wearily. 'Sandar. Forget not that we are in his camp, and within his power. And you would do well to look at the standing of the lords his friends, those who were boys with you and are generals and commanders now —'

'And it is my fault that I chose to stay in Safi at your side?'

'No, but your chance may come to share in the pickings, an you be not ill-willed towards him — consider Lakkannar. He has now a fortune five times my own, though his family were so penniless that they sold half their patrimonial lands. Gadaron governs Haramin that was a kingdom by itself. Sulakon is second in command of the army — and you will still shun the king's party?'

'I will not crawl to him to obtain money and position!'

'As you will, then. But I order you — while we stay here, you will at least keep silent an you cannot act with all courtesy, and will say no word against the king nor any of his friends, else I shall be the first to punish you — must I lock you up because you cannot behave as a man and a nobleman?'

'You may trust me,' Sandar said darkly. He slid lower into the steaming tub. 'Besides, did you not think that he looks ill? I am convinced that he suffers from a wasting disease. He looks as scrawny as a starved peasant.'

'His family have never been great of stature. And neither is it wise to go around predicting the king's sickness or death.'

Ailixond stood among the piles of gifts, looking at one then another, while the servants carried away the chairs and furnishings. He picked up the last of them, a miniature sword, perfect in every detail but made to fit the hand of a three-year-old, and tested its edge. 'Sharp as a razor. I shall have to have it blunted and the point taken off before I give it to Parri.'

Ayndra was trying to force her hand into a gold lady's bracelet. 'I think Sandar is a very vile man.'

'I can give no opinion, being excessively biased, for he wishes

378

me nothing but evil. We were rivals constantly at home, and you heard his remark.'

'It seemed harmless enough.' She succeeded in jamming her hand through the bangle. Ailixond shook his head. 'He means me to remember that his ancestors rebelled against the throne in the time of Ailixond third, and again in the time of Ailixond fifth, when one seized the throne and became Parakison fifth.'

'Your ancestors too . . . damn, I shall have to butter this to get it off again.'

'No, my grandfather came to the throne as a result of a contest and election among the lords, since Parakison sixth had only daughters, his one son having died before him.'

'I am sure that you read too much into one remark.'

'I know him. He means to remind me that kings have fallen before: be not too arrogant.'

'Then is that not treasonable?'

'It is too slender a charge, and he is too cunning to let me have any graver charge against him. And Meraptar will keep him quiet while he is here.'

'Indeed, he appears scared witless . . . curse this bangle . . .'

'Keep it.'

'No, I never use such fripperies.'

'Then wear it home and give it to your maid. There are enough jewelleries here for all the royal ladies.'

Ailixond kept Meraptar in his company all the next day, asking for news of an endless reel of persons and places in Safi, while Sandar rode in silence at the rear of the group of lords. It was only in the evening, when Firumin was serving them with a fine dinner made from the Lord Regent's presents, that he allowed Meraptar to mention the subject of his return, and then said only that he did not intend to stay long, before passing on to his plans for campaigning in South Lysmal: 'You know how short of large timber we are . . .' Sandar engaged in stilted conversation with the lords his peers, and was presented to the representatives of the conquered nations who had been invited to the dinner, who he greeted with irreproachable manners and an air of utter disdain. 'And where is this – did you say, Shgal'min?'

Aleizon Ailix Ayndra watched him from where she stood with Arpalond, she watching the company, he with his mouth at her ear. 'He has great opinion of himself as a patron of art – watch and no doubt you will see him patronising Serannin – and despises all of us here as crude military men. Consequently he has been

379

much embittered by our rise to fame and fortune, while he hangs on the cloak-hems of a gaggle of playwrights and acts as shield bearer to his father. Yet as a boy he was much the cleverest of all the noble children of the time . . .'

'Yourself and Ailixond inclusive?'

'I have always been one to hide my light under a bushel. And Ailixond in those days was, ah . . .'

'Very much his mother's boy,' she murmured.

'You surprise me! Who have you been talking to?'

'No one,' she said. 'I think more than I say; and draw many conclusions . . .' With that she broke away from him and went up to Sandar, who looked down his nose at her. She said to him, 'I do not suppose that you brought any new books from Safi?'

'New books? Why, I have one or two; what interest would you have in them?'

'Very likely I should wish to borrow them.'

'Borrow them!' he said, overcome by surprise.

'I will return them as soon as I have read them.'

'Perhaps I should lend you my secretary for the purpose – to read them out, that is. His tones are most melodious,' Sandar said sarcastically. 'O no,' she said, 'that will not be necessary – tell me, in any case, what books are they? though I will read almost any book . . .' She engaged him in a conversation on the relative merits of various dramatists and players in Safi, which was cut short only by Firumin calling them to be seated, when she was brought back to Arpalond's side.

'I did not know you to be an amateur of the drama,' he said. 'Surely it cannot be the case that you were an actress?'

'For three years come the Winter Festival I sold pancakes in a booth beneath the seats. And once I played flattanharp in the band of a group of travelling players. Most of the plays I talk about I have never even seen.' She tore a piece of bread apart and stuffed half of it in her mouth. 'But then,' she said, muffled, 'I think, neither has he.'

Meraptar had the chair of the guest of honour; he kept Ailixond occupied in conversation throughout, until the sweet wines were brought round and the meal ended, when he rose to pronounce a prolix loyal toast, to which all had to drain their cups in one save Ailixond, who must stand to reply to it and then toss off a full cup himself; which he did gracefully, and managed to sit down before he fell forward over the table coughing, just as Sandar was rising for a second round. He stood up slowly, his eyes fixed on the king, and paused, goblet in hand while Ailixond wheezed and struggled

380

to regain his breath. Meraptar looked perturbed. Ailixond shook his head. 'This time I shall not take more than half a cup,' he muttered in deprecation to the Lord Regent. Sandar raised his brows a fraction. 'The health of the king,' he said, 'is the health of the nation. Long life and good fortune to both!'

All drank; Ailixond got up again. 'And the good order of the government lies in the amity of its lords. I drink to their honour, honesty and fair dealing.' This time Firumin had supplied him with just half a mouthful, and he sat down without mishap. 'Stay an you will, and the Steward will bring any food or drink you desire; but I fear that I must retire.' Meraptar expressed regret, but Ailixond said that he was too occupied with cares of state to remain longer, and disappeared behind the curtain to his own rooms. The diners remained over their cups and fruits and sweetmeats a while longer, but within two hours the last had gone; while some, also summoned by duty, had left as soon as the king.

The second watch of the night ended between second and third hour of the morning. Lord Ayndra passed the king's tent as she was returning from the watchmaster's tent, having handed over to Golaron, when she saw a dim light glowing in the inner rooms, visible now since the servants had already taken down the big tent. She went up to the door and lifted her hat to the guards, who passed her without a word. The lamps in the vestibule were all out. She walked like a cat into the bedroom and silently lifted the curtain. Inside there were only a couple of glowlamps, shining through bowls of alabaster, and a hot brazier. Ailixond sat near the coals, stretched out on the floor with his head against the knees of the woman seated in his chair. She had a white cloth spread over her lap, combing out his hair till it spread across her knees like the threads on a lacemaker's cushion. Ailixond's face looked like bronze in the low light; it gleamed on the hard contours of cheek and forehead, and brushed over the lines round his mouth and eyes. The woman's hands moved over his forehead like a slow heartbeat, rings glinting, with an ivory comb like a ghost's face in the black locks. It was a while before Ayndra noticed that the half-hidden face was Othanë's, bent away from the door over her task; under her hands, Ailixond was as quiet as a sleeping child. She put down the comb and paused with a hand laid on his forehead, then suddenly put them either side his face and bent down and kissed him. The curtain swished. The tableau shattered.

'Who is that?' Ailixond sat up.

'I am sorry,' said a voice outside, 'I did not – I have come to say goodnight. But I'll leave now –'

'No, come in,' he said. The curtains parted and Lord Ayndra appeared, hat in hand. 'My lord – I believed you were alone –'

'I said, come in.'

'As you will, my lord.' She came a few steps and knelt down on the floor. 'My lady, greetings – I must say, it is the first time that I have seen anyone but him sit in that chair.' Othanë shrugged, reaching across her face to toy with her hair ornaments. Ailixond propped himself against her knees again. 'Well,' he said, 'it's not impossible that she sits there with the future heir of Safi.'

'O no. I never wish to disinherit Parri,' Othanë protested.

'Nor should I; but no one knows what the gods might bring.'

'I should like it to be a girl,' said the queen.

'Whichever, so long as hale and healthy.' Ailixond looked at Lord Ayndra. 'You've just come off watch.'

'And I saw the light here as I passed so I thought . . .'

'We are pleased to see you,' said Othanë.

'And I you, lady, though I was not aware that you ever came into these rough male quarters.'

'It's the first time,' said Othanë. 'You see, I could not get to sleep either – and I know that Ailixond is almost always awake, so I came here.'

'O, and do you find it excessively stark?'

'I think it a pity that you hang no tapestries on the walls. I am sure you could.'

'No, the servants spend half their lives taking tents up and down as it is,' said Ailixond. 'I'll hang all the tapestries when we reach Safi.'

'Yes, my lord, do you not look forward to returning home? I cannot abide waiting – after all these years!'

'I don't know,' said Ayndra softly, drawing idle circles with one finger on the floor. 'It's several years since I spent any time in Safi.'

'Likewise,' said Ailixond. The canvas roof snapped muffledly in the wind. Ayndra stood up. 'I must to bed; I am sure that I at least will have no trouble sleeping.' Othanë offered her hand; she took it in a gesture of formal affection, glanced down and found Ailixond's eyes like dark glass beneath her. She cast her arm round the queen's neck and kissed her convulsively on the cheek; broke the embrace, and was gone. The curtains flew in the speed of her going; their breeze swept the room like a gust of lightning. 'Aah!' said Othanë. Ailixond cast the white cloth over his face. Othanë snatched it from him. She said in a high voice, 'Is she your –?'

382

Ailixond kept his eyes shut. 'No,' he said.

'But not for want of desire on your part!'

Ailixond shook his head, rolling it to and fro in her lap. 'It has all finished,' he said heavily. 'She has no designs upon your place.'

'To be Queen of Safi?'

'To be my wife.' He felt her silent disbelief; opened his eyes. 'She refused it,' he said.

'Ha!' cried Othanë faintly. Ailixond sat up, world-weariness drawing his face in again. 'I will not cast you off,' he said, 'you know that. I shall never –'

Othanë punched her hands in her lap and drew herself up. 'I cannot help that I am a fool, that I cannot be a friend to you – I know I am foolish! Your mother chose me for it!' Ailixond began, 'I never said –' but she had seized her mantle and work-bag and flung out of the room. He heard her crying, 'Take me home!' to the guards. He remained kneeling by the empty chair.

'The Chief Clerk of the archives in Safi says that these lands belonged to Safi of old – he has a map of the days of Ailixond third, showing Safi vassals in the coastal towns almost as far as the Girran, and our dominance extending inland as far as the forest in these parts – Meraptar has brought this copy of it with him.' Ailixond spread the rolled map over his desk. Ayndra looked at it. 'I think the distances are wrong, it seems hardly more than a short walk between the marshes and the Chiaral, and from then again perhaps a few days' march to the borders of Safi – I do not think that the man who drew it can have done more than heard the names.'

'But others must have journeyed here to tell him them.'

'Sailed up the coast perhaps, and paid off once for all by the distant ancestors of the slippery lord of Gombollan.'

'But look at this. It says that Parakison third built a summer palace in the hills. It cannot be far from here.'

'It will be all ruined now, if it stands at all, surely! This is all three hundreds years ago.'

'If it was well built, and people have lived in it since . . . I wish to search for it, in any case. I should like to have a banquet there before sending Meraptar back to Safi.'

'You are going to leave him as Regent, then?'

'For a month more, a month and a half, however long it takes till I am there – then when I leave again, we shall see; he is an old man, after all . . . I shall keep Sandar with the army, though, for the time being.'

'He is plotting with Carmago.'

'Who is? Sandar?'

'You know that he lent me some books? Yester night I went to his tent to return one, and I found Carmago there, very drunk, while Sandar, though he had a whiff of wine on his breath was, I am sure, stone cold sober.'

'He is abstemious in drink, though a glutton for rich foodstuffs. Can he not invite a captain to dinner with him?'

'Will you defend him now? Carmago was a leader of the mutineers at New Hope.'

'Do not think that I forget. I think that the retention of his commission surprised him so greatly that he will not think to risk it again.'

'Possibly,' she said, getting up and fidgeting round the room. 'Also Sandar has been visiting various apothecaries in the camp, some of whom vend poisons to discreet customers.'

'Also he has had the flux lately, a good reason to visit apothecaries, do you not think?'

'Good lord, one would think the man was your bosom friend.'

'I do not acquit him of harbouring evil intentions, but I am sure that he plots nothing at present. When his father leaves . . . but even then, he will have too short a time before coming to Safi, and he has no friends in the army.'

'So long as you are confident.'

'I am. I will recommend some of my people to watch Carmago in any case. Fff! – in the past I heard or saw these things, but these days I do not even hear the gossip, let alone witness questionable goings-on.'

'Yet you still know everything sooner or later.'

'Only because I have such a network of informants – like a woman who stirs not from her house, yet knows every last happening in the town.' He slit the stitches on another packet of despatches; two more lay unopened. 'You should get more assistants,' she said. 'Cannot you give more of this to the Inner Council?'

'I do as it is.'

'Not merely for discussion, I mean to read and answer or whatever is to be done.'

'I doubt that most of them would agree to it. Consider Lakkannar trying to audit the accounts of the Lysmalish treasury – an he will count beyond ten, he has to take his boots off! I can safely leave the military command in their hands, and that is what I value them for.'

'Meanwhile you are become a glorified clerk.'

He bent over a letter. He said softly, 'Time is short . . . when I return to Safi, then I shall create all sorts of new offices and the situation will be rectified. It's not long till then.' She still looked dubious. He said, 'You may audit the accounts of Lysmal if you wish!'

'I shall, then. Where are they?'

'All these are they.' He gave her a canvas-wrapped packet weighing at least a pound. 'Go to the Treasury and ask for Master Taish, chief clerk of the Lysmalish section. He has all the records and will explain these documents to you. Report to me when you have prepared the summary.'

She imitated a phalanxman's stiff salute. 'Consider it done, my lord!'

'Thank you,' he said absently, searching in his document box. 'And call the Justiciar to me, on your way . . .'

The winter in the hills came wet and frosty, the high moors whitened with snow and the valleys awash with freezing mud; the army lumbered on complaining, no longer subject to attack but weighed down with tedium and chills; sustained only by the promise of Safi's milder climate which Sixth Month would bring them to. Messengers reached them daily now, and even a train of merchants with cheap wines and trinkets for the soldiers. It seemed as though the proximity of home slowed progress rather than speeding it, for they hardly made fifteen miles in a day. It was Lord Ayndra's turn to command the rearguard, slogging through the morass left by forty thousand feet and wheels; most of the time they rode along the valley sides, for the road was rendered almost impassable; scattered and lethargic, watchfulness at a minimum. Lord Ayndra herself did not see Ailixond until he was almost on top of her, as he appeared on the crest of the nearest rise. She sat up and raised her hand. 'Welcome – what brings you here?'

He came no closer. 'Hand over to your captain and come with me.'

She hallooed downhill. 'Douro! Would you take command until – o, until I return?' Looking up, Douro recognised the distant rider in white. 'My lord. How long will you leave us for?'

'I cannot say. All the day perhaps. You know what to do. Good day!' She brushed Anagar's sides with her spurs, and he leapt up the hill in pursuit of Ailixond, who was already galloping away.

He led her a wild chase up out of the valley and over stretches of high moor like the sea turned to mossy-soaked grasses, down again into sparse woods of ghostly white-barked trees. She caught up at last on a green lawn above a cascade. The short grass showed signs of sheep's cropping, and a faint footpath led down away between the rocks. Ailixond had dismounted. She jumped down beside him. 'How did you find this? Did you ride away yesterday –'

'This is not it,' he said. 'We can leave the horses here.' He tossed her a picket-peg; she found a stone to hammer it in with. He was a hundred yards away by the time she had finished, beckoning furiously. They chased the path through more wood-land and round the foot of a crag to another grassy lip – 'No further! There it is.'

'How did you find it?' she said again.

There was a long narrow lake taking up much of the valley bottom, its shores fringed with reeds that almost choked it in the shallows where a broad curve of marble steps, all cracked and tufted with grass, ran down to it from a colonnade in the shape of the new moon. The red tiles of the roof had faded to earth- and lichen-colour and large stretches had fallen in altogether; some had been replaced with reed thatch. There were two enclosed courtyards behind the colonnade, and a yard with a huddle of rough huts and outbuildings at the back.

'Have you been inside? Does anyone live there now?'

'I think that it's a shepherds' house in summer – that is why it has not fallen entirely into ruin, you see where they have repaired the roof – but it stands empty presently. Come down.' There was a broad path down through a number of drystone-walled enclosures, sheep pens or vegetable patches, past the middens into the yard. It seemed that no one had lived there recently, but the rubbish was not near so old as the house, and there were soot-stains on the roofs of the kitchen buildings. Ailixond pushed open a door. 'I broke the latch yesterday.' There were no pots or tables to be seen, but no one had bothered to rake out the last fire in the great fireplace and there were old clouts and potsherds on the floor. 'Come through into the king's apartments.' The room he took her to was on the south-east corner, with windows in three walls, all more or less shuttered. He went round pushing them open; she stood gazing. A crude bed with a musty straw pallet stood in one corner. 'Why do you think that this was the king's room?'

'Do you see? The walls have been painted.'

Much of it had flaked away like scurf, or faded in the dank gloom of damp-stains, and time had stripped the colours of their vigour: red borders still resembled brick, but the blue in between had faded to the colour of a hazy winter's sky, and the birds flying across it were ghosts of their former selves.

'The women's rooms are on the west side, and in the middle between the courtyards stands the hall. We shall have to put a new roof on that, for they clearly had no use for it and it's gone to rack and ruin.'

'I suppose these must be birds from the lake . . . look, there's a hawker here in the corner.'

'I imagine that Parakison third must have come up here for the hunting.'

'Is that who you think built it? Have you found his name on it?'

'No, but I know that it was a royal house of Safi.'

'How? I know it does not look like a barbarian castle, but who –'

'Come and look at the doors.'

They were barred from the inside with a roughly hewn plank, and the wood was worm-eaten under the veneer that had long since peeled away, but the bronze cladding under its coat of verdigris still rimmed them and marched in a double zigzag line across their outer face. 'Ay!' she said. 'The waves of Safi.'

'Yes, and only kings are allowed to use them.' The overgrown steps ran down to the grey skirts of the lake and the whispering reeds; the wind whined among cracked and broken columns, and chased dead leaves through the crumbled stucco at the front of the walls. Ayndra sat down on the front doorstep, drawing her cloak about her. 'It's not a cheerful place in the winter,' she said. 'And all so deserted . . . I should not like it here with darkness coming on.'

'It will be transformed if we only put a canvas roof over the hall and replaster the walls and put a new roof on. The walls, and these columns, are all stone-built.'

'They remind me of broken teeth in a jawbone . . . but what are you talking about? Do you intend to move in here and never go home at all?'

'O no! You see where the river runs out of the lake, at the far end of the valley? There's a drover's track there that goes hardly two miles to meet the road, and there's enough land there for the army to camp, while we move in here for a few days – it need only be cleaned and we'll make temporary roofs, then I shall leave some people to live here and bring it back to order – it's not so far away from Safi, but it would be a relief to come here in Last Month.'

She looked up. 'Do you intend to stay in Safi long enough that you'll want a summer palace as well as your all-the-year one?'

Ailixond shrugged with a flutter of fingers, casting the question away; he stamped his feet. 'Come down to the lake. Then we must go back. The road makes a long loop round, so it will be two days before we come to the track leading here . . .'

'Shumar! You run about so fast I can hardly keep up with you.' Ailixond was coughing into a large handkerchief when she caught up with him. 'Hagh! – I find it too cold to sit still.'

'It's not that cold. You've a bearskin cloak on!' He gave another shivery shrug. 'Have you a fever?' she said. 'You look much too bright.'

'If it is, it's no more than a touch of cold.' He set off uphill, still coughing, but walking at an unholy rate; she panted to keep at his tail, and heard his breath rasping like a two-man saw. When they reached the vantage point from which they'd first seen the palace, he had to sit down on a rock, and fell again to coughing. She was distracted by a soughing noise in the air, growing rapidly as it rushed towards them – 'Look! Swans!'

'Seven of them.'

Beating the air with a noise of a forest in flight, they bore away down the valley, southwards.

'Ah!' he said. 'Perhaps that's the old king's spirit leaving.'

'Why do you say that?'

'It's in the Book of Dreams. Swans carry the spirits of the dead away.'

'Because the new king's come to replace him?' She shivered. Ailixond turned away to spit into a bush. 'It is cold,' she said. 'Come along.'

'This is a mad plot,' Polem complained. 'I am sure that the wagons with his things in them will come up the road, even if he says that the rest cannot. And I will be bound that Lady Ailissa will not come up on the back of a horse!'

'I do not see why not,' said Diamoon. 'It makes a pleasant change.' She clasped Polem more tightly; she was riding astride behind him, her skirts bundled up over high red boots bought her for that very journey by Polem.

'I do not see why you cannot ride by yourself,' said Ayndra. 'You can borrow one of my spare horses, they are all very tame.'

'I like it this way better.'

Ayndra sniffed in disgust. 'Where is Ailixond?' said Polem.

'Already here. We should go in and look for him.'

'I must say, when he used to ride with us all day one could always find him – but these days! Since he took to sitting in a wagon half the time one never knows if he is there, or out touring the column to watch for slack discipline, or put on a dark cloak and ridden off somewhere else entirely. One of these days he will fall down a ravine and we shall lose him for ever . . .'

A couple of slaves in royal livery were lounging on the steps; they jumped up to take the lords' horses as they dismounted. Diamoon had fallen oddly silent as they neared the house. She watched the slaves leading the horses away towards the sheeppens. Polem marched up to the doors, which had been stripped down and the old bronze removed, leaving only its green shadow in the wood. 'Diamoon! Why do you wait down there? When you come with me you need not use the tradesmen's entrance.'

'I would not use the tradesmen's entrance in any case,' said Diamoon.

'Well, come then.' Polem knocked on the door. 'Where's Ailixond?' he said to the servant who opened.

'This way, my lord.' They passed a posse of slaves, three on their knees scrubbing the floor, the others slapping whitewash on lime plaster that still smelt damply fresh, and came to the room Ailixond had called the king's, when Polem noticed that Diamoon had not followed. 'Where is she? Diamoon!'

Ayndra came up instead. 'She will not come. She has gone down to camp at the foot of the lake.'

'What?'

'She says she'll not come in this house. She says there is an ill wish on it.'

'What?'

'She says that's why we found it empty yet not eaten away by time as it should be. I think if she'd not been speaking to a notorious sceptic she'd have suggested that it was hands devilish and not human who thatched the roof.' Ayndra made a quizzical face. 'I must say that this is one time when I almost agree with her.'

'What?'

'I do not like the atmosphere of this place.' But she dismissed the subject with a wave of her hands, and knocked on Ailixond's door. A secretary opened it. 'Ye gods!' she said, 'working again.'

Servants and soldiers scythed the weeds in the two courtyards, and roped canvases over the gaping holes in the roofs; to cover the hall they had to build a roof-frame out of tent poles and lash it to the ragged remnants of old beams. In the early dusk, yellow lights shone out of the latticed windows and music sang in the ladies' rooms, while smoke poured from the kitchen roof. Mountebanks from the lower camp came up to sing and dance in the hall, eat fire and conjure with coloured cloths. The weather grew very bitter and tried to snow. On the third night Ailixond held Meraptar's farewell banquet, for all the lords and officers with a table for the ladies presided over by Setha – Othanë shunned the occasion, claiming that she feared for her child's health if she indulged in rich food and excitement. Lower down in the hall, women mixed freely with the men, but Diamoon was still absent. During the dessert a servant brought Polem a message: 'My lord, Mistress Diamoon is at the door and would speak with you.'

'Tell her to come in.'

'She says you must come, my lord, she will not enter under any circumstances, but it is urgent that you come.'

'All right then. Excuse me . . . business calls . . .' Polem left the table, and picked up his fur mantle on the way out of the hall. A cold blast of winter wind met him as the door was opened for him to go out. Diamoon was huddled against the wall, muffled to the eyebrows in a vast cloak the colour of old blood. 'Why will you not come in? It's colder than a witch's kiss!'

'I will not enter that place. Look, I have something which you must give to the king.' She pushed a tiny paper packet into his hand; he started to pick it apart. 'What on earth –'

'Don't open it!' She spoke very rapidly. 'I took it from the tent where that old man with the stars on his gown who calls himself an astrologer lives. He hardly knows one star from another, his real practice is bewitchment. Lord Sandar has seen him many times and two days ago he gave him that. I know not what he meant to do with it, but I stole it, and you must take it to your king and get him to put it in the fire with his own hand, as soon as he may. Now!'

'But what is it?' said Polem. 'We are in the middle of dinner.' A loud cheer from the hall. 'See, they are just coming on to the toasts.'

'Take it to him! I do not want to wait near this place any longer than I must.'

'But what is it?'

'A lock of your Lord Ailixond's hair and clippings of his finger nails.'

390

'Good god!' said Polem. Diamoon pushed him. 'Ailixond must put them in the fire himself, this very moment.'

'All right then. But he is presiding over dinner – I do not know if he – and beside, how did Sandar come by these things?'

'Does it matter? Now take – aaah!' Diamoon let out a scream and fell to the ground. Polem, horrified, dropped to his knees beside her, just as another scream rang from the hall. He knew not which way to turn. Diamoon scrabbled to her knees. 'Put it in your pocket and do not touch it till he can burn it himself! I must go from here!' She ran away down the faintly gleaming steps, a black blot on the windy darkness. Polem turned and ran back, shouting at the doormen of the hall. They pushed the double doors open and he was greeted by a cacophony of howls – 'The king! Is he dead? They've killed him! Who was it? Is he dead?' Ailixond's chair was empty and most of the lords were on their feet; Golaron, Sulakon and Arpalond were bending over something behind the king's chair, with Meraptar leaning nervously above them. Only Sandar was still seated and looked calm, his small eyes meditatively lidded as he swirled the wine in his cup. Ailissa had run from the ladies' side to the high table and was pulling at her husband's sleeve. 'Ailixond!' she cried above the racket. Lord Ayndra jumped up on the table and held her arms above her head. 'Pray silence!' she shrieked. 'Silence! Silence!' The shouting quietened. 'Silence!'

In the sudden peace she said, 'My lord the king is not dead, merely faint. He will leave the dinner for tonight, but he will wish all of you to continue taking pleasure in the festivities. Do not, however, distress yourselves: I repeat again, he is not dead!' As she spoke, Golaron rose; he had gathered Ailixond in his arms like a child, with his head against his shoulder. The king's face was yellow-pale, his lips and eyelids purple; a streak of blood ran down his chin. The crowd in the hall started to murmur again. Ayndra clapped her hands. 'Firumin! Bring the wine round again. And call the musicians to play.' Golaron went to the side door, followed by most of the lords, but Sulakon stopped them. 'Go back and continue the merrymaking. We will only spread evil rumours if all of us leave. And you, my lady, your place is here – you will be the first to know of any change. Go now, and do your duty!'

Polem ran round the corner and almost into Golaron, who was accompanied only by Sulakon and Arpalond and the Physician. 'What is it? What happened? Is it poison?'

'He fainted after he pledged Meraptar,' said Golaron.

391

'I do not think that there has been any poison,' said the Physician. 'But I shall need braziers, and lamps, and rags to stuff all the cracks in the shutters – and hot bricks warmed in the oven – and send someone for my boy with the medicine chest –'

'I will see to it.' Arpalond slipped away. The others entered the dark chamber, barely warmed by one dim brazier. Golaron laid Ailixond down on the bed. None of them spoke; they stood round the bed with eyes fastened on him. His ribs hardly moved with his shallow breathing. Polem gripped the packet Diamoon had given him. 'This is not a faint!' he said. No one replied. The door swung open and a couple of servants rushed in with braziers, coal-bucket and lamps; while the Physician felt the king's hands and forehead, others followed until the room was a hell of radiance and growing hotter every moment. Came the Physician's assistants, who opened up a variety of bottles of stinking cordials, kitchen servants with trays of hot bricks and warmed blankets, and rags with which they stuffed the shutters; Ailixond disappeared from view under their ministrations, as they took off his boots to apply bricks to his bare feet and swathed him like a cocoon in blankets. Polem stayed clinging to the bed's foot, ignored and ignorant. Golaron had gone back to the hall to further calm the company, and Arpalond had gone off on some errand; Sulakon stood at the bed's head with his hands behind his back, watching like a drillmaster. He said to the Physician, 'Will he soon regain his wits?'

'Indeed I hope so – these passages are usually of only a few moments' duration.'

'Then it has happened before?'

The Physician coughed. 'Well, my lord, it is not unknown.'

'You realise that it is your duty to report to the lords of Safi on all matters concerning the health of the king. And you say this is not a novel episode? How long has he been subject to these fits?'

'It is not a fit, my lord.'

'But how long has it been going on? What sickness has he? And by what right have you concealed it?'

'My lord,' said the Physician, 'it is a duty of my profession to make no admissions which those we serve forbid us. I would not be acting as physician to my lord an I did not keep silent over those matters which he regards as personal to him alone.'

'You have a duty to all the lords of Safi also, sir, for we are of one body and the health of its head is –'

'My lord, I think he wakens.'

Sulakon clamped his mouth shut instantly. Ailixond moved his head, opened his eyes groggily. 'Why are all these people in the room? Send them out . . . Polem, you stay. Physician . . . the rest all go.' Sulakon bowed curtly and departed; the others scattered like rabbits. Ailixond struggled with the blankets until he got sufficiently free of them to sit up. His face was still greenish-pale; he ran one hand through his disordered hair. 'Polem,' he said.

Polem sat down on the bed and took his other hand. 'What happened? One moment you were there laughing, I go out of the hall and there is a scream and you are on the floor —'

'It was Lady Setha who screamed,' said the Physician, moving away from the bed. Ailixond drew his knees up and rubbed his feet, blinking like one just roused from sleep. 'What, so you were not there?'

'No,' said Polem, 'I had to go and see Diamoon —' he clammed up, not knowing whether this was the time to deliver her message.

'A pity,' said Ailixond, 'for most of the time neither was I . . .' he gave a sarcastic twitch of his mouth at the Physician. 'But I did well, do you not think? By the time I gave the pledge cup to Meraptar I was deaf and blind on my feet.'

'No one would have noticed it, my lord, you spoke the pledge as clearly as I've ever heard it. But you should have left before that.' The Physician was pounding something aromatic and bitter in a mortar.

'Well, worry no more; I shall not go back. Let Sulakon be master of ceremonies.' He leant back and closed his eyes. 'My lord, I order you to keep to your bed for tomorrow at least,' said the Physician.

'At the moment, certainly, I am fit for nothing else. Polem, will you go and tell Firumin to ply them all with wine and not to worry? And Sulakon and Golaron to take charge. And you, go and enjoy yourself . . . and ask Lord Ayndra to come. But not immediately.'

'I'll do it,' But Polem did not leave; he hung his head, and gave Ailixond's hand a sudden squeeze. The door opened, and Aleizon Ailix Ayndra peered round it. 'Ailix? O, thank God. Sandar has left the hall. Shall I see that he is detained?'

'Do you know where he has gone?'

'I think he heads for the lower camp.'

'Polem,' said Ailixond, 'go after him and make out that you desire his company so much that you cannot let him leave. Then privily ask Meraptar to ensure that his son remains at his side until the moment of departure, at which time I will have arranged . . . something else.'

'Whatever you say.' Polem got up, shuffled, finally waved and dashed out. 'Come in,' Ailixond said to Aleizon Ailix Ayndra.

The Physician finished pounding up his mixture and scraped it into a phial, which he sealed. 'An you feel any trouble, my lord, hold this under your nose – and of course, call me –'

'Of course.' Ailixond proffered his hand; the Physician kissed his ring, and slipped out. 'Hah,' said the king.

Aleizon Ailix Ayndra said nothing.

'How are they?' he said.

'Subdued.'

'I was just about to send Polem for you.'

'Yes?' She stood twisting one of her bracelets.

'Come closer, then.'

She approached slowly; followed his gesture, and perched on the edge of the bed. She looked at him under her brows, sidewise, like an affrighted animal. He held out his ring hand. She took it with the tips of her fingers. 'Do you want me to go?' she said.

'I never want you to go!' He flung his arm round her and kissed her hard on the mouth. She howled like a dog and burst into tears; she broke loose from his embrace and flung herself face down on the floor; racked with sobs like a child, she beat her forehead on the stone flags. Ailixond leapt down from the bed and seized her shoulders, embraced her head on his knees. She seized hold of him as if he were the mast in a shipwreck, and went on weeping open-mouthed; her tears soaked his breeches. 'Stop it!' he said. 'Stop it stop it stop it!' She shook her head. He said, 'If you don't stop it I shan't – I shan't be able to –' he closed his eyes; she looked up and saw tears in the black lashes. 'O god,' she said, and rose up and took his head on her shoulder, and they remained like that for some while, rocking back and forth as a ship does on the sea.

Eventually he said, 'Go and lock the door.'

'What?'

'Someone is bound to come soon.'

'And then what will you do?'

'You can shout at them to go away.'

'All right then.' There was an old bolt and a new one; she shut both. Ailixond got up and swayed with dizziness; he lay down on the bed and pulled a rag from his sleeve to cough into. Examining the phlegm out of habit, he found it all scarlet with new blood. He tossed it into the nearest brazier. 'I do not think that I am going to get back to Safi,' he said.

'O, surely not.' She sat down, precisely, hands in her lap. He

394

pulled her down beside him. She hid her face in his tunic and
started to cry again.

'O, for god's sake! . . . I thought you at least . . . I've never seen
you weep before!' he said.

'It's a long time . . . give me your handkerchief, I'll try to stop.'
She blew her nose like a trumpet and scrubbed at her streaming
eyes, said thinly, 'Why did you not say anything before?'

'Because I'm a fool.'

'And I'm a worse one . . . well, thank god you've said it now.'
She thrust her arms round him and hugged him against her breast.
Ailixond closed his eyes, relaxing; he smelt of spirits and wine and
winter-green oil and a faint, unmistakable tang of decay, the taint
of his rotting lungs carried on his breath. In her arms his body was
as light and hard as papier-maché and unnaturally hot to the
touch. 'Whatever shall we do?' she whispered. '– whatever shall *I*
do?'

'You'll be all right. The lords will tear the Empire to pieces, but
you will be all right.'

'Yes, but . . . I don't want to have to be lonely again.'

'You won't be.'

She gave a harsh sigh for answer.

'I'll give you the ambassadorship in Suthine, or anything else
that you want.'

'No . . . I'm not *Ylureen's barbarian* any more.'

'Ylureen's barbarian?'

'Yes. Plucked out of the guardroom and wrapped up in silks to
be presented at all the fashionable festivals . . . her noble friends
disliked me also; I never played the exotic fool to their liking . . .
no grovelling gratitude for the gift of their society . . .'

'You haven't changed, then.'

'I don't think so. Only become more blatantly what inwardly I
always was.' She giggled into his hair. 'Ylureen always puts me in
mind of sweetsmoke.'

'And why not?' He added, 'I have been such an exemplary
monarch all these years, I deserve to spend my last days in a sink
of debauchery.'

'What, shall I throw a pound lump on a brazier and fill all the
room? – if I had a pound lump to throw . . . you know why
Ylureen is so rich? She has the monopoly on sweetsmoke for the
whole of Suthine province. This comes from her.'

'And does she then sell to you at a bargain price?'

'Alas! That I should be so lucky.' She searched in various
recesses of her clothing and brought out four smokesticks all half

395

consumed. 'Eh! why am I laughing so much? . . . have some of this, then.' She sat on the floor with her knees drawn up, back against the bed. Ailixond, stretched out across it, dropped his head into the hollow of her shoulder.

'The worst thing I ever did was to send you away to Raq'min.'

'And I wondered and wondered why you ever called me back.'

'Because I missed you,' he said, muffled in her hair. Her face stiffened as if she were in pain; she said nothing, only reached up to embrace his neck with her left hand.

'Can I stay here this night?'

'I'll keep you awake coughing,' he said, 'and my breath stinks already of the charnel house. Of course you can . . . and I never sleep before third hour of morning, without I drink half a pint of Suthine firewater first.'

'Don't do that. I'll tell you a story instead.'

'A long one?'

'Thirty-one years long. But you know the latter part of it, I think.' She looked round; his eyes met hers, very sharp and surprised. She flicked her eyebrows and smiled; lit another stick from the stub of the last one, and settled down to begin. 'This is the story of a little girl,' she said, 'who wanted to be a hero with a sword . . .

'Once upon a time there was a little girl, and she lived in Safi with her mother, in one room at the top of a house not far from the Street of Dreams. Her mother worked in the Street of Dreams, because the little girl had no father. He had been a rich nobleman who found her mother when she came down from Haramin, and married her and set her up in a house, but shortly after the little girl was born he died –'

'A rich nobleman? Do you know –'

'If you interrupt, I shall not go on. All this is true as told to me, so shut your mouth and listen. Upon which all his family, who were noble and very proud, cast her out of the house without money and forced her to go on the streets for want of bread; for which reason she would never speak of him, except when she drank too much wine and then she would curse his noble wives, but she never named him at all. So the little girl never knew her father's name, although she knew that the men who lived with her mother were none of them her father. Then, when she was five years old, a sea-captain with a black beard came to the house and took her mother away to sea with him, so the little girl had to go too. And so they sailed all round North Lysmal and up to Shgal'min, and back again, until her mother found a richer sea-

captain who owned two ships, and they sailed to the far north and
went to live in Pomoan and sailed between Haramin and Great
Droagon Sea. Her mother cooked for the sailors on board ship,
and washed and mended, and helped with the business when the
ship called into port, but the little girl had no place on the ship
and slept in the sail locker with the ship's boy and ran about with
the street urchins when the ship was in port. She wore old clothes
that the sailors gave her, and no one made her take a bath for
months at a time, unless she fell into the water. The sailors fed her
their leftovers, or else she stole food and any other thing she could
lay her hands on, and swore in five tongues. By the time she was
ten she knew the receivers of stolen goods in every port they sailed
to, and filched goods from the cargo to sell to them – the money
she got, she bought sweetmeats with . . . until her mother found
out, and left her all summer in Pomoan in the charge of a wine-
sodden old priest and his housekeeper, who taught her to read and
write, for this her mother had charged them with, thinking that an
educated girl might find a rich merchant for a husband. But when
her mother came back it was not with the sea-captain, but with a
rich merchant herself, from Raq'min, who took her as a lesser-
wife, and they travelled in his land train to Raq'min. Her mother
even then was a very fine woman, with long yellow hair and an
oval face and a thin nose, while the little girl had a nose like an
eagle which she must have got from her father's family. The
merchant had a wife already, and three daughters of an age to be
married, who pulled the little girl's hair and made her fetch and
carry for them. She was very glad when the merchant caught the
bad-water fever and died of it. This time her mother made sure
that he left her some jewels and a good deal of money, and she left
Raq'min to go back to Safi where the merchant's wife's family
would not be able to sue her for the regain of his legacy. Her
mother bought a house near Yellow Temple Square, three rooms
and a shop below, and set up in business as a perfume seller,
though she sold other things to ladies who came secretly to the
back room, things to bring children or get rid of them, or to get
rid of a husband or an enemy . . . the little girl was fourteen years
old, so not I suppose little any longer, and her mother decided to
make her a lady, although she was a gawky ugly child, and still
used to run around in boy's clothing. She bought her two fine
dresses, and paint for her face, and washed her hair every week in
camomile water and ironed it with a flat-iron to make it straight.
When she was fifteen she began to visit the sons of merchants who
were looking for a bride. But the girl was sullen and with her long

397

nose she was ugly, and none of the merchant's sons chose her, and besides, although she could read and write, her dowry was only forty sols. And at night she climbed out of the window and went picking pockets and stealing in the Street of Dreams and sometimes came not home for days together. When she returned, her mother beat her with a rod and took her to a friend of hers who gave her potions supposed to make her nose shrink and her breasts grow, and asked her if she did not want to be a lady with slaves to wait on her, but the girl said I want to be a famous soldier! Upon which her mother beat her again, and locked her in, for she feared that if the matchmakers heard that she ran about alone at night they would say that she was spoiled and she would get only a poor man for a husband, or a widower with ten children. So the time passed, and the little girl was sixteen, and her mother gave a great feast with the girl all trussed up in tight laces and paint half an inch thick. And her mother drank a great deal of wine and stood up and cursed her for an old maid and a thieving trollop, and said to her, As the gods are my witness, Aleizon, you are a woman now, I will have no more to do with you. And she walked out of the house and was never seen again, and to this day no one knows if she is alive or dead or where her body lies. Now only a few months ago old Lord Parakison had come back from the campaign in Thaless where his son the young Ailixond, the one who was not going to be king, had distinguished himself in battle, and Aleizon had seen him riding in the victory parade and had been very taken with all the gold and glitter. So she sold the house – when after a month her mother had still not come back – and spent the money on a sword, which she had not the least idea how to use, and several sets of men's clothing. However she did not cut off her hair, which was yellow and down to her waist and her mother said that it was her one beauty, she merely did it up under a hat, and with her few things in a sack she went to Thaless Gate and offered herself to the guard captain, one Gamarro, saying I want to go for a soldier. He said that he was pleased to hear it, and took her into his inner room, locking the door. She understood then the jests of his men, and said I want a man's place and not a woman's. He said, there is but one place for a woman and that under a man. He kept her there three days, and then when she would do nothing but cry, he gave her to his subordinates, who kept her until she caught a fever, which they feared was the pox, and cast her sick into the street. When she woke she was in a clean bed in a warm room, and a slavewoman brought her soup in a painted cup, and she thought that she had died and gone to heaven. But when she recovered and wished to leave, she discovered the door locked on the outside, and they told her that she was in the house of Mistress Tolladi, on the Street of Dreams, and they were going to train her to work there. For they'd already spent a fortune on the physician to heal her ... so they taught her to paint her face, and converse prettily with men, and all the arts of the bedchamber, and fed her rich foods on which she grew very fat, so fat indeed that the madam accused her of dalliance with the old sweeping slave who was the only man who lived in the house, until the midwife concluded that she had been with child when she came to them, and it was too late to call the abortionist without endangering the health and life of a piece of goods in which they'd invested a good deal of money. So they set her to scrub floors and mend the other whores' gowns until her time came, which was on the day of the Summer Festival and everyone gone out to watch the merriments who could, except her and the old sweeping slave who went on his lame legs to fetch a midwife, but the only one he could find was old and already drunken, and the child presented its feet in place of its head ... they put it aside for dead, to go to the aid of the mother who was bleeding worse than Safi river in flood, but it began to cry and they found that it lived after all. Mistress Tolladi had a good enough heart after that to find a wet-nurse, for the mother lay abed sick another month, and only after that could they get any work out of her; but at least their physician said she'd never bear another child, which saved any future expense of abortionists. The child was another little yellow-headed girl ... so she went whoring nightly for a year and a half, until the child caught a fever and died. Then she locked herself in her room – they trusted her then with a bolt on the inside – while they were at supper, cut off all her long hair and climbed out of the window and escaped over the roof, into the warren of stews between Yellow Temple and the harbour. She had some bits of jewellery given her by an old man who had favoured her, which she sold to buy men's clothes and a pair of knives, and set to recovering the skills of her youth, to become the best cutpurse in Great Market by the time that she turned twenty. Indeed, she was almost too successful, for thieves have their guilds and governments as any other craftsmen do. One day someone offered her a commission to murder for money, and she took it and performed what was asked of her. Her customer must have talked, for soon came another similar, and another – but any talk is dangerous. She would meet customers for discussion and payment in the wineshop with the sign of the

Burning Pestle, and leave by the back door with the money. But on the third occasion, as she went slinking down the back alley, two men leapt upon her and managed to sink a knife in her arm before she escaped into a crowded street where they dared not follow. She thought that they must have been thieves who knew that she'd just received thirty gold sols. But two days later a friend of hers who worked on the Street of Dreams in one of the houses much frequented by the less reputable elements of Safi came and told her that the chief of the Guild of Assassins, in his cups there that night, had spoken of a woman cutpurse who had had the insolence to trespass upon his territory, and at a cheaper rate too, and though they'd missed her once they'd not fail a second time; so she took all her monies, and tied up her few things in a sack again, and went down to the harbour. The first ship she found that would take a passenger was bound for Agasthine. Now she had never been in S'Thurrulass, but they said that it was true that women ruled there, so she went with them, and from there to the city of Suthine. Where she starved honestly – except for stealing food from the stalls – for some while, since the S'Thurrulans are not very fond of foreigners whom they consider barbarians one and all, and besides she had no trade besides whoring, which she resolved never to practise more, thieving and murder. She presented herself at the hall where the rich go to hire servants, but none would take her on account of her foreign speech, until one day in the midst of winter when Lady Ylureen sent her steward to look for a new member of her bodyguard, the last one having died of a stabbing. It was a post for which she seemed altogether suited, and he took her out to the lady's estate. When Ylureen saw her, she knew that she was more suited than the steward had suspected, and within the month she was promoted from bodyguard to Ylureen's barbarian, received in every noble house in Suthine, even unto the royal palace. And there she stayed for more than two years. But she became tired of festivals and fine clothes with no work to do for them, and of watching intrigue and politicking in which she as a common foreigner could take no part. And the news of the conquests of Lord Ailixond, who by then was king in Safi and had founded his New Empire in many other lands, had reached even unto Suthine. So she told Ylureen that she wished to go and fight for her own country. Ylureen at first protested, and offered her a command in the army of Suthine, but when she saw that she was determined to go she gave her a sword and a mail coat in the Safic pattern, rich enough for a nobleman, and paid her passage back across the sea to Safi. There she asked to enlist in the artillery, but was told that she must travel to the Land-beyond-the-Mountains where the king and the Grand Army then were, for it was not the time of year for the levy. And an arduous journey it was, through North Lysmal and the Needle's Eye and up into the moors on the marches of Yiakarak, where Master Ogo had lately lost his third man from sickness and needed a new one. And so she began her military career, and encountered more success than she ever dreamed of, becoming favoured of the king, who no doubt perceived her outstanding merit, elevated to the lordship, Governor of Haramin before she was thirty years old and one of the most loved and hated in the realm.'

'And is that the end?'

'Ay . . . but it's only the end of part of it, because it's only the end of a story.'

'Why don't you ever talk about these things?'

'No reason to. All past and gone, and none of those who took part any longer living – my past selves least of all.' She felt for the last smokestick. 'You're running a fever yourself.'

The door rattled.

'Go and see who it is.'

She slid up to the door and pressed her face to the edge of it. 'Firumin?'

'My lord? Is all well?'

'Can Firumin come in?'

Ailixond was sitting up, hunched over; he shivered so violently that his teeth chattered. 'Let him in, then.'

She unlocked the door and opened it just wide enough for the steward to slip through. 'No one else is with me, my lord,' he said. 'They are all in the hall – can you hear them? – my lord Sulakon has commanded them all to drink and be merry, he says that you have retired because you have been working and needed to rest.'

'Excellent,' said Ailixond, shaking. Firumin looked horrified. 'My lord! Shall I call the Physician? He is only in –'

'No, no, no!' the king said irritably, and started coughing again. Firumin wailed. 'O my lord!' Ailixond hawked, spat furiously on the floor, and stood up. 'Firumin. For god's sake leave off your hysterics or I shall send you away to the lower camp. I shall go to bed now and no one is to disturb me till morning, or until I expressly send for them. You may go and fetch the bottle of firewater, and . . . is there anything you want?' he said to Lord Ayndra.

'If you could bring my small travelling box from my room,' she

401

said. 'Yunnil knows which it is. Tell her I shall not be back this night.'

'Bring those things, and my white fur to put over the bed. And put an end to any scaremongering rumours they are putting about in the camp.'

'Yes, lord – but Lord Meraptar –'

'Tell him not to change any of his plans, he will depart next day as arranged. Is that clear?'

'Of course, my lord. Whatever you say, my lord.' Firumin bowed and whisked out. Lord Ayndra had dropped to her knees to wipe up the bloody phlegm from the stone floor; she looked perturbed. Ailixond made a gesture of disgust as he flopped down on the bed. 'I forbid you to play my mother into the bargain,' he said hoarsely.

'I'm nobody's mother,' she said sombrely, casting the rag into a brazier and reaching for the coal bucket. 'And yours least of all.'

The Physician had his lodgings in the stables at the back of the house, hastily converted to the use of the royal household; one of his boys opened the half-door in answer to the urgent knocking. It was still dark outside, not even lightening towards dawn. 'Wake your master! Tell him to put a cloak on and come.'

Stumbling out into the frozen puddles of the yard, he found someone wrapped in one of the king's white cloaks, but knew the voice of Lord Ayndra. 'He has fallen into delirium,' she said. 'He seems to want no aid, but I think that you must come.'

'My lord,' he said, shuddering in the wind, 'I fear that my febrifuges have outlived their usefulness –'

'I know, I know, but come all the same.' She ran away ahead of him, feet flashing bare under the cloak's gold hem.

In the king's chamber, one lamp still burned, and a couple of braziers, but the rest were red eyes in snowy heaps of ash and the chill was creeping through the shutters. Ailixond had thrown off most of the furs and blankets and lay tossing his head from side to side. There were bloodstains on the pillows, and his skin, cold on the surface, was burning hot underneath. The Physician uncorked a large bottle and poured it into a basin, sopped a cloth in it and began bathing him, restraining him with a hand on one shoulder. 'I must go and dress,' said Lord Ayndra, 'I shall be back shortly.' When she returned, the bed had been made up again and the patient propped high on several pillows, wheezing like an asthmatic old man. The Physician said, 'There's little I can do now, unless he wakes enough to take medicine.'

402

'You know what is best. I must go now. If he wakes, tell him I have gone to see Meraptar, and – if he asks for the seal, tell him I have that too. As he said.'

The Physician nodded, and settled into his chair at the head of the bed.

Under the heavy pale-clouded sky, the grey wind carried a sparse scatter of snowflakes. Meraptar was in deep consultation with Sandar, while servants held their horses and the Lord Governor's retinue, already mounted, waited behind. Further up the steps, Lord Ayndra hissed in the ear of the captain of the Silver Shields. 'Six of your men, and none to leave him at any time. If he asks why, say that there has been a rumour of a threat to his life and the king does not wish him to fall into danger.'

'Well, my lord, all very well – but I cannot put a guard on a noble lord without the authority of the king, or at least the order of the Council –'

'I bring the authority of the king!' When he still looked doubtful, she dipped in her tunic and brought out with a flourish the royal seal of Safi. The captain was forced to bow his head. 'It will be as you say, my lord.'

'Remember. Let him go nowhere unaccompanied, no matter what complaint he makes. Let him complain to the king if he does not like it.'

'It will be done.'

'Good!' She stuffed the seal back into hiding and ran down the steps to Lord Meraptar. 'My lord! The king is unable to come and so I am here to bid you farewell and a safe journey.'

'Unwell? I am sorry to hear it,' said Lord Meraptar.

'No doubt we shall meet again in Safi,' said Sandar.

'The Lord Governor, yes, but as you know, my lord, the king requests your presence here with the army.'

'Does he?'

'Most certainly he does.'

Meraptar coughed. 'I must say, my lord, I had counted on my son accompanying me home –'

'No,' she said. They stared at her, the old nobility at the upstart. Sandar said, 'What authority have you? I also wish to accompany my father.'

'It is the king's express command that you do not so.' She displayed the seal on her open palm. 'Well,' said Meraptar, 'if that is how it is . . .'

403

'I suppose we must bow.' Sandar stamped away; the captain met him and they could be seen arguing, though the wind carried their words away. Meraptar made a half bow. 'Well, my lord, then I must go. Convey my most loyal greetings to the king.'

'I will do so.' She watched as he mounted and rode away down the valley. Sandar stood at the top of the steps. As she turned to go in, he scowled at her and swirled away down the colonnade, with six Silver Shields following him.

She slipped through the main doors and into the weed-choked garden between the hall and the lords' wing, to the closet between the kitchen and the dwelling rooms which had been allotted her as a bedroom; various of her belongings lay scattered on a camp bed, with a straw pallet for Yunnil beside it, but the maid was not there. She found her writing box, opened the flap that formed a portable desk, and began to write hurriedly. She covered perhaps half a sheet, and put it aside to take an unlit taper to the kitchen for a light; she melted sealing wax over it, dropped it onto a ribbon, stamped it with the royal seal, then tied up the completed letter and hid it under the other papers in the writing box. She was just locking it shut when someone knocked on the door.

'Who is it?'

'Polem.'

'O, come in, come in.'

He had to bow his head at the low door. 'Luamis, is this a dog kennel you are living in? But at least it is all your own! – do you know, I have to share a room with Sulakon? I swear he spends half each night at prayer and then wakes me rising an hour before the dawn – except last night, of course, but then –' he ran his hand through his hair and sat down heavily on the bed. 'What is going to happen?' he asked desperately. 'I went in just now but there was only the Physician and he said he has a fever and is too ill to talk – what is the matter? You were with him all last night, were you not?'

'He is very sick,' she said.

'I know, but surely – you know that they are saying already in the camp that he – it can't be true!'

'You mean they say that he's dying?'

'It can't be true!' said Polem frantically. She lowered her face over her interlocked hands. 'He doesn't think he'll last as far as Safi,' she said, her voice cracking into a whisper. 'Whaat?' cried Polem, and hid his face in his hands. 'But you must have known,' she said. 'At least, you must have thought – for a while now –'

Polem shook his head.

She kicked her writing box under the bed and moved over to put her arm round his shoulders. Polem choked and snuffled into his hands. She pulled a grimy handkerchief from a heap of discarded clothes and gave it to him; he blew his nose several times, and felt in his tunic for a creased paper packet.

'Diamoon gave me this. I know not what to do with it.'

'What is it?' Ayndra let go of him to pick it open. It contained a nasty mess of black hair-combings and scraps of dead fingernails. 'God's teeth!' she said. 'Is Diamoon resorting to common sorcery? – what on earth did she mean to do with this?'

'Not she, Sandar.' Polem blew his nose again and wiped his eyes. 'She stole it,' he said more clearly. 'From some sorcerer down in the camp. She says Sandar gave it to him.'

'I shall go and throw it on the kitchen fire this instant.' She got up to do so, but he seized her arm. 'Don't do that! She says Ailixond must burn it himself.'

'Indeed? What a pack of nonsense. The only thing that disinclines me to dispose of it immediately is that it's evidence of treasonable intent on Sandar's part – I suppose for that reason we should keep it . . . a vile thing, though! How on earth do you think he came by it?'

'Firumin?'

'O rubbish! Do you think Firumin would do anything like that? He must have suborned one of the slaves who takes out the rubbish.' She frowned. 'I suppose we should have to question them all now – but it hardly seems the time . . .'

'And I hardly want to tell Ailixond, even if he were not . . .'

'I am sure that he would throw it on the fire as soon as look at it. Still. You had better keep it for the time being, to preserve the peace of mind of those who subscribe to such witless superstitions. And I thought Lord Sandar an educated man! – a pity his father has gone now . . . where is Diamoon?'

'In the lower camp. She came with it last night, but I could not get her to come in here by any means.'

'You must admit, at least, that there's no case to connect this with the – present events.' Polem looked doubtful; she went on, 'Since we have it here, Sandar's sorcerer cannot have done whatever he intended to do with it. I am going to burn it. You know that Sandar is already under guard? – the story is that there has been some threat to his life . . . you can vouch to the existence of this horrid packet, and no one will doubt your word; we can investigate it later when things are – calmer.' She opened the door. 'No!' said Polem. 'Rubbish!' she replied, and strode into the

405

kitchen. He sat drooping on the bed. She was back shortly. 'That is the end of that.'

'So what are we going to do?' he said imploringly.

'Ailixond wants us to maintain the natural order of things. Now I think today he would have taken the cavalry out on exercise – why do you not find Lakkannar and get him to do that with you? And I believe Sulakon is commander of the watch.'

'He has gone already to see to that. I think he said he was going to drill the phalanx, if he could march them to some place where there was flat ground.'

'Ah! the endlessly reliable Sulakon. Well then! – for heaven's sake do not sit there like a wildflower out of water. Where is Lakkannar?'

'Still abed, I think.'

'Then go and wake him, and take the Companions out somewhere.' He still looked miserable. 'Get along with you!' she said. 'You help no one if you sit here moping.'

'I suppose you are right . . . you will send for me if anything . . .?'

'Of course. If I am not . . . Firumin will know where I am.'

'Yes.'

'Off you go then.' She slapped him on the back. He rolled his eyes like a sick dog; she propelled him out of the door, then picked up the heap of dirty clothes and went to look for Yunnil. Half an hour later, she returned and pulled a locked strongbox out from beneath the bed; it was full of papers and bags of coin, which she began sorting through until another knock came at the door. 'Arpalond,' said a low voice.

'Enter.'

Arpalond slipped inside and closed the door behind him. He said without ceremony, 'How much longer have we?'

She shrugged. 'I cannot tell.'

'A month?'

'Not so long,' she said. 'Not nearly so long.'

Arpalond sat down on the bed. She closed her moneybox and pushed it behind her. 'I had not realised,' he said, and saw by her eyes that she had. 'You know what, by custom, follows.'

'There is the election among the lords for the next king.'

'Yes. That in itself is not difficult –'

'Sulakon will be Regent of Safi for little lord Parakison,' she said.

'What? I wonder if I need to come here.'

'I told you,' she said. 'I think a lot more than I ever say. It is

406

what will happen more immediately that concerns me. I believe that it is usual for all the lords to come to Safi for the election.'

'That is so. Obviously we shall have to go back there, no matter what intervenes.'

'And if he dies, and the news spreads – and there's no doubt that it will, like wildfire – and all the lords governor desert their posts to run off to Safi, what then?'

'He has dealt with that. He has written letters that will go on the instant his death is announced, faster than all other news, ordering them to send proxies to Safi to vote on their behalf and not on any account to leave their provinces or institute any changes in the government until the next king has been chosen in Safi, or some form of regency or other government installed.'

'Well! I never knew that.'

'No one else does. He and I spent a night writing all the letters, two months ago.'

'God's teeth,' she said distantly.

'I have been looking through the documents in the Justiciary these last few days. There must be three books of new laws concerning provincial government and taxation, all written out since we left S'Thurrulass – he dictated all that, but all the records on the provinces have been annotated in his own hand with summaries of their histories to date, comments on the present situation and advice of his intentions for them for – o, for years in the future sometimes.'

'Ai!' she said. 'Has there ever been another like him?'

'I do not think so . . . the Physician tells me that you have been given the royal seal.'

'Why? Do you need it?'

'O no. I am sure you will use it wisely. Only – do not make it public unless you must. Certain people will take it as evidence of excessive presumption.' She looked up. 'You are going to have to watch your step,' he said.

'O, I know it. I have only used the seal to put Sandar under guard – do you know that he was plotting witchcraft against Ailixond? He had procured somehow some of his nails and hair-combings, and given them to one of the sorcerers in the camp to practise heaven knows what foolishness with.' When Arpalond looked shocked, she said, 'We should be thankful he kept to such impractical methods of attack, instead of resorting to something more . . . direct.'

'Indeed? I must say, this was one suspicion I wished to put down to old hate and fevered fancy.'

407

'When Ailixond has fevered fancies, he knows what they are – not infallibly, of course, but . . .'

'There is no end to my admiration for him,' Arpalond said with a bitter wistfulness. 'If he asked the heart out of my breast for his cure, now, I'd not deny it him.'

'I think that more than one of us would say the same.' She opened her moneybox again, then flicked the papers in disgust and slammed it shut. 'Ah! money – I can do without it . . . I shall go back in there, in case he wakes.'

'Shall I bring you the despatches? There are riders due in this day from Lysmal, Purrllum – Haramin too, I think.'

'Why not, indeed?' As they rose to leave, Arpalond said, 'Not that it will influence the end of things – to my chagrin – but you are assured of at least one vote when it comes to the election of the new king.'

'What?' she exclaimed.

'I assume, of course, that being an honourable woman you will not vote for yourself.'

'You will vote for *me*? *Me*, to be king of Safi?' She gawped at him.

'You should be the one. Sulakon will be competent, but his lack of imagination will fault him in the end, while you – you are like him. There is no end to your invention.'

'You flatter me, my lord. You are not so lacking in policy yourself.'

'Ah,' said Arpalond, grimacing, 'but I, you see, would not sully my hands.'

'You are too moral.'

'My lord,' he said, as he opened the door, 'I am too great a coward.'

The Physician ordered that the shutters of the king's room be kept shut, and stuffed even tighter with rags; slaves stoked up charcoal fires until the coals glowed scarlet and burned almost without fume, then loaded up braziers and carried them in until the room was as hot and close as the furnace-room in a bathhouse. Lord Ayndra sat by the outside wall, in her shirt-sleeves; whenever the Physician left for a moment, she furtively opened the shutters and stuck her head out for some air, only to slam them again the moment the door creaked. Ailixond drifted in and out of lucidity, but most of the time talked incoherently, when he was able to talk at all; the Physician bathed his chest and forehead with cooling liquids, and gave him glasses full of bitter cordials made up in fruit syrups to try and disguise the drugs they were laden with.

They both tried to stop the procession of well-intentioned callers and people wanting orders and advice from coming any further than the door, but whenever Ailixond realised what was going on, he would have them in. He lay borne up on a heap of pillows like an effigy in a temple, spared all but a couple of blankets by the artificial heat, and his voice was so weak that visitors had to lean over the bed to hear him. Whenever they looked across the room, they saw Lord Ayndra, in a litter of bent quills and papers and smoke-stubs, watching them. In the afternoon, he fell into a restless sleep, and as dark fell the house grew quiet; supper was served for the lords and the household in the hall, and a band of musicians and dancers came up from the lower camp to play. When Ailixond woke, about an hour before midnight, they had all gone to rest, but Lord Ayndra was still sitting among the braziers with her feet propped up; she was sharpening a short knife on a piece of stone and singing quietly to herself. On the floor at her feet lay another two knives and a sword, already polished and sharpened till they shone. The wind howled over the roof, and made the shutters batter and creak, as though the well-lit room was a ship adrift on the sea of night. He pushed some of the pillows away and sat up, but the motion disturbed the fluid which had collected in his lungs as he lay, and he fell to coughing. She looked round instantly, and reached for a bowl standing under the bed, which she handed to him, then reached behind for the pillows and put them up behind his back. Then she knelt down on the floor and stayed there, all in silence.

He leaned back against the pillows, cradling the bowl in his lap. Still she said nothing, and her eyes were as opaque as pebbles. She reached out for the bowl.

'Let me take that.'

She emptied it into a bucket in the corner and came back wiping it with a dishclout. 'The Physician said that an you wakened, and most especially an you coughed badly, you were to drink that cordial he has left you.' She indicated a covered cup on the table by the bed.

'Most certainly I shall not. Pour it out of the window.'

'Pardon? I am sure I should not –'

'No,' he said, his voice going to a dry croak as he tried to raise it. 'He has been feeding me nothing but potions full of poppy-syrup – it has the property of reducing cough, but consequently I have lain here all day in a slew of strange-coloured dreams and imagined people here who are far away – half the time my mind's unclear with fever as it is, I'll not spend the rest of the time dazed with drugs, no matter how curative their properties. And I say curative! – it's nothing but a sop to relieve the symptoms, there's no more now to be done.'

'All right then.' She took the cup over to the window. 'Perhaps I should drink it,' she said as she lifted the cover.

'Why so? You are not sick.'

She turned her head aside, hair falling over her face, and occupied herself with the twine binding the window closed. Ailixond threw off the blankets and padded silently across the floor to embrace her. Instead of turning round, she pressed her forehead against the shutter and crammed her knuckles into her mouth, shaken by suppressed sobs. Ailixond seized her shoulders and shook her. 'For god's sake!' She spun round against his grip with such violence that he stumbled and fell backward; she got one arm half under him and buried the other hand in his hair, so that they struck the floor with her astride. She hauled his head up by the hair and fixed her mouth on his with a force like the undertow of the sea, as if she would suck his heart out through the mouth. Her tears smeared wet across his face, until she felt that he was struggling for breath, let go of him and dropped face down on the stone floor, crying as noisy and open as a child. Ailixond propped himself up against the bed and waited until she had finished.

'I'm sorry,' she said.

'You must not be.'

'Have you a handkerchief?'

'I have hundreds.' He reached under a pillow, which turned out to have in its case a mine of them.

'Thank you . . . you shouldn't sit there in your shirt, you'll catch your death.'

'Come over here. You're warmer than any fire.'

'All right then . . . there's blood all over your mouth.'

'And yours.'

'Is there?' She rubbed her lips and stared at the red stain on her hand. 'Ay! – it's like after the battle of Palagar . . . that was not your own, though . . . for god's sake, put a fur on or something an you'll not get into bed.'

Ailixond got up and went over to his clothes-chest to pull out the white bearskin; it swamped him, like a stake driven into a snowdrift. In the yellow lamplight his eyes were palely bright, almost entirely iris. 'You must have been drinking poppy-syrup pure,' she said.

'I think so. That's why I want no more.' He looked around with a vague air of amazement, like one who wakes in a feather bed having gone to sleep in the gutter. 'I shall not sleep for a while, I think. But I think I'll not be able to do anything useful in that time either.'

'Yes. I've smoked the tears of the poppy, in Suthine.'

'Will you mind to stay here? I don't often sleep quietly, on my own.'

'But you're usually on your own.'

'Not as often as you might think. Or if I am, I sleep not long.' He held his hands out over a brazier, burning down to red eyes in a snowflake heart of ashes, his voice as depthless as a voice heard in a dream. 'You know that boys are put out of the House of Women after they've passed seven years. Until then I slept always in my mother's bed, and I had a key to one of her postern doors to go in to her whenever I was lonely in the night, which was commonly, until my voice broke and she decided that I could not be allowed to wander at will through the women's rooms at night, and took the key from me. So then I was kept out of the House of Women until I married, and then . . .' he shook his head slowly, suspended over the coals.

'You hardly ever talk about your mother.'

He grinned. 'But she is always present in spirit . . . you'll be meeting her soon.'

'In Safi?' He nodded. 'But so will you,' she said.

Ailixond tipped his head back, in the smoky gold gloom under the low roof. 'No,' he said very softly, 'no . . .' Aleizon Ailix Ayndra caught her breath as if at a stab of pain. 'Ah! Do you know, you look so pretty, when you stand there like that?'

'What? – o, but my dear! I'm a wreck, a veritable wreck!' He laughed out loud. She shrieked. 'Whaat? That's the first time I've ever seen you laugh!'

'No! I frequently laugh.'

'You do not. You give a little three-fifths smile, like this. Sometimes I have seen you show most of your teeth, like this. But I've never seen you laugh like that, not for years.'

He bent over and spat into the brazier. 'You speak truly. It is not a dignified act, laughing ha!ha!ha! like one applauding a mountebank at the fair. Permissible for louts, such as Lakkannar, and persons of honour but no consequence, such as Polem, but have you ever seen Sulakon laugh?'

'One could make a cat laugh before Sulakon.'

'I am sure of it.'

'Arpalond says that no one will be able to settle on a new king, so we shall have a regency for Parakison and Sulakon will be regent.'

'Arpalond is a wise man. You should listen to him.'

'I do, I do. He says also he'll vote for me to be king of Safi.'

'A pity more will not do the same,' said Ailixond, rubbing his hands together. Aleizon Ailix Ayndra gave an inarticulate cry of astonishment. Ailixond shuffled towards her, huddling into the vast white fur like a grandmother in a shawl. 'It is not my place to prejudice the election, but an I had a choice, it would be you as regent for Parakison – or as king, for that matter, let Parakison take his chance in later years. An you were noble born, I think they would have you –'

'Noble born a man, you mean to say.'

'That has not stopped you so far.'

'No, but it has strewn a thousand obstacles in my way.'

'All obstacles? Would you have fallen in with me had you been a man?'

'Very likely,' she said gravely. 'You must know that you have many male admirers – were you not much beloved in your youth?' He was in front of her now. She reached out and embraced his chilled bare feet. He shivered. 'Nothing like now,' he said, and dropped down over her in the white cloak, like a blanket of feathers.

'God's teeth! Is it not blowing up a tempest! Wa!' The wind caught Lord Ayndra's hat and would have bowled it away had she not seized it. Polem pulled his fur hood over his head and moaned. 'O, why can we not go on home? Even the natives have too much sense to come here in the middle of winter. I have had a rheum for the past week and damp runs all down the walls in my room. I am sure we should take Ailixond to some other place, it cannot be good for anyone here.'

'The Physician says he's not fit to be moved,' said Ayndra, settling down on the steps, like a crow fluffing out its feathers.

'But he was up this morning – well, not exactly up, but he had his chief secretary in there and a crowd of clerks coming and going. Besides Diamoon says he should go away from here.'

'O, Diamoon.'

'Diamoon is –'

'In general I have every respect for Diamoon, and she knows better than to lecture me on her superstitious nonsense. I think I shall go down to the lower camp and see what goes on there.' She pulled her scarf up over her hat to tie it down, and ran away

412

downhill, a black leaf flitting in the gale. Polem, hissing and muttering, scuttled gratefully back into the house.

In the corridor he met Sulakon.

'My lord cousin! I am very glad to have met you. Come and let us take some wine together.'

Polem goggled at him.

'I have some matters I should like to take your opinion on,' said Sulakon.

'O, well, I am sure –'

'Come, I have ordered a fire and spiced wine in our room.'

'O, very well then.'

Within, Sulakon busied himself pouring out wine while Polem sat on his bed like a child on a family visit.

'I am sure you know what I wish to speak about,' Sulakon said.

'In truth, I am sure I can have nothing to say which you have not thought of already.'

'My lord. You are my lord king's oldest friend, and his closest confidant – nor can you fail as a lord of Safi to feel the deepest interest in the affairs of the crown. It is for those reasons that I wish to consult with you.'

Polem hung his head, mumbling a further disclaimer. Sulakon went on: 'Excuse me then if I speak bluntly, but time is short. You are no doubt aware that he has spent the last two days and nights entirely closeted with that woman, and furthermore that he has given her use of the royal seal, at least I assume that he gave her use of it, for even she would surely not have the effrontery to steal it.'

'No, he did give it her.'

'Indeed. I have the utmost respect for my lord Ailixond's judgement, but I cannot take such an action other than as further proof of the derangement of his mind, consequent upon his illness, which cannot be aided by the poison which she has been at liberty to pour into his unguarded ears.'

'Now, Sulakon, it is not the first time, you know, that she has spoken to him, I mean, it was years ago now –'

'I may say, my lord, that I had believed their connection fallen into desuetude. Now I see that they had only become more discreet in their conduct and it is only at a time like this, when he is weakened by illness, that it comes forth – and I must add that I have been appalled that he should show so little concern for the feelings of Lady Othanë in her delicate condition –'

'No,' said Polem painfully. 'Look – I scarcely feel that it is my right to speak of this, but they had, you know, separated, before

413

he married Setha and it was all over until just the day before yesterday – you see, Ailixond thought that she – o Luamis! do you begrudge him if he wants a few days to himself at last? I am sure he is the last person to make Othanë unhappy, he would never have stayed with her all these years if he did not care for her even if at the beginning she was forced upon him as a wife. He has never failed in awarding her the honour due to the king's first wife, and now, he is ill, she is expecting a child at last, he does not want to have her in a sickroom, and instead – she is only nursing him! And have you not seen him when he – o, Luamis!' He shook his head violently.

Sulakon's face had fixed in a stony decision. 'I hold to my view,' he said, 'which is that she should be removed from his company during his sickness, and should on no account be allowed free access to the materials of government.'

'Well, he won't have it,' Polem said.

'Will he not? I have not realised that she had made her hold over him so strong!'

'O! Do you understand nothing?' Polem flung his cup down and jumped to his feet. 'You talk about feelings! Cannot you see? He's loved her for years and now he's with her at last and you say that she should be taken away from him – well! I shall not listen to any more of this.' He flung out of the door and slammed it behind him, stood in the passage trembling, open-mouthed with surprise at himself. The door remained shut. He watched it fearfully for some moments, then, when Sulakon failed to emerge, he went down to the king's door and hesitated outside it. A faint buzz of voices could be heard within, some clerk reading out a document. He pulled the hood up over his head and hurried outside, going down the valley towards the lower camp.

It was a while before Sulakon came forth; and then he went down past the main door into the west wing of the house, the House of Women.

Outside, the gale continued to rage over the mountainsides and whip up the black waters of the lake. Stunted trees bent before it, and the sky filled up with steel-coloured clouds, bringing gloom well before the early sunset. Coming up the path from the camp, the house seemed ablaze with lights, lamps placed all along the colonnade like signals to some strange mariners. The main corridor was lined with liveried royal servants, both men and women, many with additional torches; Polem was allowed to pass, but they stopped several persons of lesser degree who followed him. 'What is this?' he asked.

'The queen, my lord, she is about to pass along here.'

'The queen? Lady Othanë?'

'Lady Setha, my lord.'

'Lady Setha? Where is Firumin?' Polem strode between the ranks of servants, who must have been ordered by Setha to protect her from the gaze of the vulgar when she ventured forth from the women's rooms, though why she thought that passing down a corridor required the escort one might request in order to process through Great Market – 'Firumin? What is this?'

The steward was looking perturbed outside Ailixond's door. 'My lord Sulakon has been here, saying that Lady Othanë was much affrighted for my lord's health, and he said that he would visit her this evening, but a messenger requested that she be allowed to come to his side sooner, accordingly he sent that she could, upon which we receive an announcement from Lady Setha that she will come to see the king now, without so much as a by-your-leave! – and then all these people come out, but she delays –'

'Cannot you send them away?'

'They are all of the queens' household, my lord, and –'

'What does Ailixond think of all this? How is he? Can I go in?'

'You can, of course, my lord.' Firumin started to open the door, but someone round the corner cried, 'Make way! Make way!' and they both peered in its direction. The servants moved back against the wall, and Lady Setha appeared, dressed all in rose-coloured silk with high-heeled gold slippers, and veiled so that only her black-rimmed eyes showed. She walked very rapidly and alone. Some way behind came her twin slaves, leading – or rather dragging – Parakison between them, a hand to each. Setha did not bother to look Polem in the eye. 'You will excuse me, my lord,' she exclaimed, and he jumped aside. Firumin remained in front of the door. She stabbed gilded fingernails at him. 'Move aside, minion!' 'Aah!' he said, astonished at her insolence. 'If you please!' she said; he recovered himself and stepped backward, opening the door. Polem would have followed her in, but Sistri and Histri had come up and he was forced to give way to them; they immediately formed a guard around the queen, who had fallen to her knees at Ailixond's bedside, in such a way as to conceal them from the direct view of anyone standing in the doorway. Polem heard Setha say, 'Most beloved husband, my lord!' and Ailixond made some inaudible response, but he could not see his face. He began to move into the room to cross to the

415

other side of the bed, when there was some other commotion in the passage. A high sharp voice ordered the servants out of the way, exclaiming, 'Come along!' A second voice replied in tears, and Lady Ailissa appeared round the corner, pulling Lady Othanë by the hand. Othanë held a veil across her face, and was trying to wipe her eyes with it. 'Hush!' cried Ailissa. 'You are the paramount queen. She will make him give sole inheritance to her child if you leave her to it – come along!' She gave a curt nod to Polem, and Firumin leapt out of her path; Othanë merely sobbed into her veil. Sistri and Histri and Setha all turned to look, and it could be seen that Ailixond was sitting up, having thrown off the covers from his shoulders, while Setha passionately caressed his ring hand; he looked flushed with fever, and more emaciated than ever. Setha had frozen with her hand on his arm, but instead of devotion, her large eyes registered fury. Ailissa spun Othanë across the room and pushed her up against the far side of the bed. 'My lord!' she said. 'Do you not think that your first and noblest lady has the first claim on your attention at a time like this?' She gave Othanë a shove, which caused her to drop to her knees, cry, 'O Ailixond!' and hide her face in her hands in tears.

Ailixond shook free of Setha and took Othanë by the shoulders. 'Lady! You must not weep.' She shook her head; he bent over her, caressing her head and neck. Setha knelt like a silk-wrapped image, hands clamped in her lap, head thrown back; thus she could not avoid meeting Ailissa's eye. The king's sister flashed her eyes at her and gave a fleeting but triumphantly wicked grin. Setha snapped her veil back over her face and tossed her head furiously.

Ailixond raised his head. 'My ladies. I should be gratified if you would consent to leave us for a while.'

'As you command, my lord.' Setha rose to her feet in one smooth motion, and hurried out. One maid picked up Parakison; he peered over her shoulder, and said questioningly, 'Dadda?' 'Will you let him stay?' asked Ailixond. Sistri (or Histri) looked stubborn, but her mistress was out of reach, and Polem and Firumin looked stern. She slowly bent and deposited Parakison on the floor, then rushed after her mistress and her sister. 'Ailissa,' said Ailixond in a voice like dry leaves. She lifted her head. 'Please come and see me, later,' he said. She nodded, and came round to kiss his ring; he embraced her one-handed, and they kissed one another on the mouth. As she passed out of the door, Ailissa gave Polem another smile. Parakison stayed where the slave had left him, hands at his sides, staring at his father with enormous blue

416

eyes. 'Come here, Parri,' said Ailixond. Parakison stuck his fingers in his mouth, and looked frightened over them. Othanë sat up. 'Come along, Parakison,' she said, 'your dadda wants you.' Parakison peered round at the door, then ran at the bed and cast himself into Ailixond's arms like a miniature lance. Polem quietly shut the door on them. All the queen's servants had disappeared back to their usual quarters, and the brightlit corridor was quiet. He gasped: 'Ah! Firumin, do you not think that everyone here has gone mad since two days ago? I do not know what will become of us!'

'No more do I, my lord,' the Steward said dismally. 'Do you suppose that I should serve supper in the hall again? I have had no orders.'

'In the hall? Well, I should suppose so.'

'You must excuse me, then.' He bowed, and made off towards the kitchen. Polem stood about for a little while, and then went off to look for a folding chair, which he placed beside Ailixond's door and settled down on it. He was still sitting there, fallen into a half doze with his head against the door jamb, when Aleizon Ailix Ayndra came back. She roused him by poking his shoulder. 'Polem! Polem! Have you the key?'

'Key? O, I think it is not locked, unless he has locked it inside . . . he's with Master Tennat – where have you been? People asked for you.'

'I had to sort out some of my affairs. Has he been dictating letters all day?'

'O, no. Setha came . . .' he described the scenes. 'And then when Othanë had gone, he spent at least half an hour with Ailissa, and she brought Takarem, that's her oldest boy, to see him, and her two girls as well. And we thought Setha would come back, but she did not, and Firumin asked if he wanted to send for her then, but he said no, she would come back if she felt any need and otherwise he had nothing to say to her. I think it's the first time he has even seen her in months. Since we left the marshes, even.'

'Certainly she has no liking for his company,' said Ayndra. Polem frowned at the idea. She said, 'It's no longer necessary that she even imitate it. As the mother of his only son, she is far more secure than any best-beloved – so why should she solicit the attentions of a man whose person irks her?' Polem looked rather horrified; she shrugged. 'We all make mistakes in the heat of passion.'

'Yes, well – and he has been with Tennat and his other secretaries ever since then. Firumin says he has been dictating

417

three letters at once and so ill that he cannot talk above a whisper.'

'Yes, well.' She turned to go. Polem caught at her sleeve. 'He did ask where you were.'

'I am only gone to my room. I will come at any time. As soon as Tennat has finished.'

'No, stay.'

She halted halfway down the passage. 'I have no one to talk to,' he said.

'Who put you on guard duty?'

'I did.'

'Good!' she said, in the manner of a schoolmaster commending a slow pupil. 'We are all going to have to learn to do things for ourselves in the future.'

'I will get you a chair.'

'No need. I sit happily upon the floor.' She settled crosslegged at the other side of the door.

'You know it is not very suitable that you do that. Chairs are – well, I mean, it is proper for a lord to sit upon a chair, commoners sit upon a bench, or if they are very poor, upon the floor –'

'But only slaves squat upon their haunches. Do not worry, whenever I have to sit in judgement it is in as fine a chair as you could wish. But when I go on my own account I should prefer to be comfortable.' She drew her knees up and rested her folded arms on them.

'Sulakon wanted to see me this morning,' said Polem.

'To ask for your vote?'

'What? – o, no! He would never – no, he said that, well, he said that you had been on your own with Ailixond for days and he did not think it, well, proper –'

'No doubt he thinks that I have been pouring unutterable evil into the ears of a man now too weak to resist my blandishments.'

'Well, more or less, yes.'

'It's nonsense,' she said shortly.

'That's what I said to him.'

She extended her arms and plaited and unplaited her fingers. 'I shall have to walk most delicately from now on.'

'No more sitting on the floor.'

'O, that doesn't matter. I shall have to . . .' she fell silent, her face grim. 'Look,' said Polem, 'you know that if I can ever do anything to help you – I know I have not much power in the realm, I have never even commanded a troop of cavalry –'

'Except once.'

'All right, that was only once, but I am a cousin of the royal

418

line, and descended from Ailixond first – I know you have no respect for these things, but many people do.'

'O, I know that you are held in good repute everywhere. Not least because you have not made use of the opportunities available to one in such high and permanent favour with the king.'

'Well,' said Polem bashfully.

'I thank you for your promise. I shall need every good friend I have in the next year or two.'

'Well, I shall always stand by you.'

'I hope that you live not to regret that.' She offered him her hand; struck by inspiration, he spat in his palm and slapped it down on hers, uppermost then undermost, like two merchants celebrating a successful trade agreement, and they laughed. A few moments later the door opened and Master Selomo, one of the three secretaries with whom Ailixond trusted his most important business, looked out. 'My lords, good evening – we thought we heard your voices without. Would you like to come in?'

'Are you still busy?' Ayndra asked.

'No, my lord, we are just putting things in order to pack them away.'

'Pack them away?' Polem said eagerly. 'Are we going to move from this place?'

'Not for a while, I think,' came a hoarse croak from within. The room was still full of braziers, which had by now rendered the air acrid with smoke, and given the walls a fresh coat of smut, but Ailixond was wrapped up like a swaddled child, with the great bearskin thrown over all, so that only his head showed. He looked as if all the months of sickness, denied for so long, had taken full toll as soon as he took to his bed, sucking the flesh from the bones of his face. The secretaries were packing their document boxes, and left as soon as they had done. 'Where is the Physician?' said Ayndra.

'Gone to rest. There's no more to be done at present, so we have agreed that if I do not rise from bed, I will not be drugged into a stupor. I think I'll sleep this night in any case.'

'You look exhausted.' She sat down beside him.

'I confess I am not as lively as I might be.'

'How was Othanë?'

Ailixond turned his head away. 'Too much weeping and screaming,' he whispered.

'I am sorry.'

'No. You deserve it . . . I'd never seen you cry . . .' He slid one hand out from beneath the bedclothes; it was like a diagram of bones and tendons, only just covered by sallow skin. She took it into her lap. Polem moved back to the door. Ailixond lifted his head. 'Polem, I must spend some time alone with you.'

'Yes,' said Polem.

'Tomorrow,' said the king. 'Come next day, and I'll tell everyone else to go away.'

'O, thank you – good night, then.'

'Good night.'

He slipped out and closed the door as silently as he could.

When he came back at ninth hour of morning, Firumin was posted outside the door.

'My lord is sleeping. No one at all will go in till he wakes.'

'Yes, but is Lord Ayndra –'

'I believe she sleeps also.'

'Could you fetch her out to me? It is most important.'

Firumin looked sour, but unlocked the door with the key and peered inside. All Polem could see was shuttered gloom. Lord Ayndra came to the door in a few moments; fully dressed, but her clothes were creased from being slept in and her hair stuck out like straw. 'What is it?'

'Sulakon. He has called a meeting of the Inner Council.'

'Can he do that? Does not the king –'

'If six lords come together they can call a Council at any time.'

'I had better come, then. Where are they?'

'In Golaron's chamber.' It was next door but one to the king's. She pulled her tunic straight and ran fingers hastily through her hair.

'Come quick, they have already started.' She hurried after him. Firumin moved his chair directly in front of the door. He could hear the voices of the lords, but beyond them there was some commotion in the kitchen. Still, he could not leave his lord unattended. He craned his neck in an attempt to hear more. The door at the far end of the corridor opened, and a small and frantic potboy came running through. He trod on the hem of his greasy apron as he tried to bow, and ended up on his knees. 'O master! You must come, Master Pollin says please come!'

'What is it? – and do not shriek so! You stand outside the king's own chamber.'

The potboy looked horrified, and though on his knees, bowed three times more. Firumin cuffed him on the side of the head. 'Tell me your message!'

'The pot of hot water fell over and scalded Tessa and Lodo and

420

it knocked a pan of fat in the fire and all went burning so much that it went up and set fire to the thatch, and it is all burning, and Master Pollin knows not what to do –' Firumin still hesitated. 'O master! It is all like to burn down!' wailed the potboy.

'Be quiet! Impertinent little brat. I come.' He hesitated a moment longer, then unlocked the door and put the key in his purse, before hastening away to the kitchen. The door was warped, and would not stay closed unless it was held to it. It swung slowly across the floor in a complaint of old hinges, bringing in a shaft of grey winter light, and with it voices, small but clear.

'. . . the news reaches the barbarians both with and without the frontier, there will be rebellion.'

'And if the noble governors all depart for Safi to take part in the election –'

Ailixond opened his eyes, and pushed himself up on the pillows to hear more.

'I assure you that that at least will not happen. He has prepared instructions to all governors, entitling them to send proxies to the election, and forbidding them to come in person.' That was Arpalond. 'But will they obey them?' said someone else.

'They will go out with all the authority of the royal seal and delivered under the king's own hand. If that cannot ensure obedience, then what else may?'

'And does he warn them to prepare to put down any disturbances, and to put them down with a heavy hand? For we must not let it be thought that without the invincible Lord Ailixond the Safic army loses all its power.' That was Sulakon.

'And what of the Grand Army? Shall it sit in Safi while we argue, or can it not be sent to better use in the provinces?' Lakkannar.

'But who should we allow to lead the army away before we have a king? I for one would be unwilling to award any one of us command of such a . . . weapon.' That was Hasmon.

'I should trust Lord Golaron to do so,' said another.

'I should refuse such an appointment.' Golaron's booming bass. 'In any case, the army is but one, and must escort us to Safi, where we may disband it or else assign divisions to the defence of various provinces.'

'But we can do none of these things till we have a king.'

'It is a great misfortune that Parakison is not of age.'

'And that Lady Othanë did not fall into her present condition seventeen years ago.'

421

'My lords,' said Sulakon, 'let us not waste time over might-have-beens. I trust that we are agreed that as soon as the king has been embalmed, we march for Safi . . .'

Ailixond threw off the blankets and swung his feet down to the cold flags. He sat clutching the edge of the bed and breathing heavily, preparing to go and get some day clothes from the chest. Voices carried on seeping round the door:

'It is his own stubbornness that has killed him. If he had ever had more regard for his safety, in the person of the king –'

'An he were not so stubborn, we would be in Safi still, fighting off Thaless and Lysmal in alternate years, and bemoaning a drop of three quarits in wool prices. Do you regret what you have received these fifteen years?'

'But to die now, in barbarian lands, leaving a child as his heir and the Empire half secured – how long do you think S'Thurrulass will continue tribute payments when they hear that he is gone?'

'S'Thurrulass is the least of our worries. The barbarians in the mountains north of Haramin . . .'

His fingers were clumsy on the laces; he worked them into a rough knot, and left the ankle laces trailing. Tunic, belt, boots – he would not waste time with them. He pulled the bearskin off the bed and secured it across his chest, then got up slowly, took as deep a breath as he was able, and lurched to the open door.

'. . . New Hope. We should have disarmed the barbarians throughout the grass plains, instead of giving swords to one tribe to let them rule over others equally barbarous.'

'Far from it! Divide and rule is the best policy. We have more to fear in realms like Haramin, or even Lysmal, where they have been united in the past under their own rulers, and may try to do so again.'

The corridor was a vast highway, bleak in the grey light from the weed-choked garden. The white walls still smelt of fresh plaster and whitewash. On the wall two hands were spread-fingered, dark battered hands, the veins knotted on the backs. One wore a ring with a stone an inch across, bluish-white like a lump of ice – his ring. He pushed himself carefully upright and set off.

'. . . until the full Council of Lords meets, I must remind you that you should not engage in any communication, written or spoken which aims to prejudice the result. Particularly it is forbidden for anyone not the king to promise the distribution of offices which lie in the royal gift. We meet now only to discuss the arrangements for government during the interregnum, until we

422

have a new king who, I pray, will be as much a statesman as Lord Ailixond has been —'

The door rattled back against the wall. 'As Lord Ailixond is,' said a voice like grinding sand. Every face spun round to the doorway. Ailixond stood braced by his hands across the entrance, pale as a ghost, barefoot, hair stranding in his eyes, and he smiled at them, at the wide mouths and shocked eyes, because he knew they were his. Any time he cared to come for them, they were his.

'My lord,' Sulakon began, 'we thought it best —'

'I am aware of what you thought.' Ailixond let go of the door and walked into the middle of the room. Those who were not already standing began to rise from the beds and chairs and boxes they occupied, except Lord Ayndra, who was sitting on the edge of a table under the window. He walked up to it and turned his back, so that he could lean against it, and forced his voice to a semblance of normal volume. 'You need not stare as though you saw a spectre. I will thank you not to discuss me as I were dead until I am.'

'No,' cried Polem. Ailixond did not notice. 'You seem to believe that as soon as I am dead, even the letters in my own hand will instantly lose all authority, and the Empire will disintegrate.'

They all protested. He shushed them with his hand, and they were instantly silent. He said, 'An you believe that the provincial governors will reject my most precise orders, how well does this augur for your own obedience to my wishes and respect for the New Empire when I have left it to you?'

'My lord,' said Sulakon, 'my doubt is merely that, since this idea of proxies has never been tried before, many lords may not trust it —' Ailixond made a vicious gesture at him, and he fell silent. The king said, 'The only reason they will have not to trust their proxies is if they are not capable of finding a man whom they can trust to do what they tell him when they are out of the room. And what matter if proxies have not been written into the law books of Safi since Ailixond first? New Empire, new laws. You sit here talking about rebellion among the barbarians. I tell you that the greatest risk to the New Empire is very likely in this room, and in the governors' chambers and lords' dwellings in Safi and every provincial capital. An the barbarians see that the Empire persists in unity and firm government though its founder pass away, they will not rebel. But an they see that those who are in law its guardians have no care for its unity, but seek only to abrogate powers and lands to themselves, and spend all their time intriguing against one another instead of taking thought for the people they have been placed over, then indeed they will rebel and rightly so. When the next king comes to go through the Treasury and the Justiciary and the Provincial Administration he will find my more detailed advice there, but I say, an you do not rule with a mind to the benefit of those you rule over then you are not fit to rule at all. The nation of S'Thurrulass is as old and powerful as Safi, and we cannot expect that they will be subjects to us, but they can be partners, and teach us many things, just as we can teach them. We can build a road through the Girran marshes . . . we can admit their goods to all our new dominions, although we should ensure that only Safic ships trade to Safic ports, or that their ships pay heavily for the concession – ah!' He was gasping for breath. He went on with difficulty. 'Do you see what it is that I mean?' They were all staring at him. Sulakon began again. 'My lord –'

Ailixond stabbed two fingers at him. 'And you, Sulakon! I know that you will not err for selfish or treasonable reasons, but should you come to govern the Empire you must abandon this ludicrous reverence for the Safic nobility and its antique customs and recognise that the New Empire must use talent wherever it shows itself, whether it be among the barbarians, or the common people, or women – you would do well to admit your own wife, my sister, to your councils. There is a place for tradition, but you must be prepared to see that some customs are useful, or at least harmless, while others are pernicious and obstructive and must be put aside. Do you hear me?'

'I hear you, my lord.' Sulakon bowed his head.

'Eh . . . excellent,' Ailixond bent over, gasping; the breath rasped and bubbled in his throat. 'Now,' he said, 'I believe –' and ran out of air. 'Carry on,' he wheezed faintly, and clapped a hand over his mouth. The knuckles of the other hand were white where he clasped the table's edge, but he glared out at them with blue luminous eyes. Golaron got up. 'I am entirely prepared to lead the army back to Safi,' he said, 'especially since I am too old to consider seeking high office. When we have a new king, my lord, I should like your permission to retire to Lysmal – as governor, if you wish, but as you know my mother came from Lysmal, and I should like to spend my declining years at home.'

Ailixond looked at him over his hand, and his eyes smiled. 'The permission – is – yours,' he husked. 'It will be the place of the, new king, to choose the governor, but I should, recommend you . . .'

'And the army,' said Hasmon. 'Do you wish that we should disband the army?'

'There are many ... ah! ... veterans who will wish to retire when they reach home, who should be allowed ... but the provincial levies ... serve in part as hostages, and as schools ... it's important that we should take the best of the young men into our hands for two or three years at least, and encourage them to adopt Safi as a ... as a home ...'

'Ailixond,' said Polem, 'you should not be up.' Ailixond pushed his offered hand away and drew himself as nearly straight as he could. 'I have spoken on these subjects before,' he said. 'But it is my wish, and I want to make it known with all force, that in the New Empire, though there will be, I hope always, Safic and Haraminharn and Lysmalish people, these will be every one of them citizens of the New Empire, who may happen to have been born in one or the other part, but stand equal before the law and equal in chance of preferment. The barbarians, as you will persist in slanderously naming them, are not our natural slaves but our –' he fell forward in a racking burst of coughing. The lords remained frozen, like Serannin's painting made flesh. Ailixond choked, and spat up a great gob of bloody phlegm onto the floor. The Council jumped in a spasm as if they had all been struck by it. The king's eyes opened very wide. He said, almost in his normal voice, 'They are our natural brothers,' and his eyes rolled up in his head. He choked again and fell forward in a great spew of blood. Aleizon Ailix Ayndra sprang out of her crouch and caught him in her arms so that, when they struck the stone floor, she was under him and broke the fall. She got to her knees so that Ailixond lay across her lap, face downwards; she tried to turn him over, but he was as inert as a bundle of sticks. She flung her head back, showing her teeth like a wolf, and yelled, 'Do something! The Physician, Firumin!' Someone said, 'Is he ...?'

'He is not dead!' she shrieked. Ailixond's eyelids fluttered and half opened; he twisted against the direction of her hold, turned his head and coughed up another gout of blood, bright arterial red; able to breathe again, he slumped down in her embrace, content merely to draw air in and out in long grating gasps. From the corridor there was a scuffle, the door flung open, and an animal howl. Firumin stood there with his hands up to his face. 'O my lord! O, the gods curse me! I left him, I left him!' He raked his cheeks with his fingernails and howled. Lakkannar shook him. 'Quiet! You scream like a woman – for god's sake leave off!'

'It is my fault! O Shumar, he dies by my fault!'

Lakkannar dealt him a vicious blow across the face, slamming him back against the wall, where he shrieked once more, then covered his face and began to weep quietly, as the Physician ran in and fell to his knees by the king. Ailixond looked up at him and read the expression on his face. He shook his head from side to side and slumped unconscious.

When the sun set in a hell of brassy fires, they lit lamps at the four corners of the bed, and continued the vigil. The semblance of normal life that had been maintained for the previous days now lapsed, and no one could be found performing their usual tasks. Instead there were people everywhere, standing about in the lanes of the camp talking, going around trying to settle debts and pack up their things as if they expected total disorder to descend overnight, going up to the royal house to look for news that was not to be had. By nightfall, all the colonnade was crowded, and people had lit campfires on the marble steps and all along the path by the lake, a population of transferred stars under the cloud-paved sky. If collected wishes could save anyone, Ailixond would have been walking about by sixth hour of evening. The priests gathered in the hall outside his room, burning incense until they created a blue haze and singing continually. The modulated hum of their plainsong ran through the sickroom like a heartbeat, and each opening of the door brought a waft of cloying holy scent.

'Will it be much longer?'

'It might be days yet,' said the Physician.

'Days . . . ha!'

Polem spoke without lifting his head. He had the chair at the head of the bed on the right, the Physician to the left; he sat there continually twisting the rings on his fingers, and saying very little. 'He never wanted it to be like this. He wanted to die like his father, struck down in the middle of life —' he crammed his hand against his mouth, and said no more.

By midnight all the watchers had left except for Polem, the Physician and Sulakon, who sat without moving in the far corner under the windows, getting up only when it was necessary to put more coal on or to trim a lamp. After second hour of morning, Arpalond came in off watch and found Polem dozing in his chair. He touched his shoulder and he jerked into wakefulness.

'Do you wish to go and lie down?' said Arpalond very low. 'I can watch for you, and call.'

Polem shook his head. Arpalond nodded and looked for a seat. The only proper seat was in the far west corner, in Ailixond's folding chair. He sat down on the clothes-chest.

Between fourth and fifth hour of morning, Sulakon went out.

He came back with a bucket of charcoal, a bucket for ash and a pitcher of spiced wine that had been sitting in a haybox in the kitchen. He glanced at Arpalond, who got up to go and fetch some cups. Sulakon took up the shovel. 'Sir, is it advisable that I make no disturbance?'

The Physician shook his head. 'No amount of noise will make any difference at this time, I think. Try not to raise much dust, perhaps.'

'Have you noted any change?'

'The heat of the fever is lessening.'

A shadow passed across Sulakon's face.

'He has been very fevered,' said the Physician.

Sulakon did not look as though he believed him.

'He may wake yet.'

Sulakon turned to the brazier. It was in the form of a box, with a drawer beneath for ashes. He pulled it out to tip its contents into the bucket. The noise brought Polem bolt upright again. He looked at the tightly closed shutters.

'How long is it till morning?' he said.

'Two hours?' said the Physician. 'It gets light – when? About half past sixth hour.'

'I shall go out for a walk,' said Polem. 'You need not bother to look for me, I will be – I will be back soon.'

Arpalond, returning, found another chair empty. He said nothing, merely poured out only three cups of wine.

Outside the sky was clear, and full of stars, nor even bluing towards dawn. Several huddled groups lay under the colonnade, and, from the number of campfires still burning, many more were not going to sleep that night. Polem went down the steps to the edge of the lake. The gale had finally blown itself out, leaving the reeds to whisper among themselves above waters nearly still. He passed near one campfire with someone awake enough to be in the act of feeding it. As he bent to the flames, one could see that he was an officer of some kind, though not a Companion or a Silver Shield, since Polem did not recognise him as he stood up. Polem turned towards the light. 'My lord?' said the man. One of the nondescript bundles beside him moved to deal a swift punch to his leg. He looked down, then apologised with his hands. 'Excuse me, my lord. Merely I did not see who it was.' He returned very decidedly to his task. Polem waved his hand and went on, but he could not sit quietly by the lake, although every time he glanced over his shoulder the man had his back to him, and no one else at the fire – there were four or five cloaked bundles around it – was

427

even sitting upright. And it was cold, sitting on the ground. He got up and went back inside.

'It's not getting light yet,' he said.

'Are there many people about outside?' Arpalond asked.

'As many as when you came in, I should think. They all seem as if they have been there all night.' He sat down, and Arpalond brought him a cup of wine.

'It's no longer very warm.'

'No matter.' He drank it, and then a second and a third.

'You will go to sleep,' said Arpalond.

'No, I am wide awake now.' He went back to twisting his rings. The Physician leaned over Ailixond and peeled back his eyelids, let them fall again, shook his head. The house was no longer entirely silent; one could heard a few distant movements in the servants' quarters. The kitchen slaves would be up and lighting the fires, putting the bread which had been proving overnight into the ovens. Polem picked up the empty jug.

'I will go and get some more.'

He drank most of what he brought back. Half past sixth hour, someone knocked very cautiously. Arpalond opened; it was just getting light in the passage. Firumin stood there. 'Do my lords wish breakfast?' he said in a toneless voice.

'If you have something.'

'Yesterday's bread.'

'No matter.'

Firumin bowed and left. Sulakon stood up, stretching his arms. 'We must open the windows, if only for a few moments,' he said. 'The air in here is as stale as a wineshop, it cannot suit anyone.'

'Put that fur over the bed first,' said the Physician.

Sulakon drew the shutters back with care, but could not still the squeal of new hinges too hastily fitted. The eastern sky was the colour of fire; the shaft of ashy orange light cut through the static atmosphere of the room like slow lightning. 'What!' said the Physician. The only parts of Ailixond that moved were his eyes. They checked on each person in the room; he fixed on Polem, and tossed his glance upward. Polem sprang forward. Ailixond's lips moved, but made no sound. His eyes registered exasperation, and he attempted to move himself higher in the bed. In a sort of hiss at the back of his throat he said 'Where is . . . Aleizon Ai'ix Ayndra?'

'I'll bring her.' Polem flew out of the door. Sulakon swung round from the window, where he had been looking out at the dawn. Ailixond jerked his head at the Physician, who put an arm round him and lifted him up; Arpalond ran forward to arrange

428

the pillows. He was nodding thanks when Polem burst in again. 'She's not there! Arpalond, have you seen her?'

'I thought she was here,' said Arpalond, 'and then I thought she must be in bed —'

'No, she's not been in here since I called her out in the morning — where on earth is she?'

'In the lower camp?' suggested Arpalond, in some amazement. Sulakon looked as if he had thought so all along. Polem was not listening. 'Perhaps she's outside.'

He dashed out on to the top step. In the raw light of early morning the marble looked like the aftermath of a battle, dead fires, inert figures, one or two muffled men and women wandering among them, kicking through ashes scattering in the dawn breeze. He could see no one he recognised in the few bleary upraised faces. 'Aleizon Ailix Ayndra!' he cried. 'Aiilix!' More faces looked up. He waved his arms. 'Ailix! — has anyone seen her? Lord Aleizon Ailix Ayndra!'

Ogo was returning with a pot of lake water for porridge. He had paused to watch when the figure in a purple cloak and a scarlet tunic came out on the terrace. When he heard Polem's shout, he ran back to the campsite, but she was already stirring. He opened the sack of meal and began spooning it into the pot. 'You'll need none for me,' she said. He nodded. She gestured with her hat. 'And thank you.' Ogo looked up. 'You know that I am always your servant,' he said.

'You are always my friend — but I must go.' Polem had spotted the fair hair and the black cloak and was waving from a lower step. She flourished her hat and ran toward him. He began to speak as she came up, but she tore past him; the guards and servants who were crowding the open doorway scattered as she came up, and the king's door was being held open for Firumin who was approaching with a tray. She shot past him and landed on her knees at Ailixond's bedside in a blast of fresh air, sighing from her subsiding cloak; where she froze, gripping her hat on her knees, owl-eyed in a daze of sleep and motion. Ailixond sat up unaided as she arrived. His eyes swept the lords all ranked round the bed's foot, out to the lesser orders trying to observe through the doorway at a distance, and dismissed them. He beckoned once and said something in a ghost of a whisper, which drew her up, still clutching her hat. He seized the Royal Ring, twisted it harshly over the knuckle, and pulled it off, signed with his bare hand that she should give him her hand. She offered it like a sleepwalker. All this time they held each other in an unwavering gaze. Ailixond dropped the Royal Ring into her palm, folded her fingers over it, and turned her hand over and down on the bed. She seized his left hand. He gripped hers so hard that his knuckles shone pale, and let go with a most peculiar flash from his eyes. She fell back on her knees as if she had received a most material dart, and stared at the Royal Ring where it lay in her hand as if she'd never seen it before. Sulakon pushed the others aside and dropped to his knees at the bed's right side. He said, 'Ailixond!' Ailixond turned over on his elbow, Sulakon began, 'Do you mean to give –' Ailixond sliced the air with his bare right hand and attacked Sulakon with his eyes. Sulakon's mouth shut like a clam and he began to get up, moving back away. Ailixond flicked his brows round at the transfixed audience, and burst into a pure, fleeting, silent laugh; as he lay back among the pillows it slid away and took all the strain lines with it so that he looked almost eighteen again. No one wanted to break the silence. Golaron undid the clasp on his cloak, refastened it after he had draped it over his head, and went out. Others followed him, one by one, laying kerchiefs over their heads if they wore neither cloak nor hooded tunic. Aleizon Ailix Ayndra put her hat on and remained staring into space like an idiot child. Outside, the first howl went up, as Golaron with his head covered appeared in the doorway. He raised one hand, then dropped it; he did not need to say anything. They were running to tell the lower camp already. The Physician put the last bottles back in his box, drew the sign of blessing in the air over the bed, and left. Ayndra looked at the Royal Ring some more, then stuffed it inside her shirt. She looked around for the first time. There was no one left except Polem, who stood at the bed's head with his hands over his face, pressed against the wall. She got up stiffly, like an old woman, and put her hand on his shoulder. He groped round behind him; she reached down for his grasp. They stood so for a while, Polem pulling over her hand as he had worked his rings up and down. Ailixond's valet and the master of his wardrobe came in and started taking away pillows and straightening his limbs until he lay flat. Firumin came in, followed by the mistress of laundry with an armful of towels. He stood looking at Polem. 'My lord?' Polem said nothing; Ayndra tugged at his hand. He stood up straight and turned away from the wall. 'What do you want?' he said.

'The washing,' Firumin said in the same dead voice. 'It is the customary task of widows – and mothers.'

'Well,' said Polem.

'I think, my lord, that Lady Ailissa should be asked to do it.'

'O. Yes. Well . . . you want me to go and ask her?'

'If you could, my lord.'

'I'll do it, then.' He made for the door, but recalled on the threshold that his head was uncovered; he tried to pull up his tunic collar, but it would not do. The laundry mistress was laying out towels on the clothes-chest. He took one up, dropped it over his head and walked out. Firumin stepped out into the corridor to confer with the master of the wardrobe, and the laundry mistress followed. Ayndra looked once more at the corpse, and twisted up her mouth in a little bitter smile; stuck her thumbs in her belt with a shrug, and strutted out.

– THE END OF THE FIRST PART –